The wife of a successful banker and mother of two,
Elizabeth Walker lives on a farm in the Yorkshire
Pennines. She combines writing with keeping livestock and
has written nine previous novels, including *Voyage*,
Rowan's Mill, *The Court*, *Conquest* and *Hallmark*, all
available from Headline. She is an internationally established bestselling author.

Praise for her previous novels:

'A wonderful, romantic read' *Annabel*
'A memorable book and refreshingly different' *Woman's
World*
'The perfect holiday read' *Me* Magazine

Day Dreams

Elizabeth Walker

KNIGHT

First published in 1992
by HEADLINE BOOK PUBLISHING PLC

First published in paperback in 1993
by HEADLINE BOOK PUBLISHING PLC

This edition published 2003 by
Knight an imprint of The Caxton Publishing Group

10 9 8 7 6 5 4 3 2 1

ISBN 1 86019 6985

Typeset by Keyboard Services, Luton

Printed and bound in Great Britain by
Cox & Wyman Ltd, Reading, Berkshire

Caxton Publishing Group
20 Bloomsbury Street
London
WC1B 3QA

Day Dreams

Prologue

Her dreams were of sunshine and sunny days, in a land always at peace. Flowers grew, and never died, and if birds sang – for birds must sing, surely, in such a place? – they never stopped singing. It seemed that everything would always go on.

She lay beside water, a lagoon perhaps, for nothing flowed in or out but remained always the same. Even the pattern of ripples on the surface of the pool never changed, it was a motion repeated again and again. The land around was flat and green, and wherever she looked there was no sign of anyone living.

Sometimes she wondered about this. Where were her babies? Had there been babies? Husband, parents, surely they existed still? But in her green and pleasant land she lay in the sunshine, dreaming. The dreams, if dreams they were, filled her life. They were her life. And if some other life existed, in the far blue hills, or even in the night that never came, she remembered nothing, sought nothing, needed nothing. Living in her dream, she was happy.

Chapter One

Charles Davenport, tall, tanned and determined, walked briskly through the doors of Intensive Care, looking around expectantly for assistance. No one approached him. Momentarily nonplussed, he hesitated, caught by the soporific swishing of the ventilators, the murmuring of heart monitors, the quiet rustle of skirts as a nurse rose from her seat to attend her unconscious charge. It was the most peaceful ICU he had ever seen.

'Can I help you?'

Sister Johnson, small and calm, her hair neat under the unbecoming ICU cap.

'Davenport. Charles Davenport.'

'Oh. The new surgeon.'

'The new consultant neurologist and neuro-surgeon, Sister. I don't wish to be dogmatic, but I want people to understand right away that I'm introducing a new approach here. I intend to practise holistically.'

There was a small but telling sniff. It was clear that a doctor in his first consultancy would do well to follow well-tried paths and not blur the boundaries within which others had lived their lives. Sister Johnson said, 'Whatever you do, Mr Davenport—' there was emphasis on the 'Mr'; if he was a surgeon that was his title, and she'd hear no more about it '– whatever you do, it isn't much use today. No head injuries.'

Charles bared his teeth in a smile. 'I'm planning for the future, Sister. I should like to be shown around.'

She looked at him sardonically. His reputation had galloped to Aireborough well before he himself put in an appearance. Young, brilliant and murderously ambitious, he had strong ideas about neurology, ideas he was determined to put into

3

practice. Since no other hospital could be persuaded to take on a firebrand, however brilliant, he had been reduced to applying to Aireborough, where neurology was nothing much at all. He looked far too smart for his surroundings, she thought, noting his pinstripe suit and crisp white shirt. If he intended to impose his wild ideas here and disrupt everything, he was going to have to think again.

But it was a quiet afternoon. A bee bumped silently against the window, hinting at summer without. The year had been warm, but Davenport's tan was of the foreign variety. She smoothed her skirt and turned away from him, crooking her finger to indicate that he should follow. Instead he walked at her side, opening doors for her in a parody of good manners. She wasn't used to being out-manoeuvred and her hackles began to rise. These young doctors! Their conceit was matched only by their unbounded self-confidence.

The corridors were hushed and smelled strongly of antiseptic, the inevitable hospital smell. There were no flowers in ICU, no fluffy robes or frilly slippers, just the desperately ill, brought here after accident or surgery, stripped of everything. Charles gazed dispassionately upon bed after bed of ventilated, semi-conscious humanity, chests swathed in acres of white gauze. Heart operations, all of them. The hospital had a reputation for cardio-thoracic surgery. It seemed as if the heart surgeons had completely taken over, with all other ailments subservient to the workings of the great body pump.

Sister Johnson was right, there was nothing for him here. He wondered why that should be. He had never yet seen an ICU without a single head injury. Was it possible that Yorkshire was without young men with motorcycles, had no falling concrete, no collapsing swings, no insidious cancers pushing deadly fingers into brains? Where were the businessmen dragged from crushed cars on motorways, the toddlers whose pushchairs had overbalanced on to hard and unforgiving stone? It wasn't as if the unit was full. A four-bedded side ward stood empty, and several rooms in the private sector. If the patients went elsewhere it was not because of lack of space.

4

They stopped at the pink carpet that marked the end of NHS and the start of private practice. 'So many dicky hearts,' he remarked. Sister allowed herself a proud smile. 'We've got a name for ourselves. And we have marvellous facilities – they're planning a transplant centre next. It's almost the only reason for not closing the private beds, there isn't much demand. But, of course, once you start transplants, people come from all over the world.'

He nodded. Transplants were glamorous just now in a way that brain surgery was not. But then, neurology was all about half solutions and degrees of recovery; it rarely achieved miracles. The cardiac men did, or at least sold their work under the miracle banner. They hid their failures very well.

Charles grimaced. He was being petty. After all, if things had been different, he might have gone into heart surgery. But for the lecture. One lecture, one wonderful, damnable lecture from a white-haired old buffer with an arthritic hip, had changed everything. His interest had been awakened; more than that – his fascination. One day had changed him from a clever, idle, undirected medical student into a man obsessed by the most difficult specialty there was. It concerned the very essence of a person, their very humanity. The brain.

The human brain was so unimaginably delicate, so complex, so unforgiving of bumbling technique. He had known at once that he had finally found something that would stretch him to the limits of his abilities and nothing since had proved him wrong. It was like exploring a land where no one had ever set foot, mapping uncharted forests for the very first time. But every millimetre of exploration was dangerous. He had learned a surgical technique so refined that he could put the finest needlewomen in the world to shame, and still he had only begun!

He felt the old, familiar impatience. There was so much to do, so much to learn! Only lately had anyone begun to understand the biochemistry of brain function, and that meant a great need for research. He drew in his breath, caught again by irritation. One of the reasons he had come to Aireborough was because he had been promised research facilities. He was starting to have doubts about that now. As far as he could see, he had partial use of two laboratories plus a couple of benches in a Nissen hut behind a shrubbery in the grounds. What's more, the beds in his ward were mostly full of overflow patients from elsewhere. No patients, no money, and an openly hostile staff – he was beginning to see just what he had taken on.

Why hadn't he asked more questions? Well, he knew the answer to that one. He'd wanted the job too much to quibble. The alternative to Aireborough had been years spent licking the right boots in the hope that he would inherit a consultancy some day, and he wasn't prepared to wait. So here he was, taking over a run-down department in a great hospital which had so little interest in neurology that the patients went elsewhere.

'Where do the head injuries go?'

'St Luke's.'

'Fifty miles away? Good grief, woman!'

'We do the urgent ones,' she said quickly. 'Most of them. Mr Graham was due to retire, he'd lost interest. And isn't that why you're here? To get a name for yourself? Make your mark?'

He put his hands in his pockets. 'Really, Sister. What a cynic you are.'

Some of her frost melted into a reluctant grin. He might well prove a worthy opponent.

A buzzer sounded and she hurried away. Charles watched the muted bustle round a bed. Someone's tube had come out, and must be speedily replaced. There was nothing for him to do, and there would be nothing until the GPs began their referrals and the ambulances turned this way. The patients would come, but fresh from holiday, new in his job, young, fit and congenitally impatient, he had to do the very thing for which he was least suited: wait.

He hated activity that had nothing to do with him. Restless, he wandered again into the private unit, which he had scanned so briefly a moment before. Few of the empty rooms were fully equipped, since demand did not justify the expense. But the beds were made up with pink sheets, and pink curtains fluttered against large windows and white walls. He imagined

6

the day when all these beds would be full of his patients, brought from the furthest corners of the globe to experience his care. The cardiac men could go on with their sausage machine replacement of valves and arteries, while he attempted work of real skill.

One door in the corridor was closed. There was no name in the brass holder, no menu hanging from the handle of the door. He opened the door, wondering what secret lay inside. It was probably a cache of equipment, purloined from other departments by the heart surgeons, or perhaps it was full of balloons advertising the 'bleeding heart' appeal, or whatever new scheme they had for catching the public interest. But there was a bed in the room. And there, between pink sheets, was a golden-haired girl.

'I'm so sorry.' He spoke automatically, although the girl was clearly asleep. He half turned to go. But something about the bareness of the room alerted him. No cards, no flowers, just a trolley with the tubes and needles that denote intensive care. Although this was not intensive care. There was an oxygen bottle and a drip stand, but where were the nurses, the monitors? He wondered if perhaps it wasn't a patient at all, but a member of staff, taking an unauthorised nap in hospital time. He went a little nearer to the bed.

She was wearing a hospital gown. Taped to each wrist was a canula, to allow access to a vein. She lay on a cover made of lambswool, supported at buttocks and heels by pillows, on a bed of the latest pressure-reducing design. He took hold of her wrist and shook it.

'Hello,' he said loudly. 'Can you hear me?'

The girl seemed to stir. Her eyelids flickered, seemed as if they might rise, and sank again. She sighed deeply, just once, and resumed her regular, easy breaths. Charles reached across and put his hand over her face, stretching her eyelids, exposing irises of hyacinth blue. The pupils narrowed in response to the light. 'Hello? Hello?' he said again. Her head moved a little on the pillow. She muttered. He held her shoulders and shook her lightly, with firm insistence. 'Come on, then. Wake up!' Again, when he stopped, she sighed and resumed her sleep.

7

Behind him, the door opened. 'Mr Davenport! I'll thank you not to enter this room.'

He glanced at the Sister dispassionately. 'Why didn't you tell me you had a comatose patient?'

'I have hardly had time!' She moved to the bedside and rearranged the covers.

'You know perfectly well you deliberately avoided telling me.'

The Sister pursed her lips self-righteously. 'We don't advertise Mrs Sheraton's presence.'

He was surprised. Coma was nothing to be ashamed of. Any hospital in the country might have its tragic sleeper, doomed never to awake. 'Is there some guilty secret?' he demanded. 'Come on, Sister, you don't need to pretend with me. Was it negligence? Oxygen starvation during an operation? We all know these things happen.'

She withered him with a glance. 'It was nothing of the sort. She isn't vegetative. A car crash, merely.'

'Oh. Trauma. I see.' He moved back to the bed and lifted the girl's eyelid once more. 'Her coma's very light. Unless there's severe brain damage, the prognosis ought to be quite good.'

'They said that ten years ago.'

Davenport looked at her. 'Ten years! She must have been a child, then.'

'Not at all.' Sister Johnson permitted herself a triumphant grin. 'Mrs Sheraton is thirty-five years old.'

He didn't believe her. The girl in the bed was as fresh and dewy as a rose on a summer morning. Her hands were smooth, pink, perfectly manicured, and her skin held the fragrant sheen of youth. Her hair, coiled on the pillow, was untrammelled, lustrous gold. And yet, and yet – there was something strange about her. Her facial bones perhaps. This wasn't entirely a girl.

The Sister spoke softly. 'She was twenty-five when she came here. Deep coma. Over the next year the coma lightened until she became as you see her now. For nine years she has made no progress. No progress at all.'

Charles watched the nurse expertly smooth the long, golden

hair, lifting the head a fraction, re-arranging the limbs so that each should rest in a new and comfortable position. The girl's nails were beautiful, white at the tips like the finest pearls. As the nurse straightened the gown he glimpsed the swell of a full breast.

'You should have told me she was here,' he said again.

'We don't talk about her normally. At one time people used to come and stare. We used to worry that some man would get in. You read about such things. So we nurse her, and tell no one that she's here.'

He felt a spurt of annoyance. He wasn't a passer-by, a voyeur. He was a doctor with a doctor's dispassionate interest.

'Does she have visitors? Family? She's in the private wing, who pays?'

'Her parents are dead, Mr Davenport. They left money to the hospital on condition that she is cared for. I believe she was married with children, but after ten years, what can you expect? Sometimes a friend comes. No one else.'

Charles looked again at the peaceful face, the silken hair, the fine, healthy skin. Ten years! The woman's condition was a triumph of nursing care. 'There must be a way to wake her.'

The nurse withered him with a look. 'You won't be the first to say that. And you won't be the last. Now, Mr Davenport, Mrs Sheraton needs her bedpan. Kindly leave.'

If he had entered a thriving, busy department Davenport might have forgotten the woman. But in his first weeks he faced a few strokes that recovered well with only basic treatment, one motorcycle crash that required a straightforward operation, and very little else. He began an aggressive campaign, doing the rounds of the GPs, lobbying management, even giving talks to nurses about the treatment of neurological problems that at this rate they might never see. But he still had time on his hands. Lesser men might have played golf, but Charles had no hobbies. In the empty afternoons his thoughts turned again and again to Mrs Sheraton.

He took to visiting her after lunch most days. She was tube fed, but continent, which surprised him. It implied the lightest coma. But Sister put it down to good, reliable nursing, with bedpans provided at rigid intervals throughout the day and night. 'We have trained her system,' she told Charles, 'not her mind. That will never wake again.'

'We need a brain scan,' he said, and she laughed.

'We've done dozens. Look in the files. You don't understand. When she first had the accident her parents summoned the finest neurologists in the world. They could do nothing. She was sent like a parcel from hospital to hospital, and no one could find a cure. Ultimately she came back here. She had bedsores, she weighed less than six stone and she had a severe chest infection. We did what we could. We made her well. Perhaps we shouldn't have done it, perhaps we should have neglected her and let her die. We didn't. She's a living body with a dead mind.'

Charles went dutifully to the notes. They confirmed what Sister said. The woman had sustained a fierce blow to the head in a car crash, causing swelling of the brain, some bleeding and consequent pressure against the skull. An operation had relieved the pressure, but consciousness had not been regained. Subsequent scans had revealed a clear area of damage, small but defined, although in itself this wasn't sufficient to justify prolonged coma. But, like so many before, inexplicably and irreversibly, this brain remained inactive. He had seen it before, it wasn't so unusual, except that, in this case, she seemed so nearly awake.

So he went, every day, to the bedside. He took a rubber hammer and tested the woman's reflexes. He poured water into her mouth and watched her throat convulse in an automatic swallow. He brought a radio and played her pop music, until Sister told him to turn the racket off. 'Even if she could hear it, which I doubt, she's ten years behind! That noise means nothing to her. Leave the poor woman alone.' But he could not. Instead, he brought a CD player and filled the room with Vivaldi and Bach. Celia Sheraton simply slept.

Her recalcitrance seemed to exemplify his own frustrations. He had come here determined to introduce the latest ideas and techniques, but what use was a neurology consultant, however brilliant, if he had no patients? How could he conduct research

10

without material, without even the basic facilities? And how could he demand facilities for patients that did not yet exist? Gerald James, the hospital administrator, began to hide in cupboards when he saw Davenport approach, but eventually even Charles began to realise the futility of his position. The circle went round and round, and he searched daily, hourly, for a solution.

At present the hospital's neurology unit was housed in an old, prefabricated building in the grounds. Needless to say the heart unit had a purpose built glass and chrome birthday cake of a place with its own private car park. No one trespassed on cardiac beds, but those in neurology were constantly being invaded by geriatric patients, or maternity cases with three months to go – anyone, in fact, that the management wanted to park out of sight. In his wiser moments, Charles could hardly blame them; until now, neurology at Aireborough had been a joke.

Thwarted, he pondered his problems while digging the garden of his house. He found the turning of rank and weedy earth into dark loam very therapeutic. He had always liked physical things. The house itself was perhaps another of his follies, taking the job being his first. It was a big, rambling old rectory that had once housed a kindergarten and he had bought it in sunshine six months ago, when the long windows were brilliant with light and the huge rooms airy and inviting. Now, as autumn approached, the garden was an encroaching jungle, there was no central heating and the roof leaked. He had the roof repaired and ignored the cold. The house suited his spartan soul.

He sank his spade deep into the heavy earth, relishing the pull on unused muscles. Years of neglected leaves had rendered the soil thick and black, full of worms and goodness. He imagined plants he had never grown, strawberries and asparagus and delicious early potatoes. Things could grow quickly where nothing had grown for years. There would be new flower beds and many, many trees. He had never gardened before, but why should that matter? He was naturally ambitious. He would plan, in his garden as in his work, for a golden tomorrow.

Charles leaned on his spade for a moment. It was early days. He had hardly begun. In years to come he would establish a brain damage centre of world renown, where he could make real progress. He caught his breath at the thought of all those damaged brains awaiting his curiosity, like a car mechanic in a yard full of faulty engines. That would be the day!

A breeze struck cool through his pullover. Dreaming was an indulgence, a waste of time. He should concentrate on concrete acts that would advance his cause right now. What he needed – what the neurology department needed – was a high public profile, a spectacular case with lots of media interest. When he was in America, spending a few months at a leading hospital, there had been a careful dribble of brain tumour patients released into local television studios and fame. They were always the young and pretty ones. He had despised such things then, when finance had been someone else's problem. Now he saw things differently.

He gave up on the digging and allowed his imagination to roam. It was time the heart men were challenged. Life had moved on since the days of Christian Barnard and the first, over-rated heart transplants. Bodies were no good without minds. He imagined all that he would like to do: scanners, modern wards, an integrated and coherent system in which no new development was ever overlooked. An epilepsy centre perhaps. All he had to do was persuade the public, and through them the hospital, that he was worth it.

He needed just one outstanding case! Something that would catch the imagination, inspire people to understand what he was trying to do.

All he had was Mrs Sheraton. A young, glamorous, beautiful woman. If he could just wake her up! If he could only restore her to consciousness he could live forever on the publicity. The Sleeping Beauty whom he alone could waken. Except – he couldn't.

Charles sighed ruefully and began to walk to the house. It was late, the light was failing, but he wasn't tired. He had always had too much energy, he had been one of the few junior doctors to thrive on the hours. Suddenly he stopped in his tracks. Why was he admitting defeat so easily? He didn't know he couldn't waken Mrs Sheraton. He hadn't even tried.

'Come on, dear. Come on. Doctor says you have to sit up.' A nurse, plump and motherly, cradled the limp form against her bosom. The golden head lolled on her shoulder, but the nurse struggled on, wrestling heavy limbs until at last her patient sat slumped in a wheelchair. Her feet were twisted unnaturally, and the nurse straightened them, but gradually the woman's body began to slide. Folding her lips with the effort, the nurse pulled her straight again. Finally she tied a length of bandage around the woman and the chair. At last! She sat down, panting.

'Nurse!' Sister Johnson appeared at the door. 'Taking your ease, I see,' she said caustically. 'And why is Mrs Sheraton trussed up like a chicken?'

'She won't stay up, Sister,' explained the nurse, hauling herself to her ill-used feet. 'Keeps sliding down.'

'Next time, sit her on lambswool,' said the Sister. 'Or better still, don't sit her at all. She should be in bed.'

'Mr Davenport said—'

'I know what Mr Davenport said.' Sister quelled her with an icy stare. 'Mr Davenport has some strange ideas. It seems we must humour him. For one day at least.'

Taking the handles of the chair Sister propelled it out of the door and along the passage. The doctor had decreed that Mrs Sheraton should receive stimulation. So that was what she would get. When it had manifestly failed to achieve any result, perhaps then the silly man would realise that Sister knew best.

Heads turned as they passed along corridors. Sister felt a degree of real anger towards Charles Davenport, exposing this poor woman to the curious against all advice. In the lift one of the porters said, 'She's well away, ain't she, Sister? What's up?'

She did not deign to reply.

Their destination was the gym. The patient was to be left exposed to noise and draughts and confused activity. She was to be left there for two hours, and this was to be repeated daily until Mr Davenport saw fit to call a halt. It was nothing short of cruelty, thought the Sister, with a nasty added element of vice.

13

Celia Sheraton's beautiful, unconscious, voluptuous body seemed to give rise to certain fantasies in men. Where this patient was concerned, she did not trust masculine intent.

'Celia? Celia dear, I'm leaving you now. You're to stay here until I come for you again.'

The golden head seemed to lift a little. Imagination, of course. She never responded. It was just that after so long, she knew Sister Johnson's voice. She wasn't dead, after all. There must be some level of understanding. The CAT scan showed brain activity, she wasn't one of those unfortunates with nothing but a superficial evidence of life. Sister Johnson soothed her.

'I don't want you to be upset, Celia. Just wait quietly until I come for you.'

A boy struggling to walk between bars fell with a crash, yelling out in pain and frustration. The unconscious woman remained quite still. So of course the nurse had imagined that response. This was all pointless and cruel.

As the Sister left, Mr Davenport walked in. He smiled down at her, turning on charm like a light. As if anyone was fooled!

'How is she, Sister? Any change?'

'None at all, sir. But I imagine she'll be upset. Leaving her alone in this great, echoing place.'

'I want her upset, Sister.'

The woman drew herself up stiffly. Her thin nose quivered with outrage. 'Since when was it our duty to cause discomfort to patients? Celia Sheraton was left in our care. We are responsible for her welfare. And you are dragging her into the public view, never thinking of her dignity or her good. She looks pathetic like that. She cannot speak for herself, cannot protect herself. At the mercy of – men like you.'

A caustic reply leaped to his lips. Then he hesitated a moment. Sister Johnson had given ten years of care to this patient. Like the mother of a handicapped child, she was fiercely protective of her charge, and her charge's need of her. Sister Johnson did not know it, but she didn't want Celia Sheraton to wake up.

'Look at it this way,' he said at last. 'If she knows nothing then this can't hurt her.'

The Sister glared fiercely. 'She knows enough to be upset.'

'Then perhaps she'll wake.'

'And perhaps she won't. This is spoiling her routine. She could dirty herself, she'll be late for her meal!' But she saw that the doctor, the young, handsome, know-all doctor, discounted all that. She curled her lip. 'All you want is to be famous! I can see exactly what you're after. Bigshot doctor with cures that make Jesus look like a beginner. You don't care about your patients, they're just so many experimental animals. You don't care at all what's best for Celia.'

'Do you? To want her asleep all her life?'

Sister Johnson bristled with anger. 'I never put any interest before that of my patients' wellbeing!' she said loudly.

Her voice carried clearly across the echoing gym. Like a child, a sleeping child, Celia Sheraton stirred. Briefly, lazily, she lifted her head.

Davenport clutched the Sister's arm. 'Did you see that? She moved. She heard your voice and moved.'

Contemptuous, she said, 'She often does that.'

'What do you mean? She's done it before? My God, Sister, the woman's on the brink!'

He took long strides across the polished wood floor. Sister Johnson followed him slowly. 'Speak to her,' he said urgently. 'See what she does.'

Licking dry lips, Sister Johnson came close. 'Celia,' she murmured. 'Celia. I'm here now. Did you want to go back?'

For long seconds there was nothing. But all at once the golden head lifted. They glimpsed eyes of startling blue, and the ghost of a smile. A moment later, slumped again into coma, the movement might never have been.

'Well, Sister?' asked Davenport softly.

The woman's mouth worked. She seemed about to cry, and put up her hand to suppress tears. 'It doesn't seem right,' she muttered. 'Not after ten years. There's damage to her brain.'

'Not as much as we thought, perhaps. I shall do another scan.' He ran his hands through his hair, trying to suppress the excitement that coursed in his veins like electricity. 'OK, she could be an idiot. She could be severely handicapped. That's a risk. But anything's better than this.'

'Is it? Anything? She's happy now. She doesn't know enough to be unhappy. Her parents are dead, her husband's gone. She has no one. She's alone.'

He looked at the tight face underneath the ugly cap. Didn't the woman realise what could come of this? Medical papers, conferences, publicity, funds – his department would start to take off. He took a deep breath, trying to rein in the galloping horses of his ambition. She was right in one way; the patient was the important thing. Only through the patient could any of this come about. But he could say, and everyone would believe him, that he owed it to his patient to give her at least the possibility of recovery. All right, she could end up as a lumpish fixture in the corner of some mental home, useless and dull. But she might not. Setting aside all the dross which had accumulated since his first dreams of success, he still believed in the perfect cure. It had to be right to try.

As a concession, he helped Sister Johnson wheel the chair back up to the private wing. He lifted the patient's unconscious arm and felt the pulse – it was racing a little. The woman began moaning softly, and her feet made restless movements on the step of the chair.

'Her mealtime,' said Sister Johnson. 'And time for her bedpan.'

'You must stop giving regular meals,' said Charles. 'Stop everything regular. She needs hunger, discomfort, sound, light, movement. Tomorrow I shall take her outside and sit with her by the main entrance. I shall start a photographic record, to monitor change.'

He pushed the chair back to the private room. Sister pointedly waited for him to depart.

In the silence of the room when he had gone there seemed warmth and familiar peace. Sister Johnson relaxed a little, and smoothed her charge's long golden hair. 'The silly man wants everyone to see him sitting with you,' she murmured. 'He's going to make an exhibition of you, like a creature in a zoo. Don't you worry. I won't let him hurt you. Sister knows what's best.'

She soothed and crooned, going about the small, personal, intimate tasks that were so familiar to each of them. Suddenly,

16

a sound escaped the patient's lips. It was a sound known only to the Sister, one occasioned by attention to the patient's bodily needs, the relief of any small area of discomfort. A reward of sorts for the years of devoted care, for the endless protection. No one else ever heard it, for no one else deserved it. It was a small, contented chuckle.

Chapter Two

The abandonment of routine is against a hospital's very code of existence. There is always routine, from the moment of waking, through the meals and the doctors' rounds and the visitors, to early lights out and a troubled sleep. But for Celia Sheraton, Charles would have none of it.

Sometimes she missed her breakfast. Sometimes she was left to sleep late. Sometimes she was woken at four in the morning and made to sit up at a window in the corridor and watch the lights of planes landing at the airport. Mild stimulants were given, and spicy food in spoonfuls on her tongue. Music gave way to recorded lectures on physics and childcare, travel and religion. Had she believed in God? thought Charles. This was a living death for her. Was she, in some complex way, sitting on the threshold of the next world? And if so, did she look upon heaven, hell – or simply nothing?

True to his intention, he began taking his unconscious charge for walks in a wheelchair. They would stop by the main entrance to the hospital, next to a flowerbed, and he would read to her. At first he tried newspapers, but the stimulation of names, dates and places seemed largely irrelevant from the imagined perspective of his patient, who had last heard the news ten years ago. What about a book she might know, one she might have read? Something classic, surely? He began *Jane Eyre*.

It was in the middle of chapter two that Gerald James, the hospital administrator, arrived. A small, slightly bombastic man, he bustled about the corridors in a constant rush. Charles had decided early on that he must cultivate this man, but even James had soon realised it was the smile on the face of the tiger. Charles was only pleasant when he wanted something, and from James he wanted a lot. Their encounters were distinctly stiff-legged.

'Mr Davenport,' said James tensely.

'Mr James. Celia, this is Mr James, the hospital administrator. A very important man,' he added.

But Mr James needed no confirmation of his own importance. 'Who gave you permission to remove Mrs Sheraton from her room?'

Charles lowered the book. Sister Johnson's hand was visible in this. She must indeed be desperate to go beyond the medical fraternity to administration, the old and constant enemy. 'Mrs Sheraton is a neurology patient,' he said with chilling point. 'I wasn't aware that I needed permission to give my patients the treatment they need.'

'This is no ordinary patient.'

Charles shrugged. 'Leaving aside the philosophy in that – viz. is there such a thing as an ordinary patient, and which criteria fall within the definition of ordinariness, about which we can perhaps talk later and in some depth – so what?'

James struggled on. 'Mrs Sheraton is a very special patient! She must not be exposed to any risks, none at all.'

'I am trying to restore my patient to life, Mr James. Living is a risky business.'

'I must insist that this woman be taken back to her room. At once!'

Charles felt anger erupt within him. Those who knew him better would have recognised the signs: his sudden pallor, the slight glitter in his dark eyes, and an entirely misleading smile. James smiled back, relieved that Davenport was taking this well. His next words were therefore something of a shock.

'What in the name of your inadequate qualifications and experience gives you the right to dictate to me on patient care, James? If you wish me to call in the media to view the excesses in the cardiac wards, funded by deprivation elsewhere – in orthopaedics, or the care of the elderly who might be forgiven for thinking you wanted them all to die as they cross the threshold of this place, or indeed the neurologically incapacitated who have the potential for recovery that is never actually achieved – then just say the word. I'll have a scandal bigger than you ever dreamed of on your desk before six tonight!'

All James's worst fears about Charles Davenport seemed validated. 'You don't understand . . .' he said helplessly.

Another glittering smile. 'I'm known for the depth of my understanding, Mr James. Explain.'

'If you would just return Mrs Sheraton to her room! She's very special. Quite unique. Please, Mr Davenport.'

The woman stirred and moaned unhappily. Charles glanced down at her. James was right about one thing, this was no place for a scene. 'Of course I shall return her. As soon as you tell me exactly what it is that makes Mrs Sheraton so special. I'm all ears, Mr James.'

The administrator wrung his hands in anguish. 'I can't explain here!'

'In front of Mrs Sheraton? Indeed not. She may understand more than we know.'

Charles drew him aside. It was laughable, huddling next to a laurel bush like a couple of inept spies. He had to bend like a willow to put his head to James's. 'Yes?' he whispered. 'What is it?'

'She was Celia Braddock,' hissed Mr James. 'Old Joe Braddock's daughter.'

'You mean the tycoon?'

James nodded. 'He left us a fortune to take care of her. And here you are, exposing her! We could lose the lot.'

Charles drew back a little. 'I'm not Sweeney Todd, Mr James! I don't specialise in killing my patients off.'

James's voice sank still lower. 'We run the heart unit with her bequest. We'd close without it.'

'So?'

'We mustn't take risks. Any risks!'

The man's face was intent and concentrated. He hoped by his very stare to communicate what he dared not say. 'Is curing her a risk?' asked Charles. 'Would the money have to go?'

James shut his eyes in horror. 'We always take the greatest care of Mrs Sheraton,' he said with a gasp.

21

'But not of my neurology unit.' Charles straightened up, glaring at the smaller man. 'My patient comes first. I can't possibly put the finances of the cardiac department before her welfare.'

As he walked away, James followed. 'I'm sure we could find some extra cash for you in the coming financial year,' he called plaintively. 'Improvements . . . staff . . .'

'Indeed?' Charles softened visibly. The day was starting to improve. 'Look,' he said reasonably, 'you've been getting in a fuss about nothing. It's most unlikely that Celia Sheraton will ever make a full recovery. I see no prospect of her leaving hospital, now or in the future. But she can make progress. And that has to be good. For my department and for the hospital.'

James let out his breath in a sigh of relief. 'So she isn't going to get well?'

'She may get better. A little better. That's all.'

The administrator walked away almost jauntily. The man was nothing more than a jumped-up adding machine, thought Charles, interfering in patient care for purely financial reasons. What was medicine coming to? He looked down at Celia's golden head. How interesting everything was becoming. He had been right about Celia Sheraton. She was coming to seem infinitely precious.

But over the next weeks Charles found less and less time to spend with her. The bitter row which had long simmered between the head of neuro-surgery at the neighbouring St Luke's and his anaesthetist finally came to a head. Rumour had it that they had come to blows, although it was probably just gossip. At any rate, the upshot was that the surgeon left for America and his patients came to Charles. In between chapters three and four of *Jane Eyre* he found himself supervising three skull fractures, one serious, four post-operative tumour patients, a mental case for whom he could do nothing, and an outpatient clinic for strokes, recovering head injuries and epileptics.

Several days elapsed before he could return to Celia. When he did, Sister Johnson was scathing. 'I knew how it would be.

22

Fads and fancies, fads and fancies, that's all it is with you young men. Upset everything and everyone and then go wandering off.' She smoothed the patient's lovely hair, twisting it expertly into a plait.

'You were the one who wandered off, Sister,' said Charles. 'To administration.'

She turned a deep ruby red. 'You were upsetting Mrs Sheraton,' she said again. 'Disturbing her. I had to do something. And then everything stopped.'

'So you think she's aware enough to miss her outings?'

'I didn't say that.'

'But you think it. Sister, you know her better than anyone. If she responds to anyone then it's to you. I need your observations.'

He was challenging her professionalism. And in truth she regretted her tale-bearing to the moneymen. Not that she was any fonder of Mr Davenport. But the patient came first. Above anything that she might herself feel, the sick and the needy must be cared for. Sister Johnson folded her hands on her apron and confronted him. 'I observe a gentleman filling in time disturbing the routine of a settled patient for no good reason. We know she has some awareness. In my judgment, in my experienced judgment, it will not improve. But, in these last few days, she has shown distress.'

'How?' He was sharp.

'Mumbling. Crying once or twice. As if she's having bad dreams.'

'Couldn't she be waking? Couldn't that be true?'

'It could be true. But it is not.' She gave the bed a final straightening and walked away.

Charles lingered for a moment. Mumbling? Tears? But now the face on the pillow was as calm as death. Her skin was like marble stained the faintest pink. What should he try next? Drug therapy had never been proved effective in such cases, but he was tempted to experiment. Now that he had so little time.

He prepared to leave. 'Can't take you out today, Celia,' he said. 'No time. But I brought *Jane Eyre*. I shall leave it here

23

and get one of the nurses to come and read to you for a while. Not today, they're busy. Tomorrow, perhaps.'

He expected nothing. He was prepared for it. She reacted so rarely and in so limited a fashion that he had begun to half-believe that was all she would ever do. But in a second she came briefly alive. Her head thrashed twice on the pillow, in quick and determined objection. She muttered angrily, and one hand, clenched into a fist, a hand that he had never seen move, struck at air. Charles stood transfixed and staring. 'What did you say?' he replied. 'Speak up, I can't hear you.'

Eyelids fluttering like the wings of an injured bird, 'No. No,' she said.

Adrenalin surged in him and his heart responded with fierce beats. 'Don't you want to read the book? Say what you want, Celia.'

'No, no!' Stronger this time. The fist struck randomly against the bedcover.

Charles leaned across her, one arm either side, his face a foot from hers. He quivered with excitement. 'Well? What's the matter? Celia, wake up if you have something to say.'

The eyelids lifted. Vivid blue eyes, as clear and unsullied as a babe's, gazed up at him. 'Daddy,' she said.

He hauled her from the bed into the wheelchair. He raced with her down the corridor, searching for Sister Johnson. She was in her office, interviewing a young nurse, but he burst in regardless.

'Sister! She spoke! You should have been there. She said Daddy!'

Sister did her best to extinguish fiery enthusiasm with an icy stare. 'I am engaged, Mr Davenport.'

'Bugger that! She spoke. At first "no", and then "Daddy". She looked at me and called me Daddy.'

'But you are not her father, Mr Davenport. As I said to you, her brain is damaged. You are reviving a vegetable.'

'Vegetables don't speak. Come on, Sister! Aren't you tired of having your own life-sized doll?'

Sister Johnson froze in her chair. The nurse, young and undisciplined, giggled. The patient, apparently quite uncon-scious, moaned, and Charles realised he had gone too far. 'I take that back, Sister,' he said carefully. 'You've kept this patient alive almost single-handed. Your care has been unstinting.'

But it was too late. Sister Johnson's nose was pinched white with suppressed anger. 'I don't need your congratulations,' she said tightly. 'Nurse, get about your duties. You can take Mrs Sheraton back to bed.'

'She shouldn't be in bed,' said Charles. 'We've got to put her on a ward, she needs constant stimulus.'

'What she needs is nursing! She will be returned to bed at once. I understood you were busy, Mr Davenport. It is time you were away.'

The moment he left she would have the patient back in bed. Whatever co-operation he had achieved was gone. And the woman had looked at him! She spoke! He could not let Sister Johnson enslave her once again. 'I shall arrange to have her transferred to a ward today,' he said.

'Mr Davenport, you will do no such thing!'

'I'm sorry, Sister. I must.'

For some time after he had gone Sister Johnson sat at her desk. Then she got up and went to a cabinet. She extracted a large file, crammed with papers, and began leafing through it. Then she reached for the telephone.

'Celia? Celia, it's me, Dorrie.' A short, plump woman in a bulky red cardigan took Celia's hand and held it. She had brought with her a bag crammed with books, knitting and paper bags full of food. 'Do you like home-made bread, dear? I don't suppose you get much in here. I make a good loaf, though I say it myself.' She unearthed her gifts, looking around for a table on which to put them. In this big, bustling ward there were few resting places. A woman stroke patient learning to walk on crutches clung in passing to the end of a bed while the physiotherapist berated her. Dorrie piled everything on the locker.

She found a chair and sat down, feeling less than tranquil. It was almost a year since she had seen Celia, and the peremptory summons had come as a shock. As far as she could judge some doctor was experimenting with her, against the wishes of the nurses. It had seemed incredible, but Dorrie had come, doubtful but avenging, and found her just as she had been before. Years had passed in which Dorrie herself had grown fatter, wiser and more serious, while Celia was as lovely and immobile as she had been since the day of the crash.

The nurses, talking at the end of the ward, burst into shrieks of laughter. 'Noisy, this place,' said Dorrie. 'Do you mind, Celia? You had a lovely room before.'

No response. She delved into her bag again, saying, 'Would you like some grapes? They're delicious just now. I get them from a really good greengrocer, everything organic. Do you want some?' She broke off one or two and put them in Celia's hand. To her amazement the fingers closed. Grape juice dribbled between them.

'Miss Duncan?' A tall, dark man was standing over her. 'Hello. I'm the neurology consultant, Charles Davenport. Sister Johnson tells me you've come to discuss Mrs Sheraton.'

Dorrie got up. She felt bewildered. 'She – I gave her some grapes and she crushed them. She never used to do anything.'

He nodded. 'Yes. The coma's lightening. That's why she's here instead of in a private room. I feel she needs the stimulus.'

'She's going to wake up then? They said she'd never wake up!'

'We don't know what she'll do. But we're trying. I'm trying. Look, I really shouldn't discuss this with anyone except close family.'

'She has no family. At least – none that can come. I'm a friend. I was a friend. We've known each other all our lives.'

They moved away, talking. Suddenly there was a crash. They turned round to see all that Dorrie had brought tumbled on to the floor. Celia's head moved from side to side, and she was saying: 'No! No! No!'

'She always gets angry when I'm around,' said Charles. 'My fatal charm. What is it, Celia? What don't you want?'

Her head was up and she was looking at him. She had never been so direct before. The eyes, with their translucent vagueness, seemed almost to focus on his face. 'No?' she said in puzzlement.

'Wake up, Celia,' said Charles. 'Wake up and tell me what

you want.' Celia said nothing. Her head, on its stem of a neck, turned very slowly from side to side.

Dorrie knelt on the floor in front of her. 'Celia, it's me. Dorrie. Oh, Celia, do you know who I am?'

A faint look of what might have been recognition crossed Celia's face. But it was so easy to see in her what you wanted. Dorrie smiled hopefully, and Celia blinked, stared and looked away. Charles, moving behind her, put his hands on her head and held her, face to face with Dorrie. 'Look, Celia,' he said. 'It's Dorrie. Your friend.'

'Dorrie.' The tongue moved listlessly. Dorrie burst into tears.

Charles took her to an office to recover. 'Sister Johnson said you were torturing her,' sniffed Dorrie. 'I didn't know what to think. Drugs, perhaps. After all this time someone must have discovered something that would work?'

'Not much, no,' said Charles. 'A long-term coma such as this is very rarely reversed. But she is coming round. At first I wasn't sure, but every day now she makes an improvement.'

'So why doesn't Sister Johnson approve?'

Charles looked into the woman's gentle, weathered face. She wasn't so old, but lines and grey hairs, which she made no attempt to conceal, were abundant. She was like a sofa, sagging and comfortable, ready to enfold you. He felt warm towards Dorrie Duncan. 'Sister is very fond of Celia,' he said. 'She's become used to taking care of her. Mothering her. Now she sees her going away, perhaps to something worse than she had before. We have to face it. Celia may never be more than a long-stay patient in a mental hospital.'

'A life, though,' said Dorrie. 'She'd have a life.'

'Some sort of life, yes. She might be very miserable. We might be doing good at the patient's expense.'

Dorrie stood up and went to the window. The view was of the hospital car park, with people coming and going constantly. Delivery vans raced backwards and forwards, and porters wheeled wire cages full of laundry bags up and down. 'She's been in hospital ten years,' she said. 'We all used to visit, but there wasn't any point.'

'What about her husband? She was married, wasn't she?'

Dorrie nodded. 'As far as David's concerned, Celia's dead. He's got someone else. I'm not even sure that the children know she's alive at all. They were tiny when she was hurt.'

'How old are they now?'

Dorrie considered. 'I'm not sure. I don't see them much. I was a friend of Celia's, you see, not David's. How old were they? Two and four, I think. Both girls. Now – well, Lucy must be twelve and Ellen fourteen.'

'Old enough to understand, perhaps?'

'That their mother's coming back to life? Is anyone old enough to understand?'

She tossed back her unruly hair. Her breasts moved beneath her sweater, like rabbits in a sack. Some sort of feminist then, or a woman allergic to underwear? He imagined her as a brilliant cook but without a resident man. She was too uncaring of her appearance for that. She would have friends though. People of Dorrie's sort always had friends.

'There's no need to tell the family just yet,' said Charles cautiously. 'I see it might upset them.'

'Bound to,' she said. 'Oh God. The whole thing gets worse when you think about it. Suppose it is wrong?'

He met her worried brown eyes. 'You must know that I couldn't leave her like that.'

She turned away. 'No. I suppose not. But everything's different, everything's moved on. Did you see the way she looked at me? I used to be thin.'

He laughed and she joined in. She picked up her bag, ready to go.

'Look,' he said, detaining her at the door. 'We don't know what's going to happen. She could recover completely or stop anywhere along the road. Will you come and see her?'

Dorrie nodded. 'Of course. It's exciting, isn't it? As well as frightening.'

'Yes. Yes, I think so.'

When she had gone he went back to his patient. Celia was eating now, spoon-fed by a nurse. She chewed every mouthful like a sleepy camel. 'You're getting better, Celia,' he said. 'Every day, a little better.'

28

The woman lifted her hand and sent the bowl of food flying. Charles brushed some scraps of cabbage off his suit. 'I seem to annoy her,' he said. 'Let's hope that one day she wakes up enough to tell me why.'

Weeks went by, a month. Sister Johnson's opposition faded to occasional accusing visits. To her mind there was no improvement. Celia had moved from the normality of sleep to a distinctly abnormal zombie-like state, more asleep than awake, propelled like a defective robot from bathroom to chair to bed. Charles Davenport came daily and Dorrie when she could, bringing music and magazines, and once a child's rattle she put in Celia's hand. From then on Celia could be seen shaking her rattle, caught in what seemed perpetual childhood. Charles kept careful notes – response times, reflexes, photographs. He was considering writing a paper on the woman, and presenting it at a conference later in the year. He wondered if she might be well enough to attend in person.

He was getting to know Dorrie quite well. Once, in town, he saw her carrying shopping bags and stopped to give her a lift. She lived in a big terraced house near the river, a cheap area full of student flats and immigrant families. 'What do you do?' he asked, as he helped her get out.

'Artist,' she said. 'But not as penniless as I used to be. I sell quite a bit. Would you like to come in?'

'Thanks.'

The house was shabby, with dusty artwork all over the place. Dorrie specialised in mother and child studies, or suffering lovers, in a modernist style. Charles hated them. 'I'm getting quite popular,' she said, putting the kettle on. 'The day may come when Dorrie Duncan is famous.'

'Did Celia paint?'

Dorrie paused, teapot in hand. 'Do you know, I'm not sure? She was twenty-five when the accident happened. I didn't even paint then. I had of course, before, but at twenty-five I was too busy getting into bed with men.'

'But there's no man now.'

'No.' She sank down at the big, wormy table. 'The accident sobered us all up. I got married, but it was a disaster. We gave up on it after the fourth miscarriage. All we wanted from each other was children. That was one thing about Celia – she loved her kids.'

'How did they take it?'

Dorrie shrugged. 'As kids do. You never know. They get on with their lives and everyone thinks they're fine, until suddenly they're not. The damage takes years to show. But I'm not close to them any more, I don't know. The worst thing is – they'd have been different people if Celia had been with them. She made everyone different.'

Charles felt the stirrings of curiosity. 'What was she like?'

'Bright, funny, clever. Generous. About everything – she was a devil at parties. David was always having to drag her out of bedrooms with other men. She was – rebellious. Never bothered about rules. Never hid things. She and David had some terrible rows, but when she had the accident I thought he'd crack up. Lived at the hospital, for weeks. And after that he visited every day. But in the end – well, in the end we all gave up. Even her parents.'

'She called me Daddy, you know.'

'Did she?' Dorrie looked at him in surprise. 'I suppose he could have looked like you when Celia was small. Same height, dark hair and so on. He adored her. Both of them did.'

The tea, when it came, tasted of flowers. Dorrie gave him buns to eat, full of wheatgerm and currants. Celia Sheraton sounded quite a girl, he thought. Would she, in time, have become like Dorrie? He thought of the long, pale limbs beneath the lumpy hospital dressing gown, the blue of her slow-blinking eyes. No wonder she was trouble at parties.

'Celia hated restrictions,' mused Dorrie, munching another bun. 'David was always trying to restrict her. So was her father, actually. I suppose she was awfully wild.'

'You didn't mind then?'

Dorrie grinned. 'No. We were all younger then. You learn, don't you, over the years?'

That evening he was called to the hospital to attend a toddler who had fallen from a wall. It should have been straightforward, but was not. The X-ray led him to think that the fall was not a spontaneous event, but had been caused by a growth. His reassuring chat with the parents turned into a guarded word about tests and further examination. Their questions, their demands, irritated him unreasonably. He didn't need the burden of their fear.

Guiltily, secretly, he hoped for a tumour. Excising such a thing was one of the most satisfying experiences of his life. The gentle teasing out of alien strands required the most rigorous patience and technique. As he mentally rehearsed the procedure, he realised, suddenly, that he was wasting his time. He couldn't operate here. They hadn't the equipment. His patient would go, passed on to another hand, when his was so wonderfully competent. He closed his fingers into a fist and cursed the night.

He wasn't in the mood to go home. The walls would oppress him, the silence would fill with his frustration. He strode moodily through the corridors, plotting and planning. There was money, but it went to others. If only it would come to him! He must press his advantage with the administrator, but how to do that without something positive to show for his time here? Almost without realising he found himself going to see Celia, although it was late and the lights were out on the ward. Celia Sheraton – a golden girl, a golden woman, and now a golden goose.

To his surprise, the nurses were pleased to see him.

'She's so restless, Mr Davenport. Calling out, disturbed, unhappy. Keeps saying: "Book".'

He went down the ward and opened the curtains. Celia was half sitting up, her eyes wide open. Her hair was thickly plaited and as her head moved restlessly from side to side, the plait swung like a rope. Even as he watched and made the inevitable medical assessment, Charles was struck anew by her strangeness. She was a creature from a fairytale, once a Sleeping Beauty, tonight a Rapunzel, and sometime perhaps a Lady of Shalott.

But the patient had no use for his fancies. 'Book,' she said, when she saw him. And again, forcefully, 'Book!'

'What book? What book, Celia?'

'Book! Book!' Her face contorted and she closed her eyes as if wrestling with herself, as if searching for a word that would

31

not come. Then, painfully ducking her chin and struggling, she said, '*Jane Eyre*.'

He found the book, sat down and began reading. His thoughts were far from the words. Celia Sheraton was alive in there. An intelligent, thinking woman still lived. Memory and will remained and flourished, trapped in a body that day by day was fighting clear of its dragging sleep. He felt no caution any more, no sensible restraint. She would recover. The miracle would be done. He felt an enormous sense of triumph.

Chapter Three

It was a sunny evening in early April. Charles parked amidst children playing on bikes and roller skates, and ran up the steps to Dorrie's house. A window-box full of daffodils was gasping for a drink, and as soon as Dorrie answered his ring he said, 'There's nothing more depressing than a host of dead daffodils. Got a milk bottle? Those flowers need some water.'

Dorrie stood aside to let him go past her to the kitchen. She wasn't pleased to see him.

The flowers began to revive almost at once. Dorrie went inside and found a corkscrew and opened a bottle of Bulgarian wine, filling two tumblers to the brim. 'I've the feeling I'm going to need this,' she remarked. 'You're looking determined.'

Charles sat down at the kitchen table. A puppet was under construction and he toyed with it. 'You are pessimistic. Isn't it a lovely night?'

'It was.' She sat down opposite him. 'All right, tell me the worst.'

'You know the worst,' said Charles. 'She's better.'

Dorrie took a gulp of her wine. She wouldn't look at him. The silence felt accusing and difficult, and at last she burst out, 'You know this has nothing to do with me! It isn't fair to ask.'

'You don't know what I'm asking, yet.'

She made a face. 'You've been hinting long enough. I won't tell her husband. I won't.' She picked up the puppet, cruelly extending its legs.

'I'll come with you, of course,' said Charles. 'I know it isn't easy, but you're the only person who knows Celia and her family too. You must see that we can't go on not telling them? It's possible that she could be restored to almost total consciousness, and what then? She could arrive on their doorstep and kill them with the shock.'

Dorrie gestured dismissively. 'She's not going to be perfect. Be honest with yourself.'

'What's a little speech difficulty?'

'She can hardly put a sentence together.'

'So far! She's improving daily. All right, there may be some impediment, and residual stiffness in one side. Nothing significant.'

'Nothing significant to you. Real people think differently.'

He sipped his wine. It was comfortable here, in Dorrie's messy house, although he couldn't live like this. He liked order in his home, like a well-set-out trolley in an operating theatre. Although he wasn't all that good at living alone. He didn't so much want company as an active environment. He liked to come home at the end of the day to a house that had moved on from the morning, not to a still life. But Dorrie was different.

'Don't you ever get lonely?' he asked.

She shrugged. 'If I do I find someone to talk to. I like it on my own. No one to complain about anything. Men do complain, you know.'

'About watering plants,' agreed Charles. 'Perhaps it makes us feel needed.'

Dorrie chuckled. 'You aren't really.'

'Rubbish.'

He got up and stood waiting expectantly. She said, 'Give us a chance! I've got to think about this.'

'We've done all the thinking. Come on, Dorrie! I'll drive.'

She sighed heavily, and shuddered, as if the thought of the encounter to come was too awful to contemplate. Then she ran her hands through her coarse, bushy hair. 'I'll wait if you want to change,' said Charles, noting her red and yellow striped skirt and Greenpeace T-shirt worn without a bra.

'I'm OK, aren't I?' said Dorrie, and Charles said, 'Yes. Of course.'

They drove out of town, leaving behind the scruffy streets for lanes lined with hedges bursting into pale April leaf. Birds flew low in front of them, busy with nest building. 'Is it much further?' he asked. 'I didn't realise she lived so far out.'

'She didn't,' said Dorrie. 'David moved after the accident. When her parents died they left him the house. This is where Celia grew up.'

'Was it a happy childhood?'

Dorrie put her hands behind her head and her breasts moved hypnotically. Like a pair of hippos in bed, he thought. He liked thinking up similes for her breasts.

'She was happy when she was little. Things got a bit sticky as she grew up, but her father was a very determined man. Turn left here, Charles.'

Obediently he swung the wheel. They passed between gateposts topped with giant stone balls, and gates tipped with gold, bearing the words 'Blantyre House'. A long gravel drive lined with oaks swept into a circle of perfect proportions. The house it served was Georgian, three-storied, with a wide, hipped roof and white marble steps leading gracefully to the door. To the side, through a discreet curtain wall, were the lesser roofs of a stable and garage block. Detailing everything, subtle but insistent, were the entwined arms of a family crest, marking the fact that this was no ordinary dwelling. It was a mansion.

'My God!' said Charles.

Dorrie chuckled indulgently. 'Lovely, isn't it? The old man wasn't short of a few bob.'

'No. Well, at least they can't say they haven't got room.'

Dorrie got out of the car and went to the door with the ease of long acquaintance. The place didn't seem as well kept as in the past. Weeds sprouted through the gravel, and on the topmost floor the windows were smeared with cobwebs. She stood for long minutes waiting for someone to come to the door. Finally a woman answered. She was brown-haired and well-dressed in a blouse and the skirt of a suit, over the top of which she wore an apron.

'Good heavens,' she said stiffly. 'Dorrie. What a surprise.'

'Hello, Heather,' said Dorrie. 'May I come in? I've brought someone to see David.'

'Oh. I see. I think he's out in the garden – it isn't quite convenient—'

'Thanks a lot.' Dorrie smiled and moved inexorably forward. Heather had no choice but to move aside.

The hall was floored with black and white tiles. An umbrella stand shaped like a bear lurked in one corner and a vast oak side table dominated one wall. An impersonal place, thought Charles, and wondered if it had been decorated by Celia's parents, and untouched since. There was that feel about it. The kitchen, into which Heather reluctantly led them, was of more recent date. It was badly overdone, from the leaded panes in the cabinets to the frilly curtains at the windows. The vegetables for the dinner that Heather was preparing crouched apologetically on the work surface, the only evidence of disorder. Dorrie's kitchen was infinitely preferable, thought Charles.

He introduced himself, since Dorrie was being deliberately bad-mannered. 'Davenport. Charles Davenport.'

'How do you do? I'm Heather Wilcox. Would you like a drink?'

'Thank you.'

She fussed about finding a bottle of white wine, and in the end Charles opened it for her and waited while she dusted the cut glass. Heather looked like a person used to order, but the house, the mansion, was defeating her. He had the sense that she was sinking beneath the load. She couldn't get the glasses clean and went to wash them.

'Slosh it in cups, Heather,' said Dorrie impatiently.

'Really, Dorrie! Still just as slapdash, I see.'

Dorrie got up and looked around, although it made Heather uncomfortable. She watched every movement with the bright, angry eyes of a bird whose territory is threatened. Charles wondered if it was the intrusion she minded, or a possible discovery of bad housekeeping.

'Are the children here?' Dorrie asked, opening an unused cookery book, clearly kept for show. 'I haven't seen them in years.'

'They're in their rooms. Doing their homework.'

'Oh. Well, don't disturb them just for a long-lost

godmother, will you?' She returned the book to its shelf, upside-down.

Charles was beginning to enjoy himself. He had not realised that Dorrie disliked this woman so acutely. Her clothes, her manners, everything in fact, were planned to annoy. And Heather was becoming colder by the minute.

'If you could have let me know—' she said frostily.

'You know how it is, Heather. The unplanned, spontaneous impulse. A lovely evening, a duty to perform – we couldn't resist.'

'I'll go and fetch David.'

Dorrie pretended humility. 'If it isn't too much trouble.'

Heather changed her shoes for clean wellingtons and went out. Dorrie snorted. 'That woman! She'd have shut the door on us if she'd dared. In Celia's house. She always did have her eye on David.'

'You don't suspect her of sawing through Celia's brake cables, do you?'

Dorrie laughed and gulped at her wine. 'She's far too proper. An accountant, can't you tell? And Celia was driving too fast, she always did. She was due for an accident.'

'Did she drink?'

'Oh, yes. But she didn't drink and drive. She was just a mad driver, that's all.'

Charles went to the window and looked into the garden. Heather was coming back up the path with a tall, fair man in a mud-spattered sweater. She was talking and gesticulating, every gesture radiating annoyance. He was nodding in reply. Dorrie snorted. 'Look at the man. She's got him growing cabbages. When Celia lived here the place was crawling with staff. And they loved her. Remember that when you decide she was a good-time girl.'

He turned quickly and caught her morose stare. He grinned. 'A spoiled little rich girl, no less.'

Dorrie's gaze was unwavering.

The back door opened. David Sheraton came in first, shooting a sharp look at Dorrie and a sharper one at Charles. 'Hello, Dorrie,' he said. 'What brings you here after all this time?'

37

'You might well ask,' she said. 'May I introduce Charles Davenport? He's a doctor.'

'Oh.'

David and Heather exchanged a swift but telling glance. Expectant. Almost hopeful. Charles was suddenly aware that they were hoping he was here to tell them Celia was dead.

'I've been looking after your wife, Mr Sheraton,' he began. 'The last ten years must have been difficult for you.'

The man's face was tense and watchful. Pale eyes beneath that thatch of sandy hair, and lean, creased skin over long bones. Good-looking? Handsome? Yes.

Charles went on, 'As you know she's spent years in a light coma, showing no signs of waking. Lately we've been trying a different regime.'

'All his doing,' said Dorrie. 'Everyone else was prepared to let her rot.'

'Dorrie!' Charles quelled her. 'She was comfortable and settled. I made her less comfortable and less settled. The result has surprised us all.'

'What result? What's happened?' Heather was shrill with anticipated panic.

'Tell us what's happened.' David Sheraton's muddy fingers gripped the back of a chair.

Charles took a deep breath. 'Your wife has regained consciousness. She is still quite disabled but is moving towards what may well be substantial recovery.'

Nobody spoke. Dorrie took a thoughtful mouthful of wine, and Heather, noticing the movement, said, 'You bitch. This is all your doing. You always did have it in for me.'

'That isn't true,' said Dorrie quietly. 'After the accident you pushed me out. You never let me see my godchildren. And if you think I'd revive Celia just to spite you, then it confirms my view of your overwhelming conceit.'

David, staring at Charles, said, 'What's she like? I mean – can she talk? Remember?'

'At the moment she's still half-conscious much of the time,' he replied. 'But her lucid intervals are increasing. I thought it best to inform you now, before she's fully recovered. To allow you time to prepare yourselves.'

'A full recovery? She can actually achieve that?'

Dorrie said, 'We don't know.'

'She may retain the symptoms of a mild stroke,' said Charles. 'Or a more severe one. It all takes time. Now, I don't think she should see her children just yet but perhaps you'd like to visit, Mr Sheraton?'

Heather let out a tight, disbelieving sob. David's knuckles turned white on the back of the chair. 'I – I can't.'

'Let me assure you that I understand your problems,' said Charles. 'But remember, your wife has no knowledge of anything that's happened in the last ten years. As far as she's concerned her marriage still exists. She must expect to see you.'

'Has she said so?'

'Not yet,' said Dorrie. 'I honestly don't know if she does remember you, David. That's really why you've got to come.'

'For God's sake!' His face was pale with shock. He turned away from them, almost grey, and Heather said, 'You had no right to come here. You should have written. David doesn't have any obligation any more.'

Dorrie let out a crack of scornful laughter. 'Living in this house, you can say that? This is Celia's house! You're living off her inheritance!'

'Like hell we are!' flared Heather. 'That's you all over, Dorrie, spreading tittle-tattle. You and Celia are two of a kind – sluts!'

'I suppose someone as uptight as you would think the worst of Celia,' retorted Dorrie. 'David wouldn't look at you when she was around. But you dropped your standards pretty smartly once she was gone, didn't you?'

Charles, only half-listening, dropped a warning hand on her shoulder. He was watching David. The man was trembling, his skin clammy with icy sweat. Charles didn't know what he had expected, but not this. 'You must have known she might recover?' he said quietly. 'It must have crossed your mind?'

David shook his head. 'She was dead. They said her brain was dead and I was to think of her as gone.'

'You knew that wasn't true,' said Dorrie.

He rounded on her. 'So what was I to do? Spend every

minute of the last ten years at her side? I had children. A life. I believed what I had to believe.'

Charles said, 'Come on, Dorrie. Time to go.'

She sat for a moment as if intending to resist, but then, looking at David's face, got up. 'Look on the bright side,' she said ironically. 'She may never come out of hospital.'

'Dorrie,' said Charles. 'Out.'

In the car Dorrie was defensive. 'I never did like Heather,' she said.

Charles sighed and swung the wheel. 'My dear, that was more than a little obvious. I should have gone alone.'

'Wouldn't have made any difference. He's appalled at the thought of having Celia back. Men are so damned fickle. I could have sworn he loved her.'

Charles found himself thinking of Celia as he had seen her that day. She'd worn a dark dressing gown and her hair was once more in a long golden plait. The staff had her making baskets and she worked incredibly slowly, a smooth-skinned, dreamy beauty. She showed no sign that any time had passed since she was twenty-five, or if it had, it had passed in a reverse direction. It was as if she had been born fully formed, with skin as soft as any baby's, eyes as clear and hair as lustrous. Even her teeth seemed perfect, spared years of use. If she had looked like that at twenty-five, thought Charles, anyone would have loved her. But he was no romantic. Love was for the living, not the almost dead. It was not fear of a still burning love that beset David, but fear of a love that might begin again.

It was dark when they reached Dorrie's house. April evenings are still too short. Dorrie said, 'Are you so angry you won't come in?'

He was. But he thought of his own empty house. It would be cold there. 'What's on offer?' he asked morosely.

Dorrie giggled. 'What do you fancy? Roll in the hay? I won't shop you to the BMA.'

She got out of the car without waiting for him to reply. He followed her up the steps and into the house. She left the lights switched off, and he could hear a rustling. He reached out and encountered warm, naked flesh. The full glory of Dorrie's

40

great breasts was his, and he took huge handfuls of them, cramming the nipples into his mouth. Those breasts had tempted him from the very first.

She chuckled lewdly, and reached for his crotch. Her hands were small, well-kept, and expert. Excitement welled up in him, making him iron hard, and he began to throw off his clothes. In the dark, close to him, she was all soft flesh, and he wondered why he had never realised the attractions of fat women. She was luscious, engulfing, her breasts were like bread ready for kneading, topped with firm, round plums. Throwing off his clothes, he held her against him, a yielding mass as warm as a mud bath, a body in which he could wallow. A pile of fabric remnants lay in one corner of the kitchen, material for the puppet, and they subsided into it. There was a smell of cupboards and glue. For a second he was distracted and thought of Celia. Wife and mother. Temptress. Adulteress. Did ten years' sleep make her virgin again?

He went into Dorrie and she groaned. She undulated beneath him, absorbed in her own pleasure. What a sensualist the woman was. For a minute he wondered if she cared who she had inside her, and some of his excitement fell away. She was so obviously using his erection. The fabric pieces fell about them, he thought he felt a pin, and suddenly, too suddenly, he climaxed like an express train and it was done.

There was no awkwardness afterwards. They both knew it had been no more than friendship, a shared experience, like taking a roller-coaster ride in the same car. There was sex and there was passion, and they had shared simple sex. Charles thought how odd it was to sleep with someone who wasn't in love with him. He kissed Dorrie affectionately and said, 'We must do that again some time.'

She yawned lazily. 'I wonder what David and Heather are doing?'

They were sitting before a meagre log fire in the small sitting room of Blantyre House. There hadn't been time to talk before. The children had come down for supper, and tonight of all nights they were difficult about going to bed. David had drunk two brandies, and Heather, nerves twanging, now poured one for herself. 'You can't go and see her,' she said.

'You know I don't want to.'

'Don't you? Aren't you curious to see what she's like?'

He took his eyes from the fire and shot Heather a glance. His pulse was racing, and he felt a restless excitement that the brandy only seemed to fuel. Yet it almost seemed as if he had expected this day to come. Even Heather's dismay seemed inevitable. It had taken years to dull her anxieties about Celia, but he had always felt, always known, that the issue was unresolved. Which it was, of course. A dead wife was one thing, a half-dead wife something other. And a wife risen from the dead was something else again.

'You want to see her,' said Heather.

Why deny it? She knew it was true. 'It's only curiosity,' he said. 'Don't let it worry you. Celia and I were only married for six years, and we've been together for ten.'

'That's sixteen years, altogether,' said Heather stiffly. 'You've been married to her for sixteen years. And all through your anniversary you pretend you don't know which day it is, while you think of nothing else.'

His eyes were very pale. A muscle worked in his cheek, jumping frenetically. 'Perhaps it's guilt. You know I've wished her dead.'

'Have you? Really?' Her voice was harsh with disbelief and he felt annoyed with her suddenly. He had his own feelings to consider, he didn't want to spend hours in painstaking reassurance.

But Heather seemed to be mastering herself. After a moment she said, 'What will you say to her? She might ask about the children.'

'Yes. I suppose she might. I'll tell her what she wants to know.'

'Will you tell her about me? What will you say?'

'Heather, I haven't even said I'll go!'

She took up her brandy glass and drank the liquid down. It made her cough a little. Suddenly David remembered how Celia drank brandy, taking the merest sip, barely touching her lips with the stuff. In the end, she always emptied her glass into his. Once, after drinking brandy, he'd taken her for a drive on the racetrack they had then, driving like a lunatic one starlit, drunken night. The old, the reckless days.

'I know you want her back,' said Heather.

He ground down his irritation. Heather never left a subject, she chewed at it, endlessly. 'I don't at all. You know that isn't true. Heather, we're happy, don't spoil it.'

'I'm not spoiling it! It isn't my fault! You could have divorced her years ago. I begged you to divorce her!'

He closed his eyes for a long, hot second. 'Not that again, Heather. We thought she'd die. I didn't want the children to know. They are her children too.'

'It's guilt, isn't it? That's been the trouble, all these years, and you didn't cause the accident. She did!'

'I built the car.'

'She was driving too damned fast. Irresponsible, always irresponsible!'

'But the car was built for that! They said a tyre blew. She hadn't a chance.'

'Damn you, David! You always take her part.'

'For God's sake, Heather, you might at least try and understand.'

The trouble was there could be no understanding. It was an impossible situation. He almost wanted to laugh at the absurdity of it all. It was so like Celia, disrupting people's lives by the very fact of her charmed existence. He wondered if he could get away during the morning tomorrow, although they were up to their ears in work. Not everything had changed in ten years, the business was still struggling. What would Celia say? It was odd. He kept thinking of her as someone who had been away, to Australia or somewhere. The reality, of a life suddenly stopped, was harder to grasp. She had lost so many years. They had all lost because of it. Her life had been his life, he had wanted nothing but her. Oh God, the excitement of those years!

Heather was watching him, hot-eyed. 'Don't tell the girls,' she said. 'I won't forgive you if you tell the girls.'

Celia was sitting at the window, watching the sparrows on a flat roof below. Charles stood in the doorway watching her. It was tempting to fill every moment of her day with occupation, but surely a recovering brain needed time to reflect? The brain had two functions, one of operation and the other of storage, and Celia's brain was only slowly remembering how to assess, retain and recall information. When she was tired her previous day, let alone her previous life, appeared not to exist for her. She remembered nothing.

'Hello, Celia.' He walked towards her and she rewarded him with her brilliant smile.

'Mr Davenport. I'm watching the – feathers.'

'Birds, Celia.'

'No, no! Sparrows. I'm watching the sparrows.' She beamed at him again.

'What did you do yesterday, Celia? Remember.'

It was a ritual with them. Doing, describing, remembering. She recited the meals and activities, even the book she had tried to read, although she found reading tiring. Being read to was preferable, and she was always trying to persuade Charles or Dorrie to oblige.

Suddenly, in the midst of her recital, she said, 'Is my father coming today?'

Charles caught his breath. 'I don't know,' he prevaricated. 'Er – how old is your father?'

'Sixty-four,' said Celia.

'Do you mean he was sixty-four when you had your accident? That makes him seventy-four now.'

'Seventy-four? What do you mean?'

'That's how old he is. If he's still alive. I don't know your father.'

'He's sixty-four. I thought he was coming to see me.'

'Did someone tell you he was?'

Suddenly the lovely face fell into lines of weariness and confusion. She put up her hands and gripped her temples. To his surprise, because he was never affected by patients, Charles felt a great surge of feeling. He could almost imagine reaching out and embracing her. Watch it, Davenport, he thought. Dorrie's casual sensuality was in danger of rubbing off.

'I just thought he'd come and see me,' she said unhappily.

'In hospital. You'd think he would.'

'You've been in hospital a long time, Celia.'

'Yes. Is it long? Sometimes I feel as if it is, and sometimes – I wish I could go home.'

'Where do you live?'

She shook her head in distress. 'It isn't Blantyre House any more, is it?'

'You used to live there, I think.'

'But I don't live there now. We had a different house. Tree house – Oak House – something.' She wrestled with the thoughts, her face anguished. Then she turned to him, saying determinedly, 'Look, you've got to explain all this. I'm ill. I know I'm ill. What's happening?'

The direct question. The thing he had tried to avoid. It had come sooner than he expected, and he had no answer prepared. Sometimes patients asked for the truth when they really didn't wish to hear it. 'Tell me, Doctor,' they said. 'I can take it.' But some bad news was too terrible for anyone to bear. Death. Disfigurement. Pain. An end without dignity or repose. This was nothing so dreadful.

'You had an accident,' he said. 'A car accident. Your head was injured.'

She nodded impatiently. 'Yes. Yes. I want – I want—' Again the constriction of words. Finally she burst out, 'Was someone killed? Did I kill someone? Is that why no one comes?'

'Good Lord, no! Nothing like that. You've been ill, that's all. Unconscious. For – for a long time. It's been ten years.'

She looked at him in puzzlement. 'Somebody said that before,' she muttered. 'I don't understand this. I wish I could go home.'

'But you don't remember your home.'

She got up and stood like a deer about to run. Her breathing was quickening. In a moment she would hyperventilate. Charles wondered how long it would take to get her tranquillised. He should have set that up before he started this discussion. Her colour had drained to a chalky white, she was showing the classic symptoms of a panic attack. Who could blame her, trapped in an alien world?

45

'You're safe,' he soothed, taking her wrist and surreptitiously checking her pulse. 'You're safe with us.'

'I'm in prison! You won't let me go.'

'But you don't know where you want to go.'

'Home! Home to – I want to go – someone – I've got to go—'

At that moment the door opened. Celia spun round, Charles still gripping her wrist. She must not run out of here, she could do anything.

The man in the doorway stood stockstill, staring. It was David Sheraton – tall, fair-haired, in a pale blue jumper that seemed to leach the colour of his eyes almost to white. His wife shuddered and let out a little, helpless cry.

'Celia. Oh, my God, Celia.'

'Who – who?'

She looked from Charles to David and back again. Her face was a mask of anguished recognition. She remembered, thought Charles triumphantly. He should be recording this meeting. It would knock them dead at the Conference. He released his hold on Celia's wrist. She put her hands to her head and let out an appalled and anguished scream.

The room echoed for seconds after the sound died away. David Sheraton stood motionless in the doorway. Celia shut her eyes, as if she couldn't bear to look at him, and then turned in panic to the window, staring out at the birds, as if they would somehow shield her from terror. The muscles of her neck were as rigid as stone.

Sheraton said hoarsely, 'Celia? Darling? It's me. David.'

She whispered, 'I don't know you. This is a nightmare. Go away.'

'Of course you know me! Darling, of course you do.'

'Please go away.'

Charles said, 'What's the matter, Celia? What's upset you?'

She took a deep breath. 'I don't suppose you know, but – that isn't my husband. I don't know who he is. He's pretending to be my husband.'

'I've changed, Celia,' said David. 'It's been such a long time.'

Her voice rising, she cried, 'Why aren't my parents here? Why doesn't anyone come?'

Charles put both hands on her shoulders. 'I'm sorry, but your parents are dead.'

'Dead? Dead? You say this is my husband and my parents are dead? I saw them yesterday. I was at home. Am I going mad? And – and my – my—' she fought for a word that would not come '– my children! Where are my children? Why has no one brought them here?'

'Oh, my God,' said David Sheraton and put his face against the wall.

In a deliberate and clear voice Charles said, 'The last time you saw your husband or your children was ten years ago.'

Celia, looking from one man to the other, let out a second terrible scream.

Chapter Four

Celia lay in the bed, wrapped in a cloud of vague thought. Where was she? What was this day? In a moment her mother would come and call her for school. But gradually as the mist cleared she felt the confusion again. She knew no one. Everything was changed. Whoever it was who was staging this elaborate trick knew nothing of her family and friends, to send people who so little resembled them. She had believed in Dorrie at first, but not any more. Not after David.

A hand smoothed her brow. She looked up and saw a woman she did not know. But her voice was familiar. 'There, Celia,' said Sister Johnson. 'They've all been upsetting you. Rest now.'

'I want to go home,' she said. 'I want my father.'

'I don't believe he can come. Just you go to sleep.'

The touch was infinitely soothing. Celia wanted to let her thoughts go, releasing her grip on them to let them float away, leaving her at peace. There was no greater pleasure than this empty tranquillity. Nothing could be better than to sleep. The memories would go, she would let them go . . . Suddenly she sat up.

'They must have taken my children,' she said.

Sister Johnson said snappily, 'No one's done anything to your children. As far as I know they are growing up to be happy and confident people. Lie down again and be sensible.'

Celia glared at her. She didn't want to sleep any more, she had no thought of sleeping. 'How old are my children?'

Sister Johnson licked her lips. 'I really don't know.'

It was too much. Celia flung out of the bed and ran from the room, running across pink carpet and then brown tiles and finally the pink terrazzo of the main corridor. People stared

49

but she dodged past them, and someone behind shouted, 'Stop her! Stop that woman, at once!'

She was out of breath. Her legs were shaking. Such a little distance, too! Charles Davenport, coming swiftly out of a ward, caught her as she fell.

She cried for two hours. He told her the story once, then twice, and finally resigned himself to starting again every time he reached the end. If she knew what he was saying, if she understood it, then she could not commit her belief.

'You are telling me my life has gone,' she said once. 'I died. I'm like Lazarus, raised from the dead.'

'That's one way of looking at it.'

'Why didn't I die? My life's gone and I never knew.'

'You're only thirty-five, Celia.'

'But – that's old. Yesterday, I was young!'

He let her cry. What else could he expect? Her parents had died unmourned, and she must mourn them. Her children had grown up without her love. A great slice of her youth had been stolen from her. Whatever path she had been treading had been torn up and destroyed, and before her stretched a cavern of uncertainty. What else could she do but weep?

When at last it showed signs of abating, he asked her if she would like to see someone. 'Not David,' she muttered. 'Not yet.'

'No. Dorrie.'

She nodded. Her face was swollen and blotched, and her nose was running. He took out his camera and took a photograph, and she blinked in the light of the flash. 'Why are you always doing that?'

'You're my patient, Celia. I have to keep a record.'

She nodded, believing him. At that moment her life was like a quicksand, with deadly holes threatening everywhere. There was nothing to trust, not even her own senses. Yet Davenport told her the truth. She clung to her one article of faith, believing what he said even when it was truly unbelievable. It was all she could do.

When Dorrie came in she ran to Celia, making little clucking noises. 'Darling, darling, how awful for you! Waking up and finding everything changed. Oh, darling, don't be upset!'

'Mr Davenport says I'll be – good – gooder – better in a few days,' sobbed Celia. 'He says I'll get used to things.'

'Charles said that? He's probably right. Oh, darling, you're not too shocked by everything, are you?'

Celia gestured helplessly. 'Everyone's changed.'

Dorrie went pink. 'You mean me, don't you? I've got so terribly fat.'

'I decided it couldn't be you,' confessed Celia. 'You were – odd.'

Dorrie snorted. 'It isn't me! One day I'll be thin again. Only not yet.'

Celia tried to smile, and sobbed instead. Her distress was heartbreaking, thought Charles, taking himself off. No one who saw it – apart from himself, of course – could fail to feel for her. He wondered how long it would be before she was fit for anything more than a hospital ward. Years, perhaps. Maybe never. The administration had nothing to fear. There was plenty of time, time enough for Charles himself to feature her in a dozen studies of coma. The publicity would be wonderful. Then he would have his positron scanner, his micro-surgical video, his trauma team.

Sadly, of course, Celia must remain in hospital care. After all, if she confronted life too soon, apparently healthy but with definite residual weaknesses, in his judgment mental collapse was inevitable.

But Celia was thinking differently. 'I'm sure I'll be all right once I get home,' she was saying. 'I so want to see the children.'

'Yes,' said Dorrie warily.

Celia, alert to every nuance of speech, challenged: 'Why can't I go home? I remember now. I want to go to The Oaks. Why can't I go there?'

'David doesn't live there any more, darling. After your parents died he took the children and moved to Blantyre House.'

'Oh. Oh, I see.'

Celia felt terribly weary suddenly. It was all so hard to take in. Now they told her the house was gone. It wasn't a good house, merely the only house they could afford, marrying so

51

hastily against her father's wishes. They had decorated it together, she and David, and then, when her father forgave them, she had filled it with furniture borrowed from Blantyre House. All that was gone. What had happened to it all? The pretty mobile in Lucy's room, the stencils in Ellen's? But harder still to accept was the image of David in Blantyre House, and her parents, her mother, more permanent than any furnishings, quite gone.

She opened her mouth to ask Dorrie when her parents had died. 'Them – time – down—' she said. The words were hiding from her again. She was certainly going mad then, and who could blame her? The world had gone insane. The thought was in her head but she had no words to express it. Where did the bloody words go? 'Bloody!' she said in exasperation.

'Bloody bloody,' agreed Dorrie. 'You're tired, love. I'll come tomorrow.'

She wandered away down the corridors, unsettled as she often was after visiting Celia. All the years since the accident had been punctuated with these uncomfortable visits, and mostly she had prayed for just this event. Now it had come she was horribly afraid that this was worse than before. It was so hard to think of any future Celia could have.

As she turned the corner she met David. He was carrying a bunch of drooping flowers. To Dorrie the flowers said everything. 'You don't have to be so obviously half-hearted,' she said. 'Anyway, she can't see you. She's tired and the doctor doesn't think it's wise.'

'Did you see her?' Dorrie nodded. He stood uncertainly and then tossed the flowers into a bin. 'Come and have a drink,' he said.

They went to the Star and Garter, overlooking the park. A bowl of late hyacinths stood on the table, and there was a delicious smell of steak and kidney pie. Dorrie suggested that they eat, but David sighed. 'Heather's bound to have something on the go.'

'Don't tell me you're hen-pecked!'

He shrugged. 'Call it what you like. Heather's been very good to me. Just at the moment I don't like to upset her.'

Dorrie grimaced and took a slurp of gin. She wondered why

52

David made her so angry. Had she really expected him to stay at Celia's side for ten years? It was obviously unreasonable. But to take up with Heather – Heather! After Celia it was almost an insult.

She held up her glass and studied David through it. He looked tired, as if he wasn't sleeping. But he had always had that slightly ravaged look, as if he was just this side of debauchery. It was one of his charms, incongruous now that he was so resolutely house-trained.

Suddenly he said, 'What's going to happen, Dorrie? What can I tell her? We can't pick up where we left off. There's Heather.'

'Get rid of her,' said Dorrie callously.

'Oh, for Christ's sake!' He finished his whisky and went for another.

When he came back he sat reflecting for a moment. 'I wouldn't go back ten years even if I could,' he said. 'You know what she was like.'

'You adored her.'

'Yes.' He closed his eyes for a second. When he opened them he made an apologetic gesture. 'She was adorable! But the rows, Dorrie. I never knew where she was, or who she was with. The debts . . . We were always in debt. When I started with Heather you can't imagine the peace of it.'

'You and Celia always made up,' said Dorrie. 'I seem to remember you liked that part.'

He gave her a cold look. 'Did she tell you everything that went on in our bedroom, Dorrie?'

She grinned naughtily. 'I told her what went on in mine. It was a different age, David. She married too young. But I know she loved you terribly, and still does.'

He flinched, as if she had said something unforgivable. Suddenly Dorrie felt sorry for him. He had done his best, and no one could do more. It wasn't a crime to exclude her from his life because she was Celia's friend and she reminded him. It wasn't a crime to find another woman to share his bed. None of this was David's fault.

She put her hand on his. 'She's not coming out for months, maybe years,' she assured him. 'You're going to have time to

53

explain. We all are. At the moment she needs time and patience, we can't tell her everything at once. Charles Davenport thinks she might always need nursing.'

'Bit bloody arrogant, that doctor.'

'Yes. Young and brilliant, it takes them like that. But he's all right.'

Dorrie finished her drink and waited for David to notice and buy her another. He had the money after all. The sunshine was striking warm through the window and she wondered idly what he had done with Celia's inheritance. They should have had help in the house. Was it all in trust for the girls?

'The money's going to be a problem,' she said.

'What?' He looked puzzled.

'The money. Celia's money.'

'She hasn't any money. Her parents made a gift to the hospital on condition they cared for Celia as long as necessary, and that was all.'

'Oh. So you got it.'

The skin thinned across the bridge of his nose. 'Wrong guess, Dorrie. Try again.'

'Well, it can only be the girls! It's in trust for them, right?'

David did not speak for a moment. But the lines from nose to mouth seemed to deepen visibly. 'The money wasn't left to me, or Celia, or the girls. Joe decided – Celia's father thought I wasn't to be trusted with a fortune. And he thought it would be good for me to have to provide for the girls. So he left me the house and nothing else.'

Dorrie gaped. 'So what happened to the loot?'

'The loot, as you so touchingly describe it, went to Celia's cousin. Edwin Braddock.'

There was no disguising his bitterness. And who wouldn't be bitter, deprived of the Braddock millions? Joe Braddock had been an autocrat to the last, it seemed, trying to manipulate people even from the grave. Yet fate, that mischievous tyrant, had caused him to slight the person he had loved most in all the world. Celia. His beloved daughter.

'I thought at least she wouldn't have to worry about money,' said Dorrie wonderingly. 'Now what?'

'I thought you said she'd be in hospital for years?'

'Well – yes.'

On the way home she found herself wondering about Edwin Braddock. She had been as close to the Braddock family as anyone but she never recalled meeting him. But surely, rich as he must be, he would find it in his heart to give Celia a share? Now that she was beginning to recover.

The office was large to the point of inconvenience. The desk, a giant slab of wood dragged protesting from some tropical fastness, dominated only a corner. A trackless waste of apricot carpet separated it from a conference setting of low chairs around a smoked glass table, with mobile telephones slotted into its hollow legs. Another acre of space intervened before the bar was discovered, crammed with bottles and glass. It was the sort of room which would swallow a boardroom table seating twenty, but instead it was full of intimidating space.

Edwin Braddock had not chosen this office. It was Joe's creation, when he had flung aside the advice of wife and daughter and indulged every megalomaniac whim. He had shelves of executive toys, from replica miniaturised brass cannon to working models of steam trains and irritating table lamps running on the intermittent rays of rare gases. Without assistance, he had created an uncomfortable and threatening space, and Edwin retained it only because of that threat. In this office, only the man entitled to be there could relax. Supplicants and complainants alike were at once made insecure.

He crossed to the bar and poured himself a campari and soda. The bitter drink suited his mood. Six long months had passed since he first began to think of taking over the Marlborough chain of gambling clubs, and today he had conceded defeat. Try as he might, the last bastions of family loyalty had held; he could not persuade one more Marlborough aunt, second cousin or half-witted niece to sell their shares. Marlborough would remain in the stranglehold that had held it back for twenty years, a plaything of aristocratic nepotists. And the Braddock Consortium held only a bunch of over-priced shares.

He sat down in one of the low chairs, putting his feet on the glass coffee table. He was a man who should have been taller, broad in the shoulder and chest. Four inches more height would have given him a degree of elegance that he did not now possess. Instead he was of middle height, with a chunkiness that no tailor could disguise. His hair was brown, his skin dark, and his eyes a peculiar mixture of brown flecked with blue. Individually his features were unattractive, but taken together he was pleasant enough. The deficiencies of nature were countered by a quiet style of dress.

His drink was almost finished. He contemplated getting up and pouring another, because tonight he saw no virtue in anything except getting drunk. What he hated more than losing was the way he had lost; the snide 'I told you so's in the press, the crowing of the Marlborough family, kicking a would-be interloper off the battlements. Everyone was so eager to label Braddock enterprise Yorkshire impertinence, and to see Marlborough intransigence as the admirable stand of the Old Guard. The evening papers carried pictures of George Marlborough celebrating with vintage champagne out of superior cut glass, while one of the liveried servants of their over-rated clubs looked on. Edwin felt the iron enter his soul. Damn George Marlborough!

There came a knock on the door. 'Yes?'

A young man entered, clutching a folder defensively in front of him. 'The monthly reports, sir.'

'Take the bloody things away. I'll see them tomorrow.'

'I thought there might be one or two items of interest—'

'Tomorrow, Cartwright!'

'Yes, sir.'

But as the man prepared to scuttle from the room, Edwin remembered his drink. 'Cartwright—don't run away like that. Get me another drink.'

'Yes, sir. Of course, sir.'

He put the folder down on the table next to Edwin and took away the empty glass. A clock was ticking loudly, and Cartwright chinked bottles and glasses. He wasn't good at this, it wasn't his job, but Edwin's assistants had to be flexible. He felt a flicker of irritation. Even the little noises annoyed him tonight. The edge of one paper protruded tantalisingly from the folder and Edwin was bored and irritated by even so much as Cartwright's low, nervous breaths. Damn the man! He tugged at the paper and scanned it.

'What in God's name do you mean by this?'

Cartwright jumped and splashed soda on to the carpet. 'Sir?'

'Don't "sir" me, you incompetent jackal! Why wasn't this brought to my attention at once?'

'You said—'

'I know what I said! Clearly this is important. Far too important to be left to moulder in a file I may inspect eventually.'

Cartwright was not only unhappy but bewildered. 'I'm afraid I don't know – which report is it, sir?'

'Give me that drink.'

Edwin gulped at his glass and then read the short report again. It was from the hospital, the regular briefing on Celia. Year after year there had been nothing new except the date, and now, today of all days, it was different.

We are delighted to report that Mrs Sheraton has regained consciousness. Although still subject to periods of confusion and vocal difficulty, she has recovered substantially in the areas of memory and understanding. In the absence of further instructions we are continuing with therapies designed to improve her level of consciousness and her understanding of her situation.

Mrs Sheraton is experiencing periods of severe depression, allied to weakness on her right side. We anticipate that both these problems will diminish as time goes on, and it is our confident hope that at some point in the future, as yet undetermined, she will be able to lead a relatively full life whilst still enjoying our care and support.

Braddock looked up from the paper and registered the

shrinking form of the unfortunate Cartwright. 'Go away, man,' he muttered. 'Go home.'

'There are some letters for you to sign, sir.'

'Go home, Cartwright!'

Edwin waited until the boy was gone, waited until he was sure he had left the building. At last he was alone. With a cry like an enraged bull he picked up the smoked glass table and smashed it against the bar. Glass exploded into the room, and booze ran like lava across the carpet. The smell of spirits was overpowering. Braddock took hold of the metal frame of the table and began using it like an unwieldy club, breaking every bottle and every glass that remained. His heart was racing, and he felt drunk at last. The pleasure of this destruction was almost sexual. Finally, when there was nothing left intact, he stopped. Now he felt better. Now he felt good. When tomorrow came he would think about all this very carefully, but not tonight. Tonight was a night when he wouldn't go home.

David Sheraton was also late home that night, and he too was at work, in the small, meticulous factory that handmade the Sheraton sports car. He had a staff of ten and between them they turned out perhaps four cars a year. It was a precarious life. The motoring world loves adventure and excitement, but likes its pleasure to be vicarious in the main. And inevitably David's cars were expensive. Not many people bought Sheraton cars.

He went into his small, wood-panelled office and sat at his desk. Heather would be waiting for him, but no matter. He needed to be alone, he needed to think. As the days passed he felt as if he was living a totally false existence, with his everyday manners pasted over a maelstrom of memory and guilt. He wanted desperately to go and see Celia! And he hated himself for that desire, because in these last few years he had been happy.

Why hadn't she died? It was Joe Braddock's fault. He had railed and screamed at the doctors, he was going to keep his daughter alive through force of will alone. Nothing had been left undone, no magic remedy untried. David remembered

58

praying, long into the night. He had even prayed, one long and terrible night, that if she died he should die too. Prayers were dangerous, David thought. The greatest danger is that they should be answered. She had been so lovely. And – horribly, incredibly, cruelly – she was lovely still.

But she wasn't normal. He clung to that litany, that excuse. No one said she was normal, and he didn't believe that she ever would be normal again. The doctor's assurances were so much sound and fury. They always thought of themselves as miracle workers, and never told the truth. To Davenport it would be enough that Celia could walk and talk, he wouldn't care that she wasn't the same as before. He hadn't known her. She could never be like that again. David had come to terms with the fact that Celia was irretrievably damaged, and he wasn't prepared to alter that position now. But suppose – suppose – his mind raced away unbidden – she did get almost well?

He felt the sudden tug of sexual excitement. His body remembered. It refused absolutely to forget. She had bound him a prisoner with her long golden hair, she had kissed away his protests with lips that left him speechless with desire. He had wanted her from the very first day. To his shame, to his terrible shame, he had longed for her even when she lay in her hospital bed and knew nothing. His need of Celia, once the cement that held them together, had eventually disgusted him. He had abandoned her. He knew it now. Unable to stand seeing her, he had left her in that bed and gone away.

He got up and began to pace the confines of his office. The brass and mahogany had been Celia's idea, and had in the end proved good value, outlasting any amount of modern tat. The fights they had had over money. Over men. Eventually no doubt they would have fought over the children as well. Lucy was twelve now, and Ellen fourteen. They both had Celia's eyes.

But Heather had mothered those children and he would never cease to be grateful. She had done so much, accepting without question that she would have no babies of her own. He knew now he shouldn't have asked her to accept that. Another child would have changed everything. But Heather was an accountant, and the money she brought in was important to them, the jam on his plain bread. She had brought order and security, reassurance and support. Heather had been there when he needed her most.

He felt the familiar rage against Joe Braddock. He could have left David a few hundred thousand and never felt the draught. Even the gift of Blantyre House was a sly, round the corner sort of thing. It was David's outright, on condition Celia's children were brought up there. So, the house was worth a million and cost a fortune to maintain and he couldn't sell it. Between them, the Braddocks had stitched him up.

He flung himself down in his chair again, and slipped a silver hip flask from his drawer. He was drinking too much, but that was Celia's fault. She was a creature of excess. He should have known there was trouble the moment Dorrie turned up again. He sighed, and closed his eyes to rest them, although images played endlessly against his lids. Had he really changed so much that she didn't know him? He remembered the day he took her flying, white with fright in an open-cockpit biplane, enduring it only because she loved him and he said it was safe. Having her babies, in pain, she had wanted no one but him. Why had it all come to this?

In a minute or two he would get up and go home to Heather. There would be an atmosphere. She would suspect he had been to see Celia. And soon, very soon, he would.

Celia had decided that she wanted to wear ordinary clothes. The difference between her and the rest of the world seemed to be epitomised by her dressing gowns and their more serviceable garments. She had nothing to do, and nothing was expected of her, whilst everyone else had important business.

But nobody brought her any clothes. Every request was ignored. It was as if she was a child, wanting something outlandish and out of the question. Rage rose up in her, taking her by surprise. She had never known such anger. Now, helpless and at the mercy of others, she felt it as never before.

Eventually a young nurse came, inexperienced in refusal. 'I don't see why you shouldn't wear clothes, Mrs Sheraton,' she said helpfully. 'After all, Mr Davenport takes you out in the grounds and all.'

'I do feel silly out there,' replied Celia, mealy-mouthed and devious. 'It's embarrassing. He's a man, he doesn't understand.'

The nurse rummaged about in the cupboards on the private wing, and came back with Celia's clothes.

She recognised them at once. Her blue short skirt, knee boots and tight sweater with the roll collar. Favourite things, all of them, and the jumper only a little stained. How good it was to see her own clothes. She felt more joy than seeing Dorrie or David. They had changed while the clothes had not. They were her own still.

She went into the bathroom and stared at herself in the inadequate mirror. It was like looking at a distant acquaintance. The face was still familiar, but so much was different. It was as if all experience had been wiped away. A bland face, with an odd, mindless beauty. But, once she was dressed, she would know herself again.

She put her clothes on hurriedly, and they felt tight and restricting. For a moment she wondered if she had put on weight, but when she stood on a chair to see herself she saw it wasn't that at all. She was still slender enough. She took a deep breath and the sensation was as vivid as the very first time she had worn a bra; the same entrapment by iron bands, where before there had been freedom. Clothes were a discipline, marking the end of her formless days. As a finishing touch, a badge of adulthood for others to see, she coiled her hair on top of her head and fastened it with blanket pins filched from the linen cupboard. Now she was ready.

All at once she felt shy. If she went back to the ward everyone would look at her. So she wouldn't go back to the ward at all, but out in the long corridors of the hospital, pretending she was a visitor or someone. She felt excited, like a child taking a bus ride alone.

Celia crept from the bathroom and down the passage. No one stopped her. Soon she was in the long, central corridor that ran the length of the hospital, and walked briskly along. But suddenly she felt that the walls were crowding towards her, and the floor undulating unpleasantly. It was like a boat ride on a swelling sea, without any hope of land. She took a turning at

61

random, saw a door, and blundered helplessly out into the open. She was in the garden, full of soft air and sunshine. She staggered to a bench and sat down.

Gradually she calmed. She hadn't expected to feel so odd, that was all. But her body knew this was unfamiliar, even if she herself was unaware of it. She was truly a child again, her own child, learning to walk. Celia giggled to herself, and was surprised by a rush of emotion. Darling Lucy, darling Ellen – her adored and lovely babies. Where were they now?

A shadow fell across her and she looked up. A man stood there, in paint-stained workclothes. 'Mind if I sit down?'

She glanced around and saw a number of empty benches. 'Yes,' she said. 'I do mind.'

'Don't be unfriendly, sweetheart.'

'I – go away.'

'No need for that. Pretty girl like you.'

Celia squinted up against the sun. She often got chatted up, but not usually by the likes of him. 'I'm a mental patient,' she said in a shrill voice. 'I have fits. My doctor doesn't like me to go out.'

'Jesus wept! Sorry, love.'

He backed rapidly away, and Celia practised an off-putting twitch. Then she saw Dorrie coming across the grass towards her. 'Celia! My God, where did you get those clothes? You look like a lady of the night.'

'What?'

'Definitely got the price on your shoe.'

'Who? Me?' Celia peered down at her lovely blue clothes.

Dorrie nodded. 'Short skirt, long boots, tight sweater. Jumble sale clothes. Did the nurse find them for you?'

Unaccountably Celia's eyes filled. 'They're my clothes,' she stammered. 'The ones I had before.'

'Darling! Are they really? Oh, yes, look, there's blood on the sweater. To think they still fit. I use my old clothes as dusters.'

'I might, if I had any others,' said Celia caustically. 'Or if I had anything to dust.'

Dorrie sat down and allowed a silence to develop. She could see Celia was upset. 'Has David been to see you?' she asked.

Celia shook her head. 'I don't think they'll let him come. I behaved so badly before. No one had explained, you see. Poor David.'

'Yes,' said Dorrie doubtfully. Mentally she strangled David. He never did have any consideration. No doubt he was giving in to Heather's mean-spirited panic, and deserting Celia without so much as a backward glance. Thank God she only saw the fringes of her plight. If she saw the whole thing she'd be devastated.

'Why don't we go out for a cup of tea?' she suggested.

'What? You mean out of the hospital?'

Dorrie nodded. Charles Davenport might want to keep Celia incarcerated like a specimen in a bottle, but she saw no reason to aid and abet him in that. She looked up and saw two or three young men standing at upper windows, giving Celia the once over. How odd that clothes of cool elegance could mutate into tartiness, given ten years or so. It was a salutary lesson.

They went to a café in the High Street. Celia was suddenly very silent, and Dorrie wondered if perhaps they should have gone for a drive instead. Perhaps Charles was right and she wasn't ready for life.

'I suppose it is a bit busy,' she conceded. 'After the hospital.'

'Everything's different!' whispered Celia. 'It's all – horrible.'

She couldn't believe how the world had changed. Even the hair. Girls wore it in tangled messes, falling into their eyes. Luminous track suits were everywhere, and the café, which she remembered as chic in chrome and plastic, had become wreathed in oak chairs and dried flowers. Even the cars on the road had changed, with half of them white and all of them the same blunt shape. 'I feel like a marshmallow,' she said helplessly, and closed her eyes, because the word was wrong, as the world was wrong.

'Martian,' supplied Dorrie. 'They used to sell synthetic ice cream here. Now it's herb tea and home-made cakes.'

They had a cake apiece. Celia found hers very sweet, and her jaws were soon tired with the act of chewing. Everything tired

63

her: the noise, the bustle, and above all the constant need to think. Where am I? What is this? Where should I go? She, who had always been confident, was threatened with suffocating panic. She clung to the table, willing the fear to retreat back into her cowardly soul.

Suddenly the door of the café burst open. Everyone looked up, startled. It was Charles Davenport, in a towering rage. 'Dorrie! Who the hell gave you permission to take Celia out?'

She waved a cream-cake at him. 'I don't need permission. Celia's fine. Don't fuss.'

'Fuss? I don't fuss. But anything could have happened to her. She could have relapsed. And I'm presenting a paper on her next week.'

Dorrie made a face. It had long been clear to her that Charles had more in mind for Celia than mere recovery. 'Celia deserved a treat,' she said mildly. 'She's still a human being, even if she is your passport to global recognition.'

Charles summed up Celia's condition in a glance. 'Some treat. She's almost catatonic. Let's get her back.'

Between them they half carried her back to the ward. She was exhausted and tearful, her speech in tatters. Charles discovered the nurse who had brought the clothes and gave her a verbal thrashing. She wasn't even allowed to help put Celia to bed. He hovered outside the curtains until his patient was ready, listening to her weary sobs. At last he went in to see her.

'Let's take your pulse and look in your eyes. I'll prescribe a sedative.'

Tears ran down Celia's cheeks and into the pillow. Her hair was loose again. Charles thought suddenly that in one way it was a pity she was so beautiful, it was a distraction from her case. He had been taken aback by her in the coffee shop, and others would be too. Perhaps ten years ago her appearance was quite ordinary, or at least not so extraordinary as it seemed now. But in the long years in hospital she had acquired an almost abstract sexuality that seemed quite divorced from her consciousness.

Celia said, 'No – please – not here. Home.'

'Don't you want to stay here, Celia? You were frightened outside.'

'Home. David.'

He let his fingers rest against her cheek. 'Not yet, my dear. You've a long way to go before we talk about that. Tomorrow I'll take some more photographs and do some more tests. And if it's clothes you want, no doubt Sister can find you something appropriate. Don't worry about it. I'll take care of you.'

The tears flowed again from Celia's eyes. She was too tired to speak, or even think in words, but not too tired for anger. Today she had pretended to be a mental patient, but now they were treating her as one. They took her own clothes and promised some sack of a dress, and they tested and poked at will. Why didn't they let her family come? Where were her children? No one came and she was left here at the mercy of this godlike, autocratic man. All her thoughts centred on getting away. On going home.

Chapter Five

'Hello, my dear.'

Celia looked up and saw a man she didn't know. He was wearing dark glasses and an overcoat. 'Hello,' she said, noncommittally.

'Do you remember me?'

She put a hand to her head. 'I'm sorry – I'm not sure.'

'Don't worry. It's not important.'

He sat down beside her, and she wondered if he was some sort of psychiatrist. Every now and then Davenport would show her off to one of his colleagues, and she had to answer questions and fill in quizzes. But she didn't remember this man.

Gradually, as time went on, she was constructing two different sets of memories: now, that is after the accident, and then, before it. She judged them by two different standards. 'Now' time was easily remembered, and she rarely made mistakes. 'Then' was easy to recall too, but mistakes were common, or at least people said they were. She found it annoying, although she was ill and wasn't meant to be annoyed at being wrong. But how could anyone be as sure of themselves as these medical people, even about memory? Ten years was a long time, as everyone constantly said. It wasn't for her. It was yesterday.

'You look very well,' said the stranger. People always said that.

'Thank you.' She smoothed the skirt of the red wool dress Dorrie had brought for her. It had full sleeves and pleats, and Celia thought it dire. But Dorrie said it was fashionable enough. She had fought a battle with Davenport over Celia's right to wear proper clothes, and victory meant this red dress.

If she ever got out of here, Celia vowed, she would buy enough clothes to sink a ship.

'Why don't we go for a walk?'

Definitely a psychiatrist, then. The shrinks invariably liked wandering amidst the tulips and talking about life. As far as Celia could make out from their pointed and intrusive chats, they wanted her to 'come to terms' with her situation. She didn't know what they meant, but when she said so they looked pained. But what did they mean? Here she was, in hospital, with ten years wiped from her life, her mind precariously balanced and her body under only limited control. She was too weak to speak much, or to go out, or it seemed to be visited by her family, and if 'coming to terms' meant a bovine acceptance of all that, then she declined.

She got up and walked to the door. The psychiatrist followed slowly, and she stood waiting for him to turn the handle. He was obviously surprised that it should be expected. Manners had deteriorated in the last ten years, she decided. Perhaps doctors never had any in the first place. They treated their patients like a sub-species.

Celia led the way into the garden and began the ritual pacing of the lawn. The day was grey and overcast. 'What would you like to talk about?' she asked her companion. 'I've done childhood traumas, and your colleague had a lot of fun with maternal deprivation. I think he was saving sex for a treat, but we can do that now if you like.'

'What?'

She looked at him sardonically. It never paid to be funny with psychiatrists. 'Don't bother.'

They walked to the rose bed, turned and began the return leg. The man seemed uncomfortable, as if he found walking unpleasant. Why, then, were they here? thought Celia irritably. But then he said, 'Why don't I take you for a drive?'

She blinked. This was new. 'Does Mr Davenport say that's a good idea? He gets cross if I do something without asking.'

'He thinks it's a brilliant idea. In fact, he suggested it.'

'Oh. Oh, I see.'

If Davenport said it was all right then it would be. On the other hand, how dare he decide without telling her? She trusted him, but he made her so angry. Like her father all over again. Sometimes she woke up in the night and couldn't believe her father was dead. She remembered him that summer day, wearing his panama to play tennis. He cheated and gave bad calls to make sure that he won, and no one except her dared call him a liar. She had called him a liar and he had gone off and died. Years had separated the two events, but to her that was the reality.

Disquiet grew as she walked slowly across the car park. The sky seemed wide and threatening now she was so far from any building, in so much space. 'Are you sure Mr Davenport wants me to go with you?' she asked the doctor. 'He doesn't normally let me do much except with him.'

'He knows I'll look after you.' He had a wide, honest smile. As wide as the sky.

His car was big, with leather seats. Celia, who loved cars, sniffed appreciatively. 'How lovely! I've got a Mercedes, you know. At least – I used to have one. That and a Sheraton, the car my husband makes. When I come out of hospital I'll have good cars again.'

'They're expensive, you know.'

She laughed. 'It's all right. I'm not poor. If a psychiatrist can afford leather, then I'm sure I can too.' She slid into the passenger seat. Bliss. She was inside again, away from the empty sky.

They drove away, not talking at all. Celia was surprised. In her now considerable experience psychiatrists talked to you if you didn't talk to them. She rolled her head on the leather squabs and looked again at the man at her side. There was something familiar about him – something she recognised.

'You didn't tell me your name,' she said cautiously.

'No. So I didn't.'

Bland, uncompromising. She felt the first stirrings of alarm. 'I want to go back.'

'Nonsense! We've only just started.'

'Take me back. I insist. I want to go back right now!'

'Calm down, Celia. You're not at all well. I shall take you back when I'm good and ready, and not before.'

His voice . . . He had abandoned the objective, doctorish

tone. It was deeper. Accented. He was older than she had thought. Was he a doctor? Had he said so? Shrilly, nervously, she said, 'You haven't any right to take me away.'

'I'm doing it, though.'

She realised, suddenly, that he would not take her back at all. Panic rose like a wild animal. She was powerless in its jaws. This was what lurked beyond the hospital – stark terror. Her stomach heaved, her palms sweated, she would choke on vomit and airlessness. She had to get back! She had to get out! Shrugging off her seat belt, her fingers scrabbled at the door. He reached across and grabbed her arm. 'Keep still or you'll get hurt. I mean it.'

She bent her head and sank her teeth into him, gagging on hairs and skin. He let out a strangled cry and the car swerved madly. They mounted the kerb and he let her go, his wrist dripping blood from her teeth. She tugged at the door handle and this time it gave way. She flung herself out, into emptiness.

Dorrie was alone in her house when the doorbell rang. She was making bread, up to her elbows in flour, but the frantic insistence of the ringing made her open the door at once. Charles stood there, an apparition in the green cotton trousers and top of the operating theatre. He was wearing white wellingtons and his mask hung round his neck.

'Don't tell me,' said Dorrie. 'You're a lobotomy-gram.'

'Is Celia here? She's missing.'

'Oh God.'

He could see at once that Dorrie knew nothing. He leaned against the doorpost, suddenly overcome with weariness. This, on top of a six-hour operation and no food. In spite of all his care, no one had seen Celia go, except for an orderly who thought she might have had someone with her. 'It's all your fault,' he told Dorrie. 'She couldn't have gone without clothes.'

Dorrie said, 'You want to keep her forever. She'll have gone shopping or something, she'll come back. Come and eat something before you pass out.'

She fed him soup, and lumps of risen dough deep-fried. It

was delicious and was probably furring up an artery a minute. He speculated on the humiliation of ending up a heart patient, when he had campaigned ceaselessly for one of their theatres to be given to him.

'What's the hospital doing?' asked Dorrie, putting her chin in her floury hands.

'They've called the police and started a search. Apparently Celia's father left them a vast sum on condition that his daughter was properly cared for. If she isn't, they might have to give it back, which is concentrating everyone's minds. I'm being castigated for not putting her in a locked ward.'

'She isn't some sort of idiot!'

'And she isn't normal. This proves it.'

'There's nothing abnormal about going shopping!'

'You know as well as I do she's done nothing of the kind.'

They were silent for a moment. Charles realised his teeth were clenched and made a conscious effort to relax his jaw. He said, 'You don't suppose she could have gone home?'

'What? To Blantyre House? I think we'd know if she had.'

Charles grinned, thinking of David Sheraton's appalled face. 'Yes. So we would.' The grin faded and he added, 'If only she wasn't so beautiful. You know what hospitals are like these days. Some pervert could have got hold of her.'

'She wouldn't walk off with just anybody!'

Charles sighed and got up. Celia's mind was out of gear, and who knew what she might think? He felt angry suddenly. He had told her again and again to trust no one except him, to do nothing without his permission. How dare she disobey him?

He felt better, restored, able to think once again. He got up to go and Dorrie rose with him, dusting off her hands and fetching her coat. It was getting dark, and the street was full of soft shadows. Where was Celia? Where in God's name was she? His patient, his goddamned property, could now be in the hands of some madman . . . He stopped his train of thought. That he would not think about.

When they arrived at the hospital the place was ablaze with light. Policemen were searching the building and teams of dog handlers were out in the grounds. The hospital administrator

71

saw Charles and deliberately turned his back, excluding him.

'I'd better go and get changed,' said Charles to Dorrie. 'Then we'll drive around a bit. There might be somewhere you think she might have gone. I can't hang around here and do nothing.'

Dorrie went and sat down to wait for him, perched on a hard outpatient's chair. An ambulance roared up to the door, siren wailing, but the occupant wasn't Celia. It was a heart attack case, an old man with blue lips. She watched him on the stretcher, rushed by in a flurry of care. In all the excitement nobody noticed a woman walk in the door and stand shakily, both hands pressed against her ribs. She wore a red dress, mud-stained and torn. It was Celia.

Dorrie got up and went across, trying not to be noticed. 'What happened?' she whispered. 'Did you have an accident?'

Celia hiccupped in her effort to catch her breath. 'A man took me. I thought he was a doctor. He said Davenport gave permission, but he must have lied. I ran – no – jumped out of the car.'

'Did he chase you?'

Celia shook her head. 'I don't know. I fell on grass and there was a woman, with a pram. I should think he drove off but just in case, when I felt better, I ran.' She shook her head, still bewildered. 'The woman was in a state. Wanted to call the police.'

'She needn't have bothered,' said Dorrie. 'We've got hundreds of police.'

She knew she must surrender Celia to Charles. Anything else would mean questions and upsets that were bound to be too much. When he came through the doors a moment later, flinging them wide with a peremptory hand, she signalled to him. 'Well,' he said, when he saw Celia. 'Another fine mess!'

'She was abducted,' defended Dorrie. 'He pretended to be a doctor.'

'And I escaped,' added Celia. 'So don't go on at me! At least I came back.'

Her face was muddy and scratched. There was mud in her hair and under her lovely nails. Somehow it made her still more ethereal, a creature of the air who had tried disporting

herself in the wrong element. Relief and thankfulness made
him curt and rough-voiced. She was near to tears, but he
couldn't be kind to her. Within minutes she was despatched to
bed.

'Panic over, everyone,' he announced. 'My patient has
returned.'

The administrator said loudly, 'We never have this trouble
with the cardiac unit,' and Charles tried not to laugh. It was
hard to imagine heart patients, wired up, stitched up and
gasping, making a dash for freedom. He didn't doubt for a
moment that they would if they could.

Celia was once again in her private room. Charles had decreed
that she no longer needed stimulus, and must have calm.
Besides, it was safer. A flower arrangement in pink and cream
stood on a table, classical music played discreetly in the
background and she had some painting materials to hand. But
her dress had gone. It was imprisonment, in the name of care.

She went to the window and stood looking out. A few people
strolled across the lawns, but she was shielded from the bustle
of the main hospital entrance. Did they want her to go back to
sleep? she thought. There was no danger of that. With every
passing moment she felt more and more restless, more and
more dissatisfied, more and more sure that life was escaping
her, hour by hour. Her abduction hadn't frightened her back
into her den, whatever they all thought. On the contrary, it
had strengthened and inspired her. She had survived and
returned all by herself. It was the first sweet taste of
independence.

There was a knock on the door. It was Davenport, in his
smart dark suit, the one he wore for ward rounds. He had a
flower in his buttonhole and looked big and suave and
charming. Celia felt an unreasoning irritation with him.

'Good morning, Celia.'

'Good morning, Charles.'

He paused. It was all very well for Dorrie to call him
Charles, but Celia was a patient. 'I think we'd better keep it
formal, Celia.'

She lifted her chin, haughtily. 'Then may I remind you that

73

my name is Sheraton? Mrs Sheraton.'

'Are you angry about something, Celia?'

'Yes, Charles. About my imprisonment.'

'After yesterday, we thought it wise.'

She rounded on him. 'After yesterday? I thought he was a doctor! No one has the courtesy to introduce themselves, no one tells me anything! Why won't you let my family come? I've got a husband, children! My parents . . . You keep me here, day after day, week after week, as if I was a – a—'

'Still having trouble with the speech, I see.'

'Bugger off!' said Celia.

He got up and went to the window, trying not to laugh. She hated being laughed at. Her behaviour this morning was confirming a suspicion he had harboured last night. There was no abductor. She had cooked up a tale to explain a sudden desire for freedom, a desire that had come unstuck.

'What made you think this man was a doctor?'

'He was here, he didn't introduce himself, and he behaved as if I was backward,' she retorted. 'Oh, and he had a big car. Obviously a doctor.'

Charles said, 'You're getting very bitter.'

Celia's eyes clouded. Yes, she was bitter, kept alone here, isolated, denied her family. 'I didn't know him,' she said dismally. 'He was a stranger.'

'Are you sure? He might have been someone you knew before.'

'I – I don't know.'

'You've no idea what he wanted?'

Celia shook her head. 'I know what I want, though. My family.'

He was thoughtful when he left. In two days' time he was presenting his paper on Celia. He was about to make medical history, from the generalities of coma to the specifics of her remarkable case. All his measurements, photographs and brain scans would be open to inspection, and he fully expected publicity. He wondered if Celia was up to it.

He hoped for a television interview. He and Celia together, doctor and patient. Suppose she wouldn't co-operate? On today's showing, she certainly wouldn't, suspecting as she did that he was keeping her family from her. He was doing nothing of the kind, of course. Her isolation was all down to David Sheraton, the real villain of this piece. Charles made a decision. It was time to stop standing between Celia and her husband, to let her see just where she stood. She would come to realise that she had no choice but to rely on him.

He went to his office to telephone, settling himself comfortably at his desk, arranging his face in bland lines. He had to wait for Sheraton to be found, hanging on endlessly while the girl at the other end went to look for him. He might have known the firm would be disorganised, he thought aggressively, forgetting the hours that people spent waiting for him to come to a phone. When at last Sheraton spoke Charles was long since out of patience.

'Mr Sheraton? Charles Davenport here. The surgeon. Sorry to interrupt your important work with my small concerns.'

'I was in the factory. What do you want?'

'It's about your wife. Celia.'

A tense pause. 'Yes?'

Charles allowed a second to pass before he put him out of his misery. Let the man panic. He said, 'She's quite distressed that you haven't visited. I'd convinced her that in fact I wouldn't permit you to come, but that fiction seems to have run its course. Perhaps you could tell me what you would like me to say to her?'

There was a pause. Then, 'I don't think there's any need to say anything.'

'Do I take it, then, that you won't visit? That you wash your hands of her? Is that what you want me to say?'

'No, of course not! You're being very simplistic, Mr Davenport.'

'Your wife is going to see things quite simply, Mr Sheraton. She's going to see that you're abandoning her.'

'Of course I'm not! That's presumptuous of you!'

'Then do you mind telling me what you mean to do?'

Another pause. He could hear Sheraton's breathing. 'I shall

visit my wife as and when I feel able to do so,' he said jerkily.

'And when might that be? Today? Tomorrow? Some time? Never?'

There was a slow click on the line. Sheraton had hung up.

Charles felt an unreasoning elation. She was all his! No one had a better claim on a patient than the man who had saved her. The husband was giving up on her, of course. He could do nothing else. He probably should do nothing else, thought Charles with rare magnanimity. Where was the point in David Sheraton disrupting the lives of his children, the woman who was in effect his second wife, and himself, all for someone whose mental state might always be suspect? Celia was erratic, fanciful and moody. It took a professional to handle her. From now on, she would have to accept that Charles must be her long-term support.

He told her in the evening. He was quiet, calm and understanding. He explained that ten years was a long time, a very long time for a man to live alone, especially a man with children. Inevitably, David had found someone else.

Celia's unwavering blue stare unnerved him a little. He found himself wondering if she believed anything that he said, and once, when he was explaining how difficult it was for men living alone, he saw her mouth twist derisively. Perhaps he was being a little patronising. At the end, as he tailed into silence, she blinked once, very hard.

She said, 'I see. Thank you for explaining so clearly.'

He retreated into medical detail. 'I'll prescribe something for you. I know this must be a shock.'

'Every day is a shock.'

He prepared to get up and summon a nurse, but suddenly she turned. Her eyes blazed with unusual fire. 'Look, we've got to sort some things out. Can he keep my children from me?'

'I – I really don't know. You shouldn't see them yet. You're not ready.'

She looked away then. He felt more comfortable looking at the slender, vulnerable column of her neck. And he couldn't resist adding, 'It's all right, you know, Celia. You don't have to worry. I'm here. I'll take care of you.'

The noise met David even before he reached the front door; loud, tuneless heavy metal, played at full blast from an upstairs room. All the yelling in the world wouldn't make an impression on that row, so he stormed up the stairs and crashed into Ellen's room.

'Turn that blasted racket off!'

She looked at him with that other-worldly stare teenagers reserve for people over twenty, reached out a lazy hand and flicked a switch. Silence, blessed silence, while the very bones of his head still pulsated with the noise of a moment ago. 'You'll go deaf,' said David feebly.

'Probably. Dad, you're pathetic.'

She turned away, resuming the homework she had been doing. How she could work in the middle of noise was beyond him, but she did. Her room was lined with erotic posters: couples on clifftops kissing at sunset, a boy wearing jeans crouched over a girl's naked back. Yet there was no one more innocent than his daughter. He looked at her sprawled on the bed, long-haired and long-legged, her black tights full of holes. Couldn't they afford new tights, or was that the fashion? He felt completely out of his depth.

'Ellen—'

'What?' She didn't look up. One finger hooked her hair behind her ear.

'I wanted to talk about your mother.'

'She's gone to the shops.'

'Not Mum! Your mother. Your real mother. You remember her, don't you?'

Blue eyes, Celia's eyes, turned on him. God, why hadn't he ever noticed those eyes? He had, of course. It was Celia he'd forgotten.

Ellen said, 'I think I remember her. A bit. Lucy says she does, but she doesn't, she was too young. I remember quite a lot of things. She was very pretty, wasn't she? And always laughing. We had a game, where she was a fierce giant and I was a little girl, and I hid behind the furniture while she prowled around making her voice deep and saying: "Where's that little girl? I'm going to eat her!"'

David laughed, caught by the memory. 'You loved being eaten! You used to leap out, yelling, "Mummy, I'm here, I'm here, eat me!" And she grabbed you, and blew down your neck, making gobbling noises.'

Ellen said wistfully, 'I do remember. Really. It was awful when she died.'

David's throat closed. All he could say was, 'Yes.'

This was the moment, he thought. After all these years, he should try and tell her the truth. But the truth would change everything. It would start a long series of events that would unravel their lives in ways they couldn't begin to know. Like a domino chain, a thousand little bricks tumbling down because at first just one was pushed. And he was so tired! This was hardly something to tackle when he was tired. In a moment he would go downstairs and have a drink and in a while Heather would have dinner ready and they could go on as normal. What was the point of starting something now, and upsetting everyone?

He put out his hand and touched his daughter's hair. She didn't have all Celia's loveliness, but sometimes he would see echoes in her smile or the way she turned her head. Lucy was still too young, of course, and besides, she favoured his side of the family; curly hair and soft plumpness, like his mother.

'I'm glad you remember her,' he said.

'Why?'

He looked away, unable to face that honest gaze. Why indeed? 'She was a remarkable woman,' he said feebly.

'Yes, but why do you want to talk about her now? It's not her birthday or anything.'

'When I came up you reminded me of her. That's all.'

He escaped from the room, breathing harshly as if he had been running. Would she hate him if she knew? Would she understand why she had been deceived? It had never been a conscious thing. It had grown out of necessity, and his unwillingness to keep on confronting the same irreconcilable problem. What would they have done all these years? Gone to the bedside every Christmas, every month, every Sunday? It didn't bear thinking of. He went hurriedly downstairs, poured himself a whisky and switched on the television news.

The conference hall was almost full. As always, delegates were in constant motion, going to talk to colleagues or out to the stands or giving up on this lecture and departing to play golf. Charles tried not to resent the inattention. They didn't know what he was going to say. It wasn't important to their lives as it was to his. He glanced down at the press benches, and saw a smattering of correspondents. They were the people who mattered.

The Chairman introduced him in the offhand manner he reserved for his juniors, quite unlike his sycophancy when a senior colleague took the stand. Applause crackled like sporadic gunfire, and Charles was conscious of feeling ill. It was his usual reaction to stress, the feeling that he was coming down with 'flu. He set his papers on the podium, leaning out towards his audience aggressively. They would listen whether they liked it or not.

'As some of you will know,' he began, sweeping the hall with his eyes, 'since taking up my consultancy at Aireborough Hospital, I have been studying coma. There's a lot to learn. We know very little about the mechanisms that come into play when the brain switches itself off. I've published some work on the physiological aspects of the condition, but today I wish to present to you a remarkable case. The recovery, possibly the full recovery, of a patient in coma for over ten years.'

He pressed the remote button on the projector. The image of Celia leaped on to the screen, dominating the hall. She was asleep. Her hair was a golden fan on the pillow. She was naked except for cloths placed strategically over breasts and groin. The delegates, eighty per cent of them male, sat down and sat up.

'As you can see,' said Charles smoothly, 'a lovely young woman. But not as young as she seems. At the time of this photograph she was thirty-five years old. When I first saw her I presumed her to be about sixteen.'

He looked down and saw the pressmen scribbling madly. To his right the Chairman was craning his neck to look at the screen. Charles pressed the button to change the slide. 'Now we see the patient a month later. Note the slumped posture, drooping eyelids and sprawled legs.' The camera was in fact looking up Celia's dressing gown, into tantalising shadow. 'She is in fact still only semi-conscious,' said Davenport, 'and we discovered that her continued awakening depended on constant stimulation. She could easily slip back into coma at this point. My hypothesis, gentlemen, ladies, is that the study of this patient's unique and incredibly slow recovery gives us insights into coma that would otherwise be unobtainable. In this woman we have the process of recovery slowed down to a snail-like pace, ideal for study. The normal coma patient, if there is such a creature, moves rapidly from stage to stage, and I contest that too little attention to any one stage can result in an impaired full recovery. The brain must be encouraged to enter each stage, and complete it fully. My patient, fellow delegates, has, in the space of a few months, moved from this – ' the slumped figure ' – to this.' He clicked the switch. Celia stood in a long white nightgown, tending a vase of flowers. She was framed against the window and the sun. Her nightdress was effectively transparent.

When he stepped down from the podium, an hour later, he was engulfed by reporters. He pushed his way through, promising a press conference later in the day, fighting for the sanctuary of the bar. He wanted a beer, but not to celebrate. This was just the start.

Pint in hand, he looked around to see if there was anyone he knew. Don Matthews, a man he saw now and again, an anaesthetist from the same year at college, came across. 'Well done, Charles. Another giant stride in self-promotion, I see.'

Charles grinned. 'I have my reasons.'

Matthews knocked back a scotch. 'I bet you have. Don't know why you took the job in the first place. You might have known the heart men had it all sewn up. You could have had a consultancy anywhere in a few years.'

'Perhaps I wasn't prepared to wait.'

Matthews signalled for another scotch. 'I'll get us both another. Is this your new thing? Girly pictures to advertise neurology.'

'The work was sound. I just spiced it up a bit with the snaps.

80

Stroke of luck that she was a stunner, that's all.'

'She still in hospital?'

Charles nodded. 'Don't tell the press, but she may always be in hospital. Very panicky, and a poor grasp of reality. Not surprising, but it does spoil the story. I doubt she'll ever be able to live unsupported.'

They took their drinks away from the bar, to lean their elbows on a shelf. Charles felt a longing for a decent pub, with chairs and faded carpets. He watched his friend gulping his second drink.

'How are things at your fun factory?' he asked.

'OK.' Matthews looked gloomily down at his glass. Then he straightened, as if coming to a decision. 'That's not true,' he said. 'Things are bloody awful. I've got a negligence case coming up. We had a boy in with appendicitis. He was pumped up with drugs – some unholy cocktail, mostly heroin mixed with a hallucinogen of some sort – but we had to do him before he ruptured. I did the gas, of course, I'm the man – or at least I was. These things knock your confidence. He had a seizure and he's in a coma. Terrible accident, aggravated by the bloke's erratic lifestyle, but we can't prove that. And he would be the son of a barrister! I'm being taken to the cleaners over it. Apparently I should have used God knows what on him.'

'How long has he been under?'

Matthews sighed. 'Four months or so. You can see why I listened to your party piece. If he'd only come round! If he'd only lighten! The hospital daren't try a thing with this barrister chap looming over them. It's ruining my digestion, I can tell you.'

'The drink's doing that,' said Charles dispassionately.

After a moment Matthews said, 'You always were an unsympathetic bastard, Charles. As a shoulder to cry on you make a bloody good rock.'

'Don't whinge,' said Charles. 'Send the bloke to me. I'll do an assessment and plan some treatment. Sounds as if things can't get worse.'

'Would you?' Matthews blinked incredulously. 'I warn you, a bit of Vivaldi and a few visitors aren't going to wake him

81

up. You're not going to have a wild success.'

'We'll monitor him for a bit,' said Charles. 'The Sister on Intensive Care loves coma patients. She'll care for him like a baby, your gorilla of a barrister won't dare complain. You never know, it might be worth an operation.'

'Then the gorilla will sue you as well,' said Matthews lugubriously, although already he was looking brighter. 'Thanks, Charles. I'll remember I owe you one.'

'Always ready to oblige.' He tapped his friend's glass with a warning finger. 'Watch the sauce.'

It was a momentary impulse, regretted almost at once. Charles knew he was being wildly premature. He had no facilities, no resources, nothing. He needed a new scanner, more nurses, everything. But to be offered another case, and such a juicy one, and if he succeeded to be able to raise his standing in the profession as well as in the public eye – he mentally blessed Celia. Without her he'd still be digging his garden and praying for train crashes.

He had no doubts about his ability to do something for the patient. But no one who knew him would have found that odd. Self-doubt was alien to Charles, because he had never failed. He didn't always cure his patients, but he knew he did at least as much as anyone else for them, and usually much more. If one of his died or failed to recover, he knew no one else could have done more. It was conceit, but based on experience. He knew he was the best.

He began to juggle with figures in his head. Would half a million start him off? What about an appeal? Time-consuming. Get the barrister chappie to run one, perhaps? Out of gratitude. He made his way through the lobby, stopped a dozen times by people wanting to talk about his paper. Someone said, 'The pressmen are jumping up and down. In a day or two your patient's going to wish she'd never woken up.'

Charles grunted. It was what he had planned. Because of Celia he would have his funding and his facilities, his fame and fortune. He was using her for his own advancement, but surely she owed him that? He had given her – the words were dramatic, but appropriate – he had given her new life.

Chapter Six

'How about this? Or this?' The nurse held up a white cotton blouse, lightly trimmed with lace. In her other hand was a blue slubbed silk shirt. The clinging black skirt over her arm was, it seemed, compulsory.

'I think the silk,' said Celia nervously. 'I never was a Puritan maid.'

'I do love silk,' said the nurse, putting her face against the cool fabric. 'So sensual.'

Celia said nothing. In the last few days she had retreated into herself, like an animal hiding in its den. She imagined that everyone knew, and pitied her. Her husband, her lover, was gone. Ten years had passed, but it seemed to her that it had happened in an instant, without warning, without reason. David! How could he? David. He had abandoned her for someone else.

The shock had almost been matched by the surprise. He had loved her so. In all her marriage, whatever she did, she had known he would go on loving her. At a party once, a month before the accident, it felt like only a month ago, he'd found her on a bed with Gordon Fletcher. There wasn't anything in it, they were both married and happy. They did it for fun, that was all, at those glamorous wild parties where the drink flowed like water and the fast cars lined up outside like packs of hunting dogs. At one time she could have slipped upstairs with any of three rich men for some no-holds-barred passion in a room with a chair against the door. They were all men she might have married, if she had wished. But this time there was a lock which didn't hold, and David came in to find another man on a bed with his wife.

The worst of it was, Gordon didn't realise straight away.

83

And she just lay looking up at her husband, wondering what he'd do. In the end, an age too late, Gordon said 'Sorry, old man', and got up. She dragged her skirt down and went to get her coat.

David pulled over on the way home, and she remembered thinking, This is it! He's going to kill me! But he didn't. Instead he made love to her, as if she was a call girl, bearing the slimy taint of other men. It was one of their best times. He was so angry and she was so scared. Hours later, in bed, he asked, 'Aren't I enough for you, then?' And she whispered, 'Of course you are. It's better with you. I think I just like sinning.'

For weeks afterwards she'd expected him to ask for a divorce. It was the most horrible time of her life, waiting, endlessly waiting for someone else to decide. She had tried to imagine what life would be like without David – his enthusiasms, his obsessions, his sudden laughter and equally sudden gloom. He had taken her to Paris once, with half an hour to pack, and they'd spent the whole time looking round a car factory. Incredibly, she'd found it fun.

These last few nights she had dreamed of looking up and seeing him standing over that bed. Guilt, after all this time, when she hadn't truly felt it before. Then she had only wanted to get away with it and go on as before, enjoying herself, having fun. Why, when she loved David, had she done it? None of the happiness counted, none of the joy. She was abandoned because of that night.

Someone had chosen high-heeled white shoes for her, and she hated them. 'Did Davenport choose these?' she demanded, suddenly querulous. 'I won't wear them. Go and tell him, I won't.' They behaved as if she was stupid. Why couldn't she choose her own things? She sat in front of the mirror, her feet bare, and put up her hair on her head.

Her right arm ached more than a little, but she wouldn't give in to it. Of such little battles is my life now made, she thought, and was engulfed, suddenly, in hopelessness.

By the time Charles came to fetch her she was still without shoes. 'I won't wear those,' she said flatly, pointing at the white stilettoes. 'They're unspeakably vulgar.'

'There's nothing I can do about it now,' he soothed. 'We're due at the television studios in half an hour. Everyone wears shoes like that nowadays.'

'Do they?' She went over to the window. But in the gardens below there were only men wheeling barrows and hospital staff in stout black lace-ups. She turned uncertainly to Charles, and he thought how small she seemed suddenly, shoeless in her clothes. She still had such a defenceless, other-worldly air.

His coaxing won through. She held on to his arm while she put on first one shoe and then the other, rising to a surprising height. The shoes were an inspired touch, thought Charles. They were just sufficiently sluttish.

'OK? Want a sedative?'

To his relief she shook her head. He didn't want her slurring her words, or succumbing to confusion. He took her arm and led her down the pink carpet of the corridor towards the side entrance of the hospital. Two photographers were waiting, which was good. It would look as if he was trying to protect his patient, but the publicity would be great. He waved an ineffectual arm. 'No pictures. Please. My patient's still very weak . . .' But they ignored him, as he knew they would. Flash bulbs popped like rogue fireworks, and Celia teetered on her terrible heels.

'Come along, my dear,' said Charles, being avuncular. He felt it was the right image. Looking stunned, she let herself be pushed into his big, expensive car.

'Why are you doing all this?' she asked as they drove away.

'Don't worry.' He swerved smoothly around a traffic island. 'You're just part of my study of coma. A success story.'

'Are you asking for donations or something?'

He shrugged. 'Not from the public, especially. Not yet. It's hospital funding I want. So that people like you can be treated at my hospital.'

'Well, won't that be nice?'

'Yes, actually. It should be very nice indeed. Neurology is a poor relation in medicine, when in fact its study holds the key to almost every other aspect of medical science.'

He talked on, riding his favourite hobby horse, and Celia switched off. She stared at the people on the pavement, none of whom was wearing white stiletto heels. He was using her. Defenceless as she was, this man was manipulating her life and calling it care.

They arrived at the television studio, a graceless box of a place. It looked worn and tatty, which surprised Celia, who remembered the building going up. Concrete and glass had clearly been a mistake. It was difficult, correcting memories which were still so fresh, she thought. Ten years' absence for any other cause would have overlaid her remembrance with other experience. But she had seen the world change seemingly overnight, and felt a constant need to comment on things and point them out, to people who saw nothing abnormal.

Charles drew up in front of the building, in the middle of the gang of pressmen. He tried to look concerned.

'Celia – look this way, love.'

'Celia! Mrs Sheraton! How do you feel?'

A great gaggle of people seemed to surround her. Charles held her tight against his side, pushing through, behaving quite rudely to some. Once through the glass doors he let her go. Celia sank on to a chair, speechless.

'Sorry,' said Charles, wiping his hands on a handkerchief. 'I didn't think there'd be so many.'

'You could have warned me. What do they expect?'

'An exclusive scoop. Don't worry, it's bound to blow over. And an hour from now you'll be safely back in hospital.'

Back. After exposing her to the world and its callous battery of eyes, in clothes that weren't hers and shoes she actively disliked, he was going to take her back. She might wish to have tea somewhere, but he wouldn't permit it. She might wish – oh, daring – to go shopping. Even her greatest wish, that she should at last see her children, would be denied. She felt that surge of futile anger, an emotion she could never express. If she raged and swore they doped her, if she cried and screamed they played her soothing music and left her alone. What could she do? How could she take back her life, her independence? Her right hand was shaking, reminding her that she was ill. Charles hooked a hand under her elbow and led her firmly away.

Make-up first. They covered her lashes in sooty mascara, a look she hated, and then the hairdresser, a common girl wearing, Celia noticed, white stilettoes, took down her hair and left it loose.

'I like it up,' she said. 'More sophisticated.'

'Don't want to be too sophisticated, do we, dear?' squawked the girl. 'Not when we're not well.'

'Why not?'

'Be a good girl, eh, dear.'

Celia was amazed. What was it about her that led people to treat her like an idiot? She wondered if she was behaving more oddly than she knew. She wondered if it was the white stilettoes. She wished she could take one now and stab Davenport with it through the heart.

The unaccustomed fuss was very tiring. By the time she sat in the studio, on a sofa under a blaze of lights, her tongue was like lead in her mouth. 'All right?' Charles, with his eyebrows blacked in and his nose powdered. 'I'll talk first,' he said, 'and then you answer some questions. It's live, so do your best.'

Now they wanted her to perform. She had to try for them, and do her best. What was the point of living again if these people directed her, if she had no one of her own, if she wasn't free? Charles was hissing through his teeth, nervous as a cat. Celia longed to lay her head down on the worn blue sofa and go to sleep.

'. . . And now to a remarkable medical success story. When Charles Davenport arrived as neurological consultant at Aireborough Hospital he was startled to find a patient who had been in coma for more than ten years. According to tests her brain was relatively unscathed, but Celia Sheraton remained in the same unconscious state that had lasted ever since her car accident ten years ago. He resolved to try and waken her and, we're delighted to say, succeeded.' The interviewer turned to Charles.

'Mr Davenport, can you tell me what first led you to believe that Celia would wake up?'

'Yes.' Charles cleared his throat. 'She was in a very light coma. I believe her state had been lightening unnoticed for some time, but it is so unusual for anyone to recover after so long that we had no cause for optimism. Of course I would emphasise that we knew Celia wasn't brain dead. She was in no sense vegetative. It was a coma caused by trauma from which she had never revived.'

'What had happened to her?'

'A car accident. It so often is.'

'Is this good news for all coma patients, then?'

'Only in one sense. Most people unconscious for longer than a year have almost no chance of waking up, and I must emphasise that. But I've learned a great deal about the mechanisms of coma from Celia. It's as if the whole process of recovery has taken place very slowly, in ideal conditions. But, of course, from Celia's point of view things are far from ideal. She's lost ten years of her life.'

'Indeed.' The interviewer swung towards Celia, as if about to eat the best sweet in the box. 'What is it like, Celia, losing ten years of your life?'

The cameras loomed at her like hungry animals. The interviewer put on his most ingratiating smile. Everyone was waiting. But even as she formulated an answer she realised she'd forgotten the question. Perhaps she was brain dead. She opened her mouth. 'Er—'

'It must be quite difficult for you.'

'Er—' The words had gone. She couldn't find them. Where did the things escape to?

'How does it feel, waking up? Good? Do you like it?'

My God, if she didn't speak they'd say she was an idiot. They'd tell her children she was an idiot. She had to speak. 'Yes. Yes. But very difficult.'

'What's been the hardest thing? The thing you find most hard?'

Now they were making the questions easier. Soon they'd ask her if she had a favourite colour and did she like beans for tea. She gathered her thoughts in an heroic effort at concentration. 'I find it very difficult recognising people,' she managed. 'Everyone looks so old. And things have changed so. This television building, for instance.' Now she was launched she doubted if she could stop. 'This building. Only yesterday it was shining and new, and now I see it's nothing but cracked glass and stained concrete. Horrible. You should have built it better. Fashions as well. I was told to wear these shoes because they were fashionable, but really I can't imagine anyone of taste wearing shoes like these.'

The man looked taken aback. She shouldn't have talked about the shoes. 'What else have you noticed?' he asked feebly.

She considered. 'Telephones. Shops. Superficial things like the shapes of cars.'

The interviewer leaned forward. He had softened her up for this.

'And your personal life. You were married with two small children. What does your family think of this?'

Celia took a short, alarmed breath. She would not tell this man her husband had left her. She would not admit to him that she had woken one day and found her world shattered and brought to nothing. A noncommittal answer was somewhere in her head, but she couldn't find it, the words wouldn't come.

Charles said, 'I think we'll stop there. Celia's still having treatment in hospital, of course. She gets very tired. We don't allow too many visitors. But I do want to make the point that what we have learned from Celia can be used in many spheres. Brain damage takes many forms and they are all worthy of careful investigation—'

Reluctantly the interviewer turned away. But even as Charles launched himself on his campaign the cameras lingered on Celia, and her wondering, lovely face.

It was all over. They were disgorged into the foyer once again, their usefulness done. Charles rubbed his hands together, suddenly exuberant. 'Brilliant. Wonderful. Well done. Let's get you back, shall we?'

'I don't want to go back yet.'

'Celia, you're tired. Best you get some rest.'

She looked up into his face, darker and more handsome in make-up. 'You'll be celebrating, I suppose. Champagne and everything. The publicity must be great.'

'I hope so. Well, I've worked for it. And you've had fun too. Dressing up and getting out. It made a nice change.'

She wanted to scream at him, but the words wouldn't come. She wanted to tell him just how much she hated being stared at, hated being manipulated, hated being dressed up like a doll in his idea of PR-worthy clothes. But the words were absolutely gone. There was nothing but the hot, surging anger. So she bunched up her fist and hit him.

He reeled back against the reception desk and one of the girls screamed. Blood was seeping from the corner of his mouth. Celia's fist hurt badly. 'There!' she said. 'There. Go on then. See if I care.'

Charles said slowly, 'I suppose it's too much to expect gratitude from you.'

'Huh!' Gratitude, for treating her like a toy? If only the words were there! She couldn't tell him and she burned to let him know.

'We'd better get you back to hospital right away. I don't like to see this loss of control.'

'Won't go.'

'Come along, Celia.'

Any minute now he'd get out the straitjacket. He would drop her back at the hospital, safe in her room, and he'd go off with Dorrie perhaps, and drink champagne. Didn't he know that when her father was alive she could have drunk champagne every day of her life, if she so chose? He kept a bottle chilled for her at Blantyre House, ready in case she called. But Davenport didn't know that, Davenport didn't care, he wanted nothing but obedience and his own way. She turned on her heel, on those ridiculous white heels, and ran out of the door.

Flashbulbs popped in her face. She reeled back, thought of Charles and ran forward again. A reporter hovered in her way, a fat man with a moustache in a stained checked suit, and she said, 'Please – give me a lift.'

'What?' He looked back and saw Charles, deluged in pressmen. This was his chance to get a scoop. 'Right. Sure. Be quick, sweetheart.'

He had an old Ford Escort, one that even she remembered. They roared off into the traffic, leaving everyone behind. She closed her eyes against the unfriendly afternoon, and wished she could have gone back to hospital for a little time at least. When she looked again she saw the reporter watching her, barely looking at the road. 'Max Grindling,' he said.

'And I'm Celia Sheraton.'

'Know that, love. Had a rough day?'

She sighed. 'You could say that. All Davenport's fault.'

'Doesn't surprise me. That bloke's heading for the top of the tree and he doesn't care who he stands on. True, is it? About this coma of yours?'

She nodded. 'But I wondered if you'd take me home.'

Grindling changed gear with excitement. This was a story and a half. 'OK, love. Sure thing. Where's home?'

Celia licked her lips. 'Blantyre House.'

Heather was cooking tea, one eye on the television set. She was sipping a glass of wine. It had been a difficult day today, and she had left early in the midst of crises to be here when the girls came home from school. David didn't appreciate that, of course. Nowadays he appreciated nothing that she did. He took her for granted.

She sliced onions with energy and vigour, casting them into the pan with a swoosh of her chopping board. It was time she stood up for herself. It was time she asked him outright if he was visiting Celia, and if he was it was time he stopped. Celia Braddock had never deserved any sort of a decent family.

Heather and Celia had known each other for years, ever since they were teenagers, seeing each other across the room at parties and mutually drawing away. As Heather saw it, quiet sensible girls and wild self-indulgent ones didn't mix. Celia was a rich spoiled brat when she crashed her car, and she was no different now.

The worst thing about Celia, she decided, slicing carrots with venom, was her lack of restraint. She did everything to excess, sex, money, even the children, brought up in a wallow of erratic affection. It hadn't done them any good. It had been left to Heather to find some order in their lives, to make sense of their clothes and table manners. Celia would never thank her, but then she was an immoderate, insensitive bitch. She said the words out loud, and they made her feel better.

Obviously, since Celia was that sort of woman, David didn't love her any more. Heather's hand clenched tight on the peeler. He used to say so, she remembered it clearly.

Sometimes, in bed, he would say, 'I don't know how I can have been such a fool. But I'm so lucky, Heather. Out of it all, I got you.' That's what he used to say. Once.

She took a large gulp of wine and set about peeling some small, muddy potatoes, organic and supposedly better than the lush, plush giants she could have had. But she knew it was right to buy organic food and to forbid the girls to watch soap operas or wear jeans to school, and to insist on proper behaviour, even if everyone thought she was unnecessarily strict. Perhaps she was. But people didn't realise how hard she worked to do the right thing. Celia had never done anything she didn't think was fun. The trouble was, it seemed so difficult lately. She found it hard to remember exactly what was right. She had a constant sense of foreboding.

Heather sighed and tossed the final knob of potato into a bowl of water, chiding herself for being foolish and over dramatic. Her eye fell casually on the television set. The man on Look North said, 'And now to a remarkable medical success story.' And horribly, unbelievably, she was looking at Celia. Hair all over the place and an inch of make-up, not to mention terrible shoes – but Celia.

After the broadcast Heather went slowly to the mirror in the hall. She smoothed her own pale skin, touching the lines beneath her eyes and the incipient sagging of her once firm – too firm – jaw. From upstairs came a blast of heavy metal music, but she took no notice. Let the girls do what they want, just until she felt more in command. Would she tell David what she had seen? He might already know. All those nights when he came home late from work. He went to her.

Heather was sure, now, that he did. Suddenly tears were falling, and Heather thought, desperately, how dare she look so young? The woman was thirty-five, nearly thirty-six, only a few years short of Heather's age of forty next year. While Heather had been living, watching her hands crease with work and her face wrinkle with worry, Celia had slept. She was beautiful still.

Edwin Braddock saw the item too. He was in the drawing room of his home, Linton Place, a mansion too large for himself and his dogs, but home nonetheless. He had four German Shepherds, intelligent, watchful dogs, careful not to upset him. He had trained them to walk round the edges of his Persian rugs, and in return they lounged on his bed in the mornings and ate bacon. They treated the staff, two Filipinos, exactly as did Edwin himself; with distant good manners. Sometimes Edwin thought that if his dogs died, so would he.

He watched Celia's wooden performance with glee. She came to life like a machine with a faulty battery, a sudden surge and then nothing. But she was beautiful. He wondered if she would get taken up as a personality, and front appeals and so forth, like the first transplant patients. She was dressed for it, but people would have to overlook her sad inability to speak. Of course the doctor was trying for stardom himself, and might achieve it. Medicos always wanted to be famous.

A slight rustle at the door indicated Feodor and dinner. Roast guinea fowl, brought to him on a trolley, so that he need not disturb himself or the dogs. He sat quite still as the man arranged a walnut tray on his lap and served the meal. Edwin tucked in eagerly. He was hungry tonight, and every mouthful seemed particularly succulent.

For a moment he allowed himself to reflect on his comfort, with his good food and bottle of wine, served in such pleasant surroundings. He was fortunate indeed, although of course there was no luck involved. Edwin's life was the product of careful planning, and he was well fed and well served and well funded simply because he planned it that way. He was a master of planning, he told himself – and then he began to frown.

A small pulse was beating in his throat. He was no different from other great men, they all made a mistake at some time or another. Hitler's was Russia, Churchill's Gallipoli, and Edwin's the Marlborough clubs. An excursion that was entirely the result of an unplanned impulse.

If he had thought it through, he would never have exposed himself to public and avoidable failure. All he could say in his defence was that Marlborough clubs had been a scandal for years. George Marlborough presided over dirty premises, bad food and rigged games, and if he wasn't who he was he would have lost the licence years back. But he was who he was. The

Old Guard had stood firm, and Edwin Braddock had been sent scuttling back north with his tail between his legs.

He pushed his plate away. Marlborough intruded even here, into the pleasant luxuries of home. Even Celia had intruded tonight. It was as if problems conspired to deprive him of peace. He swore softly, and all the dogs lifted their heads, alert to whatever he wished to do. He stood up. 'Come on, beauties,' he said. 'Let's walk.'

It was a cool evening, and he was brisk. Down past the lake, where the mallards were nesting and the fish lay torpid amidst the reeds, on up the hill and through the wood to the folly. He liked to stand here in the evening and look down on Linton Place, because the sheer grandeur of the building gave him pleasure. Its wide, flat faces turned without expression to the park, the many windows glinting in the evening light like sightless eyes. If he had lived here for a lifetime, and his father and his father's father before him, would that make him better? Or, in the eyes of the world, was there nothing that could render Edwin Braddock the equal of a man like George Marlborough, and nothing that could prove him to be a better custodian of Braddock money than a beautiful fool?

He started to walk back to the house. He could do nothing as yet about George Marlborough. For the time being the shares must be held, which increased his loss on the project. But no one else wanted to buy, and who knew what changes might occur in time? As for Celia . . . He paused and dropped his hand. One of the dogs moved under it, and he fondled a thick ruffed neck. As for Celia – she was clearly far from recovered. A communiqué would go to the hospital tomorrow, from the Braddock Consortium, demanding that she be protected from media exposure. He would not permit his cousin to be exploited in such a way. She must be returned to the private wing, and close confinement.

He closed his fingers on the dog's skin, and the animal groaned with pleasure. Edwin realised he was hungry again, and began to walk with a quick, determined step. Feodor must cook once more, or persuade Tomul to some cooking. They had little enough to do, God knows.

Chapter Seven

The reporter was chewing on his stained moustache. 'So, if I drop you here and come again tomorrow, you'll give me an hour?'

'Yes. Too tired now. Can't talk.'

'They'll have you back by tomorrow though, won't they? Back in hospital.'

Celia shook her head. Her eyelids felt weighted with weariness and mascara. 'Won't go.'

'Won't you now? Dare say they'll send you anyway. Look, love, if you're not here tomorrow I'll run the story my way. Tell them how you ran away and begged me to rescue you. The blokes back at the studio have got pictures. Might even be better than a chat, come to think of it.'

Celia had ceased to pay attention. Before her loomed the great grey bulk of Blantyre House, the place she had always considered her home, even when she was married and living elsewhere. Her heart was beating with desperate vigour, because she knew her parents would soon greet her. Their death had no reality. She remembered so easily that hot afternoon and her father cheating at tennis; her mother chopping fruit for Pimms, and complaining that the knife was blunt. Someone had used it for cutting bread, new bread that she could almost taste. It was only a little time ago.

She got out of the car, leaving the door swinging wide. 'Now what?' murmured the reporter. 'One nutter, delivered to the door. Happy birthday.'

Celia went up the steps and rang the bell. It jangled endlessly and for a long time no one came. She felt a great weariness threatening her, and knew that whatever celebrations there would be must wait until tomorrow. She was still so tired. And suddenly, hearing an unfamiliar step behind the door, she remembered everything she had been told. No one here would want her. There would be no joyous welcome. But before she could turn the door opened and Heather was there.

'Oh – my – God,' said Heather. 'It's you.'

'Heather Wilcox,' said Celia. 'What are you doing here?'

'I live here,' snapped Heather. 'And you don't.'

'But—' Celia felt confused. Heather? Here? 'This is my parents' house,' she managed. 'You've got no right to be here.'

Heather looked past her, at the man in the car, watching with unnatural interest. 'Who's he? Is he a reporter?'

'What?' Celia turned. 'Yes. Yes, he is. I'm going to tell him everything.'

'You'll do no such thing!'

Heather felt certain of very little nowadays, but she was absolutely sure that this wasn't going to look good. How could Celia come here now, to the house where Heather had lived for nearly ten years, and tell her she had no rights? Panic was very near the surface. She glared at Celia's white face, the eyes as black as a panda's. 'Damn you! Damn you! Come inside.'

Just to be in the big, cool hall was exquisite. Celia walked around, touching the furniture. One side table was heavily marked. 'How did this happen? What was it?'

'That was years ago,' said Heather, grimly. 'A vase.'

'This table was fine! I remember it. How dare you spoil my mother's furniture?'

'Your mother's dead. It was left – the house and everything in it was left to David.'

Celia drew herself up. 'I am David's wife. This house is still mine. It has always been mine.'

There was a sudden chatter of voices on the stairs. Heather caught Celia's arm. 'Come in the library! Come in! They can't see you now.'

'Who? What? Heather, I'm not a criminal in my own home! Will you stop this!'

She wouldn't go and Heather couldn't make her. A gale of girlish laughter made the woman desperate. 'It's the girls,' hissed Heather. 'Your girls. You can't meet them like this.'

The girls. Her girls. Celia felt afraid. She wasn't strong

enough, this wasn't the time. She allowed herself to be pushed into the library. Heather shut the door and left her.

It was very quiet in the big, dark room. Books lined the walls, floor to ceiling, but the air was still, as if no one came here. A tired pot plant stood on the table, and Celia put it in the window, where it would catch some light. A bottle stood on a tray, surrounded by upturned glasses, and she poured herself a measure without looking at what it was. But it tasted like nectar. Good sherry, still, from her father's cellar. Under its soft influence, she began to revive.

Hesitantly, as if disturbing ghosts, she sank into her father's old chair. It had a high winged back, and a tapestry cushion her mother had made, faded now when before it had been bright. It was like watching a Disney nature film, a flower passing from seed to bud, to blossom and decay, all within a minute. The cushion was real, though. It had not faded in a moment. There was truth in all those lost years.

The quiet room seemed to tell her things that voices never could. Tears pricked her eyelids, and she forced them back. So much was changed, so much was gone. Heather lived here now. After her, David had chosen straitlaced, stiff-necked, predictable Heather. Celia almost giggled. Heather disapproved of pop music and modern novels and anyone who didn't automatically vote Conservative. She was a staunch member of some church group, and Celia and David used to imagine that they had a special section in their prayers to request divine retribution for people who enjoyed life. When she appeared at the same parties it was always unfortunate, each supposing that the evening was not what they had been led to expect. They used to laugh about Heather and her terrible dancing, like a pregnant ostrich, all stretched neck and earnest concentration. Heather!

She took a gulp of sherry and leaned her head back against the chair. It smelled of her father still. But that was imagined, smells didn't linger, not for years. She thought of David in this room, asking her father for her hand, and the explosion of parental wrath. Her father had wanted her to marry James Terrington, so she could be Lady Terrington and he could boast and buy her yachts. James had even less money than

David, but he had that title, which in Joe Braddock's eyes made it right. Thinking of her father then, of his obvious faults, she felt an enormous wave of love.

There were people talking in the hall, voices lowered. No doubt they were talking about her. It was very strange, being treated like a dangerous wild beast. Everyone wanted to cage her, lock her away, where she couldn't do damage. But what did she do, except live? She took another mouthful of sherry, though her head was spinning. Living was a sin, it seemed, if you did it when people had decided you should die. Everyone would be much happier if she was dead.

The door opened, and it was David. Her breath seemed to stop with a painful jolt. She was prepared for him, expecting him, but the shock overcame her careful preparation. Her heart raced, pounding in her ears. David's long, sinewy body, the harsh bones of his face, the eyes as pale as windows. This time she recognised them all. Her husband. David. The man she loved. At last.

'Hello,' she said.

'Celia. It really is you.'

'Of course.'

She had a great urge to run to him and hold him, to be held in return. She was here, in her father's house, and nothing had changed. She was welcome and everything would be well. But before she could move, David said, 'You shouldn't have come. The girls know nothing about you, it was wrong of you to come.'

It was like a slap, a painful collision with reality. In this at least Davenport had told her the truth. She wasn't wanted here. Her very existence was denied. She fumbled for words, for understanding. 'Haven't you told them anything?'

He came and stood over her, frighteningly tall. 'No. They believe that you're dead.'

'Why? What did I do, what was wrong? Why?'

'It seemed best. You were as good as dead. I'm sorry.'

She choked on a laugh that was more than half sob. 'Are you?'

He looked down at her, his mouth a bar beneath his nose. He was furiously angry, as if she had done something quite terrible. Strangely, she felt reassured. They had fought often enough, and David had never been so angry that she couldn't win him round.

'You don't want me here,' she said softly, picking up humility like a blanket.

'It isn't that. You shouldn't have come. Not yet.'

'When? Next week? Next month? Never?'

'I was going to come and see you.'

'But you didn't. You never came at all. You just forgot me.'

He squatted at her side. 'No. I didn't do that.'

'You didn't come. I needed you.'

'I couldn't! Can't you see that? Heather, the girls—'

Her rage, hot and painful, bubbled into the air. 'My girls! My own little girls. And don't say you care more for Heather Wilcox than for me! That has to be a lie!'

Her eyes blazed at him. Cold fire. It burned through the curtain of the years, daring him to deny her. He realised, suddenly, the full truth of what had happened. She had come back. She was his love, returned to him.

He got up and moved away. He could face anything but those eyes. 'I want you to go,' he muttered.

'This is my house. You can't abandon me and still live here.'

'Nobody's abandoned you.'

'Haven't you? You didn't come to see me. I thought you weren't allowed but Davenport told me the truth. You wish I was dead.'

But he wished only that none of this was true. He turned to stare at her, forcing himself to face her. She was a ghost, an image of the past, sitting erect in her chair, two bright flags of red staining either cheek. He had forgotten that she was so cruelly beautiful. Her very presence scattered his hard-won happiness like so much litter. He had got used to her loss, he was content with it. Yet she was here, in all her old, mocking loveliness.

'I've called the hospital,' he said throatily.

'I imagine you have,' said Celia. 'But I'm not going back. I'm not a mental patient, I can't be committed.'

'But you can't stay here!'

She spread her hands. 'Where else should I stay? In all

99

honesty, David, where? This is my home. My children are here. I have to see my children!'

'Oh, God.' David struggled with himself. He had to be calm. 'We've got to think of the children,' he began. 'They're happy. Settled. Heather's been their mother for as long as they can remember. You can't just—'

'Would you have them not know me?' asked Celia. Her voice cracked with tears. 'Would you deny me even that? None of this was my fault!'

'It wasn't mine either,' flared David. 'You were driving the damned car. Can't you see how hard this is? We had to get on with living, we couldn't stop!'

'You left me to rot,' she said in a low voice.

After a moment David said, 'Yes. But I had no choice. You never used to be stupid, Celia. Surely you can understand?'

The exhaustion of the day was beginning to tell. Her arm was aching terribly, her head was wrapped in a tight band of steel. If only she could sleep now. Sleep would blot out the need to understand. David, her lover, had no use for her any more.

But she clung, still, to hope. Surely he hadn't changed completely? If she could stay here, if she could talk to him, he would be persuaded. He had forgiven her affairs, her extravagances, her wilfulness – in time he would forgive her this. Contrite, she would be permitted to take back her life.

'Please let me stay,' she said jerkily. 'I don't need to go back, you know. When they come, say I can stay.'

'I can't do that. Heather—'

'Heather? What about Heather? What about me?'

There were footsteps in the hall. She knew it was Davenport. So the game was over, finished. Her brief escape was at an end and they had come to take her back into custody. When he came in she saw that his mouth was swollen where she had hit him and felt a sudden, sharp delight. Sometimes, just sometimes, she could win.

He glared at her, his temper firmly controlled. She realised how well she knew him, how much she had learned about him while he had been learning about her. He stood above her and took her wrists, saying, 'Come on, Celia. Back you go.'

She threw back her head, letting her hair swing. A current of electricity seemed to course from him to her. 'If I said no, you couldn't make me.'

His grip tightened. She knew that if it came to it he'd drag her away. But he spoke in his deliberate, professional voice, deceiving the others if not her. 'Don't say no, Celia. Don't make things hard for everyone. Let's take it slowly.'

She allowed herself to be lifted, she let him hold her wrist to lead her away. David said, 'I'll come tomorrow. We'll talk.'

Out in the hall Heather stood blocking a door. Behind her two girls were straining, trying to look. One was tall, with honey hair, the other shorter with a dark curly bob. Celia felt herself go cold.

'Hello,' she said shrilly. 'You won't remember me.'

'Come along,' said Charles, holding insistently to her wrist. 'Not now.'

As she went out to the car she heard a girl's bell of a voice asking: 'Who was that, Mum? Do we know her? She was terribly pretty.'

Celia had barely finished her breakfast before Davenport came in. The bruise on his mouth had turned an ugly purple, and added to his air of bubbling wrath. But the events of yesterday had steeled Celia. She launched at once into the attack.

'I had every right to go home,' she said sharply. 'I can't be kept here like a prisoner just because I embarrass people.'

Davenport cast himself down in a chair. He hadn't expected her to be quite so fresh this morning. 'You've blown everything. Your reporter friend claims you're being kept here against your will. Front page headlines, quotes, the lot. All the work and effort I've put into this and you have to go charging off and ruin it all.'

Celia glanced at the newspaper he held. It was as he said. She felt a pang, but rejected any guilt. If she thought about anything but freedom they would never let her go.

'It's true, though.' She went and stood at the window, gazing again at the tedious hospital garden. 'I want to go and you won't let me.'

His irritation was almost unbearable. After all he had done

for her, given her, she behaved like this. All he wanted was a few months' co-operation. She thought she was fit for the world and she was no more than a helpless babe. 'Celia, you have lost your sense of reality,' he said firmly. 'You don't understand the perspective other people have on things. You're – you're mentally very young.'

She turned her head then and said, 'What rubbish you do talk, Charles. People shouldn't let you get away with it.'

He had to admire the way she confounded him. She took the wind from his sails like the practised siren she must once have been. No man would have been safe from her, he thought. Her hair, against the light, was a clear, pure gold. Her breasts, swinging unrestrained within her nightdress, were like some special, tender fruit.

Suddenly he was aware that he wanted to touch her. Oh God, he thought, oh God. Let her not know that about him. It was because Dorrie was away, that was all. And Celia was a very special woman. The fates had conspired to create this uniquely lovely creature, spirited enough to excite him, yet vulnerable as a fawn. She seemed virginal too, without a virgin's innocence. No wonder he was tempted.

He got up briskly. 'I've called a press conference. You're to tell them that you're happy here. And you have to say that you are free to go.'

'But it isn't true.' She got up too, and stood close to him, her head beneath his chin. Did she know what she was doing to him? Surely not? 'Charles, you know I can't go without help. Your help.'

'There's nowhere for you to go.'

'You just want to keep me here. Like a toy!' She bunched her fist and struck at him, this time beating harmlessly against his chest. He caught her fist and held it against him, aware that his breath was coming too quickly, his heart was beating too fast. He held her for a long, long second. Gradually her hand opened beneath his, spreading out across the cotton of his shirt. Her fingertip, finding a space between the buttons, pressed against his skin. 'Oh, Charles,' she murmured, 'what a Bluebeard you are.'

To his astonishment he let her go on. He could always say

she took him by surprise, he told himself. She might look like a virgin, but this was a woman who knew her own power. His erection was out of control, straining against his clothing. Would it matter if he pulled her close – for just a second? 'Stop that, Celia.' His voice was guttural and she laughed up at him.

'Why? You know you like it.'

He pushed her hand away. 'This is inappropriate sexual behaviour.'

'Inappropriate for whom?'

She slid the strap of her nightgown off her shoulder, and then, with a wriggle, freed her breast. Charles felt a rush of saliva into his mouth. She was a goddess, a beautiful wanton, and he would give anything – anything – to touch her. Her nipple was the colour of raspberries, surrounded by a fine bristling of golden hairs. He imagined them brushing against his face as he sucked her, then, as he crammed her into his mouth, tangling around his tongue.

'Go on,' she whispered. 'Touch me. I won't tell.'

He knew a nurse could come in at any time. If he was seen, or if she told, his career was gone. But at that moment he wanted only to hold her, feel her, and the desire allowed thoughts of nothing else. As his hand reached for her some part of his mind was astonished and amazed. He would risk everything! For this!

He took the fat raspberry between his finger and thumb. She drew in her breath with a hiss, staring up at him with wide eyes. He felt a surging, erotic curiosity, and rolled her nipple, feeling it suddenly swell between his fingers as he aroused her. A moan escaped her lips, and suddenly he wanted to hear her cry out, as she must, in orgasm. There was no going back now. He had found her, he had saved her. She was his.

It seemed completely right. Entering her, filling her, she would be claimed as his own. He, who had never wanted ownership of any woman, who took what he wanted and passed on, was like a stallion with his mare. Once he had pierced her, she was entirely his possession. Even as the thought came to him, she pulled away and fell sideways across the bed.

He saw at once that she was ill, but he turned away, unable to help her, only capable of struggling with himself. He went to the basin and turned on the tap, plunging his hands in cold water, wishing he could immerse his throbbing groin. That was better. Now he had some control. He turned back to the bed. She was panting a little, her face dead white, her eyes like pools of ink. A petit mal seizure of some kind, he thought.

'What happened? Can you talk?' His own voice was still unsteady. My God, this woman was dangerous. She had nearly driven him to an act of conscious insanity.

'I – I don't know.' She was so white, like the long-time dead. She put her hand to her eyes. 'I thought I was going to faint or something.'

He went to the bed and pulled her nightgown roughly up over her breast. 'I always knew I had sexual prowess, but women don't often faint.'

'You hardly touched me. It wasn't you.'

He stood away from the bed, feeling his blood cool. A low ache stretched across the base of his belly, and the consequence of that was anger. 'I should be grateful for your infirmity,' he said grimly. 'What were you going to do, reach out a hand from beneath my pulsating body and ring for the nurse? I can see the story now, the way you struck me to defend yourself from my brutal demands, only to find that I forced myself upon you the very next day. You have my congratulations, Celia. You chose a good enough way to get rid of me. It's a fine vote of thanks.'

She closed her eyes, the heavy lashes like curtains. 'I didn't want to get rid of you. And you weren't going to make love to me. You just thought you were.'

Incredulous, he said, 'Your friend Dorrie tells me you never used to be so discriminating. I'm surprised you didn't add me to your considerable list just for the hell of it.'

The blue eyes unveiled and stared at him. He was momentarily lost for words. 'I want to go home,' she said softly. 'I want to see my children, and no one can help me but you. Please, Charles.'

'Tell me. What were you going to do?'

She half sat up. 'I don't really know. But I could see when

you came in what you were thinking. It was very easy to lead you on.'

A nurse came in with a jug of water and some flowers. 'From Miss Duncan,' she explained. 'She's coming back tomorrow. These are to cheer you up.'

'Thank you,' said Celia distantly, and when the nurse was gone she sighed. 'Even Dorrie won't visit forever. If you don't let me out of here soon I'll have no one at all.'

'You know perfectly well there's no question of your leaving yet.'

Her blue, speculative gaze remained fixed on him. A pulse was beating at the point of her jaw, and he was amazed at the strength of his annoyance. Why wouldn't she ever just do as she was told? He was going to have to run a whole battery of tests because of that seizure, and just now he wanted to be anywhere but here.

He was leaving, his hand on the door, when she said, 'You want money, don't you? For your work? I can give you that. My father was worth millions. I'll even give you money.'

'You haven't any money!'

'Of course I have. My father was enormously rich. There must be millions.'

Davenport kept his hand on the door. It gave him immense satisfaction to say, 'Celia, your father left his money to your cousin Edwin Braddock. Blantyre House went to your husband, but there's nothing for you. Not a bean.' He left while she still looked amazed.

But Charles had forgotten something. He wanted Celia at a press conference, submissive and docile, giving the lie to Max Grindling's article. Storming away from her room, determined to incarcerate her forever if need be, he remembered. Damn! Now what was he going to do?

He spent the rest of the morning in his outpatient clinic, casting a grim eye over various post-operative patients. They found him more than usually forbidding that day, and his manner wasn't helped by the newspaper they were all reading. The tale of Charles's forcible incarceration of a beautiful young woman was becoming more accepted with every passing moment. 'He looks the sort,' he heard a woman say. 'You can't never trust them with eyes like that. Killer eyes, that's what they are.'

A young girl, fascinated, said, 'He can kill me any day. He's gorgeous!'

He had a lunch date with two other consultants, but cancelled it. He did not wish to fend off ribald comments about his captives with apparent good grace. Instead, after chewing at a cheese sandwich from the canteen, he went to visit Celia once again.

She was dressed and sat by the window working miserably at an old, stiff wicker basket, with everything too dry and long since past its best. She was persisting though, as if the task had some importance, which was better than usual. Too often she worked aimlessly. When he went in, she looked up and said, 'Will you let me go if I finish this? I bet you won't. You'll say making baskets out of dry bamboo has to be insane. And you'll be right.' She tossed it aside, miserably.

'I'm sorry about this morning,' said Davenport. 'I shouldn't have told you like that. About the money.'

She pushed her hair from her face. 'Oh, that. What's a few million between friends?'

He marvelled at her calm. A symptom of the illness perhaps. Another failure to grasp what was real. But it might be that she was naturally insouciant. 'I'm sorry about – the other, as well,' he said jerkily. 'I should never have let it happen.'

'Nothing happened that I didn't wish to happen,' said Celia. Suddenly she got up out of her chair, and he saw that she was a little unsteady on her feet. A legacy of this morning's seizure? He would arrange for some tests later today.

'I'll be able to get the money back, won't I?' she asked. 'I mean, obviously my father wouldn't leave me penniless. We hardly knew Cousin Edwin – he was terribly young.'

'Perhaps your father got to know him better. After your accident.'

'Yes. Perhaps he did.' She picked up her basket and turned it in her hands.

Her façade of calm was crumbling. How odd that she could deceive him into thinking it was real. He wondered about all the other little deceits. Was he flattering himself to think that he had aroused her this morning? He must stop thinking of that! He said carefully and rather too slowly, 'You might have a good case in law. But it takes money to fight. And, honestly, you have none.'

'Anyway,' Celia gripped the basket with febrile energy, 'I want you to talk to David for me. I've been thinking – it isn't fair for me to be shut out. I want to live in Blantyre House. In the staff flat. If you help and support me, if ever I get my inheritance back, I won't forget.'

'You won't get your inheritance, Celia. It's make-believe.'

Her head came up defiantly. 'Why? No court would deny me everything. My father was going to leave his fortune to me, and if he'd known I'd wake up then he would have! And he'd want me to have it now. It was his money, and we should do what he would want. I shall live at Blantyre House and fight for what is rightfully mine, and Heather Wilcox can do what she damn well likes!'

Her voice echoed in the little room, and a nurse poked her head round the door. 'Everything all right?'

'Thank you, Nurse,' said Charles with heavy patience. She retreated, blushing.

'You are a pig, Charles,' said Celia. 'The nurses hate you.'

'Do they?' He was surprised.

'All the ones that don't fancy you,' Celia conceded. She sat down again, feeling ruffled and tearful. She hadn't felt well since this morning, and that was all Charles's fault. Her head ached. Querulously she said, 'I wish you'd talk to David.'

A thought was occurring to Charles. There had to be a way out of this situation. Celia didn't know about the trust fund set up to care for her, and since it was in no one's interest to tell her, it was unlikely that they would. If she left hospital completely then the trust fund would be forfeit – either returned to the Braddock empire, or to Celia, if a court so judged. And he was damned if his department would lose its newly increased share of the loot. Why, he was just beginning

107

to upgrade the theatre, he had equipment on order, new staff to engage – losing all that was unthinkable. But what if he encouraged Celia to leave hospital now? Obviously it was too early. She couldn't be said to have abandoned hospital care. And the chances were that she would be back, chastened, in no time.

He looked at her consideringly, taking the long view. He couldn't keep her here forever without some trial independence. And he needed her to think well of him. If she didn't, what price this press conference he wanted her to attend? But, handled right, there was no need for any upset at all.

'I'll talk to David,' he said slowly, 'if you'll talk to the press.'

A flash of humour lit up her face. 'Nobody believes that article, do they? It's your own fault. I knew you were far too autocratic.'

'Everybody knows it's rubbish, of course. But will you, Celia? Please?'

She thought how charming he could be when he wished. Without the armour plating of arrogance and ambition which overlaid the man's character, there might somewhere be a halfway decent and attractive man.

'It's a deal,' she said.

David Sheraton arrived after lunch. He was wearing a grey suit and a creased silk tie. Celia got up from her seat by the window and extended her hand, smiling formally. 'David. How kind of you to come.'

Charles felt inclined to laugh. David had expected to greet a distraught invalid, and instead she was a charming hostess. Celia was expert at discomfiting people.

David said, 'You look very well, Celia.'

'Do I? Thank you. Better than yesterday, at any rate.' She smiled again and rested her right hand surreptitiously in her lap. This was a struggle for her, thought Charles. In the afternoons Celia always flagged.

He said, 'Mr Sheraton, Celia and I have been talking. We've both agreed that it's time she left hospital. There's no need for her to be a full-time patient any more.'

Sheraton's face registered shock. 'You told me she'd be here for years. You told me – you assured me – she wasn't ever going to be completely well!'

Charles gave a bland, repressing smile. 'It seems I underestimated her capacity for recovery. She fully understands how difficult this is for you, Mr Sheraton. We all do. Celia and I have talked. She knows she has to set up home apart from you.'

'Good. Good. I'm glad that's understood.' David nodded and smiled, flushed and benevolent with relief.

'She would like to move into the staff flat at Blantyre House.'

'What?' David's voice was a bellow of protest. All benevolence was gone. 'Good God! Of course she can't.'

Celia said, 'It's my home. I don't want to live with you, surely that's enough? You and Heather can go on just as you do now.'

'Celia, you know perfectly well it's impossible. You can't just descend on us and disrupt everything! We have our lives to lead, all of us – me, Heather, the children – we can't sacrifice ourselves for you. I mean, obviously this is an amazing miracle, something for which we have to be grateful, but honestly, things have moved on!'

'I didn't plan any of this,' said Celia plaintively. 'I'm not the one who's unreasonable. You can't expect me to crawl away somewhere and not bother you again, just because it's inconvenient. I'm still your wife, I'm still mother to the girls. I can't bear not seeing them. I just can't bear it!'

David said, 'They don't even know you're alive.'

She closed her eyes very quickly. They realised that she was fighting tears. 'That was cruel, Mr Sheraton,' said Davenport. 'I'm sure you had your reasons for concealing Celia's condition, but she doesn't deserve quite such brutal treatment.'

'None of this is my fault,' whispered Celia. 'That's what's so hard. I didn't do anything wrong!'

'Neither did I,' said David. 'I did what seemed best at the time. We didn't know you'd ever recover. We couldn't spend our lives – we couldn't allow ourselves—'

'No,' said Celia. 'I'm sure you couldn't. But you could make up for it now, couldn't you? After all, you didn't divorce me, and you must have had a reason for that. Perhaps you wanted to hang on to something, perhaps you thought it was no way to end a happy marriage. Did you think that, David?'

He sighed wearily. 'I don't know. It seemed – unnecessary, almost. Cruel. And there might have been publicity, the girls might have found out.'

Celia caught her breath. But she said evenly, 'I want to come home. And it *is* my home. If anyone should go somewhere else it's you.'

David said, 'Your father only left me Blantyre House. Nothing else.'

'Yes,' said Celia. 'He always knew you'd let me down.'

David flinched and his colour came up. She had struck back at him, a stinging blow. And then he grinned suddenly, as if recognising in her the girl he had known before. No defeated invalid, this. She was still Celia. He said, 'I suppose I deserve that. I haven't been kind. But I can't lie to you, pretend things aren't as they are. Everything's been turned upside down. Nothing's the way it was, we haven't the money! We're not poor exactly, but it's a struggle. After the accident – well, your father made no attempt to hide the fact that he hated me. Everything went to Edwin.'

Celia made a face. 'Spotty little Edwin, who couldn't play tennis? I'll talk to him. I'm sure I can get some of it back.'

'Are you?' David looked at her. 'You didn't know him. None of us did. He's as tight as they come, and he won't give you a bean.'

She stared at him for a moment, as if bewildered. Then she rose and began pacing the limited confines of the room. Both men watched her, mesmerised by the swish of a borrowed skirt against the furniture, the stretching of her neck at each turn and toss of her head. 'I don't care about all of this,' she said in a low, rushed voice. 'I must get out of here! You don't understand what it's like. I've lost my life, I've lost the best years. I'm thirty-five, and everything's gone. I've got to get it back, before it's too late.'

David said, 'There's no getting it back. It's gone for good.'

'No!' She put her hands up to her face.

Her husband rose and drew her hands down. It was the first time he had touched her, Charles realised, and felt a surge of resentment.

'Stay here,' David was urging. 'You're not well enough. I don't want to be unkind to you, but ten years is a very long time! We should have divorced perhaps. It would have been more honest. Perhaps then you'd have understood.'

She said, helplessly, 'I don't see how you could just stop loving. Even if I'd died, you don't just stop.'

He looked down at her, his face quite cold. 'I changed. The accident changed me. You were right not to recognise me at first. I'm not the same man at all.'

'You are! You are!' Her voice broke.

'No, Celia.'

'Is it because of that stupid thing with Gordon Fletcher?'

He dropped her hand and turned away. A muscle fluttered in his cheek, and he was shaking. Charles watched dispassionately, surprised that the man had taken so long to crack. It was an intolerable position.

'I prayed for you to live,' said David urgently. 'You should know that. At first, I thought it would kill me if you died.'

'But when I didn't die you got tired of waiting,' flashed Celia. 'You must have been miserable, waiting for me to go. And there was Heather, at the door, ready to dry your tears. She was the real reason you didn't get the money. My father gave it to Edwin because of you and Heather, didn't he?'

David said nothing. In a voice made shrill with emotion Celia went on, 'And what about Heather? My father always said she was a prissy, self-righteous bore, and he was right!'

David turned on her. 'Your father was nothing but a vindictive bastard. He didn't give a damn about anything or anyone, and he despised most men and all women. That's how he got to be so rich – because he was a two-faced, scheming hypocrite without a decent feeling anywhere.'

Celia was pleading. 'Don't talk about him like that. Not now, not when he's dead.'

He gave her a look of weary resignation. 'We said it when he was alive. Don't you remember? Joe Braddock had only one redeeming feature.'

'What was that?'

'He loved you.'

Celia began to cry, soft tears of despair. Charles said, 'This is too much. It's unnecessary. You can rake over the coals some other time. We are here now simply to decide where Celia's going to live.'

She wept on. 'I only want to go home. It's so lovely there. It's my home.'

David said, 'There should be somewhere sheltered within the hospital. Surely something could be arranged?'

Charles lifted a hand. 'No. I think Celia's right. The staff flat's an ideal compromise. She can come first thing tomorrow.'

Sheraton drew in his breath, struggling to find a reason to say no. Charles looked at him blandly, aware that he wanted nothing so much as to put Sheraton down. But the man was in no position to resist. Charles felt Celia's eyes upon him. She was willing him silent thanks.

Celia attended the press conference. She was very tired, but today, for Charles, she would do anything. She dressed as an invalid, in nightdress and towelling robe, and appeared hesitant and lost for words. But she managed somehow to say her piece. Mr Davenport was all kindness. Mr Davenport was so good. If it wasn't for him she'd never have recovered at all, and he wasn't keeping her a minute longer than necessary. In fact, he was arranging for her to go home.

Max Grindling, chewing his moustache at the front of the room, said, 'He grabbed you back fast enough yesterday, though.'

Celia said, 'I wasn't well. He worries. He's very kind.'

Charles intervened smoothly, 'We're very anxious that Mrs Sheraton's return home should be successful and properly supervised. Officially she remains a patient of this hospital until her recovery is absolute.'

'Usual, is it? Keeping them on the books?'

Grindling was unpleasantly tenacious. Charles said, 'Mrs Sheraton's case will always be unusual.'

The reporters weren't happy. They wanted some meat.

112

Hard-bitten hacks to a man, they looked cynically for signs of abuse. They wanted to know if she was given drugs, tranquillisers, anything? Celia shook her head. 'No. I had sherry at home. It made me feel better than anything!'

'We don't prescribe sherry,' said Davenport mildly. 'People would be queuing up to get in.'

'When are you going home, Celia?' asked a woman reporter, suspiciously.

She hunted for words that seemed to be denied. Charles said, 'She's going tomorrow. It's a trial. If it's too much, she'll come back. You see, I don't believe in standard care for any patient. There's no such thing as a standard patient. Take the kids in my unit; little chap called Richard, I took a huge growth away six weeks ago. Inevitably there were large areas of damage. He could be forgiven for lying around like a cabbage, but he's up, he's fighting. If we had the resources, Celia wouldn't be the only miracle in my department. What I'm trying to say is, I'm no miracle worker. No one is. All it takes is the will, and let's be honest, the money, to try.' It was an obvious pitch, based on an approximation of the truth. Richard was a nice little boy whose large but benign growth had been removed without much trouble at all. But Charles wasn't above taking credit for his recovery. Not in this company, anyway.

When everyone had gone, Celia plucked a flower from an arrangement and shredded it viciously. 'I was an idiot,' she raged. 'I can't talk with so many people. I looked like a fool.'

Charles said, 'You'll get over it.' He came up close to her and took a strand of her hair in his fingers. It was paler than the rest, a streak of incipient white. It touched him utterly. White hair, when she was no more than a girl.

'Come and see me,' said Celia.

'Yes. All the time. You're still my patient.'

She smiled at him. 'Am I? Good. I'm glad.'

The door opened. It was Dorrie. Charles stepped away, suddenly embarrassed. 'Hi,' he said. 'We didn't know you were back.'

'Didn't you get my flowers?'

'Oh, Dorrie!' Celia ran across, full of excitement.

'Tomorrow I'm going home. I'm going home!'

She was dressed again in the clothes she had worn to the television studio. The white shoes seemed particularly horrible today, but she gritted her teeth, determined that nothing should spoil her homecoming.

'Remember,' Charles said, 'take things slowly. Don't expect too much. You're still a patient. We haven't finished with you yet.'

She grinned at him, too excited to take note.

David was driving one of his own cars, a Sheraton. It was a two-seater with a tiny back seat under the fold-down hood, and Celia slid into the leather with a feeling of intense familiarity. Yet the Sheraton was the car she had crashed in. Green upholstery. She looked at David's lean profile, at the tense set of his jaw. She felt nervous suddenly. Did he truly not want her? This was the man to whom she had once entrusted her life, willingly, with joy. She felt as if she barely knew him.

The staff lined up on the steps, waving and calling encouragement. Half the hospital had turned out to say goodbye. Charles stood in the midst of them, very tall and dark, and if she could have got out of the car then she would have run back to the shelter of his control. If only David looked as he had before, she thought. His face had thinned, and each tiny crease beneath his eyes betokened years of change. Yet he couldn't be so different, whatever he said. She was the same now as she was then. Ten years wasn't so long. The man she had loved, who had loved her, must in essence be the same. She must search for him.

Chapter Eight

Ellen flung into the kitchen and crashed the door back into its frame. Heather winced and put a hand to her temple. 'Ellen! Dear! My head.'

'Sorry.' The girl went to the cupboard and began rummaging for biscuits.

Heather said, 'Please, not before tea. You know the rules.'

'Tea's not for hours. Stop nagging.'

'It isn't nagging to expect a girl of your age to have some sense of responsibility.'

Ellen pulled a long-suffering face and gave up on the biscuits. She felt misunderstood these days, and it wasn't just the biscuits. Her parents didn't know what her life was like. What was the point in crippling themselves to send her to an expensive school when they couldn't afford to let her do the things everyone else did? Today, for instance. Riding. Fifteen pounds a lesson and everyone did it except her and Abigail, who was allergic to horses. Fifteen measly quid! And everyone would go skiing with the school that winter, and stay in a glamorous hotel, while she spent the week in freezing Blantyre House, keeping up appearances when they couldn't even afford to run the central heating. Not that she minded about the riding, or the skiing. She just minded being poor.

She became aware that Heather was hovering. Did she think she was about to stage a raid on the biscuits, despite her? Ellen picked up an apple and crunched morosely, oblivious of Heather's turmoil. This wasn't the moment to break the news, but if she didn't say something soon Celia would arrive. If only Ellen had seen the papers, or one of her friends had seen and told her. At least that would be impersonal. She wouldn't have to be standing here doing this.

She watched Ellen scratch herself inelegantly through a hole in her black tights. 'I wish you wouldn't wear tights with holes in,' she said despairingly. 'I buy you new pairs. It gives such a bad impression.'

'I like them with holes.' It was Ellen's mute protest against the kindly, jolly staff at school who never remotely suspected the torments she endured. She hated them for their determined good humour. She hated them even for their charity.

Heather was annoying her, but what else was new? Ellen went to the back door, intending to pass the time until tea in an unhappy mooch around the garden. But suddenly Heather leapt forward. 'Ellen! Don't go! There's something I want to say.'

'Yes? Well? Has the school been on?'

'No. Why?'

'Nothing.'

The interruption upset Heather. She wondered if there was something at school that she should know. Had Ellen been writing on lavatory walls again? But whether she had or whether she hadn't, there was certainly something Ellen should be told, and quickly, before Lucy came home from her piano lesson. Ellen used to have piano lessons herself, of course, because musical talent had to be fostered, but she had dropped them and demanded riding lessons and skiing holidays instead. Heather was beginning to suspect that she was hopelessly materialistic. Just like her terrible mother.

'Someone's coming to stay,' she burst out. 'In the staff flat.'

'Oh, bloody hell! We're not reduced to taking lodgers, are we?'

'Ellen, please don't swear. You know how it upsets me. Of course it isn't lodgers.'

'Is it someone to help? I could have a pony, we've got the room. I wouldn't need riding lessons if I had a pony.'

'It – it isn't anyone to help. Ellen, do sit down. I want to tell you something.'

'You can tell me when I'm standing.'

A steel band seemed to close around Heather's forehead. A migraine was beginning, just when she needed all her wits and all her strength. At work today she had made a quite uncharacteristic mistake, but was it surprising when so much was happening at home? If only she could tell someone. Someone who would understand. Someone who wasn't Ellen.

'Your mother's coming to stay,' she said, and watched the startlement on Ellen's face.

'Er – you've got one of your headaches, haven't you?' said Ellen cautiously. 'I'll go and ring Dad.'

'Ellen, listen! I'm not going mad. You think your mother's dead, but she isn't. She never was. She was ill, in hospital, unconscious. We thought she was a vegetable, and she was, she was! But a new doctor came. Ellen, she's woken up. She's better. After ten years, your mother's coming home.'

'I think I'd better go and ring Dad,' said Ellen again.

'You can't.' Heather muffled her words in her hands, pressing them hard against her lips. The headache was thundering like a trip hammer, with little pulses of flashing light on the edge of her vision. 'Your father's gone to fetch her. They'll be here any time.'

'Oh.'

Ellen just stood there. Her long, honey hair was in tangles, her stockings full of holes, there were inkstains on her fingers and marks on the cuffs of her shirt. Celia would think they hadn't even the money to be clean, thought Heather despairingly. And what did Ellen think? Her face was icy still.

'Lucy's going to be upset,' she said suddenly.

'You're upset, aren't you?'

'I'm older than Lucy. Dad always said she was dead. We talked about her. Only the other week—'

Heather gulped. 'He was trying to tell you. If only he had the courage he was born with!'

It was the first time Ellen had ever heard Heather criticise her father. Her attitude was normally one of unquestioning admiration. David was creative, David was brilliant, if the family lacked money it was simply because he wouldn't stoop to any of the degrading things that other girls' fathers did. Even when Ellen was feeling at her most deprived she never doubted this view of her father. Dissatisfaction with her lot never extended all the way to him.

'What's going to happen?' she asked tensely. 'Are you leaving?'

'No, of course I'm not!' Heather got up and went to fetch the cooking brandy. She poured herself a large measure and gulped half of it down. 'She's not still your father's wife. I mean, she is, but we all thought she'd die! If we'd known this would happen – but we couldn't know. It's never happened before and it shouldn't have happened now. She isn't – I'm not – she's going to be like a guest. Like a lodger, I suppose. She'll stay in the flat and we'll go on just as before. And probably your father will divorce her.'

'Oh. Why? He didn't before.'

'He didn't have to before. And there'd have been publicity. People would have talked – oh, Ellen, didn't you think it was odd that your father and I weren't married?'

The girl shook her head. Half her friends migrated between divorced or divorcing parents. People moved in and out of marriages in a dance that seemed to her without rules or mores. Her own odd situation didn't trouble her. She barely thought of it.

Suddenly she said, 'She was here. We saw her. That woman you said was a customer.'

'Yes. That was her.'

'She didn't look like I remember.'

'Do you remember?'

Ellen nodded. But her mother had been warm, alive, a presence so real and so substantial that it could not be like that pale and ghostly woman she had seen. She began to be filled with a deep and instinctive reluctance; she didn't want to know, didn't want to be told, she wanted to be kept safe and secure in her childish world of ignorance. There was no thought in her mind that this might turn out well. It was unfamiliar and therefore frightening. She would rather live with her present miseries than change them for any others. She did not expect to be happy.

The front door banged exuberantly. Heather shuddered, but it was only Lucy, ferried home by the obliging mother of a fellow pupil. 'He says I've got to practise two hours every day,' she declared, heading for the biscuits like iron filings to a

118

magnet. Heather was too miserable to oppose her. 'He's a creep.'

'He thinks you could be good,' said Heather absently. 'You've got talent. He wouldn't bother otherwise.'

She forced herself to look at Ellen. The girl was standing silent, eyes to the floor. So, she would not take on this duty. It was left to Heather, the step-parent, with no rights and no privileges but endless responsibility. 'Lucy,' she began, 'your mother's coming home.' And with that, the child's eyes like saucers, full of disbelief, they heard the car.

Nobody made a move to go out into the hall. Lucy said, 'Did she run away, then? Was that it?'

'She's been ill,' said Heather.

'Was she mad? Like Mrs Rochester?'

'Lucy, shut up,' said Ellen.

All three stood facing the door, as if about to be attacked by a lion. The suspense was terrible, Heather thought she must faint, she could barely breathe. How could David do this to her? And then he was saying, 'They must all be in here.' The door opened. Celia was there.

She was whiter even than before. The ridiculous stilettoes made her very tall, and she teetered uncertainly. David tried to squeeze past her into the room, studiously avoiding touching her with so much as the sleeve of his jacket. 'Hello, everyone,' she said.

Ellen felt tears pricking her eyes and blinked hard to dissipate them. How could they do this? How could they intrude so cruelly into her own inner life and stand watching to see what they could? Lucy let out a nervous cough, a habit she had when under stress.

Celia said, 'You all seem very surprised.'

'I've only just told them,' said Heather stiffly. 'We didn't expect you so soon.'

'You didn't want me at all, Heather,' said Celia. 'It's all right, I quite understand. Although why you didn't tell my daughters that I was alive is something I do not understand. They had a right to know.'

Ellen said, 'It wouldn't have been good for us.'

'Wouldn't it?' Lucy looked in amazement from one person

119

to the other. 'I don't like secrets. It's rotten to keep a secret like that.'

'Don't be rude, Lucy,' said David. 'We did what was best.'

Celia was holding herself in so tightly that she felt she would snap. But if she relaxed she thought she might fall screaming on to the floor, defeated by the closed, shocked faces of her daughters. She wished, suddenly, with violence, that Heather would go away. She had no rights here. It was like a mother-in-law sitting in on a marital row, inhibiting to the point of strangulation. Celia's head was filled with sound, the eldritch voices that screamed at her to faint. Teetering on her heels, she moved to a chair and sat down. Again everyone turned to face her. 'Can I have a cup of tea?' she demanded testily.

David went to put the kettle on. In the silence Celia found herself noting the decorations, the excessively cottagey furnishings, the over-abundance of cupboards. 'You've made a terrible mess of this kitchen,' she remarked.

'We like it,' said Ellen. 'It's nothing to do with you.'

Celia blinked. 'This was my house before it was yours,' she said. 'I was born here. We used to have a big pine table, scrubbed almost white. And a range which we didn't use, but it looked lovely with pine cones in it. And a flagged floor with lovely old rugs, and a huge old white sink. You could bath dogs in it. We often did.'

'Did you have a dog?' asked Lucy, sitting down and curling her knees up.

'Yes. Don't you remember? You saw him when we came to tea here and I used to tell you about him. Spot.' She began to sing, her voice light and easy. '"Spit, Spat, Spot, We love you a lot, Dear little Spot, With your waggly, waggly tail!"' She looked from Lucy to Ellen and back again. 'Surely you remember.'

Lucy shook her head, but began to sing the song anyway. Ellen, flushing to the roots of her honey hair, turned and ran from the room.

Heather banged the teapot down on the polished table, and it was sure to mark. It was a measure of her distress. 'You always were totally insensitive!' she hissed.

'Please, Heather,' warned David. 'Not in front of the girls.'

Celia said, 'I wish you wouldn't see all this as my fault. I didn't tell them lies.'

David said, 'Lucy, go to your room, please. Now.'

She stood her ground. 'But I want to know what's going on.'

'Lucy! Now!'

'But—'

'I'll come and talk to you later,' said Celia. 'I'll explain everything. And I promise not to tell you a single lie.'

Heather let out a crack of derisive laughter. 'You'll just distort the truth, I suppose! You're unprincipled, and devious, and you shouldn't be here. You shouldn't have come! You should – go to hell!'

It was Heather's turn to fling out of the room. Lucy stood open-mouthed, and David said gently, 'Off you go, Lucy. Everyone's upset, we can't talk.' Shocked into obedience, she went.

'Well,' said Celia, 'what a homecoming!'

'What did you expect? Flags and rejoicing?'

'Not quite. But something. A nice meal, perhaps. Some wine. Some civilised talk with my daughters.' She got up and fetched two cups from a glass-fronted cupboard, and then tried and failed to lift the teapot. She changed hands and poured two shaky cups of tea with her left hand. 'What a mess we're all in,' she remarked.

'I tried to tell you. I tried to make you see.'

Celia closed her eyes and let the steam from her cup soothe her eyelids. Hospital tea was never hot enough. She wondered how David put up with this existence. Heather, in this suburban kitchen, shut in by prejudice and lack of cash. There was no disguising the little economies they were making about the place. No gardener, no window cleaner, camping in a few rooms because there was no one to help in the house. The easy life, the luxury and fun of before had been forgotten.

She said, 'You've not done very well for yourself, have you?'

He tried to laugh. 'Indeed? I picked up the pieces. Brought up the girls. We've been very happy on the whole.'

She cast a disparaging eye round the kitchen. 'On the whole? That must be what comes of living a lie.'

'A lie? You were as good as dead.'

Celia looked at him over her cup. Her eyes were as dark as the Aegean Sea. Why did he think of that now?

'I was talking about you and Heather,' she said softly. 'David! What a mistake.'

He coloured. Looking at her disturbed him. He found himself thinking of love, on a hot island beach, the sea reflected in her eyes. Why think of that now, more than fifteen years later? He could even recall the wonderful taste of what was probably mediocre swordfish in the taverna later. 'I love Heather,' he said throatily.

'No you don't.' The same knowledgeable, seductive smile. 'You think you should, that's all.'

He felt a sense of incredulity. How had he come to be in this position? He and Heather had been as settled as any other couple, with a few problems, admittedly, but secure with each other; happy. To have Celia here now seemed like a dream, a fantasy, like his youth returned to haunt him in calm middle age. He and Celia would never have settled like this. They would have shared no mutual contentment. And now his contentment was gone.

Her tea was finished. He got up to take her to the staff flat, but of course she knew the way. She walked in front of him up the stairs, pausing on the half landing to catch her breath. He saw that she was trembling, that when she walked in front of him again the muscles in her buttocks were braced for each and every step. And the flat was cold and cheerless. The bed was unmade, with merely a pile of sheets at its side, and in the small kitchen a fly buzzed against the window amidst a dozen corpses of its fellows who had buzzed before.

Celia looked about her and felt the slow flames of anger. Somebody could have made an effort. There could have been some small measure of preparation in the last twenty-four hours. But she wasn't meant to succeed here. David, Davenport, and certainly Heather, wanted her back in that hospital within a week. She would not oblige them. She would not!

'What time is dinner?' she asked carefully. 'Perhaps we'll go out?'

'I very much doubt it,' said David testily. 'Anything decent round here is at least thirty pounds a head.'

'Thirty pounds? Don't exaggerate.'

'Prices have changed, Celia. Times have changed.'

'You used to be able to eat out for a fiver.'

'A long time ago.'

In my day we could have a week in Blackpool, fourteen fish suppers, a visit to Whipsnade and a copy of *Weekend* and still have change from a florin. She and Dorrie used to make up things like that. Now she too would be a money bore, gasping at prices. Well, she wouldn't. She would adjust – in fact, she had already done so.

'What time shall I come down?' She faced him, refusing to be imprisoned here, wanting to scream and hit him. Instead her weapons must be hidden in good manners.

'I don't know if Heather's cooking anything.'

'David dear, we must all eat.'

'Yes.'

He went out, closing the door firmly behind him. Here she was, then. Hidden in the roof, as far away from the family as was possible. They wanted to forget her, lock her away like a ghastly secret. Celia slumped on the unmade bed and closed her eyes for a blissful second. She would go down at seven, whatever they said.

Dorrie said, 'Long time no see.'

'Too long.' Davenport put his bottle of wine and bag of food on the table. Peace offerings. He should have called round when Dorrie came back from visiting her mother, but he hadn't. Why? Perhaps because Dorrie was nothing if not perceptive.

'Did you see her off?' Dorrie rummaged in the bag, finding some sticky cakes. She went off to look for a corkscrew and he knew she would drink wine and eat cake and not give a damn. He liked her so much.

'David Sheraton took her,' he called. 'Looked like death warmed up.'

Dorrie laughed. 'Don't worry, he always did. Celia sorted

him. It was what she was good at, making people different. When they were together David was a very amusing man. But now Heather!'

It was Charles who laughed this time. Heather was so earnest, so proper. He could imagine her working till dawn for nights before an exam, and still not beating the brilliant dilettante with the hangover. She would be an excellent and noble employee, but one without flair. 'Poor Heather,' he said thoughtfully.

'And poor you.'

He looked up at Dorrie in surprise. She was sipping her wine, her fingers already sticky from shop-bought icing. He waited for her to explain. 'You've lost your pretty doll,' she said.

He coughed and reached for his own glass. 'I'm too professional to fall for the patients, Dorrie.'

'Rubbish. She was your fantasy girl. And now she's gone off and you've got to come back to good old Dorrie. Aren't you glad I don't bear grudges?'

'I never touched Celia!' But he had. Oh, he had. He forced himself not to think of it, and found he was gritting his teeth. Dorrie chuckled knowingly.

They went up to her bed this time. It was as huge and soft as Dorrie herself, and Charles found himself sunk in a welter of feathers and flesh. He lay on his back, his erection the only solid thing in the bed, and Dorrie sat on him, her pretty face riding above her gathering folds of flesh. He had never relished being underneath, he hated the loss of control. But he didn't want to control Dorrie. It was too casual, too much a thing between friends for power to come into it. She closed her eyes and rocked on him, and he waited, patiently, for her to be satisfied. But the thought came again: Celia, her breast naked and exposed: holding her, hearing her gasp. He came, with a violent rush, and Dorrie was left stranded.

'I am sorry,' he said, knowing he had blotted his sexual copybook; he didn't know Dorrie well enough to give up being polite.

'Hmmm.' She lay down next to him, looking mutinous.

Charles fought off the thought of sleep and reached across. He had upset Dorrie enough lately. There was work to be done.

At Linton Place Edwin was walking his dogs. As he rounded the lake on the return leg, he saw Cartwright walking briskly across the grass towards him. He hesitated for a moment, wondering if it would do Cartwright good to be given the slip in the woods, and then walked on. He needed to know what had brought the fellow here.

The dogs bounded towards the advancing figure with worrying verve. Edwin waited until the last moment before calling them back, and the dogs returned to him, grinning. Cartwright said shakily, 'Dear me, sir. They're fierce.'

'They're meant to be.'

Edwin stood and let his employee walk right up to him. He liked these little exercises of power; they ensured that the people who worked for him remained always in a proper attitude of service, and never argued or answered back. But he wouldn't have minded if Cartwright had; he was a good-looking young chap.

Cartwright came to a respectful distance and then stopped, offering his employer a file.

'Well? What is it, man? You know what's in it, I presume.' But if he had announced what it was Edwin would have berated him for bringing a file unnecessarily, or for failing to bring it if he had not, or indeed for anything else he had or had not done.

'Mrs Sheraton has left hospital, sir. Recovered.'

A goose on the lake started to call, the long, ugly honking that Edwin found more soothing than a nightingale. His dogs, ranging in the undergrowth, put up a pheasant in a clatter of wings, and Edwin called them in while he thought.

'Is she – you say she's no longer a patient.'

'She's no longer in hospital, sir. She remains under medical supervision.'

'What sort of supervision?'

'I – I really don't know, sir.'

'Well, you bloody well should know! Find out. If it's

125

anything less than total then the hospital forfeits its gift and the money comes to us. If they've any sense they'll retrieve her at once.'

'What is total supervision, sir?'

'Oh, for God's sake! A full-time nurse perhaps. Hospitalisation. No less than that.'

'Yes, sir. Very good, sir.'

Cartwright began to walk away. He was a tall young man, quite slim, with a nervousness that only showed when he was with Edwin. Sometimes, watching him from his window, it made Edwin laugh to think that this same dapper young chap was the insecure twitcher that he'd berated ten times a day. A thought occurred to him. It was one which he had entertained a number of times before, but always discarded; in these things the moment had to be right, the situation opportune. One must never seem to be in any sense the supplicant. A man in his position bestowed his favours as a privilege, even – he thought of it ruefully, knowing himself – as a means of protection. Cartwright was the abused employee, and he could be offered the chance to be instead the beloved pet.

Edwin jogged easily after him. 'No need to dash off, old boy,' he said, and flung a companionable arm around Cartwright's shoulders. 'You can see to that little task tomorrow. Let's have a drink together. A chat. I've been thinking for some time that you and I should get together.'

'Get together, sir?'

'Yes. You'd like that, I'm sure.'

He watched the man's face intently. Cartwright wasn't inexperienced, he knew that. But if there was dismay – repugnance, even – he would have to go. Instead, the clear round eyes showed what Edwin had expected; the master's hand, instead of beating, was rubbing the cur's rough neck and it was good.

David presided over a poorly set table and a worse meal. Heather had thrown together some tinned soup, ham, bread, and an inadequate salad. He opened some wine, trying to relieve things, but Heather had a migraine coming on and couldn't drink. He and Celia matched each other, glass for glass down the bottle, while Lucy prattled on.

'It must have been terrible, asleep for ten years. Did you dream?'

'Yes. A lot. About you, mostly.' A lie, of course. David knew it was a lie, but it was so like Celia to tell it.

'I don't believe you,' said Ellen.

Celia laughed. 'Don't you? You're right not to. I was trying to flatter myself into your affections. You see, I don't know what was dream and what wasn't. Sometimes now I wake up in the morning and think this is a dream. My two girls, almost grown up, and so beautiful. That has to be a dream.'

'Are we beautiful?' Lucy's chubby face was wistful.

Her mother nodded. 'More beautiful than you will ever know.'

Heather roused herself from her state of advanced misery, and said, 'You're just making them silly, Celia. I've spent years trying to give them some vestige of sense and good manners and now you're making them silly and vain.'

'Oh, I hope so,' said Celia. 'All girls are silly and vain sometimes. But, of course, they're other things too.'

'They have exams,' intoned Heather.

'So what?' Celia emptied her glass. 'I got straight A's, with never a stroke, and I'm sure you work these two to death.'

'I've been told I could study medicine,' said Ellen primly.

Celia said, 'How fascinating. You can meet lots of people like me.'

David chuckled, and caught his daughter's eye. The determined wall she had erected against Celia was starting to crumble. Celia was so funny when she wanted, self-deprecating and sweet. But that was only one face of Celia, the face she used when she had been found out. After the Fletcher incident, she had said, 'I'm a slut, David. Beat me. Go on, beat me. I shall hate it but you won't. Expiate your rage and my guilt, and afterwards, if the bruises show, I'll tell everyone I've taken up mud wrestling for cash. See what I do for you, darling.'

She had always known how to excite him. He let his eyes linger on her now, in her ill-fitting clothes, which she somehow managed to make seem better than they were. She was exhausted, relying on willpower alone to get her through this meal. He noticed the way she retired her right hand into her lap, and managed one-handed. And as he watched, it was as if a veil was pulled slowly and carefully over her face. Her features seemed to lose their definition.

'Did you have a job, or did you just have us?' demanded Lucy, and Celia, with an effort obvious to all, staggered to her feet. 'Sorry. Tired. No words.'

As she reeled from the table and from the room, Heather said viciously, 'There's no point in thinking I'll take care of her, David! She isn't my responsibility.'

So, in Blantyre House that night, everyone was alone. Celia was collapsed on the unmade bed of the flat, while her daughters lay sleepless in the rooms below. Heather was rigid on the farthest edge of the double bed, while David lay on his back, gazing into the dark as the memories, banished for years now, played across his mind like an eternally vivid film. Life was a journey with no going back, but for some reason, some unknown and bewildering reason, they were all to step back in time. He felt there must be a reason to it. Somewhere, at some point, mistakes had been made. They were being forced to try again.

Chapter Nine

Mr James, the hospital administrator, was all unctuous charm. He offered coffee, then tea, and moved on to sherry and whisky and might have ended up at vintage Dom Perignon, if his visitor hadn't lifted a hand. 'Thank you, no. I really can't stay.'

'Perhaps I could show you the hospital? Our new heart wing's the very latest – but, of course, we're spending on neurology now that we have Mr Davenport. He's done so much for Mrs Sheraton. A wonderful doctor.'

'Indeed.'

There was a tense pause. No one from the Braddock Corporation had ever found reason to visit the hospital. This was a first, and a very unwelcome one. The visitor cleared his throat. 'Mr James, the Braddock Corporation has never before had cause to question any aspect of the running of this hospital. But we have been made anxious, in fact very anxious, about Mrs Sheraton.'

'I assure you – no need – excellent attention—'

'But the condition under which the trust operates is that she receives constant care.'

The administrator swallowed. 'We are supervising her very carefully, of course. But she was well enough to go home, and without any specific communication from the Corporation—'

'We are communicating now.'

There was a tense and unhappy silence. The administrator was experiencing a nightmare vision of closed wards, empty beds and irate doctors. His visitor stood up, pulling on a thin pair of driving gloves. He was enjoying this. 'Mrs Sheraton must return to the hospital. We expect her to remain a full-time patient, receiving the utmost care. There have been no scans for at least three months—'

'There was no need—'

'—and we wish a scan to be produced for our inspection at two-monthly intervals. We have it on good authority that Mrs Sheraton has speech problems and cannot accept reality. In the opinion of experts, this renders her incapable of independent life. Do you understand us, Mr James?'

'Yes – yes. Absolutely.'

The administrator was almost gibbering. The press would be like wild dogs once they discovered the transplant programme wasn't to go ahead, and it was only a matter of time before they found out where the money had been coming from all these years. He had done nothing dishonest, but he knew how feeble it was all going to sound. At the very least, Mrs Sheraton should have been told the terms of her care. He would be lucky to get out alive, let alone with a job.

His visitor, watching his torment, smiled sympathetically. He knew what this was like. He'd been trampled on a million times, and with a lot less cause. The woman was obviously nuts.

Collecting his briefcase and smoothing his hair, Cartwright bade his host good day.

Dorrie was painting. She had ceased to like the picture some few days ago, but she persisted. It was in a style much favoured by the smart London gallery she supplied, but it was a style she thought she had outgrown. But, when she had tried them with her new thoughts, more flowery, more relaxed, altogether less stark, they had been appalled. They said she had gone for the chocolate box image; she was not known for painting pleasantly, and should stick to her last; her pictures were meant to distress.

Dorrie didn't feel like peddling that any more. A bleak view was all very well when reality was tolerable, but her year was becoming more and more upsetting. It was all because of Celia.

The face of the mother in her work was eluding her. Try as she would to create suffering, she succeeded only in a simpering smile, hinting at well-ironed clothes, honey for tea, and Elastoplast for grazed knees. Dorrie's brush hung thoughtfully in the air. She would have been such a mother. She would have surrounded her children with warmth and love like an invisible cocoon.

A taxi drew up in the street outside. Dorrie craned her neck to see, although from her studio only the bottom third of the pavement was visible. White stiletto heels. Celia.

They repaired to the kitchen for coffee. 'You look terrible,' said Dorrie.

'Thanks.' Celia sank into a chair and let her head hang back. She had been home only two days. Her hair needed washing. She looked as if at any moment she might cry. 'They're trying to get rid of me,' she said thickly.

'Well, you knew Heather would. Obviously.'

'Yes! But David – and Ellen? Only Lucy seems pleased to have me around, and even she behaves as if I was a creature from Mars. It's my home and I'm a stranger in it. They won't let me do anything, in case I establish some sort of right to be there. They all keep out of my way. I see no one from morning till night, I can't stand it!'

Dorrie put a good big cup of coffee in front of her. 'You can always go back to hospital. Has Charles been round?'

Celia hunched a shoulder. 'He's coming today. That's why I'm here. If he sees how I'm living he'll have me back in a blink. I'm not as strong as I thought I was, Dorrie. It takes me an hour to make the bed and I can't get out of the bath.'

She shuddered, remembering. The old-fashioned cast iron tub in the staff flat had no grab handles and a smooth, shiny bottom. Climbing in on the first morning, Celia had discovered she could not get out. Her legs lacked the strength and her arms could find no firm hold. She had been reduced eventually to lying over the side and crawling out while hanging on to the edge of the door, but it was either that or sit there forever. She doubted that anyone would bother to worry enough to come to the rescue. Suddenly she was in tears. 'They don't love me!' she wailed. 'Nobody does.'

'They don't know you, love. We've all changed.'

Celia wept on.

Dorrie took charge. She put Celia in the bath and washed her hair, smoothing conditioner into the long, golden strands.

131

Celia moaned and complained as the suds were rinsed away, and Dorrie slapped her in a motherly way, hauling her from the bath and drying her as if she were no more than ten. She enjoyed caring for people. It was a side of her that received no encouragement.

'You should have children, Dorrie,' said Celia, beginning to feel more herself. 'You should get married.'

'I've tried both,' said Dorrie grimly. 'You were asleep at the time. It didn't work out. So be grateful for the little you have, my girl. Now, what shall we do?'

'Go shopping,' said Celia determinedly. 'David's new credit card arrived today, with one for Mrs Celia Sheraton. He went bright red and said it was an administrative error. I took it anyway.'

'Very Freudian, getting credit cards for you,' remarked Dorrie.

Celia grimaced. 'He probably did it to keep Heather on her toes. He never used to be manipulative. That was me.'

They took a taxi to the High Street. There was no alternative, Celia only had her terrible high heels and they crippled her to walk. So they went first to a shoe shop and bought a pair of flat black pumps and a pair of trainers.

'They're expensive,' warned Dorrie. 'Can you stand that much?'

Celia waved her credit card. 'Who cares? A hundred pounds is nothing these days. You can spend thirty pounds a head on a meal.'

'Yes, but—'

'Don't be a money bore, Dorrie.'

Celia swept imperiously down the road. The shop windows made her feel drunk. Smooth wool suits, fine linen dresses, swimwear, beachwear, lingerie – she wanted it all. The clothes she had worn recently had either smothered her in nondescription, or made statements that were patently not true. She stopped outside Chrysanthemum, a shop her mother used to use, and saw that it was still the place to go. Chic handbags and belts waved seductive buckles, and a plain dress in blue silk nodded from the model and said: 'Buy me.'

She walked through the door, with Dorrie at her elbow saying, 'Celia! Celia, are you sure this is OK?'

'I've got to have something to wear.'

'We can go to Marks and Spencer's. Even the market sells antique lace. This place is extortionate.'

'Look, I've got to have something.' She waved Dorrie aside like an irritating fly. First she would try the blue dress in the window, and then a suit in a multi-coloured weave, very summery and fresh. And no one should be without linen. She touched a jacket as dark as her eyes, with lovely gold buttons. She had to have it. It was a must.

When they emerged their arms bulged with parcels. 'Do you know, Heather's using one of my old handbags?' said Celia. She was feeling cheerful, delighted with her spending.

'Your mother got rid of most things,' said Dorrie. 'She wouldn't have given anything to Heather.'

'It must have been David, then.'

They stopped at a cafe to revive themselves. Celia had a cocktail made with creme de menthe and brandy, with a plastic monkey holding an umbrella balanced on the rim. Dorrie had a beer.

'How is David?' she asked.

Celia shrugged. 'Silent. Avoiding. Tortured.' She sipped her cocktail and giggled. 'He looks at me as if I was dangerous. I think he still fancies me, though.'

'Bound to,' said Dorrie. 'Your marriage was built on sex.'

'Dorrie, that's rubbish! We had two children and a home. We were very close. I miss that most, I think. The closeness.'

But Celia had been closer to her father than to David. They had understood each other, born of the same stock, branches of the same tree. They were each as clever and tough and undisciplined as the other.

'You going to seduce him?' asked Dorrie.

'What? David?' Celia sighed. 'He can seduce me. Or not. I don't know. Oh, Dorrie, what wouldn't I give to get Heather out of my house.'

When the shopping was done Dorrie bundled Celia back into a taxi and sent her home. She had a deep sense of foreboding; she had never seen anyone spend so much. It was spending for pleasure and spending for revenge. Celia was being ignored, and she never could abide it. Dorrie walked back to her house and her picture. She would paint, she decided, the way she wished. To hell with doing things for money.

Celia's taxi drew up at the house and she proffered her credit card once again. The plastic should have melted by now, she thought. Things had changed in the last ten years. You never used to be able to pay taxis off with plastic; you couldn't pay for much with it actually. Nowadays they merely waved your magic card through a machine and everything was done. Marvellous.

But the driver only had an old-fashioned imprint thing, and fiddled about with a biro. Celia prepared to get out. Suddenly she saw that there were people everywhere. The police. She fell back, frightened, and then she saw Charles Davenport, bearing down on her with a face like thunder. All around, in the unkempt grounds, policemen were beating at the undergrowth. Were they looking for her? Should she run? For a moment her nerve failed her and she felt sick, but then she remembered. She wasn't a patient now. She was free.

'Hello, Charles.' She got out of the car, trying to reduce his advantage. But, in her flat shoes, he towered above her. She felt a momentary pang for the hated high heels.

'Where the hell have you been?'

She spread her hands. 'Out. Shopping. Why not?'

'You knew I was coming today. It was important!'

'My shopping was more important. I had to have something to wear.'

'Two representatives of the hospital board came with me. And it seems you're so undisciplined you can't keep a simple appointment. We had to call the police. They're demanding an explanation.'

'Demands, demands.' Celia flapped her hands, and turned to collect her parcels. Charles ran a hand through his hair. She was like a child sometimes. The same immediacy, the same lack of concern for the consequences of things. The board was right, she ought to be back in hospital, and if he could find one

134

excuse, some clear evidence that she could not cope, he would take her. If she would do something mad, madder merely than going out without telling him, something wholly irresponsible – he saw the mountain of shopping.

'Where did you get the money for all this, Celia?'

She gave him a thin smile. 'A credit card, Charles. I didn't steal it.'

'The money still has to be paid.'

'I dare say. That isn't my concern.'

He thought, That proves it then. No sense of reality. She couldn't be trusted, even on a shopping expedition.

David Sheraton's car turned in at the gate. He parked and got out slowly, looking from Celia to Charles. 'As I thought,' he said, 'there was no emergency.'

Charles said, 'Not the one we expected, no. But another one. Were you aware that Celia was going to go shopping?'

'Honestly!' Celia took another four or five parcels from the taxi and heaped them on the step. 'It isn't a crime to buy clothes. David got rid of all mine, you know. He gave my handbags to Heather.'

David was taken aback. How could she know about that? It was at least five years since. Celia had owned a dozen handbags, most of them still in the tissue they came in. She always was bloody extravagant. The pile of glossy carrier bags grew. He felt a cold weight in the pit of his stomach. What had possessed him to give her that card?

He ran up the steps and caught Celia's arm. She swayed against him and he smelled booze and didn't know if she was drunk or tired. Charles was thanking the policemen and explaining that she was still officially a patient, and they went away, shaking their heads at this nightmare woman who had run off and bought a whole shop.

Celia, David and Charles went into the chill, empty sitting room. The temperature was appreciably lower than the sunshine outside, and Celia went to wrestle with a window catch. She couldn't open it. Neither man moved to help her. She turned to face the inquisition.

'I am allowed to go out on my own,' she said feebly. 'And I wasn't alone. I was with Dorrie.'

135

'Did Dorrie let you buy all this stuff?' asked Charles. 'It's way over the top, Celia.'

She shrugged. 'I've no clothes. Obviously I have to have clothes.'

'How much did you spend?' David sounded weary, as if she was altogether too much trouble. At that moment, she hated him.

'Not that much. I needed things.'

'How much?'

'About – about two thousand pounds.' She looked at their stunned faces and added, 'It isn't a lot, after all. These days eating out costs thirty pounds a head.'

David got up and began to pace the room. 'Two thousand pounds! Two thousand bloody pounds! My God, do you think if we had that sort of money to throw around we'd be living like this? I told you it was a mistake to let her go. She should never have come here. Things have changed but she simply doesn't have the capacity to understand. She'll bankrupt me!'

'It isn't that much,' said Celia in a low, controlled voice. 'You told me things had gone up and I always buy good quality. I won't buy tat. You know that, David.'

He sighed, furiously. 'Heather's hardly had a new skirt in two years!'

'More fool her,' said Celia.

David found himself losing his cool. 'Do you never learn? Has anything I've said made sense to you? Your father isn't here to bail you out this time. For once in your life, try and understand that you have to live like other people. You're poor. You have no money. And I do not possess a magic pot of gold.'

'You have this house,' said Celia deliberately. 'And you have your own talents. What a pity God didn't give you the wit to use them.'

David came towards her in a rush. He reached back his arm and struck her on the cheek, first one way and then the other. Celia's head snapped from side to side, like a beaten flower.

'Stop that! Stop that now!' Charles had David round the shoulders, he was manhandling him away. Celia's world was strangely yellow, and distant. She was vaguely aware that

136

David was hunched over on his knees, sobbing.

She woke up in bed once again. It was a moment before she realised it wasn't her hospital bed, where she had fully expected to find herself. But no. It was the bed in the flat at Blantyre House, and sitting across the room from her was Charles.

'I thought you meant to take me back,' she said.

He nodded. 'But I didn't want to move you. Not after blows like that. You're OK, though. You've been asleep.'

She struggled into a sitting position. 'He didn't take back my clothes, did he?'

'No. Not yet. Though he should.'

Linking her arms around her knees, she directed her clear blue gaze on to him. He thought how much he had missed that level stare, even in a few short days. He missed the experience of her beauty. 'What are you thinking now?' he asked.

'You're going to say I'm a loony. Just because I bought some clothes.'

He said carefully, 'The hospital wants you back.'

'Why?'

He shrugged. 'Star patient. Publicity. Don't want to be seen to be withholding proper care.'

'I'll discharge myself.'

'No, Celia. Don't.'

She lay back on her pillow once again. It was all very well fighting to stay, but she didn't like it here. Heather made sure she was always alone, Ellen resented her, and Lucy might soon learn to, as poison was dripped into her ear. 'They'll tell the girls I'm spendthrift,' she said suddenly. 'But I'm owed something, Charles. This is my house. And Heather uses lots of my old things. She had on a scarf yesterday that was mine. She's had them so long she's forgotten, no doubt – or perhaps she hasn't. She hates me enough to do it to hurt.'

'You expected that. We talked of it.'

'But – but –' Suddenly Celia's eyes filled with tears. 'I never thought they'd want her and not me. All of them. David, Ellen, Lucy – they don't want me.'

'You can't expect anything different.'

'But I do! I do.'

She was sobbing with real anguish. Charles couldn't help himself, he went to hold her and comfort her. She pressed herself into him, twining her arms around his neck. He felt her face against his throat, her tears running down his skin. In a moment he would pull away, but not yet. Her body seemed to radiate some magic chemical, drawing him in.

David gave a perfunctory knock and opened the door. Rather than leap back, Charles said 'There, there' firmly, and patted Celia's back. She moved away from him and he caught the look in her eyes; amusement mixed with something darker. Triumph, perhaps? Or something else?

'I came to apologise,' said David jerkily. 'What I did was unforgivable.'

Charles laid Celia back on the bed and said, 'Indeed it was. A head injury should never be subjected to any further trauma. What were you thinking of, man? You could have killed her.'

'That's what he wants,' said Celia.

David said, 'Of course I don't! You simply don't understand. It isn't your fault, you never thought about money, but it's all I can do to pay the girls' school fees, and you go out and spend more than a term's money on clothes! Heather and I economise, we try and make ends meet. She works like a slave to help out, an accountant, not just any old job. If I could earn more I would, but you have to taunt me, today of all days.'

'What happened today?' asked Celia. Her hair was clean and swinging, and David looked at her with gloomy resignation.

'A *Which?* report on the Sheraton. Slated it. Bad roadholding.'

Celia snorted. 'You knew that ten years ago. Don't tell me you still haven't put it right!'

Charles stood up. He wanted to be ready in case David really did try and murder her. The man's handsome, devil may care face was suffused with a dull red flush. Charles said, 'That settles it. I shall take her back to hospital tomorrow. She can't stay here.'

Celia looked from one man to the other. What was wrong

with telling the truth? She wasn't a fool about money, or anything else, yet they tried to make her believe she was. They accused her of everything, made no allowances, and she was to excuse all that. She had lost ten years of life, and was no more than an object of curiosity, while David, Heather, the children, everyone, got sympathy. They weren't locking her up for her good but for their own. Even Charles conspired against her.

'This is a betrayal, Charles,' she said slowly. 'You know I'm quite well.'

'If I thought that I'd leave you here.'

'Would you? It's very odd how keen everyone is to get rid of me. I think I'd better see a lawyer. This whole thing stinks.'

The two men looked at each other, a brief, telling glance. It was no use relying on them, she thought. They would suit themselves before her. She lay back on her pillows again, giving in to her tiredness.

'I can't afford a lawyer,' said David, wearily. 'And there's no one else can pay.'

'Believe me,' said Charles, 'we have your best interests at heart.'

Celia closed her eyes. Her head was aching. She had made a wild stab and knew she had struck home. But she couldn't think about it all now, she was so tired, a weariness beyond everything she had ever known. Perhaps she would go to sleep and wake in another ten years. But if tomorrow came and time and space had let her be, she knew she must discover what was really going on.

Chapter Ten

Celia rose very early the next morning. She felt restored once again, her mind clear and her body energised. The secret was lots of sleep, she decided, as she sorted through her bags and parcels, taking out the clothes and hanging them up, finally burning every single one of the receipts. Anyone who wished to return anything was going to have to try very hard. There was no way she was going to lose her clothes.

She dressed in a plain dark skirt, her pumps, pale tights and a sweater in crocheted cotton. She tied her hair up with a large blue silk bow, and turned several times before the mirror, admiring herself. A sudden thought arrested her – was the look too young? She was thirty-five years old. But she didn't look it, she told herself. When she gazed closely at her face in the glass she could see no wrinkles yet, although she felt as if she was changing every day. Life was touching her forehead, her eyes, her very expression. No one escaped forever.

It was Saturday, and when she went downstairs for breakfast no one was up. The house felt empty, a vessel waiting to be filled. Celia rejoiced in freedom, and walked from room to room, moving things to the places she preferred. Then, in the kitchen, she laid the breakfast table, and went into the garden to gather flowers. As always she was extravagant, and came back with an armful, cramming them into the cracked china vases that had stood on the shelf in the dog room for as long as she could remember. They were her mother's vases, antique and eccentric, long forgotten.

Ellen came down first. She was wearing jeans and a stained sweatshirt, the honey hair a tangle of unbrushed wire. She eyed Celia from the depths of its shadow. 'What are you doing? You shouldn't have.'

'Oh, Ellen!' Celia clasped her hands in front of her, and smiled her lovely, open smile. 'Don't wake up cross! You were like that when you were little, so often all grumpy in the morning.'

'I don't remember a thing about when I was small.'

'Yes, you do. You just don't want to admit it. My, aren't you mean!'

Ellen turned her shoulder and went to get some bread, ignoring her mother's laid table and fetching knife and plate from the cupboard afresh. Celia said, 'Is Heather making you like this?'

'I'm not like anything.'

'Monstrous is the word I'd use. And rude. Now, I was a naughty girl, but I was never allowed to be rude. I feel like walloping you.'

'Why don't you?' A belligerent stare.

'You might hit me back.'

'I would too!'

'Then take that!' Celia picked up a slice of bread from the plate on the table and hurled it at her daughter. It turned in the air, over and over, to miss and land in the sink. Ellen gasped. Then she picked up her own half-buttered slice and threw it back, and again it missed, this time landing butter side down on the floor.

'What next?' said Celia, her eyes alight with devilment. 'Knives? Forks? Marmalade?'

'You really are mad!' said Ellen.

'And I always was.'

Ellen came and sat down at the table. She watched as Celia made coffee and more toast. Neither of them picked up the pieces of bread they had thrown, it was as if they were quite forgotten. Ellen couldn't imagine Heather ever being like this. She was just so terribly conventional.

Sunshine dappled the table as they ate. Celia said, 'I thought last night I wasn't going to wake up today. I thought I'd sleep for another ten years, and find you married, with children perhaps, and the kitchen all different again. It was frightening.'

'Mum and Dad fight all the time now you're here,' said Ellen.

Celia crunched her toast. 'You can't expect me to be upset about that, now can you? She's got all my things. Husband, children, house – even my handbags. You didn't know that, did you? All my flaming handbags, full of her stuff. See how nice that makes you. Turn your back for five minutes and find somebody neat has got rid of all your lipsticks and screwed up parking tickets and replaced them with lipsalve and a diary.'

Ellen began to laugh. Celia looked at her daughter's suddenly bright face and thought, There then. First round to me.

Lucy came down next. She bounced in, full of weekend exuberance, and demanded to know what everyone was going to do. From upstairs came the telltale noises of people getting up. Heather and David were talking, no doubt trying to decide if they should take Celia back to hospital straight away, or be on pins until after lunch. She could almost sense their incipient relief.

'Let's go for a drive,' said Celia, and both girls looked surprised.

'Can you drive?' asked Lucy.

'Of course. I'll drive the Sheraton.' She conveniently ignored such trivia as permission and insurance.

'It'll be a squash,' said Lucy. 'I'll run up and tell them.'

'Oh, we'll be back in no time,' said Celia. She went out to the hall table and picked up the keys, and the girls followed her, as intrigued and obedient as if they danced after the Pied Piper of Hamelin.

She was a little anxious that her skill, though well remembered, would nonetheless not be there. The girls sensed her uncertainty, and giggled as she fiddled with the ignition and the gears. 'I used to drive one of these all the time,' said Celia. 'Good heavens, everything's just as I remember. You'd think he'd have moved the fuel gauge, you never could see it properly.'

'He can't do it,' said Ellen. 'They'd have to change the cast for the fascia, and that's expensive.'

Celia grimaced. 'We always said this car would be in mass production by now! Really.'

She switched on, and the engine rewarded her with a giant roar. A thrill coursed like electricity up and down her spine.

143

She had forgotten the joy of the Sheraton. Say what you liked, David had created a wonderful car. As she drove out of the gates she permitted herself a quick glance in the rearview mirror, and sure enough, there were two heads fixed at an upstairs window. So there!

The girls squealed when she did a hundred on the bypass. The wind dragged at the little car, making it twitch, although the road was dry as a bone. Celia suddenly remembered that she was responsible for these two. There was no one in the world more responsible. She slowed down abruptly. 'That's enough joy-riding. Now, girls, who can tell me where to find Edwin Braddock?'

Their expressions were blank for a moment. Then Ellen said, 'Why on earth do you want to go and see him? He hates us. He even sends us a company Christmas card instead of a proper one. "With all good wishes from the Braddock Corporation." Mum says he's a ruthless entrepreneur.'

'Your grandfather was one of those,' said Celia. 'He made millions. And they've all gone to Edwin Braddock.'

'Where should they have gone?' demanded Lucy, her eyes alight with avarice.

'Why, darling, to all of us, of course,' said Celia. 'Now, where does Cousin Edwin live? Come on, both of you. Think.'

'Linton Place,' said Ellen. 'Wherever that is.'

Celia felt a shock. For an instant she could not speak. 'Are you sure?' she managed at last. 'Linton Place? *The* Linton Place?'

'Isn't it very nice?' asked Lucy.

Celia said, 'Not in the least nice, no. It's magnificent. A palace. A stately home. My father used to go shooting there with the old duke. He used to tell us about it, though I've never been.'

'I think that's where he lives,' said Ellen dubiously. 'Near Harrogate?'

'That's right.' Celia swung the wheel of the car. 'Well, well, well. Cousin Edwin has certainly put our money to good use. The brute!'

They lost their way twice, following the garbled directions of locals, but ultimately all the rights and lefts unfurled to leave them beside a high stone wall. Celia stopped the car for a moment. The girls were hushed, gazing at this evidence of Edwin's magnificent seclusion. The wall was made of huge stones of even size, each one too big for a man to lift by himself. The stones on the top were equally massive, but sensuously curved, like a voluptuous woman. A wall like this might have been there since time began.

They drove on, looking for an entrance, and came to huge wrought iron gates. Beyond stretched a long gravelled drive, and to either side rolling parkland, where cattle grazed with slow-cudding ease, up to their knees in grass. The house was somewhere in the distance, invisible. 'A humble little pad, no doubt,' said Celia.

'It must be huge!' said Lucy. 'What a rotter never having us for tea.'

'Did he buy this with our money?' demanded Ellen, and Celia nodded.

'We ought to remember that. This is really ours.'

The gates would not open. They got in the car again and drove round the endless wall, looking for another way in. At length they came to another pair of gates, and a lodge to guard them, but the sign read: 'Linton Place. No casual callers. Admission by gatekeeper only'.

Celia checked her appearance in the rearview mirror. She was flushed and a few strands of hair had escaped their ribbon, but otherwise she seemed well enough. The girls, on the other hand, were a mess.

'Push your hair back, Ellen,' she instructed. 'And, Lucy, tuck in that shirt. We've got to try and look charming.'

'What are we going to do?' asked Ellen in a breathless voice.

'I don't know,' said Celia. 'We're going to see what he's like, I think.'

'I want to go home!' squealed Lucy. 'He'll get his gun and fill us full of lead.' She buried her face in her hands.

Celia got out of the car and went up to the lodge. She knocked, and when the door opened said, 'Hello! Would you let me in, please? I'm Celia Sheraton, Celia Braddock as was. Mr Braddock's my cousin.'

The man who confronted her was large, paunchy, and wore

carpet slippers and braces. 'He don't see no one without appointment.'

'I have an appointment,' said Celia. 'At eleven. Would you open the gates, please?'

'I don't have no appointment written down here,' he said, on a rising note of uncertainty.

'Dear Edwin,' said Celia, sighing. 'He always was such a scatterbrain.'

For a moment she thought he was going to telephone for approval. Instead, he shrugged, said 'Nowt to do wi' me', and pressed the button that swung the huge gates open.

'Thank you so much,' said Celia, and got back in the car.

'You're a terrible liar,' said Lucy, wide-eyed.

'Am I?' Celia giggled. 'I must try and improve. I'm not used to setting people an example.'

'Mum says you're a shocking example,' said Ellen. 'And you always were.'

'Hmmm.' Celia accelerated, and sent the gravel flying. 'Heather's jealousy hasn't abated one whit, I see.'

The house came into view. It was built of white stone and filled the horizon, wide and low, with the central section protruding in a semicircle of battlements and casement windows. The terrace before it was battlemented, and at the head of the lake a boathouse had been built to echo the style once more. The lake edge was carpeted with lilies, like pale jewels.

'It's beautiful,' breathed Ellen. 'The most beautiful house I've ever seen.' The others might have agreed. But they were silent, staring at the scene as if it was unreal. One thought repeated itself in Celia's head – did her father really leave money enough for this?

A man was walking in the distance, with four large dogs. Celia saw only that he wore a peaked cap and shooting jacket, but the dogs were clear enough. Alsatians.

'Guard dogs!' wailed Lucy. 'He'll set them on us and we'll be chewed up. We can't get out, they've shut the gate.'

Celia felt the same apprehension. In this wide park, she did not feel safe. 'You girls stay in the car,' she said nervously.

'Don't get out,' said Ellen urgently. 'If they get you, what shall we do?'

'They won't get me.' Once, long ago, she had been good with dogs. They were just dogs. She got out of the car.

The moment the dogs saw her they began running. She kept on, watching the man as he stood and did nothing, watching the dogs as they ran and barked. She couldn't see the man's face. Perhaps she didn't look. The dogs were close now, surrounding her in a cacophony of barking.

'Good boys! Good dogs! There's a good dog.' She made her voice light and approving. She encouraged them to approach. The first dog stopped and barked raucously, and the next sat down, uncertain. The other two ran behind her, and she felt near to panic. She could not watch all of them all the time. Again she said, 'Good dogs. Come on then! Come up!' She patted her thighs encouragingly, and the barking fell away. They came up and sniffed her, tails wagging.

Her heart was thundering. She took very deep breaths, trying to recover herself, and walked with assumed insouciance towards the watching man. The dogs danced around her, welcoming her as a friend, because nothing declared her an enemy. The sun was in her eyes and it was difficult to see. She went right up to him. 'Oh, yes,' she said then. 'So I thought. It is you.'

Edwin was absolutely surprised. He had not expected ever to see his cousin Celia again, especially not here. She was supposed to be in hospital, yet here she was, in his park, presenting a picture of sophisticated elegance. He should have set the dogs on her, he thought. He looked past her to the car, and saw the pale faces of the girls. 'Your daughters?' he asked, and Celia nodded.

'I'm surprised you don't know them. It's odd not to care for family ties. In the circumstances.'

'And what might those be?'

'My dear Edwin, I remember you as a spotty youth with nothing to look forward to except a semi-detached house in Hull. Now you have all this.' She spread her arms to encompass the rolling acres. 'These circumstances.'

He couldn't decide whether to antagonise her or not. He debated with himself. If he ordered her away that would be that, they would have settled on conflict. Not a wise move at this point. So he said, 'I've been so busy, Celia. I bear a heavy responsibility, you know. But it's time we all got to know each other again. Won't you come up to the house? We can have coffee and cake.'

She measured him with a look. 'That would be most kind,' she said.

In the car, the girls hissed, 'What's he like?'

'Scary,' said Celia. 'He's not like I remember. We used to have them over for Sundays and he was terribly shy. Used the wrong knife at table, things like that. But he learned quickly. Now he's being the English country gentleman, very tweedy. And his accent's changed.'

'He's gone up in the world,' said Ellen gloomily. 'I bet he goes skiing.'

'We should all go skiing,' declared Celia. 'Because it's our money. Not his.'

She parked the car aggressively across the front steps. They all got out and waited while Edwin and the dogs walked up from the park, and Lucy said, 'I wish I was at home.'

'Hush, Lucy,' said Celia. 'This is fun!'

'Home is going to mean trouble,' said Ellen, and glanced sideways at her mother. Celia didn't care about trouble. She was like a bright splash of colour in a world of grey. She made everything different.

The girls were surprised at Edwin. He seemed kind and friendly, and he shook hands with them just as if they were grown up. 'You take after your mother, Ellen,' he said. 'Lucky you.' He led the way into the house and the dogs trotted around them, waving their tails and being genial. Lucy plucked up her courage and stroked one, but Edwin clicked his fingers and called the animal to heel. Two servants appeared, little brown men in white jackets, and Edwin rapped out instructions to bring refreshments to the morning room, at once.

But the house itself was odd. For the most part it was traditionally furnished, with portraits and armour, marble and French mirrors, but now and then there was a touch of the truly exotic. In the hall, for instance, an umbrella stand held a collection of human-headed walking sticks. And in the morning room there was an enormous fish in a tank. The fish could not turn round, but swam in its long narrow enclosure, surrounded by artificial bubbles.

'The poor thing!' exclaimed Lucy, standing away from the glass. The fish's blank, melancholy eye upset her.

'It needs nothing more,' said Edwin.

Lucy said, 'But it's cooped up.'

'It doesn't care. It has all it wants.'

The fish's mouth opened and shut in a slow rhythm. Lucy couldn't bear to look.

They ate delicate pastries covered in icing sugar. Celia sipped at her coffee, aware as the girls were not that Edwin was watching her fiercely. She said, 'How lucky you are, Edwin, to have all this. And all thanks to my father.'

'Joe Braddock recognised my potential as a businessman,' retorted Edwin. 'I try not to let him down. He had many disappointments in his life.'

'Like what?' Celia bridled.

'Like losing faith in his daughter.'

'What – whatever do you mean?'

The girls and Celia turned their eyes on him like searchlights. The dogs lay around his chair, their long bodies relaxed and huge, and from time to time he reached down and fondled one of them. Celia felt frightened suddenly, as if he was going to say something that would change everything. And he did.

'I'm sorry to upset you, Celia,' he said. 'Obviously, after the accident your father was very – distressed. You'd been such a problem to him, marrying someone he didn't like, being so spendthrift, and having no interest in the business. And finally, through your own recklessness, you were as good as dead. He disowned you, Celia. That was his firm intention. He disowned you and your descendants, and went back to the male line. Now, I know you came here to persuade me of your claim to the estate, but truly you haven't one.'

Celia sat very still. Her lips felt stiff, with that telltale paralysis that came upon her at times of stress. The words were running away from her again. 'You – you lie,' she managed.

149

'My father loved me. He wouldn't – he didn't turn his back.'

'His love isn't in question.' Edwin was soothing her. 'That isn't the issue, my dear. Even without the accident, he knew you weren't the right person to inherit a fortune. You'd have frittered it away, and Joe knew that. He didn't give it to me because you were gone, he gave it because he knew that was the right thing to do.'

'He hardly knew you!'

'After the accident, he got to know me very well indeed.'

Celia got up. She couldn't stay. There was no fighting the man. He could say anything and she would have nothing to put up in defence. David was right, she had never understood her cousin. He was quite different from anything she had ever imagined, and he could tell her any lies and she couldn't disprove them. She couldn't know what her father had thought before he died. There was no record of it. Except – she turned to face her cousin.

'Edwin, where's the Will?'

'What?'

'The Will. My father's Will. I want to see what he said.'

'I imagine – I assume – it's in the hands of your father's solicitor.'

'You've got a copy, though.'

Edwin's fingers closed on the ear of one of his dogs. The animal yelped. 'It's not going to do you any good, Celia.'

'But it's time I saw exactly what he said. Are you going to show it to me?'

'No. It would only upset you.'

'Allow me to decide on how upset I wish to be.'

Ellen and Lucy were scrambling to their feet. The room seemed to take its tone from the trapped and mouthing fish, they wanted nothing so much as to be gone. Celia made for the door, her daughters following, although Edwin stayed where he was. But he sent the dogs after them. They heard the claws clattering on marble.

'They're going to eat us!' Lucy squealed and clutched Celia's arm.

'No. He only means us to be scared.' Sure enough the dogs only circled them. One of the servants came and shooed at

150

them nervously, and in a run Ellen reached the front door. They felt like criminals, escaping retribution, and fell into the car with a boundless relief.

'Dad's going to be furious,' said Ellen tightly.

Lucy said, 'I don't care. I just want to get away from here.'

Celia found that her hands were trembling on the wheel. Suppose the gates were locked and could not be opened? But they swung wide even as she approached. They had escaped.

Driving back, she said, 'Thank you for coming, girls. I wouldn't have dared go there alone.'

'Was he lying?' asked Ellen.

Celia said, 'I don't know. He upset me. For a moment I couldn't think. I don't know what my father felt before he died. I can't understand what happened, you see. I was as good as dead, he had no reason to leave anything to me, and there was no love lost between him and David, but surely he wouldn't desert you? My children. His direct descendants.'

'Did you quarrel with your father?'

Celia made a little face. 'Yes. All the time. But they were loving quarrels. At least, I thought they were. He knew one day I'd take over everything and run it just as he would wish. I thought he knew that. We never said anything, you see, not about love or the business. It was just – understood.'

Ellen glanced at her mother's profile. The brow was furrowed, and small creases of concentration were etched between her eyes. For a moment she looked like Joe Braddock, but Ellen couldn't know that. She simply thought that Celia was suddenly looking her age. Then, a moment later, the look was gone.

It was almost two when they reached Blantyre House. Heather and David were sitting at the kitchen table, righteously indignant. David got up as they came in. 'You realise,' he began, 'that you have taken my daughters in a car that wasn't your own, in a car that wasn't insured, without permission and without telling anyone where you meant to go? My God, Celia, you're going back to that hospital right away.'

She put her head on one side to look at him. Then she grinned. 'Oh, David,' she said. 'Haven't you got pompous?'

151

She tossed the keys on to the table.

'You had no right to take the children!' Heather was red-eyed and ugly.

Celia said, 'I had every right. Besides, we had an instructive morning, didn't we, girls?'

Ellen, caught between loyalties, blurted, 'We went to see Edwin Braddock.'

David and Heather stared at them. 'What did you – did he tell you anything?' asked David.

'What should I know?' asked Celia.

Heather went red. The colour came up from the collar of her dress and inflamed her face. She turned aside, hiding it.

Celia sat carefully down at the table. 'What's going on?' she asked quietly. 'What are you all keeping from me? Everyone says I have no money, and no hope of any, but no one will tell me why. I asked Edwin if I could see my father's Will, and he refused. What does it say about me? Is it so terrible I really shouldn't know?'

David sighed, a mixture of anger and frustration. 'If you'd just take things slowly, Celia! Why do you always rush at everything?'

'Because I've lost so much time!' She rested her hands in her lap. 'You don't know how helpless that makes you feel. I don't understand what's happened, not really. Why did my father leave everything to Edwin? Surely some provision was made for me? And what about the children? I can't believe there wasn't something left for them.'

'There should have been,' said Ellen, tossing her hair.

'We should have been rich,' said Lucy.

Heather said, 'Girls! That's enough of your greed. I'm sick of this endless materialism. Go upstairs and do your homework, at once.'

'We haven't had lunch,' said Lucy piteously.

Heather said, 'You can do without. Perhaps you may learn some sense.'

Subdued, the girls took themselves off. Celia gritted her teeth against rage. Had Heather inflicted her draconian regime all through their childhood? She imagined Ellen as a toddler, her mother gone and only Heather to comfort her.

She thought of Lucy, tiny Lucy, too young to know more than the absence of loving hands, a loving face. She could have wept.

Instead she turned to Heather and said, 'What do you know about all this? You're an accountant. I'm sure you know where every last penny of my father's money went.'

Heather, who had been stricter with the girls than she intended, snapped, 'It was nothing to do with me! David doesn't involve me in his affairs. I merely run the house.'

'How very humble of you,' said Celia. 'Well, David? You tell me, then.'

He looked at her. A rueful grin twitched at his mouth. Left to himself he wouldn't have minded about the car, thought Celia. Heather was the killjoy around here. He said, 'I suppose it's time you knew.'

He went out of the room, and they heard him rummaging in his desk. After a moment he came back with a packet of papers. He extracted a sheet and tossed it across. Her father's hand-writing, in faded photocopy, lay before her. Slowly, warily, Celia began to read:

In view of my daughter's comatose condition, she is in no way able to inherit my estate. My only concern is therefore that she be given constant and considerate care, for every moment of her remaining life. To that end I bequeath three million pounds, in trust, to Aireborough Hospital. Since my daughter's care will not require the whole of the income from this sum, the hospital may use any surplus for research into her condition, for treatment that may shed light on it, and for other projects.

She looked up. 'These other projects wouldn't be the heart programme by any chance?'

David nodded. 'But I imagine Davenport's making a bid for his share. The idea was that you would leave hospital but remain nominally in the hospital's charge. But the Braddock Corporation's the executor of the Will. They've objected. Either you remain in hospital or the trust fund is forfeit.'

'I see.' Celia looked down at her hands. Damn Davenport! She might have known. All she meant to him was a large slice of cash.

She said, 'Now that I'm better, why isn't that three million mine? It was meant for me, after all.'

Heather snorted. 'How typical! Sick people depend on that money for their very survival, but she wants it to buy clothes!'

Celia felt her colour come up, and swallowed down her rage. 'I didn't say I would take it, Heather. Merely that I could. It was my father's money. He left it to me.'

'The Braddock Corporation would fight you,' said David. 'They've made that very clear. It could take years. And think of the cost.'

She looked at him irritably. Had he always been so defeatist? She had married a man full of fun and adventure, and now he was cautious and staid.

She said, 'Do you have a copy of the Will, too?'

David hesitated. Then he tossed the envelope across. 'It's in there. It was quite a muddle in the end. In the final analysis only the lawyers really knew what was what.'

She spread the thick fan of papers on the table. Some were handwritten, some were typed, all were in the faded blue of old photocopies. Someone had numbered each sheet in pencil, and she pointed and said, 'What's this?'

'The numbers of the envelopes they were in,' explained David. 'Your father had some daft system. Obviously, before your accident he had just one Will, leaving everything to you with an allowance to your mother during her life. Then came the crash. I don't think you realise how he changed. He just sat in his room for hours, curtains drawn, doing nothing. And when it was obvious that you weren't going to get better, a number of people begged him to change his Will.'

'Edwin?' asked Celia sharply.

David nodded. 'And your mother. And the lawyers. Even me.'

He ran his hands through his hair, and Heather reached out to touch him in reassurance. 'David was thinking of the children,' she said firmly.

'Oh, I'm sure!' agreed Celia. 'Look, Heather, of course

154

David wanted a share. He had a car firm to run, he needed it. We don't have to be mealy-mouthed about needing money.'

'I might as well have been,' said David. 'He didn't change the original Will at all. He simply added bits to it, in envelopes. One left me Blantyre House, but only if I brought the girls up here. Another dealt with his cars, his chauffeur took those. The housekeeper got some of your mother's jewellery, nothing was said about the rest. And finally there was an envelope leaving everything that wasn't otherwise bequeathed to – Edwin Braddock. Almost a hundred million pounds' worth of assets.'

Celia gaped. 'A hundred million! Edwin got a hundred million! That's – impossible.'

'I always knew Joe Braddock was up to no good,' said Heather determinedly. 'No one honest has a fortune like that. Ill-gotten gains.'

'"Sooner a camel will go through the eye of a needle than a rich man enter the kingdom of God",' murmured Celia. 'Heaven's going to be full of down and outs. Don't worry, Heather, at this rate you'll get in. You'll arrive at the pearly gates burdened by nothing more than a collection of my old handbags.'

Heather, cheeks bright with colour, said, 'Do you have to be so flippant? Don't you take anything seriously?'

'Only my children's future,' retorted Celia.

David put a hand on Heather's shoulder. Celia looked away. He thought they were squabbling because of him, and she had never fought for a man in all her life. She had never had to. When he tried to catch her eye she avoided his gaze, riffling through the papers before her, pretending concentration. Her head ached. She could make no sense of what she read. She looked up and found David still watching her. 'Is some of this missing?' she asked quickly. 'How can anyone know there weren't more envelopes? I feel sure he'd have left something for the girls.'

'Do you suspect David of depriving them?' demanded Heather belligerently. 'Since you're so frank, do speak out and say so.'

David said, 'Not even Celia thinks that, dear.'

Celia looked from one to the other. 'What do you mean, not even me? I'm not a witch, David! Ten years wasn't enough to turn me into a monster, whatever you might think.'

Heather snorted, and David felt a sense of growing exasperation. In the years since the accident he had allowed a lie to grow up; he had conspired with Heather to pretend that Celia had never made him happy. The truth of it, the real, warm, turbulent maelstrom of emotion that had been his marriage, lay safe in the past – until now. And here was Celia herself, refusing to accept any distortion. She knew, and he only now remembered, how they had been in love.

He went to the cupboard and poured himself a brandy. Both women watched him, Heather's eyes red and frightened, Celia's like clouds on a rainy day. He wished, desperately, that he was somewhere else. Yes, he had loved Celia, loved her to distraction, but in these last years Heather had soothed his soul. And here Celia was, just as before, just as fascinating, demanding, difficult. Life with Celia was never peaceful; and David yearned for inner peace.

'If you want to talk about the Will you'd better go and see your father's solicitor,' he said wearily. 'All I have is in that envelope. As far as I know there was nothing more.'

Celia spread her hands. 'Didn't anyone query it? Did everyone just let Edwin take the lot?'

Heather said sharply, 'He'd got very thick with your mother. She thought a very great deal of him. The son she never had. And if your mother didn't object then no one else felt they could. It all went through quite smoothly.'

Celia tried to gather her thoughts. So much money, so easily lost. She hadn't known her father was so rich. Her mother used to work in the house, cooking on the chef's day off, polishing if a room looked dingy. Her father's roar when he got the post was always, 'Celia! These bloody bills! You're going to ruin me.' Rich beyond dreaming. And all gone.

The chug of a diesel engine came from outside. Heather got up and went to the window. An ambulance was there. Tired of waiting for Celia to be delivered, the hospital had come to fetch her.

Chapter Eleven

Celia sat in the hospital administrator's office. David was on one side, Davenport on the other, and Heather was relegated to a small hard chair by the wall. She was weeping quietly into a crumpled lace handkerchief. Celia said exasperatedly, 'Do you think someone could get Heather a cup of tea?' She was sure Heather's tears were manufactured.

Davenport said, 'Good idea. Let's all have tea. Is there anyone to make it on a Saturday afternoon, James?'

The administrator muttered and made a telephone call. They were provided with tea in pretty porcelain cups.

'I wonder if these are courtesy of my father's bequest,' remarked Celia.

'I hope you're not accusing us of anything.' James bridled comically.

'Only a very wide interpretation of your instructions.' She smiled at him, and then, as Heather's sniffling persisted, snapped, 'Heather, will you please go outside if you can't control yourself?'

David said, 'Have some patience, Celia! She's upset.'

'Why is she upset? Nobody's trying to put *her* under lock and key.'

'We were simply trying to look after your best interests,' said James in anguish. 'The Braddock Corporation seemed to feel that we weren't doing that.'

Davenport leaned back and stretched his legs. 'Well, it's all in the open now. Celia knows what a precious girl she is. As far as I can see, if this codicil stands, then Celia could go to court and get the lot.'

Mr James looked as if he might have an attack himself, then and there.

'I wasn't thinking anything of the sort,' said Celia. 'But I will not have my life ruled by the Braddock Corporation. All I can say at this stage is that if the hospital will stop trying to get me back in its clutches, then I promise to leave the three million as it is for the time being. But I must say, the transplant programme can surely manage with a little less? All those tea towels they sell. Everyone does so love a good transplant. Much better to fund Mr Davenport's brain damage unit.'

'Thank you, Celia,' purred Charles, and she looked at him obliquely.

Suddenly Heather erupted. 'Won't any of you stand up to her? Can't you see what she's like? She's going to get her hands on the money any way she can, you know how she spends. Any amount. No thought for anyone. And this morning, only hours since, joy-riding in our car – no insurance, no permission, nothing. She's corrupting the girls. Just as she always was, corrupting them, and I won't have her in the house!'

David got up and went to her. 'Heather, don't.'

She raged, 'Why won't you make her go? Look how the girls are behaving, and she's hardly been in the house a week. She doesn't care what she does, she never did! The place for her is locked up, where she can't get at people, where she has to keep away!'

'In a straitjacket?' suggested Celia. 'Down a well? Heather, you can't go on like this. You must calm down and come to terms.' Using those words, the very words used so often on her, gave her a vicious satisfaction.

David was trying to reason, but Heather was verging on the hysterical. Davenport got up and went across. He took Heather's arm and firmly propelled her from the room, taking her no one knew where. The sound of their footsteps, punctuated by Heather's sobs, faded away. James, suddenly anxious, got up and scuttled after them.

Celia looked at her husband. 'Poor Heather,' she said sardonically.

David said, 'I wish you meant that.'

She sighed. 'Actually, I do. Shall I move out, David? Is that what you want?'

He went to the window, long-legged, a little vague. 'It's what Heather wants.'

'Yes.'

She went and stood close to him, looking up at his lean, drawn face. He was exhausted, she realised. The stress of all this was taking Heather in one way and David in another. She felt a sudden rush of affection, of familiarity. It was as if she recognised him once again. She reached up and touched the lines leading from nose to chin. 'What you need is a good night's sleep.'

It was what they used to say. Their euphemism for sex. She had spoken unthinkingly, but she saw his pale eyes kindle. It had been so long. Her body knew that even if she did not. Suddenly she understood her own restlessness. There was nothing she wanted more than a man to lie on her, to take from her every thought and every freedom, to subjugate her in a way that she could not deny. For Celia sex was never a partnership, a mutual delight; it was a battle, which she hoped her man would win.

He took an audible breath and turned away. She was sharply irritated. How dare he not respond, as he had always done, as she knew he must? They had been close so often. It was like a well-remembered dance, a dance of fire.

She moved to the wall next to him, her hands behind her, shoulders back. Her breasts were clearly outlined, the nipples taut and prominent. She reached up and took the bow from her hair, and the silky, newly washed strands tumbled on to her shoulders in abandonment. She knew this man. Oh, yes, she knew him very well.

There had never been a day when they hadn't wanted each other. Desire came long before any love. He had seen her, she had seen him, and lust was born. Snatched moments alone, sucking kisses, frantic hands, a world that meant nothing but this one sweet passion. Suddenly, in the space of a breath, she was there again.

'Oh, Celia!' David reached for her, holding her hard against him. His thighs were on her thighs, her belly pressed into his. She tangled her fingers in his hair, pulling his mouth down to hers. His tongue invaded her, muscular and insistent, until suddenly he lifted his head.

'I won't betray Heather,' he whispered, his voice anguished and thick.

'You betrayed me.'

'That's a lie.'

She moved her hips in a slow roll, inflaming them both. 'Is it? Do you care?'

'You witch.'

She laughed in his face, gently mocking. There was no need to fear. David was hers again.

There was a noise in the corridor outside. At once they parted, and Celia moved to the desk, to toy with some papers there, while David gazed fiercely from the window. It was Heather and Davenport, trailed by Mr James. Heather was very pale.

Davenport's eyes took in Celia's hair, her flushed cheeks, David's pallor. She willed herself not to blush. She was married to David, she told herself. It was Heather who should be ashamed. But she felt as furtive as any teenager.

Davenport said, 'I wonder if you'd like to go and stay with Dorrie, Celia? Just until Heather feels more settled.'

David said, 'But I've been thinking. Surely Blantyre House is big enough to accommodate us all? Surely now we've talked the worst is over.'

Heather bowed her head and whispered, 'I can't stand it. I just can't.'

'I'm just getting to know my children!' Celia smoothed her hair but her hands were trembling. Surely Davenport must see how she was – surely he must guess?

'Go for a week,' he said. 'Just until things calm down. You'll feel better.'

'No!'

They glared at each other. Davenport said sharply, 'You realise this won't look good in court? But then wilful selfishness doesn't look good anywhere.'

She looked up at him. 'What court? What do you mean?'

'Well, obviously we shall have to apply for an injunction to have you restrained. With the trust fund at stake, and our duty

160

of care, we can't just let you wander off and make trouble for everyone. If you won't co-operate I fear I shall be forced to prove you a danger to yourself and others.'

Celia gaped at him. She couldn't believe this was something he would do. She looked to David, asking mutely for support.

He said, 'You can't seriously expect a court to commit her?'

'People have been committed for less,' said Charles coldly. 'Are you going to go to Dorrie, Celia? You'll find it a lot less strain.'

'Will I indeed?' Celia tossed her head. Charles was jealous, of course. He knew that she was getting David back. David was going to enjoy what Charles was so cruelly denied. She felt sure of herself now. The conclusion of all this was only a matter of time.

'We don't want to be unreasonable—' said James, embarking on slimy conciliation.

Celia turned on him with a glittering smile. 'I'm sure you don't. We leave that to Charles. All right, everyone. For the time being – just until we sort things out – I'll go and live with Dorrie. I'm sure I shall manage quite well from there.'

She cast David a look from beneath her lashes, knowing that Charles would see. Let him. Let Heather know. Let them all understand that she was her father's daughter, as determined, as single-minded, as tenacious as he. Her family had been wrenched from her, she had never given it up. And she wouldn't do so now.

Celia arrived at Dorrie's in a flaming bad temper. She felt thwarted. How dare Davenport stick his oar in just when it wasn't wanted? David was hers again, hers for the asking, and Charles had bullied her into a corner. Well, she would emerge from that corner, very soon, in fact the moment she had established herself in the eyes of the world as a rational, thinking human being. Then she could do as she wished, and damn Charles Davenport!

Suddenly her anger drained away. She was exhausted by the day, full of weariness and confusion; the world was made up of energetic, capable people, whizzing past her as she stood on the sidelines, open-mouthed. Davenport was right in one way.

This would be good for her. She could relax at Dorrie's. She could let down her defences.

Davenport put his hand proprietorially under her elbow and took her into the kitchen. Dorrie's new painting was on the table, propped against the wall. 'Oh, I like that,' said Charles, standing back to admire it. 'A great improvement.'

'What do you think, Celia?' Dorrie was cleaning brushes at the sink, making a terrible mess. Celia thought distastefully that she would have to live with it. Other people's squalor was always hard to bear.

'It's OK,' she said dubiously. 'Bit sweet.'

'I could see that up in my front room,' said Charles, and Celia turned on him. 'Front room? How terribly suburban. Where do you live?'

He ignored her venom. 'A poor little abode, but you know us doctors. Always the simple life. Don't worry, I'll find space for you when Dorrie chucks you out.'

'I shall go back to Blantyre House,' said Celia defiantly.

Charles said nothing. He really would commit her before she went back there. The very air between her and Sheraton had crackled today. It wasn't so long since David Sheraton hadn't wanted even to look at her, and now it was all glances and codes.

Celia sat at the table and rested her head on her arms. 'You should be in bed,' said Davenport.

She looked up at him with one blue eye. 'What a good idea. Why don't you put me there?'

'Not allowed, honey,' said Dorrie with decision. 'It's his Hippocratic oath. Charles can put me to bed instead.'

Celia felt a slight shock. Dorrie and Charles? She raised her head and saw that Charles was wearing his closed, excluding look. It was true then. He wouldn't let her have David, and yet he and Dorrie were enjoying unbridled lust. She put it at no less than that. She dropped her head down on her arms, feverishly imagining what they might do to each other: the kissing, the touching, the pressure of him in her. She felt lightheaded, she could think of nothing but sex tonight. When Dorrie called her, to take her up to bed, she pretended to be asleep.

* * *

Charles went home to the Rectory and tried to garden, but it was no use. His Saturday was ruined. He went into the house and scrubbed his hands, the methodical surgeon's scrub that removed grime and skin in equal quantities. He had tough skin, fortunately. The last thing a surgeon needed was a dose of dermatitis.

He put some Brahms on the stereo. Large, gloomy music that made him think of mahogany tables and dark red carpets. The front room of his youth, its only true function a vantage point for watching the street. He had done his homework there, once or twice, but it had been cold in contrast to the kitchen. He preferred it in the kitchen, in amongst everything.

He thought how different Celia's life must have been. She had lived in effortless luxury. Was she spoiled? Surely. Obviously. And yet Celia had grit, he thought, she had the ability to pit herself against odds and determine to win. Was that old man Braddock? Was it the old Celia? Or was it the new woman, risen from the ashes of the girl she had been before?

The evening stretched ahead of him. If Celia hadn't intervened he would have gone round to see Dorrie. They would have shared a takeaway, bottle of wine, roll in the hay. He thought again of David Sheraton. He wasn't a stupid man, far from it, although in Charles's terms he was undisciplined. He had allowed his life to be hijacked by circumstance, and that was something Charles knew would not happen to him. All that was required was a certain fixity of purpose.

Charles wondered what he would have done in David's place. Take up with Heather Wilcox? He looked around at his spartan, spare home and imagined it cluttered with children and disorder. He might. In a similar mess. And beneath Heather's chilly skin there lurked a woman much like any other, and more regimented than most. Perhaps David Sheraton, with his dicky company and shattered hopes, found something in Heather that made him feel secure.

Did the man really think that Celia would sleep with him? He was wrong, she would hold out until he got rid of Heather. But then a doubt assailed him. He didn't know her well

163

enough to be sure. Perhaps she'd go to bed first and make her demands later – perhaps she already had. Then he thought of Sheraton's face, and knew she had not. Davenport congratulated himself. He had done good work that day. Celia was safe, for now.

But she wasn't damned well grateful, not in the least. It seemed unfair that the woman he had revived, who owed her life to him, should resent him quite so much. He could see it in her face, the challenge, the reluctance. Whatever he suggested she tried to discount. It was automatic, a reflex – although she had supported him with James. There was no knowing, with Celia!

He could not settle in the house. He turned the music off and went to get his jacket. He would go to the hospital and do a round. One of the younger and prettier ward sisters was making it fairly clear that she'd like to get to know him better, and later, if he was in the mood, he might take her out for a meal. He was breaking his own rule, of course. Fraternising with the staff only caused trouble. At his last hospital, the one before America, there had come a point when he had been out with every nurse on the surgical floor and not one of them would speak to him.

But the hospital soothed him. He felt better just walking through the doors. He knew doctors lauded for their dedication, appearing on the wards in dinner jackets or tennis whites, devoting every waking hour to their patients. It wasn't so commendable. The ward round was a doctor's security. The problems you found there were manageable ones, and even the gravest emergency was only within acceptable limits. Protected by rank and custom, training and ability, the doctors ruled their little world like gods. Beyond, in life outside, they had to face their most painful condition; their humanity.

The pretty nurse wasn't on tonight. The nightly routine was going on without her. He must have misread the rota, or she had switched. A student nurse was clearing cups away, and there were several visitors still on the ward. Saturday evening was a good time for families, when they could visit before a lie-in the next day. He moved through to the private wing, which only contained one of his patients at present. The comatose barrister's son wished on him by the anaesthetist, Don Matthews. To his surprise, when he opened the door, Matthews was there.

'Hello, Don! What's up?'

The man looked embarrassed. 'Nothing much, actually. Just wanted to see how he's coming along. No change, is there?'

'There is if you look at the scans. We'll get some level of consciousness, I dare say. But there's damage, no doubt about that.'

'Moffat's still suing, you know.'

Charles nodded. All that he could do for Don was mitigate the disaster, he could not take it away. The barrister was a vindictive man who wanted someone to blame for his own failure. His son had been a drug addict and a waster, and had finally come to grief. It was just a pity that he was taking revenge on Don.

He had been a mainstay of the university rugby team. His battered, slightly lugubrious face reminded Charles of a hound of some sort, one with lower than average intelligence. He thought he'd better cheer him up. 'Don't suppose you fancy a drink?'

'Don't mind if I do,' said Don.

They went to the Dog and Duck and sat in the window. They talked shop mostly, and Charles outlined his planned assessment centre. 'I'm going to have physiotherapists, oculists, technicians, all working for me. No waiting around while people find room for you on a full list. Everything mine, under my own hand.'

'Bloody empire builder. Have you got the money?'

Charles grunted. 'I might have. Let's say I've got prospects.'

'Which is more than I have.' Matthews stared gloomily into his glass.

Charles wondered why he didn't feel more sorry for Don. He annoyed him, that was it. There was no need to crumble when he had a good case, when he could stand up and fight. It was the same feeling he had about some of his patients, that he was doing his share and they were doing less than theirs.

'I feel so guilty!' burst out Matthews. 'Even though it wasn't my fault.'

'For Christ's sake, Don! We're not miracle workers. You couldn't know the bloke was up to the gills with heroin and God knows what else. He'd have died if you hadn't operated.'

'But he might as well be dead. That's a life, Charles. A human life. Doesn't that ever bother you?'

He considered. 'If I'm honest, no. They're just machines. They don't matter to me. And if they did I wouldn't be so good.'

Matthews was looking at him with a bitter eye. 'You're not bloody human yourself, that's the trouble. What are you going to do when you've got to the top of the tree? It's cold up there. No wife and kids to comfort you.'

'Since when did either of those bring comfort?'

Matthews flushed. If his marriage was under strain it wasn't surprising, and there was no need for Charles to make something of it. He got up, having to talk loudly now above the noise of the Saturday night pub crowd. 'You're a bloody fool, Charles. You can sneer at me all you like, with my second-hand car and my beaten-up house and Rachel and the kids, but it's better than you've got. Even if I lose everything in this court case I'll still be better off.'

'Glad to hear it,' said Charles, and drained his glass. 'I'll do my best for your patient. Don't expect me to weep over him as well.'

When Don was gone Charles felt weary – bone weary. He might at last be able to sleep. He was getting too close to Celia, that was the trouble. She was just a patient, like any of them, like the comatose barrister's son. But his thoughts kept turning back and back. He thought of Dorrie and Celia, David and Heather. His mind turned the pairings around, infuriating him. David and Celia. Dorrie and Heather. At least Heather should be happy tonight.

David cooked dinner on Saturdays at home. It was usually spaghetti with a tomato sauce, or a stew made with beer. He wasn't a bad cook, but this evening he had slammed the food together. Heather drooped in a corner of the kitchen, and the girls made their bad tempers quite plain.

'You've sent her away, haven't you?' declared Ellen. 'She didn't fit into your boringly conventional lives, so you sent her away.'

'It was the doctor's decision,' said David diplomatically.

'And what about us?' Lucy's round little face was accusing. 'We wanted her here! She's going to get our money back. She said.'

Heather roused herself. 'She can't get anything back! We went into it at the time of Joe Braddock's death. If we wanted anything we'd have had to fight it through the courts, perhaps for years. It would have cost us everything we own, and we might not have won. Celia's talking rubbish.'

'But it is her money?' Ellen's huge black jumper made her seem like a waif. A penniless waif.

David said, 'It would have been hers. And she may have a claim now, I don't know. The cost of fighting it, though – and the time! If she does get it, you'll both be grown up by then.'

Ellen's eyes suddenly flooded with tears. The dreams she had been cherishing all day, of ponies and holidays, and at last holding her own with the rich brats at school, evaporated in a cold tide of realism. 'Nothing nice ever happens,' she sobbed. 'We never get anything we want! We got our mother back and you sent her away. We don't even have a dog!'

It had been her plea for years now, the request that ensured constant birthday disappointments. 'It's as likely as Ellen's dog,' they would say, about some improbable future event. But poking fun got them nowhere. Still she wanted her dog.

Heather was the one against it. Brought up in a dogless household she recoiled from the creatures. Weren't they noisy, dirty, didn't they harbour disease? If they got a dog she would inevitably have to feed it, clean up after it, worry about its welfare, and no doubt spend costly hours with it at the vet. She had been adamant from the start that they would never, ever have a dog.

Now, in the midst of her family, she looked at David, chopping vegetables aggressively, Ellen, in tears, and Lucy, the picture of baffled childhood. Heather was the villain of the piece, the replacement woman who had not had the decency to step aside when the old model showed up. And she would not! Never!

'Perhaps it is time we had a dog,' she said stiffly. 'Something small and well-behaved.'

'You're making fun of me.' Ellen was learning to be suspicious.

'I'm not. Not at all. We've all been so upset lately. Let's have a dog.'

David said, 'I think we should have talked about this, Heather. You know you don't like dogs.'

'Yes, I do!' She bridled, and two spots of colour stained her pale cheeks. 'I've never disliked dogs as such. I simply never thought we had the time. But we'll make the time. All of us. We'll all do our share.'

'I'd walk it!' shouted Lucy, excited.

'It's my dog,' said Ellen. 'Isn't it, Dad? Mine.'

'A family dog,' said David. 'Don't squabble, you two! As Heather says, we'll all have shares.'

The girls racketed off to find their dog books and decide on a breed. David looked across at Heather. 'I'll pour you some wine in a minute.'

She smiled, tentatively. 'You don't think I've gone mad, do you?'

'A bit. Celia makes people mad, I find.'

Heather drew in her breath. 'Don't talk about her. Not tonight.'

She wanted to make love. She was saying, to him and to fate, I will even get a dog, the thing I hate, if you will love me, forgive me, spare me. She had struggled and made sacrifices, didn't she deserve her place? The dog was a sign of her devotion, the whip with which he could lash her, if he so wished. David knew all this. But if anyone was lashed, it would be Celia. Once she had told him to do it, begged him to punish her. My God, if ever a woman deserved it – and if ever a woman needed it less. He felt again the slow burn of erotic excitement. His life had mysteries once again, promises, risks.

They went to bed early, while the girls were still calling to one another, forgetting all about a small dog and suggesting

168

wolfhounds and greyhounds or a rescued mutt from a dogs' home. To his embarrassment, and no doubt hers, Heather sat naked on the bedroom stool, consciously trying to tempt. He felt an indescribable swell of pity. Poor Heather, all goosepimples and angular bones.

'Get into bed,' he said bracingly. 'You'll freeze.'

She tried to smile. 'Don't you want to keep me warm?'

'In a minute.'

He put on his dressing gown and went downstairs to check the doors, knowing they were locked. When he came back he went into the bathroom to brush his teeth. But Heather still waited. He felt caged, suddenly he wished that he was free. Ten years of loving Heather suddenly seemed a trap of unspeakable dullness. That was Celia, of course. His head was full of memories.

Stolen kisses in the library, parting seconds before her father came in. Passionate leavetakings in the shadows by the front door, fumbling within each other's clothes. The smell of her remained on his skin for hours after, when he went to a tormented and lonely bed. Finally, the careful plans to outwit old man Braddock, to go further, to go all the way.

He had taken her virginity in a cheap hotel in Leeds, and it was raw copulation. She had kept her eyes open all the time, staring up at him as if he was raping her, although she wanted it as much as he. Every minute was etched on his memory, seared into his brain with a fiery torch. Her legs, wide open for him, her nails, like claws in his shoulders, and his whole being centred in her like a furnace about to explode. When she came she cried out, a low, guttural wail, and he felt such pride, such triumph, that he didn't care then if Joe Braddock absolutely bloody killed him. It would have been worth it. For Celia.

He went back into the bedroom. Heather was sitting up in bed with her breasts exposed, and her face set in tragic lines. David got into bed and put his arms around her. 'There's no need to be upset,' he said firmly. 'You know I won't leave you.'

'Won't you? Truly?' She twined her arms around his neck and her legs around his hips. The hair at the base of her belly grew like coarse wire, and he remembered that Celia used to oil hers. He used to help her, chasing the errant drops with his hand, pressing into her while she gasped and told him no. She never meant no. That was the sort of woman she was.

He and Celia might have done anything, gone anywhere. He didn't know what would have happened to them if she hadn't crashed. What did you do with a marriage like theirs, sexy, violent, unpredictable? The accident, coming as it did, on a bright day, in the midst of life, had left them with no need for an answer.

The present mixed inextricably with the past. He was hard, but whether for Celia or Heather he did not know. He was eager, but not for this. He pulled away from Heather and pushed her face down across the bed, her head hanging over the edge. He pushed a pillow under her hips. Now she couldn't see him, it was like having sex in private, with a stranger. The woman beneath him was letting out small cries, and he knew he should turn her over and do it differently. Heather only came in one position. But tonight, he thought cruelly, she could give him this. A small enough price to pay to keep him. The body beneath him began to rear back towards him, and he cupped the eager breasts. To his amazement, Heather had come.

They slept soon after, turned away from each other in the bed. At the front of the house the girls slept only fitfully. They were dreaming of their dog, restless, tossing and turning, until Ellen opened her eyes and thought it must be day. Her curtains were lit like a stage, with brilliant light and dancing shadows. She felt a vague, unfocused fear.

A loud bang rattled the window glass, to be followed by another almost at once. Lucy careered into the room. 'Do you see? What is it?' Ellen stood at the window, blinded by the light. 'We've got to tell Dad!'

They ran down the corridor, and the light from the courtyard was like morning. 'Dad! Dad!' they shrieked. 'The Sheraton's on fire!'

They could do nothing. They stood at the window in their dressing gowns, waiting for the fire brigade, watching the car's final incineration.

Chapter Twelve

Dorrie and Celia were annoying one another. It was a problem of housekeeping, of different levels of untidiness. Celia wondered if her old haphazard ways had evaporated while she slept and left her with her mother's distaste for dirt and disorder. Consigned to Dorrie's spare room, she began to sort out piles of junk, but when she tried to throw it out Dorrie was offended. So she reorganised, and Dorrie resented her taking charge. Confronting an alcove, into which Celia was intent on cramming all the overflowing books, Dorrie thundered, 'Leave things alone, Celia! This is my house, not yours.'

To her horror, Celia's eyes began to fill. Dorrie at once felt guilty. 'Don't look like that, love,' she said hastily. 'Come and have a drink.'

Over the gin, Dorrie said, 'Why not get on with your own life instead of with mine? What do you really want to do, Celia?'

Her friend watched the bubbles in her glass, leaping from ice cube to lemon slice and exploding. 'I want it all,' she said bleakly. 'My husband, my children, my money and my house. I want to wave a magic wand and get rid of Edwin and Heather. Shezzamm!'

'Start waving,' said Dorrie, looking out of the window. 'David's here.'

He leaped up the steps two at a time, and came in the moment the door was opened. He carried a parcel under his arm. 'Dorrie,' he said at once, 'can you swear Celia was here all night? She didn't go out? At all?'

Dorrie blinked. 'Yes. I think so. I'm not sure.'

'You must be sure.'

'I didn't lock her in her room, I can assure you.'

171

Celia perched herself on the edge of the table. She was wearing short navy trousers and a huge navy top, both of impeccable pedigree. She wore no make-up. 'What's happened, David? Is everyone OK?'

He nodded. 'But the Sheraton isn't. Someone set fire to it last night. I left it out, and it was only good luck the garage didn't catch. A foot nearer and the whole coach house would have gone up in flames.'

'You're sure it was deliberate?'

He nodded. 'The fire brigade say so. And Heather—'

Celia laughed. 'Heather says it was me. Why, for heaven's sake?'

'Because she's afraid of you.'

Celia allowed herself a small, vengeful smile.

She looked consideringly at her husband. In contrast to her own designer elegance, David was in weekend scruff. His jersey was a loopy fisherman's knit, his jeans frayed at the ankles. He might have been a university professor, or perhaps, like Dorrie, an artist. Celia looked at his hands, long and sensitive. Her father always said he didn't have successful hands. He'd been right.

'We're drinking gin. Why don't you have some?'

He accepted. 'I suppose you think it was Edwin Braddock,' he said.

'But of course it was! He's frightening me. Putting me off.'

'I'm sure he's not that sort of bloke.'

'But he is! The girls will tell you. He's exactly that sort.'

'You told me he was harmless.'

Celia grimaced. 'So I did. Wasn't I foolish?'

David sank into a chair, the parcel on the table before him. It had been a long night, with the fire brigade and the police. It was good to rest his eyes on Celia. He said, 'I think you'd better give up any thoughts of fighting Edwin. Last night proves that we can't afford it, although believe me, I wish we could. Heather and I considered it when your father died, because it wasn't fair, leaving nothing to the girls. We took advice. They said it could take fifteen years, and no certainty of anything except a massive legal bill. We couldn't take the risk then and we can't take it now. The Sheraton might be just the beginning.'

'But I've got a really good case now,' said Celia. 'Better than you would have had. Anyway, he might settle out of court. He might be going to offer. It could be what this is all about.'

'For the girls' sake, though, you ought to give in.'

She laughed at him, quite gently. 'Oh, David! It's for the girls that I have to fight.'

He felt the old, familiar irritation. He had come here determined to dissuade her. He and Heather had talked and decided it would be best. But Celia never listened. He took a gulp of his drink.

Celia said, 'Come with me to see the solicitor, won't you? I need someone who was there when it all went wrong.'

'I was there all right,' he said bitterly.

She cajoled him. 'Then come, won't you?'

'I'm busy. I'm not free.'

'You can't know that. I haven't told you a time.'

'What time, then?'

'Any that suits you. Ten? Eleven? Whenever.'

He laughed, and she lifted her glass in mocking salute.

As he left he pushed the parcel across the table and said casually, 'By the way, I thought you might like these. The albums. Photographs of the girls.'

'Oh!' Celia's face was suffused with dark colour. 'David, thank you! Thank you so much! You can't know how much this means to me.'

He stood for a moment, looking down at her.

Dorrie took him to the door. She said, 'I suppose you know you're being a fool?'

He flushed but said, 'What about?'

'Don't pretend, David. You can't have Celia and Heather, you know. You're not some Eastern pasha.'

'I'm just being kind. I thought you wanted me to be kinder to her. You've always hated Heather.'

'Heather always hated me! But David, think. Don't lead her on to believe you'll do things you won't. You know Celia. She's an everything or nothing girl.'

'So were you, once.'

Dorrie grinned. 'But I grew out of it. She's still twenty-five and wayward.'

He hesitated, not knowing if Dorrie was friend or foe. Suddenly he said, 'Did you know we're getting a dog?'

Dorrie began to laugh. Heather with a dog? The poor dog. Just as David turned to go she said, 'You shouldn't let her do it. It's cruel.'

'It was her idea, actually.'

'Yes. I suppose it might have been.'

She watched David drive off down the road, in Heather's aged little runabout. She went back to Celia and told her about the dog. As expected, Celia was furious. 'A dog? How could she! It's what I was going to do! She takes everything from me! Their childhood, their birthdays, everything.' She gesticulated at the pictures in front of her. 'She's in more than half of these. Always there, tidying hair, being careful, presiding over birthday parties with motherly zeal. Bloody Heather Wilcox that I never thought worth a light, and she's got all that's mine.' Her face set in lines of hard, implacable anger. 'I hate her, Dorrie. More even than Edwin Braddock. I hate her absolutely.'

Perhaps it was Celia's baleful influence at work that caused them to choose such a dog. Heather was determined on something small and easy to manage, so the woman at the Rescue Centre only showed them the little dogs. The place smelled of dog, ineffectually masked by disinfectant, and a tide of barking followed their progress from pen to pen. The girls were alternately ecstatic and anguished, since only one dog could come home and all the others would be left. Heather hated the place.

'This one,' declared Ellen, stopping beside a half-grown puppy that had a distinctly unctuous leer.

'He looks like a shop lifter,' said David. 'Let's have something a bit more solid.'

'Don't worry, darling, someone will come for you,' cooed Lucy, to the rejected mutt.

David paused at a pen full of Jack Russells, scrapping and squabbling amongst themselves. They broke off long enough to line the wire, yapping and wagging in equal quantity. 'No,' said Heather. 'They're an aggressive breed. I want something gentle.'

'You want a cat,' said Ellen contemptuously, and Heather thought, Yes. A cat would be better. Yet here they were looking for some horrible noisy dog.

A pen in the corner caught her eye. There was a single occupant, a small grey puppy. It sat in the middle of the floor, watching them with what seemed to Heather a benign eye, still milky with babyhood. Its feet were small and neat, its legs short and its head seemed endearingly large for its body. 'What about this one?' she said.

The woman in charge explained that the puppy had been found abandoned in a quarry at about six weeks old. Now, at twelve weeks, they could see nothing that gave a clue to its breeding. 'But obviously,' she said confidently, 'he's not going to be enormous. And he's got a lovely nature. Haven't you, sweetie?'

She rattled the wire and the puppy got up and walked forward. Ignoring everyone else, it put its paws up on the wire in front of Heather. 'Well,' said the woman, 'that's a good start.'

Heather looked at the puppy and the puppy looked at her, a measuring stare, like boxers in a ring.

'Isn't he gorgeous?' crowed Lucy, and Ellen said, 'I love his eyes. Hasn't he got lovely eyes?'

So that was the puppy they took.

They called him Tip. He was clueless about house training and wet everything, culminating in Heather's best cardigan which had fallen from the back of a chair. On the first night, left to sleep in the warmth of the kitchen, he chewed the edge of an oak door, and on subsequent evenings worked round the rest of the units, nibbling at will. Yet when they shut him in the old dog room, with its stone floor and high windows, he howled half the night.

Nobody minded mopping up puddles, but anything worse

and it was left to Heather. The house began to reek of disinfectant. Celia had wished this on her, she found herself thinking. It was a plot designed to plumb the depths of Heather's inadequacies. Celia knew all about dogs, she had been reared with packs of them, while Heather, on the other hand, only had a library book, and that was no use. She missed the start of Evening Service because the puppy had to be accompanied into the garden, and the vicar looked at her pointedly over his glasses. But all the same, when she came home there were unspeakable messes in the hall. Was God playing tricks on her? Was it a punishment? She felt persecuted.

In the chaos of breakfast next morning, the puppy everywhere, mess everywhere, and Heather distraught, David decided not to tell her that he was going to take Celia to the lawyer that day. It would have been unkind. When he said goodbye and kissed her on the cheek she looked at him tragically. He felt like throttling her. She'd asked for the blasted dog, hadn't she? He allowed his irritation to build, using it to justify his day.

When he left he saw that even this early there were plain clothes policemen examining the burnt-out hulk of the Sheraton. David stopped to talk to them. 'Find anything?'

One of the men nodded. 'Quite a bit, sir, actually. Timed device, the sort any amateur arsonist might use. No fingerprints, though. Nothing to link it to anyone – man or woman. Know anyone who's got a grudge against you, sir?'

He shrugged. 'Hard to say, really.'

The man looked discontented. They had wanted to prove it was Celia. After two pointless searches for a woman who turned out not to be missing at all it would have given satisfaction to incarcerate her as a nut. Now they had to start again. David wondered what he would gain by telling them about Edwin Braddock. Nothing, in all probability. They wouldn't be able to prove a thing.

He appropriated a new Sheraton later that day. There was a cancelled order, or at least one that looked as if it would be cancelled. The customer was abroad and couldn't be reached, and might not want the car anyway, once it was made. That

176

happened sometimes, enthusiasm waned when the wait was over a year. There was no premium on a Sheraton just now. But the new car was bright red, the leather of the seats still hard and glossy. David's old model had been a much more sober green. Newness made the engine stiff and he gave it a modest pipe opener on the way to get Celia. He was feeling optimistic; the insurance on the burnt-out car would relieve a few cash flow problems in the business. The dog was taking everyone's minds off the strangeness of recent events, and – most of all, he had to admit, it was most of all – he was going to see Celia.

She wasn't ready, but then she never was. He waited, watching Dorrie slosh paint on canvas to produce some ghastly thing that she said was going against the trend. It took him back, waiting for Celia, although in the old days he would have talked tensely with her mother. But Dorrie was sufficiently maternal to make it fit.

And Celia looked stunning. She was wearing a pale peach suit, with cream shoes and a cream silk top, against which her nipples pressed like buttons. Her hair was a sheet of satin, tempting him to touch. There was no point pretending any more, he thought. Whatever had changed about Celia, this was still the same. Between them, they had invented the word desire.

She smiled at him, and he felt as if it were yesterday. The smile was just the same. There was something about it, some element of naughtiness and allure that was completely her own. He said, 'Did you enjoy the photographs?'

'You know I did. How clever of you. Inspired. I looked at them half the night. The girls have changed so.'

'You haven't.'

'Don't you think so?'

'No.'

Dorrie slammed her palette down in mute despair.

But in the car they were alone. It was hard to know how to behave. David stared straight ahead, driving fast, as he always did when excited. On the bypass, touching ninety, he reached out and put his hand on her knee.

'Oh dear,' she said.

He glanced at her. 'Well? Isn't this what it's all about?'

'It used to be. Do be careful, David. I don't want another crash.'

'Unlike you, I'm a very good driver.'

'Even with your hand up my skirt?'

'It isn't there yet.'

'And it shouldn't be. Think of Heather.'

He withdrew his hand, and stamped on the accelerator. The engine roared in response, more animal than machine, and Celia gasped. 'I never used to frighten you,' said David.

'And you don't now. Oh, David, it's so good to be alive again. Here. With you.'

The car slowed. He pulled into the side of the road and stopped. 'Do you mean that?'

'Yes. You know I do. I know I'm asking a lot, but it's the same, isn't it? Just the same? You and me. Wanting each other.'

He unfastened his seat belt and reached for her. But the car was too small, and Celia yelped as the gear stick stabbed into her breast.

'Don't, don't! Darling David, I'm more than willing, but not in the car. It's broad daylight. And you'll make a mess of me. We really do have to see the solicitor.'

He slid her strap from her shoulder and mouthed the skin. 'Where then? A hotel? We'll have to be very discreet.'

'No, we won't. We're married.' She pulled back and looked at him. 'We are still married, David. We don't have to be ashamed of anything at all.'

A police car passed them. It was time to go. David started the engine again, feeling breathless with need. At the same time reason nudged at the corners of his vision. Suppose Heather found out? Suppose Celia told her? He couldn't dismantle his life over this. He said, 'I'm not ashamed of doing this. I just don't want to hurt anyone. The girls.'

Celia chuckled. 'Oh dear. They'd be so shocked. Well then, we'd better be discreet.'

'Yes. Just for now.'

A new hotel had been built in the last couple of years, one of those fixed-price affairs where you can pay on arrival. David drew up in the forecourt, wondering if anyone would see him.

But the receptionist was young and uninterested, the lobby empty. He felt almost foolish, getting up to this sort of thing. Such passion should have cooled by now. He used to think his had.

The room was cool and very clean. Celia went in first and was reminded of the hospital, the same sterile uniformity. She felt detached, as if this was happening despite her, although she had planned for it, worked for it, dressed for it. She was simply reclaiming her husband, she told herself. Wasn't that right? Wasn't it inevitable? But this strange place unnerved her. The plumbing clanked and the bed looked small and hard. She felt her heart hammering in her chest.

David was almost shivering with excitement. But Celia's thoughts rolled on, of Heather, the dog, Davenport – if he could see her now! Secretive, possessive, arrogant man.

David said, 'You don't know how much I need this. Ten years, Celia. Ten years!'

She took off her jacket and turned to him. 'So you did miss me, after all.'

He said nothing. The silence stretched, and he took her in his arms, trying to kiss her. Celia turned her head, saying, 'If you didn't miss me, why are you here? Be honest, David. We always used to tell each other the truth.'

He held her close and nuzzled her. 'We never used to talk when we could make love. Of course I missed you. At first. But – life goes on.' He put his hand under her top and took hold of her breast. Still Celia wouldn't stop.

'So why are you here? If life's gone on? Don't you think it's time to admit that Heather simply isn't enough?'

The hand on her breast closed aggressively. Celia kept her eyes fixed on his face, watching him smile as he used to do, when he was sure of himself, and of her. He said, 'A lifetime isn't enough to forget the sex we had. All we're doing is reminding ourselves. And I can't wait!'

He reached behind her and unfastened her skirt, slipping his hands into her clothes to hold her buttocks and press her into him. Feeling him, hard and thick, she took an audible breath. She was virginal again, afraid of his size and her own closed body. Some of her excitement was abating. Why didn't

179

he kiss her, hold her, tell her of his love?

He reached down to free himself and his sex reared obscenely between them. Celia put her finger to the tip and felt the telltale moisture. She understood the creature's ways. It was a blind and stupid thing, but David was in its power. Satisfy the creature and David would be satisfied. Whatever else she might provide, Heather could never give him this.

Her skirt was in a circle on the floor. She stepped awkwardly out of her clothes, aware that she still had not mastered every fluid and easy movement. But this was a test, a trial, in which she must prove herself, for only then would she be happy. An image from the albums came back to her; she and David, holding hands, their daughters before them and everyone smiling, smiling.

David pulled her against his skin. The contact made her head spin, she thought she might faint, but no moment of her life was more important than this. David was kissing her, and she moaned in response, aware of a rush of confused sensations; heat, cold, excitement, fear. What did she want from this? And what did David want? She became aware, in amazement, that he was taking out a condom.

'What on earth—?'

He had the grace to blush. 'We'd better not take any chances, had we?'

'If we hadn't taken chances, Ellen would never have been born.'

'So now we're older, we're more sensible. Aren't we?'

She went and sat on the edge of the bed. Suddenly she wondered why she thought she was better than Heather at this. There wasn't much to it, really. And if there was so little trust that you protected yourself with rubber, what on earth was the point? It was nothing more than a grisly exercise in self-satisfaction.

David came and sat on the bed beside her. He began to kiss her shoulders, moving down to her breasts, enjoying her with obvious relish. She felt a little better and lay back, focusing her mind on his touch, making herself aware of each new and pleasurable sensation. He moved to cover her, and she gasped. The weight of him. The power. It was new and it was remembered, it was right and it was wrong. He lifted himself up and entered her.

All restraint was gone. He began to move in her, vigorous and purposeful, pushing his face into her breasts. But Celia was still frail, she lay doll-like beneath him, letting out weak cries on each thrust. He looked at her face, the eyes closed, small beads of sweat on her lips. She excited him utterly, more by her weakness than her strength. He thought he must explode or die. The intense, sharp pleasure flooded out and was gone. Too late now for regrets. It was done.

They showered together in the tiny bathroom. Celia was very pale. David said uneasily, 'Was it too much for you? I'm sorry, I knew you wanted it. I thought—'

Celia said, 'It's all right. I'm fine. I get tired, that's all. It was wonderful, wasn't it?'

'Yes. Wonderful.'

He looked away and Celia felt sharp dismay. He was wondering what they were doing here, why he had ever come. She reached out and took his arm, as if she could go further, and touch his heart. He said, 'I'll pick up the albums next week, if that's OK. Heather doesn't want to lose them.'

Celia drew in her breath. 'But I want to keep them. I thought they were for me.'

'Just as a loan, Celia. They're our family record. All we have.'

'Really?'

She went back into the bedroom and began to dress. She took care, smoothing every crease and fold. What a terrible mistake she had made. David had not come here to do anything more than slake a passing lust. She gathered the rags of her pride about her, determined that he should not see how much she had hoped. Why, she had even imagined what she would say to Heather! 'I'm sorry, my dear. I know how hard this is for you. But David and I have always known we must be together.'

She watched her husband straightening his tie, every inch the businessman. He cast her an obliquely guilty glance and she said in determined tones, 'Hadn't we better go? It's nearly twelve.'

181

'Is it? Damn, we'll have to rush. Ready?'

She nodded and stood up. Her legs were trembling. David, in the aftermath of passion, thought of this morning's breakfast, messy, disorganised, warm. Why had he come from that to this? What was he risking? No more and no less than his happy home.

The solicitor's office was in a Leeds courtyard, high in an elegant building sheltered from the traffic by yards of newly laid cobbles. David parked the Sheraton where the doorman could watch it, and led Celia inside. The place surprised her. The last time she had visited her father's solicitor this had been a depressing and rundown street.

But her heart sank when she confronted Mr Lowndes. Ten years had worked the opposite miracle on him. He was old and thin, stooping a little as if to walk upright would pain him. Her hospital experience came into play; he was ill, and probably with cancer.

His thin face stretched into a smile. He took her hand and clasped it warmly. 'Celia, how lovely to see you. I can't believe you look so well.'

She returned his greeting and they chatted, about her father, about old friends. 'I'm retiring soon,' said Lowndes. 'My son Hector's taking over. I've not been well.'

'Perhaps you'd like us to talk this over with him?' said Celia anxiously. 'It's going to be quite a long haul.'

'My dear.' He folded his hands on the desk. 'In my view you should not even begin.'

He began to speak about her father, his energy and drive, of his sadness when Celia was hurt. 'He turned very much to your cousin,' he said. 'You see, Celia, he didn't leave his wealth to Edwin Braddock because there was no one else. After all, there was David and the girls. He left it to him because he thought he was the best man for the job. The person best equipped to take care of all that your father had created. Your revival like this isn't going to alter anything. In my view, you should appeal to Mr Braddock for an income and drop all thoughts of inheriting. I have no doubt that he'll happily, on that basis, oblige.'

182

Celia felt her heart sink. David said, 'Mr Braddock hasn't shown any signs of generosity so far. I don't know if I agree with her, but Celia still feels she wants to fight the case.'

'Does she?' Mr Lowndes smiled at her. 'Do you, Celia? Knowing the trouble it could bring? You've been given your life back again, my dear. A precious gift, the most precious thing in all the world, worth far more than money. Why not make good use of that, rather than go chasing off after something you may not win?'

Through the mists of weariness, like clouds in her brain, Celia forced herself to think. 'Didn't you consider it odd that nothing was left to my children?' she said. 'Not even my mother's jewellery. I understand the Will was in a series of numbered envelopes. Don't you think that one of the envelopes, the one about the children, was missing?'

'Everything was in order, Celia. We kept everything together and brought it out after your father's death. All parts of the Will were adhered to most carefully. We missed nothing.'

'Perhaps it wasn't with the rest.'

He spread his hands. 'Then where else would it be? Your father was a careful man, Celia. His Will wasn't made up as I should have wished, but it was adequate. He couldn't face redrawing it, you see. He merely scribbled a few notes. If he excluded the girls I think it was because he wished to exclude them. It wouldn't have been an oversight.'

Celia turned to David. 'Did you search the house when my father died? Who cleared it out?'

'Your mother,' said David. 'I believe Edwin helped her.'

'Edwin! He would.' She tried to speak calmly. 'Mr Lowndes, do you think it right that Edwin Braddock should have assisted my mother at such a time? Shouldn't you have gone through the papers?'

He said stiffly, 'We do like to leave such things to the family at a time of grief.'

'I bet you do.' She tried to hang on to her temper. The man was ill, and had been less than well for years.

A thought occurred to her. 'Are you my cousin's solicitor too?' she asked bluntly.

Mr Lowndes looked momentarily discomfited. 'We – we used to act for him, yes. Not so much recently. I hear he has a London firm he prefers to use.'

'But you acted for the Braddock Corporation when you advised against suing them, didn't you?'

'Celia, that would never have influenced me!'

'No.' She dropped her eyes. 'I'm sure it would not.'

He saw them out into the reception area, and bade them goodbye with somewhat less warmth than when he had welcomed them. He went back into his office and they stood in the hall waiting for the lift. Celia swayed slightly.

David said, 'Are you all right?'

She lifted her head. 'Yes. Fine. And we do have a case, I'm convinced of it. The Will was a mess, it would have been child's play to take something out. Old Lowndes won't admit it, though. He just wants a quiet life and a nice big retainer from the Braddock Corporation.'

His face took on the cautious look she hated. 'I do think we should be careful. He might be right, you might be wasting time and money. Why not try and persuade Edwin to give you an income?'

She shifted from foot to foot. 'He isn't persuadable. And I won't let him win.'

The lift began to whirr up from the floors below. David jabbed the button again, unnecessarily. 'You always were vindictive. I thought you'd lost that.'

She eyed him coldly. 'Then you thought wrong.'

The lift came and they stepped forward. But a voice called them. 'Mrs Sheraton! Mr Sheraton! If I could detain you?'

A young man was emerging from the offices. He was short and square, with thick-rimmed glasses and a balding head. He should have been unprepossessing, in his dusty suit and scuffed shoes, but somehow the inner man had triumphed. He had a rumpled charm. 'I'm Hector Lowndes. I wonder if we could talk?'

'How do you do?' Celia was cool. She suspected the Lowndes family. She followed him reluctantly to his office.

Unlike his father's uncluttered space, this was overflowing with paper. Books and files were everywhere, even the visitors' chairs were piled high. So they stood on the small square of open carpet. Hector Lowndes said, 'I think we should have a stab at getting your money back, Mrs Sheraton. We could make a good case.'

'You realise Mr Braddock cheated?' said Celia. 'I think he destroyed a part of the Will.'

'We can't prove that,' said Hector. 'But, yes, I think so too.' He beamed at them both, and began to polish his glasses. His weak eyes blinked with a spurious vulnerability. Celia felt her sagging spirits rise like a helium balloon.

'You see,' he went on, 'I hadn't qualified then, but I remember the salient facts. My father and I disagreed about them at the time. The Will was in numbered envelopes. Lots of them, with pencilled numbers.'

'I've seen photocopies,' said Celia absently. 'Anyone could have altered the numbers, it seems to me.'

'Indeed they could. The thing is, the bequest to Edwin Braddock was no more than a tidying-up affair. Joe left him the residue of his estate. In other words, your father had dealt with most things and was leaving the crumbs to your cousin. Not the main meal. Oh, no. That had been bequeathed elsewhere. But where? That part of the Will is missing.'

David said, 'That's all conjecture. There's nothing to prove any other papers ever existed.'

Hector Lowndes made an arch of his fingers. 'Do we know that? As far as I can see, no one has ever even looked.'

In the silence, Celia said, 'Why on earth didn't anyone look into this at the time?'

Lowndes bowed his head in apology. 'There was quite some delay. Your mother was very distressed, and these things are always complex. The full position only unfolded gradually, by which time your mother was emotionally dependent on Mr Braddock. In one sense, so were we. I believe my father wished to retain the Braddock account. It was vital for us at that time. We lost it soon after, though.'

'Do you still receive money from them? Any money?'

Hector Lowndes forced himself to meet Celia's eye. 'None at all, Mrs Sheraton.'

David leaned across the desk. 'Really, is there any point in

185

pursuing this? We haven't the money for a long legal battle, and it could take years.'

'Perhaps only two years,' said Lowndes. 'As for the money— well, obviously it will be costly. Barristers' fees and so forth. Those are unavoidable. But we would be prepared to set our fees aside until the case is settled. Nonetheless, there are no guarantees.'

David thought for a moment. Then he looked at Celia. 'You could claim the money left to the hospital. It's yours, after all.'

'I decided I wouldn't,' she said tightly. 'I know Heather would love me to take it, just so she can despise me, but I won't give her the satisfaction, thank you very much.'

Hector Lowndes coughed diffidently. 'That money isn't exactly Mrs Sheraton's, to do with as she would like. It is in trust for her care in hospital. If she no longer needs such care, then the Braddock Corporation could make a legitimate claim that it should be returned to them. You would of course be able to contest that in court.'

'And I'd win,' said Celia.

Lowndes spread his hands. 'Probably. Who can tell?'

She tapped a finger against her lip. All this money, and none of it to hand. She had never been without funds in her life, the situation was utterly unfamiliar. How did people usually manage if they weren't born with her brand of silver spoon? She looked at David.

'You could take a mortgage. On the house.'

'What? On Blantyre House?'

'Yes. Why not?'

David exploded. 'A mortgage! No! Heather and I have worked ourselves stupid to avoid getting into debt. I wouldn't take a mortgage to expand the business and I won't do it now. Not for some idiot pursuit of money you'll never get.'

Celia was bewildered. 'You mean you've thought about a mortgage before?'

'Yes. Obviously. Heather and I made a decision. The risk was unacceptable.'

The words 'Heather and I' flicked Celia on the raw. 'Oh, I bet you decided,' she sneered. 'That's Heather all over, too cautious to blow her own nose. You don't have to be quite such

186

a coward, David. If you'd mortgaged the house at the start you could have put the money into the business and made it a success!'

He turned on her a look of weary and unpleasant recognition. 'You are so like your father,' he said bitterly.

This time, they were silent in the lift. They only spoke when they reached the car. Celia said, 'I won't tell Heather about the hotel. I can see you want to keep it a secret.'

He made a vague, uncomfortable gesture. 'It would only upset her.'

'And how we should hate to see Heather upset.'

Celia drummed her fingers on her bag. She was miserable, and her only refuge now was in anger. Yesterday she had been sure that he would love her again. Was she asking too much too soon?

David was starting the car. He said, 'I'm glad you're being reasonable. A court case like this isn't something people like us can just rush into.'

She sat bolt upright in her seat. 'What do you mean, people like us? I'm me, David. An individual. Not some ordinary, dull, unambitious little nobody, constantly living in fear!'

'I only meant—'

'I know what you meant! Be damned to you. If you want me to keep secrets you can take out that mortgage. You should have done it years ago, you should thank me. And Heather should thank me for letting her keep her illusions. Those are my terms, David. I almost forgot what sort of person I am. People like me don't give something for nothing. Not to people like you.'

David said, 'Why are you angry? What on earth is this about?'

She glared at him. 'Money. That's all. You know where you are with money.'

He started the car and rammed it into gear. Celia's rage began to dissipate, leaving her strangely weak. Even her thoughts weighed heavy, tumbling in her head like stones. Suddenly she was afraid. She tried to speak, tried to move, but the weight in her head, enormous now, denied her. She tried to breathe, but even the air was leaving her. Even life. The world raced away, a receding light in a tunnel. She was left in the

187

dark, floating, motionless. All alone.

David said, 'Celia? Celia, are you all right?' But she was utterly unconscious.

He drove straight to the hospital and once there, dragged Celia from the car. She hadn't moved since her collapse. He was imbued with sudden strength, enough to pick her up and carry her. Her head hung down and one arm trailed limply. Everything came back to him: the accident, the months of hope, the final acceptance that her life force was spent. Had she gone? This time, had she really gone?

They put her on a trolley and took her away. David followed, at a distance, and suddenly Davenport came flying through a door. He went straight to the trolley. 'She's breathing, but only just. Get a ventilator on her, we've got to keep her gases up. Celia? Celia, can you hear me?'

No reply. He demanded a pencil torch and shone lights in her eyes, he threw off her shoes and tested reflexes. 'I want a CAT scan,' he said tersely. 'Right away.'

I've killed her, thought David. It was the sex.

People bustled about the trolley, preparing a mask, trying to insert needles, tapping a hand to bring up a vein. Suddenly the comatose figure stirred. One of the nurses let out a little cry, and David said tensely, 'Did you see that? Did you see?'

'Yes.' Davenport snapped his torch off. 'Panic over, everyone.' He took a deep, calming breath before saying lightly, 'Hello, Celia. Nice to see you again.'

Looking up through mist and confusion, she saw Charles, as always. There was sweat above his mouth. She reached up to touch his lips, although her arm seemed barely to belong to her.

Another face moved into view. It was David. She looked at him bemusedly.

'Are you all right? I thought you'd died.'

'I'm still here,' she said weakly.

'We'll need to do some tests,' said Davenport. 'You'll be staying the night.'

She closed her eyes in relief. Charles and the hospital. She could rest.

Chapter Thirteen

Celia was in hospital for two days. She was subjected to a battery of tests, blood samples, brain scans, the works. On the morning of the second day Charles came to see her. He sat on her bed.

'You look very much better, my girl.'

She grinned at him. 'I needed a rest, that's all. I'd been overdoing it.'

'What did you do that day? Tell me.'

She turned her cheek into the pillow. 'Oh. You know. Things.'

'What things?'

She looked at him then, her eyes a challenge of blue. 'I think you know, don't you?'

'Do I?' He was bland and unforthcoming. Yet she knew David must have told him. Surely, with her health at stake, David would have come clean?

'I thought David had spoken to you.'

'He said you went to see a solicitor, and spent some time standing around waiting for a lift. Did you do something else, Celia? Something – physical. It's important. I must know.'

She picked at the bedspread nervously. This was not something she wanted to say. He would think she was the sort of woman who went around trying to get men into bed with her. A woman without shame. But David was after all her husband! She licked dry lips. 'I – I wanted to re-establish the relationship with my husband. He isn't nearly as settled with Heather as he led you to believe, you know. He felt the same, that we were still very close, very much attracted – so we went to a hotel and made love.'

He met her stare, unblinking. She had the sensation that he

189

was absolutely furious with her, and yet nothing betrayed it. 'Did you reach a climax?' he asked bluntly.

Her face flamed. 'That has nothing to do with you.'

'It has a lot to do with your brain.'

'And rather more to do with your voyeuristic instincts.'

'You can screw who you like, Celia, it's your health I'm interested in!'

'You're just upset because I wouldn't screw you.'

He said harshly, 'Watch it, Celia. I'm not above committing you for your own good. Rampant sexual appetite is a recognised side effect of brain injury.'

'Rampant? Rampant?' Her voice rose to a shriek. 'Dorrie tells me that if anyone's rampant it's you!'

She had surprised him. Celia had a sudden desire to drive her advantage home. 'Do you enjoy your lovemaking?' she demanded. 'Does it have a bearing on your health?'

His voice was firmly controlled. 'My sexual activities have nothing to do with our doctor–patient relationship. Yours do. Tell me what happened.'

It was the ultimate invasion. There was nothing else. She stared at him defiantly. 'If you must persist in this, I regret to say that there's nothing interesting to tell. Normal sex. The only abnormal thing was my own weakness. I felt ill and tired. I couldn't get into the mood.'

'Are you telling me the truth?'

'I can't think why I should hide anything from you, Mr Wonderful.' Heavy irony.

'Did you take anything, were you drunk?'

'Only with desire,' said Celia flippantly.

He snorted. 'A desire for revenge.'

She lay back against the pillows like a sulky child. Her eyes were shadowed, her lips pale and bloodless, but he was aware of her attraction as at no time before. Deep inside, hidden from anything but his conscience, he knew he was jealous of David Sheraton. He had enjoyed what Charles could never have. She had given herself to a man who had abandoned her for ten long years, while her saviour, the man without whom she would have no life at all, was fit only for teasing. He was finding it hard to look at her without imagining how it had been. Yet Sheraton hadn't even had the guts to admit what he'd done, even for Celia's health.

He forced his mind into other channels. 'Right,' he said briskly. 'No more sex. At least until we get the results of the tests.'

'Don't tell me what I can and can't do! You know as well as I do that sex had nothing to do with it.'

He lost his temper with her. Sometimes she was no better than a child! 'Celia, when you left here you accepted that your marriage was over. You knew your husband had another life. But you let him use you, let him have a quick poke, and why? To try and get him back. Don't you think that's a little degrading?'

'He's my husband.'

'But he won't leave Heather. Accept it. The most you can hope for is more of the same, his bit on the side.'

She put her hands up behind her head and glared at him. 'If he'd rather have Heather than me, I'll be surprised! All the practice I've had has made me quite a good lay, so I'm told.'

'Then you'd better learn to be a bit more discriminating! This is the Aids generation, Celia. And you are not the young thing you once were. Women of your age do not sleep around.'

She sneered at him. 'Don't worry. Once I've got my husband back I won't sleep with anyone but him. Promise.'

'Has it occurred to you that your husband doesn't have to leave Heather any more? You gave him what he wanted. On a plate.'

'Is that the way you do it, then?'

'You randy little bitch.'

They stared at each other, anger almost visible between them. Then Davenport left.

He stormed into the administrator's office, only to find it empty. He cursed, and went to his secretary to demand an appointment. 'Can I tell him what it's about?' she asked nervously. Davenport was obviously in a towering rage.

'A patient transfer,' he snapped. 'To another hospital. Any other hospital.'

'Oh. Oh, I see. Can you tell me who it is?'

'Mrs Sheraton.'

He began to walk out. But the girl said in amazement, 'Not Mrs Celia Sheraton? Mr Davenport, you know we can't transfer her!'

Of course he couldn't. In the heat of the moment he was behaving like a fool. He couldn't deprive the hospital of three million pounds just because she annoyed him. Besides, they'd get rid of him long before her. He sighed, utterly dispirited. 'No. We can't have her transferred. Forget it.'

He walked glumly back to his office. She was going to haunt him, perhaps for years, perhaps forever. He had summoned a spirit, hoping for treasure, and instead was in the grip of something which would not let him go. He hated the days when he didn't see her almost as much as those when he did, but it was only sex, he told himself! He was suffering one of those odd, irrational assaults on the senses that happen to men sometimes. Obviously Dorrie wasn't enough.

When he opened his door she was sitting on the desk, waiting for him. Her dressing gown was tightly closed, her feet encased in respectable slippers, her hair caught up in a clip. She looked about fourteen.

'I came to apologise,' she said. 'But no one knew where you were.'

'No.'

'I think you made me so angry because you were right. I shouldn't have slept with David. It was a cheap, silly thing to do.'

'He is still your husband.'

'I'm not sure that he still wants to be. Except for the sex, that is.'

'Yes.'

He went to sit down and she got off his desk and stood in front of it, like a schoolgirl about to be told off by the head. He wondered if she knew how she aroused him, and thought that she must. He busied himself sorting out his papers. 'You've got to understand,' he said suddenly. 'You've got to be careful, Celia. I know you feel quite well most of the time, and you are well. Of course you are. But – I must be honest. I was waiting for some sort of problem.'

She stared at him. 'You mean, you knew I'd collapse?'

'I thought you might. You've got a brain injury, Celia. Sudden blood surges aren't safe.'

'Are you saying I can't ever have sex? Even the dismal sort?'

'Not really, no. I'm saying that you should be very sure of what you want to do before you do it. Everything carries a risk for someone like you. Anger. Fear. Exertion. And sex. They're all things you should treat with caution. You need to take life quietly and calmly. For now.'

'Do you mean – forever?'

He looked up into her lovely, chiselled, timeless face. 'I don't know.'

She sat down in the hard little chair he kept for visitors. He realised that he had shocked her and was angry with himself. He had told everyone that she wasn't cured except Celia herself. She had believed herself whole.

In a low, penitent voice, she said, 'I thought I could be happy again. I wanted my husband and children. I wanted to make up for all the things I did wrong before and do it right.'

'You can still do most things. Just—'

'Just remember that I could die. I nearly did, I know. For a second, before I went, I knew I was dying. What am I going to do, Charles?'

'Wait. Take care. Take notice of yourself. In time you might be much better. You took ten years to get here, Celia. In another ten years you could be altogether well.'

'Or dead.'

'We could all be dead, sweetheart.'

The endearment surprised them both. Celia got up and tried to grin, her mouth twisting a little as she fought against grief. She said, 'I've been squandering my days, haven't I? Wasting my time. I really must do better.'

'You're my star patient. You can't do any better.'

She put her hand up to her face, snapping, 'Charles, will you stop being nice to me? I hate you when you are. Just be arrogant and objectionable, as usual.'

She walked away, leaving the door swinging wide. He watched her to the end of the corridor, saw her halt, sway and gather her breath. And he wished suddenly, fiercely, that he had never brought her to life at all.

Celia went to her room and sat in a chair, staring at nothing. She had been foolish, she knew that now. She had thought all she need do was oust Heather, by fair means or foul, and resume her rightful place. But suppose she succeeded? What then? If she died, or worse, slipped back into that nowhere land in which she had spent so many years, she would have dealt her family a brutal service. They didn't deserve such a thing.

A nurse knocked briefly, and then came in. 'It's your husband, Mrs Sheraton. Is it all right?'

'What?' Celia felt bemused. 'Yes. All right.' Why had he come now, when she had decided such a terrible thing? She didn't want him now.

He entered, carrying a large bunch of flowers. 'Hello, Celia.'

'David.'

They were embarrassing each other. Celia wondered what he had said to Heather on the night she collapsed. Perhaps he had said nothing. As Davenport pointed out, she was just David's bit on the side.

He began babbling about the girls and the dog. They were fighting for the privilege of holding the lead, and kept trying to smuggle him into bed, much against Heather's wishes.

'What did you tell her?' asked Celia.

He hesitated. 'Nothing. Just that I heard you'd fallen ill. How are you? Better? You don't look too well.'

'I'm well enough.'

The conversation died into nothing. Celia stirred herself. 'We haven't talked properly, you know. How is Sheraton Cars? Does it need money?'

He shrugged. 'Yes, I suppose so. We're not going anywhere, you see, each year's very like the last. Some aspects of the design are perhaps a bit dated now, and we can't improve those without cash. But that doesn't mean I want to risk my home.'

'It was my home first.'

He dropped his head. 'Yes. Yes, I have to concede that it
'

was. Would it make you happy, would it make you feel better, if I lost the house and the girls had to live in a hovel?'

She sighed. Trust David to leap to the extreme and irrational conclusion. She had once asked him to change out of grubby jeans for a visit to her father, and he had come down in his dress suit, complete with bow tie and varnished shoes. She never criticised his clothes again, of course. David had his own brand of weaponry.

She said, 'You wouldn't lose the house. The mortgage would only be a fraction of its value. I could use some for my legal fees and you could have the rest for the firm.'

'And if I don't agree you'll tell Heather I was unfaithful?'

Celia giggled. 'You can't be unfaithful with your wife. No, I won't tell Heather anything. But I will ask you, again, to do this one thing for me. Mortgage the house. It's the least you can do.'

David got up, as if he wanted to rush from the room. Celia realised she had confounded him by a simple request, when he had come here ready for blackmail and confrontation. She felt sad suddenly. David never used to shy away like this from a challenge.

He turned to her. 'You don't realise what's involved. Heather would have to know.'

'Heather's an accountant. She ought to see sense. We both need money and this is a surefire way of getting it.'

'But a mortgage has to be repaid. We're struggling as it is.'

'When the business expands you won't be struggling! You'll update the car and sell twice as many. Honestly, David, does Heather make you so defeatist? What does she think's going to happen to Sheraton Cars?'

He said, a trifle huffily, 'I don't involve Heather in my work. She knows nothing about cars.'

'But she knows about money.'

'For God's sake, Celia, I was relieved enough to have an end to your meddling. I was damned if I was going to have Heather airing her views! Sheraton Cars is mine, I started it and I will run it. I don't need a pack of women telling me what to do.'

Celia was silent. After a moment David said, 'I'm sorry. When I'm angry I don't mean half the things I say. I'll talk to

Heather and then go and see the bank. They've been urging me to borrow against the house for years.'

'Thank you for coming to see me,' said Celia with formal restraint. 'And for the flowers.'

'What? Yes. Look, I really must go.'

Left alone, she lay down on the bed, letting the cool pillow soothe the chaos in her head. Davenport was right again, it seemed. David did not want her back.

They called the dog Tip, because one of his ears had a faint white edge. He answered to it spasmodically, abandoning his early cultivation of Heather and ignoring her calls as if deaf. She found him utterly dislikable. As far as she could see, owning a dog was all mess in the kitchen, exuberance when she wanted calm, wanton destruction and compulsory walks in the rain.

After the first terrible days she had suggested a kennel, or failing that a muzzle, but she'd been shouted down. The family harmony for which she strove seemed in danger of foundering. 'We knew you didn't really want a dog,' said the girls, bitterly. And Tip had yawned and been sick on the floor.

But for the first time this evening Heather had come home to find the kitchen clean and no new toothmarks on the cupboards. She and the dog eyed each other thoughtfully. Was it possible that they could come to an understanding?

'Good boy, Tip,' said Heather. He wagged his tail and grinned, and she threw him a doggy choc. The worst was over.

She made an effort with supper that night, hoping to eradicate some of the worst effects of the word 'kennel'. The girls, as always, were forgiving. 'We knew you didn't mean it really,' said Lucy. 'Jesus wouldn't want you to. There isn't anything in the Bible about putting dogs in kennels.'

Heather said somewhat frostily, 'I don't need divine guidance for everything I do, Lucy.'

'Don't you?' Lucy looked surprised.

Privately, Heather decided to let the girls miss Sunday school for a week or two, and prove to them she wasn't a religious bigot. Her own faith, of course, was unshakable. It had supported her through many difficult years.

The girls took the dog for a walk, and Heather and David settled down by the fire. David poured them both a brandy. 'Feeling happier now the dog's settled down?'

She nodded. 'I'm fine.'

'Good.' David rested an elbow on the mantelpiece. 'I rather wanted to talk to you.'

Cold fingers of fear touched her heart. What now? Was he leaving her? Even after the dog?

He said, 'I've decided to mortgage the house.'

Her relief was almost tangible. It was as if she had stepped into thin air, and just as she began to fall encountered warm, solid earth.

She took a sip of her brandy. 'I didn't know you'd been to see the bank manager. What did he say? Does he think it's a good time to expand?'

'I didn't go and see him, actually. I talked to Celia.'

Her feet slipped again, violently. The brandy in her glass almost spilled. If he confessed to one meeting with Celia, how many had he really had? And what did they do? She imagined everything, and worst of all that they talked about her, and laughed between themselves. Silly Heather Wilcox, with her dull clothes and duller religion, the stopgap until Celia returned. How they must laugh about her efforts with the dog!

David said awkwardly, 'She's in hospital again. They telephoned me, she had a turn.'

In a low, passionate voice Heather said, 'You're going to mortgage my home and give the money to her?'

'Some of it, yes. For legal fees. The rest really is for the business. Heather dear, you know how often we've talked about expanding! You were all for it, last year.'

'You wouldn't do it when I asked. Why when she does?'

He let out an incredulous laugh. 'You don't really expect me to answer that childish remark! Heather, I have to support Celia somehow. She's expensive and she's determined to take Braddock to court. At least this way she won't have endless calls on us for cash. She can be independent, up to a point.'

'And when she's spent up to that point? She'll be back here, demanding more, taking away from us! And you'll give her everything, just as you always have.'

David drained his brandy and put down his glass. He never could stand scenes, especially with Heather. She had none of Celia's zest for a battle, none of her steel. She retreated too easily into hurt and shuddering silence. 'I'll go and see where the girls have got to,' he said stiffly. 'I've decided, Heather. I'm going to the bank in the morning.'

When he was gone and the house was her own, rich in its silence, she sat very still. Then she rose and went to the telephone book, leafing through for a number. Before she dialled she went out into the hall and looked about, but she was quite alone. No one would hear.

Nonetheless, when a voice said 'Hello?' she instinctively whispered.

'Mr Braddock?'

'Yes. Yes, this is Edwin Braddock. Who is this?'

'Heather Wilcox. We met once, I don't suppose you remember—'

'But of course! Heather. How are things going? You must have had a very upsetting time of late.'

She choked on a giggle. 'You could say that. Mr Braddock, I wondered if you would like some information. About Celia.'

A pause. As it lengthened, she wondered if he was there still and said, 'Hello?'

'What about Celia? Why should there be anything I should wish to know?'

Heather burst out, 'I'm sure you'll wish to know it when I tell you. David's been seeing her, you see, although he swore to me that he hadn't. The hospital won't supervise her, they let her do just as she likes. Did you know she'd been ill again?'

'How ill?'

Heather laughed bitterly. 'Not ill enough. Even the hospital can't control her, she has fits the moment they let her go. And mentally she's all wrong. She's planning to take you to court over the money, and she's persuaded David to mortgage our house so she can do it. And I can see what's going to happen, she'll take more and more until we've got nothing, and she runs rings round David so he doesn't understand. I want you to stop her.'

Braddock said, 'He never did see what a schemer she was,

198

behind that pretty face. But what can I do to help?'

Heather let out her breath. 'I thought, if I kept you informed – who she's seeing, what they've decided and so on – then you can take steps.'

'What sort of steps?'

Heather's voice was suddenly very shrill. 'I really don't know. The sort you usually take. Only against her this time, and not us! Goodbye.'

Her hands were trembling and she went to pour herself another brandy, taking deep breaths to calm herself. She had made a fool of herself to no purpose. But then the telephone rang again.

'Hello?'

'Heather, this is Edwin. It was kind of you to call. Just to tell you that I'm very grateful. And if you find out anything else I'll be more grateful still. Don't worry, my dear. I won't let her win. An early and spectacular defeat would suit us both.'

Heather said, 'I'm just afraid that she'll take everything and leave us bankrupt. That's what she's like, you see. And David—'

'It really is time he stood up to her, isn't it? Call me again, Heather. Any time.'

The next morning, at work, a brown envelope was delivered to Heather by motorcycle despatch rider. It contained £500 in crisp new notes, and a letter written in a neat, upright hand. 'Just a token of my appreciation, Heather dear. I have today taken steps to forward our mutual interests. Best wishes. E.'

Celia and Dorrie were sitting watching television when Charles called. He strode into the room on a blast of cold air, suddenly making the place seem small and cluttered. 'Have you heard?' he demanded.

Celia blinked at him. 'Heard what?'

'I've been suspended.'

Dorrie got up and put out her arms, but he evaded her. He didn't want comfort, he wanted revenge! 'This is all your fault,' he said to Celia, in disgust. 'You insisted on leaving hospital. You invited a collapse. Because of that collapse the Braddock Corporation has declared the hospital in breach of

199

its duty of care. They've obtained an injunction. The trust fund has been sequestered, pending a hearing. The hospital says it is all down to me.'

'What's going to happen?' asked Dorrie.

Charles paced the carpet, full of agitation. 'There's not much can happen. I shall probably be the scapegoat and lose my job.'

Celia dropped her head in her hands. 'They want me back under lock and key,' she said softly. 'You're just an innocent bystander.'

Charles said, 'Thank you so much for your concern. I wish I had stood innocently by. One thing's for sure, if I knew then what I know now I would have left you in that bed for eternity.'

She looked up at him, her eyes that startling blue, bright with the suspicion of tears. Charles felt an urge quite unfamiliar to him.

'I'm sorry,' he said gruffly. 'That was unnecessary. I apologise.'

Chapter Fourteen

The weekend of Charles's suspension was a busy one. His first task was to get in touch with a solicitor, which was next to impossible out of hours. When he did at last run him to earth, in the bar of a golf clubhouse judging by the telephone noises, the news was bad. He could not oppose his suspension; he could merely wait for his case to be heard.

Thwarted, he turned his attention to his colleagues, but it was difficult now to appeal for support to men who had felt threatened by him. Charles's expansion plans had been an open secret. If, by his downfall, others could feel more secure then no one would reach out a hand. Medicine was so political, he thought angrily, who had been the most political of them all. It shouldn't be like that.

He went to see his special coma patient, Martin Moffat, the barrister's son. He was improving, responding now to Sister Johnson's voice. 'You've got a rare skill of some kind, Sister,' said Davenport. 'I only wish I knew what it was.'

'It's called dedication,' she said frostily. 'A word not much used by your sort.'

He caught his breath. 'Are you saying that I don't give my patients proper care, Sister?'

She fixed him with a gimlet stare. 'Not at all. They receive all the care that an ambitious young man can provide. After all, they are rungs on the ladder of your career, are they not?'

He wondered what she expected. Sobbing at the bedside, perhaps? It was amazing how the wolves gathered around the doomed stag. He glanced again at the young man lying on the bed. 'You can't expect me to care too much about someone who addled his own brain with adulterated heroin mixed with alcohol and cocaine. He has earned his coma, Sister.'

She smoothed the sheets and pillows, and patted the unconscious shoulder in a mute gesture of reassurance. 'Perhaps his father earned it for him, Mr Davenport. Have you ever thought of that?'

He should have been used to Sister Johnson's acid tongue by now. No doubt he was feeling vulnerable. At any rate, he was especially charming to all his patients that day, as well as their endless relatives. A frisson of anxiety was running through the wards as gradually they realised that from Monday he would be gone.

'What shall I do?' asked a nervous and unhappy epileptic. 'You might not have much of a bedside manner but at least you know your job. Now I'll never get stable.'

Charles grunted. 'I admit, it's going to be difficult. I'll talk to my juniors every day from home. With a bit of luck we could have you back at work by the end of the month. Insurance, isn't it? Probably half the trouble. Hellish job, bound to give anyone a seizure.'

The man laughed, and Charles was surprised to find himself comforted. Just because he didn't spend hours patting hands didn't mean he ignored his patients' needs. He felt a renewed surge of anger against James and the rest. Look what they were doing to him! He was losing his confidence, when this was all about money. If a financial wrangle destroyed his function as a doctor then he was not the man he believed himself to be.

When Monday came, a dark day full of rain and wind, Charles paced the rooms of his big, old house like a caged lion. There was a week before the preliminary hearing, a week in which he could do nothing but wait. He imagined cabals and cliques ranging against him. The heart men wouldn't say a word in his support. But were such words even necessary? All that mattered was whether or not he had given Celia Sheraton adequate care.

As the short day slid into a wind-tossed night, he went upstairs to shower and change. Rain rattled like pebbles against the ill-fitting bathroom window, and air roared in the drainpipes, howling around the Victorian bathtime pipework like a squadron of banshees. The weather suited his mood. He pulled on a thick sheepskin coat and went out into the night.

Celia opened the door to him herself. The wind almost dragged it from her grasp and he stepped inside quickly. 'Dorrie's not here,' she said. 'She takes a life-study class at the college on Mondays.'

'Does she? Damn,' said Charles, who knew it perfectly well. 'I was going to take her out somewhere, I'm going mad with nothing to do. Why don't you come instead?'

She lifted an eyebrow. 'I thought I was supposed to be taking things easy.'

'I'll take you somewhere easy. Come on, I'll drive.'

She went to change into a skirt and soft, scoop-necked pink cashmere sweater. She had folded her hair into a complicated knot on top of her head, and he was caught anew by the long inward curve of her throat, swelling out at its base to the fullness of her breast. But there were purple shadows like thumbprints beneath her eyes.

'You've not been sleeping.'

She pushed her arms into a voluminous mackintosh of Dorrie's. 'No. I don't like sleep. It feels dangerous.'

'You must sleep. I can give you something.'

'Don't be a bore, Charles.'

They ran to the car together through the storm, and drove in silence to a restaurant in the country. Charles played a tape of a violin concerto very softly, and the rain swished beneath their wheels. He felt some of the day's tension begin to ebb, and saw that Celia too was sliding a little lower in the seat. He was almost sorry when they drew up at the restaurant door.

The place was virtually empty, due to foul weather and the time of year. Perhaps because of this and to create a feeling of intimacy, the dining room was lit with candles, reflected in silver and glass, making shadows of infinite depth. Celia spread her linen napkin and said, 'It's so good to touch things of quality again, after hospital. Dorrie's house isn't very stylish.'

'What's Braddock's place like?'

She grimaced. 'The other side of style. He has ambitions to be a potentate.'

He ordered a light white wine, and wouldn't let her drink more than a glass. It was enough, she was tired tonight, and her brief store of energy was giving out. The food revived her; quail and delicious vegetables, and a pudding of brandied summer fruit in a froth of cream. They talked about Edwin Braddock, and in talking, Celia realised how much she didn't know. She recalled her father advising him to abandon art, declaring it to be a nothing subject for nothing people – he often talked like that. So Edwin must be artistic in some way. She thought back to the house. Her clearest memory was of porcelain, standing in delicate groups on tables and mantels. He must collect.

Charles listened to her dreamy, sleepy voice. She changed when she was tired. He felt a sudden panic, as if she might at any moment slip away into sleep, and keep on slipping, until she was gone. He said, 'Do you think I gave you proper care, Celia? Should I have kept you in hospital? You were so desperate to go.'

She put her head on one side to study him. 'Really, Charles. Self-doubt, at this stage? Not like you.'

'At what stage? What stage am I at?'

'Now that is a very interesting question.' Leaning forward in the candlelight, she was a beautiful, merciless judge. 'With or without this latest upset, you are a successful doctor about to achieve his heart's desire; which is, if I'm not mistaken, a huge salary, mass adulation and influence where it counts. At the top. The very top. In a little while you'll probably give it up and go into politics.'

'Rubbish.'

'Oh, the old Charles! I thought you were crumbling. You know you gave me the best possible care. You do it with everyone. Despite yourself.'

'And what's that supposed to mean?'

She shrugged and sipped at her wine. 'You don't like the patients.'

He felt himself flushing, a long suffusion of blood from toes to hair. Thank God for the candlelight. 'I like you.'

'I hope you do,' said Celia. 'After all I'm putting you

through. Don't worry, Charles. I'll speak up for you. And I shall fight Braddock and win. It's up to you to keep me going long enough to see it through.'

'You're not going to die tomorrow, damn it!' Horrible, terrible thought.

She downed her wine in one last, long swallow. 'That's wishful thinking, Charles, it isn't fact. I could, couldn't I? Be honest.' He bowed his head. When she demanded honesty he couldn't hold out.

'Yes. Indeed you could.'

And she smiled, as if he'd given her a present. 'Thank you, Charles.'

Dorrie was at home when they went back. Celia invited Charles in for coffee, and when he saw Dorrie he said, 'Hi! You were out, so Celia and I chummed up. How was the life class?'

Dorrie shrugged. 'Dead. Look, Charles, I'm a bit tired, I'd rather you didn't stay.'

He hesitated. He had been planning on staying the night. An evening with Celia, followed by a night with Dorrie, appealed to him more than a little. 'Oh, come on, Dorrie! I've had a hell of a day.'

'And so have I. I'll see you out.'

On the doorstep he put his hand on her great, soft breast. 'Come on, Dorrie. What's up? I'd have taken you if you'd been in. I wanted some company.'

She gave a rueful laugh. 'Oh, yes. It's all right, Charles, I'm not jealous. But I won't be your surrogate lay. If you want to have it off with Celia you'd better get over it or get on with it, but you don't take it out on me.'

He was utterly taken aback. Dorrie watched him with calm clear eyes. At last she said, 'It's OK, Charles. You're allowed to be human.'

'She's my patient.'

'And she's my friend. So what? These things happen.'

'Does everyone know? I mean, is it obvious?'

'I don't think so. But I couldn't help noticing that if you went from Celia to my bed you were like a raging bull.'

He leaned his head back against the door. 'That obvious,

eh? But we don't have to finish, surely? I need you, Dorrie. I need your good sense.'

'And I don't need your frustrated passion. Be off with you. Take up jogging.'

'Thanks. Another time.'

But she still stood, watching him, and he got in the car and drove quickly away.

The encounter had left him wide awake, not in the least ready for sleep, although he never needed more than six hours at the most. Normally he used the late nights and early mornings, doing paperwork at a garden window, or in winter, muffled up in jumpers beside a smouldering log fire. His habits had annoyed everyone he had ever lived with, and now there was no one to annoy. And he had nothing to do. Alone in his big, quiet house, in the dark of the night, he could imagine himself the only living person in the world.

On impulse he stopped the car and turned round. He was sick to death of talking about Edwin Braddock and never seeing him. It was as if he was a wizard, weaving mysterious spells to confound the rest of mankind. He was only a man, thought Charles. He would go and see this place where he lived, now, before morning turned everything dull. The rain was slackening, leaving a clear, starlit sky marked with clouds scudding in the breeze. He thought of Dorrie, and of Celia, and drove quickly, cornering too fast. It was nearly one when he began to circle the high stone walls surrounding Linton Place.

The gate lodge was in darkness, so he drove on, but all the entrances seemed locked and probably disused. The place was like a fortress, but Charles wasn't deterred. He fancied the exhilaration of illegal entry, the deliberate step that would take him outside proper behaviour. He was being pilloried for being a good doctor, let them try and catch him now for determined trespass. It was a long, quiet night, what else was he planning to do?

He parked and walked round the wall until he came to a place where a tree grew inside the park, hanging its branches over the stone coping. The wind was cold, but his coat was too heavy to climb in. He took it off and left it by the wall, then made a jump and missed, and jumped again, this time putting effort into it. His hands caught one of the branches and he swung, trying to find holds for his feet. The toes of his shoes scuffed against the wall, but the mortar was old and crumbling and he kicked up securely. Soon he was on top of the wall, looking down into blackness. Far away across the park a light glimmered, and it was like a beacon, calling him. The whole episode was reminiscent of childhood, full of daring and improbability. How strange it was to find his body grown so heavy and disorganised. He tried to recapture the old, careless competence of his boyhood, tried to let himself down lightly, slipped and fell. He landed amidst damp leaves. That was lucky. Anything could have been down there.

The moon came up as he walked. It shed light on the lake and the mist, like a ghostly ballet with no dancers. His shoes were soon soaked through, and he was growing ever colder. Charles found himself wondering what he was doing there, trespassing in the grounds of a house belonging to a stranger. Didn't Celia say there were dogs? They might be out. Or instead there might be some elaborate security system that was even now watching his stumbling progress in the dark. He walked more briskly, thinking up some tale or other, something not totally implausible.

But all was quiet. He came to the terrace, and saw that the light shone from one of the rooms overlooking it, casting squares of yellow on to the stone flags. For the first time, going up the steps, Charles felt like a burglar. He felt the same illicit excitement. He put his back flat to a pillar and eased himself round, to look into the large, lighted room. He could hear the faint buzz of voices, and as he looked he saw two men, both in dinner jackets, standing together.

There were dogs in the room. Charles felt the sweat start on his forehead. Suppose the dogs heard him? They could be let on to the terrace in a moment and he'd be had up in court, the wayward medic who had finally flipped. The thoughts distracted him, and he jumped when the two men suddenly laughed. They had been out somewhere and were more than a little drunk. 'Go and stand at the window,' commanded one. 'Don't watch.'

Obediently the younger man came and stood, looking out into the night. Charles held his breath. Did his silhouette show against the pillar, like an unnatural excrescence? He tried to shrink himself into a hard, stony line, while at the same time refusing to draw back an inch from his view of the room. The man at the window was young, with shining hair. He had a ring on his little finger with a dark red stone, and he toyed with it as he looked out into the night.

'Aren't you done yet?' he called. He sounded nervous, as if he was being presumptuous.

The other man, smaller, slightly nondescript, was crouched by a cupboard set discreetly into the panelling. 'Be patient,' he said. 'It takes time.'

For an instant, Charles wished he was truly a thief. He would linger in the park for an hour, perhaps longer, until he could break in and rob that safe, opening it with a brilliance that would confound any locksmith. He would use his surgical tools.

He was imagining the technique when the man at the safe stood up, shutting the door firmly. Charles stared hard, for this must be Edwin Braddock. But he was certainly a disappointment. His hair was thinning prematurely, and his jacket was mostly padding. Celia's villain was a very ordinary chap.

He had taken something from the safe. 'Here,' he called, and the man at the window turned not a second too soon. The object flung at him, and jerkily caught, was a triple rope of pearls.

'They should sort us out, don't you think?' said Braddock cheerfully. He crossed the room to a silver tray and poured two brandies. 'Don't try and sell them in Britain, my boy. Take them to Romanoff in Strasbourg next week. If he's not there, he could be in Vienna. Let's be very discreet.'

Charles watched as the pearls were ritually admired. Even one of the dogs rose to his feet and lifted an elegant nose to sniff them.

'Leave,' said Braddock, and the dog at once subsided. Finally the pearls were laid with a rattle on to the silver tray.

The two men sipped at their brandies, chatting quietly. The younger of them was a little nervous, deferential almost to the point of servility. But, as Braddock continued in high good humour, he began to relax. At intervals Braddock leaned a hand on his shoulder, or patted his arm. It was obvious how the evening was developing.

Charles shifted his position, and his foot scraped against the pillar. It was a small enough noise, but enough to bring two of the dogs to the window, growling and staring out.

'There's something there!' The younger man came towards the glass again. Let there not be a light, thought Charles fervently. One click of a switch and he would be revealed. He rehearsed the idiot phrases: 'So sorry – lost – midnight walk.'

'A fox, I should think,' said Braddock. He yawned, capaciously. 'Come here, Peter. Don't be so jumpy.'

He reached out an arm, and his friend went to him. Charles seized his chance and took a step away, and the dogs, knowing he was there, began to bark. He bent down on all fours and scrabbled back to the shelter of the night, praying that the terrace was too wet to reveal a trail of mud, and the dogs barked frenziedly. He glanced back to see if they were following, if someone had let them out. No. The men in the room were uninterested, locked in a passionate kiss.

He stayed in bed for much of the next morning, something he had only ever done half a dozen times in his whole life. But he was tired, the events of the night before seemed unreal and after all, what was there to get up for? What was there to do? When at last he rose the house seemed stale and unwelcoming. His sheepskin coat lay in a sodden heap on the kitchen floor, the fridge held nothing but mousetrap cheese and sour milk and there was a letter from the hospital board, hedging their bets. It seemed they didn't hold him to blame at all, not at all, but to be on the safe side warned him completely off the premises while they sorted it out. He wasn't so much as to look at the place. Damn them, he thought. It would look bad at the inquiry. The hospital should have given him its support.

The telephone rang and he grabbed it eagerly. It was his

junior, wanting advice. Charles gave it, detailed, exact, wishing that he could just pop in, only for half an hour, to cast his own eye over the patients. 'He seems quite OK,' said the junior, and at once Charles imagined pain stoically endured, some frightening symptom that the patient would not acknowledge. People weren't straightforward, that was the thing you couldn't teach the young. They defended themselves against their doctors like soldiers under siege. 'Go and check him again, would you?' he said curtly. 'Don't ask him how he feels. Ask his wife.'

'Right. Yes, sir. OK.'

The conversation made Charles feel better. He looked anew at the sheepskin coat and tossed it over a chair. Last night was a lifetime away, he hardly believed it had happened. But he must tell Celia. He went upstairs to shower.

He felt a certain restraint when Dorrie answered the door, although she smiled with her usual generous welcome. 'Really, Charles, you must be bored. All this socialising.'

He came into the kitchen. Celia was sitting at the table, reading through a pile of papers. 'My father's letters and things,' she explained, scooping them up to make space for Charles. 'The solicitor thought I might want to see them.'

He picked up a sheet and read. It concerned an investment on Celia's behalf, and demanded, curtly, that Lowndes liaise with the accountant for it to be curtailed and the money disposed of. 'I am not interested in any more damned trusts,' wrote old man Braddock. 'They did Celia not a bit of good, so I shall give the girls what they need when they need it. None of this waiting around for years that may never come.'

'I knew he didn't mean to cut them out,' said Celia.

'He could have changed his mind later.'

'He didn't. I know he didn't. He was my father, I should know!' She glared at him, daring him to contradict her. He shrugged.

Dorrie brought a plate of biscuits and some coffee, and Charles tucked in with real appetite, since he'd had no breakfast. He said, 'I've got some news. From the front.'

'The hospital?'

'No. It's ominously quiet there. Last night – in a mad fit of

210

bravado, for which I can think of no reasonable excuse – I went to Linton Place.'

Celia was incredulous. 'What? You mean you went and talked to Edwin?'

'Not exactly. I climbed into the park, walked to the house and skulked on the terrace in the dark.'

Celia stared at him in disbelief. But of course that was so like Charles. He tackled everything head on.

'Did you see him, then?' she asked. 'Did he see you?'

'I observed him secretly,' said Charles, a trifle smug. 'Him and his friend. Did you know your cousin is gay?'

'Yes.'

He was taken aback. 'How?'

'They haven't invented homosexuals in the last ten years, Charles. I don't know how I know, but he just looks gay. His expression or something. To be honest, we wondered when he was a kid, but you know teenagers. They grow out of things.'

Dorrie said, 'In the case of girls, they grow into them. I know an amazing number of women who are sort of political lesbians. It's like joining the Labour Party, a left-wing gesture.'

'A refuge for ugly women,' said Charles.

Dorrie went a deep and enraged red. 'What a disgusting thing to say.'

After a moment he said, 'I apologise. That was very chauvinistic.'

'You're telling me! Really, Charles, you are absolutely unreconstructed caveman. I don't know what I ever saw in you.'

Celia looked from one to the other. She wasn't surprised they were finished. It seemed that Dorrie had raised her standards so high that no man could come up to scratch for more than a month or two, and Charles was obviously a no-hoper. Much too self-opinionated. But he grinned at Dorrie and said, 'You're getting narrow-minded, Dorrie. Fight it.'

Celia tensed for the reaction. Let Dorrie not have changed so much that she no longer laughed at herself. Everyone had become so grown up and pompous in the last ten years, so unwilling to like people different from themselves. To her

211

relief, Dorrie merely swiped at Charles with a teacloth. 'Go on. Tell us what happened last night.'

At first they didn't believe him, but as he went on, the immediacy of his story established it as the truth.

Celia said, 'He could have set the dogs on you or anything.'

'I forgot about the dogs. Until I was on the terrace. They were in the house.'

Dorrie said, 'Didn't you once balk at spying? It's the most terrible invasion of privacy!'

'Not nearly so terrible as depriving a hospital of cash. Braddock deserves all he gets. You can go and reason with him if you like, Dorrie, dole out some camomile tea and a few organic buns, but it's going to take a bit more than that to persuade him to get his paws off three million quid.'

'All you care about is your job. Be honest, Charles.'

'I am trying to be honest! I saw something of very great interest.'

'Braddock's sex life, in all its glory?' Dorrie was scathing. 'That was a coup.'

Charles felt a flicker, more than a flicker, of irritation. 'That was just incidental. As you so rightly say, the man's nearly cost me my job, I don't owe him a thing. And I saw something. Braddock opened a safe. He took out some pearls, and told this man, his lover or whatever, to sell them. There were three great loops of the things on what looked like a diamond clasp. Advised him to try and sell them privately in Strasbourg or Vienna. Know anything about them? Or are they stolen?'

Celia looked at Dorrie, and gave a strangled little cough. 'Oh God. They were my mother's.'

She remembered the day her father brought the pearls home. It was her mother's birthday, and Joe Braddock had gone off in the morning promising great things for the night. He came back at ten, long after anticipation had turned into disappointment. Celia and her mother were sitting in the kitchen, still dressed up, eating cheese.

'There you are, then,' he said, and dropped the pearls across the cheese board. His wife burst into tears.

It turned out that he'd gone that day to London to pick up some special piece of jewellery. But just as he arrived so did a messenger with the pearls, and the shop was agog. It seemed they had been in the same family for generations, but impoverishment finally meant that they must be sold. It was all supposed to be secret.

Joe, with his natural curiosity, wanted to know what was going on, only for the salesman to put him firmly in his place. Northern industrialists did not put their great dirty paws on pearls like these. They spent their trivial sums, ten thousand or so, on flashy trinkets for their uninteresting wives, while other, greater men were ushered into velvet rooms and sold these pearls. So Joe summoned the manager, whistled up a banker's draft of unimaginable size, and bought them. 'It didn't half make that jumped-up load of snobs look sick,' he said.

But the pearls hadn't often been worn. For one thing they were ostentatious, and for another the insurance company virtually insisted that armed gunmen be present all the time, which diminished the pleasure of an evening somewhat. They lived in a bank vault, and Celia had forgotten them. If pressed she would have said they might have been sold. Her father was like that, buying and selling on an impulse. But it seemed the pearls had been a fixture, until somehow, undetected, Edwin Braddock had acquired them. They represented a sizeable fortune.

'His ship really came in,' said Celia bitterly. 'No one even knew we still owned the pearls, and he can't have paid tax on them when my father died. That must be why he wants to sell them out of the country. He must be in trouble, though, to need the cash.'

'The Marlborough thing,' said Dorrie. 'I told you, remember? He tried to take over the whole chain of gambling clubs. And now you're getting ready to take him on in the courts, and that won't be cheap. Money's tight, and he's overstretched.'

They all sat in silence, turning over possibilities. 'I keep wondering why he doesn't offer to pay me off,' said Celia at last.

'Looks as if he hasn't got the money,' said Charles. 'What would you settle for?'

She looked up in surprise. 'I wouldn't. Not after what he's done.'

'Perhaps he knows that,' said Dorrie. 'Well, what do we do? Call the police?'

Celia snorted. 'We can't tell them how Charles came to see the pearls. And Edwin would just have to give up the pearls to pay the tax. We wouldn't get them. I've got a much better idea. Let's steal the pearls back.'

'What?' said the others in unison, and Celia looked round at them, all large-eyed innocence.

'Steal the pearls. It should be easy, if someone's wandering around Europe with them in a bag. We just have to go to Strasbourg.'

'Or Vienna,' said Charles.

'Well, yes. Now, what did he actually say? Word for word.'

Charles cudgelled his brains. 'I don't know exactly. Take them next week to Romanoff in Strasbourg. But he could be in Vienna.'

'Who's Romanoff?' asked Dorrie. 'Jeweller? Crook?'

'We'll find out when we get there,' said Celia determinedly.

'Get where?' demanded Charles. 'We're talking either of two huge cities, my girl! God, but you're impossible sometimes. You're supposed to be leading a quiet and regular life.'

She looked at him, but without recognition. Her mind was elsewhere, wrestling and tugging at each successive problem. She would telephone Hatton Garden and see if they knew of Romanoff. She would go to Strasbourg first, and then to Vienna. What of money? David must pay. She'd tell him she was incurring legal expenses.

'I'll need at least a few thousand from David,' she murmured.

The others exchanged glances. Celia was proving conclusively that she wasn't operating in the real world. They didn't argue with her, or remonstrate, they simply turned the conversation to something else.

'I am going, you know,' said Celia, looking from one to the other.

'Rubbish,' said Charles, abandoning his brief flirtation with diplomacy. 'I forbid it.'

'Horrors!' Celia put her hand up to her head in mock dismay.

Dorrie said, 'Even if you did go, you couldn't go alone. Not after last week.'

'Coming with me then?'

'I can't,' said Charles. 'I've got a hearing at the end of the week.'

'I was asking Dorrie,' said Celia pointedly. 'Come on, Dorrie. Let's.'

Celia went to see David at work. The little factory was a totally male environment, the only female presence the posters of impossibly busty girls pouting down from the walls. Nothing had changed from ten years before. Three half-built cars stood around, and the atmosphere was gentle and unhurried. A man with a pencil behind his ear was marking out leather for a fascia, and another was working the metal lathe. One or two of them recognised her, and her very presence caused a flutter. She knocked quickly on the door of David's office.

'David? It's me.'

She went in. His desk was covered in balance sheets and folders, and sheets of scribbled calculations. When he saw her he fixed his face into blankness, got up and gave her a perfunctory kiss. That in itself annoyed her.

She wound her arms seductively around his neck. 'David, David,' she whispered.

'For God's sake, Celia! We've caused enough trouble.'

'We haven't caused any. You've got a guilty conscience, that's all. What was it you said? Celia, Celia, you're so good, you're so sexy, oh – oh – your beautiful body!'

She felt him unbend a little, and told herself that he never could resist her. 'I never said anything of the sort.'

She put up her face. 'What did you say, then? I can't remember.'

'Not that. Are you forgetting things now?'

She pulled quickly away. 'No, of course not. But I passed

out. It left – gaps. Whatever you do, don't tell Charles.'

David went to his desk, needlessly rearranging things. Celia remembered when she had bought them, and saw that the leather edge of the blotter was worn with age. David said, 'Are you well, though? Better?'

She sat down in the old leather chair, nervously crossing her long legs. The oddness of her situation was never stronger than when she was with David. 'I'm OK, yes. Thank you for asking.' But despite herself, she couldn't repress the recrimination. 'You could have been concerned! You dumped me in hospital and ran. And I could have died.'

He didn't meet her eye. 'Yes. I'm sorry. It – it shouldn't have happened.'

'What shouldn't? You and Heather? I couldn't agree more.'

'For God's sake, Celia. Life moves on. We couldn't wait forever. And we can't go back.'

She felt again the outrage that always welled up in her when she remembered how her life had been parcelled out to others. No one had hoped for her. No one had waited. They had all been so willing to consign her to the grave! Her heart thudded in her chest, the blood rushed noisily in her ears. She must keep calm, always calm. She must remember why she was here.

'I need some money,' she said. 'Have you arranged anything?'

'I haven't even seen the bank yet! You've not been shopping again?'

'No – no.' She wondered how much she dared say. 'There are expenses. Legal ones. Mr Lowndes wants to be sure there's something to pay the bills, investigators, lawyers, that sort of thing.'

'I thought he was going to try and do it for you on the cheap?'

'He is. But we need something. I thought ten thousand to start, don't you?'

He looked into her guileless eyes and felt untrusting, suddenly. He remembered that innocence. He thought of Heather, working for half a year to earn what Celia wanted given. Why couldn't she too go out and get a job? But he sighed gustily, letting her see his displeasure, and telephoned the bank. The manager was busy, could he wait five minutes and they would call back? David replaced the phone.

'They'll call back,' he said unnecessarily. 'Would you like a coffee or something?'

Celia shook her head. 'What did Edwin do when my father died?' she asked suddenly.

'What has this to do with anything?'

'I want to know. Did he help my mother?'

'Are you thinking of the Will again? Yes, he helped quite a bit. She was – well, she and I had had our differences. Over Heather, of course. I wasn't welcome. So Braddock stepped in and went through the papers. I had some small amount of correspondence with him, all very official. Then the Will was published, and that was that.'

'Why didn't my mother object?'

He looked puzzled. 'Object to what? He seemed – in the early days he seemed harmless. Young. One of those nice young men of dubious sexuality who get on well with old ladies. They didn't get on well for long, though. I had a call one night – but it was a long time ago.'

'Tell me.' Celia was very calm, and David sighed, remembering.

'She was in a state. Said that Edwin had deceived her. That he'd taken something she didn't wish him to have. Everything was cut and dried by then, I knew that I couldn't expect anything, and neither could the girls. So I was a bit shirty – she'd been impossibly rude a few times. In the end I said I'd call round in the morning. It was almost three, the middle of the night. And in the morning—' He turned away, walking restlessly to the window. 'In the morning, she was dead. Heart attack. She'd been under enormous strain.'

The blood seemed to pound in Celia's head. She willed it to calm and to slow. There was no space in her life now for unconsciousness. It was important that she think, make connections, use her mind. Edwin had taken the pearls and the shock of it had killed her mother. Suddenly she felt angry, but with her mother, not Edwin Braddock. Why hadn't she stayed alive and fought him? Why wasn't she alive now to tell Celia just what should have happened to the money?

'She must have hated you a lot to stand by and watch the girls get nothing,' said Celia. 'She adored them. Presents all the time.'

'She was an absolutely stupid woman,' snapped David. 'All she cared about was punishing me. Whatever she thought, or you think, I did not desert you, Celia!'

But her gaze was implacable. Suddenly, unexpectedly, she found it in her to despise David. He could never stand up to women, not her mother, not Heather, not her. If she got up now and tempted him, lifting her skirt or showing him her breasts, would it be just as easy as before? Seduction, satisfaction, guilty aftermath. He wanted the sex to be all her fault. If Heather ever found out, and he was terrified lest she should, he wanted to be able to tell her that he had been powerless to resist.

The telephone rang. David went to answer it. She sat and brooded while he spoke, hearing the forced laughter, the uncomfortable pause. He was never any good with money, was David. She wondered if she was in danger of hating him. No. Not yet. She was angry and she was hurt, but ten years wasn't long enough to sleep away love.

He put down the receiver and smiled at her, that old, boyish grin. She had her money.

She and Dorrie spent the afternoon looking for Mr Romanoff. It was surprisingly difficult. When they rang the international directory and asked for the Romanoffs of Strasbourg they uncovered three dozen names. So they abandoned that line of enquiry and moved instead to the jewellery trade. Celia telephoned the shop from which her father had originally bought the pearls, playing the grande dame for all she was worth, and demanded to be put in touch with Mr Romanoff of Strasbourg.

'Of – Strasbourg, madam? Is the gentleman in the jewellery trade?'

Celia sighed in exasperation. 'The name is Romanoff. Romanoff. Of Strasbourg and Vienna. Please don't tell me that you are really so parochial that you don't know of Romanoff! This is—' she groped for the date only to find that it eluded her, and instead substituted '– this is the twentieth century and you did sell my father the Madonna pearls, did you not? Or have you become one of those vulgar places that pretend to be jewellers and sell nothing but tat?'

The poor man on the telephone gulped. 'One moment, madam,' he said uneasily, and left to find someone more senior. Celia curbed any latent soft-heartedness. This same company had sneered at her father's brashness, and should be sneered at themselves.

A few minutes later an unctuous voice came on the line. 'Miss Braddock, I conjecture?'

She corrected him. 'Mrs Sheraton. It seems you employ untrained fools nowadays.'

'My apologies, madam. You enquired about Romanoff, I understand. Would this be in connection with the Madonna pearls?'

'Would you expect it to be?'

'His expertise is highly regarded, madam. But if you wished to dispose of the pearls, I can assure you of no more diligent service than we would provide. Your father often found us more than helpful. We obtained many fine pieces for him over the years.'

Celia resisted the urge to scream down the phone. She must think calm and beautiful thoughts, she told herself. Instead, little demons of aggression prickled on her tongue. She drowned them in a gush of charm. 'So you did, so you did! No piece finer than the Madonna pearls. But if I could just trouble you for Mr Romanoff's address – for a friend only, never, ever for myself!'

The details, lengthily, were given. Celia gushed her way off the phone. 'A pearl dealer,' she declared. 'Nothing else. How does Edwin know about him?'

Dorrie considered. 'He must have had them valued at some time. He plans ahead, doesn't he?'

'In contrast to our welcome spontaneity,' declared Celia. 'Don't tell Charles we're going, don't tell anyone. Let's just go.'

They were waiting for the Manchester flight to Strasbourg. It

219

was the only one from Manchester that week, although of course it was nothing but a guess that he would fly from there at all, let alone direct. But if Charles had reported correctly, Edwin's man wasn't in so much of a hurry that he would airport hop to get there.

Dorrie was wearing a cartwheel hat in pink crepe, and looked like a misplaced racegoer. Celia had all her hair pushed up into a brown toque, and should have looked like her grandmother. Instead she had all the appearance of a film star in a period drama.

'I don't think we blend in too well,' she murmured to Dorrie, looking round at all the travellers in business suits or sportswear. She remembered flying with her father, and it had always been an occasion. Now, trying to disguise themselves, they were hopelessly conspicuous.

They found themselves eyeing the other passengers expectantly. Davenport had given them a fair description of the man he had seen, and Celia was almost sure she didn't know him, her main anxiety being that he should know her. Of course he might not be on this flight at all, there was no reason why he should be. And yet they looked from one person to another, anxiously.

'I'll swear that's him,' said Dorrie suddenly. She was staring at a tall man with a moustache. 'He's like us. In disguise.'

'He doesn't need to be. And I don't think that man's English. What about the blond one?'

Dorrie eyed him suspiciously from beneath her hat. 'Yes. Could be. Too smooth, do you think?'

'I don't know.'

The plane was delayed, they had been waiting at their gate for an age. Their chosen suspect had only one black leather bag, bulging with overnight gear and with a side pocket for business papers. He held on to it firmly, and that decided them. Celia hid her face in a tabloid paper someone had left on a chair. 'Sexy Susan And Her Secret Swinger!' proclaimed a headline. And the very next page was crammed full of scurrilous tales about aristocrats. She decided to read this paper more often.

When at last the flight was called they were not confident

enough to hang back in the queue, and bustled forward with the rest, in case the plane went without them. Celia found herself shoulder to shoulder with the suspicious man. He bumped her with his bag and said, 'Sorry. Late, aren't we?'

'Prego?' said Celia.

He looked surprised. 'I'm so sorry. I thought you were English. The paper—'

'Prego?' She shuffled in front of him and ran up the steps to the plane.

She and Dorrie were at last settled in their seats. The stranger was further forward, with his more expensive ticket, and they were safe.

'I didn't know you spoke Italian,' said Dorrie, taking off her hat.

'I don't. It's the only word I know. How can we find out who he is?'

'Could be anyone,' said Dorrie. 'Let's not talk for a bit. I want to prepare my soul.' She folded her hands and closed her eyes, beginning the low hum that helped her to meditate. Other passengers shifted in their seats, wondering if something was wrong with the aircraft.

Celia leaned her head back against the seat. Much as she loved Dorrie, she wished Davenport was here. She wasn't used to confronting life without him. Bossy men had their uses, she thought, taking away all necessity for independent thought. And she didn't feel very brave today. Yesterday, when she was young, she had lived thoughtlessly, and then in the night her youth had been stolen, and she must learn to think, as if for the first time. Most people came to this gradually, but she had been flung here, unprepared.

The engines of the plane began their usual screeching, and Dorrie began to hum a little louder. Celia looked out as they began to move – at the rushing tarmac, the passing buildings, the air, the clouds. I don't want to die in a crash, she thought. I don't want to die at all. I've got so much to do! Had she felt that ten years ago? She didn't think so. Then, with the world full of other people to take care of her, there had been nothing to do but have fun. The plane levelled out and the seat belt sign was switched off, Dorrie stopped humming and that was that.

221

They didn't see their suspect again. He had no checked baggage and rushed away as soon as they touched down, while Celia and Dorrie waited at the luggage carousel. They hadn't considered this likely event and stood glum and depressed. It was early evening and a cold breeze was blowing up. Dorrie put on her hat again and held it on her head with one hand. With the other she summoned a taxi.

'Take us to an hotel,' she said peremptorily.

'Which hotel?'

Celia stepped in. She could not bear to go somewhere unwholesome, she thought. Not tonight. 'A nice one. A good one. Très bon.'

Twenty minutes later they were disgorged on to the flagpoled steps of the best hotel in Strasbourg. Porters in white gloves took their luggage and the doorman swept them to the desk. They ordered two rooms with a connecting door.

'This is going to cost an arm and a leg,' murmured Dorrie as they were ushered into a glass-lined lift.

'I didn't understand the rates,' said Celia. 'I don't think it's more than fifty pounds.'

'A hundred and fifty,' retorted Dorrie. 'Per night. Each.'

Celia was unsettled. Surely there were an awful lot of a hundred and fifties in ten thousand? Until she got married all the hotels she had ever stayed in had been like this.

'Can't we stay here?' she asked. 'Where else can we stay?'

Dorrie saw Celia's white, drawn face. They would stay, at least for tonight.

In the privacy of her room Celia began to recover. She took off her brown cloth hat and threw it on one side. There was a television and a coffee maker and a fridge, and even the bathroom had a telephone. She ran a bath and soaked herself, wondering where the man on the plane had gone. If she had been a sleuth of any standing she would have talked to him and discovered everything. But he might have discovered her. And probably it wasn't him at all.

They went down to dinner shortly before the dining room closed. Dorrie was wearing a shapeless green dress, and Celia a skirt and sweater with a blouse with the collar turned up. Her hair was put up too, and she felt like Heather, everything tidy.

But still something about her attracted stares. It was as if she was less than flesh and blood, as if she was more ghost than real.

The man from the plane was in the dining room. He was sitting two tables away, finishing some cheese. Dorrie made big eyes at Celia, whispering, 'I know he's the one! Charles said he was dapper. How many dapper Englishmen fly to Strasbourg?'

'But he looks so ordinary! So does Edwin. I can't believe a man looking like anyone has got my mother's pearls.'

'He's got something in his pocket,' murmured Dorrie. 'Something big.'

'A gun. He's a crook. A gangster.'

'If you can believe that, then you can believe he's got the pearls.'

They giggled at each other. Celia felt better, with food inside her, and a glass of wine. It was good to have Dorrie's kind face across the table. She thought of all those endless days and nights in the hospital. She had earned this, at however much a night. By God, she had!

At a neighbouring table some businessmen were roaring with mirth, drinking schnapps and beer. Their suspect from the plane was reading a newspaper as he ate, as if he expected to remain alone. Which was surprising, since a moment later a man in a smart, double-breasted suit came in from the bar and went across to him.

'Someone about the pearls,' said Dorrie.

'Or a hotel pick-up,' murmured Celia.

Dorrie stared at her. 'You do have a dirty mind.'

'But an honest one. They're so tense. So – expectant.'

They sat and observed a stylised flirtation. Unlike the raucous businessmen, these two were discreet and civilised. At no point did they touch each other, and yet the air was redolent with desire. After about five minutes the two men got up and went out.

'Thank you, Mr Cartwright,' said the head waiter with a bow, practising his English.

Celia and Dorrie both stared hard at the wall.

They did not speak again until they were safely back in

223

Celia's room. 'Cartwright,' said Dorrie. 'Does it mean anything?'

'Yes. Peter Cartwright, Braddock's right-hand man. Lots of letters in the hospital file are signed by him. Oh, Dorrie, he really does have the pearls. I thought we were just being silly. Now I don't know what to do.'

'Just what we were going to do before. Go to see Mr Romanoff.'

'And?' Celia looked expectant.

Dorrie said, 'I thought you had a plan.'

'Yes. To steal the pearls. But how shall we do it?'

Dorrie lost her temper. 'Celia, this was your idea! How should I know how to steal something?'

'You used to shoplift chewing gum.'

'Once, when I was twelve.'

'Well then.'

'Well nothing.'

Celia went to the window and leaned her face against the glass. Strasbourg lay beneath her, a pattern of light. People hurried far below, muffled against the wind, and it seemed colder by far than before. A flake or two of snow swirled past her window, but the room was heavily double glazed, and she felt no chill. It was an end to autumn and the beginning of winter. The telephone rang.

Dorrie picked it up. 'Hello?'

'Ladies? Would you like to haf a drink in our room? We observed you. We would like to extend our hospitality.'

'You must excuse us. We're tired,' said Dorrie, and put down the phone on the man's blandishments.

'The drunken businessmen,' she explained. 'That's what comes of staying at an expensive hotel. You need never sleep alone.'

Celia thought of her father, who had always stayed in hotels like this. She could imagine discreet liaisons. Even her mother might not have been the paragon she had once thought. Suddenly the whole place, the whole world, seemed dangerous and difficult. At twenty-five she had been up to this, her steel carapace intact. But the years had stripped her of certainty, taken away all her convictions. Every day that passed showed her more of what she had lost. At first she had thought it due to her accident, but now she wondered; everybody changed. Even Dorrie wasn't the same. It was like a maze, solving the puzzle easily and arriving at the centre, only to realise that it wasn't the centre at all. The puzzle was more complex and more threatening than they had thought. If they had known what it was they might never have entered at all, and here they were, in the maze, blundering about looking for the clues that would tell them which way to go.

She turned to look at Dorrie. 'I wish life still had rules,' she said. 'Then you knew what you had to do.'

'Rules are for children,' said Dorrie. 'Look, I'll take myself off to my room and let you sleep.'

Celia came away from the window. 'I don't feel very sure of myself here. I was better at home.'

'What aren't you sure about?'

She made a vague, touching gesture. 'The point of it all. Beating Edwin and getting back the money. Is this really what I should be doing with my second chance? Why am I in this hotel? Dorrie, tell me I'm doing the right thing.'

'Would you stop, even if I said you should?' asked Dorrie shrewdly.

Celia thought for a moment. Then she shook her head.

'There you are, then,' said Dorrie. 'Good night.'

Left alone in the bedroom, Celia went to the window again. Above the alien lights of Strasbourg there was nothing. No stars lit the snow-filled black of the sky. There wasn't even a moon, or anything by which anyone could guess his position. There must be others, like her, who wandered in the night. They must all just keep on, hoping for a ray of understanding.

Chapter Fifteen

The sun was shining when Celia woke. The snow of the night before had vanished, and in its place was a clear, bright morning, the sky a cold and vivid blue. Celia dressed in short brown boots and a short red dress, her expanse of leg covered in thick white tights. She was still out of tune with fashion, but it didn't seem to matter. People always thought she had come from somewhere else.

Dorrie was in tweeds gleaned from some second-hand shop catering for Scottish cast-offs. The effect was oddly Germanic, munching her cold meat breakfast. 'A morning's work, then we'll assess progress at lunchtime. Aren't you going to eat something? It's freezing outside.'

Obediently Celia forced down lumps of bread, although she wasn't hungry. The coffee was delicious, hot and strong, heating her through to the tips of her fingers. Then the cup froze, halfway to her lips. Peter Cartwright was entering the room, looking around in case there was someone he might know.

He began to move towards an empty table on Dorrie's left. Celia put down the cup and ducked over her plate.

'He's here. He's coming over.'

Dorrie had her back to him. 'Pretend we're Germans.'

'He already thinks I'm Italian.'

'Mama mia. Spaghetti bolognese. Tagliatelle verdi,' muttered Dorrie.

'He'll think we're the Italian version of the *Michelin Guide*.'

'Firenze! Roma! Napoli!'

'Scouts for an AA road map?'

They vibrated with muffled laughter. Cartwright, seating

himself at the next table and shaking out his napkin, smiled and said, 'Good morning.'

'Guten Tag,' said Dorrie, and rose to her feet. Celia took a last gulp of coffee and followed her.

'Suppose that man did come for the pearls last night?' she said urgently to Dorrie as they went back upstairs in the lift.

'He still had a bulge in his pocket.'

'It could still be the gun. Oh, Dorrie, this is all a bit stupid, isn't it? What do we do now? Hang around outside Romanoff's and pick his pocket?'

'We could talk to Mr Romanoff. Explain that the pearls aren't Edwin's to sell.'

'We can't prove they're ours. And he'd talk to Edwin and then everything would be quite obvious and terrible! I don't know what to do.'

They got out and wandered the long carpet to Celia's room. The maid had already been, and everything was neat and orderly. Dorrie remembered when it was like that at Blantyre House. You left your room for a moment and the fairies came. Celia sat in the armchair and swung her long white legs. 'We must follow him,' she declared.

'Don't you think we're a little conspicuous?'

Celia waved a hand. 'I'll change. I brought a raincoat. And you look wonderful, like the female villain in a film about Berlin.'

'But we know where he's going. What are we following him for?'

'To – to impede him. Somehow. I don't know.'

But neither of them could think of anything else to try. Dorrie went to the mirror and put on the hat that matched her outfit, an upturned flowerpot in brown tweed. Celia changed into flat shoes and a mackintosh, with her hair stuffed in the collar of her coat.

They went to the foyer and sat down to wait. The hotel was hummingly busy, with businessmen moving in and out, flowers arriving, luggage carts and departing visitors. They wondered if they might miss Cartwright in the throng. But barely five minutes later they saw him, briefcase in hand, pockets apparently empty, coat held neatly folded over his arm. He left his key at the desk and marched out into the morning air, pausing to take two or three deep breaths at the top of the steps. Dorrie and Celia rose as one woman and followed him.

'Taxi, s'il vous plaît,' he said to the doorman.

Celia gulped and stared hard at Dorrie. 'Taxi, bitte,' she said.

Cartwright turned towards them. 'Perhaps you'd like to share mine?' he asked, making elaborate hand gestures to convey his meaning to the foreigners. 'Share? I am going to the centre. The Cathedral.'

'Jah. Sehr gut. Sank you very much,' said Dorrie, in her best pidgin English.

In the taxi Celia was frozen into silence.

'Your friend is Italian?' said Cartwright, conversationally.

'Jah. From Sicily,' said Dorrie.

'Ah. Mafia country.'

'Jah,' said Dorrie, and gave a heavy, meaningful wink. Cartwright shot Celia an amazed look, and she dropped her eyelids to give herself a hooded, menacing air. Dorrie spluttered. She had all the appearance of a sleepy camel.

'Ve are travelling,' explained Dorrie. 'My friend's family hev all been kidnapped.'

'All?'

'Jah. Are you von of them? After her too?'

'Not in the least. Not at all.'

'Gut.'

Dorrie was getting over-enthusiastic. Celia kicked her hard on the shin. The briefcase was resting tantalisingly on Cartwright's knee, and for a moment she had the idea of seizing it, running off with it, and letting him worry about laying claim to the pearls. The idea took root. Why not?

The taxi stopped outside the Cathedral. Dorrie flung a vast German note at the driver, was given it back and muttered something about her failing eyesight. She and Cartwright came to some sort of financial agreement on the pavement, and he gave them a wave and walked away.

Dorrie collapsed on to a stone lion, placed at a convenient spot. 'My God! What a terrible ten minutes!'

'Get up at once,' ordered Celia. 'As a fully fledged Sicilian bandit, I must keep track of my victim. We're going to rob him.'

'I'll do nothing of the sort! I'm not a violent person.'

'I shall rob him, then. Dorrie, come on!'

Cartwright was almost at the corner. Celia scuttled along the pavement, trying not to break into a run, but the moment he was out of sight she sprinted. She stopped at the corner and saw him further along, looking up at the street names. How to get hold of the briefcase?

Dorrie puffed up behind her. 'Where is he?'

'Down there. Looking for the address. We've got a few moments, let's go and buy a briefcase like his and swap them.'

'How?'

'Dorrie, you're being obstructive! Somehow. Where's there a leather shop?'

She hurried up the street, looking. The district was very expensive, with glossy consumer goods for sale on all sides. Cartwright, further ahead, turned left and they followed him. They saw him glance at his watch, hesitate, and turn into a shop selling chocolates. He was early for his appointment and was wasting some time. Celia dived into the leather shop across the road. 'Watch out for him,' she ordered Dorrie. 'I'll buy the bag.'

The shop had shelves full of briefcases. Celia chose one at random, that appeared to her untutored eye to be most like Cartwright's. It was made of calf's leather, and cost nearly two hundred pounds. The assistant was at great pains to explain all the wondrous features, but Celia said, 'Yes, yes, I'll have it. I'll give you the cash, but please, hurry!'

She even rejected the wrapping. Hurt and dismayed, the man took the proffered cash and gave her the case. She rushed out into the street.

'He's just coming,' said Dorrie. 'Didn't take any time at all. He's bought some chocolates.'

They shrank against the leather shop as he came out and set off down the street, a little square parcel dangling from his free hand. Celia began to follow, shaking her briefcase, trying to make it look well-used. It retained its flat and expensive appearance. She hurriedly bought a newspaper from a stand and crumpled pages, stuffing them into it.

'And you want to be inconspicuous?' demanded Dorrie. 'Half the people of Strasbourg will report you to the police, and you haven't done anything yet.'

'We've got to knock him over,' said Celia. 'Then we grab the case in the midst of apologies, and make our escape.'

'He'll report it to the police.'

'He won't tell them about the pearls!'

'He won't need to. We'll have dumped him with a case full of newspaper, so they'll know we meant something by it. He just reports that his bag was stolen.'

Celia stopped and confronted her. 'All right then. What do you suggest we do?'

Dorrie thought of several things, mainly that they should go home. But Celia's determination was affecting her too. She didn't want to quit without even trying.

'Which one of us knocks him over?' she asked.

'Me,' said Celia. 'I'm going to faint. I've had a lot of practice.'

A taxi passed them and they hailed it. The whole thing seemed unreal, something that wouldn't happen. They passed Cartwright, striding along purposefully, the briefcase held firmly in his left hand, and as soon as the taxi had rounded a corner they stopped it and got out. They began to walk back, towards their victim, and Celia held her case in her left hand, ready for the swap.

'This is madness,' muttered Dorrie.

'That's going to be my defence,' said Celia. 'You knew nothing and I was temporarily deranged. Watch it. I'm about to come over all peculiar.'

She stopped, leaned against the wall for a moment, and put her hand briefly to her head. Dorrie was full of concern, but Celia made as if to insist that she was recovered. They walked on. Cartwright was no more than ten paces away.

'Well, hello again, ladies,' he said.

'Buon – buon—' Celia slumped against the wall in an incipient swoon.

'My good sir,' said Dorrie, urgently. 'My friend, she is ill.'

'Oh dear,' said Cartwright, with the reluctance of an Englishman who would very much rather not get involved. 'Shall I call a taxi?'

'I do not know – I cannot—' Dorrie had not envisaged her Good Samaritan backing so resolutely away.

Celia resolved the problem by taking a step forward and collapsing on to him.

People and briefcases descended to the pavement. Dorrie was all solicitude, fastening her hand firmly on Cartwright's case. 'Taxi! Taxi!' she yelled. This time no taxi appeared. Celia was moaning theatrically, Cartwright was swearing underneath his breath, and concerned passersby were offering to call an ambulance.

'We will get a taxi,' declared Dorrie, although still none had appeared. It was like a bank robbery when the getaway car's been wheel-clamped.

Celia was on her feet, leaning groggily against the wall, muttering 'Prego' and 'Tagliatelle' at intervals. And praise be to God, a taxi turned the corner. Dorrie was so anxious to get inside she almost forgot her fainting charge. But Celia too made it through the door, and they left, waving with feeble gratitude to the little crowd on the pavement. 'If you picked up the wrong one you can just go back and change it,' said Celia.

'It's the right one. Let's get to the hotel and check out.'

All the time they stood at the desk, settling their bill, they expected Cartwright to walk in and challenge them. Even when they were speeding away, heading for the airport and safety, they expected at any moment to be overtaken by a police convoy. 'The pearls can't be here,' said Celia suddenly. 'He must have left them somewhere. The chocolate shop was a cover!'

'We can't check now,' said Dorrie. 'At the airport.'

'Where at the airport?'

'I don't know! Somewhere quiet.'

They settled themselves in the bar, in a well-padded corner. By now they were convinced that the pearls were elsewhere. The case was locked, but Celia stabbed it viciously with a nailfile and the clasp flicked open. 'I left him a much better model,' she declared. 'This is really cheap. Look. A filofax, a map of Strasbourg, a plane ticket, and – a jewellery box.'

Dorrie erected a cocktail menu on the table to conceal them. Celia brought the box into view. It was dark blue leather, just as she remembered it, egg-shaped with a neat brass catch. A patch on the top showed where the original owners had removed their initials. She snapped open the catch. Suddenly, unexpectedly, she was eighteen again, getting ready for her party. Her mother was wearing dark blue silk – and the pearls. These pearls. For the very last time.

They were not as lustrous as she remembered, for pearls gain their lustre from human skin. But the clasp was brilliant still, aflame with diamonds. When she lifted the three strands she was impressed again at their weight. Every pearl was an exact degree smaller or larger than the one next to it. Each strand hung an exact distance from the one above. They were magnificent.

They left the briefcase under the seat in the bar, and put the pearls in Celia's bag. There was no flight to Manchester that day, so Dorrie skulked at the ticket desk and booked them through to Munich, from where they could leave for Manchester later that night. Every minute's wait seemed like a lifetime. They kept telling each other that no police force in the world would close an airport for something so trivial as a snatched bag. Cartwright couldn't admit to having the pearls. They had to be safe.

Driving home from the airport at midnight, exhausted and utterly stressed, they realised they had no idea at all what they were going to do next.

The next day, Dorrie took to her bed with a feverish cold. Celia put it down to stress, and wished she could stay in bed too, but the pearls were under her pillow. She couldn't rest while she still had them. The burden of secrecy was intolerable. She considered telling David, but rejected the idea at once. He would be shocked by the theft, and even more shocked by her extravagance. If anyone was to be told it must be Davenport.

He grabbed the phone at once, as if he was sitting next to it in constant anticipation that it would ring. 'It's only me,' said Celia. 'Who were you expecting?'

'No one. Anyone. I'm going stir-crazy here.'

'Well, come and see me. I've got some news.'

She got dressed while she waited for him to arrive. After her daring escapade, she was feeling wild and wacky, so she borrowed one of Dorrie's navy artist smocks, with a huge wide neck, and wore it off one shoulder, revealing the snowy strap of her bra. Then she scraped her hair from her face and tied it up in a huge, navy bow, and finished it all off with a pair of Dorrie's jangling earrings.

When Charles arrived and she opened the door to him, he said, 'My sainted aunt! If your clothes get any stranger I'll have no difficulty in having you certified.'

'That isn't funny, Charles.'

He went to slump down at the kitchen table. 'I wasn't being funny.'

Unemployment was clearly very bad for Davenport. He hadn't shaved or, it seemed, slept. His eyes were bloodshot and sunk into his head, and his shirt hadn't been ironed. 'Are you all right?' asked Celia tentatively. 'You look—'

'I'm OK. Now, tell me. What happened?'

For answer, Celia reached into the breadbin and took out a box. Within lay the pearls.

He took them out and held them for some seconds. Finally he said, 'Celia, are you going to get arrested?'

'I don't think so. Perhaps. We stole them but he won't dare say.'

'Could he recognise you? Could you be traced?'

She picked up the jewel box and opened and closed it nervously. 'I'm not sure. If he saw us again he'd know.'

As he still gazed at the pearls, hanging like a cluster of perfect eggs from some exotic species, she sank into a chair. Now she had told him she felt better. 'Do we dare sell them, do you think? Edwin might claim they were part of the estate, a part he never got his hands on. But he'd have a right to them, under the Will. So I thought we might sell them in secret.'

'In Strasbourg or Vienna,' said Charles, with a sigh. 'My God, Celia, you do take some risks.'

'If they caught me I was relying on you to say I was mad,' she said. 'Would you have done that?'

234

His head came up. 'You bet. Like a shot. I'd have you in a locked ward in a straitjacket before you could blink.'

She laughed, nervously. Let him be joking. He had the power, that much was certain. 'Don't – don't ever get so cross with me you'd do that,' she murmured.

'Why not? Don't tell me you like it out here. You've shed more tears in the last few weeks than ever in your life before. Who do you know who's having fun? Me? Dorrie? Your precious David? From where I'm standing you'd be better off in your little white room, Celia my girl. This life is nothing but misery.'

He flung the pearls across the table and they skidded almost to the edge. She wondered if they would shatter if they fell. She stood quite still, saying nothing. He got up, came around the table, took her in his arms and kissed her.

It was the hungriest kiss. He tasted of old whisky and salt, and his tongue was a muscle, strong and invading. Celia's first surprise was suffused in a rush of sensation; heat, and an almost electric charge. He groaned and took hold of her breast, rubbing the coarse weave of the smock against her, startling her nipple into prominence.

He was mouthing her, bruising her lips, one kiss leading to another. Then his mouth slid away to the neck of her smock, to her shoulder. He closed his teeth on her skin.

She recoiled quite violently, breaking free and putting a chair between them. Her shoulder was clearly marked with his teeth, a circle of bright indentations. He stood, swaying slightly, holding on to the chair, his face quite unlike himself. Gently, slowly, he crumpled up.

He was asleep. She couldn't move him so she fetched a cushion and a blanket and sat, wondering what she should do. He wasn't a man who could take idleness, that much was clear. He would never find it in him to live with failure. His short sojourn in the wilderness had found him wanting, as responsibility, work and unpopularity had never done. Suddenly Celia felt sorry for him, and she almost laughed. Never in her wildest dreams had she imagined feeling sorry for Davenport. But she did. Now, the grounded eagle, he was a sorry sight.

She wondered if he had known what he was doing when he kissed her. Perhaps not. He would never know that he had aroused her, stirring in her the very sensations he himself had said she must not feel. Charles was such a disciplined man, you became used to observing his discipline, and its absence changed him completely. If he broke any of the rules he broke them all. Underneath that iron exterior lay a seething mass of humanity.

Her heart was thumping hard. That wasn't supposed to happen, she was supposed to keep calm. How, when she lived like a nun? All her life sex had been like a choice sweetmeat, that she delighted in when she pleased. Only now, when she had been told it was bad for her, did she realise that it wasn't just a pleasure; for her, highly sexed and used to love, it was a need, a release, an affirmation of life. Only in love did she reach out and touch the central flow of her existence, the river on whose surface she was carried. Alone like this, unable to love, she felt locked already in her cold white room.

She paced the kitchen restlessly. Charles hadn't slept for days, he might not wake for days more. She picked up the pearls and fitted them carefully back into their satin case. They must be hidden before she was traced, when she could deny it all. How? Where? The house felt flimsy and unsafe.

And she didn't want to hide the pearls away. She didn't want the pearls at all, in fact, she wanted their value in cold hard cash. David's money wouldn't last. She had spent more than a thousand already, and legal bills would be thousands more. She faced the eternal dilemma of the crook – how to turn ill-gotten gains into a bank balance.

She pondered the problem irritably. Everyone always said stolen goods were sold in pubs, but since she had never seen anything more than a bunch of flowers and a plate of whelks sold in a pub that avenue didn't seem promising. What did people do when they needed money and owned something valuable they couldn't sell? The answer was obvious. They went to the pawnshop.

She racked her brains for what she knew about pawnshops. Very little, in fact. They asked no questions and charged punitive rates of interest, but they kept their pledges safe, she was sure. She would have cash in hand and a secure haven for the pearls. As for redeeming them, she would worry about that later.

Celia felt very cold suddenly. The artist's smock did not envelop her like warm wool, and it was late in the year. She folded her arms around herself. These cold spells kept on descending, like a sudden ebbing of her life. She looked down at Charles, his face smooth now in sleep. He hadn't cured her enough.

She looked through the Yellow Pages and found an address in Bradford. The thought of the drive made her feel weak, but she was determined now, anxious to see the pearls safely out of the house. She changed into her pale grey suit, folded her hair into a French pleat and set off.

The pawnbroker surprised her. The shop resembled a discreet jeweller's, with only the three golden balls declaring its purpose. Celia walked past twice before entering. It seemed almost more disreputable than to be seen going into a betting shop or a brothel.

A gentleman in a dark suit greeted her as she entered. 'Can I help you, madam?'

Celia put up her chin. 'Yes, I believe so. I have a valuable necklace which I wish to pledge. Very valuable.' She laid the jewellery box on the counter's velvet cloth.

One look and she was ushered into a booth. The broker rubbed the pearls with a worn cloth. 'We don't often see a piece like this,' he remarked. 'One hesitates to imply—'

'My father was Joe Braddock,' said Celia quickly. 'They were my mother's pearls.'

'Braddock. Yes. I see. Well, I'm sure we can help you, madam.'

Celia struggled to conceal her relief.

She emerged an hour later with the pawn ticket in her handbag. Contrary to expectation, it was enormous, a great sheet of paper covered in legal jargon. They had given her a cheque for two hundred thousand pounds, which must mean that the pearls were worth at least twice that, or even twice that again. The interest was nearly four per cent a month, which she calculated to be over fifty per cent a year. Extortionate.

What's more, she had just six months in which to redeem her pledge, which was a worry. Still, the pearls were safe and she had money to play with at last.

Halfway home she began to feel cold again. The hammering in her head felt like Beltane the Smith, forging the weapons of heaven. Her mouth was dry and stiff, and her thoughts, let alone her speech, were a jumble of confusion. Only one clear aim remained – to get home.

When she arrived all was peaceful, as before, with Charles stretched out downstairs and Dorrie up. Exhausted, beyond everything, Celia crawled away to bed.

Edwin felt a certain pity. Standing on the vast expanse of rug in the wholly unwelcoming office, Peter Cartwright was so obviously mortified. As he deserved to be. The man had fallen for a basic ruse, used by street thieves the world over.

'You say one was Italian?'

'Yes. She didn't look it, though. Blonde, very glamorous. No English. The other woman was fat. German.'

'What names did they use at the hotel?'

'I couldn't find out. I offered money but the manager was called. He said I should approach the police. I did, of course, but they were very unhelpful. As far as they could see, nothing valuable had been stolen.'

Edwin went to the mirror at the end of his office. He saw that his jacket was creased and smoothed the fabric. Then he took a key from his watch chain, went to his desk drawer and unlocked it. He extracted a photograph. 'Was this one of the women?'

Cartwright scanned the picture. The colour rose and fell in his skin like the fluttering wings of a butterfly. 'How do you know her?' he said at last.

'That is my cousin,' said Edwin softly. 'Celia Sheraton. Quite a looker, isn't she?'

'I don't – I'm not—'

'Someone's been spying on me. Did you see anyone while you were away? I mean – see anyone?'

'I wouldn't ever betray a secret. Not even—'

'Did you sleep with her? Or someone else?'

238

Cartwright was trapped. A secret had been discovered, and what Edwin didn't know he would suspect. It would be worse to deny and be discovered than to confess.

'It was nothing,' he said jerkily. 'Someone in the bar. Dutch, Danish, an engineer. We had a drink in my room, that's all.'

'Liar!'

The shout echoed in the room. Cartwright felt a desperate urge to run, to escape, to get away from here. Instead he remained where he was, glued to the carpet.

'You are a fool,' said Edwin softly. 'That necklace was worth over a million pounds, and you've allowed it to be stolen from you by a deranged woman. But worse than that, far worse than that, the moment you are free you abuse my trust. How dare you betray me? With a stranger. Someone you don't even know. You could be infected, you could pass it on to me!'

To his shame, Cartwright was crying. 'We took care,' he snuffled. 'I'm not that much of a fool!'

Edwin came across the room to him. 'You are all of one.' He drew back his hand and slapped the man lightly across the face, a contemptuous insult. A rictus of anguish contorted Cartwright's smooth and boyish features.

Edwin felt aroused. He imagined the coming pleasure, with Cartwright humble and anxious to atone. The boy was an innocent, of course. If every good relationship broke up because of a casual fling or two, there'd be no one together at all. Peter really was so inexperienced. Edwin put his hand on his shoulder, in a solid gesture of support. 'Don't worry,' he said kindly. 'I shan't abandon you, Peter. You've been foolish. We both know that. But now it's time to go home.'

Before they left, Edwin wrote a brief note. He addressed the envelope himself and stopped the car to post it. Cartwright gave way to curiosity. 'Is that something important?'

'Very important,' said Edwin. 'You must atone for your mistakes, but I must put them right. Learn this of me, Peter. I never allow myself to be defeated.'

He was conscious of the younger man's silence. Poor Peter. To be still so very young.

Chapter Sixteen

Celia awoke quite bewildered. She didn't know where she was. What's more, an unholy noise was erupting outside the door. She sat up, her head filled with marshmallow, or something equally soft and useless. Her brains had been scrambled.

There was a foul taste in her mouth, a thickness, a lack of air. It was dark, with only a faint light from the window – not the window. The door. Beyond the door, flickering between the cracks, was a mass of flame.

She wanted to scream, but hadn't the breath. Foolishly she reached out for the light switch, and felt a wave of panic when no light came. She was lost in a room, in the dark, with the world on fire! The crackling and crashing that had woken her was becoming lost in another, wilder sound. The fire was roaring, like an animal, beating hot breath against her door. Terrified, she began to blunder her way to the window, and then she thought of something. The photographs! They were all she had of her children, all that remained of their childhood. Fearful, sobbing, she ran back to the bed and crouched down to scrabble underneath it. One album was easily found, the other was out of reach. She lay on the floor, conscious that the carpet was hot and pained her skin, even through her nightdress. The album was gone – she wouldn't find it – but if it burned then so would she!

Her fingers touched the leather edge of the book. In a second she had them both, held tight against her breast, and instinctively she made for the door. But it was blistering in the heat, and she thought suddenly of Dorrie, and Charles, in that inferno.

Fear for her own life gave way to terror for theirs. Help. She

241

must get help. She ran to the big sash window and stared out, and there were flames from the windows below. She put down her photograph albums and picked up the bedroom chair. Imbued with sudden strength, she flung it through one of the panes. And Charles's head appeared.

'For God's sake!' he yelled. 'Get over here, will you!'

The door was starting to flame now, but the room seemed more secure than the emptiness beyond the window. Charles said, 'Come on. Down the ladder. Quickly now.'

The calm of his voice communicated itself to her. She turned and picked up the albums again and Charles said, 'Leave them, Celia. They're not worth dying for.'

But they were. Her children existed within these covers, and she would not let them go. 'Celia, I said leave them!'

'I won't come without them.' She stood framed against the room, and behind her the door erupted in a gout of flame.

'Celia, come on! Give me the books, damn it. I'll carry them.'

She passed the albums to him, and he held them between his chest and the ladder, obviously awkward. Then she climbed out, scratching herself on shards of glass, clinging to the wavering ladder. Charles was below her. 'Don't drop the books,' she said.

'All right! Now you've got to climb down. Quickly but steadily. I can't help, I've got the luggage.'

She was unsteady and slow. In the end he climbed up to her, jamming the albums between his chest and her back, holding her tight around her waist. They descended together, still not speedily enough. As they passed the flaming window the heat was unbearable, and yet it had to be borne. Even before they reached the ground people were beating at them, putting out the flames on their clothes. And there was Dorrie, in a nightshirt, quite distraught, while the flames licked and crackled and a high, wailing screech told them that at last the fire engine had come.

They were given tea in a neighbour's house, and blankets, like a televised disaster. A fire officer came and spoke to them, and talked of arson, since the fire had started in the hall. Or so it seemed. Charles had woken first to find the hall and stairs ablaze, and the telephone not working. He had roared enough to wake Dorrie, who had crawled out of the bathroom window on to a flat roof. Celia needed Charles and the ladder, though.

'You nearly killed me with the chair,' he said ruefully. 'What a night! I wake up not knowing where I am or why, to find the house on fire and the distressed damsels fighting back.'

'You came round to talk about something,' said Celia, sipping her tea. She looked meaningful. 'Remember?'

'Oh, yes.' He was inscrutable, and she wondered how much he recalled.

Dorrie said, 'It's all gone. My home, my work in progress, everything. Oh dear!'

Celia put an arm round her as she wept. For herself she had saved the one thing she cared about. Everything else had gone. The house was no more than a burned-out shell, and on either side the houses were uninhabitable. She wondered if the pawn ticket, not to mention the cheque, had gone up in smoke with all the rest. Her clothes had, and some of her father's papers, and so would the pearls too, but for her timely idea. The pearls, which might have been the point of all this, were safe.

'I bet I left my handbag in the car,' she said hopefully. 'I often do. I might even have a cheque book in it. Perhaps I could book us into an hotel.'

'Money shouldn't be a problem,' said Charles. 'You were insured, weren't you, Dorrie?'

She looked bewildered. 'Yes! But the policy was in the house. Oh God, what am I going to do?'

They were silent, stricken by the enormity of what had happened. It was terrible to think this might have been intended. Charles said, 'You'd better come to me. It's going to take months to get everything sorted out. I think it's best.'

Both women looked at him doubtfully. He wasn't the sort of man to do anyone a casual kindness. Dorrie had been stiff with him since they stopped sleeping together. Celia thought of all the quarrelling they would do. But Charles wasn't a happy man these days, he had clearly been drinking his nights away.

Perhaps it wasn't kindness at all, but necessity. He needed two women in his life.

It was still dark when a police car dropped them at the house. Dawn was still an hour away, and they shivered in the wind that had whipped the flames of the fire to the merry blaze that had left so little. Celia looked up at the big, rambling Rectory that was Charles Davenport's and felt acute surprise. It was neglected, spartan. Trees crowded in on it, their arms like wild women against the sky. Inside, the kitchen held only an Aga and a huge pine table, set foursquare on the cold flagged floor. A whisky bottle and a glass stood on the table, and another, empty, lay by the sink. No wonder he had passed out.

Dorrie was still in shock, and dripped tears uncontrollably. Celia put the kettle on the stove and went to find beds, while Charles rifled cupboards, saying, 'There must be something to eat around here!' Why did he live like this? she wondered. Perhaps he didn't, always. But the house must have been bare and shabby for a long time, waiting for the pictures and rugs that would turn it into a home.

She found Charles's room, big, bare, with a giant double bed and a table covered in various ties and collar studs. Looking elsewhere Celia came upon a room overlooking the garden, only dimly seen in the grey of a winter dawn. There were curtains, threadbare but clean, and a high iron bedstead. The light would be good, she conjectured, and allotted this room to Dorrie. For herself, from the remaining six rooms, she chose one small and white, with a window leading on to a verandah. No more fiery horrors for her, she decided.

She made tea, without milk, for the milk was days old and definitely off. With Dorrie safely in bed and the sky at last beginning to lighten, Celia felt some of the night's terror recede. She wondered why she, like Dorrie, wasn't in shock. And Charles was thinking the same thing.

'I suppose after what you've been through, the odd fire's nothing special,' he remarked.

Celia sipped her tea. 'Thanks for getting me down. I could understand it if you hadn't.'

'Why?'

She shrugged. 'I've got you into a mess. But I suppose if I

244

was dead Edwin would certainly get the money.'

Charles's face became oddly stiff. 'I wasn't thinking about the money. I quite genuinely didn't want to see you fry.'

'Why, thank you, Charles. That's very kind.'

They eyed each other, wary but well-disposed. She said, 'Do you remember what happened? Before you passed out?'

'Do you?'

She nodded and he looked rueful. 'I wasn't at my best.'

'Is that an apology?'

His rare grin lit up his face. 'Good God, no. Did you apologise when you tried to dishonour me in hospital? No, you bloody did not.'

'Yes I did.'

'No you didn't. Did you?'

'Yes.'

He leaned back, as if victorious. 'Well then. There you are.'

She had a sudden memory of David, sharp and painful. He had always apologised, and never meant a word. It had come to seem, to her if not to him, as if when he apologised, she should feel guilty. She thought back to their last row, something stupid, about who did what. Why hadn't she done everything and never complained? If she had known that one day she would have nothing, no one, never have to wash another baby sock – she would wash them all again now, just to have her life back. Tears, unexpected and unchecked, rolled down her cheeks.

'More shock,' he said. 'Inevitable.'

'It isn't.' Celia wept on, unable to tell him that memory had trapped her again.

'I'll put you to bed.'

'You just want a bit of the other.'

He held her shoulders and squeezed. 'Come on, love. I can want all I like but it wouldn't be good for either of us. Would it?'

'Wouldn't it?' She looked up at him. How she yearned for warmth and closeness. How she longed to lose herself, for a little, in love. He bent his head and she waited, expectant, for his kiss. But he brushed her lips merely, and put her to bed like a child.

They woke up in the afternoon, the girls dressed in what they could find and they all went back to the house to assess the damage. Dorrie had lost everything and Celia almost everything, although she couldn't get upset about a few clothes. Fortuitously, as she had thought, her handbag had been in the car. There it lay, with most of her papers, and most important of all, the pawn ticket and cheque.

'Oh, good,' she said and folded the papers up small enough to squeeze into the coin pocket in the pair of Charles's old trousers she was wearing. She looked like a clown, or a waif. Dorrie merely looked miserable.

'All my things,' she said softly, starting to cry again. 'All my life was in this house.'

'Only the visual element,' said Charles firmly. 'Don't be a bloody materialist, Dorrie. No one died, nothing wonderful was lost. And in that I include your paintings. Do something different, make a new start.'

She turned away sobbing, and Celia said angrily, 'Charles, if that is the tone you take with your patients, I'm not surprised you've been given the boot. You're a heartless pig.'

He looked aggrieved. 'But you're taking it better than Dorrie, and you've lost a fortune.'

'No I haven't,' said Celia, and instinctively touched her pocket. 'All is well. The pearls are in a pawnshop, and on the strength of what I got, I think Dorrie and I should go shopping.'

They both looked amazed, and Celia found herself wondering why they thought her so useless. Any sign of adult competence was greeted by everyone as a miracle.

The shopping cheered everyone up. Celia remembered the last expedition, her own vagueness, the feeling that she and the world no longer understood each other. This time it was different. Charles carried the parcels while she and Dorrie misbehaved in changing rooms.

They went again to Chrysanthemum, and bought every thing, even thigh-high leather for Dorrie. And Charles said, 'Wow! Wear that home, Dorrie. Let's live!'

They were on an unnatural high, survivors of the flames and ready to make the most of every moment. As they swept out of the shop, laden with parcels and giggling like children, they ran into someone. James, the hospital administrator.

'Hello, Mr James,' said Charles, trying to pretend that he did not know either of the mini-skirted women hanging on his arms. Celia, conscious of acres of bare leg, tried to sidle back into the shop.

'Mr Davenport. Mrs Sheraton.' James raised his voice to ensure that Celia had heard.

'Mr James,' she called back. 'Excuse me, I believe I've forgotten something.'

'Me too,' said Dorrie, and retreated, wondering how on earth anyone had persuaded her to display her thighs in public. But she hadn't been persuaded. She had done it all by herself.

James and Davenport eyed each other. 'I see that you and Mrs Sheraton have something of a relationship,' said James.

'It's called doctor and patient,' said Charles coldly. 'Are you insinuating anything else?'

James said, 'I always wondered how she managed to get her own way so much. I suppose it was inevitable. A beautiful young woman and a doctor unused to the responsibility of consultancy—'

'Mrs Sheraton survived a house fire last night. I was merely helping her replace her lost clothing, and at the same time maintaining a level of vigilance. Try and make anything more out of it at Monday's inquiry, James, and I'll tear your head off.'

James looked up into Davenport's dark face. He nodded curtly and walked off.

'Damn,' muttered Charles. 'Damn, damn, damn.'

'Don't worry, Charles. I'll speak up for you,' said Celia, emerging from the shop.

He grunted. 'Much good that will do. They'd expect you to defend your lover. They'd all imagine I was buying your silence with nightly rogering.'

She put her hands on her head and struck a pose. 'What a delicious thought!'

Charles caught her arm and hurried her away. 'Not in public, Celia. From now on we're going to have to be very discreet.'

'But we're not doing anything!'

'That won't make a blind bit of difference.'

It suddenly occurred to them that they had left Dorrie in the shop, changing her skirt. They walked back, more slowly. Celia saw someone watching them, a face in the crowd. 'I'll swear that's Heather. Yes, it is. Heather! Heather!'

She waved frantically, and Heather, unable to escape, stood resignedly. 'Hello, Celia.'

'Hi. Look, I've got a new address, the house burned down. Can you tell David and the girls? They might want to talk to me.'

Heather blinked and said, 'Burned down? How? Was it arson?'

Hesitating, wondering why Heather should immediately think that, Celia said, 'The fire people have to file a report.'

'But do they suspect it?'

Charles, standing doctorishly to the side, said, 'Yes. Actually, they do.'

Heather's face was a study. Then her eye fell upon the bags and parcels Charles was carrying. 'Have you been shopping, then? Replacing everything?'

Celia said, 'Yes. Dorrie and I didn't have a stitch.'

The colour surged into Heather's cheeks. She said stiffly, 'I'm sorry about the fire, of course. But you really must be sensible, Celia! David's taken a terrible risk with the house, and he didn't do it to give you money to fritter away. We have to economise, you know. I don't give nearly as much to the church as I would like. We gave you money for legal costs and barristers, not clothes!'

Celia let out an exasperated sigh. 'I don't think I'm exactly your pensioner, Heather. I don't have to justify everything I spend to you. But you can put your mind at rest. You won't have to shortchange the Sunday collection just yet. I've come into enough money to keep me in shoes for quite a time.'

Questions were writ large on Heather's face, which she would have died rather than ask. She fished for paper and pencil in her well-ordered bag. 'I'd better make a note of your new address.'

'Indeed,' said Celia. 'I wanted to come to dinner one day this week, actually. Would tomorrow do? I haven't seen the girls for an age.'

'I don't think – I'm not sure – the girls find it so unsettling.'

She found the paper and Celia scribbled: The Rectory, Raikes Lane.

'Tomorrow then? I'll come about eight.'

She thrust the paper back at her rival. They left her, standing in the crowd, the address crumpled in her hand.

Later, eating cakes around the big kitchen table, Celia said, 'I wish you hadn't told Heather about the arson. She thought I burned the car. She'll think this was me too.'

Dorrie said, 'Obviously it was Braddock. He knows we got the pearls. He's a nutter, that man.'

Charles said, 'You should give his name to the police. Even if they can't prove anything they can warn him off.'

'I'd rather we didn't say a word,' said Celia. 'We're not innocent enough.'

She sipped her tea and wondered why Charles had never put a single decorative item on his kitchen walls. They were as plain as an unmarked page.

'Mr Braddock?' Even though she was alone in the house, Heather felt furtive. 'Mr Braddock? It's Heather Wilcox. I just thought you should know that Celia's house burned down last night. The one where she was staying.'

There was a slight pause. Then, 'Oh dear. I do hope she wasn't hurt?'

Heather couldn't contain herself a moment longer. 'Was it you? I know you burned the Sheraton. Did you do this?'

'Heather dear, don't be silly.'

'It was you, wasn't it?'

Edwin chuckled. 'I neither deny nor confirm silly rumours, Heather dear. Besides, why should I do such a thing? I can't think of any reason. Can you?'

'If you wanted to—'

'Kill her? But she didn't die. And I know we live in a world of televised makebelieve, but in real life, my dear – do you really imagine that murder is easily committed? I might want to murder Celia, but no more than you. We're neither of us murderers.'

His quiet, clipped words calmed her. The slight tremor that had affected her hands ever since she lifted the phone suddenly stopped. Of course this man wouldn't do anything terrible.

'I'm sorry,' she said stiffly. 'It was the shock, I suppose. I wondered – I thought you might like her new address.'

'Heather! How very thoughtful.'

'I shall need rather more than last time, I'm afraid. I do have expenses.'

He choked on what might have been a giggle. 'I'm sure you do! I shall be generous, I assure you. I know your penchant for good works.'

As Edwin finished writing the address, Heather burst out, 'I'm only doing this for the girls, you know. It's so bad for them to be exposed to someone like Celia. She's unprincipled. Spendthrift. She makes them terribly greedy.'

'I do see your point,' said Edwin.

Heather had the vague notion that he was laughing at her, and charged on. 'She says she's come into money. Obviously David gave her some, but it isn't that. I think you should talk to the hospital. That doctor's completely useless, he lets her do anything she wants. She might be spending the trust fund, and legally that's not hers.'

Edwin didn't reply for a moment. Then he said, 'That is interesting. Thank you, Heather. Thank you very much.'

When Celia arrived for dinner the dog, Tip, was in the hall, tied to a pillar by his lead. Celia bent down and stroked him, and he hammered his tail on the marble floor. 'You're the oddest-looking thing,' she murmured. 'Does she leave you tied up all the time?'

He sat up and grinned at her, and she thought how much she would like this dog. He was a rogue and a liar, she could see it at a glance, and she loved the badness in him.

Ellen came down the stairs and said, 'Hello. Do you like

250

him? Mum won't let him loose when we have company.'

Celia got up and dusted her hands. 'Isn't he super? I won't mind if you let him go, really.'

But Ellen said, 'Mum would be cross.'

Celia looked at the dog again. Poor mutt. But he looked anything but vulnerable. She said, 'Hasn't he got some bull terrier in him? I bet he grows up to fight.'

'What? You mean dog fights?'

'Looks to me as if he was bred for it. Do be careful when you're near other dogs. But you can always say it's the other dog's fault, and yours has never bitten anything before!'

Ellen tossed her honey hair and laughed. 'No wonder Mum hates you.'

'Why? It isn't so awful knowing about dogs, is it?'

'You seem to know about everything fun. And you always look so gorgeous.'

Celia's spirits, previously at low ebb, took off and soared. She didn't care that Ellen was being obviously manipulative. She was happy. 'I thought she'd stolen you for good,' she said bluntly.

Ellen said, 'But you'll always be our mother.'

'Do you think there's something in that? Something special?'

It wasn't a fair question. Ellen coloured to the roots of that lovely hair. 'I understand you a lot better than they do,' she burst out. 'Is that what you mean?'

Celia nodded. 'We do understand each other. We're alike. In lots of ways. Lucy too.'

David came out of the kitchen. Ellen watched him closely, but he seemed his usual relaxed self. Suddenly her world felt insecure and threatening. Her parents looked so right together.

David said, 'Heather told me what happened. Any idea who it was?'

'Lots of ideas. No proof,' said Celia. 'It's OK, though. Our friend doesn't know where I am now.'

'Will you be wanting some more cash? You must have lost everything. I don't want to be unreasonable, but—'

Heather hadn't told him all she had said, then. Good. She'd

251

regretted her little boast. 'I'm fine.' Celia smiled reassuringly. 'Insurance and all that. Look, does Heather want some help with the meal?'

'I think she'd rather get on by herself.'

They went through to the sitting room instead. David began to talk of his plans for the business, and Ellen sat with her knees to her chin, listening. After a while he opened a bottle of white wine and they all had a glass, Ellen's with a splash of lemonade. All at once Ellen felt adventurous. It was wonderful to have two such beautiful and charming parents; to live in this lovely house; to own a dog, and for things to be happening, at long last to experience change.

'Now we've got money to invest, I dragged out those old designs we did for the Sheraton's fascia,' said David. 'We were ahead of our time there. But I've revised the plans for the body shell. Technology's moved on, we need to reduce the profile. It's inherently unstable. But if we smooth everything off we look like every other car.'

'That's not on, then,' said Celia. 'David, everything's computerised nowadays. Why don't you go for all-wheel drive and link up with some computer man who can magically alter the drive to individual wheels when they start slipping? Can't you do something like that?'

'The Germans do,' said Ellen.

David looked from one to the other. 'Yes, but how do you two know about it? I thought I was the technical wizard.'

'I just made it up,' said Celia. 'It seemed like a good idea.'

'I read the technical press,' said Ellen, and held out her glass for more wine.

David began talking about the vast sums involved in that sort of new development, but Celia wasn't listening. She was indulging a lovely thought. She imagined Ellen as the first lady head of a car firm, rich and incredibly famous. Obviously an engineering degree was essential, but other considerations came first. If the company was going to continue under Ellen, or even Lucy, then it had to be in better shape.

'We shall have to get more money,' she murmured, chewing a nail. 'Go public or something.'

'I think we'll walk before we run, thank you,' said David in quelling tones.

She felt a great and impossible frustration. She had married David because she adored him, but he had never been anything of a businessman! In the early days they had fought like tigers to keep Joe Braddock out, when they should have welcomed him in and to hell with pride. The business would be coining money by now. David would come round, she told herself. It all took time. But her ten lost years filled her with wild impatience.

Dinner was good, in the food sense. Heather had whipped sauces and piped cream with a vengeance, only to be excluded from conversation.

The girls and Celia chattered like magpies, laughing and telling each other things, because there was so much to tell. Over the pudding Ellen said, 'Celia thinks Tip's a fighting dog. In fact she's sure he is.'

Heather let out a gasp of horror. Celia said gently, 'I'm not absolutely sure, Ellen. But he looks like one. Don't you think, David?'

David thought of the dog's chunky, nondescript physique. 'Oh my God,' he said, laughing. 'You might be right.'

Heather put down her spoon. 'We can't possibly keep him. Not if he's going to be a killer. We'll have to take him back to the dogs' home. David, you must take him tomorrow.'

Lucy looked at her with horror in her face. 'You wouldn't! You couldn't!'

'Of course she wouldn't!' Celia put a hand on Lucy's arm to soothe her. 'Heather doesn't understand, that's all. You must train him, teach him that fighting's not allowed. And keep him on a lead when you're not sure. He's a lovely dog.'

'Yes,' said Lucy, tearfully. 'He's a lovely dog.'

Heather said, 'Since I'm the one who'll have to pick up the pieces, I'm the one that decides! The girls could be bitten, some child we don't know. I won't have a dog I can't trust.'

Lucy burst out, 'If he goes, so will I. I hate you! You're not my mother. I've had enough of things around here.'

There was an awful silence. Heather's cheeks flamed and David began to say, 'Lucy, I will not have behaviour such as this—' but Celia cut him off. She laughed, a determined musical chime. 'Don't be silly, all of you,' she said happily. 'If Tip gets too much for you all I'll have him. He can keep me company. A little bit of you when you're not there.'

'We could still come and see him!' said Lucy with relief.

'It wouldn't be the same,' said Ellen darkly.

Heather, watching the situation cartwheel out of control, said shrilly, 'I think I should point out that Tip is my dog. I look after him. He – he loves me. He's staying here. I was – I was alarmed, that's all. For a moment.'

Celia, cool and unpleasant, said, 'Let's hope you don't get alarmed too often. You gave us all a terrible fright.'

Celia drove herself home, although she was tired and wished David had taken her. Charles was sitting up in the kitchen, drinking whisky. The house felt cold, although the Aga ensured it was not. But the uncurtained windows and bare floors made the place feel unfinished and unloved. She went to the windows and tried to draw what curtains there were, discovering that they came from other houses and were too small. She said, 'What a mess this place is in. You should be ashamed.'

He sighed. 'I've got worse things than that to be ashamed of.'

'What?'

He shrugged, but she persisted. 'What?'

'All in all I must have been a bloody awful doctor.'

She was dumbfounded. But then, gathering herself, she said, 'This isn't like you, Charles. You were a good doctor, and you will be again. You needn't talk as if you're finished. Are you worried about tomorrow's hearing?'

He looked down at his hands, cupped around the whisky glass. 'They're going to bust me. I just know it. They're going to say I was high-handed and dictatorial, that I alienated the staff and was rude to the patients. And I got sexually involved with you.'

'But you didn't.'

'They'll want to believe it. So they will.'

She sat down at the table next to him. The hearing was at ten the following morning, and by rights Charles should be in bed getting some sleep. If he appeared bleary-eyed and rumpled the impression given would not be good. She put her hand over his. 'You're a good doctor. A very good doctor. Look at all your cures.'

He sighed, heavily. 'Look at all the failures. You don't often get clear wins in neurology. All right, some of my patients might have done better with me than with someone else. It's possible to think that. But they might have done worse.'

She thought hard. 'The concussion, with the depressed fracture of the skull. Complete cure. I saw him.'

'Easy case.'

'What about – what about the child with the bulging eye? You took away the tumour and she was completely cured.'

'Could have gone either way. That was luck.'

'Me, then! What about me? No one else had any luck.'

He looked at her lugubriously. 'That just demonstrates my Bluebeard tendencies. Damn it, Celia, stop trying to cheer me up!'

She sat back, exasperated. Then she took hold of his glass and gulped the contents. 'Whisky tastes better now,' she remarked. 'I hated it before.'

'You weren't old enough before.'

'I wasn't old enough for a lot of things. I must have been the most immature twenty-five year old in history. I didn't value what I had, I took it all for granted. I looked only at the negative, bossy father, demanding children, moody husband. And here you are, doing the same. Brilliant, successful, searching for the downside of life.'

He watched her sitting there. She needed that whisky. She was very tired, and her face was losing its definition. He had waited for her tonight, longed for her to come home. He was sitting here now, luxuriating in her sympathy and concern. If Celia liked weak men he would show her weakness, he thought.

'How was David?' he asked disingenuously.

She grunted. 'Harassed by that terrible woman. She keeps

the dog tied up when people come. Really, I despair of David! He's got such a conscience about her. I'm telling you, if I was well, if I was absolutely sure I'd stay well, she wouldn't last a minute. They wouldn't stay with her. Not if I insisted.'

They were brave words. She looked up and met Charles's dark gaze. He had told her she had no chance against Heather, and she had believed what wasn't true. She was handicapped, that was all, by uncertainty. Her uncertain future. She felt again the heavy weariness that detached her from life, that kept her apart from all the careless, happy people in the world. 'I wish you could cure me altogether,' she said desperately. 'If you could do that you'd be the best doctor in all the world. And everyone would know.'

He got up and threw his whisky down the sink.

Next morning, Celia was heavy-eyed but Davenport was in fine form. He dressed carefully, in a dark suit and crisp white shirt, while Celia tried on this and that, searching for a balance between formality and style. She was not used to her new clothes and they seemed to look at her rebelliously, like foster children. Finally she chose a navy wool skirt with matching jumper, enlivened by white arrows. She put up her hair in a tangled, falling knot.

'All right?' she asked Davenport.

'Penitential, with a touch of the penitentiary. You'll do.'

'What do I say?'

'Whatever seems best. But don't obviously try to defend me.'

'I might not want to defend you.'

'Ungrateful bitch.'

Dorrie came in, muffled in her dressing gown. She listened to the others sparring, but did not join in. Instead she leaned on the Aga, taking comfort from the warmth.

'I thought you were coming,' said Celia.

Dorrie shook her head. She was dispirited beyond words. She put it down to the loss of her paintings, and knew it to be an irrational response. In the scheme of things the paintings weren't important, but to her, their creator, they were a tangible mark of her achievement. Without them, she felt rubbed out; worthless. There would be no recovery until she had made more.

'I'll stay and work,' she said, her voice rough and husky. 'I'll be all right.'

Charles grunted. He wasn't sure about Dorrie. Years as a clinician had taught him to spot the seriously off-balance. But at this point, certainly, there was nothing for him to do.

The car drove away and Dorrie was left alone in the house. It was very quiet, without so much as a ticking clock. The floorboards creaked and settled and the wind filtered in to cause papers and curtains to flutter. Dorrie felt spooked and was annoyed with herself. The fire had changed her, made her aware of her own weakness. She wasn't confident any more.

She went upstairs and got out the brand new paints and canvas that she and Celia had bought. Today, in her new and shaken mood, she couldn't think of the human face. Trapped in her own insecurity, she had room to think only of herself, and objectivity was denied her. But there were other subjects: from her bedroom window she could see the neglected vegetable garden, left to run riot in late summer and now a jungle. Runner beans had grown enormous, onions had bolted to seed and leeks were giant and slug-eaten monsters. They suited Dorrie's inner turmoil, matching her sense that evil was abroad. She began to paint, with absorption and skill, experimenting with a new technique.

She was colour-washing carrots when she heard a car approaching. To begin with the noise did not register, but when the engine stopped, she realised she had a caller. She did not go down at once, because to stop painting would have meant a splodge of colour she would always dislike; instead she waited for the jangle of the doorbell but it didn't come. Rinsing her brush, the wash completed, she opened her bedroom door, ready to go down.

A man was in the hallway. He had his back to her. Dorrie felt the most violent rush of adrenalin she had ever known, and her heart crashed into action, like an engine suddenly going full blast. The man was moving steadily along the passage, opening each door, looking in. The rooms at that end were empty. In a moment he would turn and come back. Dorrie took a careful breath. 'Do you have a right to be here?' she asked.

The man turned, and it was a face she didn't know. He's going to kill me, she thought. He'll knock me out and set the house on fire and burn me alive. But in the instant that she prepared to scream her useless scream, the man turned and fled.

She followed him down the stairs and into the kitchen. He had turned a pile of papers on to the floor, and in the sitting room she could see more paper, the contents of Davenport's desk.

'What do you want?' she demanded. 'What are you looking for?'

But he was through the door and away.

The car drove off with a scream of tyres on loose gravel. Dorrie sat in the kitchen for a moment, wondering why she didn't feel more scared. But she didn't. The fear had been in not knowing her enemy, and once she knew him, and saw that he was afraid, she feared him no more. She began to tidy the mess, all the bills and letters and bank statements. Then she locked the doors and windows and went back to her work.

Celia sat outside huge double doors, waiting her turn. Charles was within, permitted to hear the evidence, but excluded from discussion of it. Celia was next to go. Her stomach churned with nervousness. A buzzer sounded and Celia tensed. 'Mrs Sheraton?' a smiling secretary asked. 'They're ready for you now.'

'Thank you.' Get up smoothly, walk absolutely straight, don't hold the door with your right hand, you know it's too weak. She entered the room and saw them all, eight men behind a table, and Charles at the side, on his own. He avoided her eyes completely.

'Good morning, gentlemen.'

'Mrs Sheraton, do sit down. How are you feeling nowadays?'

'Very well. I – I get tired quite easily, but that's all.'

'Speech difficulty? Confusion? I notice you have a weakness in your right hand.'

Damn them. 'All those things are getting better,' she said defiantly.

All eight men smiled in that way doctors had, that said they would humour her and make up their own minds. Step by step they took her through all that she knew of her care. Suddenly one of the men tossed a folder towards her. 'Look at those photographs,' he said. 'Do they offend you in any way?'

They were photographs of her. Clinical, but suggestive. Soft porn crossed with research. She glanced at Charles. 'Did you use these at the conferences? Good heavens.'

'They are somewhat offensive, are they not?' said the primmest and most brittle member of the panel.

'Who to?' asked Celia.

'To yourself, Mrs Sheraton.'

'But I'm not offended. Mr Davenport used these photographs to publicise his work, and really I can't fault that.'

'Did you give your consent?'

'I really don't remember.'

'I must press you, Mrs Sheraton.'

Trapped. She said, 'I don't believe that I did.'

They moved on, to her absences from hospital. She blustered, claiming confusion and loss of memory.

'Don't you think you should have been protected from wandering? Kept more closely confined? When at last you were released you suffered a serious relapse I understand.'

She could see Charles's nostrils going white. They had him. Surely they had him. He would be fired. Celia put her palms together and summoned her wits.

'Gentlemen, I don't think you quite understand,' she said softly. 'I wasn't an easy patient. I was desperate to get back into the world, back to my family. My – husband. My children. Mr Davenport had to slow me down, keep me contained. I wasn't well enough to do what I wanted, but I wasn't ill enough to be kept confined to bed. I was like a child, a teenager, needing freedom to learn. He gave me that. Admittedly, I gave him a few frights, but what child doesn't? If my medical help had come from someone too worried about my trust fund to allow me to learn, then I wouldn't be sitting here today. Mr

Davenport put aside the question of money, and for that I am more than grateful.'

James, the hospital administrator, suddenly leaned forward. 'But you're living with Charles Davenport, aren't you, Mrs Sheraton?'

She shook her head. 'No.'

'The Braddock Corporation lawyers tell me that you are.'

She felt a slight shock. 'I don't know where they get their information from. I'm staying with my friend, Doris Duncan. Her house burned down last week and we are temporarily in rooms at Mr Davenport's house. We are not living together.' She paused, looking at their sceptical faces, and went on. 'I think you should understand the depth of Mr Davenport's concern. After the fire I would have been readmitted to hospital if he could have attended to me there. But because of this stupid suspension he couldn't do that. So, he generously provided accommodation for us in his own home, although he hates sharing his extremely spartan house. And he's a great deal too self-opinionated to be a comfortable host, I can assure you.'

A ripple of laughter went along the line. This was a Davenport they could understand.

She was dismissed soon after. This time, as she went to the door, she could not avoid a certain wobble in her step. Charles got up, blank-faced, and held the door for her. She nodded in acknowledgment and passed the Braddock lawyer, on his way in. Now the fun would start.

She took lunch alone, in the canteen, while the tribunal ground on, with coffee and sandwiches for the main protagonists. Forced to stay, she was ignored, although the standard of her care was supposed to be the central point at stake. A slow, steady anger was beginning to burn inside her: she was nothing but a pawn in a game of power politics.

At nearly four o'clock, they said she could go.

'What about Mr Davenport?' she asked. 'I came in his car.'

Her query was taken back into the room and the answer emerged that she was to take a taxi home. Mr Davenport did not want her waiting around any longer than necessary. He

260

must have loved issuing that instruction, she thought. The concerned doctor, to the last.

There was a smell of baking when she went into the house. Dorrie was in the kitchen, serenely mixing and rolling and spooning.

'You look as if you've had a better day than I have,' said Celia, collapsing into a chair.

'I don't know about that,' Dorrie replied, pouring them both a cup of tea. 'There was a bit of an upset this morning. Someone broke in. I found them searching the house.'

Celia's face stiffened. 'Braddock. Somehow he found out I'm here. But what's he looking for? If he even knew I had the pearls, he must think they were lost in the fire.'

'Someone's talking to him. It couldn't be Charles, could it?'

'Charles?' Celia felt a thud of shock. 'Charles? No. Could it? Why?'

'I don't know. Who else could it be?'

'I said to Heather that I'd come into money. I wasn't sure she even believed me, though. Surely Heather—'

'Heather,' said Dorrie.

An hour later Charles came in. He had a bottle of champagne. 'I'm back in my chair,' he said, flinging himself down as if this was the very chair of which he spoke. 'But the case is going to court. The trust fund's frozen. Braddock's got an injunction.'

'He's got more than that,' said Celia. 'Someone came here today. Looking for something.'

'What do you mean?'

'Braddock thinks I've sold the pearls. Someone came here to look through my papers. Dorrie caught him.'

She could not help the suspicion that made her watch him. She could not put her faith in anyone's innocence. Suppose Dorrie had lied? Suppose Charles was wholly venal? Suppose they were all in league with Braddock? But if that was so, she didn't want to believe it. There had to be some certainty in a treacherous world. Come what may, she would believe in her friends.

Chapter Seventeen

Mornings were always cold in the big, empty house. Celia lay in bed, watching her breath form clouds above the coverlet. Ice had frozen on the windows during the night, for this was the first deep frost of winter. Her feet were freezing. She leaped from the bed, grabbed her dressing gown and ran down the stairs to the kitchen. It was the only warm room in the house.

Charles was there, dressed and buttoned, reading the paper. He was a different man since he had got his job back. No more late night drinking, no more sob sessions. He was crisp and competent, and as unforgiving as ever.

'I've told you to wear slippers,' he said, barely lifting his eyes from the print.

'And I've told you to get central heating. And some carpets. And curtains. Honestly, Charles, this house is primitive!'

He ignored her, as he always did, and went on with his reading. Celia put the kettle on and stood over it, moving from one bare foot to the other as the cold of the flags struck home.

Suddenly Charles lifted his head. 'It's cold today. You'd better stay in.'

'Can't. I've got to go and see Hector Lowndes. He thinks it's time I filed an official claim to the hospital trust fund.'

'I thought you weren't going to do that?'

'I wasn't. But if Braddock's going for it, I've got a better claim than him. I can always re-donate it if I win.'

'The way you spend you'd need the lot.'

She was taken aback. 'What? Charles, are you saying I'm extravagant?'

'Wildly. You can't buy a vegetable that isn't out of season. Last night's asparagus must have been flown in from the moon.'

'Israel, actually. Didn't you enjoy it?'

'A packet of frozen peas would have done as well.'

'Rubbish!'

Celia felt flustered. It hadn't occurred to her that the asparagus was expensive. She resolved to be more sensible, and try and live as ordinary people did, every day of their lives. Shifting from foot to foot, she wondered if it would indeed be easier to buy a pair of slippers than to heat and carpet the whole house. But on that, Charles was simply being mean.

The exchange irritated her sufficiently to make her late. She couldn't settle to putting up her hair, and took four attempts to achieve smoothness. Her arm ached, and her mind seemed to be diving in all directions at once, a sensation she only had when not at her best. She wondered if Charles was right, and she should stay at home. She didn't even have the car today. Nonetheless she found herself queuing at the bus stop, and when the bus came was confused by the strange fare system that had developed. She had neither change, nor some ticket strip that had to be stamped, nor even the endless passes that people flashed at the driver. Instead she was cursed for offering a five pound note, as if it was some arcane artefact of little merit. When at last she arrived in town she felt as if she had unravelled one of the mysteries of the universe.

Hector Lowndes was fizzing with impatience. 'I've been waiting this half hour,' he declared.

She was immediately on the defensive. 'I'm sorry. I had to get a bus. Taxis are so expensive.'

'Have you decided, then? What you want to do?'

'Everything. As much as it takes.' Celia sat herself down, making it clear that she intended to stay. Lowndes was irritated, drumming his fingers, taking off his spectacles and polishing them. It was intimidating and unexplained. He had been so helpful before.

He was talking about applying to the Court for a hearing. It sounded very slow and very tedious. Celia cut him short, saying, 'I came to begin all that. I came to tell you to get everything moving.'

'You realise you might not win?'

'You said before you thought we would.'

'It could cost you everything – everything.'

He looked down, away from her. Something had changed, she thought. Something had caused him to lose his nerve. She wondered what it could be. 'Has Mr Braddock threatened you as well?'

'As well? Have you been threatened?'

She nodded. 'I believe so.'

Lowndes took off his spectacles and polished them. 'Clients don't threaten solicitors, Mrs Sheraton.'

'Don't they? It must happen. By the way, how is your father?'

It was a random shot in the dark. But the man before her paled and seemed to sag in his chair. The spectacles were removed once again, but this time he mopped at his eyes with his handkerchief.

'I'm sorry,' said Celia, haltingly. 'So sorry—'

He gestured myopically. 'It's not you who should apologise. My father's dying, I'm sure you know that. The damned illness is taking so long, giving him hell, of course, and he has too much time to think. I wanted to put this case right for you, Mrs Sheraton, but I'm not sure I can.'

'Why not?' She spoke softly, fearful of stemming the flow of words.

'He's been talking to me. Confessing, I suppose you'd call it. It seems – it seems he knew that the main part of the Will was missing. After your accident Joe took to keeping a lot of documents at home, the Will amongst them. When he died your mother was distressed, obviously. She brought the papers to this office. And my father saw at once that the main Will was not among them.'

Celia said, 'You had a copy. You must have had a copy.'

Lowndes avoided her gaze. 'It seems that copy had gone astray.'

'I bet it had!' She got up, furious now, losing all her hard-won control. 'How could he? My father was his friend, he was trusted! Did Edwin pay him, was that it?'

'Please – please.' Hector shook his head miserably. 'Your father and mine might have been friends, but we didn't prosper. We only got the personal business, none of the company work. I imagine your father doubted our competence. And so it seemed did the rest of the business community, following his obvious lead. So we were poor. Not working-class poor, of course, no meat for dinner and hand-me-downs, but miserably, genteelly hard-up. Thin carpets, school fee hassles, better than usual meals when friends came to tea. We always had to pretend. My father – my father realised he could change all that. Set us up, set me up, for life. He simply assured your mother that the Will she saw was the Will your father meant to write. And Edwin Braddock rewarded him. These offices, our home, everything, all came from that.'

He put his glasses back on and met Celia's eye. She gave a half smile. 'I suppose after that people patronised the prosperous firm. When you have money, more comes rolling in.'

'Exactly. I don't want my father's name blackened, Mrs Sheraton. I don't want to drag all this through the courts, adding to my mother's misery. But you must decide. If you'd been well, my father would never have done wrong, but as it was – he knew there was bad blood in the family. Your husband and your father hated one another, so perhaps he did mean to leave it all to Edwin. Any rate, he convinced himself.'

'He never believed it,' said Celia softly. 'He knew my father would never let me down.'

Hector Lowndes slowly bowed his head.

She asked for coffee, and while it came she got up and went to the window. The square below was bustling with people passing from office to office, getting into and out of cars. Old man Lowndes must never have expected his sins to find him out quite so conclusively. Clients did not often rise from the dead to berate you. She tried to think what she really wanted, what must be the result of all this. Money, yes – but for what? To put Sheraton Cars on a firm footing, so that it would always provide for the girls; to allow the people she loved to live comfortably, without worry. And for herself? She hesitated. Lately, she didn't know. To be well perhaps. Quite well. And then to have David back again!

She turned to Lowndes. 'We must chase the hospital trust

fund,' she said decisively. 'That's quite clear-cut. It was intended for the hospital, and my cousin must not get his hands on it. Do that and do it for free.'

Lowndes nodded, pouring coffee for them both. Confession had restored him, he was calm again.

Celia went on, 'As for the Will, I think we had better disregard your father's part in things. I've no doubt it would be disputed, and we'd have stirred things up to no purpose. My father always thought of him as a friend, and perhaps he wasn't such a good friend after all, but he's sorry. We need to find some copy of the original Will, Hector. Talk to your father. Make him search his memory. Edwin Braddock got the Will itself, and no doubt destroyed it, but there may be some record. If there is, then we must discover it.'

Lowndes nodded. He was beginning to reassess this woman. Some of her elegance was gone, and her hair was coming down. She was visibly tiring. But he was conscious of a warmth that had been absent before, and an earthy sexual attraction. It was strange that he hadn't felt that earlier. She hadn't come back to life all at once, he thought. Perhaps she returned in stages, acquiring first this and then that quality, concentrated, like perfume, by their long sleep. She was exceptionally vivid, in all things. He was almost relieved when she got up to go.

He put her in a taxi, and tried to settle back into work. Not much could be done until he spoke to his father, he thought. But all the records remained, heaped in files on the top floor of the building, dumped there when they computerised everything. Hector had wanted to burn the lot, but his father had always resisted. It might be that in his heart he had wondered if this might arise. One day, he might be called to account.

He abandoned the tedium of a company law suit and told his secretary to field any calls. He went up to the attic, to the stacks of dusty boxes and grimy files, kneeling in accumulated years of muck, getting up to wipe the skylight clean before he had light enough to begin. He was atoning for past sins, doing penance. And there was order of a sort. Each year had been piled separately, and subsequent years had been dumped on top. But there was no way of knowing in which year Joe Braddock had made his Will, in which year he had altered it, and when he had finally decided what would stand. He must guess at the year following Celia's accident, when he was learning to live without hope. From then on nothing was certain. With weeks of work ahead of him, he began his mammoth task.

The headache that had begun in the office magnified outside it to a rhythmic, pile-driving thud. Celia's taxi was held up at some lights, and in the distance a road drill echoed the tumult in her head. She leaned forward and spoke to the driver. 'Will you take me to the hospital, please? I don't feel so well.'

He turned the taxi in a squeal of rubber, and raced back the way they had come. Celia leaned her head against the seat, utterly spent.

She had no idea how much time passed before she awoke. She knew only that she was here, in hospital, and that at last the pain in her head had ceased. She looked up and saw Davenport, armed as always with his pencil torch. 'You again,' she said.

'Here again,' said he. 'What did I tell you about staying home?'

She struggled to sit up. 'I'm not so ill. A bus ride, and the lawyer, and then a taxi.'

He sat on the bed and held her hand. There was a clock in this room, ticking loudly. Or was it simply that she could hear every sound, every whisper, like a shout? The smell of Charles, that mixture of antiseptic and good soap, and the darker end-of-the-day tang of his sweat, seemed unbelievably strong. She looked at the clock, but could not make out the numbers. 'What time is it?'

'Nearly nine. Do you want to stay?'

She shook her head. 'I'd rather go home.'

'Why? It's freezing in that house.'

'You admit it at last. At least I'm alive in there. Here – I know I'm going to die in a place like this. I can feel it.'

'Don't get all fey on me, Celia.'

He wrapped her in blankets and had her wheeled

downstairs to his car. She felt utterly drained, her head rolling on the seat as if her neck was a wire, with not enough substance to support even her damaged brain. But as they drove from the hospital, she couldn't leave foreboding behind. Life was slipping from her grasp. She couldn't hold it, she was too weak. Soon she would be cold, cold forever.

Dorrie, anticipating her arrival, had lit fires and made soup. Celia sat by a blaze, eating from a tray, trying to shut out Charles's looming displeasure. He had changed into jeans and thick sweater, and ignored her and Dorrie alike. When she was sure Celia was settled, Dorrie took herself to bed.

There was no light in the room but a table lamp and the glow from the fire. Shadows lurked in the corners, surrounding the light, encircling them with unreal but visible walls.

'All right, Charles,' said Celia. 'Tell me.'

'What?'

'Tell me what's so terrible. I do what you say, I do less and less in fact, and I'm getting worse. Don't deny it. I'm inside this ailing body and I know.'

He crouched down in front of her, looking up into her face. 'Yes.'

'Am I going to die, Charles? When? Tonight it feels very close.'

'No closer than any other night.'

Celia rubbed a hand across her eyes. 'I want to live, more and more. I'm only just getting to know people again. The girls. David. Dorrie. I've got things to do, I don't want to die yet. Why can't you operate, Charles? I want to be better.'

The question hung in the air between them. He sat back on his heels and gazed into the dying fire, wondering why she asked this now and never before. 'If you were unconscious and there was no other hope, I might try,' he said. 'You'd have to be good as dead. It isn't my job to turn a woman I – to turn any woman into something else.'

'What else?'

'A creature without sight, speech or hearing. Perhaps even without a sense of smell. A creature whose thoughts we could only guess at, whose movement we couldn't understand. The chance of that – I can't take a chance like that.'

She turned the thought over in her mind, wondering where her thoughts would go when her mind stopped functioning. They would exist somewhere, she was sure. To cease to exist was unimaginable. She shivered and pulled her dressing gown a little closer. The worst of this, the very worst, was the steady detachment she felt from the people around her. She felt as if they were all on the same meandering paths, while she alone had her path to herself and had no company. How much she wanted a companion, she thought. How much she wanted heat.

She looked up at Charles. His face had the familiarity of long association. In all the world, he was the person closest to her plight, who knew most of what she faced. And he was a big, dark, utterly virile man. Such a man would shelter her. Such a man would shield her from the dark.

She said, 'I wish you would make love to me, Charles.'

His head lifted and he stared at her. 'What?'

She reached out and took hold of his wrist, the black hairs curling over her fingers. A shiver ran through her. Tonight, more than any night, she needed him. She whispered, 'I want you – to be close to me. I want to be touched. You don't know what it's like, half dead and half alive. I can't go on like this, waiting to die, too frightened to live. I need you, Charles.'

His face, in the firelight, was all lines and shadows. As she held his wrist, he took hold of hers, turning it to look at the pale purple of her veins. 'But you really want David, don't you?'

She drew in her breath. 'He's not here.'

'And if he was?'

She turned her palm towards his, and linked fingers, squeezing with all her might. 'I'm safe with you. I know you'll take care of me. What does it take, Charles? This?' She let him go and slipped her robe from her shoulders, exposing her breasts. She leaned back a little and reached up to cup herself, putting back her head.

He rolled forward on to his knees, a foot away from her. He reached out and touched her hair, where it fell across her nipple. She opened her own knees, letting him come closer, her nightdress hiding her. He moved on, forcing her legs wide until his torso was pressed against her opening. Now she was

270

groaning, pushing her pelvis into him with small, insistent thrusts. He pulled off his shirt and felt her heat against his skin. He pulled up her nightdress and felt her moisture. A madness seemed to overtake him, he writhed and twisted against her, and she against him, her vulva against his belly in unlikely eroticism. Her head fell back again. Orgasmic shudders began to shake her. He gripped her breast, cramming it into his mouth, the nipple like a stone.

She was crying out, convulsing, her arms waving like seaweed, her face amazed. He was hard, huge, and conscious of a great exhilaration. She wouldn't want Sheraton once she'd felt this! But her muscles were tight with orgasm, her flesh engorged. Charles forced his way into her, making space where there was none, and she began to gasp as he thrust up and in. This is it, he thought. This is where I shall stay forever, and never want more. At that moment his whole body was swept with feeling. He hung above Celia, his face anguished, while his whole being seemed to pump itself dry. Her fingers gripped the skin of his buttocks as her orgasm fluttered again. A moment more – surely it need not end? – but the end was inevitable. They subsided into peace.

In the firelight, sleepy, Celia felt restored. The flame of his life had restored the flicker of hers. She had been right to follow her instincts and turn to this. If she wanted to live she must take hold of life, live vigorously, with joy. If she wanted to die she need only lie in wait.

They lay together, but did not speak. It was as if they had quarrelled unforgivably, as if they had had enough of each other. When the fire died they went up to bed, she to her room and he to his. There was the sense that something momentous had happened, and they each needed to be alone. They were separate people still. As she settled to sleep, filled with the strange calm that follows sex, she wondered if tomorrow she would have a slight distaste for tonight. It was usual, in her experience, to regret the night before. But waking to another grey dawn, with fine drizzle spattering the windows, Celia lay and took stock. She felt better. She felt good.

Charles and Dorrie were both in the kitchen. Celia went and hunched on a chair, cradling her bare feet from the stone floor, and saw that Charles was embarrassed. 'You should rest in bed today,' he said briskly. 'Dorrie's coming into town with me. She needs some paint and stuff.'

Celia was aware of reluctance. She was afraid of being alone. 'I'll be bored,' she prevaricated.

'Read a book,' said Dorrie, and put a plate of toast on the table.

Celia nibbled at it, aware of Charles standing away from her, forbiddingly cold. She looked up quickly and caught him watching her. She manufactured a grin and he blushed.

Left in the kitchen, with only the soft hiss of rain to distract her, she knew she couldn't stay here alone. The house was so comfortless, the silence so menacing. Edwin had no reason to hurt Charles or Dorrie. He had every reason to hurt her.

Dorrie had left her car behind, and Celia had the keys. No one had thought to ban her from driving yet, although they would if they remembered, no doubt. She got up and went upstairs. She wouldn't cower at home, waiting. She would beard Edwin Braddock in his den.

She put on dark trousers and shirt, knowing that against them her skin was like parchment. Edwin might suppose her at her last gasp, she thought, wrestling with the gears of the car. She drove quickly, as she always did, although the roads were wet and the tyres squealed on corners. When she reached the offices of the Braddock Corporation she parked aggressively behind Edwin's Rolls-Royce.

Everything was so achingly familiar. Daddy's work, she thought suddenly, looking up at the solid, stone building. This place had been as much part of her life as the house, her parents even, it had made up the fabric of her world. She went in, and it wasn't the same. The girl at the chrome reception counter seemed absurdly young. Celia felt her certainty waver, and mentally shook herself. 'Mr Braddock, please,' she said crisply. 'I'm his cousin.'

It was some time before she was admitted. She sat in the foyer, watching people come and go, until there was someone she recognised. Her colour came up, unbidden. It was Peter Cartwright.

'Mrs Sheraton? If you'd like to come this way?'

He was stiffly polite. He knew her as much as she knew him. Her face grew hotter and hotter, remembering her dreadful Italian, her worse acting, her perfidy. In the lift, standing together in silence, she couldn't bear it.

'I'm – I'm sorry,' she burst out.

'For what, Mrs Sheraton?'

'For getting you into trouble. I'm sure there was trouble. But it was worse for us. I mean, we had our house burned down.'

'What?'

She wondered suddenly if he had been responsible. But he looked too shocked, and was altogether too nice. 'Yes,' she said feebly. 'It burned down.'

'You're not suggesting – you don't suppose—'

'The fire people said it was arson.'

They went in silence up the stairs into the executive suite, exactly the same as always. Nothing had changed, except that her father's comfortable secretary wasn't there nowadays, and his voice didn't boom out, calling, 'Celia? Darling, why didn't you tell me you were coming? Someone get us some champagne!' He would call for champagne even if she visited four times a week, as if he must celebrate, and would always celebrate, his lovely daughter.

The memories were too much. She found herself blinking furiously, in no condition to confront Edwin Braddock. But she couldn't delay. The door opened and there he was, smooth-skinned and smiling, protected by his vast desk. Used to the place, Celia did not stand as others did, stranded on the expanse of carpet. She went at once to the bar.

'Hello, Edwin. Can I have a drink? Champagne.'

'Champagne? At this hour?' Despite himself he was drawn from behind his desk.

Celia rewarded him with a glittering smile. 'Don't tell me you have none? My father bought fifty cases of Krug every year, and we never drank it all.'

'I'll send for some.'

'Thank you.'

She sat on her bar stool, swinging one high-heeled leg. She sensed that her femininity annoyed him, and to prove it, he

273

took the battle to her. 'Peter Cartwright tells me you met him in Strasbourg.'

'Yes. We fell over one another.'

'Profitably?'

She met his eye. 'Justifiably. Wouldn't you say?'

He returned her gaze quite steadily. 'No. Most definitely not.'

The champagne arrived, not properly chilled, but he opened it just the same. Celia sipped her glass, and was amazed. The bubbles exploding in her mouth, the flavour, the textured finish, all transported her in an instant to yesterday. Let Edwin say what he might, she knew the truth. It was in the champagne. She drained her glass and held it out for more. 'Please.'

This time she sipped slowly, aware that her silence was making Edwin progressively more uncomfortable. So she remained silent a little longer.

'Look here, Celia,' he said suddenly, swinging angrily towards her. 'There's no point in behaving as if I took anything that wasn't mine. No, I leave that entirely to you. Your father made his Will in my favour, and that's the way it is. I will not be treated like some robber baron.'

She looked up lazily. 'A rather profligate robber baron, if all I hear is true.'

'What have you been hearing?'

'I gather you've overstretched somewhat. A failed takeover. The Marlborough gaming clubs, someone said.'

He was silent for a moment. She could almost see his thoughts. How much to tell her, how much to hold back? How can I draw her poison? Finally he said, 'We're overstretched at the moment, yes. That's common knowledge. We could sell the Marlborough shares now and take a loss, of course. But I'd rather not. When the upturn comes, they'll reward us. It's a short-term problem.'

'But you borrowed to buy the shares,' said Celia. 'And there's Linton Place, and everything. If you're reduced to fighting for my trust fund as well as selling the pearls, then things must be bad.'

'Not in the least,' said Edwin tightly.

274

Celia sipped her drink again. She doubted that he was totally strapped for cash. Perhaps it was as he said, the trust fund and the pearls would simply ease things. While he waited – for what?

'Do you still mean to get Marlborough?' she asked.

He said nothing. A muscle at the corner of his mouth jumped and twitched. Celia thought, There is something in genetics, just as Ellen said. They shared the same blood, she and Edwin, neither chased a mouse and let it escape with its tail. The City had laughed at Braddock's impertinence, and nothing was more certain to harden Braddock resolve.

Celia slipped off her stool. 'I see you do,' she said. 'Good luck to you. In the meantime, Edwin, will you please stop threatening me?'

He gave her a measuring look. 'Hallucinating again, I see.'

'Do you think so? You can't hallucinate a burning house. I'm thinking I might take the press into my confidence. Do you know Max Grindling? A sleuth of the dirty washing brigade. He's always been interested in the more dramatic elements of my story.'

'Tell who you like!'

'What? About arson and burglary? Really, Edwin, you must have a thicker skin than I gave you credit for. Because I'll tell everything.'

'We do have laws of libel in this country!'

'Another court case? You're determined to go broke.'

He stood, quite flushed, in the centre of the room, making a visible attempt to gather himself. He shot his cuffs and adjusted his tie, restoring that image of perfect order which he so admired. Celia could sense him calming and coming to terms. He wasn't a man to act emotionally. His fires smouldered very deep, permitting his intelligence to live in cold, hard isolation. He went to his desk and pressed a button. 'Peter,' he said, 'telephone a journalist for me. Mr Max Grindling. I wish to speak to him.'

Celia swallowed. 'What are you doing?'

He said 'I won't be blackmailed. I shall tell Grindling exactly what you accuse me of. And I will be believed. Not you.'

Celia went back to the bar stool. Her hands were shaking. 'Do you really want to wash all our dirty linen in public?'

'Not in the least.' He was smiling now, in control of himself and the situation. 'I think I've been a little too kind to you. Perhaps you treasure the thought that I will give in to your demands – at least to the tune of a million or so. But I won't. I tell you here and now, Celia, you will get not one penny from me.'

'Don't you think you ought to be reasonable?'

'And when were you reasonable?' His voice rose to a shout. 'You were a stupid, wilful girl. You dodged university, yet you wouldn't go into the firm. You married to spite your parents. Finally you crowned your brief and inglorious career with a car smash, in which you didn't have the decency to die. It was left to me, the insignificant cousin, to pick up the pieces. I comforted your father – helped your mother – put the firm back on the rails. I deserved what I got. I've put my sweat into this company. It's mine by right, not yours by medical miracle!'

'You stole everything. Even my mother's pearls.'

'Don't you accuse me! Don't you dare accuse me!' He approached her, the length of the room, his finger held up threateningly. 'Don't think I forget my enemies. Don't think I ever let them win. Some people are worth something and some are no more than the dust beneath my feet, and so help me, I'll trample you, Celia! Just wait!'

His face was an inch from hers. Spittle was on his lips. She was suddenly terrified, seeing a new and different Edwin, the tyrant whose opinion was holy writ, to contradict it a sin. Celia dragged the shreds of her courage about her. 'They were my mother's pearls,' she whispered. 'Not yours.'

He spat, full in her face.

She gave a strangled gasp and fell back. The telephone rang. They both looked at it, and Edwin cleared his throat. Celia turned away, taking a napkin from the bar to wipe her face. 'You needn't tell Grindling a thing,' she said softly.

The telephone rang again. Edwin picked up the receiver and put it down again, severing the connection. Celia walked the length of the room to the door, loaded with defeat. But then she turned. 'You haven't won,' she said clearly. 'Now I know where we stand I shall fight you all the way. I'll see you in court.'

His mouth was a hard, straight line. Suddenly, deliberately, he picked up the half empty bottle of champagne and threw it at her. It turned in the air, its contents showering, before crashing against the closing office door.

Chapter Eighteen

For once Charles Davenport was unsure of himself. But then he had never been to a gambling club before and didn't know the form. He had to confess to being fairly disappointed. The room was dim, each table in a pool of light which diminished to nothing only a yard away. But even this could not disguise the slight shabbiness of the place; baize worn smooth, carpets losing their colour, polished surfaces bearing the marks of months of damp glasses. If Charles had been a regular he might have heard people commenting on the fact. 'Good God, Bertie, this place is getting dreadfully grim. Someone really should say something to George. One half expects to see mice!'

Nobody did say anything to George, of course. He was known for his irascible temper. He presided over his clubs determinedly, brooking no criticism, excluding whom he wished. The food was disgusting, and exorbitantly priced, so no one actually ate there if they could avoid it. What's more, nowadays the Arabs had deserted, and some of the wealthy Americans, defecting to smarter, sleeker places, where one didn't see the cloakroom girls obviously soliciting. The people who remained, prepared to put up with the sub-standard croupiers and the ill-attended tables were George's sort: public school; landowners mostly; old and diminishing money; but unquestionably out of the top drawer.

Charles was more than a little surprised to be there at all. He had attended the medical conference with something like relief, able to lose himself once more in the safe world of science. Lately he had felt himself to be wallowing in deep water in every other aspect of his life. It was all Celia's fault – and yet the blame was his own. He had wanted to make love to her, and he had. Always before with women he had felt an immediate and refreshing relaxation, and a certain loss. Of interest.

All right, he admitted it to himself. Fascination, for him, rarely lasted beyond bed. But with Celia, his patient, his charge, almost his property, there were bound to be complications. Afterwards, the next evening, she had been so obviously depressed and upset, and that had had the strangest effect on him. He had felt – hurt. Rejected. If Dorrie hadn't been there he might well have had it out with her then and there, so it was a very good thing that Dorrie was around. And an even better thing that he should come to this conference.

Politically it was well advised too. It gave the lie to all those who thought his suspension might have been deserved. What's more, Sir Geoffrey Moreton, one of the Great Men of Medicine, had surprised him with an invitation to dine at the Athenaeum, which had put a stop to much back biting.

The dinner itself was formal, the company distinguished. Charles had the distinct impression that his companions were marking his card. Keep on as he was, keep his nose clean, let this little unpleasantness die down, and he too might be blessed with greatness. The Establishment was keen to have the thrusting men of the future firmly on its side.

As the brandy went down, so did the inhibitions. Moreton said, 'This place is getting a bit damned sleepy, if you ask me. How about going on somewhere?'

For an awful moment Charles imagined he was going to be taken to a strip club by a royal gynaecologist, but thankfully it was not to be. Lord Royston, big in thoracics, was a member of the Marlborough.

It was on occasions like this that he knew himself to be a total innocent. He had never gambled in his life, except for the odd pound on the Derby. Charles had worked nonstop since he was eleven years old, and this new, dim world was a revelation to him. A woman loaded with diamonds lounged across a table, her breasts impeding the croupier's wooden sweep as he gathered cards and chips. She was drunk and almost insensible, but continued to play. She was younger than she seemed, thought Charles, and watched as a man she seemed to know came and blatantly fondled her. 'Come on, Lindy,' he said. 'Let's go and screw.' But still she continued to play.

Lord Royston was talking to a large, florid man who had spilled something down his dinner jacket. It was George Marlborough, the owner, and Charles was called over to be introduced. 'Meet our up and coming brain scrambler. Bash your noddle one night and this is the man. Brings them back from the dead.'

'Nothing of the kind,' said Charles, privately amazed. If even the great and good of his profession believed newspaper fairy stories there wasn't much hope.

'In private practice, are you?' asked Marlborough, gazing at him blearily.

'Not at all,' said Charles.

'Soon will be, if he's got any sense,' said Royston, and he and Marlborough burst into guffaws of laughter.

Some gambling chips appeared, from somewhere. Charles wondered if he would wake in the morning to find a bill for thousands pinned to his pillow, but there was no point in worrying. Moreton had wandered off and established himself in a corner playing cards, and Royston was pawing the drunken girl, falsely avuncular. The place had the ambience of a nightmare.

The rattle of the roulette table attracted him. He went across, and a beauty in a long white dress, feverish with cocaine, draped herself on his shoulder. 'Wow, aren't you the hunk? You playing? You look lucky to me.'

She helped him play, or rather to lose. The chips went, some faster, some slower. Sometimes he won a small sum, only to lose it again. The woman at his elbow was pressing her thigh against his, until at last she said, 'Oh, good. There's no more left. Now we can go.'

He thought, Why not? At least she wasn't a patient. At least she wasn't going to lead him on to something that wouldn't be there. Moreton was deep in his game, Royston too drunk to care. Charles knew he had done his duty as an up and coming star. Quite suddenly he thought of Celia. He wished she was here. This sort of place was the stuff of her youth, she could lead him and teach him – he caught himself up short. Celia had used him. Be honest and admit it. Stop trying to build on a foundation of lies.

He took hold of the girl's arm, and walked away from the table. He had been brought here to lose money and paw girls, after all. She pretended to stumble in the gloom, and her hand groped at his groin, finding him semi-erect. He grunted and she let him go. He said, 'I'm in a hotel. Want to go there?'

'No. Come to my place.' She had the telltale sniff of the habitual cocaine user. He felt a rising distaste, and suppressed it. This sort of sex was all about sleaze.

They took a taxi, stopping first at an all-night chemist's. Charles felt he would have been happier with a blood test than a condom, but needs must. He must not allow his medical squeamishness to put him off pleasure. This encounter was meant to be cathartic; he was in the business of changing his sexual landscape, widening his sensual horizons. When they reached her block of flats in Mayfair they stopped in the doorway, fumbling at each other's genitals, and he kept thinking that on no account was he going to do it to her here, with the condoms still in his pocket. One breast was free, the nipple cold as a frozen berry. He began to lick it, humming some indeterminate tune. She began to giggle wildly.

The night took on a surreal, almost comic quality. He was outside himself, watching his own debauchery. She lived in an upstairs flat and they ran up the stairs, until she crashed through the door saying, 'Christ! I must have a snort.' He watched her, dispassionately, and then, when she offered some to him – accepted.

He remembered the night as red in colour. The carpet, her membranes, his own. She had a flatmate who was woken by the noise, and she joined in, quite merrily. Two women, straddling him. There was no pretence of anything, it was raw, and probably corrupt. But that was the inevitable result of sexual sophistication. The hours had a desperate clarity, which afterwards he longed to clothe in haze. Towards morning, as the drink subsided, as the cocaine cleared his system, he wondered how he had ever come to be knowingly in bed with two prostitutes.

He left them before seven. They were the wrong class to be

professional, they merely picked up what they could, round about. They mumbled about the rent and so on, bleary-eyed, much younger than he had supposed. In the sour aftermath of his orgy he had a bleak vision of the headlines if all this came out. He gave them cash, amazed to find himself doing it. The whole thing was unbelievable.

The car was approaching. They could hear the buzz of its engine, the abrupt coughs that meant gear changes, every few seconds on this twisting, slippery test track. David was anxious. The track was wet today and treacherous, but they had hired it and the test must therefore go ahead. The driver was new to them, an ex-Formula man who had never driven a Sheraton before. David felt foolishly protective, as if his child was being judged.

The Sheraton appeared as a button on the horizon, grew to matchbox size, larger, and was gone. They were left with a hole in the air, filled with sudden silence. The car had never been driven so fast.

'Christ,' said one of the mechanics. 'What have we done to it now?'

'That equalled the lap record,' said the man with the watch. 'Unofficial, like.'

Half a minute and the car was round again, but this time it slowed and stopped. David went to the driver's door and squatted, bareheaded in the fine grey drizzling rain. 'That was quick,' he said. 'You surprised us.'

The driver, Adam Partridge, took off his helmet. 'It's a good car. Is this engine set going to be standard? I'll have one.'

'We're putting it in as an option. Bit hairy for some customers. How about the stability?'

Partridge unfastened his belt and got out. As always, David was surprised at how small he was. This Titan of the racetrack barely made a chunky five foot four. Partridge kicked one of the tyres, fat racing treads at hundreds of pounds apiece. 'Hell of a waggle on corners. Without these tyres I'd have been doing the rumba. What do you plan to do?'

David said, 'Computerised all-wheel drive,' and Partridge snorted.

'Not on mine you won't! You ought to modify this car. Do some racing with it.'

They went into the caravan that served as hospitality on this windswept Yorkshire test track. But the coffee was cold and they couldn't talk freely. David invited Partridge to dinner that night, with his wife. Only on the way back, his head filled with thoughts of racetrack victories and rally success, did he remember that he hadn't cleared it with Heather. She had less than six hours in which to produce a dinner party.

Heather ran from her office the moment she put down the phone. She hit Marks and Spencer at a gallop, only to find they had little left. So she raced to the butcher and bought some veal, although what she would do with it she couldn't imagine. In the supermarket she threw food into the trolley, cream, cocktail cherries, booze, anything that might be relevant. She never cooked on impulse, it wasn't her style. Heather's meals were never other than meticulous.

She drove home, wondering if she should use the prawns for the first course, or if that was banal. Perhaps she should put them in a sauce with the veal – it might be disgusting. They weren't even first quality, she might poison everyone. And what were they having for pudding?

The dog was tied in the kitchen, and he had passed the time by chewing a hole in a cupboard. She hit him, furiously, and he showed the whites of his eyes. She thought he might turn and savage her, so gave him a biscuit to make up. The dog grinned, reminding her of Celia, quite sure of himself. She pushed him willy-nilly into the garden.

Alone in the kitchen she tried to pull herself together. Everything she had bought was ranged about, jumbled, confusing her. She sat at the table with paper and pencil and tried to think coherently. It was after five o'clock! She had done nothing and they were coming at eight.

Ellen and Lucy sailed through the door, squabbling noisily. 'It's my Walkman! Geroff!'

'It's my tape, and no one said you could have it. Give it back.'

'I'm owed your tape, you pinched my skirt without asking.'

'I did ask! I asked Mum.'

Ellen confronted Heather. 'Did you give her permission to borrow my skirt? You know what she's like. She ruins everything of mine. You'd no right to say she could.'

'It's only an old skirt,' said Heather.

'I don't care how old it is! It's my favourite. I don't go around ruining other people's things without asking. All I ask is the right to have my things treated with respect. It isn't as if—'

'Ellen, do shut up!' snapped Heather. 'I've got to do a dinner party and I can't.'

'What do you mean, can't?' asked Lucy.

Heather waved her hands frantically in the air. 'I mean, I can't! I had absolutely no notice and I couldn't get half the things and they're coming at eight and I haven't begun. It's Adam Partridge and his wife. They've travelled the world, they must be used to wonderful food. All my recipes call for things I haven't got.'

The girls were silent. It was slightly alarming, seeing Heather in this state. They were used to someone bossy and self-opinionated, ruling them with inflexible certainty. The ebbing of her confidence had been gradual, and now to see her brought down by a simple meal was shocking.

Ellen said, 'Can we help? We could peel things.'

'No, we can't,' said Lucy. 'Celia's coming to take us there for the evening.'

Heather looked up. 'You didn't tell me that!'

'No. She arranged it with Dad.'

The last straw. Celia having cosy little chats with David, everyone knowing what was going on except Heather. They were all lying to her. She got to her feet, picked up a box of groceries and sent it crashing to the floor. 'So there,' she said with satisfaction.

They all stood looking down at the mess of smashed bottles and cornflour. Celia, coming in at the door, stared too. 'Have you had an accident?' she asked.

Heather's colour came up. For Celia to appear just then was beyond everything. For once restraint was out of the question. She let fly.

'It would be you!' she declared, taking in the clear skin,

shining hair, the immaculate clothes. 'Come to gloat, no doubt. You wouldn't be in this mess. Not you. There'd be no money in the bank and a dozen strangers in your bed, but you'd manage to have a little woman slaving down here, producing wonderful food at a moment's notice, while you shagged away upstairs and turned up looking glamorous. And there you go, chatting away to David behind my back, making arrangements, and you don't have to do a single bloody thing that doesn't suit you! Well, I've been raising your children and caring for them, bringing them up as Christians in a Godless world, doing the best I could! I don't expect thanks. St Ignatius Loyola told us to give and not to count the cost. But if this is the reward I get, then I've had enough.'

She fell into a kitchen chair and put her head in her hands. Celia gave a shaky little laugh.

'Adam Partridge is coming to dinner,' said Ellen in explanation. 'Mum didn't know.'

'He's a racing driver,' added Lucy. 'Dad's hired him to test the Sheraton – he was really pleased he agreed to come. But he's used to posh hotels and things. And he's bringing his wife.'

All was clear. Celia looked at Heather's bent head. Serves you right, she thought aggressively. That's what you get for invading. She thought of taking the girls and just leaving, letting Heather stew in this mess. But of course she couldn't. This was a business thing, and the business was important. So dinner must be provided, somehow.

She turned the knife a little. 'Why didn't David suggest you all go out?' she asked, pretending innocence.

Heather snarled, 'Trust you to think up the spendthrift solution! Do you know how much it costs nowadays?'

'Thirty pounds a head,' said Celia. 'Cheap at the price, I'd have thought. Don't worry, I'll sort you out. Girls, get some newspaper and clear up the floor.'

Heather sat, bemused, while Celia made an aloof inspection of the foodstuffs. There was salad, and the peculiar prawns, and of course the veal. 'We could do French prawn salad to start,' suggested Celia to the girls. 'With deep fried croutons, all mixed in.'

'The prawns looked a bit iffy to me,' said Heather, forced into speech. 'Everyone might die.'

'Who cares if they do? Let's live dangerously! We'll make the dressing with lots of vinegar and pickle the bugs.'

Ellen and Lucy began to giggle, getting into the spirit of this meal. Celia flourished a salad basket and showered them all with water.

Heather sat up. 'Don't make everything a mess! Can't you be sensible for once?'

'Look where sense has got you!' trilled Celia. 'Miserable and sour. Now, for the main course – what?'

'I thought a sort of blanquette for the main course. Vegetables and things – the freezer's full.'

'Oh, I'm sure it is,' said Celia. 'You spent all summer filling it, I suppose. Hours and hours of labour. Weeks and weeks of digging. I do so admire you, Heather. Such solid worth when I'm so flighty. But do get on with your blanquette. I shall do a hot pudding. Jam roly-poly and custard. If there's some fresh fruit as an alternative you should be all right, even if his wife's a Jewish vegetarian with an allergy to wheat.' She struck a pose to make the girls laugh.

'Or a Muslim diabetic with a weight problem,' added Ellen. 'We'll do the table.'

'You haven't even finished the floor,' said Heather. 'You girls have no idea what thoroughness means!'

By the time the floor was mopped and the meal begun it was nearly seven. Ellen and Lucy laid the table erratically, and Heather insisted on teaching them exactly how to do it right, quite regardless of the time. In the flurry that followed, everyone rushing, someone let the dog in. He stepped on an unseen shard of glass and bled dramatically. Heather screamed, abandoned her cooking, and had to be restrained from calling an ambulance. Instead she was sent to find a tennis sock which could be sacrificed as a bandage.

Celia, first course concluded, moved on to the blanquette. Heather's sauce was lumpy so she threw it away and made fresh, adding herbs and chopped mushrooms, a bit of green pepper she found mouldering in the fridge, a handful of grated cheese to add zest and some mustard, because it occurred to

287

her. By a quarter to eight the vegetables were done, and Celia was wrestling with jam roly-poly. Heather was persuaded to stop searching for little lace mats for the backs of all the chairs and was despatched upstairs to get dressed.

'What about us?' asked Ellen, licking the jam spoon. 'We were going out.'

'We'll still go,' said Celia. 'Fancy fish and chips?'

'Pizza. It was jolly nice of you to help.'

'Yes. Wasn't it? I'm amazed at my own helpfulness.' She wondered a little at Ellen's trust. She could hardly disguise the cold, hard rage she felt for Heather. And yet Ellen didn't see it at all.

She heard a car, David and the Partridge couple. Heather came downstairs and, peeping, Celia saw she had overdressed. David and the Partridges were in casual clothes, while Heather was done up in taffeta. That was the trouble with Heather, she thought. She took everything so terribly seriously.

But Heather was out there, being seriously charming, while Celia hid in the kitchen. The skivvy. The help. There was no justice in this world, she thought, putting the plates and dishes to warm, checking on the pudding, stirring the sauce. When they were all safely in the sitting room she and the girls would sneak quietly away. The girls would tell David who had really created this meal, and the credit would be doubly hers.

She hadn't bargained on David's bonhomie. Searching for ice, he flung into the kitchen, closely followed by the guests, with Heather in the rear trying vainly to hold them up.

'If we can get the suspension sorted,' David was saying, 'then of course a racing model's a possibility. Now we're investing – good God, Celia!'

She raised a hand in mock salute. 'Hello, David. Just – helping out.'

'So I see.' He turned to the Partridges, both smiling expectantly, awaiting the introduction. Mrs Partridge was very small, dressed with casual ease in jeans and a silk shirt.

'Adam – Jane—' said David. 'This is my—' He hesitated, and Celia shot out her hand. 'I'm the girls' mother,' she declared. 'Do call me Celia.'

'Hi, Celia,' said Jane, and Heather added icily, 'I believe Celia was just on her way out.'

With becoming modesty, she began a tactful sidle to the door, only to find David's arm on her wrist, restraining her. 'Stay for a drink, at least. We've been discussing one or two modifications to the Sheraton. I know you'll be interested. We beat the lap record today. Or rather, Adam did it for us. The new engine.'

'The new set? Marvellous!'

And somehow Celia found herself in the sitting room with a drink, listening to the story of the day. It seemed so natural. After all, it wasn't so long since this was her role. She was the charming company wife, glamorous, relaxed, while Heather sat in her stiff dress and looked daggers. Celia hauled herself bodily back to the present. She had made an effort to save this evening from disaster, there was no point in sabotage now. Besides, Heather was easy to beat on this ground. It was in the area of solid worth that the battle must be won.

As soon as her drink was finished Celia put down her glass and got up.

'Look, I promised to take the girls for a pizza. Must dash.'

'You haven't heard the best bit, yet,' said David. 'You know the oversteer problem?'

'Yes, but I've got to go! This isn't my party. Remember?'

'We certainly do,' said Heather bitterly.

Celia retreated, laughing, and David laughed too, going with her to the door. He came back into the room with the laughter still in his face.

The dinner was excellent. It bore all the hallmarks of Celia: the lack of pretension with the salad merely tossed anyhow in a glass bowl, the odd flavours in the sauce as she reached for this or that at whim. Even the pudding was all Celia, the erratic bit of fun. The Partridges, experienced and conscientious socialites, made it their duty to draw Heather out, and David relaxed as she relaxed. They talked politics, and Heather held the economic corner. David wondered why she so rarely showed this side of her personality, the intelligence, the confidence. But she was always stiff and shy.

He had felt critical of her tonight, and was ashamed of

himself. But Celia's glamour and charm extinguished Heather. They reduced her to nothing. This evening, under the influence of wine and kind people, he glimpsed again the clever, good-hearted, slightly timid woman who had given him a reason, years ago, to go on living.

It was late when Celia took the girls home. She dropped them off and waited until they turned at the door, and waved. They would be tired tomorrow, and Heather would be angry. She would write a stiff note of complaint. Celia drove away, tired herself, dreamily following the road until it arrived at the house. A single light burned in the kitchen, and everywhere else was dark. Charles was away still, but Dorrie might be up. But when she went in she saw that Charles had come home.

'Oh. I thought you were Dorrie.'

'She's in bed. You're very late.'

He sounded accusing. Celia lifted her eyebrows and went to the stove, putting the kettle on. 'Yes,' she said provocatively.

'Have you been out with someone?'

She laughed. 'What do you think?'

He stood watching her, his face very hard. Celia was nervous of him suddenly. 'I took the girls for a pizza,' she said, too cowardly to tease him any more. 'We were late setting off.'

'You didn't have to pretend, then.'

She shrugged. 'I'm not a child, Charles. You didn't have to ask.'

A vase of late roses stood in the window. They were windblown and shaggy, refugees brought in from the storms. The reds were like blood. He wondered why he felt such a terrible need to tell her he was sorry, what indeed he was sorry for. Seduction? She had asked to be seduced. Betrayal? There was nothing to betray. Oh God, he thought suddenly, on a rising note of panic. Oh God. How had this happened? Despite all his vigilance, how was it possible? He was on a downhill slide into love.

The kettle had boiled and Celia was making tea. He stood watching her, the careful protection of her weak side, the touching way she cradled her right wrist against her body. She

290

was very tired tonight, he could always tell. She glanced up and saw him watching her.

'I'm sorry, Charles. I know you feel guilty about what we did, but it can't be undone now.'

'Does – does Dorrie know?'

Celia shook her head. Her hair skimmed the back of her neck and he felt a surge of real desire, as if he hadn't had enough of that, as if he didn't still feel tainted by it. He wondered who she had really seen tonight. David, or someone else? He knew the slow, hot gnawing of jealousy.

'Where did you take the girls?'

'I told you. For a pizza. What is it, Charles?'

'Which restaurant?'

'I know you're not writing a guide to pizza eating. Where do you think I was?' He said nothing, but held her gaze. She looked away, into her teacup. 'I was with my daughters,' she said quietly.

He felt a great wave of relief. He couldn't have borne to know that she would sleep with other men! He took hold of her shoulders and held her, knowing he was exhausted, that she was weak, that he had resolved only that day never to touch her again.

She said, 'I hate you to be angry with me. I don't understand why you are.'

'I know you don't.' He pulled her close to him, and she slid her arms around his neck, resting her head against him like a weary child. Still sore from the night, still guilty, he felt the beginnings of desire. He moved against her, hinting at sex, and she put back her head for his kiss. He tasted pizza and a soft, smoky red wine. Then, denying his own obvious arousal, he let her go. She stared at him in puzzlement. 'What a strange man you are.'

He brought her a mug of tea and sat on the bed while she drank. She studied him through the steam. Deep furrows ran from nose to mouth, quite straight. Everything about him was straight, thought Celia. He thought in straight, logical, unforgiving lines.

'Sometimes I think you despise your patients,' she said.

291

'Rubbish!'

'No it's not. You do. It's what protects you from them. You tell yourself that you would never be so stupid as to be that ill.'

He tried feebly to defend himself. 'I never despised you!'

'But you did. Admit it. You thought I was a fool.'

'Never.'

'Admit it! You thought I was a rich bitch. I got what I deserved from driving too fast.'

'I don't think that now.'

'Then what? With your new softness. Your human understanding.'

He sighed, as if he was giving up. Letting go. Releasing his hold on resistance. 'I don't know. I think you should sleep.'

She stretched back in the bed, her arms above her head, her breasts heavy against the lace of her nightgown. Charles felt a new and frightening despair. Drained as he was, sated as he was, he still wanted her. This was a disease he could die for! He leaned down and kissed her again. If she asked him what he had done he would tell her everything, he decided, each stupid and lustful thing. But her mouth was cool and pure, the touch of her lips a benediction. He felt cleansed.

Chapter Nineteen

Celia awoke heavy-eyed, to the sound of a shrilling telephone bell. She staggered out of bed, wondering where everyone was, and saw that it was half past ten. Charles would be at work and Dorrie painting, oblivious to telephones. Rain was lashing the windows, and she stood on the cold floor of the hall. 'Hello?'

'Is that you, Mrs Sheraton? Hector Lowndes here. I've found something.'

'Something? What?' She was still befuddled from sleep.

'I can't talk over the phone. Can you come into the office after lunch?'

She agreed, and put the receiver down. Then she stood for minutes, wondering what Lowndes might be going to say.

He was in more than his usual chaos, with paper everywhere. Dusty files lay in heaps on the floor, and an old set of golf clubs was propped against one wall.

'I found those,' he said cheerfully. 'Amazing what turns up when you have a clear-out. Feather-filled golf balls. Quite a find!'

Celia smiled politely. A pile of yellowing documents lay on the desk, riveting her attention. She pulled them towards her and began to leaf through.

'Most of it's irrelevant,' said Lowndes. 'Ancient tax dodges. But this – well, take a look.'

It wasn't in her father's hand, which was disappointing. The typed sheets were on ordinary paper, so it was clearly a draft. But Celia read it with increasing excitement:

> My beloved daughter Celia, following her accident, is
> not in a position to inherit my estate. I am assured that

293

she will never be in such a position. Since it has always been my intention to leave her as my sole beneficiary (notwithstanding the personal bequests I may make, detailed elsewhere), I find myself in difficulties. A bequest of this magnitude is not one to be made lightly. I have decided, therefore, to leave the majority of my estate – that is, my companies, properties, shareholdings, personal effects including vehicles and jewellery, insurance monies and monies in hand, to my grand-daughters, Ellen and Lucy, divided equally and in trust until each reaches the age of twenty-five. Application may be made to the estate by their father, David Sheraton, for the following:

1. School expenses. A list of designated schools is attached. Such expenses to include fees, clothing, entertainment and any activity that can reasonably be considered educational. Both girls are to receive sound scientific and business training, since it is my fond hope that they will each wish to partake in the management of the businesses I leave in their care.

2. Ponies. As required, capital cost and upkeep. Not less than two thousand pounds to be spent on each animal. I will not have my grand-daughters mounted on some scrub animal that cannot be trusted. Hard hats to be worn at all times.

3. Cars. On their seventeenth birthday, each girl is to receive a motor vehicle. It is to be of the make at that time considered safest by a reputable motoring organisation. All running expenses will be borne by the estate.

4. Clothes. To a maximum of ten thousand pounds annually, per girl. Nothing to be made of leather except shoes and accessories. I will not have fifteen year olds prancing about in skintight leather trousers.

If any of these matters is neglected, or if it is felt that
David Sheraton has departed in fact or in spirit from
my clearly expressed intentions, the estate will revert
to my residual beneficiary, Edwin Braddock, my
trustee and executor.

The paper was unsigned. Celia looked up from it, bewildered.
'This is it, of course. But anyone could have written it! No
date, no signature, nothing. Just a piece of typing.'
  'Read the copy letter,' said Lowndes.
  Celia did so.

  Dear Joe,
  I have pleasure in enclosing the final draft of your Will,
  for your approval. Should you have any wish to alter
  anything, please do not hesitate to telephone me, but I
  am sure that this time we have covered all eventualities.
  Unless I hear to the contrary, then, I shall bring the
  finished copy to you on Friday evening as arranged, for
  your signature and retention. I would once again remind
  you that it is often advisable to lodge a Will with your
  legal adviser, in order to avoid misunderstandings, but
  of course I leave that entirely to your discretion.
  With all good wishes,
  Yours,
  Jeremy Lowndes

Lowndes said, 'I believe a copy of the final document was
lodged in our strongroom. It went missing.'
  Celia looked up, fiercely. 'So it was your father?'
  A pause. Lowndes said, 'I don't know.'
  She sat back in her chair. It was what she had hoped, what
she had expected, but now that she read the words she felt it
was more than she deserved. Her father hadn't deserted her.
In his grief he hadn't turned away. The wind sent another
rainshower clattering against the glass. She stirred and said
dreamily, 'What now? Can we take this to court?'
  Lowndes nodded. 'It's the basis of a good case. I'm sure

you'll win, or at least force them to make a settlement out of court. After all, if you throw Edwin Braddock's business record at him it's going to seem as if your father left his life's achievement in the hands of an incompetent.'

'It's not that bad, surely?'

He tossed a pink newspaper across to her. There was a two-page analysis of Braddock Corporation. The last words were, 'The failed takeover of the Marlborough Gaming Group has left Braddock highly geared, over-borrowed and vulnerable. Against this we must set the innate profitability of some sectors of the business, and the large holding in Marlborough, although this stock declines daily. Braddock's, this once proud group, is clearly under pressure, and any investors fearing to take a loss must hope the company's lenders feel similarly, and take a generous view.'

'He should sell Linton Place,' said Celia dully.

'He'd rather have your trust fund.'

'And—' She stopped, thinking about the pearls. All she had intended was to snatch back her mother's jewels, and in so doing had painfully tweaked Braddock's nose. For years now he had kept the pearls as rainy day money, and here he was in a downpour with the umbrella gone. No wonder he was angry.

She took a copy of the papers Lowndes had shown her, stuffing them in her handbag. 'You have further copies?' she asked anxiously. 'You'll keep them safe?'

'Yes – yes.' He wasn't taking her seriously and she felt a rising panic.

'Keep them in the strongroom,' she advised. 'Really, Hector! It's important. This isn't a game.'

The light was fading as she left. The dark afternoon was giving in to evening without a fight. Her raincoat felt heavy and cumbersome, even her head felt heavy on the inadequate stem of her neck. She knew she shouldn't have come this afternoon. But she would soon be home.

She got into the car and switched on the heater and the wipers, forgetting that Dorrie's battery wasn't up to such things. The starter whirred miserably and she switched everything off and tried again. This time the engine fired, and she could run the wipers. Some of the money from the pearls must go to buy Dorrie a new car, she thought. But first things first. She had to collect evidence from the time of her father's death, and evidence too of Braddock's mismanagement. Together, those things would sink the man.

In the small confines of the car her coat was too bulky for comfort. She shrugged her arms out of it, shivering, and peered through the smeared space on her windscreen into the gloomy night. The traffic lights were green and she accelerated, but at the last moment they changed to amber. She trod on the brakes to stop, but the coat, its length gathered on the floor, got in the way. The lights were red and upon her, she had to stop! She stamped again, and the car twisted sideways in a murderous skid.

Instinct saved her. Years ago, when she was seventeen, her father had sent her on a safe driving course. She had learned to skid before she learned to reverse, and she swung the wheel automatically, catching the spinning motion and controlling it. At the same time she touched the accelerator, and the little car slid into the kerb. The oncoming traffic swished past, and a man knocked on the window.

'You all right, love? Could've been nasty.'

She nodded. 'Yes. I'm OK. It was the wet.'

'You were lucky.'

She got out on shaking legs and folded up the raincoat, putting it in a bundle on to the back seat. When the lights changed again she drove carefully away, longing without reason to get home.

Over dinner, a bean thing Dorrie had prepared, she foolishly told them what had happened. Charles was suddenly furious. 'Bloody hell, Celia, you could have been killed! That's it, then. You're not to drive.'

'I won't be a burden to people. I won't be a prisoner. It was the rain and my mac, nothing else.'

'It was your own damned incompetence! Have you any idea how many people I treat who have been run down by idiots like you?'

'I didn't run anyone down.'

'By your own admission, that was luck. You've got no sense of responsibility. Let me tell you, it's time I had your licence revoked. I'm damned if I'll let you career about, risking everything.'

Her anger rose up to meet his. Nothing had changed between them. This was the old Charles, dictatorial and opinionated. 'Don't you dare try and stop me driving,' she flared.

'I will do what I must. For your safety and other people's.'

'God, but you're pompous! I'm safer behind the wheel than most people. Probably safer than you. You don't own me, Charles. You're not my Svengali. You didn't buy the right to my life with your miracle cure, and you didn't buy it in bed, or by letting me stay here, or any other way! You don't own me, you don't control me, and I won't have you think that you do!'

Dorrie said, 'He might be right about the driving. He is your doctor.'

Celia turned her fierce blue stare on her friend. 'Don't you take his side too! I made a slight mistake, that's all. I corrected it. I am not a bad driver.' She got up and left the room.

Charles and Dorrie looked at one another. 'Are you really sleeping together?' asked Dorrie.

He shrugged. 'Don't know. Probably not, judging by that.'

'Don't look so miserable!' Dorrie began to clear the plates. 'She doesn't like being crossed and never has.'

'She's like a wilful child.'

'Don't be silly, Charles. She's no more childish than you, because you each want exactly what suits you, and nothing else will do.'

He felt a spurt of irritation, like being flicked with a lead-tipped whip. 'It's hardly broad-minded to let her drive around as if she was well. She could kill someone. Her victim could end up on my operating table.'

Dorrie considered him. 'But she's right in one way. You want to own her, if you don't think you already do. How you cling, Charles.'

They were silent for long minutes. He went to the fridge and fetched a beer. 'She's making it impossible for me to do my work,' he said abruptly.

Dorrie snapped, 'Don't exaggerate.'

'I never exaggerate. Give me some credit for scientific method, please.'

'There's nothing scientific about your need for sexual domination. In charge and on top, that's you, Charles.'

'Bloody hell, Dorrie!' He was blazing with anger now, and it took him beyond discretion. 'Don't you think I have a right to be paid back for what she's done? Before her I had everything under control. All right, I had little private life, but so what? I had a career, and that was important to me. It still is. But when I woke her up I really opened Pandora's box. I found I couldn't stop thinking about her, worrying about what she was doing, bloody caring! Which was OK to start with. She was in the hospital, under my control, and it wasn't even too bad when she left at first, because she needed me. But now, all she thinks about, all she sodding cares about, is what went before. David. Her children. Her other life. And she doesn't give a damn about me.'

'Why should she give a damn? You were doing your job.'

'But you ought to give a damn about people who love you.'

The word hung in the air between them. Dorrie gave a quizzical little laugh and drained her wine glass. 'Poor Charles,' she said.

When Dorrie went off to bed, Charles began drinking. He felt miserable tonight. He, who fought with all and sundry, couldn't rest while Celia was angry with him. His third whisky made him no less miserable, only miserably light-headed. He couldn't bear to go to bed like this.

He went slowly upstairs, and paused outside her room. He wanted to knock, but thought that Dorrie might hear. From the silence he imagined Celia asleep, so he slowly turned the handle and went in.

She sat up, and he saw that she was naked. She had been crying. The photographs of the children, much thumbed, lay by the bed.

'I was waiting for you. You won't really stop me driving?'

He shook his head. 'No. But you've got to tell me where you're going. It's dangerous, no one knowing where you are.'

'You just want to keep tabs on me. You can't stop me, you

know. If I want to see David, I will.'

David. Always David. He stood at the foot of the bed, looking down at her. Her skin was as pale and delicate as the wing of a butterfly. He would bruise it with kisses, mark her as his own. The notion excited him, and he began to unfasten his shirt. It was the whisky, freeing him to do as he wished. Would she think about David? He felt a sudden surge of power, of sheer virility. In this bed, tonight, there would be no room for anyone but them.

Edwin Braddock lay sprawled next to his companion. He was relaxed, in that rare mood of tranquillity that comes after sex. He leaned across and ran a hand down Peter Cartwright's back. The boy recoiled, and Edwin felt his mood shadow a little.

'Didn't you like it?' he asked suddenly.

'You don't care if I did or not.'

'But you did like it. Admit it. What's a little pain between – friends?'

Peter turned his face into the pillow. He had shamed himself tonight. Braddock had discovered some need in him, for approval and humiliation at one and the same time. He was beginning to despise himself. What flaw was there in him that he could not resist pain? The fist would strike him, bring him to tears, and then, in an instant, caress.

Edwin said, 'You worry too much. Don't you see how free we are? People like us can do anything we want. No one's made any rules, and God, if there is a God, doesn't know that we exist.' He slid across the bed, pressing himself against Peter's naked back. 'We're free. Entirely free. We can forget guilt, forget about namby-pamby love. Find out about this!'

Beneath him, Peter groaned. In this unequal partnership he had no choice.

When it was over he got up and went to shower. Edwin didn't like him to stay, not all night, he had to be up and gone, leaving his employer to greet him at work as if he had seen nothing of him since five the night before. Edwin called this freedom, but Peter knew he wasn't free. He was shackled by need.

He and Edwin were both outcasts. They were forever doomed to wander, meeting and parting, using and discarding, discarded themselves.

Letting the shower cascade over his face, he wondered despairingly, why didn't Edwin care about his loneliness? Wasn't he lonely himself?

As he dressed and prepared to leave, Edwin lay on the bed, apparently sleeping. Peter's resentment grew. Since this thing had begun he had lost touch with other friends, letting Edwin fill his life with this sterile and bitter connection. It was time to strike out again. He thought of a club he used to go to, small and rather seedy, the first place he had ever found where a man like him could know he was not alone. He glanced at his watch. It was late, but not so late. He would go there.

Edwin lay in a half sleep listening to the car as it drove away. He wished he had not let Peter go. The boy was unhappy tonight, a little out of his depth. After a moment, when the noise had died away into heavy, constricting silence, Edwin got up and let the dogs back into the room. They climbed on the bed and stretched on the floor, wagging their tails in satisfaction, and he was jealous of them suddenly; they were each other's companions before they were his. Why had he sent Peter home?

He tossed and turned for almost an hour, but it was no use. He got up and dressed, while the dogs watched him blearily, not in the least anxious to go out at this time of night. Edwin left them in the bedroom, clattering out of the house with a fine disregard for noise. As he drove away he saw Feodor's face at one window and the dogs watching from another. He grinned.

He drove to a small, neat bungalow on the edge of a village. Most of the houses were in darkness, but here a light was burning. Edwin took out a key and let himself in through the front door, calling out, 'Hello! It's me.'

The air of the hall smelled cold. He went through to the sitting room, where the gas fire burned, but there was no one there. He looked about with a sense of weary familiarity. Everything was tidy and well polished. The *Reader's Digest* was neatly set out on a shelf, held up by an amateurish bookend. Edwin had made that himself in woodwork, years ago. He picked it up to look at it and the magazines slid down with a gentle sigh. He put everything back, carefully.

'Edwin.'

'Hello, Father.'

The older man was tall and grey, his hair parted exactly in the middle and swept back over his ears. He was wearing a smoking jacket over a shirt, neat grey trousers, and slippers. 'Why are you here?'

'I couldn't sleep.'

'That doesn't surprise me. I'll make a cup of tea.'

Edwin followed him through to the kitchen. The counter was pale yellow plastic, rubbed almost white in places, but again there was the remarkable neatness. The teabags were stacked in precise rows in a small wooden box. Edwin got out two mugs and waited for his father to make the tea.

'I saw that article,' said Mr Braddock, warming the pot.

'In the *FT*? A set-up. Marlborough trying to weaken us.'

'I considered it impartial.'

Edwin turned away. There it was again, unrelenting. The constant pressure, the endless demands. Edwin remembered the time he had made a miracle catch in school cricket, he who had never had any ball sense, and his father had said, 'Next time, do it with some style, Edwin.'

When the tea was made they went back to the fire to drink it. The clock in the hall struck three, but neither the old man nor the younger one seemed weary.

They talked desultorily about the firm. Edwin's father got up to fetch the newspaper cutting, and began to read paragraphs. The scene had a grim familiarity, it was like a re-run of every year end, with Edwin's report card under scrutiny. He got up when the tea was drunk, although his father had in no sense finished.

'I'll be off then.'

The older man looked at him, his eyes unfaded by the least glimmer of age. 'So. What do you mean to do?'

'I haven't decided. I didn't come here to talk business.'

'What then?' He looked at his son uncomprehendingly. And Edwin despaired.

He went to the door, leaving his mug where it was, although that was another black mark. He never left this house without anger. It was part of him, part of his life. He wished, as he always did, that he had never come.

His father said, 'Let me know next time. I'm sick of having you turn up whenever you please.'

On the way home, restless, he decided to go to a club. He parked discreetly some distance away, and walked in the shadows of the pavement. It was never sensible to be seen openly frequenting such a place. But then, as he drew near, he saw Peter Cartwright, standing under a light, talking with animation to a short little bloke in a checked jacket. Peter. His Peter. He felt a sudden surge of white-hot rage, the anger he had felt at his father, distilled and concentrated. He stopped and waited, emotion rolling and tossing inside him like a volcanic sea. He watched Peter talking, gesticulating, tossing back his head to let forth a guffaw of honest mirth. Why did Peter never laugh like that with him? Because he was the butt of their jokes. To think that he had looked tenderly upon this man, and was betrayed. First the man in Strasbourg, and now this. Every time, the wheel came full circle and crushed him. He turned and ran back to his car.

Chapter Twenty

Heather was in her office, working conscientiously through yet another balance sheet. Essentially numerate, she couldn't help but extract sense from the columns and columns of figures she was required to assess. But somehow, she never became a partner.

They excused themselves by saying she was only part-time. She did the work of two, but since she left at three-thirty every day it was conveniently assumed she wasn't serious about her career. Younger and less able men and women used her as a sounding board, picking her brains for clever ideas. Before Celia, she hadn't minded, her priority had been hearth and home. Now, newly insecure, she wished she had been less generous.

One of the secretaries buzzed through. 'Miss Wilcox? There's a gentleman here. A Mr Cartwright. He wants to talk to someone urgently, and no one else is in.'

Heather sighed. It was probably a bankrupt. They usually turned up in a panic at a moment's notice. Neglected, they were quite likely to jump off a bridge. 'Send him in, please. And bring some tea.'

'Yes, Miss Wilcox.'

Heather cleared a space on her desk, and was sitting, looking efficient, when the man came in. Young, younger than she expected, with a swelling bruise on his cheek. He looked nervous and very much on edge. 'Mr Cartwright?' Heather stood up and extended her hand. 'Do sit down.'

'Thank you.'

He was twisting and untwisting his fingers, and he was deathly white. Heather felt a little uneasy, you read such things nowadays. But the poor man seemed on the verge of

305

collapse. Heather said, 'A financial problem, I take it? Do take your time. I can assure you I've heard them all.'

'I bet you haven't,' said Cartwright. 'Not like this, anyway.'

'What's so special about it?'

He looked at her for a long, tense moment. 'Can you tell that I'm gay?' he said at last.

Heather was taken aback. Nonetheless her analytical mind took in his neat haircut, smart clothes, his general air of self-awareness. That was unusual in a man. Given time, she might have suspected. 'I wouldn't have noticed anything if you hadn't said,' she managed at last.

He grinned, miserably. 'Wouldn't you? I often wonder. I always think everybody knows. Odd, when they don't.'

'Yes.'

She wondered if he was mad, and if so, how she could get out of this. But he didn't look dangerous.

She said, 'Does being – homosexual – have anything to do with why you're here?'

'Oh, yes.' He nodded vigorously. 'It couldn't have happened otherwise, so there must be a lesson there somewhere. I've been having an affair with my employer. It was going OK, if you can call it that. We weren't – close. But something's upset him and he's sacked me.'

'Because of work, or – not?'

He grimaced. 'Not. The thing is – obviously I can't appeal against the sacking, not if I want to work again. And he's left me in a fix with my tax. He gave me presents.'

Heather pulled her note pad towards herself. 'How much?'

'I can't remember exactly.'

'Rough figures.'

He shrugged. 'I don't know. Five hundred here, a thousand there. It mounted up. I bought a car, things like that. He said he'd see to it that the payments went into the books as something else and I wouldn't have to pay tax. Now he says he's going to shop me to the Inland Revenue, and make it seem as if I evaded paying altogether. I don't see what I can do.'

Heather looked down at her blotter. She must relate this tale at her Bible study group. It would be a salutary lesson, especially to the pimply young boy she had long suspected of

306

effeminacy. 'How much have you had?' she asked.

'About – about five thousand in all. I can't exactly remember.'

'He might be bluffing. He might not say a word.'

Cartwright nodded. 'I know. And he was in a state, he might change his mind when he calms down. But he's going abroad any day. He's trying to get control of some gambling clubs, and if he's shopped me already I'm done for!'

Heather kept her face absolutely still. Cartwright. Yes, she knew that name. Braddock's right-hand man. 'Can you tell me who you worked for?' she asked casually. 'In strictest confidence, of course.'

'I really don't want to say. It is highly confidential.'

She inclined her head. 'Of course.' Anyway, she was sure. David had always said Braddock was unnatural.

And the first task was to extricate this foolish young man from the situation in which he found himself. He must volunteer his payment and claim that he believed tax to have been deducted at source. She explained her strategy quite carefully.

'You realise I haven't a bean?' he said, with his charming smile. 'I'm useless with money. Spend it the moment it comes in.'

Heather blew down her nose, her habit when annoyed. 'You're going to have to find some from somewhere,' she said tartly. 'In fact, if I may say so, this is the moment to think about what sort of person you are and where you mean to go in life. We are all God's children, you know. It does us no good to cause our Father grief. Come along. Let's make an assessment of your position.'

Over dinner that night, amidst the girls' chatter, Heather decided against telling David about her visitor. She toyed with the idea of telling Braddock, but put it out of her mind. The young man today had been cruelly used. Braddock was more of a devil than she had supposed, and if she supped with him she must indeed use a long spoon. Yes, she would keep her own counsel.

'Miss Phillips is going to go completely bonkers one of these days,' Ellen was saying. 'She's obsessed with knickers. Green knickers. She thinks the world will end if we don't wear them.'

'She's only trying to uphold the standards of the school,' intoned Heather, taking the party line.

'Celia says she's a frustrated spinster with piles,' said Lucy.

There was a stunned silence. Heather managed, 'I'm sure Celia said nothing of the kind.'

David gave a snort of laughter. 'Don't be so sure. Sounds just like Celia. Don't repeat that sort of thing, girls.'

As soon as the meal was over and they were both at the kitchen sink, Heather hissed, 'You've got to talk to her, David! She can't go on saying things like that to children. She's quite mad herself.'

'Then she always was,' said David. 'You know she won't listen to anything I say.'

Heather's cheeks flew bright spots of colour. 'I know nothing of the kind! If you must know I think she does everything you want, and you're so stupid you can't see what she's at. She wants to get you back, you know. Yes, she does!'

Groping for words, David said, 'I don't think that at all. She knows that I won't change my life. Not now.'

Heather twisted a tea towel in her hands. 'Why not? Do you just feel sorry for me?'

'No! No, of course not. Heather, what is the matter tonight? I've never seen you so on edge.'

She gathered herself. 'I'm fine. Really. It's just – oh, David, why do we have so many secrets nowadays? I can't talk to you. It's as if she's there all the time, listening.'

He said, 'What did you want to tell me?'

Turning back to the sink Heather let it out in a rush of words. 'Braddock's assistant came to me today over a tax problem. He and Edwin have been having an affair. He happened to say – he told me that Edwin's going to Europe to get control of the clubs over there. And I don't want you to tell Celia.'

After a moment he said, 'Damn it all, Heather! We've mortgaged our house to help her fight Braddock. And you won't tell her something this vital. If Braddock gets control of Marlborough, it could seriously weaken her case.'

'So you do want her to win.'

'Yes! Yes, of course I do.'

'And then she'll not only be young, beautiful and charming, she'll be rich! What are you waiting for, David? Why don't you pick your cherry now? I'm sure she's more than willing.'

Ellen's head appeared round the door. She was supposed to be doing her homework. 'You're not having a row or something, are you?' she asked anxiously. 'I mean, Lucy didn't say anything to Miss Phillips. It's not as if we repeated what she said.'

David glanced briefly at his daughter before returning his gaze to Heather. 'It doesn't matter at all about Miss Phillips. Go upstairs, Ellen.'

'Are you having a row?'

'Go upstairs!' Heather screamed at her, and Ellen, terrified, retreated.

'I want you to talk to Celia,' said David.

'Never!'

'But you must! This is really important.'

Heather glared at him. 'See how she's changed you! Now it's all money, money, money. So she doesn't win. So what? We'll just go on as we used to do. Calmly. Sensibly.'

David's pale eyes were fixed on her. He was wondering how it was that Heather seemed to have changed. She had been his rock, his certainty, her principles solid. Only now she seemed unsure.

He said, 'You know we're both sick of scraping by. What is it, Heather? I won't leave you for her, I promise.'

She turned and flung hungry arms around his neck. He held her, patting her shoulder dispassionately. After a moment he put her away from him a little. 'We'll go and see her together,' he said. 'Tonight.'

They interrupted the Davenport household whilst they were eating. Charles opened the door and grunted, 'Oh. It's you. Come in, if you must.'

David and Heather stepped into the room, looking curiously around. Even the short time of Dorrie and Celia's stay had changed the house. The kitchen was warm and smelled of good food, there were curtains at the windows and a

309

rug on the floor. Light fell on the table, but all around was in shadow. The room seemed cosy and welcoming.

'Hello, David. Heather. Is everything all right?' Celia's first thoughts sprang to the children. She put down her fork.

'Everyone's fine,' said David. 'We just wanted to talk something over. Finish your meal.'

'Get a glass and pull up a chair,' said Charles, helping himself to more of Celia's casserole.

Perching uncomfortably on her chair, Heather wondered why on earth she went to such trouble over food. The pine table was bare of any cloth, and dishes stood on old and tattered rush mats. The wine bottle presided like a mast above salad and bread and good, thick stew, and a tray of baked apples stood on the Aga, cooling enough to be served. It seemed to her just then that in everything Celia seemed to come out best. Charles opened another bottle of wine, and Heather consoled herself with the thought that they were all obviously alcoholics.

Celia was only too glad of the drink. She felt flustered. Her life in this house was separate from her family, and she liked it that way. What's more, she wasn't prepared for David. She wasn't at her best. When she saw him she liked to have every hair in place, every nail varnished, even her underwear neat and uncreased. And now he saw her without make-up, the table bare of any cloth, bohemian to the point of slovenliness. She felt at a complete disadvantage.

When the meal was done, the table cleared but for coffee and wine, Charles leaned back in his chair. 'Now, to what do we owe this honour? Has dear Edwin burned your house down too?'

'What?' Celia squawked in horror.

David had the effrontery to laugh. 'Nothing of the kind. It's Heather's story. She had a visitor today.'

'I'm sorry. I don't want to say. It was David's idea that we come.'

'Heather,' said David gently, 'we agreed.'

Celia said, 'I'm sure we don't want to hear anything that contradicts Heather's principles. I'm not up to divine retribution.'

'I should think you've had your share already,' said Heather nastily. Celia confounded her by laughing.

Charles said, 'If we could get to the point, ladies. We don't have to fight World War Three.'

Heather sniffed and shifted in her seat. 'My client was Peter Cartwright,' she said frostily. 'He's been sacked.'

Celia looked puzzled. 'Why did he come and see you?'

'I *am* an accountant. Braddock's threatening to shop him to the Inland Revenue for tax evasion. Cartwright was given presents which weren't declared, and of course it's all been spent. His only hope is to say he thought the firm had paid the tax, or his code was going to be adjusted or something, and cough up now. But he hasn't the money. He came to me in a flat panic.'

Dorrie and Celia exchanged amazed glances. 'Poor Peter Cartwright,' said Celia.

'He seemed like a nice boy,' said Dorrie. 'What's going to happen to him?'

'He'll probably spend the next few years under a load of debt,' snapped Heather. 'Isn't that what usually happens to people who get out of their depth? Ordinary people, that is. People like Celia just persuade others to pay.'

'Do you have to be such a cow?' Celia got up and put on the kettle. She kept her back to them all, visibly fuming, and David shifted in his chair, uncomfortably.

Dorrie said, 'Why don't we offer to pay his tax? In return for – well, inside information.'

'I'm not some sort of spy,' flashed Heather.

David said, 'He's already told her one thing. Braddock's going to Europe to try and gain control of the Marlborough clubs there.'

'What?' Celia spun round. 'But he can't! He mustn't!'

'Why not?' asked Charles.

She gestured angrily. 'Because it's the right thing to do. If he gets the clubs then he could turn them round, and when I stand up and say my father never intended that he should inherit, because the man's a fool and has made a mess of it now he has, Braddock will be able to point to his shining successes and make nonsense of me. And if he's doing OK he won't have any

311

incentive to settle out of court and we might have to fight it to the death. Can't you see? It's a disaster!'

'He might not succeed,' said David, mildly, and Celia turned on him with scorn.

'We can't just sit back and hope for the best! Now, was this planned, or is it a spur of the moment sort of thing? A winter offensive. Heather, where's he going first?'

'Good heavens, I don't know,' she said and Celia replied, murderously, 'Then you'd better just go and find out.'

When they had gone, and Dorrie had gone to paint, Celia sat for a long time at the table. Her thoughts were like arrows tonight, thudding into a target. Her aim was improving, she felt herself coming nearer and nearer to the bull. There was only one thing to do for now – confound Braddock. He must not be permitted to take over the Marlborough clubs. She must stop him.

At last, with a yawn, she came back to the present. Charles was at the other end of the table, working.

'What are you doing?' she asked.

'What?' He glanced up. 'Nothing much. I've got a patient transferred from another hospital. Intractable epilepsy following trauma. I'm trying to see if there's something they missed. The notes are terrible, tell me nothing at all.'

'Will you cure him?'

'God knows.'

Celia pondered the short reply. He wasn't being flippant. God was the only arbiter. In her own case, Charles had taken the trouble but God had done the work. Why? What was the purpose of her untimely return? Perhaps there was no purpose and she was simply a death gone wrong. A heavenly oversight – even, perhaps, a devilish intent. She said to him, 'Do you think I'm wrong to chase my money?'

He looked up. 'What else would you do? Good works?'

'Yes. Possibly. Don't you think I should be more spiritually inclined?'

Charles looked at her. Because she was rumpled tonight, she seemed more overtly sexual. Her blouse was stained near the buttons, on the lower slopes of her breast. This was no nun.

'I think you should get your money back,' he said. 'You can

think about what you do with it after that. Should you decide to live under a banyan tree, wearing sackcloth and chanting mantras, I shall simply commit you to a mental institution and be done.'

Celia laughed at him. 'Fool! Your idea of a worthy life is a knighthood and a Rolls-Royce.'

'What's yours?'

She blinked at him. 'If I knew that I'd live it.'

They sat in silence, as the house sighed and settled for the night, as the owls in the trees stretched their wings and prepared to go out hunting. Celia yawned again, ready now for bed. 'If Heather does find out Edwin's plans, will you come with me?' she asked.

'Come where? You don't mean to chase after him, do you?'

She nodded. 'I must. I know what he's trying to do, you see. I looked into it.'

She moved to his end of the table, and perched next to him, enumerating points on her fingers. 'Edwin holds about thirty-five per cent of Marlborough. He needs over fifty to win. Most of the remaining shares are held by family, but there's a slice in the hands of the individual managers of the clubs. They were given them a few years ago, when Marlborough couldn't afford a salary increase. Now, the shares held by the managers are the most vulnerable holding, perhaps the only vulnerable one, everyone else is sitting very tight and won't let Edwin buy. He's going to offer for those shares in person. And so am I.'

Charles put down his work and folded his hands on top of it. His doctor stance. 'You know, that's not sensible, Celia. You're not up to it.'

'I know. I want you to come with me.'

He took a short, surprised breath. She was a constant source of amazement to him. 'There are people depending on me, Celia! I've got work to do.'

'You're owed masses of holiday, so you could take a week.'

'Think of the gossip!'

'No one need know.'

'And you're not fit!'

'But I'd have my doctor with me. Please, Charles.'

She pouted and fluttered her eyelashes, funny and arousing at one and the same time. He had to admire her style. 'Hussy.'

'Prude. Come on, Charles. One week, that's all. In a minute I'll think you don't fancy me.'

He thought of all the ways in which he could stop her, and none of them would work. He thought of all the things that could happen to her, if she fell ill on foreign soil. Could he stand the anxiety of not being there? Hardly. He really hadn't any choice.

Celia scanned the rushing crowds anxiously. Cartwright had said Edwin was travelling from Heathrow, so there was no reason for him to be in Manchester. Nonetheless she half expected the throng to part and reveal him, watching her. He had the hard, masculine Braddock stare.

She turned to Charles. 'Do I have hard eyes?'

'Nobody has. You have two spheres of gelatinous membrane, just like everyone.'

'Don't be pedantic, please! My father had. And his brother. And their father too. Perhaps I've developed the look. With age.'

Charles sighed, and lowered the scientific paper he'd been studying. 'The only thing you might be developing is long sight.'

She snorted. 'You really are tediously literal, Charles.'

She looked again across the teeming concourse. Of course Braddock wasn't there. Peter Cartwright hadn't known what he was telling, and had no reason to lie. But Heather might have done. Celia's stomach knotted again.

The flight was called, and they made their way to the gate. An Austrian woman, obviously pregnant, waddled along beside them, and Charles muttered, 'I thought airlines forbade travel after seven months.'

'Perhaps it's twins,' said Celia. 'Can you deliver babies?'

Charles grinned. 'No! It's too damned messy. When I was on the wards nurses always poured scorn and shouldered me out of the way.'

They amused themselves making up heroic ways in which he could deliver quins to the Austrian woman during take-off.

But all went smoothly, and Charles settled down for the flight with a gin and tonic and his scientific journals. Celia looked out of the window, wondering why George Marlborough had established a club in Vienna. All she knew about the place was waltzes and cakes.

One of the stewardesses bent down and whispered to Charles. 'Oh my God,' he said despairingly. 'Tell her I'm a brain surgeon.'

The stewardess smiled, a little anxiously, and Celia said, 'He is, actually. But he can do deliveries. He's done hundreds.'

'A mere few dozen, in actual fact.' Charles got gloomily up from his seat.

The Austrian lady was lying on the cabin floor at the front of the plane, beringed hands clasping and unclasping, her face a lather of perspiration. The staff rigged up a curtain while Charles went to wash his hands, watching ruefully as the trolley with his meal went by. This was what happened when you tried to play truant from work. It followed you, like Nemesis, intent on your destruction.

He knelt beside the Austrian woman, saying, 'How many weeks are you? Honestly.'

'Thirty-eight. Please – do not tell!'

'I think they're going to guess, don't you?'

Nonetheless it was a relief. No struggling to rig up an incubator from a meal container and a life jacket. The last birth he had attended had been of a child thought to have sustained rubella damage, and there had been serious complications. He hoped and prayed he would see none of those here.

The examination was reassuring. In all probability the child wouldn't even be born before they landed in Vienna. But that just showed how out of touch he was, because suddenly, while everyone else was tucking into the pudding and considering another drink, she went into second stage.

Time passed. As her contractions progressed the woman developed the disconcerting habit of suddenly shrieking. It was a sign of stress more than anguish, Charles felt, but the surrounding passengers were reduced to pulp. One woman fainted and a man had to be escorted to the rear of the plane, from whence he could still hear the shrieks but less plainly. Finally Celia poked her head around the curtain. 'OK? You're causing terrible consternation out here.'

'We're doing fine,' said Charles. 'Five minutes, I should think.'

'We're all putting on seat belts for the landing. Do hurry up.'

The Austrian woman moaned and muttered in German. Crouched half under a seat, Charles thought his back would break. But the head was in view, topped with a mop of black hair, and within seconds he had extricated a brand new human being. It was a boy, but his airway was blocked. Charles used a straw and sucked out the mucus, and the baby coughed, spluttered, and began living. His mother burst into tears.

Charles left the plane amidst applause, hungry, his papers unread and his trousers covered in unspeakable slime. 'What a hero,' mocked Celia, as he gritted his teeth against the fulsome thanks of the aircrew. His patient was taken off on a stretcher, smiling beatifically, her bemused husband summoned from the air terminal to escort her.

'What a bloody mess,' said Charles, striding away from the plane. 'Hello Vienna.'

Celia stopped in her efforts to keep up with him. 'You're the most unfeeling man I ever met. You've just delivered a baby, for God's sake! It was wonderful. Everyone except you felt like cheering.'

'They didn't have slime all over them.'

He saw their cases on the baggage carousel and dashed off to get them. When he returned he met Celia's stare with one of his charming but meaningless grins. 'Don't expect me to bleed for my patients, Celia. I don't. It's not me. I'm a mechanic for bodies and a mender of minds, and you don't expect the man at the garage to be moved by his work. I look after machines. That's all.'

It began a chill which lasted long into the evening. They had a vast room in a grand hotel full of red plush furniture and mirrors a storey high. The baths were on huge clawed feet, and the taps were shaped like fishes. The rates were extortionate, of course, but Celia didn't care. There was too little time for economy.

Lack of food made Charles grumpy. He showed no sign of good humour until Celia rang down for a tea-tray, and it arrived laden with cakes. He munched his way through three of them, and drank a pot of tea, before leaning back in his chair.

'That's better. Stop glowering at me, Celia. Would you be happy if I'd insisted she call the child after me?'

'You don't deserve to have children, or to deliver them.'

'And you do, I suppose.'

'Yes! At least – oh, Charles, you don't understand. Sometimes I ache for my babies.' She folded her hands across her bosom, for that was where it hurt. She had lost her children's childhood, and it was gone forever.

Outside there was a bell striking the hour. Pigeons cooed on the cold window sill, as if it were spring. Charles was getting changed and Celia went across to him, running her hand over the smooth skin of his back. It was like marriage, the easy companionship, the relaxed and easy sex. Marriage was safe, she thought, bending to press kisses to the ridges of his spine. And she was safe with Charles.

Chapter Twenty-One

They were to visit the Marlborough Club that evening. It was well known in the hotel and Charles had arranged a visiting membership with the clerk on the desk. But as they were dressing, Celia went pale and sat down. Charles took her pulse and said, 'I knew it. You're pushing your luck. Time to stay home.'

'No!'

'Yes! Why bring your medical adviser if you don't do what he says?'

She tried to pout, but failed. 'I had my reasons.'

'Enough of that. Look, I'll go to the club by myself. You never know, it might be best. I gather from the man on the desk that it isn't the sort of place men take their wives.'

But it was the snow that decided her; cold, silent flakes drifting down from a heavy sky. The warm room and soft bed seemed infinitely more inviting. She let Charles tuck her in, wondering how it was that her father had so signally failed to pass on his incredible grit.

In dinner jacket and crisp wing collar, Charles was very smart. He poured Celia brandy, and that at least seemed to put some colour in her cheeks.

'You really are gorgeous this evening,' she said. 'I ought to be coming with you. To save you from rapacious women.'

He grinned and sat on the end of the bed. He didn't quite know what he was supposed to do tonight, but he couldn't say that to her. In the face of her weakness he was obliged to be strong. He felt moved by tenderness towards her, when at other times she could inspire him to rage. Was this love? he thought. He had professed that it was when it was less than now. He felt such a great urge to take care of her.

He closed his eyes for a second, thinking that he had never felt such a threat to his sense of self, his independent, unfettered progress. Celia, watching him, said in alarm, 'What is it, Charles? Don't you feel well either?'

He opened his eyes. 'I'm fine.' He tapped the brandy bottle. 'Drink more of this.'

The club was near the city centre, down a narrow street off a wide boulevard. Vienna was beautiful in the snow, quiet and fairylit. Charles's taxi left him at the end of the street, and he walked the last yards on a coating of thin white fluff. From a distance, in the cold, the club seemed to cast out a yellow, welcoming glow, a beckoning finger of light.

But the impression was false. The place was very down at heel. The girls looked like prostitutes, the man on the door a failed boxer. Charles bought a drink, something sticky and unpleasant, exorbitantly priced. If ever a dive existed, this was it. The room was shabby and smelled of stale smoke, and any one of the customers looked as if they should be in the hands of the police. Bored croupiers pushed cards and counters this way and that, while the roulette wheel clicked and whirred and men haggled over sex with the girls. It was all incredibly seedy.

A man at one of the tables was winning too much; Charles watched as a girl moved either side, distracting him sufficiently for his cards to be observed. The whole set-up amazed him. Presumably there was glamour here once. Now, everything was rigged and everything for sale.

He bought some chips and ordered a whisky. He recognised no one, so he settled himself at the roulette table to begin losing slowly. It was almost midnight and the place was filling up, he hadn't known so many shifty characters existed.

One of his numbers came up unexpectedly, and Charles found his fortunes restored. He changed tables, going for a card game he only vaguely understood. He bet while the croupier dealt, and his haphazard guesses paid off again. He moved on, conscious that the two housegirls were getting ready to make him their next target. And then he saw Edwin Braddock.

He emerged from an inner sanctum, small, very dapper, his eyes missing nothing. Behind him came a perspiring hulk of a man, mopping at his face with a large white handkerchief. Charles shrank back into the shadows, watching the men move slowly through the throng. At the door they stood and talked for ten minutes or so. Charles went back into a game at the far end of the room and won again, despite his inattention. The housegirls clamped in on either side, and after that he lost incessantly. At last Braddock was gone. Charles cashed in and got up.

He intercepted the fat man in the middle of the room. 'Excuse me. May I introduce myself? Charles Davenport.'

The fat man glared at him from beneath bushy brows. 'You have a nice evening?' he demanded.

'Wonderful. Perhaps we could talk in your office.'

'You are from the police?'

'Not at all. I am acquainted with Mr Braddock.'

There was a distinct, telling pause. Charles couldn't decide if acquaintance with Braddock had put him up or down in the fat man's estimation. The heavy face gave nothing away, and Charles felt his first stirrings of anxiety. Who was he to be adventuring like this? Nothing but a cloistered doctor, whose world began and ended in the safely defined corridors of a hospital.

They went into the fat man's office. Another man was there, smallish, thinnish, with a face that Charles instantly distrusted. He was the wrong size and shape for a bouncer, but he had the air of a street tough. Charles's guts contracted, imagining a fist crashing into them. He thought of all the battered men he had ever patched up when he was a junior doctor in casualty. He wondered how best to protect his spleen.

'What you want?' demanded the fat man, pulling out a pack of cigarettes and thrusting one between his blubbery lips. He wore rings on every finger.

'Braddock wants your shares,' said Charles. 'So do I. I will pay more.'

'Marlborough send you?'

'No.'

Another endless pause. Why hadn't he set up an alarm system of some sort? Celia wouldn't think to call the police until morning.

The man puffed out a cloud of acrid smoke. 'I like my club like it is,' he said.

'If Braddock gets control it won't be like it is,' said Charles. 'You'll be out, for a start. I'm only interested in doing down Braddock. If you want things to stay the same you can either keep your shares and make no money, or sell them to me. What did you tell Braddock?'

The man chewed his already mangled cigarette. 'I don't tell you a bloody thing.'

'I'll double his offer.'

'Give me fifty thousand English pounds.'

Charles felt his stomach drop. Could Celia afford so much? Was it worth it to her? 'Thirty,' he said hoarsely.

'Get out,' said the fat man. 'I have work to do tonight. If you want my shares you bring me fifty by midday tomorrow. Braddock comes at night.'

'I'll give you a cheque now,' said Charles, and the man laughed in his face. 'Cash. That is all that interests me.'

The smaller man suddenly grabbed him by the arm. 'Time to go,' he said. He jerked his knee and jabbed at Charles's leg, implying a jab somewhere else if he didn't obey.

Charles said, 'I'll be here at twelve tomorrow. I shall bring a lawyer. I warn you, I won't stand to be deceived.'

The fat man laughed at him. 'Who are you? Who sends a man like this? What do you know? Bring your lawyer and bring the money. And don't come to my club again.'

Out in the street the air was clean and cold. Charles walked for a while until he could hail a taxi, there were few about at this hour of the night. He felt good suddenly. This was the life, danger and deceit in a snowy foreign night, and Celia waiting for him. He half turned to look up at the sky.

In that moment the blow fell. It missed his skull and struck his shoulder, bouncing harmlessly off his thick coat. Shocked, Charles let out a yell, kicking at his assailant. Then he saw

322

there were two of them, in leather jackets and jeans, their faces white blurs in the darkness. Fear made him strong. He flung a fist at a face, a boot at a shin, and felt another blow graze his temple. They were using a blackjack. He struck out again, wildly, and hit something soft. In the next instant, miraculously, they were gone. He leaned against a wall, his heart thumping like a steam hammer, exhilarated, triumphant.

He got a taxi in the next street and went straight to the hotel. He checked his face in the mirror in the lift, but he looked quite normal. Inside he was a mass of jitters and excitement. The light in the bedroom was still on.

She was sitting up in bed, looking pink. 'It's the brandy,' she said. 'It's woken me up. You look pleased with yourself.'

He sat next to her on the bed and told her what had happened. At the end, she said, 'Fifty thousand. I didn't think he'd want so much. Did you haggle?'

'I tried. You didn't see the bloke. An air of quiet menace. One wrong move and you could find yourself in the river.'

'Do you think his men attacked you?'

Charles shook his head. 'Just muggers. They got more than they bargained for.'

Celia leaned back and put her hands behind her head. The satin of her nightdress was clearly stretched across her nipples. 'Oh, Charles! You hero.'

He laughed, and she laughed too. The laughter died away into watchful silence. He was so close to her. Thin satin was all that hid her from him, and tonight, especially tonight, he wanted her so much. At that moment she was the most desirable woman in the world. His erection, suddenly powerful, was a hot weight of blood.

He said, 'I want so much to make love to you.'

She said nothing. But she drew her hands from behind her head and slowly, lazily, ran a finger down his chest. When she came to the waistband of his trousers she hooked one finger inside. 'Let's,' she said.

One strap had slipped from her shoulder. He watched himself reach out and draw the nightdress down and away. He touched her lovely, roseate nipple. Celia sighed, softly, gently, and he put his mouth to her breasts, still so heavy, still so firm. She twined her fingers in his hair until at last he pulled free and kissed her mouth, tongue against tongue. He put his hand on her throat, stretching her neck, holding her still while he kissed her.

They made love slowly, as if each moment was worth the savouring. Celia eased her body free of the nightdress, relishing the feel of skin against skin. There was nothing more sensual than a man's naked body, she thought; his weight pinned her down, his body hair set up delightful ripples in her own smooth skin. She held to his shoulders, eyes closed, feeling him go far into her. This was perfect pleasure, a warmth in her body's deepest core. She turned her head and groaned, wishing only that this could go on and on. But he looked down at her closed eyes, and felt a great horror, a great dread. Let her not be thinking of David, he thought. On this night, when he had triumphed, let her for once love him.

When it was over and she slept, her heavy, frightening sleep, he lay beside her, still charged, still restless. From time to time he reached across and took her pulse, feeling it labour. At night she hovered on the border of her former state, exhibiting many of its signs. In the dark, eyes wide open, he seemed to see the channels in her brain, energised in vivid colour, with somewhere, and where he did not know, the fatal, telling distortion.

Charles was subdued in the morning. Celia ate breakfast in bed, and mocked him. 'I feel better than you. Have some more toast, it might do you good. Have some brandy.'

He said, 'I should take you back to hospital. You need a CAT scan at the very least. I should be working harder to make you totally well.'

'But you might kill me,' said Celia lightly. 'How much nicer to die with you in my bed instead of gazing at me loftily from the foot of it.'

She bathed and dressed with sensual satisfaction. She felt better today. It was Charles, and love, and adventure. But she pondered the ease with which he had made a deal with the club; she had expected to talk for hours, even days. Perhaps if you offered enough that was the way things worked. Charles came and stood in the doorway.

'We ought not to give anyone fifty thousand pounds. For a few shares?'

Celia glanced at him. 'If the worst came to the worst we could sell them to Edwin. He's playing cat and mouse with the club manager, but he's desperate, the shares are worth twice that to him.'

'Where can we get that much cash?'

She swung round, the epitome of elegance. He couldn't believe that after the night she could look quite so cool. 'I arranged it before we left. I knew we couldn't use cheques or anything, and I wouldn't want to. We don't want Edwin to know for certain that it's us.'

He was dumbfounded. Up to now he had seen himself as several rungs in the ladder above Celia in intellect, qualifications and achievement, although he allowed her to be quite bright. Was it possible that she was in fact clever? He leaned against the door. Obviously she was. Joe Braddock's daughter had an effortless grasp of most subjects, and for months he'd been treating her like a fool. He wondered if she'd noticed.

'Where do we get the lawyer?' he asked.

She turned on one slender spiked heel. 'No idea. The bank can suggest someone. You know, I'm really looking forward to this morning, it should be fun!'

Vienna was beautiful that day. A fugitive sun turned the dusting of snow to diamonds, as if all the rooftops had been jewelled overnight. Women wore huge fur hats and long, fur-trimmed coats, beneath which tight black boots tripped and bustled. Celia felt a charge of excitement, as if for once she could believe that the world was hers, that she truly belonged, and would not suddenly be whisked away.

But her mood could not survive hours at the bank. It was after eleven by the time they had both an official and the money. Celia was being deliberately open with everyone, as if it was the most natural thing in the world to do such a deal. 'Takeovers are always so dramatic,' she confided to the lawyer, a quiet man who seemed unsurprised by the need to supervise a share transaction for cash in one of the seedier parts of town. He murmured politely.

'The Marlborough Club? Yes, I understand. We have much trouble from this place. How good that it should no longer be run by such people. So much violence, so much drugs.'

Charles and Celia exchanged a glance.

They were at the door of the club prompt for twelve. The small, thin man opened to their knock and ushered them inside. The place was tawdry in daylight, the tables rubbed, the carpets worn. The lawyer brushed dust ostentatiously from the fabric of his good black coat.

They went into the office. The fat man was there. He stared at them all, still seated, his little eyes grim and unpleasant. 'You have the money?'

'Of course.'

Charles opened the briefcase, showing the stacked piles of notes. At a nod the small man began counting. The lawyer said, 'I have a form that must be completed—'

'Wait!'

They all waited until the counting was done.

A nod of confirmation. The lawyer extracted a folder from his bag. 'A form of agreement, no more. You have the documents?'

A folder was pushed towards him, stuffed with paper. The lawyer began leafing through, turning up a sheaf of certificates and contract notes.

'This will be legal?' asked Celia. 'These are British shares.'

The lawyer nodded. 'The form is binding. I shall take it and register it at once with your Stock Exchange. In the meantime you have the copy form and the certificates.'

'And I have the money,' said the manager. He smiled, horribly.

After a while the small man left the room and did not come back. The lawyer took a long time to be satisfied. At last, Celia and the fat man signed a document and all was done. The fat man was becoming intrigued by Celia. 'You want to come to my club tonight? I give you a good time.' His pudgy fingers held her arm.

In the street, everything safely locked away in the briefcase, Charles said, 'Both of you, into the cafe across the way. We'll telephone for a taxi.'

'This is not a dangerous place in daytime,' said the lawyer. 'A taxi can be found easily.'

Celia shivered. 'I don't want to walk around here. That man was—'

'Yes,' said Charles. 'Until we register this deal, the only proof is in this briefcase. If they get that we've spent fifty thousand pounds for nothing.'

The taxi was a long time in coming. They sat and waited, watching the shoppers and business people in the street. Charles noticed a man across the way, watching them. The bouncer from the club. He dropped a hand on the lawyer's shoulder. 'Let's get out of here. The back way.'

He glanced at Celia, but she was quite calm. She got up, as if to go to the cloakroom, and drifted towards the kitchen door. The lawyer, suddenly decisive, said, 'I shall wait for the taxi. Take the documents. If they catch me at least they won't get those.'

It was calm, practical heroism, from a man of whom they knew nothing. Charles didn't know what to say. 'It isn't worth getting hurt over,' he said at last. 'It's only money.'

The lawyer grinned a little. 'And I am only a lawyer. But I am also a student of T'ai Chi. Call me when you get to your hotel.'

Charles got up then, as if he too was going to the lavatory. The lawyer sipped at his coffee once more, assuring the watcher that his birds had not flown. But a second later, slipping out of the kitchen door, they had.

Celia's high heels slid on the snowy cobbles of the back yard.

'You'll have to climb,' said Charles, and at once she hitched up her skirt to scramble on to a dustbin. He put his shoulder under her to help her to the top of the wall, and she sat there for an instant slipping off her shoes. Then she jumped down. By the time Charles had scrambled over she was putting her shoes on again. They were in a dingy back alley, walled in on either side by the backs of offices and shops.

Charles pushed a half-open door. It was the basement of an

office block, stacked high with old newspapers on their way to the incinerator. They crept through and up the stairs, emerging into a bare corridor. Celia straightened her skirt, and they walked on, emerging unexpectedly into a reception hall. 'Guten Tag,' said Charles to the surprised girl. Celia treated her to a dazzling smile. They stepped brazenly out into the street.

It was difficult not to run. They turned left, only to see that the street veered the way they had come. So they went back, seeing no taxis of any kind. It was snowing again, large soft flakes that muffled the world in silence. If someone came up behind them they would scarcely hear. 'So they weren't muggers last night?' said Celia tensely.

'No. Are you all right?'

She swallowed. The extent of her own fear had surprised her. 'Yes, I'm OK,' she said at last. She thought, if she must die let it be in bed, not on some cold and foreign pavement at the hands of a thug.

'Oh my God,' said Charles. She looked up. The small man from the club was walking down the road towards them.

They turned as one into the neighbouring building. It was a block of flats and the hall was bare except for a list of names and appropriate bells and intercoms. The door to the higher floors was locked. They were trapped in a marble-floored box.

'Did he see us?' demanded Celia urgently.

Charles nodded. 'Must have done. We saw him. There isn't even anywhere to hide the bloody papers!'

Celia, in an agony of suspense, went to the door and peered out. The man was no more than ten yards away, walking purposefully towards the building. She fell back, terrified. Her only possible weapon was her shoe.

Charles was ringing the bells for the flats. But this was a business area, and the flats no more than a dormitory, so no one answered. The small man was on the steps, reaching into his pocket. Celia gave a small, frightened squeak.

Charles hit the man as he stepped through the door, and except for the scuffle the night before he had never hit anyone in all his adult life. In fact, the only violence he could remember was when he was five, scrapping over a toy with the boy next door. After that he grew tall and no one bothered him. Now, fuelled by fear, he was suddenly strong.

But the man he fought was experienced. He brought out the blackjack and struck into his opponent's side. Charles grunted, more in surprise than in pain, but when the man struck again the sudden surge of anguish overtook him. He roared, like a primitive beast, and bore down on his attacker. Now, in pain, he didn't care what damage he inflicted. He seemed to look through a red mist of pain and rage, sending his fists thudding into unresisting flesh. The man crumpled and fell. Charles stood astride him, shaking.

'Let's go,' said Celia, tugging his arm. 'Quickly.'

'He might come after us.'

'He's unconscious! Come on, Charles.' She dragged him into the street and hurried him away. At the corner she saw a taxi and hailed it wildly. She had to push Charles inside, and he slumped in the corner, like a drunk. When they reached the hotel she experienced a flood of almost tearful relief.

Chapter Twenty-Two

Charles stood in the hotel bathroom, looking at his ribs in the long mirror. It was intended to reflect the torsos of the wealthy and well-fleshed, since they were the usual patrons of this establishment. Broken and battered skin was not its customary fodder. He fingered his side gingerly, amazed that it should hurt so much. He had always been offhand with the broken ribs he met professionally. He wished he could go back and make profuse apologies to all his past patients.

Celia came in. She was wearing a dressing gown and no make-up. He thought how much he loved to see her like this, as only her intimates must see her. Let others have her made-up beauty, her elegance, her sophistication; he would have her ruffled from bath or bed.

She stood in front of him and took his hand. The knuckles were bruised and cut. If anyone saw them they would know instantly that he had been fighting. She looked up at Charles, and he saw only misty blue eyes. Behind them her imagination ran riot; the man was dead, the police determined; they would find the taxi driver and soon, very soon, there would be an arrest. No one would ever believe their side of it.

'I always seem to be running from the police,' she said.

'We don't have to run from anyone. We were attacked.'

'All the same, we've got to go. Suppose you killed him?'

Charles grimaced. He tried to think back to the hall, those fevered, frantic minutes. 'I hit him here.' He indicated the point of his jaw. 'Couldn't have done it better if I'd planned it. Instant unconsciousness, little lasting harm. He'd have woken up in a minute at worst.'

'Oh, Charles.' Celia put up her hand to cover her mouth. It was because she felt like smiling. It was incredible, Charles as a

331

rough-house fighter, he of the lofty disdain.

They packed and checked out in the next half hour, took a taxi to the railway station, paid it off and went to a hire car office. They left the city as it was getting dark, driving off into the snowy countryside, heading for Strasbourg, home of another of the clubs. She saw now that the point of sale for the pearls had been no random selection; Edwin had done his homework well, and knew his ground.

They stopped for the night at a charming Austrian inn. No doubt in the skiing season it was crammed with hearties in salopettes, but tonight, as the first snow fell, it was firelit and welcoming. Their hostess fussed over them, which surprised Celia at first. Then she remembered. She was in her thirties now. She and Charles were at an age when they could be expected to be well-off and luxury-loving. In their smart clothes, with their smart car, they looked as if they might scorn simple pleasures.

Instead, they relished the table drawn up to the crackling log fire, the soft white wine that tasted still of flowers. They ate veal and apple tart, their plates heaped high with good thick cream. 'We deserve a treat,' said Charles. 'Today was amazing.'

Soon they felt drained and sleepy. Charles took Celia's hand, tracing the veins and sinews. It was still a young hand, unused for so long. When the lady of the house came to take their plates, he let her go and hid his own scarred knuckles beneath the table. They each accepted a glass of plum brandy, and sat in the firelight, watching the flames flicker in each other's eyes. They both knew that it was time to go to bed.

They slept under the eaves, beneath a huge feather quilt. It was like another body in the bed, alternately smothering them and letting in the draught. Charles hung over Celia, the quilt draped across his shoulders, like Lucifer's cape. His ribs were utterly painful, he could not lie on her. She held his arms, like a wrestler, while he made cautious thrusts. She felt the hot beginnings of excitement, lifting her hips to bring herself up against him. He was whispering to her, enfolded as they were in a tent of bedding, and she could scarcely hear him. All she knew was the heat, spreading, growing, engulfing her in a final, glorious convulsion. She fell back and her hands dropped down.

'Darling,' whispered Charles, within her still, wanting some words of love. She said nothing. A slow realisation came to him. She could not hear.

She came back to herself long before dawn. Charles lay beside her, propped on his elbow, staring into her face. He was holding her wrist, taking her pulse. 'Seven hours,' he said.

She put her hand up to her head, although the effort was immense.

'Better. It was ages, before.'

'Can you remember?'

'Last night? I don't know.'

Charles lay on his back, with the finality of exhaustion. She realised he had watched her for every minute of those seven hours. Suddenly she didn't feel brave any more. 'Oh, Charles, why won't it stop? Why won't it go away?'

She turned to him and despite his ribs he held her, hurting in body as he knew she was hurting in mind. He had never known why illness came, why it tormented and destroyed. He didn't concern himself with such questions. If God had invented disease, as a trial to be nobly borne, then he despised such a God. There was no God, if suffering was his invention. There was only the world, made perhaps too hastily, with this and that mistake. Charles's job was to put right the mistakes, to undo the accidents. Man was a machine, and he the mechanic. When confronted with something beyond his power, he had no words of comfort.

'If you keep calm and don't exert yourself it might go away,' he whispered.

'You know it won't.'

'I don't know anything! I only suspect. There's a weak vessel, near the site of the accident. When blood flow increases – and occasionally when it doesn't – it sometimes shuts off.'

'Can't you operate? Can't you make it bigger?'

He took a long breath, deep in her hair. 'I wouldn't dare. No one would. The risk is too great.'

'Are you sure? There must be something you can do.'

'Yes. More tests. You wouldn't take the time before, remember?'

She was silent for a long, long time. At last, she said, 'I'll take the time. Soon. When I can't go on. Oh God, Charles, I've only just started! Perhaps it's a sign, that I'm wasting what I've been given. I won't waste it any more. When I've finished this, I'll – I'll meditate. Study philosophy. Go to church!'

He blinked at her. 'Do you really think this is some weird attempt to swell the numbers at Evensong?'

'How the devil do I know? If it's just for nothing, for no reason – I can't believe that. It can't all be pointless.'

'Why not?' Charles spread his hands in a gesture of resignation. 'Just because we would like there to be a point doesn't mean there is one.'

'Yes, it does! Purpose is one of the fundamental things. Our purpose isn't God's purpose perhaps, but us having a purpose means that He has one too. Don't you think?'

He shook his head. 'No. I'm not so conceited as to think there's God in me. I might just be here. I might be an accident. Or the world could be a prison of some kind in which the inmates can riot and kill, or love and hope, but as long as they keep inside who cares? I'm on the side of love and hope, I'll grant you that. But I don't think I've got any divine supporters.'

Celia felt affronted. He was so against goodness, he wouldn't allow himself the luxury of imagining it. But surely she had been nearer to understanding than anyone? She who had spent so long on the shores of that distant land. She tried to think beyond it, tried to imagine an eternity of stillness, in which her soul, the essence of herself, was no more. But her dreamworld had been a sanctuary! She had felt no need of rescue. A little of her fear drifted away. Why be afraid? If she travelled where she had been before, then what matter? All that must concern her now was what must be done.

Charles reached out and enfolded her. His breath was on her cheek, her eyelashes in his hair. They could have been no closer. She wondered which of them was most in need of comfort.

* * *

They were each subdued at breakfast. They drank coffee as if it was lifeblood, and Charles ate bread and plum jam, although Celia could touch nothing. Their hostess beamed on them as they left, presuming their weariness due to their passionate night, and they were glad to get away. As they drove out of the valley the sun came up over the horizon, bathing them in a sheen of gold. Charles reached out and took Celia's hand, and she touched the scars on his knuckles.

They reached Strasbourg the following night. It might be that she was remembered at the grand hotel, so they booked in at a place of discreet elegance near the cathedral. Only when they saw the room, awash with antiques and marble baths, did they look at each other.

'Did you check the rates?' asked Celia, when the porter had gone.

Charles grimaced. 'No. But I can guess. Don't you like it?'

She went to the window and looked out into the garden. The snow on the lawn was quite untrodden, and the statues had incongruous snowy additions to noses and breasts. In the distance a tall spire was a finger pointing into the darkening evening sky. She turned to Charles.

'I want my daughters to know places like this. I don't want them always to struggle. David never had it in him to make money, he wouldn't see a chance if he fell over it. If I hadn't crashed – it was my fault, you know. Everyone always said I drove too fast. And it cost them everything, all the chances, all the ease . . .' she drifted into silence.

Charles said, 'It does children no good to have everything. Indulged children never make anything of themselves.'

'I was indulged!' She bridled at him, and then, thinking, laughed. 'And now I'm a thief and a rogue. And I've made you one too.' She put her hands in his, affectionately. 'Perhaps you're right. Good things don't make for good people.'

That night they stood and marvelled at the cathedral, its façade a riot of gargoyles and statuary. It spoke of a simpler age, when men believed in spirits and devils, when they knew themselves to be part of a thronged eternity. After a time they

335

went inside, and listened to the choir. It was as if angels stepped out of heaven, filling the stone vaults with sound like a stream of pure water, sending it in fountains into the air, to billow and swell like the sea. Afterwards, they went in search of the Marlborough Club.

It was in a respectable sidestreet, well-lit and clean. A jeweller's was opposite, and a restaurant further down was doing a roaring trade. When Charles approached there was much argument before he was allowed in, but Celia's presence tipped the balance, lending him a spurious respectability.

'I thought you said all these clubs were rundown,' she murmured, taking in the chandeliers, the heavy drapes, the smiling and bright-eyed girls.

'They are.' Charles bought them both a drink, a bottle of champagne for the equivalent of sixty pounds. He tried to look as if such prices were nothing to him, although he wasn't easy with money. His impoverished student days had never left him.

'See anyone we know?'

He meant Braddock. But the man was nowhere to be seen. Instead, the manager circulated unctuously, a word here, a word there, a brief reprimand to the man paying out chips to straighten his bow tie and brush his hair. A woman in a red velvet frock came up to him and kissed him with enthusiasm. 'Yuri! Dearest. How wonderful to see you. As always, everything is divine.'

She was American, with long diamond earrings. They watched in fascination as she moved from table to table, losing steadily and without regret. Friends and acquaintances met and parted in a constant ebb and flow, and waiters walked amongst them bearing trays of delicious little snacks, like the best sort of cocktail party. It was obvious to the least tutored eye that this place was making pots of money.

'I'll go and talk to the manager,' said Charles, accurately divining that Celia was too shy to make the approach.

She said, 'It's all right. I'll do it.' But she didn't move. Finally Charles got up and walked across. Celia watched him, and knew she should have done it herself. Charles was so used to being known and respected, he could not divest himself of the consultant's natural arrogance. To those who did not know him, it looked rather like aggression. The manager was waving his hands in deprecation. He couldn't talk now, in the midst of the evening, with so many people to attend to! Another time – if he might be excused – some other time.

Celia got up and went across. She said, 'I'm so sorry. Mr Davenport was talking to you on my behalf. I'm interested in buying your shares. I imagine you've already had an approach from Braddock.'

A look of amazement passed across the man's face. 'How can you know such a thing?'

'If we could talk in private?'

They moved into the office, a small plushy room furnished with a desk and two gilt sofas. Celia reclined elegantly, consciously trying to give a good impression. Charles was too large for the other sofa, and sprawled somewhat, looking for all the world like her minder.

Celia said. 'You are Mr—?'

'Wulf. My name is Yuri Wulf.'

'And I am Celia Sheraton. This is Charles Davenport.'

'Does Mr Davenport need to stay?'

Celia tried to look enigmatic. 'I do prefer to have him close at hand. I can ask him to stand outside the door if you'd prefer?'

Mr Wulf waved a deprecating hand. 'People would notice.'

He was perspiring gently, and Celia found herself wondering if there was more than Charles to make him nervous. From the moment she mentioned the shares he had been on edge.

She said, 'Can I ask what Mr Braddock has offered for your shares?'

'I permitted him to make no offer. My shares are not for sale. I have a pride in my club, it is the best. My members are my friends, I have no enemies here. There is no need for all this!'

Celia let his words fall into silence. Wulf pulled a handkerchief from his pocket and mopped his glistening face. She said, 'I imagine the Marlborough management takes a great interest in your club.'

'They – they permit me much freedom.' He sighed, and his face suddenly contorted. He let out a small sob. 'Tell me the truth! You are from England, you have come to spy on me? There is no need for such treatment, I do only what I must for my club.'

'And for yourself,' said Celia. 'Mr Wulf, I am not from Marlborough. Neither am I from Braddock. I am acting on my own behalf to prevent Mr Braddock taking over the Marlborough clubs, and anything you have been doing which may or may not reflect on Marlborough profits is no concern of mine. As long as Marlborough remains independent your – management – can continue. If Braddock gets control it will not. Now, what did Braddock say?'

Wulf looked at her miserably. 'He tried to threaten me. I told him I would inform the police.'

'But you dare not do that.'

'I have a friend in the police. He takes care that my club is not inconvenienced.'

'I see.'

Celia tapped her teeth with her nail. She could see Charles watching her out of the corner of his eye. His expression, deliberately thuggish, threatened to induce a giggling fit. She dragged her mind back to the matter in hand.

'You ought to buy the freehold of this place and run it independently,' she said. 'Why let Marlborough profit from your good sense?'

'I have tried to negotiate. Marlborough will not sell.'

'I'm sure twenty thousand pounds would help your offer. They are very short of cash.'

His head came up. 'Are you offering me twenty thousand pounds? English pounds?'

She nodded. 'For your shares.'

They left the club shortly before one. The certificates were in their possession, a banker's draft lay in the manager's drawer. At the hotel they sat for a while in the bar, sipping brandy and talking.

'He's obviously pocketing most of the profits,' said Celia. 'I don't know how he's got away with it.'

'Lax management,' said Charles curtly. 'Happens in the

338

health service too. We once discovered an orderly selling the effects of patients who had died. Watches. Pairs of Marks and Spencer pyjamas. Weird.'

'Not in the same league, exactly.'

He leaned back in his chair. 'Same principle. Don't argue with your minder, I could turn nasty.' He took her hand and bent the fingers back, just far enough.

Celia made a face. 'He could tell that if Braddock got the shares his own days were numbered. Braddock exudes control. The end of his gravy train was in sight, he must have been worried.'

'By my calculations,' said Charles, 'your current share-holding means that Braddock can't possibly win a takeover. Now, why don't you talk to him? He ought to pay you a small fortune for those shares. You've got him over a barrel.'

She shook her head. 'You don't know him. He'd go down rather than lose.'

'Surely the man's not that much of a fool!'

Celia blinked at him. Charles didn't know how much this meant to Edwin. He would never admit the justice of her claim, by giving her so much as a penny piece.

They went to bed, tired and companionable. Charles glanced through a medical journal before settling to sleep. Celia felt warm towards him. She rested her cheek against him as she slept.

A summer's day, hot and heavy. The car was like an oven, her skirt sticking horribly to her bare legs. Flat shoes, her driving shoes, clammy on her feet. She braked for the corner; the back of the car jumped and twitched, like the tail of an angry cat. She corrected, automatically checking the car's lurch across the road, and braked again, more gently now. The same thing. The boys at the works had set it up wrong, she thought, and resolved to be angry with David.

The problem was getting worse. Perhaps it was the tyres, or again the forward wishbone. She decided to pull over at the next call box and telephone for help. But the rain was beginning, a heavy summer shower, like a fountain from a sky turned black. She slowed, the car twitched, she used the gears

339

to slacken speed, cornering without brakes at all. The tyres squealed, losing traction on a glassy road. She dared not brake. But a tree loomed. She cadence braked, foot stamping on and off the pedal. The skid, screaming, inevitable, took her past the tree, spinning, spinning – into nothing.

She was sitting up. Her heart was pounding, her hands wet with the sweat of panic. Charles was holding her. 'You're all right. It was a dream, you're all right.'

'It wasn't a dream. It was real.'

'You were asleep. None of it happened.'

'It was the accident. My accident. The crash.'

She couldn't stay in the bed. It seemed to harbour the memory of horror. But outside, pacing the room, she was soon cold. Charles was irritated, and insisted on drawing her back between the covers, and she felt better. Calmer. Able to talk.

'I was driving away from Blantyre House. My father was being infuriating, and I was cross. Not that cross. I was used to him. But the car was odd. It had been into the works for something, and I knew at once it was strange. Suspension. Tyres. Something. It was wagging all over the road. It started to rain then, and there was this corner – I did everything right, Charles. I know I did. I even remember the skid.'

'You only think you remember. It was a long time ago. Besides, the accident trauma would have blotted all that out.' He was tired, and his ribs hurt. He longed to go back to sleep.

'I'm sure it was real! Charles, listen to me. Will you please listen! The car was wrong.'

He said patiently, 'Everyone knew it was the suspension. The Sheraton's notorious.'

'Not that notorious. Charles, it was deliberate. The car had been changed. I didn't have an accident. Someone wanted me dead.'

He reached out and took hold of her wrist, feeling for the pulse.

Celia felt a great surge of rage. He thought everything about her was a product of some physical state. He doubted her mind, her rational thought, as if she had nothing of her own any more and was just a damaged machine. She fought for calm. 'I dreamed it. I can remember it. I know what I know.'

340

Charles raised a cynical eyebrow. 'And who do you want to blame? Your father? David?'

'Edwin Braddock.'

'Celia, he wasn't much above sixteen!'

It was true. She leaned back against the pillows, weak suddenly, and shaken. Only sixteen. Young and unprepossessing, a nobody. It couldn't have been Edwin Braddock. She looked sideways at Charles and saw that his eyes were closed. She knew she could never sleep. She turned off the light and lay in the dark, willing herself to stop thinking. If not Edwin – who?

She must have dropped off towards dawn, a troubled and restless sleep. She woke to see Charles almost dressed, in jeans and trainers.

'What are you doing?'

He pulled on a sweatshirt, cautious of his bruised ribs. 'Going for a run. Stay there, you need the rest. We'll breakfast later.'

She lay back in bed, remembering the horrible night.

Her eyes closed, and she tried again to sleep. Almost at once the dream began again, playing like a film across the blackness within her head. She opened her eyes and sat up, and the film stopped, whirring, as if the projector was set at pause. Celia clenched her hands in her hair. How to make it stop? She got out of bed and went into the bathroom, leaning on the basin to look at herself in the glass. Pale, paler than usual, and her eyes like blue windows in her head. Behind and beyond the dream waited, ready, in mid-frame.

She closed her eyes, and again she was there, the heat, the trees, the terrible sense that certainty was gone. She pressed the brake, again, and still the car – she opened her eyes and hung gasping over the taps. It was like being there again. Perhaps, like a film, it would only stop at the end. She shut her eyes, watching the action unfold, right to the point of impact. She cried out, in sudden and excruciating pain – and then opened her eyes once again. There was no pain. It was remembered, not real. Celia folded her hands to her breasts, and sank down against the bath. Would the film come again, was it on an endlessly repeating loop? But nothing happened.

341

She could conjure it by remembering what she saw, no more than that. The dream itself was ended.

When Charles came back she was still in her dressing gown drinking coffee. He peeled off his sweatshirt, noting her pallor, the tremor in her hand, the air of slight vagueness. He reached for a bottle of pills, but Celia shook her head at him. 'No. I don't want anything.'

'You need to calm down. Do as you're told, Celia.'

'Damn it, no!'

She blazed at him and he drew back. It was so bad for her to get excited. He said, 'There's something you should know. The Marlborough club burned down last night.'

'What?' For a moment she didn't believe him.

He gave her a grim smile. 'The club. Someone burned it. Someone's dead.'

They went out as soon as Celia was dressed. The street was closed to traffic. Three fire engines blocked the way, and gendarmes prowled the perimeter, moving people on.

'Madame. Monsieur. S'il vous plaît.'

'The Marlborough club?' asked Charles tensely.

'Il est incendie, Monsieur. Completement.'

'Le directeur?' demanded Celia. 'Monsieur Yuri – Yuri—'

'Wulf,' supplied Charles.

'Il est mort,' said the gendarme matter-of-factly.

They turned away. Celia's face felt stiff with shock. They walked blindly through the chill streets, the wind suddenly icy. Charles pushed her into a cafe, and they sat at a table, looking at nothing.

'Are you going to tell me it wasn't him?' asked Celia in a low, throbbing voice. 'How many more things does he have to do? We haven't proved any of them. But I know what happened here. We bought the shares, and Wulf telephoned Braddock and told him that there was no deal that could be done. He was negotiating to buy the club outright and his Marlborough shares had gone elsewhere. So Edwin revenged himself. It was just the same over the pearls. He was angry and he took his revenge.'

'You still can't say he caused your accident,' said Charles.

She glared at him. 'Can't I? He was there that day. I remember that he was there. What do you bet that something upset him, some confirmation that I would inherit, that nothing would be his? I'm getting to know him, you see. He has cold, hard rages. When they come upon him there is nothing he will not do. But he isn't usually impetuous. He likes to move carefully most of the time. I'm ready to bet that nothing about this fire will link it to him. He won't have been seen near here because he wasn't here. Edwin can always find someone else to do the dirty work.'

Charles said, 'But you have nothing that really links him to your crash.'

'No. Nothing.' The waitress came with coffee and Celia stirred herself. 'But then, there's nothing that links him to my mother's death either.'

Charles, taking a sip of coffee, choked. 'Will you please have some sense of proportion? Not every misfortune that ever befell your family can be put at his door!'

'Don't you think it strange, though? Some time that evening my mother had some sort of showdown with him. She called David and asked him to come round. Before David got there she'd had a heart attack.'

'The shock. She had a weak heart.'

'Aren't there drugs and things people can be given?'

'Celia, in all my years of medicine I have never once come across someone murdered like that.'

'Have you ever once looked?' She waved a hand at the waitress and asked for tea and some cakes. Charles, exasperated, said, 'Is there something wrong with the coffee now? Did he poison it?'

'I'm off coffee, that's all.'

'Oh, Christ! Appetite disturbance too. I don't know why I have other patients, Celia. You are a complete lifetime's research project.'

But he was amazed to see how much better she looked. It was as if she too had doubted her own sense. Now she knew she wasn't mad or paranoid or deceived. She was right.

'What do we do?' he said softly. 'Go to the police?'

'So you do agree with me?'

'I don't believe in too many coincidences. You know we can't prove a thing?'

'I know.' She lifted her head and her eyes were like cold, blue glass. 'We'll go to the police when we can prove something. I know one thing for certain, though. I'm not going to let him off. Not now. Not ever.'

Chapter Twenty-Three

David was taking Heather and the children for a rare day out. They went in Heather's car because the Sheraton was too small, and took a picnic and Tip the dog. They had bought a muzzle for him recently, although he only ever chased the odd cat, and Heather insisted he wear it in public. Passersby stared and murmured and sometimes even demanded to know why they kept a dog so obviously dangerous, but Heather had decided on a muzzle and a muzzle it would be.

The day was sunny but chill. The girls squabbled mildly about who was on which side of the car, and who had the privilege of cuddling the dog. Heather wondered how long it would be before the animal killed one of them. It seemed inevitable.

They drove up into the dales, where dry stone walls mark the landscape like ruler-drawn lines. The winter grass was losing its colour, as grey as the walls in places. The rising hills, with here and there the white scar of an abandoned lead mine or the little square of a shepherd's hut, lifted David's heart. This was the place to be when the world crowded in on top of you. This was the anteroom of heaven.

So late in the year there was no one else at their picnic spot. They fell from the car and the girls at once took Tip for a walk, exhorted by Heather not to let him off the lead and on no account to unfasten his muzzle.

'Shall we walk?' asked David, who knew that Heather disliked strenuous hill climbs. 'We haven't been out on our own together for ages.'

They set off up a gentle track. Rowan trees grew in the hollows, laden with berries this year. Perhaps they presaged a hard winter, or merely told of a good summer past. At the first rise they stood at the top for Heather to catch her breath and look down on the sunlit village below.

David said, 'There's something I want to tell you. About the firm.'

She said sharply, 'Has it to do with Celia?'

He grimaced. 'No. Not at all. It's just that – well, the British Motor Group have made me an offer. They want to buy Sheraton. No price mentioned as yet, they want to negotiate. I don't know what to do.'

Heather turned to stare at him, her face the picture of amazement. 'Are you serious? You must negotiate. Of course you must. David, this is your big chance!' She felt breathless with excitement and pressed her hands to her rib cage, struggling to contain herself. All the years of worry, all the years of want seemed like a heavy weight that she could suddenly, blessedly, put down. They were to be free! They were to be happy! The future, that dark and fearsome place, was all at once turned magical.

And David said, 'No. I don't think so. They wouldn't keep me, you know. I'd be out. The Sheraton wouldn't be mine any more. And if they can develop the car, then so can I.'

'You don't mean that! They've got vast resources, millions. All we've got is the money from the mortgage and when that's gone there's nothing! Think, David. You don't get a chance like this every day.' She held on to his arm, imploring him.

'Oh, I know, I know. But what about the girls? Either of them might want to go into the business. When it comes down to it, money's not as important as you think. It's what you do that matters, and what I do is build cars. Good cars, bearing my name and my crest. Sheratons.'

Heather took a deep breath. She knew David too well to speak hastily. He was a man of great pride, all of it vested in his one enthusiasm: the Sheraton. 'It won't be lost entirely. They'll keep the name, everyone will know it was your idea. But the new development's costing more than you thought. Suppose you can't finish, can't follow through? We'll lose the house, and all for nothing.'

'It's not like you to be defeatist, Heather! Of course I'll finish. The car's going to be a worldbeater, become a cult. And

346

then we'll be rich. By hanging on and working, we'll have the money and the car. There's no need to sell out now, when we're within inches of success! That is for the best, darling. Honestly. You do agree?'

He looked at her as he had years ago; pale eyes, flaxen hair, bones that might have been chiselled out of some angular, fleshless mountain. She loved to look at him. The first time she had seen him, at some do, he was with Celia and noticed Heather not at all. But she noticed him, oh yes. Her heart had jumped like a rabbit, she had tingled from head to toe, and from that moment on she was in love. Dear David. Unworldly, unrealistic man.

She said, 'If that's what you want, darling. I know you can turn the Sheraton into a super car.'

'You don't mind about the risk?'

She shook her head, bravely. If this was what David wanted, if this was what he insisted upon, then so it would be.

He reached out an arm and hugged her. 'You know, I love the way you support me. Celia never gave in without one hell of a fight. You've no idea how that undermines someone's confidence. She always wanted me to follow her ideas, mine were never quite good enough. But you – dear Heather!'

They kissed. A small flock of birds twittered in the hedge, and a gust of wind rushed soughing through the bushes. Heather was conscious that for once she had some sympathy with Celia. It was a disloyal, pernicious thought and she stamped on it at once.

Celia and Charles arrived back early. After Strasbourg there was no more to do, and somehow they had lost their taste for a casual holiday. They had read reports of the fire in the newspapers, and no one spoke of arson. It seemed there might have been a fault in a heater, although Celia wondered how much of the fault was due to a petrol-soaked rag. Yuri Wulf was popularly supposed to have been overcome by smoke, since he appeared to have made no attempt at escape. Sadly his remains were too badly charred to allow for an accurate post-mortem.

In their absence, Dorrie had given up housekeeping. Celia

moved paint-soaked cloths from the sink and made coffee, while Dorrie sat bare-legged at the table and waited for all their news. When they had told her everything and asked, as an afterthought, what had happened at home, she said, 'I'm thinking of moving out. The insurance company have made me an offer for my house. I'm looking for somewhere new.'

Charles glanced at Celia. She looked surprised and asked, 'Are we really in that much of a hurry to leave?'

Dorrie said, 'I don't know. I just think all this communal living's a bit tedious. I'll be better on my own.'

'Oh,' said Celia, and was silent.

Dorrie said, 'I assumed you'd be staying here.'

'You want me to stay here, you mean.' Celia's voice wavered and Dorrie looked uncomfortable.

'Not exactly, no! But I was just a stopgap. Someone to keep an eye on you. And now you've got Charles.'

'I've been a burden, haven't I?' Celia ducked her head, and over it, Dorrie and Charles exchanged glances. They weren't used to Celia in self-pitying mood.

'I'm here when you need me,' said Dorrie. 'I'm always your friend.'

'But I'm too much trouble to have around. First David, now you. Brilliant.' To the amazement of all, Celia burst into tears.

Charles couldn't stand to see her cry. He offered a handkerchief and a perfunctory hug, then took himself off to the hospital. Dorrie, watching Celia try to control shuddering breaths, said, 'What's up? Really? This isn't like you.'

Celia mopped her eyes. 'I'm glad you think so. Sorry. It's the trip and everything. More strain than I bargained for. I can be so stupid sometimes, Dorrie.'

'Stupid?' Dorrie eyed her cautiously. Tears, shining hair, and a need for reassurance in Celia used to mean just one thing. 'Celia, what have you been stupid about? You're not – you're not pregnant, are you?'

Celia's colour came up and she blushed a deep red. 'I don't know. I suppose – I could be. I've been ill, I'm bound to be a bit irregular.'

'Were you careful? Charles is a doctor, surely he made sure?'

348

Celia looked at her ruefully. 'He asked all the right questions, yes. I just forgot to take all the right pills.'

'Celia! Celia, how could you?'

She folded her arms around herself and rocked helplessly. Conversely the motion seemed to steady her tumbling thoughts.

'Perhaps I wanted it,' she murmured. 'I go to bed every night and remember my girls. They were so lovely when they were small, and I lost them. I so much wanted them back.'

For a moment Dorrie was dumbfounded. Then she said, 'I never would have believed you could be quite so irresponsible. You don't have babies on a whim! You don't produce them for something to cuddle!'

Celia put her hands to her head, wailing, 'Don't yell at me, Dorrie! Tell me what to do. What am I going to tell David?'

Dorrie snorted. 'More important, what are you going to tell Charles?'

Celia began her rocking again, moody and preoccupied. 'He'll only yell at me. I don't feel well enough to be yelled at. I won't tell him yet.'

'But you will tell him?'

Celia hunched a shoulder. She nodded.

How like Celia, thought Dorrie, absently shredding a dishcloth. The wish, the need, the fulfilment, what she wanted she had to have. But there was a credit side. Celia never dodged the fall-out, and never shirked the blame. Dorrie thought for a moment. Then, slowly, she said, 'What would happen to this baby if you died?'

Celia glanced up at her. She forced a smile. 'Ever the optimist, I see. Perhaps I won't die. Perhaps I'll live to a cantankerous old age. If I didn't – if I don't – well, Dorrie, there's always you.'

'And Charles,' she said, but Celia grimaced.

'He's career mad. I won't have my child chained up in a hospital corridor, parked until Charles goes home. No, Dorrie. I'll put my trust in you.'

Charles was in an unusually buoyant mood that evening. Several new cases had turned up while he was away, and he was enjoying a feast of diagnosis. But no sooner had he sat down to dinner than the telephone rang. It was the hospital again, a road accident victim with head injuries. There was a terse, technical conversation; it was clear that Charles meant to operate. 'I'll be there in half an hour and I want him ready. No hanging around for someone to develop an X-ray, for God's sake. What? Oh, right. I'll bring her in. Yup. That's great.'

He came back into the kitchen. 'Sorry, Celia, but they want you in tonight. I asked them to find a slot for you to be scanned, and you're booked for tomorrow at nine.'

'But – I can't.'

He paused, mildly irritated. 'Of course you can! It's time we found out exactly what's wrong.'

'There isn't anything much. I feel better, you don't know how much better I feel!'

'This afternoon you were tearful and sick. I won't have it, Celia. The time has come to face up to things.'

Dorrie removed his untouched meal and put it to one side. 'You don't scan pregnant women, I take it?'

'What? No, of course not.'

Celia got up and stood behind her chair, like a naughty schoolgirl. 'Dorrie!' she said warningly.

Charles said, 'I hope you don't mean to say—'

'Dorrie!' said Celia again, in panic and despair.

'Yes,' she said. 'Celia's pregnant.'

He remained silent for at least a minute. Dorrie put the lid back on the potatoes. Celia held to her chair, a nervous giggle welling inside her as she waited for the explosion. Instead there was tight, controlled venom.

'How dare you tell me that now?' said Charles at last. 'I've got an operation to perform! Does either of you have the least idea of the concentration involved?'

'I'm sorry,' said Celia.

He ran his hand through his hair. 'You're not in the least bloody sorry!'

'About being pregnant? I'm not sure. No, probably not.'

His eyes seemed to burn a hole in her head. She looked away, feeling sudden fright, wondering if he might hit her.

'Is it mine?' His voice was raw, as if he had been shouting.

Celia ventured a glance and saw that his face was drawn, his upper lip beaded with sweat.

'Yes, of course it is! But really, you don't need to bother.'

'Why not?'

She almost shrugged. 'Because I'm all right. Not as sick as all that. Just pregnant.'

He looked at Dorrie, who still stood, saying nothing, and then at Celia. He said, 'Didn't you think about my career? You know this could finish me. Babies don't come under the heading of discretion, I'll have you know.'

'It was an accident,' said Celia softly. 'I haven't decided what to do. I didn't mean you to know.'

He glanced at his watch, the doctor still, calm and in control. 'We'll have to think about this. Look, I've got to go. Don't wait up for me, I'm going to be late, but—don't wait up.'

He picked up his coat and his briefcase, ready to leave. Celia realised, suddenly, that he impressed her. He was taking this so much better than he might. She wondered what people would think when they saw him tonight, the great, the revered surgeon, putting everything personal aside. He might seem cold, she thought. He acted sometimes with great coldness. But she knew, with certainty, that he burned.

Driving to the hospital, Charles's thoughts were chaotic. They fell over one another in a jumble of emotion. Some part of him maintained a thread of coherence; he must handle this carefully. Celia was unbalanced or she would never have done this – the damage to his career could be terminal – how to get out of it?

But above that, bouncing around like a rubber ball, was an emotion he found hard to understand. Incredibly, it felt like – joy. He, who had kept himself free of ties as deliberately as a wily rogue elephant, rampaging through the gardens of other people's hopes with no thought for them, was shackled at last. He was surprised at how good it felt. It was a reciprocal capture, of course. There was no way now in which Celia could be free of him. They were linked forever, indivisibly joined in a new being. His child.

At the hospital he was at once caught up in the emergency

351

routine. He felt the familiar surge of adrenalin, he could focus and concentrate. Through a door he glimpsed the relatives, made hunched and unattractive by anxiety. He didn't want to see them yet. He would do his best and no more, without the burden of their hopes to oppress him. Instead he went straight to the patient, a man, eyes almost closed with bruising, heavily unconscious. Pressure was building in the brain and must at once be relieved. 'How old is he?'

'Early forties. Married. Two children.'

Two children. Two days like today, when he knew he would be a father. Charles dragged his mind back to the task in hand, and went to scrub up. His juniors were silent and respectful, as he liked them to be, but for once he wondered why. Today he wouldn't mind a bit of chatter in the scrub room.

The brain he worked on was a mess. He had known it would be. Even as he laboured, sawing and draining, putting in a shunt, removing a tatter of something fibrous, a piece of a hat perhaps, or some of the car's upholstery, he wondered how much handicap there would be. Some, certainly. But only last year he'd done one worse than this and the bloke was back at work, with only some memory loss and a tremor. A thought impeded him; to think that this battered machine had been created by two people, creating in its turn, had developed its complexity from the union of two people in love. It was a stunning reflection. He paused, unable to go on, and his junior, surprised, said, 'Sir?'

Charles said, 'I'm OK. How's the pressure?'

'Fine. Better. He's holding on.'

Charles resumed his work, resolving to philosophise no more.

When it was over and he was tired and hungry and anxious to get off, he still had to talk to the relatives. He went to them still in his greens, knowing that they hoped for less when they saw that he was just a mechanic in a mechanic's overalls, with only the skill in his ordinary, human hands. It was his practice to be frank, to disguise nothing, to offer no false hope. Surgeons were so often falsely optimistic. 'He's doing well so far,' he said. 'If he gets through tonight he'll live. But he has a severe brain injury. There's no way of knowing what that will mean. Go home, have some sleep, and in the morning we'll talk again.'

They turned and went, quite meekly. He used to be surprised at how obedient these people were, but now he expected it. And yet he felt a sudden and overwhelming surge of feeling for them. As they turned at the door, to bid him farewell, he heard himself saying, as he had never said before, 'I want you to know that I did my very best.' Seeing the blankness in their faces, the incomprehension, he wished he had kept silent.

On the way home, driving carefully as he often did after a crash victim, he wondered why on earth he felt suddenly like giving thanks. What for? His skill? It was learned. His child? There was no species in the world that could not reproduce. But the feeling remained, buoyant, intoxicating, that he was blessed beyond all reason, far beyond what he deserved.

Braddock sat with his accountants, listening intently to all that they said. They weren't encouraging. All he had achieved in his further pursuit of Marlborough shares was a large bill for expenses. Meanwhile, bank charges mounted, and the lake at Linton Place was going dry. There was a leak somewhere. He had set in hand repairs costing thousands.

'The business is sound,' he was assured in cautious tones. 'But you are seriously over-borrowed. If you could realise some assets and reduce that borrowing . . .'

'You mean me to sell my house,' said Edwin thinly.

'It would be the best option.'

'For everyone except me.'

He drummed his fingers on the desk. Damn that woman! Damn her! He should now be planning a rights issue on Marlborough to raise money for improvements, he would be selling off some of the clubs, even closing some and redeveloping the sites. Instead he was still in this bind, and without even Peter to console him. Damn him too.

When he was alone again, the office silent but for the murmur of his secretary talking on the phone, he decided to call Heather. She was at work and it took some moments to get through. She answered cautiously, sounding nervous. 'Mr Braddock?'

'Heather. Dear Heather. Why didn't you tell me Celia was travelling to Europe?'

She drew in her breath. 'I'm afraid I don't know what you mean.'

'Don't lie, dear. I always know.'

She tried to control her voice but it rose despite her. 'I can assure you I know nothing! Celia tends to dash off here, there and everywhere. She doesn't keep me informed.'

'But I'm sure she tells David. And he tells you. So how did she know I was going? I wish to know, Heather. If you don't tell me I shall put down this telephone and call David. Do you really want him to know you've been selling Celia's secrets?'

Heather's heart began a jerky, uncomfortable flutter. 'You mustn't tell David,' she whispered. 'Please don't.'

'I won't. If you tell me how she found out what I was doing.'

Heather wondered if she might faint. At that precise moment it seemed more than possible. David would think she was a traitor. He would see her as a stupid, jealous, vindictive woman. He would see through all her compliance, all her support, and see her for what she was: grasping; fearful; terrified lest he leave her.

Her hands were shaking. She gripped the telephone as tight as she could and said, 'I gather she got in touch with someone who used to work for you. A Mr Cartwright.'

'How? They don't know each other.'

'I believe – I think they do.'

Braddock replaced the receiver very softly. He was outwardly quite calm, although his centre boiled with white rage. So, Peter had betrayed him in every possible way. The pearls hadn't been stolen, Peter was in league with Celia and between them they cooked up an implausible tale. Celia in disguise, a bag snatch? How had he been deceived by it? He could hear mocking laughter even now.

He opened his drawer and got out Celia's photograph. He often looked at it, searching for clues. All he saw now was a lovely woman. What had Peter seen? A desirable woman? Had

354

Edwin been deceived in that too, had Peter gone to Celia and told tales about his employer's funny little ways in bed?

He looked out into the cold afternoon. A car was entering the office car park, striking away from a steady stream of passing traffic. He thought of Celia, going on, winning at every turn. It was time she found out just what she fought.

Celia stood in the sitting room, surrounded by baby paraphernalia. There were bags and boxes – a cradle, a pram, a large and frilly Moses basket, several packs of disposable nappies and a bottle-sterilising unit. She reached out and touched the pram with one distasteful finger. It rolled soundlessly across the carpet and bumped into a chair. A pile of baby clothes fell with a small sigh.

'Charles,' she said patiently, 'this has gone too far.'

'Pram too big? It is rather Royal Baby, I must admit. I'll send it back and get something smaller.'

'Send it back and forget it,' snapped Celia.

He viewed her from the elevation of his considerable height. She wished she didn't feel quite so weary just at present and could summon the energy to oppose him. But pregnancy sapped her. She sank into the chair so recently vacated by the baby clothes.

'You don't know what the hell you're doing,' said Charles, in his flat, you-really-are-an-idiot voice. 'Who got all the stuff before? David?'

'There are seven months to go,' said Celia, her patience becoming strained.

'I don't care if it's seven years! This baby is on its way and we have to be prepared.'

Celia looked up at him. 'Not we, Charles. I. I have to be prepared. Nobody ever said you were going to be involved.'

He took the pram by the handle and wheeled it back and forth, marking the same six inches of the carpet. 'Don't be stupid, Celia,' he murmured.

'There's nothing stupid about it. I got pregnant. My fault. As you said yourself, it's hell for your career. The best thing for you to do is deny all knowledge and let me get on with it.'

'You wouldn't say that if David was the father.'

355

'What?'

'Is that what this is all about? You're disappointed that you didn't land this on him?'

She said, 'This has nothing to do with any man. It's me. What I want, for me.'

'Then you made a big mistake. I'm the father and I won't let that go.'

She turned her head away, deliberately shutting him out. After a moment or two, when he saw she wasn't going to speak, he said, 'You'd better get a quickie divorce. David won't mind. It must have been hell for him all these years, hanging on.'

'I don't want to be divorced!'

'For once you'll do something that doesn't suit you, then. We've got to get married. It's the only way out.'

She had a lump in her throat which she couldn't swallow down. Damn Charles. She shouldn't have told him anything, should have kept it a secret, told him she'd slept with someone else. 'I don't want to marry you. You're only doing it to protect yourself.'

He went on as if she hadn't spoken. 'The hospital board might turn a blind eye. I hope to God they do. I can't afford to have things go wrong now.'

'You always thought I should divorce him. It was always what you wanted. Then I'd have no one but you.'

'It's time you grew up, Celia. The old life is gone. And this is the new.'

The room was full of cold, hard light and baby things. She put her hand down to her stomach, feeling it firm to the touch. What did Charles really want? The baby? Her? Or did they simply represent for him a controllable unit? She had no doubt that Charles really wanted control. He allowed her only as much independence as suited his purpose. He had taken over more and more of her life, reviving her simply to have her as his own.

She faced him across the room, full of challenge. 'I don't love you, Charles,' she said.

'I haven't asked you to love me.'

'No. That's the strange part, it seems to me. You don't care what I think or feel, you just want to own me. You don't care if I get my money or not. In fact you'd rather not, because then I'd be truly dependent. What is it with you, Charles? Can't you get a real, free, capable woman? Why pick on me? The only thing I've got is that I'm too damaged to run away.'

He turned to the door, but she moved to stop him, getting in his way. He said, 'This is getting us nowhere. You just want to sharpen your claws.'

Celia laughed in his face. 'There you are! You don't even like me! And you talk about marriage and a baby, as if we were going to live in wonderful, loving harmony! I won't be taken as a job lot, Charles, the necessary adjunct to your child. Go and father a child somewhere else, and leave mine to me.'

He took hold of her shoulders as if to move her from his path. But he held her for a moment, the heat of his hands clearly felt through her shirt. She fixed her eyes on his chest, where she knew the hairs curled in tight coils that resisted her fingers. She wondered how she could desire a man she could not like.

'You're so beautiful,' he said.

Celia murmured, 'Is that it? You like the way I look?'

'Yes. Partly.'

'And the other part?'

'I don't know. It seems to me we neither of us know what we're doing here. But let's do it anyway.'

He moved his hands from her shoulders to her buttocks, bringing her close, closer, until his hips and hers were tight together. She could feel his arousal, rigid against her small hard belly, and she put up her hands to pull his head down to hers. They kissed like enemies, rough and untrusting, and she felt the first hot flames of excitement. But, as if at a signal, they parted, and stood looking at each other, in wary acknowledgment that in this at least they were as one.

357

Chapter Twenty-Four

David was not having a good day. It began to go wrong at breakfast when Ellen announced her firm intention of leaving school and becoming a hairdresser. Heather had taken it quite well, merely remarking that there were exams in hairdressing too, she believed, which had given Ellen pause. David had taken leave of his senses at that point, telling his daughter that if she aspired to tend other people's hair she could do a lot worse than learn to brush her own, since she looked like a badly made haystack, at which Lucy had laughed and Ellen had thrown the butter dish. Lucy was now in Casualty, having stitches.

David and Heather sat either side of Lucy, her head swathed in a tea towel, blood congealed in her hair. Ellen was at home, her head under her pillow, full of remorse. David wondered if he should tell the school the truth of the incident. He knew he would not. Lucy was going to have a fall down the stairs.

A face he recognised passed across in front of him. Davenport. Damn. Charles, recognising the party, came over. 'Good Lord, is that Lucy under there? Ellen take a swipe at you, did she?'

'Yes,' said Lucy.

Heather's face flamed. 'It was nothing of the sort! An accident. She fell.'

'Down the stairs,' said Charles laconically. 'Look, I'm quite good on heads. Why don't I do the honours?'

They looked doubtfully at his immaculate suit and crisp white shirt. But he waved a hand at a nurse and in no time they were all in a cubicle, Charles in an apron and gloves, a little coterie of staff gathered round to see the master at work. They

359

behaved as if Michelangelo was doing a bit of painting by numbers, thought David sourly.

Charles viewed the inch-long gash, lost in the midst of Lucy's hair. 'What did she throw?' he asked.

'The butter dish,' said Lucy. 'It was a mistake. She always misses.'

Charles laughed. 'Well, you're going to lose a bit of hair. Sister?'

A pair of scissors was taken from a trolley by a nurse, handed to the Sister, and thereafter placed in his extended hand. He snipped, observed and admired by everyone.

The gash was exposed in all its gaping glory. A small pulse of blood welled up, soaking into Lucy's dark hair. Charles began swabbing, deft, efficient. 'I can't bear to look,' gasped Heather, and rushed out.

'My charm never fails,' said Charles, and the nurses all laughed like surgical groupies.

But despite himself, David was impressed. Charles could sew like no one he had ever seen. He used some sort of complicated running stitch, pulling the gash together without a pucker or a crease, calling another doctor over to demonstrate just how it was done. 'You want to join my firm, don't you? Get some practice in. Stitchmarks of any kind annoy me.'

When it was done, Lucy studied herself in the mirror. There was almost nothing to see. 'Will you tell Celia?' she asked Charles. 'Tell her I'm really ill. She might bring me something.'

'I'll tell her you're dying for lack of chocolates and comics,' said Charles.

'Anything,' said Lucy avariciously. 'Anything.'

'It was very good of you,' said David stiffly, as Lucy dashed off to show her scar to Heather. 'Thanks.'

Charles stripped off his gloves. 'You don't have to go just yet, do you? I wanted to discuss something.'

'Oh?'

'Celia wants a divorce.'

David was conscious only of confusion. His emotions rolled around inside him, like a tidal wave racing across an island, bearing in it the solid forms of houses, bridges, trees. Out of all of it, finally, he extracted a thought. 'Why are you telling me this?'

Charles said, 'Celia and I are going to get married.'

They must have been sleeping together. While David stood aside, someone else had slept with his wife. Anger came to the surface, just as if it was years ago, and he was discovering again, unbelievably, that his young wife, the mother of his children, was unfaithful. 'You unprincipled bastard!' he burst out. 'You're a bloody disgrace!'

Heads turned, but Charles said quietly, 'Do you really want to make a scene here? In front of Heather?'

David took out his handkerchief and wiped his hands. What an appalling thing to do, to spring this on him now. He should have known Davenport wasn't someone who would do him any favours. 'Does Celia want to marry you?' he asked suddenly. 'You've been after her from the first, but I didn't think she liked you very much.'

Charles said, 'You had your chance with her. Actually I think you've made the right choice. You're much better suited to Heather.'

'What do you mean by that?'

'Only that Celia's a handful. Be honest with yourself, Sheraton. If she hadn't had her accident, you'd only have been divorced.'

David didn't trust himself to reply. He turned and strode quickly from the building, his family trotting bewildered in his wake.

That evening, Celia came to see Lucy. David was working late, deliberately no doubt, and the patient was reclining in state in the sitting room.

'You do look wonderful,' said Celia, delivering a bag of sweets, a copy of *Just Seventeen* and a set of silk underwear.

'Fantastic! Super!' shrieked Lucy, and gave Celia a spontaneous hug. 'I knew you'd get something good. Mum only got me some library books.'

'You're not going to be laid up long, are you?' asked Celia. 'You look well enough to go back to school to me.'

'Do I?' Lucy considered. 'It's hockey tomorrow.'

'Oh. Perhaps you'd better have the day off.'

'Can't. I'm in the team.'

Celia felt slightly stunned. Never in all her life had she imagined a daughter who would glory in hockey. Perhaps it was the new wind that had blown across the world. Girls weren't languid any more, they did aerobics and tennis, swam and played hockey, even apparently lifted weights. Celia thought back to her own tennis-playing days. Her mother used to warn her about being too good. She said it put men off and caused a girl's shoulders to overdevelop. It seemed ludicrous now.

After ten minutes or so she left Lucy reading the angst in *Just Seventeen*'s agony column, a mixture of moral tale and eye-widening revelation, and went in search of Ellen. She found her lurking upstairs, in voluntary seclusion. When Celia looked round the door her daughter set her face in a rictus of a smile.

'Cheer up,' said Celia. 'Charles says he'll testify in court. "The blow must have been accidental, m'lud, Miss Sheraton could easily have brained her sister with the milk bottle, if murder was intended."'

'Heather doesn't have milk bottles on the table,' said Ellen morosely.

'Well. She wouldn't. What did Lucy say?'

'I don't know. Really, I can't remember. But she makes me so mad!'

'Perhaps it's your hormones,' remarked Celia. 'Everyone tells me I'm suffering from mine. Personally, I think it's Life.'

'Mum says it's exam nerves.'

'Oh dear.' Celia sat on the bed, looking rueful. 'I might have to admit that she's right.'

She opened her bag and brought out some more goodies. Ellen took them silently, and crammed her mouth full of chocolate, in an obvious and childlike attempt to comfort herself.

'Have you apologised?' asked Celia. 'You won't feel better until you do.'

'Everyone at school's going to know.' Ellen's voice rose hysterically.

'Rubbish! You're all going to lie. And a jolly good thing too. It doesn't do to let these people feel superior. Did you know I went to the same school? Have you still got Miss Briggs?'

'Batty Briggs? She's a hundred and ten!'

'Yes, she would be by now. Tell her Celia Braddock sends her love, would you? She always thought I'd turn out a bad lot. And look how right she was.'

Ellen giggled delightedly, and Celia found herself wondering how on earth she would ever tell her about the baby. Why, oh why, hadn't she behaved better? It was terrible, seeing your actions through the eyes of your children, behaving badly at an age when you were supposed to be setting an example. Moralising was useless when you yourself were so visibly in error. Charles was right. The only thing to do was to shuffle towards marriage and respectability.

She said, 'Would you mind if your father and I got divorced?'

Ellen, alert to all the nuances in Celia's manner, said, 'I don't know. Have you met someone else you want to marry?'

Breathily, blushing, Celia said, 'Not really, no. But poor Heather – your poor father – after all this time—'

Ellen got off the bed. 'I'll go and say sorry to Lucy now,' she said.

Celia drove home, wrestling with despair. She and Ellen had seemed so close, only for the shutters to be slammed down. She needed to explain, but there was danger in that. She would be revealed for what she was, human, fallible, indulging herself in the most selfish way. She wanted, she needed, a baby. So she was having one. For herself.

Suddenly, out of nowhere, a car appeared, shooting in front of her. Instinct saved her. She stamped on the brake, at the same time swerving hard. Her car mounted the pavement, and a tyre blew. She stopped inches from a high stone wall.

She could have been killed. She could have lost her baby. She spun round in her seat, to see what had happened to the other car. It was still in the road, doors wide, and two men were running towards her. Her subconscious prompted her; she leaned on the door lock. The men dragged at the handles, vicious, determined. One of them stood back and kicked at the back window. Celia was showered with crystallised glass.

She flung the car into reverse, not looking, not caring what was there. Its flat tyre groaned and squealed, but she rammed her foot to the floor, back into space. Why had she come this way, between old and deserted mills, with no one nearby to help her? She stopped, changing gear, and a hand came in at her. She drove forward violently, the car lurching from side to side, going the way she knew. Side turnings tempted her, she could lose herself there, but again she might be trapped and they could find her. She could hear shrill, terrified sobs, and was amazed at her own weakness. Surely she had always been brave?

Traffic lights loomed, at red. She went through them without hesitating, and the car behind, gaining on her every second, blasted through too. But a van was crossing. Horns screamed, the van braked, while the car swerved right, skidding into the lights. Celia looked back to see it crumpled and dead, and her pursuers running away. She kept on, driving fast, wanting nothing but the security of home.

Dorrie was in the kitchen, and Charles had just come back from a late visit to the hospital. 'Hi there,' he said, as Celia came through the door. 'You're early.'

She licked dry lips. 'I – I think you should know,' she said carefully, 'I think someone just tried to kill me.'

At first, they barely believed her. But then they looked at Dorrie's car, and at Celia's insistence rang the police. Yes, there had been a crash at the Hollingtree lights. A stolen car. An officer would call upon them at once.

When the police had gone, they talked. 'They can't really believe it was a robbery,' said Dorrie. 'In that car, you don't look worth a light.'

'It might have been kidnap,' said Charles. 'If they knew who you were.'

Celia put her hands together. 'I think they meant to kill me. Edwin's behind it, of course. He wants rid of me and he doesn't care how.'

Charles took a long, thoughtful breath. 'I don't think it's likely,' he said at last. 'We don't know he set fire to Dorrie's house. We don't know he killed the manager of the club. And for God's sake, Celia, Braddock can't be this obvious. For one

364

thing, how would he get away with it? He'd be a prime suspect.'

'Yes,' said Celia. 'He is.'

Dorrie folded her arms across her breasts, as if to protect herself. 'Stop it, Celia,' she said grimly. 'Stop everything. Give him the shares, give him the pearls, let him have the blasted money. You're pregnant, you've got a new life to consider. You can't afford to have enemies, and nothing's worth this.'

'Coward,' said Celia. 'Charles, do you think I should give in?'

His face was quite without expression. The long nose, arrowing so fiercely, gave him in relaxation a look of slight contempt. Tonight it seemed very pronounced, as if he could see Edwin Braddock and despised him. 'I don't believe it was more than a scare,' he said thinly. 'But obviously we must be careful. And if the opportunity arises, attack in our turn.'

'Now you're being really foolish!' said Dorrie shakily.

She looked round at them both, her soft face bewildered and slack with fear. Everything around her seemed to be dangerous all of a sudden.

'I've had enough,' she said. 'I'm telling you, Charles, I don't want anything to do with any of this. It's all gone too far! I've lost my home, my pictures, and now it seems we could all be killed. I really don't want to know!'

Celia reached out and touched Dorrie's hand. 'Poor Dorrie,' she said. 'Don't worry. I do understand.'

Dorrie looked at her hopelessly. 'No, you don't. You think you'll talk me round. But I just want to get on with my life, with my painting. Is it so much to ask? I've been offered an exhibition, but I get no time to paint. I feel as if you've taken me over!'

Celia said, 'I have been through rather a dramatic time, you know!'

'I know all right,' said Dorrie. 'Why don't you think what it's like for me? I'm a childless woman, I will always be childless, and you expect me to sit around watching you grow a baby while disaster and mayhem follow you like chains! I've had enough. I'm going to see my sister in Cornwall. If you need me, if you really need me – the baby or anything – then I'll come. But not otherwise. Not if it's just wanting good old Dorrie around.'

Celia said, 'I didn't know you felt like this. You never said.'

'Didn't I? I'm saying now. This is the last straw. I'm giving up.'

Celia sat with bowed head. She felt helpless. Had she abused Dorrie's friendship? It seemed that she had drained the pot, drinking too often without replenishment. Had it been the same with David? Did she always, in the end, ask too much?

'I've ruined your car,' she said humbly. 'I'll get it mended. I'll buy you a new one.'

Dorrie flared at her. 'Celia, have some sense! You can't buy cars or anything else. You've spent all your money! And you've got to redeem the pearls. What are you going to do, persuade Charles to re-mortgage his house and spend that?'

'I wouldn't do it,' he said.

Dorrie looked at him darkly. 'You will. I'd lay money on it. In the end, Celia can make anyone do what she wants.'

She got up and left the room. In the silence, already lonely, Celia felt afraid. 'What am I going to do?' she asked. 'Do you think she'll feel better tomorrow?'

Charles shook his head. He looked weary suddenly, as if the day had been very long. He got up and stood over Celia, running his fingers through her hair. Small crystals of glass tinkled down, nestling in her clothes like jewels. 'I was so scared,' she told him. 'I really didn't want to die.'

'Did you talk to David?'

'He wasn't there.'

Charles allowed himself a small, contemptuous chuckle.

She pushed his hands aside and looked into his face. 'I know how he feels, Charles. It isn't so terrible. There's nothing harder than telling your children that you're not perfect, that things have gone wrong. It's hard to face.'

'He's a weakling, Celia.'

'No, he's not. He's sensitive. More sensitive than you.'

There she went again, refusing to see what David Sheraton was made of. Charles put his hands on either side of Celia's head, closing his fingers. The grains of glass that remained felt

366

rough against his skin. He tightened his grip, wishing that he would bleed.

'Don't.' She reached up and took hold of his wrists. 'There's no need to be angry. I've only got you now.'

'I'm the one you don't want.'

'Tonight I do.'

She couldn't bear to sleep alone. They went into his bedroom, cold and sparse and empty. Celia undressed and lay down naked on the bed, shivering. He saw that her breasts were already veined in blue, that her belly was minutely swollen. He put his face to the swelling, in praise of her fecundity. She moaned, pushing herself into him, trying to drive out fear and loneliness. The smell of her was intoxicating. He put his hands on her breasts, watching her nipples push stiffly between his fingers like bolt ends. His own bolt was solid, thick as iron. He couldn't hold back. In one hard thrust he invaded her.

Sound seemed magnified. She could hear him grunting, her own softer breath, even the pulse of blood in her head. She felt the long, darting fire, arrowing from groin to heart, and she thought, The celibate don't understand. She was made for this. It wasn't pleasure, it was a need, a fundamental necessity. On this dark night, she had to know and feel that she was part of someone else, that he was part of her, that she wasn't alone.

He came, and she let out a strangled cry. But it was no use. This was one of those times when she couldn't be satisfied.

'Oh God,' said Charles.

Celia said, 'It's all right. I don't need any more. I just wanted you inside me.'

He pulled back the covers and wrapped her up in them. They were both very cold. 'Are you frightened?' he asked, watching their breath steam in the icy air.

'Yes.'

He pulled her close to him, her face in his neck, her breasts like cushions between them. At intervals a shudder ran through her, though of fear or arousal he did not know. What would she do if he did not protect her? She had nowhere else to go. In the quiet, he wondered if he cared that she didn't love him, and decided that he did not. She would never leave him now.

Dorrie did not change her mind. In the morning she packed and took the lunchtime train, leaving Charles and Celia waving on the platform.

Charles said, 'I've been thinking. You're not safe in the house alone. I think you should hide.'

Celia pushed her hair back from her face. Talk of change unnerved her, she had suffered too much change. 'Where would I go? I can't leave everyone! The girls—'

'Get a flat. Just for a little while. Somewhere in town.'

He dropped her at an agency on the way to the hospital, but the only place available at once was pricey. She thought of her dwindling resources. Money fled from her these days, racing away down the cracks in the pavement like water down a drain. She went to see the flat anyway. It was at the top of a low-rise block, with huge windows offering views of Roundhay Park. The other tenants all drove Porsches and Jaguars, and in the day it was sepulchrally quiet. Celia stood in the vast, white-carpeted sitting room, with black leather chairs and a circular gasflame fire, and thought how impressed the girls would be.

She went through to the kitchen, all steel and white light, with a marble floor, and then to the bathroom, with a bath shaped like an oyster and big enough for three. It was glossy and cold and strange.

She telephoned Charles at the hospital. He took an age to come to the phone, and when he did he was brusque. 'What is it? Are you all right?'

'Fine. I don't know about this flat, though. Are you going to be here?'

'No, of course not. Everyone's going to think you left town with Dorrie. Why, don't you like it?'

'I don't know. It feels – it doesn't feel like home.'

'Is that all? I have been dragged from my work for this? Celia, are you ever going to grow up?'

She slammed the receiver down. Damn him! Just damn him. She thought how much it would cost. She could only afford the deposit and a month's rent. Dorrie was right, she was going to have to turn to Charles for money and she couldn't care less.

She went back to the agency, paid the deposit and collected the key. Then, because she hated the thought of being in the house alone, she sat in a tea shop for an hour, got up and went to another, to sit for an hour there too. Finally, when she thought Charles would be home, she went out and caught a taxi.

He took her to the flat that night. The block had an underground garage, and Charles made her stand in the shadows while he piled everything into the lift. She felt cold and miserable, in need of somewhere cosy and familiar. The flat, with its gleaming surfaces and polished opulence, didn't feel like home.

Charles stared at the place. 'This is horrific! Can you afford this, Celia?'

'Don't be banal.' She walked through to the bedroom, throwing off her coat and shoes, deliberately marring the glossy, filmstar perfection. She could sense his fulminating rage. Why on earth did she make him so angry? That was the hardest thing about Charles, to understand what he wanted from her when she so clearly enraged him. She turned on her heel, to face him.

'Is it the baby?' she demanded. 'Is that what's upsetting you?'

'Damn it all, Celia!' He went to the window, and prodded the button that opened and closed the curtains. He did it several times, like a little boy experimenting. The motor whirred unhappily. 'What a place to take. As if you couldn't find anywhere else. You're mad.'

'It was short notice. The best I could do. I'm sorry if it makes you so cross.'

'I'm not cross.'

'Liar!'

He pressed the button again and the curtains trundled open once more. 'I don't know how I shall manage without you in the house.'

Celia was dumbfounded. Charles needed her.

She said, 'You ought to have a housekeeper, perhaps.'

'Bugger a housekeeper! I don't need someone to boil me an egg!'

'Then what, Charles?'

369

He sighed, heavily. She noticed how tired he was looking, and realised that she too was exhausted. They had eaten nothing that night and it was almost ten.

'Shall I telephone for a pizza?' she suggested. 'You can do that, you know. The girls told me.'

A grin lightened his face. 'Of course you can do it. It's one of the great discoveries of the last ten years. On a par with the invention of penicillin.'

'They had that before. But now you've got lots of new diseases. How do we order this pizza, is there a central number or something?'

He went to the little varnished telephone table and extracted the Yellow Pages. 'We're not that advanced. It isn't yet a national service. What do you want, pepperoni?'

'I don't know. Whatever's good for me.'

He dialled, and issued instructions in his usual brusque manner. Celia took time to ignite the fire and draw the curtains properly. She went into the kitchen and made a pot of tea, and brought it to the fireside where they could sit in comfort. When the food arrived, Charles said, 'I don't even like pizza much, actually.'

'Eat it for me,' said Celia. 'Then I don't have to feel bad about you. My mother always said a woman's first duty was to feed her man.'

He eased his slice of pizza from the rest, leaving long mozzarella strings. 'That makes a number of assumptions.'

Celia said, 'Don't be so analytical. People never say what they mean.'

'So you admit you're a liar.'

'If I said yes I could still be lying.'

'Are you? Lying to me?'

'I don't know. I can't find the truth. Not in anything.'

They were soon finished. There were crumbs on the carpet and the gas fire quietly hissed, waving blue pretend flames. Celia thought of Charles going back to his house, cluttered with baby things but empty of people, and she in this elegant, empty flat. How she wished he could stay. And she knew he wished it too.

Chapter Twenty-Five

The flat improved the next day. Celia revelled in its comfort: hot water at the turn of a tap, heat at the flick of a switch, thick carpets and soft chairs at every turn. But by mid-morning the novelty had palled. Living here, she had time to dwell on things: the baby; Charles; the girls. She picked up the telephone and called David.

'David? Hello, it's me.'

She heard him catch his breath. 'Celia. What's the matter? I'm busy.'

'Don't be unfriendly. You can't still be feeling guilty about your little lapse, can you? It was ages ago.'

'And it shouldn't have happened.'

'We are still married, you know.'

She leaned back against the sofa, enjoying herself. In her mind's eye she saw David start to fiddle with the things on his desk – the letter opener, the papers, the blotter. 'I thought you wanted a divorce,' he said at last.

Celia said, 'I thought you wanted one.'

'I didn't say so. You're still the girls' mother.'

'Yes.' She sighed heavily, obviously. 'I don't see enough of them. Will you bring them round one night? We could have dinner. Like a family again.'

'Heather wouldn't like that.'

'Oh, David, why tell her? What's there to worry her if we're getting a divorce? Come on. Say you're dropping the girls off here and going on to the office to do some work. Please, David.' She dropped her voice to the breathy, sexual whisper she used to tease him with before. They used to have the most sexy conversations.

The line went very quiet. Then David murmured, 'Tell me what you're wearing.'

'Oh, David.' She giggled. 'Nothing very much. Stockings. A pair of lace panties, with the suspenders outside, because I really get so hot and uncomfortable. Should I take them off, David?'

'Yes.' A low, seductive whisper.

Celia panted a little. 'They're off. I'm still terribly hot. My blouse is sticking to me.'

'What does it look like?'

'David,' she whispered, 'if you want this sort of thing you're going to have to be helpful. Very helpful.'

'How?'

'Bring the girls for dinner tonight. I'm in a flat now. Number eight, Grosvenor House, near the park. Seven-thirty. If you do this for me, I'll do a lot for you.'

David's voice snapped at her. 'Bitch!' He hung up.

Celia sat for a time, doing nothing. In the old days, after a call like that, David would come rushing home; they'd spend the afternoon in bed. Now what was he doing? Going into the lavatory for five minutes? Sadness rose like a grey mist and coloured all her thoughts. That she should be reduced to taunting him like this. That she should need to do it! Heather was to blame, she told herself, blinded suddenly by tears.

When she had calmed she stuffed her hair under a hat, put on a coat and went out shopping. In this part of the city she felt anonymous, knowing no one and expecting not to be known. So she was amazed when a woman stopped her. 'Celia, isn't it? We met, do you remember? At David Sheraton's? Jane Partridge.'

'Jane! Yes, of course I remember.' Celia forced herself to smile. It was the wife of the test driver David had hired.

Jane said, 'I was puzzled about what was going on, you know, when you didn't stay that day. But then I heard all about your accident. It must be terrible for you, trying to put everything back together.'

'I've given that up,' said Celia, with a brave grin. 'Everyone told me I shouldn't try, you see, so I'm making a new life and forgetting about the past.'

The other woman looked at her shrewdly. 'I bet the past hasn't forgotten about you. We've seen David a few times lately. He seems to us very – unfocused.'

'In business, you mean?' Celia's heart jerked a little.

'Yes. We put it down to all this upset in his personal life. He knows what he wants but he doesn't seem able to get there.'

'Oh.'

Celia took a deep breath. She had been here before, she thought. Year after year when she and David were together someone would tell her that David wasn't putting what he should into the business. Her father had once said that David never understood one fundamental truth – the business was more important than him. It was the lifeblood on which all else depended. Yet Celia knew that for David it was more than anything his personal hobby.

'He's such an enthusiast,' she prevaricated. 'Sometimes he doesn't concentrate as he should.'

Jane said, 'It's such a pity when the product's so good. Look, why don't we have coffee somewhere? Are you in a rush?'

They went to a small, refined coffee shop full of ladies like themselves. Celia had the odd sensation that she was pretending to be her mother. She wasn't the sort of person who shopped and had coffee and lunched.

But Jane, often a stranger in strange cities, was used to passing time. She leaned back and said shrewdly, 'This is all a bit odd for you still, isn't it?'

Celia shrugged. 'I'm getting more used to things. Tell me, how did you find the Sheraton's road holding? Good? I mean, good enough, for a car of that power?'

The other woman looked at her speculatively. 'You were driving a Sheraton, weren't you? When you had your accident.'

Celia nodded. 'Except now I don't think it was an accident. Please don't tell anyone you saw me round here, will you? I've been having more accidents lately. Frightening ones.'

There was a silence. Celia knew Jane Partridge was trying to decide if she was a loony or not. Catching sight of herself in a mirror she wondered if she looked like a loony, white face, dark eyes and all.

'Who do you think's behind it?' asked Jane. 'Your cousin? I

read something in the papers over the weekend. You're suing him and his company's in trouble.'

Celia looked at her sharply. 'Do you know my cousin?'

Jane smiled. 'Not really. He was at a charity do we went to a year or so ago. There was an incident, nothing much. One of the waiters spilled tomato juice down his suit, and this man Braddock – well, he exploded. Quietly. The most venomous, vicious public exhibition I have ever seen, and all over in about five seconds.'

Celia breathed deeply through her nose. 'That's Edwin,' she admitted. 'More coffee? I think I'll have a cake.'

In the evening, she cooked dinner, although she didn't know if David would indeed bring the children. But at seven-thirty, just when the pastry of her steak and kidney pie was starting to brown, the carrots were glazed and the potatoes coming to the boil, the intercom buzzed and they were there. Celia felt a great swell of pleasure as she ushered them into her flat. The girls began to explore, opening the curtains, playing with the fire, going into the bedroom and making each other up. They were children again, boisterous and playful. Celia went into the kitchen and turned down the oven.

'Drink?' She offered David a glass of white wine.

'Thanks.' He was stiff and formal, a little antagonistic. She reached out and put a finger on his wrist. 'Don't worry. I'm not going to misbehave. Do you remember when we had phone calls like that all the time?'

He grinned wryly. 'Seems a lifetime ago. I can't believe it was me.'

'I can,' said Celia. 'You haven't changed all that much, you know. You're not nearly as staid and boring as you pretend.'

'I don't pretend anything!'

She went to the stove and adjusted the heat under the potatoes. Tonight she was cooking plain, ordinary food, but doing it as she knew Heather could not. It was pretence, as if they were all meeting at the end of the day as they always did, as if they were truly a family. She said, 'I saw Jane Partridge today. She says you're having trouble producing the new castings.'

'Not us. The foundry.'

'Well of course the foundry!' She stamped on her impatience. 'Have you been to see them? Can they suggest anything?'

'They want the design changed, but of course we won't.'

'Why not? If it makes casting easier?'

She turned and met his eye, saw again the irritation with those who thought his car should be in any respect different from his vision of it. 'I designed the car as I wish it to be, Celia! I'm not having some useless load of metal bashers tell me it can't be done. They can do it. They must.'

'I bet it's costing a fortune.'

He coloured. 'Well, these things do.'

Frustration welled in her. Once again she must confront the reality of David's money sense, standing by as the pounds were leached uselessly away. She had never had it in her to economise, but she never wantonly watched money go. 'Why don't I come in and see if I can't suggest something?' she said brightly.

'Don't be foolish, Celia. You are not an engineer.'

She said nothing, simply checking on the potatoes and taking a fruit fool out of the fridge. 'What are you going to do if it doesn't work out, then?' she asked. 'Sell?'

'I've already had offers.'

'Which you won't take. Why, David? You can't blunder on watching it all go wrong.'

'I wasn't aware that I blundered, as you so tactfully put it.'

'Oh, really! Has all the money gone, then? Is there anything left? Now you've mortgaged the house you have to make repayments, the business has to make more than before! And it isn't, is it?'

David said stiffly, 'I might remind you it was your idea.'

'Not to fail, David! Never to fail!'

She went back to the stove, experiencing a tremendous sense of déjà vu. They always rowed if they talked business, as night follows day. She might have been twenty-two, with a small baby and her father nagging that David simply wasn't going to make things tick. But why not? Why couldn't this clever, charming man make money? The frustration was as bitter now as it had ever been.

The girls came in, chattering like magpies, going through the cupboards as if this was truly their own home. 'Yum, peanuts. Can we have some, please? And crisps too, I'm starving.'

'Dinner in five minutes, don't fill up on rubbish,' said Celia automatically. 'David, help yourself to more wine. Ellen, get drinks for you and Lucy, would you? There's some Coke somewhere.'

Soon they were all at the table. Lucy giggled, because it was so ordinary and yet so secret. 'Mum would be furious if she knew Dad was here,' she said.

'Don't you tell her,' said Celia. 'She'd be upset. But it's lovely to be all together again. I dreamed of this when I was getting better in hospital.'

'You couldn't dream a flat like this,' said David. 'Did Davenport choose it?'

Celia shook her head. 'No. He – he's more into cold showers and rattling windows. I can do things without his say so, you know.'

David grinned, and his eyes crinkled. He was still a most attractive man. 'Your Svengali.'

'Who's Svengali?' demanded Ellen.

'A sort of wizard,' said Lucy. 'Really, I'd think you'd know that, Ellen! I suppose you're too busy throwing things to read.' Lucy was easily the more academic of the two.

'None of that,' said David. 'That's over and forgotten. Girls, why don't you watch television while your mother and I have coffee and talk?'

They went off, squabbling a little. Celia looked at him under her lashes. 'You don't want more telephone teasing, do you?'

David took in his breath. 'What would you do if I said yes?'

'Tell you to come back tomorrow, of course! Honestly, David, you don't change. Still just as randy as ever.'

He looked at her, marvelling as he always did that he had ever made this woman his wife. She was in a white dress, cut low at the neck, its loose fit completely negated by its tendency to cling. If she turned her shoulder the fabric at once stuck to her and fell away, treating him to a view of her breast and torso. 'Are you all right now?' he asked. 'Last time you passed out.'

'Oh. That. I'm fine now. Only a little sexually frustrated.' She lifted her glass of mineral water, and extended her tongue to its surface. She kept her eyes down, because David never liked boldness in women. Damn Heather! She had trapped him with feebleness.

'I thought the doctor chap was – well, that you were sleeping with him.'

'Charles?' Studied amazement. 'He's my doctor! Really, David, the things you think.'

'He rather implied it was true.'

'Well, it isn't. I sleep here alone.'

She could feel his eyes on her, moving over her skin like heatlamps. And she alone knew how to please him. At that first awkward family dinner, when her father was so unpleasant, she had taken David to see the garden. They made love in the twilight, yards from the house, against an apple tree. There had been nothing she would not do for him – including, she thought suddenly, sleeping with other men.

How had it happened? The first time was a party, with David angry with her even before they arrived. He had seemed to encourage her flirting, almost pushing her into the arms of men he knew she liked. After an hour or so she had gone to him and tried to make up, but he was impossible. He humiliated her in front of her friends. So she humiliated him, in secret, in a swimming pool changing room with a man who told her she was the best lay of his life.

Was he thinking of that night? She felt his eyes on her, knowing she excited him, knowing that in some complex way he was diminished by her. The affairs always came at times of David's stress; he almost demanded it of her, so he could witness and punish her disgrace. Suddenly the pieces clicked into place. David was jealous of her wealth, her brains and her courage. But he couldn't be angry with her because of that – he needed a focus, an excuse. He pushed her into affairs, so his rage could be justified and taken out on her. She was the guilty one, the sinner. Naturally she must repent. A husband must surely be justified in abusing his unfaithful wife.

377

Why hadn't she remembered those nights? What subtle system had come into play? His accusations and her pathetic denials. She had shut them out, ignored them, wiped them from memory. Those nights – she remembered bruises and fear. Those were the nights when he debauched her, taking his revenge for what she was and what she had done, until at last he fell asleep, and she could crawl away, sobbing and ashamed. And in the morning she always promised that now she would be good.

'Shall I come tomorrow?' he asked throatily.

She blinked, trying to bring herself back to the present. It was long ago. Years had passed. David had changed. She wondered what would happen if she told him she was pregnant. Would he think it was his? Celia felt herself go cold.

'What's the matter?' asked David. 'I thought you wanted it. Part of your battleplan.'

'I don't have a plan,' she said. 'And, anyway, why do you want to come? You don't mean to leave Heather.'

He looked at her across the table, his eyes hot with arousal. 'Sometimes I do. When I sit here with you and think about how it was, I don't know what I've been doing the last ten years. Do you remember the apple tree, Celia?'

A smile tweaked at her mouth. 'Actually, I was thinking of that earlier. We must have been mad.'

'Only for each other.'

He got up and came behind her chair. He crouched over her, sliding a hand into her dress, his mouth on her shoulders and neck. It was the old David, demanding, peremptory, as if she owed him her compliance. Her body was surprised into arousal, responding to the old, familiar touch. She arched back against him, willing, brazen. He let her go as abruptly as he had taken hold.

'I'll come tomorrow.'

As they were leaving, and the girls went to fetch their coats, David said, 'This place is really amazing. Can you afford it?'

She said, 'I can for a bit. I was meaning to ask. I know the business has problems, but what if I wanted some cash? Any chance?'

'Good Lord, Celia, no! We've had to claim against the

foundry and they're fighting it, so we've no spare money at all. I've given what I can, you can't really want more.'

She forced herself to laugh. 'You know me, David. There's never enough.'

At the door she kissed the girls. David, her husband, stood watching. Then he bent, put a hand on her waist and kissed her flushed cheek.

'Tomorrow,' he whispered in her ear. 'Wait for me.'

He turned and went out, briskly, without looking back. Their voices came back to her as they went down in the lift.

She found it hard to sleep that night. Thoughts kept pursuing her, and when she dozed she jerked awake, thinking herself trapped somewhere, lured back unawares into danger. Finally, exhausted, she turned on the light. She was afraid of something. David? Herself? The person she might find herself to be?

David had her dancing to his tune. He had only to hint that he would take her back and she was ready to let him use her, like a mistress kept sweet on promises that one day he would leave his wife. Well, she *was* his wife! She wasn't just a body, to be fumbled or invaded whenever he chose, having to perform, come up to standard, in case he was considering changing his life. If she wasn't pregnant – she put a hand on her belly. Was this all that prevented her from giving in? Was she really so weak that she would let David have her as he wished, accepting the degradation as her due? All right, she might well deserve guilt, she had become pregnant carelessly, without any proper thought. But David was not the man to punish her!

She lay back again in the bed, trying to cudgel her brain to remember things it was determined to forget. How was the business when she crashed? Was it failing again? She remembered, or thought she remembered, going with David to the works in the dark, with no one there but them. They had argued about something, a late delivery perhaps, and he had pushed her down across a car, spreadeagled painfully across the engine while he symbolically conquered her. And afterwards they had stopped at a pub and been charming and funny with each other. How on earth could she have forgotten all that? The marriage she remembered was only half the tale. They had lived two lives, she and David.

She wanted one of those lives back. Even now, pregnant and ill, she longed for the serenity of their happy times. If all David wanted to give her was the reverse side of the coin, then she had to refuse. In her youth she had thought herself capable of anything, and it was hard to give that up when she was suddenly ten years older. But even she had to admit that she couldn't have David, happiness and this baby. It might be possible to choose any two and live with the choice, but the third would always be denied her.

Sadly, wearily, she closed her eyes and thought of sleep. She would escape into oblivion, and face the end of her marriage with the dawn.

But morning brought something of more pressing importance – a phone call from Charles.

'Celia? Me. There's a letter here for you, I opened it just in case, it looked important. The payment on the pearls is due next week.'

Celia said, 'What happens if I don't pay?'

'What you knew would happen. You lose them.'

She said nothing for a moment. Then, coaxingly, 'Charles—'

He laughed. 'Don't bother, sweetheart. The answer's no.'

'But you've got stacks of money. If we just pay the interest it won't be much. It's only a loan. In fact it's an investment. The pearls will be worth a fortune one day. We can't turn our backs on millions of pounds.'

'Well, I'm not turning my back on a few thousand of mine. When we get you properly divorced I've got a baby to support, remember?'

Celia lost her temper with him. 'I'll have you know I don't want to see or hear from you ever again.'

'Oh, Miss Independent! Aren't you the poor loser.'

'It isn't as if you haven't got the bloody money, is it?'

'Celia, the one thing I've learned about you is that you can spend millions. You don't spend them foolishly, I'll grant you that, but I've been poor too long to be poor again. I'll feed you

380

when you're starving, but I'm damned if I'll clothe you in pearls. Got it?'

'No. You have.'

She heard him chuckle.

She flung down the telephone and paced the carpet. Her thoughts were taken up with financial calculation. How was she to redeem the pearls? Redeem them she would, and if Charles wouldn't oblige, and David couldn't, then she must find a way. She sat down to do her sums. Bank statements lay beside credit cards and lists of bills. Next to them she put a list of her assets. Apart from shoes, clothes and handbags, she owned only one thing: the Marlborough shares. Dropping her chin in her hands she lost herself in thought.

The buzzer sounded. She looked at her watch and saw that it was almost twelve. She was still in her bathrobe, but the morning had gone. David had arrived.

She pushed at her hair and let him in. He had brought flowers and she took them into the kitchen, flustered and ill at ease. She ran a bowl of deep water and cooled both her wrists and the flowers. He was here for sex, of course. What was she going to do?

He stood at the door and said, 'I've thought about nothing else but you since last night.'

She glanced at him. 'I thought a lot, too. I don't think this is such a good idea.'

He came over and stood behind her. He smelled like no man she had ever known, a tang of lemons and engine oil. 'We both want to,' he whispered, and put his hands on her shoulders. 'We both need it.' In one swift movement he pulled her robe to her waist, pinning her arms at the elbows. He reached to cup her hanging breasts, mouthing her neck, kneading and grasping her with all the frenzy of a man who has at last succumbed to temptation. He was groaning, open-mouthed against her skin.

'Oh God,' he whispered, 'oh God, why can't I ever forget what you're like?'

'Don't. David, don't!' She dragged her arms free of her robe and moved away. He followed her, hands reaching, pinning her against the cold chrome of the fridge. His mouth was slack and needy, searching for her nipple, while reaching fingers pushed between her legs. She wondered if it would be easier to give in. He was her husband. For years she had satisfied his needs. Why not once more?

His hand forced her thighs apart, bruising tender skin. The pain jolted her out of compliance. She wrenched herself away, feeling his teeth on her nipple, and she hit out in revenge. This was another thing she had forgotten: how David could hurt.

'Stop it! Get off me. I don't want it.'

He stood a foot from her, aroused and bewildered. 'You wanted it last night.'

'Did I? Last night we were pretending we were a family. I know we're not. Tell me, David, if I let you make love to me, will you leave Heather?'

He said, 'Who knows? Who cares? You love it, you know you do. Come on, I know what you want, we'll do it here and pretend we didn't.' He pulled at her robe, and the tie gave way. She was naked. She put her hands to her groin, covering her bush of pale pubic hair. 'Oh God!' He began tugging at his own clothes, trying to free himself, desperate for his own brief satisfaction. Afterwards they would pretend it hadn't happened. Her throat closed up in misery.

She pushed past him and ran into the bedroom, leaving him wrestling with his zip. She began pulling on clothes, trousers, a top, anything. She even kicked her feet into boots. He stood in the doorway, the fervour visibly dying. He said, 'Damn you, Celia! What now?'

Almost hysterical, she shrieked, 'If you touch me I'll tell Heather! I won't have you come here and – and – I'm not your prostitute! I won't be used.'

'You offered yourself to me. You arranged it.'

She glared at him, her eyes hot with rage. 'I offered myself as a wife. Your wife. Mother of your children. I offered to make you happy! If all you want is a body, you can go and find someone else's. Mine – mine isn't available part-time.'

He turned and went back into the sitting room. She heard him pouring a drink, fastening his clothes, regaining his balance. After five minutes or so she went in. 'I'm sorry,' she said dully.

'Are you sleeping with Davenport? Really?'

'Yes.'

'I can't say I admire your taste. I should have known, of course. You and chastity always were complete strangers to each other.' Celia's cheeks flamed. He had struck her on the exact point of her own weakness. She reached out for a missile and her hand closed around a glass. She threw it hard, only for it to shatter against a wall.

'I see where Ellen gets it from,' said David coolly. 'You were right. I won't leave Heather for you. You're not worth it.'

'Bastard! Cruel bastard. My father said as much!'

'Do you always have to drag him up? If it hadn't been for him we might have had a halfway decent marriage!'

Celia stared at him. Her rage began to trickle away. 'I thought we did. I always thought that. Didn't we?'

David shook his head. 'I don't know. I can't remember any more.'

He began to leave. Celia was shaking, on the verge of hysterical tears. As David reached the door he said, 'By the way, I think you should know. I won't divorce you. There's no way I'm saving Davenport from a charge of improper behaviour.'

'He's never done anything to hurt you.'

'Who else is behind what you're doing? Chasing the money. Raking open old wounds. Insisting I mortgage the house. I know you, Celia. When a man like that turns up, you're nothing but his toy.'

When he had gone she closed and locked the door. She felt threatened and unprotected, even though she knew she was safe. David's insults were like fishhooks, impossible to shake off. She crouched on the sofa, as if surrounded by unseen enemies. Edwin, Heather, and now David. She, the golden girl, was finding herself suddenly in a hostile world. You never knew who might turn against you next.

Chapter Twenty-Six

Charles was in the laboratory. He had been watching the development of a series of tests on brain tissue from different organisms. Hormones of various kinds were introduced to see what effect they had, and the results were measured, charted, calibrated, computerised and marvelled over.

He tried to visualise the brain, something he saw in reality so often and yet had never really related to the data he learned about its function. The organ lived in a constant bath of substances, toing and froing like miniature tides, causing action, reaction, and inhibition of both. That he should interfere so crudely with the workings of such a thing seemed presumptuous in the extreme, and yet malfunction did occur, and must be tackled. Again he had the sense that he was nothing but an ill-trained mechanic, working on a machine of exquisite efficiency without going on the course from head office.

He turned to one of the researchers, John Barnes, whom he had known since medical school. 'What you are telling me is that you believe you have found an inhibiting substance that prevents waking. Too great a production of this could be a cause of extended coma.'

'Some extended coma,' said Barnes. 'One patient in a million, perhaps. Now, I know this must hurt, Charles, but it could be that your star patient revived simply because her brain produced less of this inhibitor. You provided stimulation at just the right time. We know where this substance is produced, so if you could surgically interfere with that production – Bob's your uncle. Coma patient wakes.'

'Or dies under the knife,' said Charles laconically.

'Well, there you go,' said Barnes. 'Never worried you much

before, I see. How come you're suddenly concerned with human emotion? Could it be our lovely, libidinous lady patient?'

Charles grunted. 'No, I wasn't thinking about her. I've got another one, very stubborn. Stewed his brain with every illegal substance he could get his hands on, and quite a few legal ones too. Father's a barrister. I'm just wondering if I dare try to experiment.'

Barnes clutched his head theatrically. 'God, how you pick 'em, Charles. Tired of medicine, are you? Oh, well, when you're sacked come and get a job here. We don't mind how many lab technicians' hearts you break. Within reason, of course.'

Charles laughed and went back to the graphs he was studying. But his thoughts kepts drifting to his coma patients. You couldn't assume an untried technique would help them, particularly when your judgment was clouded by the urge to try it. It was possible that injury caused an over-secretion of hormone, of course. The tissue was scarred, and perhaps lacked the usual inhibiting triggers. Would reduction of the flow cause permanent wakefulness? Would it cause death or worse? Was it even worth reviving a human being who had brought his condition so determinedly upon himself?

Back in the hospital he found himself walking the corridor of Sister Johnson's Intensive Care suite. She acknowledged him with a lift of her brows. Their truce was never less than wary. He stamped past, grimly entering Martin Moffat's room. At once the Sister was at his elbow.

'I trust you won't disturb him. He's been restless today.'

'Better restless than a living corpse. Or perhaps you don't think so. Tell me, Sister, what do you think is worth trying, in the cause of his revival? Anything? Nothing? What do you say?'

She said primly, 'You may attempt anything which does not positively cause his condition to become worse.'

'But can anything be worse? Who's to say?'

'Me.'

It was the boy's father, the barrister, who had come quietly into the room. He stood looking down at his son.

386

'I'm sorry, Mr Moffat,' said Charles stiffly. 'Sister Johnson and I were merely continuing our long debate on the rights and wrongs of coma treatment.'

'I'm glad someone sees fit to discuss it,' said Moffat. 'The man who caused all this seems to want to ignore the condition altogther. Look, you're the expert. I need a medical witness. Could I call on you?'

'My God, no.' Charles viewed the barrister with grim eyes. 'The anaesthetist is a friend of mine. Of course I'll give testimony on your son's current state, but no more.'

'How you medicos stick together! You're nothing but a bunch of crooks!'

Charles considered for a moment. Thus far he had been unusually kind to Mr Moffat, less from an impulse of charity than an urge not to get sued. But the time had come. He said, 'Mr Moffat, you have to realise that your son brought a lot of this on himself. He was abusing his body to a considerable extent. I imagine you blame yourself for the way he behaved – perhaps you bullied him too much, as you try to bully me and anyone else you come in contact with. But let me tell you this. If the appendicitis had never happened he'd probably now be dead from drug abuse, and if my colleagues hadn't operated he'd certainly be dead from septicaemia. The point is that life isn't safe, Mr Moffat. We don't have a right to get through it unscathed. Face what really happened. Your son wasted his life when he had it, and is paying the price.'

There was a silence. Sister Johnson broke it, saying, 'That was unnecessarily harsh, Mr Davenport.'

Charles, thinking privately that once started he had gone too far, decided to brazen it out. 'It's the truth. We've been avoiding truth here. It's time to confront the realities of this situation. There's no mileage in trying to blame people for what must be considered as much the patient's fault as anyone's.'

For a moment it seemed as if Moffat would explode. The skin around his eyes seemed to inflate, and Charles found one part of his mind assessing the blood flow changes while another imagined the inevitable court case. He should have kept his mouth shut. Now he too stood ready to be accused.

But as he watched, Moffat seemed suddenly to diminish. He rubbed his hand across his face, a brisk, grey-haired man who suddenly seemed to sag. 'You're telling me I'm simply being vengeful,' he said helplessly. 'Trying to pass the buck.'

'That's not for me to say,' said Charles. 'But I can assure you I'm not just closing ranks here. As it happens I've been expert witness in two negligence cases, both of which were won. But this wasn't negligence. It was bad judgment, caused by the necessity for speed. They couldn't test your son for everything he might have taken, not in the time. That's what the court will find.'

'Don't tell me my job!' snapped Moffat, reviving a little.

'Of course not.' Charles wrestled with himself, since Moffat so often tried to tell him his. But the man was overwrought. He had to be excused his behaviour. Charles said, 'I think this might be time for a discussion, Mr Moffat. We have to talk seriously about your son.'

They repaired to Charles's office. It was strange, he thought, but he had never really spent time with the barrister before. It was the threat of court proceedings, frightening everyone into silent efficiency, lest they too should be caught in the scattergun of accusation. The man had gone on, aggressive and unforgiving, quite unchallenged.

'I hope you're not going to attempt to intimidate me,' snapped Moffat.

Charles almost grinned. It was difficult to imagine anyone intimidating such a belligerent man. 'As far as the court case is concerned, you can do as you wish,' he remarked mildly. 'But your son's care is another matter. I've got an idea for treatment that might not work. It could kill him. If I do, or if he wakes and he's fit only for some institution, I don't want you screaming that I could have saved him if I'd tried, or I didn't tell you we were experimenting, or we used your son as a human guinea pig, or any of the other little tricks you might try.'

Moffat blinked at him. 'What if you do nothing? Will he recover?'

'Not a hope,' said Charles. He sat back, throwing a leg over the arm of his chair. 'You can leave him here, of course, costing a mint. Sister Johnson loves coma patients, she'll keep him going for years. I doubt if he'd appreciate it, though. From what I hear he must have been something of a live wire.'

'He was a bloody young fool who never listened to a word of advice except to do the opposite!' Moffat dropped his head to his hand for a second. 'If you knew how angry he makes me. Just lying there, as if he knew it was the one thing I couldn't stand! His mother can't bear to see him now, you know. His sister never came. She gave up on him when he was on the drugs. But – but I remember how he was. Ten years old, bursting with excitement because we'd given him a new bike. And then we gave him everything. Yes, I was strict, yes, I demanded standards, but I owed him a decent upbringing – discipline – something achieved. We never stinted. Never denied him. And he turned on us.' He was fighting tears. Charles felt great irritation with him, and swallowed it down. The man had a right to his emotion.

After a moment he looked at his watch. Moffat was blowing his nose, wondering how to continue. Charles said, 'Fancy a drink? It's way past opening time. We could grab a sandwich.'

'What? Well – yes, all right.'

They sat in the pub, and at once the atmosphere was different. Charles was no longer the doctor, Moffat no longer the aggrieved relative. They were two professionals, choosing roast beef sandwiches and a pint of real ale. A couple of office girls wiggled in, wearing tight skirts and high heels. They sat on stools at the bar, whispering and giggling.

'Just my son's type,' said Moffat. 'We used to think the worst he could do would be to marry the wrong girl.'

'Is it going to be worse for you if he ends up in a mental institution?' asked Charles. 'At least now he doesn't seem to know what's happening to him.'

'Don't they have dreams?'

Charles hesitated. 'Perhaps they do. It is a dreamlike state. But there's nothing to say those dreams are unpleasant.'

'There's nothing to say anything, is there? They don't respond.'

The beer and sandwiches arrived. They ate in silence, while the lunchtime traffic ebbed and flowed about them. Suddenly

Moffat said, 'What is this treatment, then? Do you mean to operate?'

Charles nodded, automatically bringing out the sketchpad with which he always approached relatives. He began to draw the brain, as seen from below, labelling the frontal and temporal lobes, the cerebellum, the optic nerves, olfactory bulb, and the nerves to the head and face. In the centre, close to the pituitary gland, he pinpointed the hypothalamus.

'That's your problem,' he said, tapping the page. 'Your son's hypothalamus maintains him in a state very similar to sleep. It's been triggered by something, possibly by a substance produced in the brain that we have only just begun to understand. Why is your son producing so much of this substance that he never wakes? We don't know. Possibly because a few cells have been damaged. It might be an area about the size of a matchhead. I would like to try to eliminate those cells and see what happens.'

Moffat licked dry lips. 'An experiment.'

'Absolutely. A dangerous experiment. I need your whole-hearted understanding and consent. If you don't want me to proceed, I won't.'

The girls at the bar were looking at them. They seemed to recognise Charles. 'You've got quite a fan club since you went on television,' said Moffat. 'You want to make a name for yourself, I suppose.'

'Indeed I do,' said Charles. 'Which is why I'm prepared to take this sort of risk. We could wait twenty years until the research is watertight, but your son will be dead by then. He won't have lived a minute more than he has now. Really lived, I mean. You'd have been spared the necessity to adapt to whatever he becomes, of course, and that's not to be despised. Have no illusions. You are the one who'll suffer if this goes wrong. You, not me.'

'And my son?'

Charles shrugged. 'Life at any price? I don't know.'

Absently, although Charles had barely touched his beer, Moffat went to the bar and ordered more. The two men sat in silence, sipping their drinks, while the office girls chattered and the barman turned on the radio for the sports news.

Charles thought of all that he had to do that day, and knew he should not be sitting here dulling his senses with beer. But Moffat seemed in no hurry. 'If I bring my wife, will you talk it through with her?' he asked. 'Or perhaps you'd like to come to dinner.'

It was an honour. Charles had been granted favoured person status. He thought of going on his own and mentally winced. 'Thank you. I'd enjoy that. I wonder if I might bring someone? You might like to meet another of my coma patients, Celia Sheraton.'

'The woman who recovered? You can't imagine – we've often said – if she would come, we'd be delighted.'

They parted soon after. The beer had given Charles a slight headache. He went back to the hospital, but found he needn't have hurried. Since Celia's trust fund was frozen everyone was short of cash. He couldn't even run as many tests as he wanted. He wandered the corridors for a while, savaging any of his juniors who crossed his path, before deciding he might as well call it a day and go home.

He hadn't been in the car more than ten minutes before the idea of visiting Celia came into his head. He wondered if that was what he'd been intending all along. He couldn't trust his own motives nowadays. He could tell her about the dinner engagement with the Moffats, and perhaps she'd go out with him tonight. Never lonely in his life, he was discovering a need within himself for company.

He turned the car, losing himself in a welter of sidestreets. He was beginning to doubt that he could get through this way when he found himself in a shopping area, full of jewellers' and old clothes shops. Charles glanced at the street names, and realised he was near Celia's pawnbroker. On impulse he began looking for it, half imagining that the pearls would be exhibited in the window, half curious to see what would really be there. Soon he saw the three golden balls above a shop of surprising distinction. The window display was a disappointment, though, with nothing of interest. Somehow Charles had imagined seeing if not the pearls, then at least evidence of financial degradation. Wedding rings perhaps, or war medals.

Deprived of that, he looked instead to see if anyone would enter or leave the shop, but the door remained closed. Then a taxi drew up. Charles parked briefly on a double yellow line across the road, waiting to see which poverty-stricken duchess or blackmailed lord would emerge. But it was Celia.

She went quickly into the shop, as he imagined a customer might, head down, looking neither to right nor left. His mind raced, and for a moment he almost followed her. Then he paused. He thought of all the things she could be doing; someone might have given her money. David? Surely not. Perhaps she was negotiating for an extended loan. At pawnbroking rates it wouldn't be long before redeeming the pearls was utterly out of the question. It was probably so already.

He drove around the block, looking for somewhere to park, but when he passed the shop again he saw Celia once more. She was some way down the road, hailing a taxi. Charles cut in, causing the taxi driver to curse and lean on the horn, but Charles ignored him. Celia stared at him, colouring to her hair. Charles opened his window. 'Get in.' He drove away in a flurry of litter and dead leaves.

She was flustered, a little breathless, obviously guilty.

'Why are you here?' she demanded. 'Are you following me?'

'No, I saw you by chance. You're supposed to be in hiding, remember?'

She turned her face away from him, the profile smooth and firm. Then a shiver racked her. 'Actually, I'm glad you came. Will you take me for tea? I'm cold.'

'How cold?' He cast his physician's eye over her.

'Slightly cold. It's a cold day. I want a cup of tea. Don't fuss, Charles!'

He took her to a small, dark tea shop where the cakes were second rate enough to keep the custom down. Celia complained, until Charles said, 'We can't go anywhere more public! If you really thought you were in danger you'd be taking this a hell of a lot more seriously. Don't you think it? In which case move back home.'

'With you? No.'

An uncomfortable silence fell. 'I didn't think you were

trying to get away from me,' he said at last. 'At least, it didn't seem obvious.'

'I wasn't. I'm not. Anyway, without Dorrie there's scandal.'

'I've decided to forget about that. And you won't move back?'

'Charles, your house is freezing cold!'

He laughed, as she had intended. She reached out and stroked his hand, a light pressure of a single finger. He said, 'You look beautiful today.'

He had never complimented her before. He never paid compliments. She went a little pink, glancing down at her black coat and skirt, enlivened by fake ruby brooches, knowing that the hat with its curling feather had been the perfect rakish touch. Now, because he had remarked on it, she would wear it more. What Charles liked, others would too.

'I got the pearls,' she said, when the waitress had brought them the tea.

'What?'

'I got them. Here. Look.'

She brought a box from her bag. Charles sat and watched as she snapped it open and casually draped the pearls across her hand. No one could mistake them for anything but the real thing. They glowed with an inner light, like newly caught fish still wet on the slab, brilliant with life. Celia let the rope fall to the table, and the pearls rumbled gently on to the wood. 'Put them away,' said Charles in a hoarse whisper. 'Someone will see.'

'It's too dark in here,' said Celia casually. 'What shall I do with them now? The bank?'

'Yes. Just as soon as you tell me where in God's name you got the money to redeem them. Was it David?'

She studied him with a clear, blue gaze. 'You always want to know everything,' she said. 'It's one of your least attractive traits.'

'Don't try and wriggle,' he retorted. 'You've done something and you don't want to tell. You'd have said nothing if I hadn't seen you.'

'I don't have to keep you informed.'

'For Christ's sake, Celia, you are pregnant with my child!'

'So what? It gives you no more rights than before.'

He wondered who else in the whole world had as much power to enrage him. Even his juniors, whose vacillations and lack of dedication sometimes drove him to roar irascibly, never created in him this fulminating, impotent rage. Impotence. That was the key. Only Celia was beyond his power. She caused anger, and he could not revenge himself. He was shackled, endlessly, by gentleness.

'I wish you wouldn't do this to me,' he murmured.

'Do what? Charles, don't be silly. I didn't mean to upset you.' She was looking at him with alarm. He never showed weakness to any degree, she sometimes thought him incapable of human emotion. 'Charles?' she said again.

He took her hand. 'Tell me where you got the money. Please. If you don't I'll think terrible things. You might have another man.'

'I haven't. There's just you.'

'And David.'

'I don't know why you're jealous of David. He won't leave Heather.'

'But you want him to.'

She made a face at him, keeping her secret, saying, 'I didn't get the money from him. It was stupid, really. I had what I needed in my own two hands, and all I had to do was tell someone I had it and they'd pay what I asked.' He didn't understand, she would have to spell it out for him. 'The Marlborough shares. I sold them back to George Marlborough. I got more than I paid, and then some.'

She pushed the plate of scones and dry gingerbread away. The pearls still lay on the table, and she ran them through her fingers as she spoke.

The Marlborough shares; whoever held those documents had control. Edwin wanted them, of course, and she wouldn't sell to him – although Marlborough couldn't know that. They must be waiting daily for the news that Edwin had his controlling interest. So, why not sell to Marlborough?

Her first thought was that they wouldn't have the cash. But the clubs, although badly run, weren't bankrupt; and if they

394

knew (or thought they knew) that if they didn't buy, Edwin certainly would – well, she could virtually name her price.

She contacted George Marlborough by telephone at his London club, and he was drunk. 'My dear, what is all this? Do I know you? Are you someone I'd like to know? Money, money, what's the world coming to when even the women want to talk about it all day long?'

She got nowhere and hung up. No cash and no pearls, and all because Marlborough was run by a drunken fool. She began to see Edwin's point of view; if George Marlborough could make money out of his clubs, anyone else could make a fortune.

She was in despair. But an hour or so later, the telephone rang. It was the financial manager of Marlborough, the shares were of more than casual interest, and if she would be so good as to lodge them with a solicitor she would be in receipt of a banker's draft by the end of the day. And the man was as good as his word.

It had all been so easy. Too easy. Charles felt his thoughts turn round and run back on themselves. 'I thought you said Marlborough was drunk.'

'He must have written down my number, so he can't have been as drunk as all that.'

'Apparently not. Was anyone else on the line?'

'Not that I know of. You don't think—'

'Have you anything that says it was Marlborough who paid you? Anything at all?'

'I was paid by banker's draft. They're like money, signed by the bank. There's nothing to say who they come from.'

'So you need not have sold the shares to Marlborough. They could have gone to a holding company, or to a friend – in fact, to anyone.'

'You mean Edwin, don't you?'

He nodded ruefully. 'So easy. All he needed was a spy in the camp.'

'Oh God.' The ramifications were plain to them both. Had she really sold Edwin the shares? It was possible.

She said, 'Now he's got my telephone number. He'll know I'm still in Leeds.' Her mind whirled helplessly. It was at moments such as this that she knew she wasn't well. The dynamic, direct pathways along which her thoughts used to run seemed now to lead to dead-ends. How could Charles see so clearly what she could not? She felt a fool, as if this at last proved that she was no longer a woman capable of controlling her own life. What a mess she had made of everything!

'He'll make a fortune,' she said at last. 'I've given it to him on a plate.'

'You've made a packet yourself,' said Charles.

'How? I've put it all into these damned pearls, and I can't sell them. The moment I offer them on the market Edwin will come down like a ton of bricks and claim that they should have been his. I've wasted all that money.'

They sat in silence, the pearls clutched in Celia's hands. It seemed so foolish to be short of cash when she held a fortune in her palms. She sighed heavily. 'Hector Lowndes wants to hire a barrister to deal with my case. We'll have to do it on tick. They don't demand cash on the nail, do they?'

Charles shrugged. 'Don't know. But you can always ask. We're having dinner with one. Wear the pearls.'

Celia dressed with infinite care. It was so long since she had been taken out with the intention of impressing people. She chose dark blue silk, a long skirt with an oriental cheongsam top. It made her look very tall and thin, and the high neck was a wonderful backdrop for the pearls. They gleamed against the blue as if in a jeweller's shop window, and she put up her hair in a long fall from crown to shoulders.

On her feet she wore high-heeled sandals, the straps bejewelled, as if she was in a harem. Charles was waiting in the sitting room, curbing his impatience with a scotch. Celia came in and turned round for him, saying, 'Do you remember those terrible white shoes? Why those shoes?'

He shrugged. 'They were in the hospital store. I don't know where they came from.'

'I thought you wanted me to look like a tart.'

'I liked you looking tarty.'

She made a face. He would.

The Moffats lived in one of the leafy suburbs, in a big house set well back off a main road. The house had latticed windows and panelled rooms, and it was near the tennis club and the golf course, with shops and buses only minutes away. Yet the son of this household had burrowed relentlessly down. Charles felt depressed suddenly. Fate lashed out at success, as if it was unworthy. He looked at Celia. Was she to be the cause of his own ruin?

Both Moffats greeted them. 'Good evening, good evening.' Much rubbing of nervous hands. 'I'm Barry, this is Theresa. My daughter Susan, and her husband Frank. We thought – we're all concerned – social occasion of course—'

'Be quiet, Barry,' said Theresa, quelling him.

They went into the sitting room. Celia was the object of all eyes: her skin, her hair, her pearls. She sat in a low chair, her legs at an elegant stretch, while the conversation limped desultorily around her. Finally Charles said, 'If we want to talk coma, why don't we do it now? It's a big subject, it needs time.'

'Yes. Yes, indeed,' said Barry Moffat.

His daughter said, 'What is there to discuss? Celia here may look a million dollars but Martin never will. He was a mess before he even got ill.'

'At least he's off the heroin now,' said Charles cheerfully. 'You could say that he's well and truly cleaned up. The wonders of modern science.'

An uncomfortable laugh ran round the room. Celia said, 'Please don't mind Charles. He may not be sympathetic, but he's a good doctor. Such a pity no one taught him anything about bedside manners.'

'Don't be cheeky,' said Charles, and Celia looked at him quizzically. They exchanged a wry grin.

'I didn't realise you were on intimate terms with Mrs Sheraton,' said Barry Moffat stiffly. Charles froze in his seat.

'I'm sorry?' Celia lifted her eyebrows. 'Charles and I know each other very well by now. Is that intimate? It sounds quite obscene.'

Theresa said, 'Barry didn't mean – of course no doctor . . .'

'I have a family,' said Celia.

'Apologise, Dad,' said Susan. 'You've got the wrong end of the stick, as usual.'

The unfortunate Barry Moffat grunted the undeserved

397

apology. Charles gritted his teeth. Moffat was a lawyer, used to seeing through lies. And Charles knew that his glance softened when he looked at Celia, that even his voice changed. In the hospital he compensated with brusqueness, but here, in a social setting, he wanted to relax. He dared not. Celia was dangerous! If she had made his career, she might well destroy it. He had eaten of the fruit, and the Garden of Eden was not for such as he.

His refuge must be medical. He began his usual dissertation on the structure of the brain, noting the temper of his audience. They wanted everything known, everything cut and dried. All the unproven theories and interesting sidelights were not for them. They wanted facts, immutable facts, they didn't want reality. They wanted to believe he was some superman, more brilliant and more knowledgeable than any before.

He turned quickly to Martin Moffat's particular case. 'He is damaged,' he said. 'There's no question of that. But the damage as we see it is slight. If he woke now he ought to have fair motor control, and I suspect some visual problems. His mental abilities, his emotions, his capacity for pleasure or pain, are all things on which we can only speculate.'

Susan said, 'You could damage him terribly, though. Just by operating.'

'Indeed.'

'But you don't often damage people, I know that. Everyone says.' Theresa Moffat, clutching at the hem of his garment. She wanted her miracle.

Celia said, 'Charles tells me you don't go and visit your son, Mrs Moffat. Why not?'

'It's just – it's too awful. I can't bear to be so upset.'

'You wouldn't rather he was dead, would you? Perhaps you imagine he's dead.'

Theresa Moffat swallowed. 'It would be easier.'

Charles said, 'Mrs Sheraton's husband spent many years pretending she was dead. People's lives go on. The place someone occupied is filled up by other people and other things. There might not be room for your son if he revived. Emotional room, I mean.'

Nobody spoke. Charles knew that he had entered a dark corner, the place they wished no one to go. If Martin returned, and was as before, then they would rather he was dead. Susan said, 'We kept a place for him before. We want him back. Not as the person he was, but as the person he should have been, if things hadn't gone wrong. We want another chance. To do it better this time.'

The meal was ready. At the table they thankfully abandoned brains and talked of more everyday things.

Charles turned to Barry Moffat. 'I suppose you've heard about Celia's trust fund. Braddock's trying to take it from the hospital.'

Moffat nodded. 'Hasn't done Braddock's image any good. People are saying he must be desperate. Is it true?'

Charles took a sip of wine. 'No one knows. One thing's certain, the hospital's going to suffer if he wins. We really should all back Celia, because if she comes out on top she's going to redonate the entire fund, mostly to the benefit of my department. Brain injuries don't get much money in the normal course of events. But fighting Braddock's proving pretty expensive. Legal fees.'

It was the most blatant propaganda. Moffat glanced at his wife, and then at Charles. Celia, across the table, said, 'I didn't hear you say that, Charles. I don't care how many cancelled operations there have been, you shouldn't pressure people over the dinner table.'

'Cancelled operations?' Theresa's eyes widened. 'For lack of cash? Brain operations?'

'Afraid so,' said Charles. 'But, of course, none of this would affect Martin. He's a private patient, I always have cash enough for them. It's the others. The people like Martin who haven't got parents like you. Fathers with young families. A young girl whose parents are dead. They lose out.'

'Charles, you will stop this,' sang out Celia, between clenched teeth. 'Eat your broccoli and shut up.'

Susan said, 'Isn't he supposed to tell you to eat the broccoli?'

Celia chuckled. 'He has minions to do that for him. Let me tell you, difficult as it may be to believe, when he's like this, Charles is a very Great Man!'

They dissected the evening in the car on the way home. Generally speaking they had pitched it pretty well.

'You shouldn't have asked if his mother wanted him dead,' said Charles.

She glanced at him. 'I wanted to know. When you've been presumed dead yourself it's interesting to see things from the other side. It's easier when people die. Coma is so terribly untidy.'

He reached for her hand and held it. 'I like your untidiness. I don't regret a thing, even if Barry Moffat runs off and shops me to the BMA for unprofessional conduct.'

Celia blew down her nose. She wanted to move her hand, because nowadays Charles was always trying to move in on her, make progress, stake claims. 'I won't tell anyone the baby's yours,' she said. 'And Dorrie won't breathe a word.'

'It's going to be obvious in the end. We'll be married once you get a divorce.'

'Yes. The divorce.' She took her hand away and nibbled at the side of her thumb.

Charles changed gear and accelerated hard up the road. It was a wet night with a stiff breeze sending clouds scudding across the moon. Few people were abroad at this hour, although it wasn't so late. Celia knew he would want to come up. He might want to stay. She balanced the pleasure of his body against the pressure he would apply. Could she ignore the nagging for the sake of the sex?

It was odd how even thinking of the act could make all the nerves and blood vessels, neurons and ganglia, the undefined and indefinable substances of which Charles had spoken only tonight, begin sparking and conspiring together. Her body wanted him. A low throbbing was beginning, she was heavy with anticipation. The perfect end to an evening.

Her head rolled on the back of the seat as she looked at him. Charles reached out and put his hand on her belly, pushing over the hard swelling to the moistness between her legs. He pressed and she groaned, writhing against him. Then she reached out and gripped him, an experienced woman who knew what a man couldn't stand. He let out a cry and the car swerved.

'What the hell was that for?'

'Fun. You make me so angry. You assume so bloody much.'

'What do I assume? That I'll sleep in your bed tonight? Yes, I grant you, that is what I intend to do, and it would take a herd of wild elephants to stop me.'

She looked at him beneath heavy lids. 'Let's do it in the car and sleep alone.'

He pulled the wheel hard and turned a corner. 'Let's not. I won't be added to your list of other men. I am telling you, Celia, here and now, that you are not shaking me off. You can try and you can wriggle, but you're not getting any way out.'

She sat in her seat, fulminating with anger. But still she wanted to make love to him. Would she never learn? Time after time desire had betrayed her. All the problems in her life had been because of it. She had slept with Charles because he was attractive, desirable even, and she needed what he had to give. And now she couldn't escape him.

They came to her flats and Charles drove into the basement car park, reserved for residents and their guests. Celia wanted to deny him permission, refuse him access to the residents-only lift, but you didn't refuse Charles things like that. She got out of the car, the pearls heavy around her neck, wondering if she wanted to fight Charles, make love to him or both. In the lift he stood against the far wall, looking at her. The light was very harsh, turning them into ghosts of themselves, a hundred years old.

On the landing, thickly carpeted, Celia fished for her key. Then Charles gripped her arm. 'Someone's here,' he whispered.

She went cold as ice, and looked frantically around. It was just like the last time, a lobby, danger, no escape. There was escape. She backed towards the lift. But Charles was dragging at her, pushing her towards the stair. He pushed her through the heavy fire door and crouched down.

'What did you see?'

'Light. Under your door. Did you hear talking?'

She shook her head. 'It could be David, or the girls.'

'Do they have a key?'

'No.'

The top of the door was reinforced glass. Charles peered cautiously through, and Celia could sense his anticipation. Since the fight, his only fight, he had begun to relish proving himself.

'Let's get away and call the police,' she muttered, tugging at his arm.

'Not yet. Let's see who it is. By the time the police get here they could be long gone.'

'If they come this way so will we!'

'Go down now if you want.'

'No!'

He glanced back at her. She was standing on the stairs, hands tightly gripping the rail. She wore the pearls and he held out his hand.

'Give those to me and go down. You look exhausted.'

'I'm fine. I won't go and not know what's happening.'

He was about to insist when the door to the flat opened. They both crouched again, and Celia realised she should have given him the pearls. People would kill for those pearls.

But nothing happened. They stayed motionless, and in a moment there came the whine of the lift. They waited a long few minutes, giving the lift time to reach the bottom and return. It did not. The raiders had gone.

They went into the flat slowly, cautiously. Someone might still be there. But the place was empty, with only ransacked drawers and cupboards to prove that burglars had been. If they were burglars. Celia went from room to room, checking on her things. She had so little. Nothing was gone.

She returned to Charles. He was pouring himself a scotch, surveying the broken door lock. 'What were they after?' she asked.

He looked at her. 'The pearls, perhaps. Most probably you.'

She sat down by the unlit fire, holding herself together. 'They must have known I wasn't here. Why didn't they wait?'

'Don't know. They might want to flush you out. Drive you back to me, where they can get at you.'

'You're so comforting.'

'There's no mileage in lies.'

She wanted to cry. Again she was driven out, again she was hunted. Braddock had the measure of her. He had only to click his fingers and she lost. This proved that he had bought her shares. He was in triumph tonight; he had Marlborough, and he had her on the run. When would she ever turn the tables?

She said, 'I'll go to Blantyre House. He won't expect that.'

'But you must come back to me. We'll get a guard, something.'

She shook her head. 'I want to be near the girls. How did Braddock know where I was? He only had my telephone number.'

'You can't expect children to keep secrets.'

'They're not stupid! I told them not to tell. Somehow it got out. Could it have been David?'

'Probably.'

Celia thought for a moment. Suddenly she said, 'You know, I've never been sure if David wasn't in some sort of deal with Edwin.'

Charles looked at her. It was the first truly critical thing he had ever heard about her husband. And it might be true. She went on, 'It seems as if he made so little fuss about the Will. Between them, he and Edwin convinced my mother that the girls were supposed to be left out. She agreed, partly because she was persuaded and partly because she had the pearls, which the girls could have. She didn't think that Edwin would try and get those too. Edwin's a very greedy man.'

'He leads an expensive life.' Charles considered the possibilities. This piece slotted into the jigsaw with a little, satisfying click.

'So, Edwin offered David a cut if he didn't oppose the Will?'

She nodded. 'He might have done. That way, David got something in his own right without an endless list of conditions. But he didn't get any money, and since he loathes Edwin Braddock he must have been cheated in the end. It's so like David!'

'The man's a complete fool,' said Charles with satisfaction.

Celia turned from him. Charles would never understand David, never see that a man's intelligence wasn't measured by his worldliness. As an inventor, as a designing engineer,

David was brilliant. But if she was right – he wasn't much good as a crook.

Chapter Twenty-Seven

Heather's face, bare of make-up and covered in a thin film of night cream, was not at its best. In contrast Celia swept past her, long hair swinging, her skin reflected in the fabulous pearls. David, at war with her and unable to admit it, felt a subdued and admiring rage.

'Those pearls,' he said, grimly. 'Your mother's pearls.'

'Yes.' Celia swung on one heel, and didn't explain. She was desperately tired, longing for nothing so much as a bed. Any bed. She felt the telltale blurring of her thoughts.

Charles said, 'Celia needs to stay here tonight. There have been developments. One or two unpleasant things. Someone broke into her flat tonight, she can't stay there.'

'Edwin?' David was incredulous.

'We think so.'

Heather laughed, an eldritch cackle that made everyone turn and stare.

Celia put her hand to her head. 'Don't – don't—' She swayed and almost fell.

Charles helped her to bed in the staff flat. Her right hand was shaking and she couldn't unfasten the pearls. He unhooked the clasp, letting the rope fall in her lap. He began to undress her for bed, sliding her arms from her blouse, and she thought of David, who might come in. 'Don't,' she said again.

But he kept on, until she was curled naked on the bed. She felt like a child again, helpless and trusting. His hand, warm and strong, rested on her shoulder. The door opened and David was there.

'My God,' he said. 'You never lose an opportunity, do you?'

Charles stood up, reaching for a blanket to cover her. 'In future I suggest you knock.'

David ignored him. Celia lay on the bed, her eyes half closed. 'I don't know how you have the gall,' he said. 'She looks half dead.'

'Just how you like her,' retorted Charles, and shook out the blanket. But he didn't at once put it over her. The woman before them was a sculpture, remote and inviolate. Early pregnancy had made her voluptuous. Her skin ran like silk over rounded flesh, her breasts were as heavy as marble.

Suddenly Charles reached out and covered her, tucking the blanket securely as if she was truly a work of art and might break. He looked up at David Sheraton. He said, 'I don't know why she wanted to come here tonight. Perhaps it's the house, it's still home to her. You'd better take care. She's precious to me.'

David looked from his dark, alert face to Celia's sleeping one. He licked dry lips. 'I should have you struck off.'

Charles let a pause develop. He found another pillow and lifted Celia's head to rest more comfortably. Sheraton watched him. At last Charles said, 'You know more than you pretend about how Braddock got the money. You were left a packet, but it was tied up with string, and you didn't want that. So you let Braddock alter the Will, no questions asked. Later, he was to pay you what was owed and you'd have thumbed your nose at Celia, the old man and his wife who didn't like you, and got your fortune after all. When Braddock didn't pay up, there wasn't a single thing you could do. God, but you're a fool.'

David, white and sweating, said, 'You're the fool, Davenport. Falling for a woman whose loyalty only lasts for the time it takes to screw her!'

Charles came up off the floor in a rush. But Sheraton stood his ground, and at the last moment, reason prevailed. He couldn't hit him. Not if he wanted to keep his reputation. And he had a patient under his care.

He turned from Sheraton's infuriating face, taking up Celia's wrist to feel her pulse. He was suddenly aware that her eyes, bright slits beneath her lids, were watching him. Conscious then. Was she merely exhausted? He rubbed her hand, holding it tightly, aware that he had betrayed her confidence, said too much.

Behind him, Sheraton said, 'I pity you. I really do. At least I got free.'

'Free?' Charles mocked him openly. 'Your whole life revolves around Celia. Her children, her money, her own self. She can stir you up any time she pleases. Your freedom extends only to the length of your lead.'

David said nothing. But the door opened gently, and they saw Heather standing there. She could have been there forever.

Celia awoke late the next morning. Her memory of the night was blurred and indistinct, as if she was remembering a dream. She felt slightly sick, and got out of bed in search of a glass of water. She wondered if Charles was here.

There was no glass nearby and she went out into the hall. Its well remembered lines reassured her. Blantyre House was as solid and as polished as it had been all through her life. But it was not as warm. Celia looked down at herself and saw that she was stark naked. She ran quickly along to Ellen's room, and fell through the door. Ellen was doing her homework.

'Help!' she yelped. 'Is there a fire?'

'No such luck,' said Celia. 'Have you got a dressing gown? Quick.'

Ellen went to the cupboard and gave her the outsize towelling cover-up she liked to lounge in. Celia wrapped it around herself. 'Very bohemian. You may have seen the last of this, my girl. I love it.'

'Mothers aren't supposed to borrow their daughters' clothes!'

'Why not?' Celia climbed on the bed and tucked in her toes. 'Could you get me some water, do you think? I feel a bit odd.'

'I've got some breakfast juice, would you like that?'

'Thanks.'

She sipped gratefully. It felt odd, in Ellen's room, almost as if Ellen were the older. As if Ellen might judge. Her daughter said, 'Mum says you've been having an affair with Mr Davenport.'

'Oh.' A buzzing began in Celia's ears. Damn Heather.

Would she never keep her mouth shut? 'Charles and I – well, yes.'

'Mum says you won't divorce Dad, though. She says you'll cling on.'

'Cling on! Cling on? If you must know—' The urge to tell Ellen everything almost choked her. But she swallowed it down. 'Your father and I have to agree. We haven't. Yet.'

She watched her daughter, trying to judge her thoughts. Ellen was so young to be asked to confront this turmoil of adult emotion. But then, was Celia herself old enough? The confusion went round and round in her head. She had underestimated Heather. That woman would do anything.

'Did you tell Heather where I was living?' she asked suddenly.

Ellen blinked. 'Well – yes. Shouldn't we? I know you didn't want everyone to know but it was only Mum. She sort of likes to find out what's going on. If we've been to visit she asks all sorts of leading questions, and in the long run it's easier if we just tell. All the kids from divorced families say it's always like that, the third degree dressed up as casual interest.'

'We are not a divorced family,' said Celia stiffly. 'We're a very unusual family. Suffering because of something which was absolutely not my fault!'

'Mum says you were always a wild driver,' said Ellen laconically.

'Does she? Does she?' Suddenly Celia was angry. 'Let me tell you, my girl, that I crashed because someone was trying to kill me. And they're still trying to kill me, and in all likelihood Heather, that wolf in sheep's clothing, is helping them on their way!'

There was a shocked silence. Celia got off the bed, saying, 'Sorry, sorry, don't listen to me. Ignore it.'

'Are you ill?' asked Ellen shakily.

Celia confronted her. 'No, darling, not that ill. Angry. Someone is trying to hurt me, and I think Heather may have given them my address. I don't suppose she realised.'

Ellen reached out to her. 'But – you're going to be all right?'

'Darling, yes. Of course. Nothing really bad can happen, I promise.'

She left the room and went slowly downstairs. Heather was in the small sitting room, shaking cushions and dusting. A cleaning lady was brushing the hearth, and Celia said, 'Could I have a word with you, Heather?'

They went into the library. It always smelled of disuse nowadays, and Celia went at once to open a window. Heather, dressed in a thin lambswool sweater, said, 'Please don't touch things in my home, Celia. If you don't mind.'

'I'll do what I like,' said Celia belligerently. 'You gave Edwin Braddock my address. Didn't you?'

The colour sank from Heather's skin, leaving it like aged parchment. Celia thought dispassionately that Heather was one of those women whose looks completely reflect their mood. She only ever looked pretty when she was happy and relaxed. She felt a sharp satisfaction that those conditions were nowadays so rarely fulfilled. 'You Judas,' she said.

Heather looked wildly around, as if searching for escape. 'What did you expect?' she said shrilly. 'You came here, flaunting yourself just as you always did, determined to get David, not caring at all about anyone else. What was I to do? Stand by while you wrecked my life? I knew you'd do anything you could. I thought – I thought you'd try and get him to bed, try and get pregnant, something like that. But he wouldn't listen. I couldn't just wait for it, could I?'

'You could have got me killed,' said Celia.

'You were supposed to be dead. That accident should have killed you. We'd all be happy if you'd only damned well died!'

It was too much. Celia felt emotion, held tight inside her, begin to boil up to the surface. She turned and walked quickly away, going out into the garden, still in the dressing gown, her feet bare on the cold, damp earth. Once at the tennis court, standing on the tussocky grass that used to be silky smooth, she uttered long, dry, guttural sobs. It was terrible that people wished her dead. Edwin. Heather. Even David.

Lucy was coming across the grass towards her. She was carrying a golf club. 'What are you doing here?' she called. 'You're not dressed.'

Celia tried to get a grip on herself. 'I haven't any proper clothes,' she managed. 'They're all at my flat.'

Lucy, cheerful and incurious, said, 'I bet Mum can lend you something. Let's go and see.'

In the face of Lucy's childish good humour neither woman could bring herself to spit venom. Heather found a jumper and a pair of slacks, and some tennis shoes she said she no longer wore.

'They won't fit over your talons, I suppose,' said Celia under her breath. She hated to wear Heather's clothes. They smelled of lavender bags and were sharply creased from the neatness of their folding. Nonetheless she combed her hair, catching it up in a scarf of Ellen's, and pulled the sleeves of her jumper to her elbows. There. She looked better in Heather's cast-offs than Heather ever had.

'You're putting on quite a lot of weight,' said Heather sharply.

Celia felt the telltale flush creeping up her neck. 'How kind of you to be concerned, Heather.'

Under Lucy's eye, Heather had to surrender. 'It – it suits you.'

'How fortunate.'

Lucy was sent to put her golf club away. The cleaning lady was banging ineffectually in the hall. In a low voice Celia said, 'So, what else have you told him? Everything about my court case too?'

'He – mostly he doesn't need to be told.'

'But you confirm every vague suspicion. Thank you so much, Heather dear.'

Celia picked up Heather's car keys, daring her to complain. But she stood in absolute silence while Celia stalked to the door. She waited until the car was driven away, until at last she knew the enemy was gone. Then she crumpled into a chair, hiding her face in her hands. This was the end. She was quite sure that Celia was going to tell David everything.

George Marlborough was in his usual morning condition. He sat slumped in a corner seat in his club, surrounded by upturned chairs on tables, a vacuum cleaner whining somewhere to his left, on his right the barman stacking bottles with a painful clatter. His cigar smouldered in one hand, his 'reviver', three parts gin and one each of tomato juice and Worcester sauce, in the other. He gazed out at the world with gloomy resignation, waving his cigar at his companion.

'Sorry about the noise,' he muttered. 'Place is a hellhole until lunch. Tables open at twelve. Always get a few. The Lucan type. Well, with a club like this, bit of class, bit of style, the right sort can't keep away.'

Edwin murmured noncommittally. He had never met Marlborough before, the man hadn't bothered to find out what sort of northerner he was rubbishing. Now, in one of his best handmade suits, jewellery discreet gold with just one very good diamond in his tiepin, he looked the right sort himself. The lies had come easily. Prospective member – quick look round – mutual friend to vouch for him – and here he was, watching the veins in Marlborough's nose turn bluer by the minute.

'Hans!' yelled Marlborough suddenly. 'Bring me another. Pronto! And something for my friend.' He lifted an enquiring eyebrow.

'Champagne,' said Edwin.

Marlborough blinked. People you didn't know didn't normally ask you to open bottles of champagne after breakfast. 'Who did you say you knew?' he asked.

'Lamberhurst,' said Edwin easily. 'And Cumberworth.'

'Cubby Cumberworth?'

'God knows.'

He sat back, waiting for the champagne. Marlborough's confusion was very satisfying, and quite understandable. He had set about pickling himself some forty years before and was now reaching utter saturation. Edwin could almost feel sorry for him – until he reminded himself of what Marlborough had said. It had been printed everywhere. 'At the end of the day, it's up to people of our sort to keep out people of his. Who does this vulgar, jumped up little pipsqueak think he is?'

The champagne arrived, slightly too warm. Edwin sipped, nodding to his host, and Marlborough peered at him blearily. He couldn't remember why the man was here. 'Sorry. Can't remember your name,' he said. 'Bit early for me. I'm a night owl. Have to be, with the clubs. Nothing like a convivial host

411

for making things go with a swing.'

'My name's Braddock,' said Edwin, twirling his champagne glass. 'Edwin Braddock.' The famous Marlborough look, confused and belligerent, passed across his companion's face. Edwin leaned back comfortably. 'I'm so sorry, I should have explained myself earlier, perhaps. I have just acquired a controlling interest in the Marlborough clubs, and I am here to inform you that I intend to take over at once. My team of auditors is waiting outside, ready to come in and begin the inventory. But please do finish your drink.'

Marlborough gaped at him. His mouth opened and closed, so much like the huge, imprisoned fish Edwin kept at Linton Place. 'You're lying,' he said at last. 'We've got all the shares tied up – was it my sister Julia? Damn the bloody woman!'

'I shall leave you to make your own enquiries,' said Edwin. 'There are going to be some changes, I'm afraid. You won't be permitted on the premises except during normal club hours, and all drinks must be paid for. We'll serve a decent champagne in decent condition in future. And as for this place – ' he looked about him with distaste '– the carpet ought to be taken up and burned. If this attracts the right sort, as you call it, then they're people we can do without.'

Marlborough flailed for some solid structure in an unsteady world. 'The board – we have to consult—'

'I've asked the members to attend here in precisely ten minutes' time.' Edwin got up, dusting flecks from his immaculate suit. A commotion in the lobby caught his attention. It was Julia Marlborough, in a fluster.

'George? George!'

He rose unsteadily from behind his table. 'This is all your bloody fault!' he roared.

'Mine? When you're sitting here, drunk, at ten in the morning?'

'Traitor! Betrayer! What did he give you? A quick half hour in the back of his bloody Japanese car?'

'George!' Julia's face flamed. She was a large, unattractive woman, with mild blue eyes, now filling with tears.

Edwin said, 'Please, Lady Julia, I don't want this. Have some champagne. Come and sit down.'

412

Unsure who he might be, she accepted. Marlborough roared, 'I knew you'd let him in your knickers! If you were that desperate I'd have hired you someone. Always some young lad doesn't care where he puts it.'

His sister began to sob. Edwin gestured to the man behind the bar and he at once came over. 'Hans, be so good as to remove this gentleman from the club,' said Edwin in clipped, cold tones. 'He isn't the type of person we want on the premises.'

'Certainly, sir.' The barman put an iron hand on Marlborough's arm. The older man began to bellow and struggle, his shirt came out of his trousers, the drink in his hand spilled like so much blood. To Edwin's entire satisfaction, George Marlborough was propelled into the street and left there, under the startled eyes of the board members arriving for their meeting.

'Well done, Hans,' said Edwin to the barman. He offered him a long white envelope. 'My thanks. Tidy up at the bar, would you please, and join us? I think we can find you something much more interesting to do from now on.'

The others in the room were gathering in knots to whisper. The staff were milling about, openly confused. Edwin sipped again at his champagne, enjoying even the roughness that denoted less than perfect vintage. It was right that he was here. He was born to depose the unworthy, to step into shoes that they believed were theirs, but which fitted him to perfection. Another wonderful day.

Celia stopped the car under overhanging trees near one of the locked gates of Linton Place. She reached behind her seat, extracting a pair of heavy bolt cutters. They were hard to lift, and would be harder to use, but she was determined. She staggered to the gate, and fitted them round the chain. Let no one come now, she thought. If they did she would have to bluster her way out of it.

The handles of the cutters needed to be brought together with a fair amount of strength. Her right arm lacked the necessary force, she could bring no pressure to bear. Instead she wedged the cutter against the gate, using both hands to

413

force the left blade down and through. It wouldn't go. The teeth bit and chewed, like a dog with a tough carcass. She kept working and working, growing hot with sweat, taking off her coat to give herself more freedom to move. At last, her strength almost gone, the chain gave way.

She had to go and sit in the car to recover. After ten minutes or so she went back and gathered up the broken chain, scuffing the telltale swarf into the dust. Then she swung one of the gates wide, with a great screech of rusty metal. She drove the car tentatively through, parked, and closed the gate carefully behind her.

From what she could judge, this road did not lead to the house at all, but to the wood behind the lake. She only felt calm when she was in the shelter of the trees, away from the park's blank exposure. There was a house here, a small cottage, but it seemed empty. She left the car beside it and got out. From here she could look across the lake at Linton Place itself.

All was peaceful. She was about to walk through the wood, to get as near as possible to the house before stepping into the open, when a figure appeared. Someone was walking the dogs. She strained her eyes, trying to see if it was Edwin, but the distance was too great. She waited until they were closer, and saw that it was one of the servants. Tomul? Was that what Edwin had called him? Her confidence surged. Edwin wasn't at home.

The man moved away from her, briskly, as if intent on a long walk.

When he was out of sight Celia began to move, imbued with a sense of urgency, almost running. The ill-fitting tennis shoes hurt her, but she took no notice. She was tired of powerlessness, sick of waiting. Everything she did depended on others, and she wanted, for once, to take charge.

The yards from the wood to the house, open to a sea of blank glass windows, seemed to take forever. She knew that she was tired already, and her head hurt. But she reached the house without incident and walked around it, wondering where she would find an open door. The French windows on the terrace were locked, and a door from a disused service room, but the next handle she tried turned easily. She was in.

It was one of those concrete-floored, mildewed rooms that crouch at the back of great country houses. There were leads and dog bowls, a pile of old garden chairs, a tennis net rolled up and folded away. Celia was reassured. It was the sort of place she understood. In the passage beyond, thinly carpeted, she guessed at the doors. The kitchen would be at the end, with access to the main house. She opened the door a crack and peered in.

A big, old room lined with pine cupboards. Some vegetables lay on the table but no one was there. She didn't know how many servants Edwin employed. Was there a cook somewhere who would find her? No one came. The house ached with silence. In the great, polished hall there was the scent of out of season roses.

She was disorientated suddenly. She couldn't remember where the rooms were. On her one brief visit she had never expected to need to recall. Sure now that the house was deserted, she opened door after door, unable to find the room which she sought. Suddenly she froze. Footsteps. A voice called, 'Tomul? Qui est là?'

She opened a door and went in. She stood behind it, facing the wood, waiting for the servant to discover her. What would she say? Something. Anything. And none of it would be any good. What would she tell the police?

The footsteps were coming nearer. Small, crisp feet in leather shoes. They came to the door – and passed on. Celia's heart, which seemed almost to have stopped, began thunderously beating. Charles had told her to avoid anything like that. What would happen if she collapsed? There was no time to think about that now. She turned into the room.

It was the room with the fish. There it was, in the huge tank, its mouth opening and closing in a silent cry of pain. She had intended to steal, vandalise, do something to inflict on Edwin some of the fear he created in her. But the fish – if she did nothing else she had to save the fish.

The tank couldn't be moved, she could never move it. As for the fish – she lifted the lid and stared down. Bubbles fizzed ceaselessly past its gills, and it fluttered its fins and mouthed. How could the man keep it like this? A prisoner. Even a fish must feel something. Even she had felt something. In her lost world, there had been elements of pleasure and pain.

She picked up a heavy brass doorstop, in the shape of a bell. She hit the tank, once, twice. Buttressed by the water, there was no great crash. The glass fractured, the water fell in a giant cascade, and the fish lay on the floor, flapping with desperate energy, gasping for life. Celia reached down and enfolded it, hugged the great wet body to her, feeling its huge muscles struggle and fight. She staggered from the room and down the hall, going to the front door this time, knowing she hadn't got long.

She rested twice, once at the door and once on the lawn in front of the house. The fish's struggles were growing ever weaker. Desperation imbued her with new strength, and she clasped the fish for the last time and staggered to the lake. It fell heavily from her arms on to the shale at the edge. Celia went into the water, past her ankles, feeling the tennis shoes fill horribly. She held the fish and guided it, knowing it was limp, its strength was gone. Was it dead? Had it forgotten how to swim? She pushed it towards deeper water, watching for some sign of life, some last flicker of consciousness. The fish floated lopsidedly, like the discarded catch of a deepsea trawler. At least it was free, Celia told herself. It would die in open water, its torture ended. All at once the fish opened its mouth, gulped, and with a flick of its tail was gone.

She stood there, covered in fish slime, laughing. Her feet were wet, and she must stink. When she turned she saw a small dark man watching from the house. The servant.

'What you do?' he asked nervously.

'I set the fish free.' She waved a hand to the lake. 'It's free. Now it can live.'

'Mr Braddock say you can?'

She nodded. 'Yes. Don't worry, I'll leave a note.'

She went back into the house and went to Edwin's desk. The things on it had all belonged to her father. Selecting a sheet of Edwin's headed notepaper, she wrote:

Dear Edwin,
Sorry to have missed you. We keep visiting each other at

416

such odd times, don't we? I have freed your fish. It
seemed by far the best thing to do. If things go on as they
are I shall certainly call again.
Yours,
Celia

As she left, leaving the little brown man holding the letter, she
saw the dogs come racing back across the park. She kept on
walking and they bounded round her, unsure what to do
without any command. 'Good dogs,' she said, and they sat
down, barking. The two servants were talking animatedly,
and a shout carried to the dogs. One of them, more aggressive
than the rest, gave a menacing growl.

By the time she reached her car her legs were weak and could
barely hold her. Her vision seemed blurred, she heard ringing
noises, and her right hand shook without pause. But she had to
drive. Somehow she managed it, and got back through the
gate, this time leaving it swinging wide. When at last she
arrived back at Blantyre House, she felt she had been gone
half a lifetime.

Chapter Twenty-Eight

Blantyre House was very quiet. Celia lay on the sofa, watching Charles play with his stethoscope. She knew he was giving himself time to think. He said, 'Have you any idea where Heather might have gone?'

Celia shook her head. 'She just went. She was the one who gave Edwin my address. She's been talking to him right from the first. Perhaps she thought I'd tell David.'

'And did you?'

Again she shook her head. Then she swung her legs over the edge of the sofa and prepared to stand up. Charles restrained her. 'You're not in any condition to do anything useful around here. If necessary I'll admit you to hospital.'

'Under the Mental Health Act?' Celia was rousing herself.

'Of course not!'

'Anything else is optional. I wouldn't go.'

'At least you could think of the baby.'

Her eyes flew open and she blazed at him, 'I won't have you blackmail me! The baby has nothing to do with it. You just want me out of this house!'

'You know perfectly well that you shouldn't be here.'

'I'll have you know that my husband and children need me.'

Charles settled his face into the mask he reserved for patients he disliked. At that moment he loathed Celia, for still, after everything, hanging on. Would she never learn?

He said, 'You might show some concern for Heather. The woman who selflessly cared for your family all these years.'

'Oh, really, Charles!' She got up. There were dark blue circles beneath her eyes. 'Selfless she was not. She jumped into my bed, into my shoes, into my everything, just as soon as she could. She had nothing and she wanted my life. She got it. It was my life, Charles! I lived it, I made it, those were my children! She stole them. She just came along and bloody stole them.'

'Would you rather no one had loved them?'

'Of course not!'

She sank to the sofa again and dropped her head into her hands. 'Damn you, Charles,' she muttered. 'Look at it from my point of view. I don't have sympathy to spare. At the beginning I tried to see things from the point of view of everyone else. I didn't demand, I didn't expect. I thought someone might look at things my way. And no one did. It was like living beyond a glass wall. There was my life, going on as before, and I was shut out from it. No one made any attempt to let me back in, not even for an instant. Least of all Heather.'

There was a low whining at the door. It was the dog, Tip, moping since Heather's abrupt departure. Celia reached down and tickled his nose and he licked her obligingly. But he wasn't happy. Everyone in this house was accustomed to Heather's rules, Heather's standards, Heather's prejudices. Without them, even the dog, least loved of them all, was bereft and unsettled, and he wandered the corridors searching for some semblance of normality.

Since he couldn't persuade her, Charles got up to leave. He felt depressed and angry. Celia had longed for this day, lived for it, worked for it; David and the girls, once more her own. The only thing now standing in her way was the foetus he had implanted in her, the cuckoo child growing in her hidden inner nest. He felt a sudden searing pain, quite unexpected. Heart, he thought. Damn it all, a heart attack. But it was nothing of the kind. It was a searing shaft of anguish.

He couldn't go back to work. He would take an hour off, go for a walk, take solace from the bare trees against the pale winter sky. Crows were in the fields, rising and falling like a ragged blanket, and he walked to the river, where he could look at the swans. But they too were in winter plumage, stained and rather worn. At this time of year, the months passed so slowly. It was as if spring would never come and the world would go on

420

getting barer and muddier, colder and darker, until it was all over.

He wasn't dressed for walking. His overcoat was too smart, his shoes too polished. What's more, the open air was cold, after the hothouse atmosphere of the hospital and the still chill of Blantyre House. So he walked briskly, trying to stir his blood, trying to rouse his spirits from the slough into which they had sunk. For the first time he felt that he was truly going to lose. The day would come, not too far distant, when there would be no Celia in his life. She would be gone.

A woman was sitting on the bank. He saw at once that her posture was unnatural. She was sitting with her legs stretched out in front of her, like a very young child on the schoolroom floor, and she was digging her fingers into the sticky mud, clawing up handfuls. Her coat was stained and torn, her hair full of leaves, as if she had slept out in a wet wood. Charles went and crouched down beside her.

'Hello, Heather,' he said. 'Are you trying to pluck up courage to drown yourself?'

She looked at him. Her face was stiff and angular. 'I can swim,' she said. 'I should float and get hauled out. Everyone would think I was such a fool.'

'Actually, I think they'd understand. You've been in a terrible position.'

'I'm glad that someone sees it! The situation was unique. I really hadn't any choice.'

'You didn't have to try to get Braddock to kill Celia. Although I don't suppose you really thought he'd do it. Did you?'

'I never meant him to kill her. Although why anyone should care! She's been a parasite all her life.'

Charles grimaced. 'Just at the moment I might agree with you. We're in the same boat, you and I. They won't leave go.'

'She won't leave go, you mean!' Heather banged her fist again into the mud. 'I've been good all my life,' she said angrily. 'I'm a regular churchgoer. I teach the girls the Bible. I did not do wrong! Anything I did was justified. Absolutely justified. For the good of all.'

Charles said, 'I suppose you know that sounds rather smug.'

She sighed impatiently. 'That's what people always say about goodness.'

'It's often a way of getting one up on other people,' said Charles. 'If you can't be as clever or as good-looking or as charming, then at least you can be better at being good. Face it, Heather. You hated Celia and you wanted her gone.'

She glared at him. 'I haven't done anything I'm ashamed of! Nothing! I leave that to people like her.'

Charles was silent for a moment. Heather's principles couldn't live with her guilt, so one of them had to be denied. What was he to do? One thing was certain; he couldn't leave her to work this out by herself.

'I haven't behaved badly,' she insisted, staring at him. 'You do accept that, I trust?'

'Do you think David will accept it?'

Her mouth twitched a little. He had a brief glimpse of the strain under which she laboured. 'I – I think I should like to go now,' she said carefully.

'I don't think you should go home just yet.'

'No. No – not just yet.'

They agreed that she would go with him to hospital. He got her to her feet and led her shakily along the river bank, and a couple walking by saw them and stood staring. Heather pushed at her hair. 'I must look like a madwoman. Perhaps you could go back to them and explain—'

'It really isn't necessary. I'll get in touch with David from the hospital. He's been looking everywhere.'

'Has he?' The first hint of insecurity. 'Was he – is he angry?'

'Worried, I think. You gave everyone a terrible fright.'

'I don't think you can possibly blame me!' Heather walked determinedly towards the car.

The news that Heather was in hospital surprised everyone. Lucy, looking dubiously at Celia, said, 'At least we've got you to take care of us.'

Celia fought the weariness that seemed to drag at her nowadays and replied, 'I'm sure we'll manage perfectly. We'll throw Tip's muzzle away for a start.'

422

'We'll put it in a drawer,' said Ellen. 'For when Mum comes back.'

By lunchtime Celia was halfway to wishing she had never gone. Even the dishwasher defeated her, a forest of buttons and racks. She put things in anyhow and they came out smeared and unpleasant.

'Didn't you wash dishes when you were young?' asked Ellen incredulously, and Celia admitted, 'We had a maid.'

The house seemed inexorably chaotic. As she walked from room to room, gathering glasses and discarded books, clothes and newspapers, the girls followed behind, discarding more. Finally she couldn't stand it. 'Have you two spent your whole lives being waited on?' she thundered. 'Don't you know how to be tidy?'

Ellen blinked. To her certain knowledge they were no more and no less messy than their contemporaries. 'Mum manages,' she said vaguely. 'She doesn't make it all a big deal.'

'I suppose you're out of practice,' said Lucy kindly, kicking off her shoes and curling up on the sofa. Celia knew with certainty that she would later get up, abandon the shoes, and find another pair.

It was mid-afternoon and there was nothing for dinner. She realised she should have gone shopping. The telephone rang, and it was Heather's firm, wanting some advice about something. 'She's ill,' said Celia. 'I don't know when she'll be back. Who called? Mr Braddock? Yes. I'll tell her.'

She sat down at the kitchen table. So, Edwin was looking for her again. Coming back to find her note, his fish away in the murky waters of the lake and his tank in pieces on the floor, he was once again appealing to his usual grass. The dog whined. He needed walking. For a moment Celia found herself lost in admiration of Heather. How had she managed it? This house, the dog, the girls and a job, as well as a hotline to Edwin Braddock, all at once. Amazing.

They got through somehow until evening. Celia let everything go except the cooking, and produced a version of osso bucco, with salad and crisp brown bread. But David didn't appear. She felt angry, and then anxious. Had he gone to Heather? Had he been hurt? Was she to be left endlessly in command of this place with no hope of relief?

The dog needed walking again. She flogged the girls into accompanying her, and because they were as unsettled as she, they squabbled. Lucy stood in a cowpat and expected Celia to wipe her shoe, but the smell of it, under her pregnant nose, made her heave.

'You're a terrible wimp,' said Ellen.

'I'm not usually,' defended Celia. 'And why you came in those shoes, Lucy, I shall never know. Where are your boots?'

'You moved them,' said Lucy. 'I left them by the back door.'

'That isn't the proper place, though.'

'Well, you didn't put them there. I looked.'

The dog put up a hare and set off across the fields like a rocket. He hadn't a hope, but ran anyway, and the three of them yelled and chased, quite ineffectually. Celia soon gave up and left the children to it. She felt mentally battered by constant demands, and physically wearied by effort. She wasn't up to this. She simply wasn't. Charles had done nothing to prepare her for real family life.

When they got back, David had come in. 'She's fine,' he told the girls. 'Sleepy. She needs a rest. They've given her something.'

'Is she hurt?' demanded Ellen.

Her father shook his head. 'Just upset. She thinks she did something – said something – for which I won't forgive her. And of course I will.'

Lucy pushed at her hair. It was Heather's gesture. 'It wasn't anything awful, was it?'

'No.' David threw an arm around her shoulder. 'It wasn't so awful. Fortunately.'

He felt Celia's eyes upon him, and looked away. She said, 'I wish you'd let me know. Your meal's keeping hot in the oven. Shall I get it?'

He said, 'What's wrong with the microwave?'

'I don't understand it.'

He looked exasperated. 'It's perfectly simple, I can assure you. Look, don't bother about the food. I'll have something later.'

He poured himself a whisky, offering Celia nothing. She could feel his anger, enveloping them like thick mist. So many evenings in the past he had sat with her like this, until the anger found its outlet in their bed. Sometimes he was gentle, sometimes he was fierce, and sometimes it was as if she touched a fury that never existed for anyone else. Afterwards, he was always wonderfully calm.

Ellen came in. 'Is Mum in Mr Davenport's hospital?'

David said, 'Yes, she's on his ward.'

'That's good of Charles,' said Celia. 'She's really a mental case.'

'What?' Ellen's eyes were like saucers.

'I mean – she's in need of a rest. Not really ill. Sort of.'

Ellen said, 'I wish you wouldn't be so mean about her. It isn't her fault any more than it's yours.'

They heard her stamp up the stairs to bed. David got up and poured himself another whisky. A pulse started in Celia's throat, she could feel it steadily throbbing. She said, 'There's something I should tell you.'

He sighed. 'What now?'

'I'm pregnant.'

He turned and stared at her. She said, 'I'm sorry. I don't know how it happened really. But I missed the girls so much – missed what they used to be. I've made rather a muddle.'

'You're not trying to pin it on me, I hope?'

She grimaced. 'Hardly.'

He poured himself more whisky. She wondered if he always drank so much. 'Do you mind?' she asked.

Glass replenished, wavering a little, he strolled towards her. 'What is there to mind? You always were a slut.'

'Don't call me that. Please, David. We used to be happy.'

He stood over her, those pale, cold eyes fixed on her face. 'Were we? I loved you, I don't deny that. We were never happy, though.'

Celia felt her heart begin to break. Not happy? Ever? 'We were terribly happy,' she said, her voice starting to crack.

'Sometimes. You've forgotten, she's made you forget.'

'I haven't forgotten the rows. I haven't forgotten the way your father never ceased trying to humiliate me!'

'But David – that wasn't all of it.'

'It's all I remember.'

She ducked her head. And suddenly he was bent over her, kissing her hair, her neck, catching her hands and pressing her fingers to his lips. 'David – David, don't!'

'You want me to remember, don't you? And you sit there, just like before, so I can't damn well forget!' He sank to his knees in front of her, almost beside himself on whisky and despair. 'Why do you do it? I'd got over loving you. And here you are again, beautiful, lovely – and pregnant with another man's child!' He took hold of her shoulders and shook her, back and forth, back and forth. She opened her eyes and gasped, her head rolling on her neck. Then, abruptly, he stopped. 'Why do you do it?' he asked again. 'I think you must like to torture me.'

He began to move away, but she put out her hands and stopped him. 'Do you wish we could try again? Do you wish the baby was yours?'

He closed his eyes, unwilling to face her eagerness. 'No. No, I don't wish that. I just want you to leave me in peace.'

In the middle of the night, rousing Celia from a troubled sleep, a cry rang along the corridors. One of the girls, having a bad dream. Celia got up at once and went to see, and found it was Lucy again, grinding her teeth and tossing in her sleep. She woke her, and the child lay with dark, troubled eyes, trying to escape from whatever it was that had caused her so much fright. 'Shall I turn your pillows?' said Celia. 'I can get you a drink if you like.'

'Mum always makes me hot milk with honey,' said Lucy.

'Do you often get bad dreams, then?'

'Sometimes. I saw an accident at school once, when a girl broke her leg, and I dream about that. Sometimes Mum reads me a story.'

Celia got the drink and settled down to read some childish tale. Her thoughts were not on the words. What a lot she did not know about her own children. The years had been crammed with happenings, and she knew nothing of them. Her instinctive understanding of her children, as people out of

426

the same mould, formed by the same influences, was tempered by Heather's practical knowledge. The girls missed their stepmother. Celia could only satisfy by pretending to be her.

Lucy was becoming sleepy again. Celia smoothed the tangled hair, and bent down to kiss her cheek. Lucy murmured, 'Is this going to be the way it is, then? Forever?'

Celia hesitated. 'Do you want it to be?' she said at last.

Lucy let out a long, weary sigh. 'Everything's so confused now. Nothing's simple any more.'

'It never was,' said Celia slowly. 'It never was.'

David rose late the next morning. Alone with the girls, Celia struggled with the morning routine – food, clothes, dishes, the car. Battling through the traffic to school she felt tired and rather forlorn. 'Have a good day,' she called, as the girls got out.

'Mum always tells us to take care,' said Ellen. She waited, as if for a talisman.

'Look,' said Celia slowly, 'do you want to go and see Heather tonight? I'll take you.'

Ellen stood on one leg. 'I didn't think you would. We thought we'd have to go on the bus.'

'Well, you were wrong.'

On the way home she bought a paper, and scanned the business pages. There it was, at last. A huge picture of Edwin Braddock, with the words 'Gamble Finally Pays Off'. She sat in the car and read the article, a eulogy in praise of Edwin. The final words were: 'A modest man, Mr Braddock is clearly very astute. His tenacity in fighting for Marlborough, overcoming failure and facing ruin, must make him one of the country's most watchable entrepreneurs.' She drove slowly back to the house.

To her surprise, David was still there. 'I wanted to talk to you,' he said. 'We're doing a test at the track this morning. I thought you might like to come.'

She turned away. 'We don't seem to get very far when we talk. Is it the divorce?'

'To an extent. It's money.'

'Oh.' She knew she must face up to things. Inevitably,

predictably, David was in a mess again. She went to fetch a sheepskin jacket.

David drove fast, as always. He had first got into cars as a boy of fifteen, with a few drives in juniors on the local track. He was good, but not brilliant, and soon turned his attention to building cars instead of racing them. But, deep inside, he was still the boy who wanted heads to turn as he raced past.

As they topped a rise, doing ninety, Celia said, 'Oh, wonderful!' He chuckled, changed down and threw the car into a series of bends. Exhilaration took her breath away. She felt wild again.

It was very cold at the track. The wind was blowing from Siberia, laden with flakes of snow. Someone's hat cartwheeled across the stony ground, and a car raced by in the distance. A Formula car, the mechanics clustering like flies, while the Sheraton had such a little group of supporters.

'Didn't you bring a team from the workshop?' asked Celia.

David said, 'We're behind on production. Can't afford it.'

Her mood began to darken. She knew the story without being told, the delays, the overspends, the disasters. She nodded to Adam Partridge, elbowing his small frame into the car. The Formula car, whose time had expired, was doing a bit extra, and David went to remonstrate with the officials. But no one wanted to offend the paying customers, so flags were waved somewhat half-heartedly. Partridge stamped on the gas and sent the Sheraton hurtling into the chicane. The Formula car followed, going like hell's chickens, but incredibly Partridge held him off. There was a pitched battle for almost a lap, before the interloper gave in to the flags and came off. Partridge pulled up, glowing with righteous victory.

'Bloody hell! You've done something to it this time, all right! Did you see how he couldn't make ground? What is it, the wishbone?'

'We twitched it a bit,' admitted David. He was quietly smug.

Celia said, 'So you did get a decent casting after all.'

'Oh, yes. Eventually.' He shot her a speculative look, and she wondered again what he wanted.

David took her to a pub for lunch. They sat before the fire, gently thawing, eating steak and kidney pie. Celia, toying with the food, said, 'You need more capital, of course. I haven't any.'

David looked up. 'Of course you have. The pearls. You were wearing them the other night.'

'Oh. Yes. The pearls.'

He said, 'Don't you dare tell me they're of sentimental value, or some such claptrap! I need the money to support our children. The pearls have got to be sold.'

Celia pushed her plate away. 'They can't be. They aren't really mine, at least not in law. A breath of publicity and Edwin can claim them under the Will.'

'Then do it without publicity. People sell things all the time. I'll see to it.'

She was aware of considerable unease. David selling her pearls? He'd be rooked. 'We ought to wait,' she prevaricated. 'The court case starts soon. We could be selling for a fraction of what they're worth. You don't need money that urgently, do you?'

'Yes.'

A pulse was beating next to his mouth. He said, 'It was your idea to mortgage the house. Your idea to expand. It was all an excuse, wasn't it? You wanted cash, so I had to raise it, and the only thing I'd do it for was the business. Now, when I need money from you, it's no go. When I think of what Heather's given me over the years! The love. The sheer, solid loyalty!'

It was a knife in her guts. Celia closed her eyes against the pain. 'You've been cruel ever since I woke up,' she said at last. 'Is it just because of Heather?'

'I only asked you to sell the pearls! That's not cruelty.'

'I wouldn't have gone to Charles if you'd been kind.'

The pulse was beating still harder. He said, 'I'm glad you did. After the accident I used to imagine things about you. That you weren't – what I knew you were.'

'But you liked me to sleep around,' she said jerkily. 'It gave you a stick to beat me with. It gave you a thrill.'

He didn't say a word, simply went to the bar and bought more drinks. When he came back he looked straight at her. 'I liked the idea of it. When I actually saw you it wasn't an idea I

429

liked any more. And you didn't have to do it, for God's sake! A woman like Heather wouldn't do it in all her life!'

'Oh, the wonderful, virtuous Heather,' said Celia in contemptuous tones. 'She wouldn't end up pregnant by the wrong man. Her very virtue would protect her. Angels would descend from heaven to hold her knickers up.'

She went out to the car, but it was locked. David took his time, leaving her in the wind, at last coming out. She said, 'Charles has got the pearls but you can have them. They're all I've got but I shall give them to you, so the girls at least can inherit a decent firm and not some half-baked, crumbling mistake. But believe me, David, this is the end between us.'

He looked at her, across the car. Her scarf had come loose and rested on her shoulders, above the bulky jacket. Her eyes were luminous, her nose reddened from the cold. He could never be free of her! Whatever he did, she rose up again, in her old beauty, in her old power. She had an endless hold over him, just as Davenport said. Would it never be finished? 'You should have died,' he said helplessly. 'You were meant to die, and let us all get on with living!'

She looked away and got into the car.

Chapter Twenty-Nine

When they returned to Blantyre House they found the front door swinging wide. The dog, locked in the kitchen, was beside himself, hoarse from barking, the window sill scratched to sawdust by his claws. Celia soothed him. 'There, Tip. Good boy, Tip. What did they take, then?'

But nothing was gone. Instead, in state on the hall table, rested a goldfish bowl. One large, stately fish swam round and round in it.

'What in God's name is going on?' demanded David. 'Is it some sort of joke?'

'It was Edwin,' said Celia calmly. 'Not in person, but sent by him. Poor Tip's beside himself. Here, boy, have something to eat.' She fed the dog some corned beef out of the fridge. He wolfed it down, still upset, still on hairtrigger nerves. Celia wrapped her arms around herself, not as calm as she pretended. He had found her again. He never failed. She went upstairs to lie down.

When the girls came home they found the house much as they had left it. There was no shopping, no washing, the books and papers lay as they were left, the breakfast things remained out of the dishwasher, the clean things still within.

'You can't just go to bed in the afternoon and do nothing,' remonstrated Ellen. 'I mean, we all have work to do.'

'I felt ill,' said Celia, who certainly felt ill now. There was too much to do, too much to think about. 'I'll cook something.' But there was nothing to cook. Tip had eaten the last of the corned beef, and the freezer held only worthy vegetables, like broad beans, that no one liked to eat. Her purse was almost empty, the banks were shut and even if they weren't, she had hardly anything in her account. And now she had promised the pearls to David for the business. A sense of hopelessness oppressed her.

She created a meal out of tins and made a white sauce for the beans. It was a creditable effort, given her disadvantages. Afterwards, David drove them all to the hospital. The girls were puzzled that Celia came, since David was taking them. 'I've got to see Charles – and collect something,' she prevaricated. She guided David through to the staff car park, and saw that Charles's car wasn't there. Her heart sank a little. She told David to park in his place.

They had to wait to see Heather. David said sotto voce, 'I can't wait, you know. And you agreed. Hadn't you better ring him?'

She nodded. 'Later. When you've all gone in.'

They sat in silence. The place seemed so terribly familiar. Celia felt she knew every crack and blister in the walls, every meaningless picture, every carelessly placed trolley, every door that wouldn't open without a squeak. Sister Johnson passed by, and Celia almost rose to say hello. But the Sister passed on. She only liked sick people, Celia remembered. Once well they lost all their attraction for her.

When they all went into Heather's room Celia went to the phone, but there was no reply. She began seriously to worry. Suppose Edwin had sent his heavies round? Charles thought he was quite a fighter nowadays, but no one won against odds. She imagined Charles bleeding and beaten on the floor, with a head injury perhaps, one which needed urgent care. She thought of all the procedures that had been enacted on the wards she had been in; trepanning; shunts; that chopping of arteries with which businessmen made up for all their expense account meals.

Standing by the telephone, wondering what to do, she saw him. He strode down the corridor, obviously cross. 'That damned man parked the Sheraton in my space! What does he think he's doing, there could be an emergency.'

'But there isn't.'

'There could be.'

She smiled, and he saw himself through her eyes; a little ridiculous. He could have parked anywhere. He smiled too.

'You look whacked. I thought you'd ring, why didn't you?'

She shrugged. 'Things. I tried just now and you weren't there. Edwin's tracked me down again.'

'Well then, time you moved out.'

She shook her head.

It seemed so final. She had achieved her end, the very thing for which she had been struggling from the moment she first knew what had happened to her. He felt a great helplessness, and with it a great rage. 'It'll just serve you right if he does bloody well murder you!'

A couple of nurses bustled past, shooting covert looks at them. Charles looked very forbidding, as he often did when upset. Celia wished she could touch him, reassure him a little. Everything wasn't as it seemed. He wasn't entirely shut out.

'I'm giving the pearls to David,' she said, intending to go on and explain. But the words died in her throat. Charles's face was suffused with dark, angry colour.

'You are doing what?'

She hushed him quickly. 'It's for the business. He's desperate. The car's going brilliantly, it has to be good news, and he insists!'

He met her eyes, and hers were the first to fall. 'He insists?' he said slowly. 'What else does he insist upon, may I ask?'

'Nothing.'

'Indeed.' He took two or three long breaths, the sort of trick he taught the more tense among his patients. 'I warned him, and I meant it.'

'What do you mean?'

'I'm just bloody sick of being polite to David Sheraton!'

He started for Heather's room and Celia hung on his arm, trying to stop him. But he went on as if she wasn't there, and people stared, so she ran beside him, trying to reason. And then, just as he neared the door, the bleep in his pocket went. He stopped, even his anger arrested by his training. He marched down the corridor to the nearest staff phone. 'Davenport.'

An emergency. A boy had come off his bike and was comatose with vomiting and depressed reflexes. He was to go at once to Casualty, with the possibility of an emergency operation. Celia stood aside as he strode away, wondering again at the immediacy of his response, when he really cared very little for the people he saved. He must care, she thought. Somewhere in that complex and forbidding personality there was an element of compassion that could be activated for people he did not know. Perhaps that was the secret; Charles felt for anonymous humanity, not for anyone he knew well. Once he knew people, turning his searchlight intelligence on their foibles and stupidities, he disliked them.

Ellen was outside Heather's door. When she saw Celia she said, 'Mum wants to have a word with you.'

'Me?' Celia was aware that she was backing away. 'Surely not.'

'Afraid so.'

David and Lucy left as she entered. Heather wanted to see her alone. Taking a deep breath, Celia approached the bed, noting that Heather looked better than for weeks. 'I gather you wanted to speak to me,' she said frostily.

'Yes.' Heather plucked nervously at the quilt. 'David thinks – David thought – that is – I wanted to apologise. For talking to Braddock.'

'Oh.' Celia took a deep breath. Did she really have to kiss and make up? For the girls, she thought. Only for the girls. 'It's very good of you,' she said stiffly. 'Apology accepted.'

An uneasy silence fell. Then Celia said, 'I think perhaps I should make an apology on my own behalf. I never thanked you for all you did for my girls. You've brought them up to be lovely, intelligent people. I am grateful, Heather. Despite everything, I'm grateful for that.'

'Well. I'm glad that at long last you realise the commitment I made.' Heather's contrition dissolved into a smirk, and at once Celia's good intentions evaporated. She took a seat by the bed and leaned back expansively. 'Tell me, Heather. Did David have much to do with Edwin Braddock at the time of my father's death?'

'I don't know what you mean.'

Celia met her eyes. 'Oh yes, you do. David was supposed to get a pay-out, wasn't he? In return for not contesting the Will. Edwin kept my mother quiet, so there was no problem there,

434

and at the end of the day he was supposed to share the spoils. But he didn't. He kept the lot. So poor old David was left with nothing, all because he was too proud to dance to my father's tune. That's right, isn't it, Heather? That's how it was.'

Heather's colour ebbed and flowed. 'It really had nothing to do with you. You were dead! As good as dead. It didn't involve you at all.'

Celia sighed and rose to her feet. 'I know. But somehow it doesn't make it in the least bit better.'

She left, and the others went back in. They would be at least an hour more. She sat waiting in the hall, restless and upset. She had been right about David, then. In paying her back for each and every betrayal, he had offered her birthright to a thief. She got up and began to pace the corridor. It was no use. She had to talk to Charles.

He might not yet be operating, these things took time. Knowing the hospital as she did, she went up in the staff lift to the theatre floor, empty of people but ablaze with light. If she was seen here she would instantly be asked to leave. On impulse she turned into the scrub room, where gowns, boots and hats hung in rows. Would it matter? In greens no one would question her. She grabbed a gown and dressed.

Catching sight of herself in the mirror as she left, hair scraped tight under a theatre cap, she paused. She looked anonymous, and rather beautiful. She pulled the mask over her nose and hurried out.

A nurse passed her in the corridor. 'Theatre Two,' she called. 'He's mild as milk today, he won't mind you watching.'

'Thanks,' said Celia, but paused at the door. Nurses were setting up trolleys in the lobby.

'Take this in, would you?' said a voice, and Celia found herself with a trolley to push. There was nothing to do but go through the door into a throng of people.

The trolley was taken from her with an impatient hiss. She sidled round a wall of green backs, lined in an impenetrable row beside the patient, unable even to distinguish which one was Charles. But then he began singing to himself: 'Oh, dear, what can the matter be, Cranial damage is not what it used to be . . . Get that for me, would you, Stephen? Thanks.'

His assistant mopped at something. There was a huge fixture set over the table, with microscopes, lights, even a camera. Celia slid away into a corner, wondering how on earth she could escape. Now and then Charles would pull the microscope down and study his work. Despite herself she longed to see what he was doing.

She shuffled towards the head of the table, straining for some view of what was happening. Everything was swathed in sheeting, except for a nose, incongruously poking out. It seemed a very young nose, spotty and undeveloped.

Charles was singing again. 'Oh, dear, what can the matter be, Clotting of blood is a sodding catastrophe . . . You doing anything this weekend, Stephen? More of the terrible dinner parties?'

'Another one,' admitted the junior. 'She knows she's a bad cook, but if we entertain we get asked back and then we eat decently. And it's an incentive to clean up the house.'

'Sister?' Charles held out his hand for an instrument and it was instantly there. 'I have mess beyond your wildest dreams,' he went on. 'But I am installing central heating.'

'I thought you'd done all you wanted to the house, sir?'

'Yes. But a certain lady found it cold, even in bed. Let it be a lesson to you, Sister. Never sleep alone.'

'I'll remember that, sir,' she said.

'The only alternative is a house full of pipes. Bugger! He's a real little bleeder, this one. How is he?'

The anaesthetist looked up from his dials. 'Not bad. I'm happy with him.'

'This'll teach him to ride no hands. This looks like the last. We'll be closing in fifteen minutes. Too late for your seats at the ballet, Sister?'

'Afraid so, sir.'

'We shall have our reward in heaven. Let's give it all up and become accountants instead. That's what the Health Service wants these days, isn't it? Oh, look at that. A tidy job, if I say it myself. Right, Stephen, you can do the honours. I'll hang around. Call me if you get stuck.'

'Yes, sir.' Stephen was heavily ironic. Clearly he was unamused at being thought incapable of coping.

Charles walked out of the theatre, throwing his gloves at one nurse, his mask at another, striding to the scrub room at a million miles an hour. Celia followed at a discreet trot. But of course Charles was headed for the surgeons' sanctum, where she could not possibly go. He turned at the door, and said, 'Come on in, Celia. We have it all to ourselves.'

She stamped past him in her too big wellington boots. Taking off her mask, she said, 'OK, how did you know?'

'You hovered. People who know what's going on do not behave like uninvited guests at a funeral. You getting changed or do you fancy yourself in that?'

She viewed herself in the mirror. 'I do, rather. What a wonderful life you lead, I'm terribly envious. Waited on hand and foot.'

He ran a towel under the tap and wiped his face and neck. She realised he was very tired. She put out a hand and took hold of his shoulder as he bent over the basin. He said, 'Isn't David waiting for you?'

'Probably. I don't care. I wanted to see you.'

'You wanted the pearls.' He moved away from the basin and stripped off. Wearing only the loose surgical trousers, he seemed very big and very hairy. The muscles of his chest were flat plates, covered in a dark scrub of hair. She remembered lying on him, her hands across those muscles, feeling them tense as he moved in her. All at once she wished she could go home with him now, to his house and the mess of his central heating. Instead she had to go with David.

'Can you come tomorrow?' she asked. 'It's the case. First day in court.'

'I'm busy tomorrow. Sorry.'

'Couldn't you come for an hour? I wanted some support.'

He gave her a look. 'You've got David, haven't you?'

'I wanted you.'

He wanted to hit her, then. He wanted to show her what he thought of her primitive manipulation. She was only happy when she had them both on a string. When she lived with one she spent her days tempting the other. He took hold of her arms and brought her close to his naked chest, he held her against the unforgiving hardness of his body. She put her

437

hands on him and said, 'Don't be angry with me, Charles. I couldn't bear it. I've really had enough today.'

His hold on her relaxed a little. She wondered if he knew how much she needed just to stand like this, so close, and know that he would not hurt her. She needed to touch another person, to prove to herself that she existed in the physical world, that she had a place there. She put her face into his neck and rubbed her cheek against him. He said, 'Aren't you ashamed to come from David to me? You've got what you wanted. I've no doubt at all that you'll get rid of Heather in the end.'

'He thinks more of her than you imagine.'

'Oh, so you've discovered that at last! Don't worry, she'll be here for at least another fortnight. If you can't turn him off her in a mere fourteen days then I've badly underestimated you, Celia. I have never known a woman so capable of getting what she wants.'

She pulled away from him, fetched her clothes and got changed. Charles was fastening his tie, looking neat and spruce, smelling of antiseptic. It was no wonder he always looked so clean, thought Celia. All this scrubbing and rubbing – he ought to perish in the outside air, falling victim to a million unfamiliar germs.

He turned and looked at her. 'Don't come in my theatre again unless you're properly scrubbed. If you want I can show you something really interesting. But not many people like brain operations. We have a very high fainting factor.'

'I didn't see anything of this one,' she confessed. 'There wasn't enough room.'

'There never is.'

She still waited. He went to a cupboard and picked up briefcase, overcoat, the hat with which he intimidated lesser men. It made him look dashing. 'Charles—' she began.

'No.'

'You don't know what I was going to ask, yet.'

'You want the pearls. And I've decided. No.'

'Charles, they are my pearls! If you keep them, it's stealing!'

He fixed her with a grim stare. 'I view it as safe custody. If you give them to David, he'll try and sell them, because that's the kind of prat he is. Braddock will hear of it and claim them under the Will, and even if the Will is set aside in your favour, which is debatable, it's going to look as if everyone had their hands in the till. You will all look equally dishonourable. Be grateful to me, Celia. I am protecting you from your own stupidity.'

Once again she was powerless. Once again her life seemed out of her control. Charles thought she couldn't see what would happen if David had the pearls, but that wasn't true. If he didn't have them, though, this might be the end of Sheraton Cars. David was stretched beyond anything before. Blantyre House was at stake, the girls' future, David's future. He needed that firm. He had clung to it through everything. It embodied his self-respect.

She put out her hand. 'Charles, I will decide if I want to take a risk with the pearls. It isn't up to you.'

He held the door for her, but she didn't go through. 'I know where they are and you don't,' he said simply. 'Come along, dear. Your husband will be waiting.'

She raged at him all the way down in the lift. He listened, impassive and disinterested. Two nurses finishing a shift joined them on the third floor, but she didn't stop. Let him be embarrassed. Let everyone know just how difficult and autocratic he was. 'You have no right to keep my possessions!' she bellowed.

He gave her one of his professionally tolerant stares. 'Mrs Sheraton, you know very well I don't have anything at all of yours,' he said soothingly. 'Perhaps you're a little confused. Is it likely that valuable jewellery would be in the hospital's possession? Consider.'

The nurses exchanged glances. The more senior said softly to Davenport, 'Would you like us—'

'Nothing I can't handle, Nurse. Thanks all the same.'

They all got out on the ground floor, and Charles took Celia's elbow in a caring, sharing way. When the nurses were gone he let her go. 'You'll end up in the psychiatric wing if you go on like this,' he said. 'Next thing you'll be telling people I got you pregnant.'

He grinned, rather amused by the thought. Suddenly, so was she. 'You bastard,' she murmured. 'I really hate you sometimes.'

'Only sometimes? I am honoured.'

She brushed a hand gently across her stomach. 'It couldn't be always, could it?'

His mouth set in a hard line. She realised she had touched him, and moved swiftly in on her advantage. 'It is up to me what to do with those pearls.'

'And it's up to me how much I give in to you. No, Celia. If you want the pearls you get out of Blantyre House, for good. That's my condition. And I mean it.'

He flung out through the swing doors, and the doorman intoned 'Night, Mr Davenport' before announcing to anyone who would listen, 'Charles Davenport, that. Best neurosurgeon in the country. Brilliant.'

Celia thought of Charles in the theatre today. Neither she nor the doorman knew anything at all about it, but she wasn't going to disagree. Sadly, Charles's brilliance was exactly counterbalanced by bossiness, obsession and pride. He was used to getting his own way, and saw no reason ever to compromise.

David and the girls came out of the lift behind her. 'Celia! At last. The girls are way past their bedtime, and visiting's been over for an hour. What on earth have you been doing?'

She sighed. 'Talking to Charles. He's being – difficult. He won't hand them over.'

'Hand what over?' Ellen, alert to adult talk, was at once all ears. 'Nothing to do with you,' snapped David, but Celia said, 'Some jewellery, darling. I gave it to Charles for safekeeping. He thinks it's safer with him than with me.'

'He hasn't stolen it, has he? You could go to the police!'

David said, 'Celia, none of this concerns the children. We'll talk about it later.'

'He thinks we're too stupid to know he's got money troubles,' said Ellen in ringing tones. 'He thinks we don't notice that we never go skiing and eat cheap meat.'

'That's probably half Mum's trouble,' added Lucy. 'She's sick of trying to manage. She can't, you know. It's inflation. Every week the prices go up. I blame the government.'

David was looking beleaguered, and Celia was seized with the desire to laugh. Her children delighted her. Perhaps, one day, the child growing in her would delight her too.

Chapter Thirty

Celia slept badly that night. A sharp wind was blowing and the windows of the old house rattled alarmingly. When the alarm shrilled at seven, she rose heavy-eyed, only for David to start again about the pearls, over the breakfast table. He wanted the pearls. He needed them. Didn't she care what happened to her family, didn't she have any proper feelings at all?

In the end, she threw up her hands. 'All right, David, all right! I'll get them from him. Somehow, I'll get them.'

'You'll say anything,' said David suspiciously. 'I know you.'

'They're my pearls, and I'm going to get them,' Celia assured him. 'Honest. I can persuade him.'

David laughed bitterly. 'Oh, yes. I bet you can.'

She left him in the kitchen and went upstairs to change. She dressed carefully in a navy blue suit with a pale blue blouse. It was chic and restrained, just the thing for court. Her heart was thumping rather more than she thought it should. Nerves, she told herself. Anyone would be nervous today.

She had been asked to arrive just before eleven. She found Hector Lowndes waiting for her in the lobby, looking unusually sombre in dark suit and black tie. She remarked on the tie. 'Was it your father?'

He nodded.

'I'm – I'm sorry.'

They stood uncomfortably together. She asked, 'Do we have any sort of chance, do you think?'

He shifted from one foot to the other. 'As far as the trust fund goes, yes. I don't think anyone can dispute that it was intended to finance your life, however that was lived.'

'But you don't think they'll accept a challenge to the Will.'

'It's bound to go to a higher court.'

'That's not what I asked.'

'No.'

He moved her to a seat in the corner. She didn't want to sit, being filled with restless energy, but she did anyway. She suddenly had the thought, one she had not had before, that Lowndes was only going through this to protect his own firm. After this it would be difficult to sue them for fraud, or negligence, or whatever. Perhaps she should have done that. Her confidence in Lowndes took a wild dive.

'You haven't discovered anything new?' she said unhappily. 'I bet you haven't even looked.'

'That isn't fair. I've been through the files with a toothcomb.'

'And still you haven't discovered anything. What about your father's papers? He's dead now, there's nothing to worry about there.'

'He only died on Sunday.'

'Oh. Oh, I see.'

She was constrained by good manners. At last she said, 'So when is the funeral?'

'This afternoon.'

'But what about my case?'

'They won't go on for more than an hour. They'll adjourn, I've requested it.'

She had dolled herself up and steeled herself for only an hour's work. They would hardly even begin. She felt helpless again, and very alone. She didn't trust Hector Lowndes any more. But then he took her hand and patted it reassuringly. 'Don't worry,' he said jerkily. 'I promise I'll do a good job. It all rests on whether it's thought likely that your father would forget your children. The common sense view is that he would not, but the legal position has to be more stringent. You've got to be prepared to fail.'

No one ever prepared her to win. She had been a winner all her life, up to the accident. Winning begets winning. She had ridden her confidence like a fast horse, with never a tumble. A small commotion made her look up. It was Braddock.

He was wearing a pearl-grey suit with black shoes of a shine so brilliant it seemed improbable. There was a white carnation in his buttonhole, and a smile of welcome on his lips. He looked for all the world like an actor of the old school, who never stops performing. A girl was with him, with a shorthand notebook.

To her surprise he came across. 'Celia! My dear, how well you look.'

She licked dry lips. 'Edwin. Thank you for the fish.'

'What fish? Has someone sent you fish? What an odd present.'

'I thought so. So did the dog.'

'What a preoccupation you do have with the natural world, Celia dear. A comfort in your darkness, no doubt.'

He was going to say she was unbalanced. At once, she began to feel it. Wasn't she showing evidence of paranoia? Everyone seemed to be moving position, Charles, David, Hector Lowndes. No one had her interests solely in mind, they each worked to their own hidden agenda. She dragged her thoughts back to the plank of normality. She must seem calm, reasoned, without flaw.

'Poor Edwin,' she said softly. 'This must be so distressing for you. A man like you is so vulnerable. Alone as you are.'

His colour came up. If he taunted her with insanity, she would retaliate with hints at his abnormal life. 'I'll see you in court,' he said stiffly, and turned on his heel.

Lowndes, exhaling noisily, said, 'Round One to you, I think. Don't let him make you angry. He's up to all the tricks.'

A barrister rushed in, robes flying. He came over, wearing his professional smile. 'Mr Lowndes! A pleasure. Mrs Sheraton – a delight. We'll go all out for the trust fund initially, and hope that our momentum will carry us through on the Will. We're only making a start today, so don't be disappointed. Boring technicalities for the most part.'

The usher began to call them. Celia rose, feeling her palms begin to sweat. Her head was fuzzy too. Let her not faint, not here, not now. But fighting it was never any good. She forced herself consciously to relax.

It was better in the court. Scene of so many television dramas, she felt she had been here before. Small, wood-panelled, it had none of the sausage-machine anonymity of the corridor outside. The judge entered and they all rose, sinking again almost immediately. And at once Braddock's barrister got up and went forward. 'If you please, my lord, my client has given me further instructions . . .'

The judge, dressed up in wig and gown, grumbled a little. Then he commanded that the court should be cleared.

'What's happening?' asked Celia, being pushed once again into the corridor. 'What's going on?'

'I'll let you know,' said Lowndes, and turned to push his way back through the crush. The doors of the court closed and Celia, Braddock and the rest found themselves excluded.

She could feel Braddock's eyes upon her. She looked up and caught his gaze. He was pulling a fast one here. She could tell. Her throat was dry, again the pressure in her head. She wanted to reach down and cradle her womb, touching a known source of comfort, but not here, not now. All these men. Between them they were betraying her.

Someone was striding purposefully down the corridor. She looked up and saw that it was Charles. A beam of relief lit her from within. She went forward, waving. 'Charles! Charles.'

'I thought you'd have started.'

'We had. Then we stopped. They're plotting something.'

'Oh. Nasty. Well, there's one sure thing. You'll be the one to get screwed.'

'That's what I think. Oh, thank you for coming.'

'I had a free couple of hours. No big deal.'

The doors of the court swung open. The little gaggle of people emerged, and the barrister and Hector Lowndes advanced at once upon Celia. 'Mrs Sheraton!' boomed the barrister. 'Good news. They've withdrawn over the trust fund.'

'And the Will?'

'We've adjourned until tomorrow on the Will.'

'Tomorrow?' Celia looked wildly round at them. 'That's too soon. We wanted to set the scene over the trust fund first, we aren't ready. And what about this settlement? Do they pay costs? Or is the trust fund supposed to do that?'

'It is a very large fund,' said the barrister soothingly.

'Which finances a very large hospital,' retorted Celia. 'I can't take my costs out of that fund! Braddock's doing wonderfully. He's saved himself a packet on costs and soured the case I really need to win. And you two let him. Hector, whose side are you on?'

'I find that very offensive,' said Lowndes after a moment.

'She's got a point,' said Charles. 'You have been out-manoeuvred. Are you prepared for the next case?'

'We will be,' said Lowndes stiffly. 'I admit they've rushed us, but we can cope.'

Celia's silence made it clear she had her doubts. The barrister made encouraging noises. They had begun well, she mustn't look on the black side . . . Lowndes suddenly said, 'I wonder – could you possibly come to my father's funeral, Celia? My mother always believed that my father and your family had a sort of – special relationship.'

She was aghast. Go to the funeral of the man who had helped swindle her? 'I think we could have wished for a relationship less special and more everyday,' she said tartly. 'Really, Hector! Are you serious?'

'My mother would see it as healing old wounds,' said Lowndes. He was clearly unhappy at having to ask her. His mother must have nagged impossibly.

She looked at Charles. 'Could you come? I'd want some moral support.'

He nodded.

On the way out, he murmured, 'When did I ever support your morals?'

Celia chuckled. 'You're sorry, aren't you? Well, have you brought the pearls?'

'Of course not. You know my terms.'

'I can't leave David and the girls to fend for themselves!'

'They can get a bloody housekeeper. You look exhausted, you're not up to it.'

'I'm not up to Braddock and his cleverness. He's a real weasel.'

She stopped at the top of the steps, swaying a little. Charles

445

caught her elbow and steadied her on the way down. There was a restaurant nearby, retreat for the courtroom beleaguered, be they lawyers or the common man. Charles took her there and ordered an early lunch. Celia drank soup with relief.

They talked about Dorrie. Celia had received a letter, telling of a lover. He was an artist, quite uncommercial, living in a cold, dark, dank little cottage with a pig in the garden and a dog in the bed. Dorrie was making a threesome. She wrote: 'Sorry to have been so sour. The insurance has come through and I'm thinking of settling down here. Shocking my sister at such close range is absolutely irresistible.'

'You could go and stay,' suggested Charles.

Celia made a face. 'I wouldn't be welcome. And I'm not running any more. This time I stand and fight.'

'Pregnant women with brain problems don't do much fighting.' There was a note of real anxiety in his voice.

Celia smiled. 'Don't panic. I'm safe for now. And if I lose the case, I'm safe forever. We only have to worry if I win.'

Charles looked away for a moment. He worried all the time. Jealousy, worry . . . they took up all his emotional space. Yet she sat there, serene, a little weary, and tormented him. He stood up and said, 'Let's get off, then. Time we got this fellow buried.'

The funeral was held in a small suburban church, surrounded by trees whose leaves littered the gravestones and the paths. Mourners, and there were distinctly few, slipped and slithered on their way to the door. One of the undertakers, resplendent in a top hat with a draping of crepe, stood behind the hearse surreptitiously smoking. Celia and Charles slipped into the church at the back.

She hoped to be discreet, but she hoped in vain. All through the service the widow kept looking round, taking stock of those who had felt themselves to be close enough to attend. When she saw Celia she nudged her son, and murmured to him. Then she lifted her black-gloved hand in a little wave.

'She's going to talk to me,' said Celia between gritted teeth. 'I can think of absolutely nothing to say.'

'You don't have to talk, only listen,' said Charles, veteran of a thousand encounters with relatives in various states of elation and distress. 'They run out of steam and feel better.'

Celia privately thought that if anyone came out emotionally restored after an interview with Charles they must be warped indeed, but it was time to sing the last hymn. It was Love Divine, All Loves Excelling, which she presumed had been sung at the Lowndeses' wedding. Although she had barely known the man, and had good reason to feel bitter, she found herself saddened suddenly. He had done wrong and had suffered for it, punishing himself far more than any outside agency would countenance. It must be terrible to live with guilt in old age, she thought, to suffer an illness that seemed no less than a visitation from beyond the grave.

There was to be a cremation, but the crematorium was at a distance and the family would not attend. The coffin was removed with due state, and they all stood outside and watched it depart, awkward, sombre, not knowing what to do. There was a distressing urge to wave. Celia suddenly thought of her parents' funerals, of which she knew nothing. Had someone gone with them to the crematorium? Had they had to go alone? All at once she felt as if this was their funeral. That she was watching the departure of the people she had loved best in the world.

Tears welled up and she tried to blink them away, and as luck would have it, Mrs Lowndes chose that very moment to come up to her.

'Mrs Sheraton? Oh – please – I hope you're not upset.'

Celia swallowed. Charles, beside her, blew down his nose. She gulped for breath. 'It's just – I never attended my parents' funerals, you see.'

'My dear, I quite understand.'

Mrs Lowndes took her hand and squeezed it. She was a small, grey woman, with that air of sparkle that sometimes attends the bereaved after long and painful illness. It was transitory, a reaction to the sudden relief of suffering, and it carried them through. Celia was surprised, but Charles, more experienced, said, 'You must feel quite strange now it's all over. Are you managing to sleep?'

Mrs Lowndes looked surprised. 'Not much, no. Is it usual?'

'Very. Don't take pills, they're not good for you.'

'He's a doctor,' explained Celia.

'Oh.' Mrs Lowndes looked from one to the other. 'I was hoping to talk to you privately,' she said.

Celia looked at Charles, who was not used to being dismissed so promptly. She lifted her eyebrows. 'Charles? Would you mind?'

'I shall wait for you by the gate.'

Mrs Lowndes drew Celia back into the porch. 'I've had absolutely enough of doctors,' she declared. 'I never want to see another. They pretend to work miracles, but in the end they can't save you.'

'Sometimes they can,' said Celia. 'But obviously not in the end.'

Mrs Lowndes waved her gloved hand. 'Charlatans, the lot of them. Mrs Sheraton, there's something I want you to have. I told myself if you didn't come to the funeral I wouldn't bother, but if you came, then I would. My husband was such a great friend of your father. They were so close as boys. And then your father made all that money and poor Frank just plodded along – it was very hard for him. Very hard.'

'You knew,' said Celia softly.

Mrs Lowndes lifted her chin. 'Most certainly I did. Not at the beginning – but later. We were married for forty-seven years, Mrs Sheraton. You know someone after all that time. You know their thoughts. And I decided – if you came – that I would give you this.'

She held out a long brown envelope. Celia stared at it, mesmerised, as if it might be dangerous. It was. It surely was. 'Is it the Will?' she asked tensely.

Mrs Lowndes shook her head. 'I imagine that's destroyed. It's a copy. Initialled by your father. I know Hector has found a draft, but there's nothing to prove your father ever acted upon it. This does. He could always have changed it later, of course. That's up to the court to decide.'

Still Celia hesitated. 'Does anyone else know that you have this?'

'I don't think so. Mr Braddock used us and discarded us, Mrs Sheraton. He thought we were too slow and old-fashioned to keep up with him. He isn't quite as smart as he likes to believe, you know.'

Celia took the envelope. It felt stiff and old, as if it had spent years in a dark, dry place. Where had it been hidden? She imagined a shoebox in a wardrobe, out of sight but never out of mind. 'Did your husband want me to have this?' she asked suddenly. 'When I saw him he never gave any sign that he did.'

Mrs Lowndes seemed to fade a little. Some of the shine was going. She was starting to look as she would a week from now, weary, a little disorientated, a little bleak. 'If he could have undone it all I know he would,' she said. 'It wasn't in him to confess.'

Charles was waiting by the lychgate, stiff and forbidding. Celia could tell that other mourners had tried to engage him in conversation. He said, 'Three women have supposed me to be the undertaker. Should I be flattered, do you think?'

'It's a calling you could consider,' said Celia. 'If you get struck off.'

They walked to the car. 'When I get struck off,' said Charles. 'What in God's name are we going to do about this baby? You're beginning to show.'

'Am I?' Celia glanced down at herself. 'Don't I just look fat?'

'Fat doesn't accumulate in one round ball,' said Charles. 'OK, what did she say?'

'Not a lot. She gave me an initialled copy of the Will.'

He was in the process of starting the car. His foot hit the accelerator and it roared throatily. 'Are you sure? Have you checked?'

'I didn't spread it out on the coffin, no.'

'Right. Let's get away from here.'

They stopped in a quiet road with long gardens stretching up to large, old houses. Snowdrops gleamed by the flagged pathways, and daffodils, yet to flower, poked bravely through the winter soil. Spring was coming, thought Celia. Her first spring. She felt a burgeoning, heady excitement.

Charles was opening the envelope. The stiff, legal pages resisted him, and crackled their way out. But there it was; tied with red ribbon, as solicitors often did, initialled, on every page, and dated in her father's own scrawling, distinctive hand. 'Now will we win?' asked Celia tensely.

'I don't know. You must have a chance.'

It was after four by the time she returned to Blantyre House. The girls were in, ravenous and short-tempered. She had again forgotten to provide anything to eat. 'I'll go and shop,' she promised them hastily. 'I'll get something – chops or mince.'

'It had better be quick,' said Ellen menacingly. 'We're not used to waiting hours for a meal.'

'And I'm not used to being bullied,' retorted Celia. 'Take the dog for a walk, can't you? And – tidy up.'

'Not when I'm hungry!' wailed Lucy. 'Why didn't you put something in the freezer? You've got to plan ahead!'

Celia slunk off to the shops, aware that even her children would be better at this than she. It was already dusk, and soon it would be night. She thought of her childhood, returning home late from a show or a party, and finding delicious little snacks set out in the fridge. But then there was a housekeeper, and sometimes a cook. Life had been easy and untrammelled. The days had stretched to a limitless, never reached horizon.

She threw things into her supermarket trolley, paid with her plastic card and left. Her stomach felt heavy and burdensome. Charles was right, the day was coming when everyone would know. She loaded everything into the car, hating the endless baggage handling, knowing that she had to do it twice more before the task was ended. Men should do it, she thought rebelliously, humping all the tins and packets and boxes. Women should lie on sofas and leaf through cookery books, deciding on tonight's culinary sensation.

When she got home, ready to cook the less than sensational pork chops with apple sauce, David was there. He was drinking whisky.

'Had a hard day?' asked Celia.

'You could say that. The bank wants to foreclose.'

'Oh.'

She was absolutely shocked. Bad as she knew things were becoming, she had never once suspected they were terminal.

'Is that all you can say?' demanded David. 'Oh?'

450

'I don't know what else I can say. I didn't think things were so bad.'

'You wouldn't, would you? You never think. It's all fantasy with you, all imagination. You never thought that it would come to this.'

She tried to still her whirling thoughts. 'But it needn't, surely? I mean – you could sell up, or talk to someone. You could sell just a share—'

'And you could give me the bloody pearls!'

She was silent. David went to get himself another drink and she realised that he was beyond being drunk, he was at that stage of despair when nothing can send you further down and nothing can bring you back up. There was no point in reasoning with him now.

'I'll get you the pearls,' she said softly.

'Will you? I doubt it. There you stand, quite calm, as if none of this had anything to do with you. My wife, my bloody, beautiful wife. So beautiful. Even now. Pregnant with another man's child!'

'There's no point trying to blame people,' said Celia. 'Not now.'

'Trying to blame you, you mean! Can't you face it? Can't you take it? You've ruined me. You made me take out that mortgage, you made me run the risk. Before you came back – before you sprang so eagerly into life – Heather and I had a good thing going. We were happy. Peaceful. And then you come back, and you're not thirty-five, you're more like fifteen. Irresponsible. Just like before. Why did I listen to you? Why did I let you ruin my life?'

Celia turned and went into the kitchen. She started to unpack the shopping, hearing a pulse bang unnaturally in her head. Then a flutter came, deep inside. The baby. Stirred by its mother's turmoil, it was giving its only response. She rested a hand against it, for the moment unable to go on.

Ellen, coming into the room, said, 'We heard.'

'Did you?'

'I didn't know you were pregnant.'

Celia stirred herself. This was going to be a terrible night. She said, 'I didn't want you to know yet.'

451

'It really isn't Dad's, then?'

'No. It's – it's someone else. Someone very – nice and kind.'

'The doctor.'

'I didn't say that!'

'You don't have to. We've seen the way he is with you. Honestly, I think you're absolutely foul!'

Ellen flung out of the room, and Lucy, in the passage listening, stood anxiously to one side. Celia felt her head start to pound again, as if it would explode. If ever she would like to black out it was now, to hide from this, forever if need be. But consciousness refused to leave her. Reality remained.

'Would you like to set the table, please, Lucy?' she asked jerkily. Her voice sounded harsh and raw.

'I don't think anyone wants to eat.'

'I don't care what they want! Everyone will eat. I insist on it!'

The meal got made, somehow. By the time it was ready Ellen had cried herself into a jelly and David was almost beyond speech. But they came to the table, aware that in some way life together had to go on. They were linked, inextricably, until death and possibly beyond. It was a horrible thought.

Somewhat restored by hot food, Ellen blew her nose. 'What's going to happen to the business?' she asked at last.

David groaned but Celia said, 'Nothing terrible. I won't let it. I've got some jewellery to sell. We'll give all that money to the bank.'

'It's not enough,' mumbled David. 'It'll never be enough.'

Celia said, 'It's very valuable jewellery. We'll see.'

After dinner, the evening fragmented. It was late and the girls went to bed. David went back to his whisky and Celia sat in the kitchen, amidst the debris of the day, and tried to make sense of it all. Was she really to blame for all this?

When she awoke, and more importantly understood what had happened, she had wanted nothing more than to regain her former life. She was like a horse in a long race, stumbling halfway through, making desperate attempts to catch up with the leaders before the winning post arrived. But life didn't have a winning post. There were no victories, except perhaps personal ones, defeating the demons in one's own soul. She had imagined that happiness, once lost, could be snatched back by brute force. And all the faults she had possessed when she slept were still there when she woke – selfishness, impulsiveness, pride, sexual greed. Now, pregnant and bewildered, she was reaping her own whirlwind.

But it wasn't all her own fault. She strove for balance, for fairness in her thinking. Edwin was a thief and a trickster, and David – well, what was David? He confused her now as he never had before. A poor businessman, that was self-evident, but this paralysis, this inability to grasp reality and wrestle with it – she didn't remember that. The mortgage on Blantyre House had given him a chance to send his car rocketing into the front rank of exclusive sports cars. Everything was there, in place, waiting. Delays, rigid thinking, indecision, had all played their part. And now this. Assuredly, this wasn't her fault.

She got up and went into the sitting room. David was slumped on the sofa, morose and bleary. Celia stood looking at him for a moment, trying to recall those things about him which had so shocked her when first she saw him again. He was faded, less bright. The shining gold of his hair was dimmed by grey. She remembered him as tanned, smiling, a different person from this worn individual. What had she wanted back? This man? Or the other, distant, lover of her youth? They were not at all the same.

She sat down on the end of the sofa. 'David, I'm sorry you're in such a mess.'

He dropped his head and his shoulders began to shake. Celia reached out a hand to him, and then withdrew it. She didn't dare touch him, and she didn't want to. Drunk and weeping, he repelled her. She tried to think what to do, what to say, and could think of nothing. Charles was right. She wasn't up to this.

It was late by the time she got to bed. She felt shaky, on the verge of some terrible breakdown that she could not permit herself to have. Lying in bed, looking into the darkness, she felt demons gathering about her.

In the morning she was late setting off for court, and drove quickly. Only after some ten minutes did she realise that someone was following her. She took a wrong turning and had to go back. An anonymous green car turned with her, braking when she did, changing lanes at the same time, following her erratic course through traffic lights. Anxiety began to make her heart flutter, and her palms became wet on the wheel. Not again. Not now. Edwin couldn't know she had the copy Will, he wouldn't attack her. He thought he was winning. But the car kept following. She kept to main roads, ignoring any of the short cuts she normally used. The traffic was light today, and the green car worryingly obvious. She began to cherish a vague hope that it might be the police, keeping her under surveillance for her own safety. It was possible. They might be taking her more seriously than she thought.

The idea became more convincing by the moment. It was the police, keeping a fatherly eye on her progress, making sure she arrived safely at her courtroom destination. She turned right alongside the canal, and saw that the follower was coming closer. She was calm, waiting for the car to come alongside, for a copper to give her a friendly wave before setting off on his daily round of preserving the honest citizen from harm. The green car came up to her, swung hard in her direction, and dealt her car a swingeing blow. The world spun before her eyes, a confused mêlée of wall, railing, sky. Noise filled her head and then suddenly, as if a giant hand had grabbed her in the middle of flight, all was still. Her car hovered on the edge of the canal, front wheels over the edge, the back still safe on dry land. All that held her, all that saved her, was a rusty iron stanchion. Where others had broken, it alone held.

Some workmen rushed out of a nearby house. 'Are you all right, love?' A big burly man was helping her out. Another, younger, very excited, shrieked: 'Did you see him? Deliberate, it were. He drove right off.' A third, enjoying it all and anticipating a fun morning, said, 'Anyone get his number? Someone should call the police.'

She sat down on the pavement, unable to persuade her legs to be anything other than useless jelly.

'Can we call your husband, love?'

She nodded. 'Yes. I mean – actually, would you call my doctor? Charles Davenport.'

Chapter Thirty-One

He found her sitting in the workmen's hut, trying to drink tea. He took in her condition at once, and that of the policeman, trying to make sense of what she said.

'It's all right, Officer,' he said. 'I'll take care of her. Perhaps you'd like to talk to her later on.'

'She keeps saying someone tried to kill her,' explained the bemused bobby. 'This car tried to drive her into the canal.'

'Did it indeed?' Charles squatted down in front of Celia. 'You're in shock, but apart from that, any visual disturbance? Pain? Obvious injury?'

She shook her head. He nodded and got up. 'I'll be taking her into hospital for the time being. Come and see her this afternoon.'

Safe again. Back on the warm, undemanding sidelines. In hospital, she lay in the bed Charles had found for her, letting tears of fright seep into her pillow. He sat down on the bed and stroked her hair. 'Just cry. Let it out. You'll feel better soon.'

'I don't know who it was,' she said thickly. 'I thought I was safe.'

'We'll get you protection. The police have got to be involved.'

'I daren't! What about the pearls? I stole them, and David's got to have the pearls.'

'He's got to have nothing! Whatever he has he fritters. If you lose the court case, the pearls are all that you have. Why do you have to feed them to David's inadequate ambition?'

Her sobs became fewer. She was calming, trying to think, not about the pearls but the accident. 'It wasn't like the other times,' she said slowly. 'Much more inept.'

'So?'

'It could have been David. He's so angry he hasn't got the pearls.'

Charles let out a crack of mirthless laughter. 'Well, it could have been Heather for that matter, sneaking out of her room for a quick bit of murder. Be honest, Celia. We under-estimated Braddock yet again.'

'Why not David? He's had enough of me, I'm sure of it. He wants me out of his life.'

Charles got out his torch and began peering into her eyes, as if he could detect the turmoil of her thoughts. She tried to push his hand away, but he held firm. She gripped his wrist, and he peered into her, blinding her with the light. 'What do you want to see? Clear evidence of my insanity?'

'I don't know. You look different. Shadowed.'

'Death, walking at my elbow,' she retorted, without flippancy.

Charles snapped off the torch and stood back. 'How do you feel? You've been better, better than I hoped. No fits, no fainting.'

'I – I cope better,' she confessed. 'Sometimes I can ward it off.'

'Now? Are you warding it off now?'

'All I feel now is – my thoughts are jumbled. I see enemies everywhere. Am I going mad, Charles? Don't let me go mad!'

He knelt down and held her. Her breathing, tense and desperate, was loud in his ear. He thought how often he had heard breathing stop. The first time, a medical student sent to a hopeless case on a dark ward at night, he had suffered a real thrill of fear. And he was a man who was very rarely frightened. Bizarre though it was, the moment was one he had enjoyed. Emotion, real emotion, had touched him. And now, suddenly, he knew that if Celia's breath stopped, if she suffered that jerking, gasping, racking last inhalation and was still – he could not bear it. She feared madness, but he had no concern over that. In her right mind, or out of it, Celia was Celia. It was her absence he could not withstand.

She moved her head, bringing her lips almost to his. 'Don't you crack too,' she murmured.

456

'Why?' He felt her warmth, her softness, like a caress.

'Because I need you. Don't you let me down.'

He opened his mouth and kissed her, gently, lovingly. It was a kiss without passion, and full of trust. But the door of the room opened and a voice said, 'Good God! Davenport! What on earth is going on?'

It was Moffat, the barrister. He had suspected them from the first, and now, before his eyes, he had the proof.

Celia was the first to recover. She pushed herself up in the bed, saying, 'Get up, Charles, do. How do you do, Mr Moffat? I've had a car accident, I'm afraid.'

'So I gather. I came to offer my sympathy. But I see Mr Davenport was before me.'

Charles put out his hand and Celia grasped it. She didn't know what she should do. Charles could lose his career over this. The work he loved, the work at which he excelled, could all be lost to him.

Charles said acerbically, 'It would have helped if you'd knocked.'

'Helped whom? This is obviously something long-standing.'

'Not at all,' said Celia. 'I was upset. I thought – you don't know what someone like me might think. Charles is my friend, my good friend, he was simply—'

'Don't, Celia,' said Charles. He lifted her hand and kissed it. 'Don't. I won't pretend. I'm your lover. If he wants to bring me down over it then he will.'

'And his son won't have a hope,' said Celia in a shrill voice. 'You realise that, don't you, Mr Moffat? If your son is to be cured you can't have Charles struck off. Not for something as – as trivial as this!'

Moffat took off his glasses and polished them. 'I came here today to offer my assistance,' he said stiffly. 'With your court case, Celia. I have a full caseload, but in a few weeks I should have some time. I heard what happened yesterday, and it wasn't good. I thought – I wanted to help you. Wanted to assist you in your struggle to be the person you once were.'

She said, 'I've stopped trying to be that, as it happens. I

want to be someone new. I couldn't be the same, and your son won't be the same, because this whole thing is much harder than it looks!'

'Calm down,' said Charles urgently. 'Don't excite yourself. You've had a shock and you must calm down.'

Moffat said, 'I just find it rather hard to countenance lechery masquerading as medicine. You're a vulnerable woman. I don't blame you, believe me, I do not. I have to blame the man.'

Charles said, 'I did not take advantage of her. I truly feel that.'

'She's got a family! She was ill, dependent! My God, what sort of man are you?'

Charles's bleeper went. Moffat said angrily, 'If I believe anything it's that you've got those things trained to get you out of awkward situations.'

'Think what you like,' said Charles. 'I've got to go. Celia, if he bullies you, ring for the nurse. I'll make sure he's chucked out.'

He went out, leaving the door swinging. Moffat reached over and shut it.

Celia said, 'He's the only person who can save your son. At least, he's the only one prepared to try.'

Moffat ran a hand across his face. 'I was impressed by you,' he said at last. 'And by him. I wanted to believe that you were as you seemed. Does that surprise you? An idealist, still, at my age? Robbers, murderers, rapists . . . I've had them all past my desk. And yet I wanted two good-looking, intelligent people to lead wholesome lives. I still believed it was possible.'

'Making love isn't quite such a sin,' said Celia quietly. 'Not if you don't betray anyone. And we don't. Didn't. Our affair isn't exactly on at the moment. I look after my family, though they don't really want me back. And Charles works. It's all he does, all he ever did. And that makes him vulnerable to someone like me. Don't blame him entirely, Mr Moffat. I never did lead a wholesome life.'

'I came here to help you,' said Moffat again. 'To offer my professional skills.'

458

Her face was pale and strained. The hospital nightdress she wore was too big, and she looked like a waif. 'Then offer them,' she said. 'But if you love your son, don't ever turn Charles in.'

The car was returned to Blantyre House later that day. Hard on its heels came Heather.

'Mum!' yelled Lucy, who had been picking her way through the wreckage of the kitchen, trying to salvage some food. 'Are you all right? You're not supposed to be here.'

'I couldn't stay away. Not when I knew you were on your own. How are you, darling?'

'Fine. Really. Celia must be a terribly bad driver, mustn't she?'

'I don't know. Perhaps.'

Heather was pale, but better. Some of the strain was gone from her face. She had grown thinner, too, in the last days and it suited her, as did her new haircut. Charles had sent the hospital hairdresser to her, whether she wanted it or not. Her mouth curved a little in a grin. He was a very peremptory man, was Charles Davenport.

The air of relief, of normality, pervaded the whole house. Ellen gave up adult airs and took to her bedroom to play loud music, and David opened a bottle of wine. 'Better? Happier?' he asked.

She nodded, but said, 'We can't go on like this, you know. Me and Celia, fighting. We've got to make some decisions.'

'She's the one who has to do that. She still hasn't given me the pearls. Honestly, Heather, we could be bankrupt and she wouldn't lift a finger to help.'

'Are we? Bankrupt?'

'God knows.'

She immersed herself in domestic concerns, refusing to let herself think. The evening passed in a mêlée of housework and homework. David, who seemed unnaturally tired, took himself early to bed. Alone downstairs, Heather sat for a while, watching television with the sound turned down. People mouthed meaninglessly, a silent accompaniment to her thoughts. At last, she flicked the remote control and turned the pictures off. They meant nothing to her. She had no interest outside herself. She reached out and picked up the telephone.

'Mr Braddock. It's me.'

'Heather! My dear, what a pleasant surprise. All my efforts to contact you have been in vain for so long that I convinced myself you were avoiding me.'

'I was. But something happened today. Someone tried to kill Celia. Was it you?'

There was silence. She could almost have sworn that Braddock was surprised. At what? The news? Or her accusation?

He said, 'Can you tell me what happened?'

'I should think you might know. Someone tried to drive her car off the road into the canal. They'd been following her, they knew her route. Was it you? You tried before. I know you want her dead.'

'Leaving aside the validity of that accusation – so do you.'

'Not enough to kill her!'

'But enough to have her killed. Be honest with yourself, Heather. Don't shelter behind suburban squeamishness. You hate dear Celia as much as anyone.'

Heather replaced the receiver. Her hands were shaking, and she had sworn never to let herself get so bad again. She drained the last of her wine, left over from dinner. It tasted very good, a strong draught of pleasure. She was glad she had come home today, despite the hospital's warnings. She had the sense that her life was entering a crisis, and she needed all her wits to encounter it. The dog, lying at her feet, groaned and rolled against her. She reached down and tickled his tummy and he groaned again in ecstasy. It was odd how you could grow to like the most improbable things, she thought. It was odd how your loyalties shifted.

When she went up to bed David was fast asleep. She stood for a moment, looking down at him, seeing the lines and anxieties smooth away in sleep. She had felt herself to be the main victim of this tragedy of no one's making, but now she wondered. David seemed torn almost in two. He was running the business so badly, even by his arbitrary standards. Would

460

the pearls make everything right? Wasn't it better to wait until the court case was over, and see where they stood? David didn't want to wait. He was in desperate need of cash. All the puzzles and questions crowded in on her. They hadn't gone away during her time in hospital, they had merely sat down and waited until she returned. This time, she thought, they would not defeat her. She would fight and struggle until she found a way through.

Braddock looked out across his park, to the still water of the lake, where the wind stirred the surface into a textured sequence of ripples. He was puzzled by Heather's call. It was another element in the complicated game he was playing, and he wasn't sure what it meant. Had she given up working against Celia? Why? He tried to think objectively, free to do so now he had Celia so completely on the run.

He felt good tonight; strong and capable. Giving Celia the trust fund had been an inspiration, and one, since Marlborough, that he could afford. Now, when the court looked at the running of the business, they would not see it as overstretched and overburdened but orderly, profitable, with no need to grub for cash. He had shown the same entrepreneurial spirit and flair as old man Braddock, while Celia just showed herself up.

He called to the dogs and they rose in a body and came to him. He would go for a drive and take them too, in the Range Rover. He opened his desk and punched a series of buttons, de-activating the alarm. Since Celia's little visit he had seen fit to install a great many devices to protect his home. It was as well, in a case such as this, to be more than prepared.

As he left the moon rose above the trees. It sailed in the sky like a balloon made of glass, shedding a light so brilliant that he could read the clock on the stables. Half-past eleven. The gates, electric now, with the gatekeeper sacked and gone, swung inaudibly wide. He was very pleased with their efficiency.

His father's road was absolutely silent as he drove up. He parked, and shushed the dogs, who were eager to get out. 'Not tonight, children,' he murmured, ruffling coats and soothing

461

anxious noses. 'You just came for the ride.' His father's sitting room showed a gleam of yellow between the curtains. He was still up, then. Edwin went to the door and let himself in.

'Father?'

'Oh. It's you.' The older man was dressed in a grey suit with a patterned pullover underneath it. He was working on a photograph album, surrounded by stickers and labelling strips. He tapped the page. 'This should be your job. But you never were thorough.'

'You enjoy it, don't you?'

'There is nothing in this that I am likely to enjoy.'

Edwin took hold of a photograph. It was of Celia, aged eleven or so, gawky and long-legged in an old-fashioned swimming costume. There was little to say that she would ever be beautiful. She was just an awkward, thin little girl. 'Have you been out in the past few days?' asked Edwin, with assumed casualness.

His father took the photograph from him with a determined twitch of arthritic fingers. 'What do you mean?'

'Have you been out anywhere?'

'I live my life, Edwin. Constrained as it must be. I see no reason to account to you for my movements.'

'Father, this is quite important.'

'Your concerns so often seem to be. But then, your values always did lend themselves to distortion.'

It was no use. It was never any use. Edwin blinked rapidly, infuriated that he should be so unmanned by his father. How old did his father have to get, how old did a son have to be, before a father's opinion didn't matter any more? Crossly, defiantly, he said: 'Do you remember what we talked about last time? The Marlborough clubs? I got them in the end. It was in the press. They were very complimentary.'

For a long moment his father said nothing. Instead he concentrated on his photographs, putting a caption in place with a pair of pointed tweezers. 'I saw,' he said at last.

'Did you agree? I mean – it's made all the difference. The management was terrible. I'm selling clubs and making money every day—'

'The risk was unacceptable. You faced ruin. It was only luck that saved you.'

The muscles in Edwin's jaw ached with tension. He wanted to scream, to smash things, to smash his father into oblivion. He went to the cupboard in the corner and dragged the doors open, revealing his father's meagre stock of booze. There was some sherry left over from Christmas. Edwin poured himself a large measure in one of the old, brown glasses he remembered from childhood. His father watched, mouth pursed in disapproval.

'You still haven't told me if you've been out,' said Edwin again, his nerves beginning to steady. 'It's important.'

'Why?'

'Someone made an attempt on Celia's life.'

His father let out a crack of laughter. 'And you thought it might be me? I'm impressed, my boy. And I marvel at your estimation of me. Might I remind you that I am nearly eighty?'

'It was a car. Someone tried to force her into the canal.'

'Why me?'

'Why not?'

The two men stared at each other. Edwin saw the veins standing stiff and prominent on his father's head. He was so old, and yet so indomitable. Edwin felt the age-old resentment that still his father stood so immovably in his way.

He said, 'For once, I'd like to know the truth.'

'Would you? Your mother and I always thought you the most consummate liar. Truth never meant much to you as a boy, and even less since you left boyhood.'

'Father, I'm not a liar!'

'We both know that to be a lie in itself.'

Rage clouded Edwin's vision. He made for the door, falling over a little table on the way. Once in the hall, he waited to see if his father would follow him, but there was no sound. Edwin flung from the house, got in his car and drove away.

Moffat was at his son's bedside. It was very late, perhaps two in the morning. He should be at home now, his wife was waiting. But he stayed here. Looking at his son.

Martin had moved a little in the bed. He sometimes did, said Sister Johnson, but that shouldn't raise hopes. Moffat knew better than that now. In the early days, torn between rage and pain, he had constantly expected to arrive at the hospital and find Martin had woken up. He used to plan what to say to him; sometimes he would rehearse a diatribe in his head. After so long, though, what was there left to say? Life had moved on. Everyone had changed. They no longer spent weekends touring the squats looking for him.

He was going to drop the case against the anaesthetist. He knew that now. When people like Davenport were seducing the patients it proved just how far standards had sunk, and how tough it would be to make any sort of prosecution stick. They all had their skeletons to hide. And a thought came unbidden. Who didn't?

Years ago he had successfully defended a man on a rape charge. It was a vicious case, involving a knife, and he'd got the chap off. Trouble was, he knew he'd done it. Something about the man's manner, some air of triumph, had alerted him. He never said a word, not even when the bodies started coming in. Same style, same handiwork. Three of them, before he was caught. Yes, everyone had something they wanted to hide.

Martin stirred again. He would shake him, except he feared it would dislodge the drip. What sort of sleep was it that wouldn't allow waking? Was it deliberate? Was Martin in there still, refusing to come out and face his own future? The boy was a coward, an utter coward!

He felt tearful suddenly. That was the trouble with these visits, they leached away your control. No wonder the boy's mother wouldn't come. But he found himself wondering, not for the first time, if there was more to it than that. Women were such realists, underneath all the froth. They were so much more resilient than they seemed. Sometimes his wife seemed to be constructed out of strands of metal, twisted into a great rope of steel. It was a thought he wanted to share with Martin, which was incongruous when they had been almost enemies for years.

He touched his son's hand. They could have been close. There was a day somewhere, lost in the past, when he and his

464

son began moving away from one another, and if he could get back to that day he'd do things differently. When was it? Which of the times when he'd been too busy, too lazy, too uninterested, had been the one? All the small failures of parenthood lay stored up in his memory, and he could recall each one.

A nurse came in, taking blood pressure, moving the body in the bed to a new and more comfortable position. She was a young girl, pretty in a plump sort of way. Moffat said, 'Do you like my son, Nurse?'

She looked askance but said, 'We all think he's very sweet. Such a kind face.'

A diplomatic response. Moffat went on, 'Do you have any trouble with Mr Davenport? I mean – trouble.'

The girl laughed. She didn't understand. 'Loads! He's terribly bossy. He and Sister Johnson are always having fights. But it's bound to be like that, really, isn't it? When someone's as clever as him. We all want to do theatre when we know he's on, although he won't have beginners – he swears at them. But we love watching him work. You wouldn't think a big man like that would be so – deft.'

He hadn't expected a eulogy. Moffat said, 'How does he get on with Mrs Sheraton?'

The girl made a face. 'No one's quite sure. She answers him back, you know. The only person who dares, and the only one he takes it from. It's a pity she isn't as well as she might be. We thought at one time they might get married, because her husband forgot her, you know, over all those years. We don't think it's going to come to anything, though. He's got her down for more treatment, but he wants to wait until it's absolutely necessary. So, no wedding bells.'

Moffat said stiffly, 'Isn't it rather disgusting, getting involved with a patient? For a doctor, I mean?'

She grinned. 'You can't expect people not to get to know each other, can you? Like Martin, here. We care about him, even though he can't talk. Lots of nurses marry patients, you know. Why not doctors?'

'He's in a position of trust! He has a responsibility to her!'

Bewildered and a little worried, the girl said, 'I don't think

465

you realise – Mr Davenport takes wonderful care of all his patients. And half of them he doesn't even like!'

When the girl left, Moffat felt bewildered. He looked at Martin's sleeping face. Martin always used to accuse him of silly idealism that bore no relation to life in the real world. And Moffat still thought it appalling that Davenport should so abuse his position as to seduce a patient, however beautiful and willing she might be! But that was nothing to do with his surgical skills. Everyone said he was brilliant. Moffat took a long breath. 'All right, Mr Davenport,' he murmured, 'prove how good you are.'

When Davenport came into the unit later that day, Sister Johnson met him with a stare of molten fury. 'Really!' she exclaimed and stalked past him.

Charles felt a tightening in the pit of his stomach. Was this it, then? The final breaking of the scandal? He glanced at one of the nurses. 'Well? What sin have I committed this time?'

The nurse smirked. 'Mr Moffat's given permission for the operation on his son. I talked to him and he came right out a minute later and signed the forms. Sister wouldn't speak to him. And she's had me giving blanket baths for hours.'

He laughed. 'Keep trudging the steep and rugged pathway, nurse. When we're old and grey and I dodder back to the hospital and find you Chief Nursing Officer, we'll talk about Sister Johnson with affection.'

The nurse coloured, grabbed her bowl and ran off. Charles sank his hands into his pockets. He was nervous suddenly. He'd suggested the operation, but it had never been tried before. Had he the right? Had he the skill?

Sister Johnson came past him again. He said, 'Tell me it's worth the risk.'

She sniffed. 'You've told me that for long enough. But I console myself with the thought that you'll probably get sued. The father's quite unpredictable.'

'I would have said rigid. Firm in his views. Probably drove young Martin mad.'

'Which he could do again. Imagine, Mr Davenport, that boy, mentally impaired, in the hands of his father.'

466

'He might not be mentally impaired.'

She gave him an old-fashioned look. 'Good as you are, I very much doubt that you can perform this operation without some damage to function. He will wake to find himself handicapped.'

'So you do acknowledge that he'll wake!' He clapped his hands together, in a surge of triumph.

Sister Johnson pulled on a pair of plastic gloves, preparatory to some procedure. 'One thing that cannot be said about you, Mr Davenport, and there are many things that can, is that you attempt the impossible. But, like all surgeons, you have a limited view.'

'Unlike nurses,' said Davenport dryly.

Suddenly, the Sister stopped and turned to him. 'I'm not optimistic,' she said honestly. 'I understand what you're doing, and why you're doing it, but I can't pretend to hope. You want to see if this case can have any bearing on Mrs Sheraton. We both know she hasn't got long.'

Charles took in his breath, feeling it sear like a flame. He put his hand to his face, trying to control himself, reassemble the mask. 'Don't say it,' he whispered. 'Don't even think it.'

'We're both too old not to know the signs,' said Sister Johnson. 'She had the look, didn't she?'

'I imagined it. I didn't see a thing.'

'We never do. It's never tangible. They just look as if they're dying.'

He went to sit in Sister's office. She left him there, getting on about her business, only sending a nurse with a cup of tea. After half an hour she came in. 'You have work to do, Mr Davenport. I can't have you cluttering up my office all day.'

He looked up. He was a little pale, a little strained, but in command. 'I'm sorry to have inconvenienced you, Sister. Could you – could you convey a message, please, to Mrs Sheraton? Tell her I won't be seeing her this week. My registrar can attend to her.'

Sister nodded. 'Of course. Now, when shall I prepare young Martin Moffat? It's a big operation. You'll want to be at your best.'

But he felt so very weary. Why hadn't anyone told him

neurology would be so hard? He felt as if there was a mountain before him, and he must dig it away, armed only with a very puny shovel. All he could do was hack at this stone or that, and even when there was a little fall and the mountain was less, he knew eternity would not be long enough to shift it.

He said, 'I'll do him next week. I'm going away for a few days. I'm sick of the whole damn thing.'

The Sister stood aside to allow him to leave, wondering how she was going to explain to the patients that he had forgotten them. But he went into the ward, and snapped out a greeting to one of his recovering surgeries. The woman smiled tentatively, and Davenport pulled down her eyelid and grunted. 'You'll be in here for six weeks,' he grunted. 'Don't start bellyaching at four. I know Sister Johnson's a trial, we all have to get used to her. Believe me, it hurts less with time.'

And to the next patient, who had thought himself doomed, 'I know you're surprised to see me. You have my permission to ask the solicitor for a refund on your Will. You're going to be around for a lot longer than you supposed.'

Although desperately ill, a rustle of laughter went round the beds. Charles strode on, and halfway through his coterie of juniors came through the doors and gathered about him. He grunted and they looked at each other uncomfortably. Word had spread. The old man was fulminating about something. And Charles clung to the misconception, knowing that beyond it he was breaking into pieces.

Chapter Thirty-Two

Celia was bewildered by the suddenness of Charles's departure. She waited all one day, expecting him to come and see her at any time. But when he still hadn't come, and the registrar had made two visits for blood tests and paid prolonged and tedious attention to the blood flow in her neck, she said, 'Where is Mr Davenport, please? Isn't he in today?'

The registrar was a little embarrassed. 'Didn't he tell you, Mrs Sheraton? He's taking a few days' holiday.'

'But – what am I supposed to do? Did he say? I mean – can I leave?'

'I don't think so. In fact, I'm sure he wouldn't like that. Why don't you try and get some rest?'

He slid out of the room, and she was alone. And already she was missing Charles. She lay back against her pillows, feeling her headache begin again, wondering what she had done. Charles was gone, Dorrie was gone, and Heather was back in Blantyre House. Life was cartwheeling away, out of control. She asked for the telephone and it was brought to her. She rang Hector Lowndes.

'Hector? What's happening? I'm in hospital and you haven't told me a thing.'

'Nothing serious, I hope?'

'No, nothing much. But what's going on?'

'Actually – ' she could hear the apology in Lowndes's voice '– the judge is studying the papers. He didn't allow the copy Will. It wasn't registered in time.'

'It wasn't what?' she shrieked down the phone.

'Our barrister had another case booked. He wasn't in court. We didn't expect this to come up so soon, of course, and he – he made a mistake. The evidence wasn't submitted at the proper time, and is therefore inadmissible. We can have another go, of course, take it to appeal.'

'Costing a fortune I haven't got.' She brought her knees up to her breast, feeling the baby flutter as she compressed herself. She stretched out a little, giving her infant space. 'We've got to stop it, Hector. We've got to put it right. We're giving this to Edwin on a plate!'

'I applied for an adjournment! But without counsel we got nowhere. The judge thought it was an excuse to let our barrister off the hook. I'm sorry, Celia.'

'Yes.' She lay back against the pillows. 'I bet you are.'

Willing but disorganised, Hector had excelled himself this time. And she felt too weary to carry on. But her father's face, sometimes so vague, suddenly seemed very clear. He looked quizzically at her, as he had when she came home from school with an average mark. 'Average isn't for us, my girl,' he used to say. 'In this family, we always excel. If everyone in the world always tried their best we wouldn't have any problems. There'd be enough food, enough money, enough everything. Learn to do your best, Celia, even when it isn't important, because you'll get in the habit. And one day, when you're tired and sick of it all, when it really matters, that habit will stand you in good stead.'

She was tired. She was absolutely sick of it all. She was alone. But the habit of trying was one she couldn't shake off. She got out of bed and put on her dressing gown and slippers. The walls of the room seemed to slip and slide about her, and she sat down on the edge of the bed for a moment, to gather her wits. When everything steadied and she felt stronger, she got cautiously to her feet and opened the door. In her weakened state, feeling inadequate, the corridor seemed to stretch into infinity. Nonetheless, one hand on the wall, she began to walk down it. She was going to see Moffat.

Charles booked himself into an hotel. It was a small, warm place, with low ceilings and sloping floors. On the first night he drank a whole bottle of wine at dinner, followed it with two brandies and crawled off to bed. Just the same, he woke in the early hours, and lay dry-mouthed, listening to the birds under the roof. Get used to it, he told himself. This is what life's going to be. No Celia, no baby. Their tiny store of days was almost used up.

It kept occurring to him from time to time that the baby might live. It was possible, if Celia went beyond six months. But he didn't think she had so long. As Sister Johnson said, she had the look, as if a point had been passed, a commitment made. As the old soldiers used to say, if your number was up there was no use bleating. And Celia didn't bleat. It was left to him to rage and despair at the unfairness of it all.

The hotel was in Devon, near Dorrie. It was a deliberate choice, he felt in need of Dorrie's brand of good sense. But when he went to her house her artist friend was there, and he felt awkward. They sat in the small, dark kitchen, with herbs hanging from the low ceiling and dangling in your hair, and a duck in the corner sitting on a clutch of eggs, and tried to make conversation.

'You don't look very well,' said Dorrie uncomfortably. 'Are you convalescing, or something?'

Charles wondered if she thought he was going to impose himself on them, and make the little house untenable. 'It's just a rest. Nothing more. By the way, Celia's back in hospital.'

'Anything serious?'

He tried to form the words. He told people things like this every day, he didn't find it hard. But all he said was, 'No, no. She's been overdoing things. We both have.'

Dorrie laughed dirtily, and the artist joined in. Charles decided he didn't like him. The man looked like a caricature of the impoverished creator, right down to his soggy, open-toed shoes.

'Do you remember that legal bloke with the comatose son?' he remarked. 'He's considering having me struck off.'

'What? Because of Celia? Honestly! Don't worry, Charles, I could find a dozen character witnesses more than willing to tell everyone you hadn't a chance. We all know Celia.'

'That's what I like! A liberal spirit,' said the artist, lighting up some disgusting herbal cigarette.

Charles got up and took his leave. Dorrie came with him to the gate, her face pale in the daylight, thinner. 'You worry me,' she said suddenly. 'I don't know why.'

Charles said, 'I think she's going to die.'

A minute passed. A robin hopped from one damp branch to the next, watching them beadily. 'What if she is?' said Dorrie at last. 'What then?'

He shook his head. 'Don't you care?'

'You forget, we've all mourned Celia before. It was more dreadful than you can imagine. A real death can't be so bad.'

He said levelly, 'I can't bear it to be over. I imagine what it's going to be like. When it happens. Each day, each hour. No different probably to the days and hours I spend now. Busy. Worthwhile. But I spend them now in the knowledge that she's there, that there's the possibility of seeing her. If that was gone – Dorrie, there's something I didn't understand before. People talk about love and it's trivial, a liking, an enjoyment of sex or another's company. But it isn't that. It's fundamental. A need. Like something animal, basic, a need for water, like a flower turning to the sun.'

Dorrie pushed her hair back from her face. She seemed embarrassed, as if he had made some slighting reference to her casual romance with the artist. 'Most people don't want your sort of deal,' she said.

Charles tried to laugh. 'I don't want it! It's like some rare infection, unknown in science, a sort of emotional Black Death. Perhaps I'm genetically susceptible or something. All I know is that I need her. And I can't even tell her how much.'

Dorrie touched his hand, aware that Charles was the least tactile of men. 'She's a lot stronger than you think,' she said.

'Yes.' He looked back at the little cottage, thatch sagging over the porch, a stack of canvases, half-finished, unfinished, under an inadequate sheet of flapping canvas. An ill-prepared, half-finished idyll.

When he got back to his hotel, he ordered dinner and then sat in his room, drinking whisky. He drank more with his meal, and still more later on, until he fell into bed at midnight. It was his first good sleep in days.

There were advantages to Charles's absence, Celia discovered. For one thing, when she announced that she was leaving there was only his registrar to contend with, a man of undoubted brilliance but little courage. Celia assumed that he was sapped by the constant strain of Charles, although her last interview with him caused her to change her mind. He was a diffident young man, probably best suited to the supportive role, and quite unable to face her down on his own. So she behaved badly, demanding her clothes, insisting on a taxi. When she left, Davenport's staff hovered miserably on the steps, and as she drove away James, the administrator, joined them at a run. He waved after her, hopelessly, pathetically, as if the trust fund itself was running away. If Celia had felt strong enough, she would have laughed.

She felt very tired and weak. Her shape had changed while she lay in bed, and minus the drapery of her nightgown, she looked pregnant. That was the cause of everything, she decided. Pregnancy always took its toll. But she knew she couldn't appear in public much longer, and keep her condition secret. Without Charles, on her own, she felt vulnerable and a little lost.

The taxi driver turned in his seat. 'Got your bearings now, love? Where's it to be?'

'The law courts, please.'

She assessed the contents of her handbag during the journey; two pounds in loose change, an expired credit card and a key to Charles's house. She looked at it with pleased surprise. That was fate, if ever fate took a hand. Charles was away, and she could sneak in, like Goldilocks, and eat his porridge. She felt no obligation to tell David or the girls. They had made their position very clear. When it came down to it, they wanted Heather.

It was a bleak thought. But what else could she think, when neither David nor the girls had visited? She didn't blame the girls, she decided. They wanted the known, the familiar life. She had landed on them like an exotic bird, dazzling and a little unreal. But they could at least have visited.

She dabbed at her eyes with the remnant of a tissue she found in her pocket. There was no use moping. She had work to do, because if her family didn't need her they certainly needed her money. She wasn't about to give up and let Edwin have that. Not after all he had done.

The taxi drew up and she scrambled out. The fare came to two pounds fifty. She apologised to the driver and said if he wanted to wait, she was sure she could borrow some cash – but he sighed and let her off. 'Seeing as you're expecting, love.'

She felt dishevelled and obvious. Her clothes didn't fit any more. Even her hair was untidy, because her right hand was being difficult and she hadn't liked to ask a nurse. She unfastened her jacket and pulled it forward, and took her blouse from her skirt and bunched it over the waistband. She still felt nervous and uncertain. She hurried up the wide steps and into the building.

Moffat was in the corridor, talking with animation to Hector Lowndes. 'You must have known the man wasn't competent! Mrs Sheraton seems to have doubted him from the first. I hear what you say, but ignorance in this case is something I cannot accept.'

'Hello, Mr Moffat. Hector.'

They both turned in surprise. Moffat said, 'Mrs Sheraton. Celia. You don't look well.'

'I'm not. But I had to come. Look, don't shout at Hector, I know he's done his best. Can we save it, do you think? Or is it hopeless?'

Moffat said, 'Very near hopeless, I'm afraid. And due to nothing but inefficiency. Not on Mr Lowndes's part, at least not entirely, but a member of my own profession. Fortunately I have some sort of standing. I may be listened to. I'm going to ask the judge to admit our new evidence, but it's quite against the rules. Even if he permits it and we win, you have to realise the case will probably go to appeal. Your cousin will have grounds to contest it, you see.'

'If we win conclusively though – then they'd lose at appeal too. And they'd have to pay. Wouldn't they?'

Moffat shrugged his shoulders. 'In theory, yes.'

Celia smiled in relief. She was sure she would win. As it was, she hadn't even the money for the taxi fare home. She went into the court and sat at the back, watching the comings and goings of officials. Moffat came in and inclined his head. Braddock's men entered. And Braddock himself.

474

Edwin saw her and waved. She had the oddest feeling, that she was closer to this man, who had plotted her death, than to anyone else in the world. Attacker and victim, understanding each other perfectly; safe together, for the most part; workers at the same last. She lifted her hand and waved back.

There were a number of spectators today, old age pensioners who wanted to experience something at first hand. There couldn't be any murder trials, she supposed, for them to attend something so steeped in legal argument. But it might be the attraction of her counsel. Moffat's small, belligerent figure was strangely hypnotic. He had the decisive, theatrical air of a star.

They rose and the judge came in. When everyone else sat, Moffat remained standing, a Napoleon of a man. 'If it may please, Your Lordship, I have a request of the utmost importance.'

The judge looked owlishly over his spectacles. 'And what brings you, Mr Moffat, before me today? I believe that only yesterday I had the pleasure of Mr Parsons's advocacy.'

'Indeed, My Lord. Mr Parsons is otherwise engaged and has kindly asked me to take over this brief. And I find that due to some misfortune—'

'—not unrelated to Mr Parsons's lack of concentration,' broke in the judge.

'As Your Lordship pleases. But the proper conduct of this case must require that new evidence be admitted. It is of material importance, and non-admission, if my client loses this case, will make an appeal inevitable. I must ask for your indulgence, My Lord.'

The judge took off his glasses. Celia realised he was much younger than she had supposed, of the same age as Moffat perhaps. 'Really, Mr Moffat,' he murmured. 'We are both aware of the technicalities in this issue. To appeal, or to be appealed against.'

In a gravel voice, Moffat said, 'The proper examination of the facts must surely come before any such considerations, My Lord. If you will permit me.'

'Thank you kindly for your instruction,' said the judge.

Gravely, Moffat said, 'My Lord, I wouldn't presume.'

'I'm glad to hear it. Request granted. Let's proceed.'

The court was to be shown the copy Will. Celia sat back, heart thumping. Lowndes pushed into her row, red in the face. 'The judge knows him. I think they're old friends. Braddock's side are furious.'

She looked across. They were all talking together in hurried whispers. Edwin lifted his head and Celia met his eyes. A blaze of anger, transmitted across empty space. Her heart fluttered against her ribs and she was conscious of the urge to run away, to run anywhere, but just to escape.

Lowndes said, 'I doubt he'll do anything. There's no need to be afraid.'

'Isn't there?' She turned her face back to the body of the court.

Moffat was talking. The bare bones of her father's life and death were being laid before the court. A rich man, a very rich man, deprived of his beloved heir, who had suddenly decided to leave his grandchildren destitute. Was this likely? Was it the action of a loving and family-minded man? Celia began to relax. She had been right about Moffat. He was good.

They broke for the day shortly after three. Braddock's side would begin early the following morning. Celia caught Moffat in the corridor and thanked him. 'You were wonderful. It all seemed to make such sense.'

He said, 'Wait until you hear the other side. They've got good people too. He's got a worthy argument – that your father left his estate in the hands of the most competent member of the family he could find.'

'He wasn't competent then. He was just a boy.'

'But your father was a good judge of men. I don't subscribe to that view, you understand, but there are those who will.'

'Can you tell what the jury thinks?'

Moffat shook his head. 'But they're mostly men. My instinct is that they'll incline towards Braddock. Look your best tomorrow, if you please. A little less – tousled.'

She flushed. She was falling down on her task of charming the jury. She turned to leave, but Moffat caught her elbow. 'By the way, have you heard from Davenport? I wanted to talk to him – it seems he's gone away. The operation's next week.'

'Yes.' She tried to smile reassuringly. 'He's resting. It's a tough job. I'm sure he'll get in touch in the next day or two. By the way,' she added, as if in afterthought, 'could you possibly lend me five pounds? I've left my purse behind and I haven't a bean.'

'What? Why, yes. Certainly.'

She closed her fingers round the note. That was two taxi fares. What she did after that she simply didn't know.

When she arrived at Charles's house she found it cold with emptiness. Even the Aga was out. She pressed knobs and switches ineffectually, finally persuading the heating to come on and the cooker to begin its revival. There was little to eat; she found some crackers and a piece of hardening cheese, and made a cup of black coffee to go with it. Afterwards she wandered from room to room, thinking what a lovely house it could be, with a little bit of care. In a back bedroom she found all the baby things Charles had bought. For some reason, looking at everything, tears threatened her. She picked up a teddy, small, fluffy, exorbitantly expensive, and took it with her to bed.

She slept poorly that night. Partly it was the cold, and partly nerves. The house felt exposed, with too many windows and too many doors. If someone wanted to break in they would. Towards dawn, not wanting to put on the light, she lay on her back and wondered how she was going to clothe herself in the morning. She had looked scruffy yesterday. Even her style was deserting her, she thought, and hugged the teddy, tight. It was a small comfort in a very comfortless world.

She found herself wondering about Lazarus. Revival was such a tricky thing. He was only dead four days, that was the secret. No one had begun to share out the loot. But even then there must have been mutterings about the money they'd spent on the funeral, and what was he good for, anyway? Once you slipped from the world the surface closed over, and it was as if you had never been.

She felt herself hovering on the edge of despair. 'If it wasn't for the baby,' she found herself whispering. 'If it wasn't for that—' What? She wouldn't kill herself. There was no need for that. She would simply – let go. It felt as if she could surrender herself quite at will. And the whole, dreadful mistake would be over.

But not yet. Baby or no, she would finish the court case first. People remembered money, and revered those who had left it to them. She was living again, simply to make a bequest.

Dozing in the early light, she began to wonder where she was. Blantyre House, perhaps – or her flat – or an hotel in a rundown part of town? She stirred and tried to sit up. She couldn't. For long, long seconds, she was nailed to the bed, wanting to move, willing herself to move, and lying still. Panic came on in a rush. She tried to struggle, tried to flail, and achieved – nothing. She just lay there. Very still.

The baby moved. It was a fluttering, turning disturbance. I function still, thought Celia. There is simply a small hiccup in my brain. She looked at her hand, stretched out above the bedclothes, already stiff and cold. So, her eyes still worked. She tried to swallow, and after a moment, achieved it. There. She looked again at her hand, and willed her fingers to curl – once, twice – gradually, stiffly, they responded.

Some of her fear subsided. This wasn't a permanent state, then. She waited, ten minutes, perhaps twenty, and tried again to move. Her left side – no problem. But her right hand remained stubbornly immobile. It will come, she told herself, crawling off the bed. It will come.

Dressing was torture. She was incapable of doing her hair in any style, and was forced to leave it loose around her shoulders. And she could not manage her blouse. She went slowly round the cupboards in the house, seeing what was there. She found an old opera cloak, which might have been Charles's, or more likely his father's. There was a dress too, one of Dorrie's, a loose blue caftan thing. Celia struggled into it and topped it with the cloak. The effect was strange to say the least, but it would have to do.

The kitchen was warm now, but no less empty of food. She had some more black coffee while she waited for the taxi, wondering how she could persuade Hector Lowndes to buy her something to eat. Perhaps hunger was the cause of this paralysis. A sandwich might put everything right.

478

Tears of fright welled up, but she swallowed them down. Courage was reserved for times like this. She would get through. When the taxi came she pulled her cloak one-handed around her and walked out.

The expression on Hector's face told her how strange she looked. 'Celia! Are you sure you're all right?'

She stretched her mouth in a smile. 'Of course, Hector. But could you possibly get me a sandwich or something? I didn't have time for breakfast.'

'Actually we're not allowed to eat in here. You could go to the canteen.'

'But aren't we about to start?'

'Yes.'

She gave up all thought of the sandwich. Her right arm was like lead, dragging on her shoulder, and sometimes she had to look to see where it was. What's more, her head felt empty. Thoughts echoed in it as if in a vast, vaulted church. I'm going mad, she decided, walking into the court. Everyone will be delighted to put me away. The only paralysed, pregnant madwoman in history.

Braddock was there again. He was staring at her across the banks of seats but she wasn't strong enough to return his stare, or calm enough to smile. Perhaps she was going to faint – but she very much feared she wasn't. She was going to be trapped in her body, in a waking nightmare.

Braddock's counsel was putting his case; a young man, much admired by his uncle, his comfort in a desperate hour, entrusted, wisely, with the control of a fortune. Against his claim there stood only the inadequate business abilities of Mr Sheraton, the claims of two girls – the word was emphasised, as if girlhood alone was a slur – and a few pieces of paper that might or might not have a bearing on a man's intentions. For years that fortune had been in safe hands. For years all had been well. Why should a woman with a trust fund worth millions be entrusted also with such largesse?

Moffat leaped to his feet. They were in the thick of it now, squabbling and arguing, casting slurs and retracting them, all in calm, well-modulated tones. Celia was bewildered. In the midst of all the jargon, there seemed no place for the truth. She got to her feet, not knowing that she did so. She pushed past several people in the row. Moffat looked up at her, and his expression told her all she needed to know. He had requested a mannequin and she had appeared in fancy dress.

Braddock got up at the same time. As she pushed her way into the corridor he followed her. She hadn't time or strength to be frightened, she knew that something terrible was happening to her, something she couldn't control. An arm was around her. It was Braddock's.

'Celia? Shall I call a doctor?'

She shook her head, stiff and uncoordinated. Any doctor Braddock called would not want her to live. One of Braddock's assistants came out of the court behind them, and he and Braddock talked in low voices.

'She looks terrible – doesn't seem to be in control – I'm not sure what to do.'

She knew they were going to take her away. She wanted to scream but could not. With an agonizing effort she turned her head, willing Hector Lowndes to come out of the court, for someone, anyone, to rescue her. But everyone thought Braddock was being kind.

'Take her to my house,' he said thinly.

Celia was propelled bodily from the court.

Chapter Thirty-Three

The car paused before tall gates. Celia stretched her neck as far as it would go, and recognised Linton Place. They were almost there. She felt a great sorrow, that all her struggles, all her turmoil, had come to nothing but this. She was defeated.

When they came to the house the Filipino servants came out on the steps to welcome them. When they saw her state they chattered to each other, and looked amazed. Between them, they carried her up and into the house, and down a corridor to a small sitting room. A log fire blazed cheerfully in the grate. A sofa was pulled up before it, and they laid her down, with the utmost care.

A servant rushed off to fetch food. Celia let her head fall back against the sofa, unable to feel anything except thankfulness. She was at rest, however briefly. When he came back with some soup, she let him spoon it into her, as if she was a helpless babe. Soon she felt better. They wrapped her in a blanket and she lay in the heat of the fire, drowsy and warm. If they were going to murder her it was a very pleasant end. She thought of all that Edwin had done before: the fires, the attempt at kidnap, and the last, unmistakable car crash. Now he was sure to succeed.

After a while she realised she had to go to the bathroom. She sat up gingerly. Her legs felt as if they were trembling, but when she looked at them they were still. If only Charles were here, she caught herself thinking. She wanted to understand what was happening to her, what disaster was taking place in her brain. He at least could quell some of her fear.

She crept from the room, holding on to the door, and found a small cloakroom. In the mirror above the basin she saw a face she half remembered; it was the old Celia again, the one she had first seen when she woke up. The vitality of her living self had given way to ethereal strangeness. When had it happened? Last night, this morning? The basin felt cold against her hands. She could still feel then, even her right hand still possessed sensation. She laid it against her stomach. This poor baby had trusted its life to a vessel with terminal cracks.

She returned to her couch, wondering if anyone had heard her. But all was as it had been. She lay down, thankful to be back, wondering if she could summon the strength to get out of here, even if she knew for sure that Braddock would burst in at any moment with a blood-stained axe. She doubted it. At that moment comfort and rest were all she required.

There came a knock on the door. It was Tomul and Feodor, bearing a trolley laden with goodies; there were smoked salmon sandwiches, quails' eggs, toast spread with anchovy paste and a hot mulled drink which Tomul said was, 'Ver' good. Restore person. Old remedy from old home.'

Celia tasted it dubiously, and found it delicious; a mixture of honey and wine, with a raspberry taste as well. Drinking it, and nibbling a fraction of the spread, her person was indeed restored.

What style Edwin lived in, she thought. Even in its heyday, Blantyre House was never like this. Her father was too close to his origins to be truly lordly in his day-to-day living, and so should Edwin be, she decided. But somehow, he had moved from his dull and spartan childhood to Linton Place with the aplomb of the true aristocrat. Not for him the neat, over-furnished, apologetic overspending of the usual new aspirant to the status of landed gentry. He had created here a home to rival the greatest. She remembered the fish, and the devoted, finely controlled dogs; yes, he even had the right element of thin-bladed cruelty to boot.

Perhaps his sexuality was behind it. Such people grew up in two worlds, and lived in many more. It encouraged a chameleon-like sensitivity to their environment. He had seen how they lived at Blantyre House, and even while he envied he maintained a critical judgment. No half-good paintings by local artists for Edwin, no home-made cushions and too bright silver plate. He had only the old, the good, the beautiful. She resented finding it admirable.

Dozing in the firelight, she was only vaguely aware of Feodor and Tomul removing the trolley and making up the fire. It was heaven, lying here, with the thick scent of wax polish and old roses. She sighed, and turned her cheek a little more to the pillow. A moment later she became aware someone was watching her. She lay still a minute longer, feeling her heart begin to pound. At last, unable to bear it, she looked. Edwin was standing there.

'Celia. Hello. I'm told you're better.'

She tried to sit up, and made a deliberate hash of it. She pushed her hair out of her eyes. 'Your people have made me wonderfully comfortable.'

'My people? My dear Celia, I have servants. No people.'

He was shadowed against the firelight. Looking up as she did, his features were indistinct.

She said, 'Why did you bother with me? You could have called an ambulance. That would have been the easy thing.'

'But I'd rather have you here. Surely you understand that? With so much of importance going on, it's as well to have you close at hand.'

'Does anyone know I'm here?'

'No. I said I'd put you in a taxi. It's assumed you found the court proceedings too much for you. No one is even alarmed.'

That was it then. She was a prisoner and no one in the world cared one jot where she was. It was a salutary thought. In her first twenty-five years she had been surrounded by people who loved her. Now, there was no escaping her own lovelessness. This time round, she had nothing to offer. No youth, no wealth, no prospects. It was a cruel reckoning. All she had achieved in her life was being shown to her at its true market value – and it was worthless.

'Are you going to kill me?' she asked. 'You've tried often enough.'

'Don't be melodramatic,' said Edwin, and moved to sit down by the fire. Celia could only see him by turning her head uncomfortably far. She gave up trying, and spoke to him without looking.

'Fires. Burglaries. Car crashes. That's the stuff of melodrama, isn't it?'

He chuckled. 'Possibly. My dear girl, you can't complain at my determined efforts to take back my pearls. They were mine, you know.'

'They're mine now,' she said. 'You might as well get used to the idea.'

'I never get used to unpleasant ideas!'

She saw his hand move and press a bell. Feodor appeared magically in the doorway and Edwin ordered a whisky and soda, and some more of the mulled wine. 'By the way,' said Celia, as Feodor withdrew, 'let me congratulate you. This house is perfect. Now the fish has gone.'

'You always were so sentimental,' said Edwin contemptuously. 'Your father was the same. Ruthless, but with this sickly overlay of sentimentality, going all soppy over children with impetigo at Christmas.'

Celia giggled. 'No one can be sentimental about impetigo! You do exaggerate, Edwin.'

'Do I? Perhaps you're right.'

When the drinks came Edwin leaned on the mantel to look at her. 'My God, you look deathly,' he said.

She nodded. 'I know. Perhaps I'm going to die and save you the trouble of killing me.'

'Now who's exaggerating?'

'Don't pretend, Edwin. You've been ineffectually trying to wipe me out for months.'

'How do you know it's me?'

She lifted her eyes to his face. 'How do I know it's not?'

The question hung in the air. After a while, like a dog turning from punishment and scratching himself instead, he said, 'Now, you've put me in a quandary. Do I settle with you or not? If you're going to die it hardly seems worth the bother. My counsel tells me that the court seems to be leaning towards giving you the money. Grandchildren don't have the same clout.'

'My counsel wouldn't agree,' said Celia lightly. 'And he's very well regarded.'

'Can't entirely undo the mess the first chap caused, though,' said Edwin. 'You really should watch me a little more closely. I left old man Lowndes because he was useless, and his son's not much better. They couldn't find a good lawyer if their lives depended on it.'

'You left because they knew what you'd done,' said Celia. 'You and David.'

'David?' Edwin's voice rose in surprise. 'What have you heard about David?'

'Nothing. But I know him.'

'So it seems.'

His face had lost its brightness. She wondered why. And then she thought, He might believe she had proof. If he and David had truly been in league, and she was on bad enough terms with her husband not to care what happened to him, she could go public. No question then of a settlement. She would have it all, leaving the conspirators to the tender mercies of the police. If he thought that, he might kill her and be done. 'I can't prove it,' she said quickly. 'Any more than I can prove you burned out that nightclub in Strasbourg and killed the manager.'

Edwin put up a hand. 'Believe me, I didn't know he was there.'

'You wouldn't have stopped if you had.'

'What a terrible opinion you have of me, dear girl.'

He came close to the sofa and looked down at her. Celia found she was beyond fear. It was a sensation she was leaving behind. In the dreamworld, further on, such things had no meaning. She was giving up on life, strand by strand.

Edwin said, 'I've had a room made ready for you. We'll talk when you're stronger. Don't be stubborn, Celia. A deal's going to benefit us both.'

'You'll cheat me. Just as you did David.'

'Remember, my dear. You are, as it were, in my hands.'

A moment later the servants came and carried her up the broad stair to a warm, tapestry-hung room overlooking the park. Undressing her with dispassionate hands, they gave her a nightdress of unbleached linen, and tucked her between smooth, cool sheets. But when they left, with little clucks of concern, she heard the unmistakable turn of the key.

Charles drove straight to the hospital on his return, early on Monday morning, filled with a new resolve. Martin Moffat was to be operated on the following day, and somehow the task to come concentrated his mind. He felt more in control of things. What was the use of his training, his experience, if all he could do was stand by and watch Celia die? He would fight for her as he fought for Moffat, starting that very day. Any treatment, however dangerous, however untried, was better than none. So when he breezed in, demanding of his registrar 'Got Mrs Sheraton's notes then? I'll see her first', and heard that she was gone, he felt total surprise.

He relieved his feelings by stamping on his registrar, the hospital administrator and Sister Johnson. Sister responded by saying acidly that his holiday had obviously done him a power of good. He glowered at her. 'You know where she's gone, don't you? Back to her husband.'

'I doubt it, Mr Davenport. Her husband hasn't visited. As for the children, they telephoned yesterday in case she was here. They were anxious too.'

Charles felt the first stirrings of alarm. He went into his office, closed the door, and telephoned her apartment. No reply, and the letting agents told him she'd sent back the key. He rang his own house, and again the phone wasn't answered. And when he rang her solicitor's, the secretary said that in actual fact Mr Lowndes was looking for her as well.

He went to talk to Sister Johnson, closing the door of her office. 'Vanished,' he said curtly. 'I don't know where she is.'

'Did she have any money?'

He shook his head. 'I had – I've still got something she wanted to sell. I wouldn't let her. She's got no cash to speak of.'

'That is worrying,' said the Sister. 'She isn't well.'

'She could have collapsed, be in another hospital. If they didn't know who she was.'

'I'll get someone to ring round.'

But all enquiries proved fruitless. Charles worked around the search, seeing this patient and that, his conscious mind completely engaged while his subconscious wrestled with panic. The day dragged on. He had intended to go home early and prepare for the operation in the morning.

At four he gathered his theatre team around him, and talked them through the next day's procedures. 'I want you all to understand,' he said carefully, 'this is highly experimental surgery. The patient is quite likely to die or be seriously damaged. He could die on the table. If you all do your jobs correctly, with maximum concentration, it's no reflection on any of you if that happens. I want no nightmares, no "if onlies". I want an adult appreciation of the risks.'

One of the younger nurses gulped. His registrar giggled, a habit of his in times of stress. That giggle would certainly stop him becoming a consultant, thought Charles with grim satisfaction. That and his diffidence. It pleased him to think he had such an able but unpromotable lackey.

Walking to the car park, as soon as the meeting was over, his anxieties began again. Where was she? How was he to know? He drove home quickly, thinking that she might be there, that she might be collapsed in a heap by the door. The heating was on, roaring away, the house was an oven. Relief coursed through him. He went from room to room, calling her name, becoming gradually less exuberant. She wasn't here. She hadn't been for hours, perhaps days. All that was left of her was a teddy in her bed.

He scrawled a note and left it on the table, in case she had gone somewhere and might be back. Somehow he doubted that she would return. There was an emptiness about the house that alarmed him. A sense of abandonment. He got in the car and drove quickly to Blantyre House.

He arrived during dinner. David answered the door with a napkin in his hand, and said aggressively, 'What do you want? You never bring anything but trouble.'

Charles said nothing. But when David still barred the door he asked, 'May I come in?'

David stood reluctantly aside.

Charles went straight to the kitchen, and sure enough, the family was gathered there. They were eating a casserole, one of

Heather's standby dishes, nourishing but dull. Lucy was kicking rhythmically at the leg of her chair.

'Stop it, Lucy,' said Heather automatically.

Ellen said, 'Have you come about Celia? We don't know where she is.'

'None of you?' said Charles, with forced innocence.

Behind him, David said, 'No.'

Heather was looking hard at her plate. 'Do you know?' asked Charles, staring at her directly. She coloured. 'David said she was in hospital. We decided – we thought it was best not to tell the children. They've had so many upsets lately.'

'She had not a single visitor, I understand. And now she's gone.'

The girls looked at each other. Ellen's wide mouth stretched to a line across her face. 'That was disgusting,' she said flatly. 'You had no right not to tell us. You might not want her, Dad, but we do. She's our mother. And she'll always be our mother. And when she's ill or unhappy we've got a right to know!'

David stood with his back to the window. 'We didn't want you upset,' he said.

'Were you in it too, Mum?' Ellen turned her gaze like a searchlight on to Heather, but without result. She sat quite still, gazing down at the food on her plate.

Lucy began to cry. Charles said, 'I want you to think, girls, where she might be. She discharged herself from hospital. She wasn't well. Did she say anything to you? Anything at all?'

Lucy said, 'We made her ill. It was our fault. We made a fuss when things weren't right.'

Still David stood with his back to them. Charles was puzzled. Who was he hiding from? What did he know? He walked to the back door and opened it. 'Let's talk in the garden,' he said.

David nodded and followed him out.

The evenings were getting longer. Winter was in its last throes. They stood by an apple tree on which there was the suspicion of a bud, and in the grass underfoot were purple crocus and aconite. But it was still cold and cheerless in the open air. David, in a sweater, shivered.

'You've been cruel to her from the first,' said Charles. 'In the beginning I made excuses for you. I don't do that any more. Celia makes you feel just so guilty, and I want to know what for.'

David put his hands in his pockets. 'I don't have to explain myself to you.'

'If you don't I'll go to the police and tell them I suspect that you've hurt her. Perhaps you have. At any rate, they'll take you and your home apart.'

For the first time, David faced him. 'Why shouldn't I feel guilty? I deserted her. I told the children nothing about her. I found someone else. I behaved as if she was dead!'

'We can all forgive you that,' said Charles. 'But what else?'

'Just what you thought. The Will. I admit, I trusted Braddock and he cheated me. My fault.'

'So what do you know about where she is now? About her car crash? About her accident the other day? I think you know a lot.'

David swung round on him. 'Like hell I do! How dare you insinuate such things? I'm no murderer. And you should be careful who you accuse. You're pretty damned vulnerable yourself.'

Charles chuckled. 'Dear me. What a prospect. Struck off for an affair with a vanished woman. From where I'm standing you've got a great deal more reason to worry. All I can see is a dozen motives for wanting to get rid of her.'

David said, 'Have you been to the police? They won't believe you.'

'I think they might. The police aren't noted for the depth of their insight. What do you bet they'll think it must be you? The Sunday papers are going to love just tearing it all apart.'

Suddenly Charles saw that he had gone too far. It was the fading light that had tricked him – David's expression was no more than a blur in the dusk. He moved a fraction too late, and a punch grazed his cheek. He twisted hard, and David rushed past. When he turned the first, wild surge of anger was spent. 'Go away,' he said, in a low, throbbing voice. 'Get away from me and my family! You meddled in my life without anyone asking that you should. You took it upon yourself to play God, and what right did you have? What authority? Celia was dead!

489

She was better dead! I wanted her dead!'

The words hung on the air between them. Somewhere, in the silence, a blackbird sang, mockingly. Charles turned on his heel and walked quickly from the garden to his car.

After a while David went back to the house. The table was clear of dishes, and the remains of the stew had gone to the dog. Heather had the bills spread out before her, and was listing them in an accountant's meticulous way. When David came in she put the pencil down and sat, waiting for him to speak.

'I – sent him packing,' said David vaguely.

'I didn't think he was that sort of man.'

'Above himself, like all these medicos. Want a drink?'

'No. And don't you have any more, David. Please.'

He paid no attention. When he had poured his whisky, she said, 'We should have told the girls. They don't trust us now. They wonder what else we keep secret.'

He sat down in one of the hard kitchen chairs. 'The only secrets I have are worthless. Everything's worthless. It's all been a terrible, terrible mistake.'

'What has?'

He opened his eyes. 'You're looking at the figures. I let Celia bully me into ruining the firm. If that wasn't a mistake then what is?'

Heather rested her hands on the piles of paper before her. Household bills, endless and unremitting. She hadn't looked at the firm's books for weeks. 'How bad are things? Can you still sell out?'

'I don't know. The bank could foreclose before we could get anything off the ground. We'd be sold then all right, for nothing.'

Heather looked down at her hands. She was used to saying nothing, used to compliance. David never liked her to meddle in the firm, never wanted to hear criticism. But tonight she had to speak. 'Is it really her fault? Or yours?'

He sat up and stared at her. That Heather, loyal and workaday Heather, should say such a thing was intolerable. 'Are you suggesting – are you saying that it was me? That I'm incapable of running Sheraton Cars? Come on then, out with it! You obviously know so much more than me about the matter. What am I doing wrong, in your expert, objective eyes?'

She glanced up at him and away. She should take it back, she knew it. But somehow she couldn't go on, not admitting the truth. Did it matter, anyway? 'I just think you could have compromised. Or sold. Or done the things the test driver suggested, without wanting it all in gold plate! You're just so impractical, David. And no one can ever tell you anything. You won't take any advice.'

His hand clenched, shot out and hit her on the side of the head. She fell away from him, utterly stunned. Her head echoed like a belljar. The sound of water seemed to rush at her and away. She pushed herself up from the floor and clung to the edge of the table.

David began to sob harshly. 'Oh God, Heather, I'm sorry! Davenport made me lose my temper, I took it out on you. It was an accident. I didn't think. I didn't hit you, truly I didn't. Why did you make me so angry?'

'It's – it's all right,' she said slowly. 'I shouldn't have said what I did.'

'I'm going mad! It's her fault, I haven't been sane since she came back to life. Don't leave me, Heather. Don't leave me in this mess.'

'It's all right,' said Heather again.

She sat heavily in the chair, her elbows in the midst of the piles of bills, her head resting on her hands. She felt sick and very shaken. David, wanting comfort, knelt at her side and clung to her, although she was the one with the aching head. She remembered conversations she'd had with friends, years ago.

'If he ever lifted a finger to me, I'd leave. At once. I'd be up those stairs and pack my bags and be gone. No second chance. I'd go.'

But here she was. And she wouldn't go. Her life was here, and without it she was nothing. David, sane or half mad, was everything to her. 'It's all right,' she repeated, patting his shoulder. 'It's all right.'

Charles drove home slowly. His imagination was playing him

491

tricks. Every shadow looked like a body, every tree a person hiding from him. He went through every strange and rare delusion anyone had ever had after brain injury, and wondered if it could apply to Celia. And then he thought about murder.

Had Edwin done it? Had Celia been right and he had finally succeeded? It appalled him that he considered this as the last possibility. It proved how little he had believed her. Delusion was something he lived with, something he expected from patients, he automatically sifted reality from fantasy, quietly ignoring the things he knew to be untrue. Now he was being asked to think again. Someone could have murdered Celia.

He thought about each separate incident. Dorrie's house fire; an attempt at kidnap, or worse, and he had seen for himself the state of her flat. And an attempt to drive her into the canal. None was in the same league as the usual stuff, the phantom smell, or the strange tales of persecution by men from outer space. A popular one seemed to be instructions from the queen. The psychiatrists always encouraged that. They said it made for sensible dress and impeccable, if slightly bizarre, behaviour. People sat around a lot, taking tea.

But there were so many remarkable things. He remembered the man who, in the aura of epilepsy, had constantly recalled someone cartwheeling to their death. After months of discounting it, his mother revealed that at the age of three he had seen a trapeze artist fall at the circus, in just such a way. The patient had been much less relieved than triumphant. 'There you are, then!' he'd declared. 'Now you know I'm not round the bend.' And Celia seemed to be about to prove that she wasn't either.

When he got home he sat by the stove and tried to decide what to do. Nothing was clear. Perhaps he should call the police. He got up, went to the cupboard and opened a canister of rice. He fished about with his fingers for a while, and then hooked the pearls. Rice scattered in a shower across the floor. If he went to the police now there was this to contend with. And David. And the whole convoluted mess. She wouldn't thank him for leaving that as her legacy.

He considered the facts of the matter: Celia had been living in his house, had attended court and decided to return home early because she felt ill. Which was the most likely? That someone had murdered her or that she had decided, for whatever reason, to visit a friend, or a nursing home, or even to book herself into an hotel for a rest? If, on her journey home, she had fallen into a river or off a bridge, someone would notice. He felt a horror come upon him, a sense of dread. Twice before he had been called upon to identify bodies. An unsettling experience, whatever the cause, and tomorrow was the operation. He had to wait.

He made a pact with himself. He would wait until after the operation. Moffat needed calm concentration, he couldn't work with the police outside the door. Let the operation be over, he thought, and repeated it like a mantra. After that he would face what must be faced, and decide what to do.

The telephone rang, jangling him into action. 'Yes? What? Oh, Moffat. Yes, we're going ahead.'

He often got a call like this on the eve of major surgery. It was usually one of his staff, checking some small point of procedure.

Moffat was simply adjusting his timetable. 'I've got to be in court at eleven. When will you be done?'

'It's at least six hours,' said Charles. 'Possibly more. Two o'clock, four o'clock, I don't know.'

'I see. His mother worries, you know.'

'Yes. It's a worrying time.' The clichés, the meaningless responses.

Suddenly Moffat said, 'Has Mrs Sheraton turned up yet? I've been concerned.'

'Have you?' Charles fought down the note of scepticism. 'As it happens, I'm very concerned. If I don't hear anything by tomorrow night, I'm calling the police.'

'You don't think you should call the police now? It was very odd.'

In a gravel voice Charles said, 'Look, Moffat, I've done all I can for now. I don't know where she is and if I had my way I'd turn the world upside down looking for her, but your son's operation is tomorrow and I can't, simply can't, let personal considerations interfere with my capacity to work. At the

493

moment your son is my first priority. When he's been dealt with, then I will find Celia.'

Moffat said, 'Do you always flaunt your dedication so obviously?' Charles gripped the phone and hung up.

He slept fitfully that night. Images of Celia kept floating across his consciousness. But he couldn't recall her at her best, when she was well and happy, climbing over that wall perhaps, or in the hotel, drinking plum brandy. All he saw was the paleness of her, the strange otherworldliness of her expression. Nothing else seemed real.

He rose at six. It was still solidly dark, as if dawn was hours away, although by the time he got into the car the sky was lightening. He was hungry. He'd have to grab a sandwich at the hospital, beef perhaps, or fish, something high in protein. He always drank tea before a long job, to combat the inevitable dehydration of the operating theatre. It was a carefully balanced calculation; enough liquid to keep you fresh, not enough to send you to the bathroom halfway through, with an obligatory rescrub. A tingle of excitement ran up and down his spine, and he thought of all the chemicals sending their messages to his peripheral nerves. He was an amazing piece of biochemical engineering. All people were. Until Celia he'd thought that was all they were. But he had no place in the world of emotion, in any sphere of the immeasurable, he knew that now. He couldn't cope in it.

An air of excitement pervaded the theatre floor. It wasn't often they performed a new and experimental procedure. One of the junior nurses dropped a tray, and there was no reprimand, just a clipped and telling command to: 'Clear it up, Nurse. At once.'

'Good mornings' rained down on all sides. Charles thought, I shall imagine that Celia is in bed downstairs. I won't think of anything else. That's where she is.

His registrar said, 'No news of Mrs Sheraton, sir?' and Charles snarled at him.

The swing doors opened and a trolley appeared. The patient, the star of the show. Charles went to glance down at him, face chalk white under the theatre cap, hands with the telltale thinness of the longtime coma. Sister Johnson waged a ceaseless war against wasting, but it couldn't be entirely eliminated.

The anaesthetist came in. He wasn't there to induce sleep but to check the patient's gases, a vital part of brain surgery. Damage to the brain could be much reduced with regulated oxygen intake. Charles had considered whether it was worth giving the scalp a local anaesthetic, and had decided against. Neither skull nor brain had the capacity to feel pain, and he sometimes operated on a conscious patient, although it was a strain for everyone. He did not expect this patient suddenly to sit up and take notice. It wasn't in the least likely.

Charles began his ritual scrubbing. He always did it in precisely the same way, although he would have poured scorn on anyone who accused him of superstition. The rhythm, the repetition, comforted him. The sensation had something in it almost of meditation. His mind cleared, his hand steadied, and he felt that calm certainty of purpose without which he could never do this job. It was right to be here. It was intended. If the body was mechanical, and he was a mechanic, then he had been given his orders by the chief engineer. For Charles, the scrub was the nearest he came to praying.

'Right, let's get on with it.'

'Righto, sir. Would you like some music?'

'Yes – what does everyone fancy? Rhapsody in Blue?' It was a favourite in theatre, everyone hummed along. There was a murmur of agreement.

The music began. Charles asked for the patient's face to be covered, he never liked to see an expression beneath a brain. The cap was removed, revealing the pale baldness of a skull. On this occasion there were no X-rays to help, no scans, no helpful little maps. It was an uncharted journey. Sister swabbed generously, and placed a glittering tray of scalpels at Charles's disposal. Nothing to wait for now. He picked one up, and drew a perfect freehand line across the head before him. The skin peeled away on either side, as if a zip had been unfastened, revealing the white bone beneath. A little blood oozed, not a lot, and was instantly sucked away. The music began to gather pace, the anaesthetist settled himself more comfortably, and Charles picked up his drill and began to get

495

seriously to work. He was entering the skull from the rear, with the patient upright and slightly forward in a chair. It wasn't a position of much convenience for anyone, but the nature of brain surgery made it inevitable. A microscope was fixed above the chair, with one eyepiece for the surgeon and another for his assistant. There was a video camera too, which could be activated by a foot pedal, to record the operation on tape. Some American surgeons used video routinely, to protect themselves against law suits, but Charles just liked to have an image in the theatre that everyone could see, and a record he could use later. In this instance, it was doubly important. When all this was over, and the results known, they would need to do a lot of thinking.

The drill was making a whirring noise, as if it was overheating. 'Bloody thing,' said Charles, and tapped it on his gloved hand. The whirring subsided somewhat.

'Would you like a new one?'

'No. It's OK. Now, isn't that neat?'

He had made a series of burrholes in the skull, joining them together with neat sawn lines. The bone was lifted carefully away, to be preserved and later reinstated. The brain's opaque protective membrane was revealed to view. Charles looked at it carefully; no signs of damage, no indication at all of anything untoward. But his patient remained quietly sleeping.

Now the real work began. Once through the membrane and the brain itself was revealed. The inexperienced often fainted at this point, although they might have been stoic through hundreds of other surgeries. But the brain was different. Even to Charles, who loved its complexity, it was vaguely repellent. There was something about the texture, even the shape, that seemed to forbid touching. Indeed, every touch, every cut invited irreparable damage.

They began to ease their way through the complex structures. Everything was delicate and slow, even retracting the brain was dangerous. Instruments were padded, every last blood vessel carefully excised, nothing left to chance. Charles realised the music had long since ended.

A nurse mopped his face. 'How long have we been going?'

'Three hours, sir.'

Amazing. It felt like ten minutes. 'Put some jazz on,' he said, and his registrar sighed. He hated jazz.

'It's Billie Holliday,' said Charles, and the man cheered up.

Charles crept ever nearer the reticular formation. 'Good God,' he said suddenly. 'This never showed on any scan. He's got a clot here. Or at least, he had one. Take a look at this, everyone.'

He pressed the pedal of the video camera, and the image was put up on the screen. A tiny area of darkness was visible, sharp against the pervading greyness of the brain. Without being instructed the registrar activated suction and swept the little clot away. Charles began instinctively to tidy the debris. A clean cut was always preferable to a ragged scar on the brain. Healing was always more satisfactory.

Charles was humming along to the music. His staff relaxed a little. When Mr Davenport hummed it meant all was going well. 'How's breathing?' he asked.

The anaesthetist checked his instruments. 'Better, actually. I'll bring his oxygen down. He's getting lively.'

'Is he now?'

Charles looked at his patient's hand. He reached down with the handle of his instrument and ran it across the palm. The fingers clenched with sudden and wholly unexpected violence.

'Wow!' said Charles. He stood back and laughed.

'Heart rate increasing.'

'Slow him up a bit, for God's sake.'

There was a pause while the anaesthetist worked. Charles took some orange juice through a straw. It tasted very strong and delicious, as it always did in theatre. He realised how stiff and tired he was becoming. He never noticed while the work was going on.

Back at it. Endless meticulous probing. He glanced at the transparent sheet on which he had made his notes, and in his mind went again over his journey here, what he had expected and what he might find. This piece of brain, this unmarked spot, was where he intended to be. Now he was about to do damage. 'Let's have the probe,' he said.

His registrar giggled nervously. 'Shut up!' snapped

Charles. 'God, if you don't do something about that giggle, so help me I'll throttle you one of these days.'

'Sorry, sir. I can't help it, somehow.'

Charles took up the tiny electric probe. Using it, he was about to burn and destroy an area of brain smaller than a matchhead. 'I wonder which cells cause your giggle,' he said idly. 'We could cure you overnight. Fizz them – just like this.'

His hand was utterly steady. His registrar, choking on another giggle, took in his breath. All eyes were fixed on the monitor, while the blues, still playing, told of misery and vanished hopes. And it was done.

'Right,' said Charles. 'Let's get out of here.'

They began their careful withdrawal. But odd blood vessels began to pop, tiny points on the surface of the brain. Charles snapped at the anaesthetist. 'Lively, did you say? Slow him down, damn you!'

'He's beating me to it, sir.'

'Shit!'

He increased his pace of work. Now the team really was on its mettle. To be neat was easy, and they were naturally exact, but to achieve all that under pressure was something else. Charles muttered and swore, demanding more and yet more lubrication. The brain was drying, they had to close. The anaesthetist said, 'He's slipping.'

'Stir him up, then. Don't mind me.'

Sister dropped an instrument, but Charles took no notice. Another was instantly in his hand. Fluid coursed over the odd, slimy contours beneath his fingers, everything was slippy and difficult. At last he was able to close the dura mater. The flap of skull slipped neatly back into place. The job was done.

'OK. How is he?'

'Not good.'

'Going to lose him?'

The anaesthetist grunted. 'Not yet. We'll make a fight of it. Leave him to me.'

'Right.'

As the trolley was wheeled from the room, Charles looked for the first time at Martin Moffat's face. He looked ill, desperately ill. And Charles thought how odd that was. It was the first change in expression he had seen since Moffat first came under his care.

He glanced at the clock in the corridor outside. It was nearly four. Charles knew that he was exhausted, and wanted nothing more than a stiff whisky and a moment's peace. But his theatre staff were waiting. He took off his mask and said, 'Thanks, everybody. It was a bloody good job. No mistakes, none at all.'

Theatre Sister said, 'I dropped something. Sorry.'

'That was me,' said Charles. 'I took it wrong. And, Perkins – I was bloody rude. That does deserve an apology.'

He giggled, and Charles at once regretted his big-heartedness. Try as he might, he just wasn't any kind of a saint.

He threw off his gloves and hat. Now was the time to get on and see the relatives, while the adrenalin still pumped and the energy still flowed. Moffat would be waiting. Still in his greens and wellington boots he pushed through the doors and out into the ordinary life of the hospital. Noise crashed about his ears. People and colour seemed everywhere. His brain felt numb and unable to cope.

They were waiting downstairs, in a small carpeted room. Moffat, his wife and his daughter. Charles was surprised, he had expected Moffat alone. But here they were, hopeful and expectant. He cleared his throat. 'Well. He's still with us.'

'You were so long,' said Moffat.

His wife said, 'Eight hours! What went wrong?'

'Actually it went according to plan,' said Charles. 'It was never going to be quick, you know. There were one or two problems. I found a small clot and when that was gone he sharpened up quite a bit and we had to put him down. I was glad to find that actually, because even if I hadn't been going deep I'd still have liked to get rid of a clot. And then we went on and destroyed those few small cells.'

'And?' The daughter, wide-eyed and tense.

'He's not well. Breathing's poor, heart erratic. But those needn't concern you too much. His system's undergone a terrible shock. If he makes it through the next twenty-four hours then he's got a chance.'

Moffat said, 'Is he going to wake up?'

Charles nodded. 'To some degree, yes. By that, I mean his level of consciousness is obviously increased. That doesn't mean a miracle. Not by a very long way.'

They all stood there, looking at him. They were like cows in a field, a battery of liquid, uncomprehending eyes. And an image of Celia caught Charles as sharply as if he had been stabbed. Her eyes delighted him. In their dark shadows he could see forever.

He turned quickly away and went out of the room, not caring what they thought of him. If he didn't get a drink soon he'd be nothing but a quivering heap of jelly. There was a bottle in his office. He went straight in, past his bemused secretary, and poured himself a good solid slug. He took it down in a gulp, like medicine.

And now what? He sat at his desk, drinking more slowly. In a moment he would return to theatre and get changed. Throughout the night he would call the hospital, and ask how his patient was getting on. Sister Johnson might answer, she often did nights when a special patient came in. They didn't make them like that any more, he thought, and put his head back to stem the rush of pointless tears. What was he afraid of? What was he hiding from? Sooner or later he had to confront the terror of knowing that Celia was dead.

Chapter Thirty-Four

Celia was feeling distinctly better. It might have been the food or the comfort, but she strongly suspected it was the drink. Whatever Feodor and Tomul put in their concoction had properties unknown to Western medicine, she was convinced. Three times a day her door was unlocked, and she was supplied with food and the potion. Strange as it might seem, she was beginning positively to enjoy staying here.

In the evenings Edwin joined her. She found she looked forward to his visits, now that he knew her better and could relax. He was less the great man, was less anxious to be seen to be imperious. He asked a lot of questions about David, which Celia always deflected or ignored. It was dangerous ground.

On this night, though, he was not to be deterred. And he caught her on a tender spot. A spot, quite literally, of tenderness. 'You must have loved him very much,' said Edwin.

'Who?'

'David. To give up so much. I remember, you see, when you married him. Your father cut you off with a shilling.'

She laughed. 'For about five minutes.'

'You didn't know that then. I was impressed, you know. You were so beautiful together. And you left all your father's wealth, just for love.'

The memory came back to her, like the scent of roses on a warm summer's night. Passion had caught her up like a twig in a stream, she had been powerless to do anything but rush on and on, joyfully, with no looking back. David's hair had been golden; his laugh made her laugh too; they could spend all their days together and never once feel the need for more.

She became aware that tears were running down her cheeks.

Edwin said, 'Why are you crying?'

She shook her head. 'I don't know. Because it was beautiful. Because I was happy. Because it's all gone.'

'I thought you were going to get it back. David never could resist you.'

She sighed and pushed her hand through her hair. 'If you're talking sex, then that's true. But that's not everything. You must know it's not. Even you.'

He laughed bitterly. 'Even me? My dear Celia, even me?'

'Well. Especially you. Don't you think?'

Edwin looked at her. He had a face that disguised itself, thought Celia. A nothing face, through which you glimpsed tiny flashes of the real man. Now, fleetingly, he seemed – sad. 'I never know if it's love,' he said. 'None of us do. We don't put the same price on faithfulness as you. Or at least, some of us do, and some of us don't. And some do when some don't, and never at the same time. It's a difficult life.'

'We're no different,' said Celia. 'Look at David. He doesn't want me now.'

Edwin got up and came over to the bed. Again she felt no fear. The room was so quiet and warm. He picked up a lock of her hair and held it between his fingers, those delicate, elegant fingers that should be so much more a surgeon's than Davenport's thick, workmanlike hands. He wound the tendril tight, tighter, until it dragged against her scalp. And he wound it tighter still.

The pain awoke her. She let out a cry. 'You're hurting me! Edwin, don't!'

'Why not? You deserve it, damn you! How dare you try and take what's mine?'

'It was mine first! You stole what was mine!'

'But you should have been dead!'

His face was an inch from hers. His eyes were green flecked with brown, lit from within by a strange yellow glow. Tiger eyes. A creature unused to the civilised world, lost in the concrete streets. She put up her left hand, her strong hand, and raked her nails hard down his cheek. And Edwin laughed.

'Of the same blood, you and I,' he whispered.

'You are dangerous and mad.'

'But you knew that before! Why do you think you are here?'

'Because you want to kill me. And you daren't.'

'Dare I not? Are you so sure?'

'Yes.'

She didn't believe it. But he got up and moved away from her and the baby in her womb began to struggle and kick. It was Celia's urge to run, transmitted to the only creature free to act. If only she could leap from this bed, make for the door, escape! But she sat there and endured. Because she had to. Because in all her life she had never felt so unprotected.

When he had gone she crawled from the bed and went to the window. It was very high. And in her bathroom, standing precariously on a stool, she could see only sky and trees through the narrow skylight. If she was strong, what would she do? Smash the window, climb the tree, knot the sheets into a rope and be gone? Anything. Everything. If only she could have her strength back again, if not for her then for the one creature who depended on her. The baby.

In these days she and the baby were starting to understand one another. With Ellen and Lucy, born in love, there had been no need for it, but she and this baby had no one else. Their destiny was absolutely entwined. Celia whispered, 'If I could save you I would, baby. I'll try and hang on. For you.'

But would she? The weakness was too much to bear. They needed help, she and this baby. They needed Charles.

Charles sat in the police station and tried to marshal his thoughts. The officer said, 'Have you been drinking, sir?'

Charles said, 'Yes. You bet I have. I spent eight hours in the operating theatre today.'

'You had an operation?' Incredulity.

'No, damn it! I'm a brain surgeon.'

'Are we now?'

'Yes, we bloody well are! Or at least I am. I was under the misguided impression that you were a competent officer of the law.'

He tried to gather his wits. This was not going at all well. In a moment they would do him for driving while under the influence, and then what? 'Look,' he said carefully, 'I'm the head of neurology at Aireborough Hospital. One of my ex-patients is Celia Sheraton, and she's gone missing. I've reason to be worried about her safety and I want you to look for her.'

'Mental case, is she, sir?'

'No! I'm a neurologist, not a shrink! God, doesn't anyone know the difference? I deal in physical problems of the nervous system, including the brain. Epilepsy. Injury. Tumours.'

'Has fits, does she?'

'What have fits got to do with it?'

'You said she was epileptic.'

'I did not, officer. If you think a little you'll find I did not. She's got a brain injury, she has some small measure of – she isn't quite—' He became aware of the impossibility of explaining. He said dully, 'Yes. She has fits.'

The officer beamed. 'Well then. Now we're getting there.'

'Are we? I had rather the opposite impression.' To think he'd been worried that they might discover a theft. This bloke couldn't find his own front door without assistance.

But the door opened and another man came in. Charles sat up in his chair. Sharp, intelligent face, wary eyes. The last of the whisky fog curled lazily about Charles's brain, mingling with tiredness in a dangerous cocktail.

'Hello, sir,' said the new man. 'I gather it's about Mrs Sheraton. Mrs Celia Sheraton.'

'Have you found her?' Charles felt a tightening of his guts.

'Not yet sir, no. But we have been concerned. She's been involved in a number of incidents lately, hasn't she?'

'I thought she invented half of them. Or at least – she's brain injured, you see. Some residual disability. Look, the thing is, she might have been kidnapped. If she's in some ditch that's as may be, but she could be a prisoner somewhere. I believe that could be it.'

'If it's Mr Braddock that concerns you, I've spoken to him on the telephone and he assures me he knows no more than you.'

'And you believe him?'

'I've no more reason to believe him than you.'

There was something steely about the man's stare. Quite

suddenly Charles felt threatened. The man suspected him of hurting Celia. And a moment later the question came: 'It was a very sudden decision of yours, sir. To go away.'

'How do you know about that?'

'You'd be surprised, sir. You really would.'

An hour later, Charles reeled out on to the street. He was supremely thankful to be there. Never before had every word he uttered been subjected to this and that scrutiny, been openly discounted, openly disbelieved. In the end he hadn't known what was true and what was not. The lies he was telling came back at him, the truth sounded like lies. And in the end he had achieved nothing. They merely suspected that he had murdered Celia, and was trying to shift the blame. They would do nothing before tomorrow, and would then drag lakes for her body.

He sat in his car, utterly drained. What a day. What a hellish day. Then he got out again and went back into the police station. The desk sergeant looked at him askance, but Charles merely leaned across and picked up the phone. 'OK if I call the hospital?'

'Certainly, sir. Urgent case, is it?'

'Not at all.'

Charles dialled and waited. A long ring, but it always was on Intensive Care. Nurses had better things to do than answer the phone. At last Sister Johnson's voice said 'Yes?' frostily.

'It's me. How is he?'

'Mr Davenport. Well.'

'You mean he is well?'

'Not exactly. It was a figure of speech.'

'How is he, Sister? This isn't a difficult question!'

'But it is, I'm afraid. Mr Moffat regained consciousness half an hour ago. He exchanged several sentences with his parents and sister, before lapsing into coma.'

'What?' Davenport squawked in horror. 'You mean he came out and went back?'

'Yes. That is so.'

'Any rise in intracranial pressure?'

'Nothing significant. And – ' she forestalled his next words ' – if there is we are more than capable of dealing with it. I've

505

told the family to go home. Are you at home, Mr Davenport?'

He let out his breath in a long, weary sigh. 'Not at the moment, Sister.'

'You've had a long day. Go home and sleep, and we'll talk in the morning. Don't worry, Mr Davenport. You've done what you could.'

Don't worry. She said not to worry. But he thought of Moffat's family and, damn it, he thought of Celia. This was to be her chance. This was to be her operation. And it didn't bloody work!

The desk sergeant was looking at him quizzically. 'All right, sir?'

'No! That man in there thinks I murdered a patient. And I might have done. But not the one he thinks.'

A shocked inhalation. 'Do you want to talk to someone, sir?'

'Oh, go to hell!'

This time he drove quickly away. If he stayed any longer they'd arrest him and he'd never see the light of day. He turned towards home, but his foot lifted involuntarily from the pedal. He wouldn't sleep. He couldn't sleep. There was nothing in sleep but dreams.

So he turned the car and began driving again, aimlessly at first, but then with increasing purpose. In twenty minutes he was outside the walls of Linton Place, and he didn't know why he had come there. It was simply that it was the one place he hadn't tried, and if anyone was behind Celia's disappearance, Braddock had to be the man.

It was late. He looked at his watch, and saw that it was nearly one. But he had broken in here before, and he could do it again. He walked around the wall, looking for the place he had climbed before, and found it easily enough. But he was tired and the leap was difficult. He roused a surge of determination, and forced himself upwards, until his fingers found their grip. Then he hung, gathering himself, while his joints ached and his fingers went numb. At last he kicked himself up and rolled from the top into the soft wet earth. He lay there, and felt the day's keenest pleasure. He lived too false a life, he thought. He wasn't natural enough.

He began the walk across the park, just as before. But that

506

had been months ago, and things had changed. Invisible beams crossed and recrossed the park. Quite unaware, Charles broke one. Instantly a bank of floodlights switched on round the house. A klaxon began to sound, braying and insistent. Charles froze. Now what? After tonight, if the police came, he'd never walk free again.

Acting on instinct he ducked into some bushes. Crouched there, he looked about, and saw the sensors set high on stakes above the ground. There would be others, of course, set lower. And sometimes animals must cause all this. He remained where he was, still and quiet, while the klaxon died and he heard voices. The servants, twittering to each other, and separately, Braddock.

'Is there anything to see?'

'I think, sir – the deer.'

'Possibly. I'll let the dogs off, anyway.'

Cold, atavistic terror. Charles felt his tongue dehydrate and cling fixedly to the roof of his mouth. Some part of his mind registered amazement, that really happened, a true physical sign. But the rest of him was appalled. Dogs. He was to be hunted like a runaway slave. What was he to do? He wanted to leap from his hiding place and run for it, back to the wall and safety. But they'd get him. And if he stayed where he was, the dogs would find him in a moment. He had to move, to find safety. Where?

He could hear a scuffling in the undergrowth nearby. He slid away backwards, able to see better now. The ground was a tangle of roots and dead bracken, every step made a noise. The dogs were coming closer, in a moment they would have him! Again he wanted to turn and run, but suddenly a great crashing almost startled him to a shout. The dogs began barking, racing away after the quarry. Charles crouched, his throat tight with suppressed sound, wondering what on earth it could be. But Braddock's voice came clearly across the wood. 'There he goes! A stag. Now we'll never get the dogs back.'

Charles could hear them moving away. His limbs were suddenly heavy, almost leaden with weariness. He leaned against a tree for a moment, letting his heart slow and his breathing subside. He didn't know when he had been so frightened. It was the thought of the dogs, an irrational dread of being hunted as prey. His mind was very clear and lucid. It was time he got away.

Not for a moment did he think of going back. Instead he moved forward again, slowly now, searching for sensors set high or low in the undergrowth. At first he almost walked into several, but then he saw a pattern and could anticipate where the next would be. A hundred yards from the house and all seemed clear. Perhaps it was aesthetics; no one wanted a security system they could not ignore.

He wondered about pressure pads set in the paths, and instinctively walked on the grass, sheltering against trees and shrubs in case the floodlights should once again click into life. He tripped over the raised edge of a flowerbed and cursed under his breath. He was too tired for this; if he could have done anything else he wouldn't have hesitated. This was a pointless, dangerous errand.

The downstairs rooms were all in darkness. What had he expected, to find Celia sitting at a window? There were lights upstairs, though. Faint ones at the very top, where the servants must live, and several further down. Why so many? He felt the first light stirrings of hope.

But the options before him were daunting. He could break in, although he was no sort of a burglar and the house was bound to be alarmed. He could call the police, and be arrested for trespass and wasting police time. Or he could climb a tree and peer in at the lighted windows, like Peeping Tom. The tree was the only sensible course. He sighed. Exhausted, at night, in a good suit, he was going to climb a tree.

It started badly. He couldn't reach the bottom branch. But there was a seat nearby, unnoticed in the gloom, and after a while he saw it. He pulled it across although it weighed very heavy, and at least then he could scramble into the lower branches. The tree was greasy with moss and his shoes, smoothly soled in leather, slipped alarmingly. He whispered curses under his breath, and thought that at least it was too dark to see how far he had to fall. He thought of the garden seat neatly positioned to catch him and break his back. Paraplegia seemed a certainty. He clung on tighter. Ye gods, he might get Sister Johnson as nurse.

His head was on a level with the sill of a lighted window. He paused to catch his breath. What would he do if Edwin Braddock looked out and saw him? Wave? An untimely laugh threatened to finish him. This whole thing was getting totally out of hand. He struggled up a further slimy foot, and hung there, the branch across his guts, winding him. The room seemed empty but for an enormous four-poster bed. And in the bed, diminished by its size, was Celia.

He called, but his voice was a croak and she didn't hear him. He dared not shout louder. He broke off a twig and threw it at the glass, but missed. He lurched in the tree and clung on again, this was no time for boy scout heroics. The ground seemed far away and infinitely desirable, now that he knew for certain that Celia lived. There was no time to waste. In fact, he had to get down.

It was an undignified, noisy scramble. When he felt he had been climbing down for hours he looked and saw he was still ten feet from the ground. But he had lost patience and let himself hang by his hands from a creaking branch. Suspended like that, he felt patient again, but the moment was upon him. He had to let go. The branch sagged beneath his weight, he could fall with it or without it, and his hands lost their grip and the decision was made. The ground punched him like a giant fist and he crumpled and lay gasping.

His first thought was to test himself for sensation below the waist, but since his knee was killing him it was pretty evident it was intact. He sat up, and observed that his spinal cord was undamaged. Not his knee joint, unfortunately. He decided it was ligaments, and took off his tie to strap the leg up. With his trousers tied at knee level he looked vaguely piratical, or at least a candidate for the masons. He got up and tried to stand, and it was possible to hobble quite effectively. It would take a while, but he would make it out of the park and call the police.

Out of the darkness to his left, unseen and unexpected, there came a low and increasing growl. The hairs on his neck rose vertically. He turned and saw the dog.

It was close to the ground, yellow eyes fixed on him, body

steadily advancing as the growl rumbled again. The dog's lips were curled back from its long, wolf nose in absolute, unreasoned loathing. In an instant, Charles knew, it would spring.

He made a dive for the chair beneath the tree. As he moved the dog came for him, erupting in a torrent of sound and exploding aggression. Imbued with strength he had never before possessed, Charles swung the heavy garden seat between him and the dog, his back against the tree. But the dog was the more agile. He lunged and fastened his teeth on Charles's shoe, exerting pressure even through good leather. Charles kicked and the dog let go, taking a snap at his calf. Charles swung the heavy seat and the dog yelped, and then the lights came on. Everything was white and stark. The combatants looked at each other warily. The dog backed away a pace, snarling.

'Come here, Lupus! Good dog, Lupus!'

Braddock came out of the house, barefoot and in silk pyjamas. Behind him came a servant, carrying a shotgun. But Edwin called, 'It's all right, Tomul. No need to shoot. It's only that bloody fool doctor.'

Charles said, 'What the hell do you mean letting vicious dogs roam loose?'

'What do you mean prowling around my house? Go and call the police, Tomul.'

'Yes,' said Charles. 'Call them. You spoke earlier this evening, I understand. How is it that Celia's suddenly resident in a bedroom in your house when two hours ago you knew nothing of her whereabouts?'

Braddock said nothing. But he clicked his fingers and the dog crawled to him, one leg dragging. 'Damn it, you've hurt the dog!' he said furiously. 'Poor Lupus. Good Lupus.'

Charles said, 'I insist you call the police.'

'Insist all you like, old chap,' said Braddock. 'My other dogs are still at loose in the park, you know, so why don't you walk out and call the police yourself?'

The prospect was unattractive, and besides, it would give Braddock time. 'Why have you got her here?' Charles leaned wearily against a stone urn. 'Have you threatened her?'

'I wouldn't do anything so crass.' Braddock looked back at his servants. 'Don't just stand there, damn you! Get some water and bandages. I've got to see to Lupus.'

As he went in he said to Charles, 'Come in if you must. But I won't be responsible for what happens to you. I hate uninvited guests.'

The park and its dogs were behind him, a dubious welcome before. Charles hobbled into the house.

Celia picked up the hairbrush again and resumed her rhythmic hammering on her bedroom door. The commotion in the garden, in which she was certain she had heard Charles, had given way to silence. No one came near her room. No one listened to her cries. The house could go up in flames and no one would come for her.

She imagined the worst; Charles ripped to shreds by the dogs, and finished off by her cousin. Idiot Charles! Full of his own importance, sure he could do everything himself. He had walked into the lion's den, armed with not so much as a feather duster.

After a while, her arm began to ache. She gave up her banging and went back to the bed. She was cold and rather shaky, on the edge again. The baby was restless and she talked to it, trying to communicate calm she did not feel. If only she could get out of here! If only there was something she could do!

The key turned in her door. She sat up, in total surprise. In came Edwin, and Charles. 'Oh, Charles,' she said.

'Hello, Celia.'

She had to smile at him. His suit was in ruins, there were teeth marks in his shoe and his tie was knotted incongruously around one knee. But he looked remarkably cheerful all of a sudden. Their eyes met again and they laughed.

'Fancy seeing you here,' said Celia.

'Not half. You OK? Headaches, vomiting, lapses?'

'Just the usual. You look worse.'

'Appearance so often deceives.'

Braddock said, 'Will you sit down, please? I don't wish to extend hospitality for any length of time to someone who broke my dog's leg.'

511

'Charles! You didn't!' said Celia.

'It was Lupus,' said Edwin.

Celia said, 'Not Lupus?'

'It's only bruising. The dog's a ham actor. And did you really expect me to let the animal bite at will?' The question was rhetorical. Charles had the feeling that they did.

Celia leaned back against her pillows. Charles watched her anxiously, seeing nothing to reassure. He said, 'Sorry to raise the matter now, but you appear to have kidnapped Celia.'

Edwin yawned. 'It was more a case of taking her into safe custody. She was in a state of total collapse. If you're so unwise as to involve the police I shall simply say that she needed complete rest and I respected her wishes absolutely.'

'I could tell them different,' said Celia.

Edwin turned his gaze upon her. 'I'm sure you could. But are you sure you can survive all this truth? We have the pearls to consider. Your – condition. It hasn't gone unnoticed. And, of course, dear David.'

'What about David?'

Edwin ignored the question. He got up and went to the wardrobe, pulling out a large tartan rug which he wrapped around his silk-clad shoulders. He said to Charles, 'You really should not have done that to Lupus! You're supposed to be medically skilled, not some thug with a blunt instrument. The dog may never be right again.'

'Next time, I promise to let him bite me,' said Charles thinly.

'The dog was in the right. You people never understand. Protecting one's own is an absolute, fundamental right. It's even admirable.'

'In a dog,' said Charles.

Celia said, 'Actually they've looked after me so well. I've enjoyed it. After all, no one else cared.'

'Except me.'

'You went away.'

'I couldn't – I didn't want to wait around.'

'For what?'

Charles didn't reply. After a moment Edwin said, 'I think we've got to come to some conclusions here. It's all quite straightforward. Clearly, Celia's life expectancy is – shall we say, limited? There's no way that she could control her father's business empire. And I am doing somewhat better than might have been hoped.'

'Thanks to me,' she flashed. 'I bought the Marlborough shares. I saved your bacon.'

Edwin inclined his head. 'Unwittingly, you did. Now, what would happen if you died? Everything would fall to David, in trust for the girls. And he has proved incapable even of running a little car factory with anything resembling success. The thing you never saw about him, Celia, the thing you still don't realise, is that David can't follow through. It's his one great fault, and you never saw it. You always thought he'd change, and he never has. He never will.'

Celia felt her face stiffen. 'Business acumen isn't everything,' she murmured.

'I wasn't only talking about business. Always a vacillator, David. Surely you can see that now?'

The tears pricked her eyes. 'You sound just like my father,' she said bitterly, and Edwin erupted in unkind mirth.

'The girls will inherit!' blazed Celia, roused to anger. 'Who are you going to leave it to? Lupus?'

'I've got rather more time to think about that than you,' said Edwin. 'I could marry. I could have children. It's not an impossibility.'

Charles said, 'Let's keep to the here and now. Are you going to settle out of court?'

'No.'

Celia's colour came up. She looked suddenly well. 'Damn you, Edwin! In all conscience you should quit. You defrauded me and my children, you colluded against the wishes of the man who made the money in the first place. If you don't pay me out I'll take it as far as I need. I won't rest until I get everything.'

'You already have the pearls,' said Edwin genially.

'You know I can't sell them for anything like their true value.'

'My dear, you should have thought of that before.'

He gazed at her dispassionately, and sighed. 'Now that I

know I shall fight I can assure you it won't be clean. It's all going to come out, you know – the arguments you and your father used to have; the unwise marriage; the affairs. The girls will hear everything. Why not make do with the pearls? If you fight, you might not live to see a result. Sell the pearls. I won't say a word. Promise.'

'I imagine David could tell us what your promises are worth.'

He winced. 'What a nasty tongue you do have. Don't you think it's unwise to antagonise me?'

'I'm not afraid.'

'But – mightn't you worry about the others?'

Celia felt very cold and very ill. 'Are you threatening my children?' He did not reply.

'This is unbelievable. I don't believe it. No one can be so dedicated to money.'

'What has money to do with it?' Edwin took a turn about the room, tartan blanket like a cloak. 'This is my own place. These are my own things. I have a right to protect them.'

Celia said, 'I won't give up! I won't! You took everything away from me, didn't you? Everything! My whole life!'

He swung round to face her. 'You gave up everything. You threw it away. You were so careless of what you had, so sure it would all go on forever. No one else mattered to you. You cared about nothing but your own foolish gratification. Be grateful that I'm even willing to throw you this crumb.'

The room was becoming darker. In the centre the light was strong, but the periphery was becoming sunk in deeper and deeper gloom. Yet she alone could see it. She felt fear, and was grateful. Not so far gone, then. Edwin was right, she hadn't much time. She said, 'I want to go now. I want to be out of here.'

Edwin inclined his head. 'As you wish.'

Celia and Charles drove away at about four in the morning. A servant had fetched Charles's car, and between them the men carried Celia downstairs and put her in. Charles himself could hardly walk, his knee was stiffening into a fluid-filled balloon. Nonetheless he crawled behind the wheel. They were desperate to go.

Edwin leaned on the car door for a last farewell. 'I'm glad you came to stay with us, Celia,' he said kindly. 'Don't mind my temper. You're really rather extraordinary, you know.'

'Do thank Feodor and Tomul for me,' said Celia. 'And I'm sorry about Lupus.'

'I do so hope it's not a fracture,' said Edwin, and slammed the door.

Charles drove erratically away. 'You look terrible,' said Celia. 'And your knee needs attention. Shall we go straight to the hospital?'

He shook his head. 'I just want to sleep. I want to get into bed with you beside me and sleep.'

She reached out her hand and took his. 'Don't feel so much,' she murmured. 'You were safer before.'

'Yes. Wasn't I?'

He took his hand off the wheel and took hold of her fingers. To Celia's embarrassment she started to cry. 'I didn't know if I'd ever get out again,' she said tearfully. 'And nobody cared, except you.'

'Would you rather it had been David?'

'David!' She almost snorted. 'If you knew what I know about David!'

'Want to tell me?'

'Not now.'

She fell silent. What was there to say? Perhaps other people had always seen the truth about her husband, if it was the truth. She was beginning to doubt the evidence of her own eyes, her own experience. Her mother had once said, 'David's a very ordinary sort of chap, isn't he, dear?' And Celia had been cut to the quick. But he was ordinary. He had settled down with Heather to be ordinary and dull.

'Call the girls in the morning,' said Charles at length. 'Don't speak to him. Not until you're better.'

'But I'm not getting better. We both know that.'

Charles said, 'Well then. Don't talk to him at all.' He felt a quiet, intense victory.

The house was quite dark when they returned. Charles helped her into the kitchen and up the stairs to his bed. They sat on either side, equally weary and spent, until Charles at last summoned the strength to get undressed. When he was naked he lay down and put his arm around Celia, and at once she relaxed and rolled against him. Gently, slowly, Charles eased her clothes away until they were lying skin against skin. In the last few days she had swollen like a plum, her body was three firm globes pressing into him. He put his hands on her back and held her very close, hearing her heart, the whisper of her breathing, the soft brush of her eyelashes against his cheek.

'I love you,' he murmured.

'I know.'

'I never meant to.'

'I know that too.' She eased away a little, to rest her palm against the warm hairs of his chest. His nipple, hard and berrylike, pressed against her fingers. Her hair was like silk against him and he held her close, discounting his own erection. In a little while he would love her. But all she wanted now was tenderness.

Celia slept more soundly than for many a night. When she woke and breathed the smell of him, the warm tang of his skin tasting salt against her lips, she felt a great thankfulness. She had been so alone for so long. She had forgotten how good it was to subsume her own self like this. For a little time only, her life was his life too. Lying like this, they seemed to break out of the skins that contained them. Their souls seemed to meet and understand one another. It was more than liking, almost more than love. In each of them there was an emptiness which only the other could fill.

She pressed a kiss against his lips, soft at first. He whispered to her, she didn't care what he said. It was enough that he was there. She moved against him, stretching her body, rejoicing in all that it could offer this one last time. How magical it was, this spreading warmth, this desire to give all, take all, lose oneself. He was hard against her, and she bit him gently. He moaned, and she moved her mouth to his for his kiss. Outside, in the early morning, the wind chased leaves and rattled windows, but here, encased in the dark tent of the bed, they were safe. She lifted her leg to let him come into her, and it was absolutely new. He was heavily engorged, a weight of blood and flesh finding its rightful place inside her. And briefly, gloriously, she touched paradise. For the first time in her life she was giving everything and holding nothing back. She had nothing that she wished to retain, she was used up, without a future.

Charles, sensing her desperation, tightened his hold, but it was no use. Every nerve, in welcoming him, seemed to bid him farewell. He moved ever closer to ecstasy and release, taking her with him, knowing he should leave her behind. Her arms reached up around his neck, and her breath came in quick, sharp gasps. He spoke her name, once, twice, but she said nothing in reply. Then feeling rushed upon him, he shouted her name: 'Celia!'

He felt her tense, felt the shudders begin, felt them die away into stillness. But when he looked at her face he saw that she was gone.

Chapter Thirty-Five

Charles limped uncomfortably down the corridor and every head turned surreptitiously to look at him. He wondered what showed. Grief, perhaps? Scandal? Or only his damnable limp?

His knee was encased in plaster, and would remain so for a fortnight. He fancied the patients smirked at him, recognising their own disabilities, which he had now inherited. But of course it might not be that at all. There was enough gossip.

The administrator was lurking ahead of him. Charles thought cravenly about diving into a side ward, but it was no use. Like a mountie on the range the man would get him in the end.

'James. Are you waiting to drag me down?'

'Er – in what sense, Mr Davenport?'

'That's up to you. Well, what is it?'

'The Moffats. They've made a complaint.'

'What? After all I said to them? They've no bloody right!'

He moved heavily to the window and stood looking out at the grounds. A porter was moving a trolley with a long covered shape. A body to the mortuary. Charles wished, suddenly, that he too could be lying under a long green sheet.

'I told them I couldn't guarantee a cure,' he said between gritted teeth. 'I should have got it in writing, no doubt. In triplicate. Or better still, left their worthless son to rot!'

'They're not complaining about the operation,' said James. 'It's the time since then. They think you've given up.'

Charles turned and blinked at him. 'Given up? How?'

'You've abandoned all forms of active treatment. You've decided there's no hope for their son when they feel – they believe – that another operation could cure him.'

'What would they like?' asked Charles thinly. 'Why don't I

just do a frontal lobotomy on the whole damned family and be done with them?'

James put a hand on Charles's arm, saw the look on his face and removed it again. There was no getting close to this man. He said, 'I know it's difficult for you, Davenport. Believe me, I do understand. But you were near success! The boy woke, he recognised his parents, he even spoke a few words. So Moffat feels you were too cautious in your surgery. You could have done more. He wants you to go back in and repeat the procedure.'

'Just like that,' said Charles.

'No! There are risks, and they understand them. I said I'd talk to you and ask you to consider what can be done. Make no mistake, you have the clinical authority here.'

'Delighted you feel that way,' said Charles in icy tones. 'Is there by any chance some financial incentive? Are the Moffats about to endow the hospital with some well-fleshed fund?'

'There has been talk of a Law Society fund, yes,' said James stiffly.

'Wonderful,' said Charles, and hobbled away.

The meeting had darkened his mood, if that were possible. James had hit the one area of vulnerability he had left – his professional competence. In suggesting that Charles was neglecting one of his patients, failing to consider that patient's needs and showing cowardice in post-operative care, he was considerably beyond his area of responsibility. And he was also right.

He stamped up to Intensive Care. Sister Johnson bustled from her office, all starch and briskness. 'Right, Mr Davenport. Your registrar's tumour isn't too good. I should like you to take a look at him. And the fracture needs a drain, in my opinion. It's a tricky one, I don't think Mr Perkins is up to it.'

Assuming, rightly, that Sister referred to a tumour Perkins had operated on, rather than one he had grown personally, Charles said, 'Flattered as I am by your concern, Sister, I am not indispensable. Perkins can excise a benign tumour perfectly well.'

'But his never recover quite as well as yours, do they, Mr Davenport?'

Beneath his breath, Charles hissed, 'I am not about to shoot myself, Sister. I don't need this obvious manipulation.'

The Sister shot him one of her ice-cold looks. 'It is the truth, Mr Davenport. I merely felt that this was the time for you to hear it.'

She led the way to the tumour's post-operative bed. A young man was lying semi-conscious, with a dribble of saliva oozing from the corner of his mouth. Charles felt the pulse, checked the notes and peered into the patient's eyes. When he moved away from the bed, Sister said, 'Well?'

'We'll have him back into theatre as soon as we can. Something's not right. He's probably bleeding, but I don't want to waste time on tests. Bleep Perkins for me.'

'Yes, Mr Davenport.'

She hurried away, and he moved on to the skull fracture. Sister was right again, of course. A number of patients would be made miserable today, their operations delayed while these two desperate cases took their place. His knee throbbed terribly. He wouldn't be able to stand for long, and much as he disliked it would have to ask for a stool.

The X-ray machine was being wheeled in, he needed a final shot before operating. He limped gloomily out into the corridor. Moffat was waiting for him. 'Go away,' said Charles sourly.

'Mr James said he'd talk to you.'

'He has.'

'Well?'

'No.'

'You haven't even thought about it. I ought to have you up before the GMC for negligence!'

Charles turned and glowered down at him. 'I could kill your son. You don't nip in and out of the brain at will. It is – it's meant to be a sealed, contained system. Operating on the brain is always ham-fisted, I'm going back again now to a man who's haemorrhaging purely as a result of an operation. Yes, I agree your son showed positive signs. But we need to do research before we go blundering back in. If he's still alive in five years' time I might then have the knowledge to try again.'

Moffat took off his spectacles and polished them vigorously. 'What are the chances he'll live that long?'

Charles wasn't in the mood to prevaricate. Martin Moffat was very prone to respiratory problems. 'Slim.'

'Well, then. We've got nothing to lose and everything to gain. I want you to operate.'

Charles said nothing. If he could have given up right then he would have done it. He would take a suitcase and throw it in the car, drive away from all this, somewhere cold and distant. He would tramp wild moors and high mountains until the pain that burned even in sleep was frozen to solid ice. He was so tired of other people's problems. Where were the healthy, happy people in the world? He was surrounded by need and he had given all he could. There was nothing left.

He began to walk away, and Moffat said, 'When Celia came to me I didn't say no.'

Charles turned and said vaguely, 'What?'

'I'm fighting on.' Moffat looked embarrassed. 'I haven't let it drop. I must get something for the children. In trust, so their father can't waste it.'

'That's – that's decent of you.'

'I'm not doing it out of kindness. I want you to save my son, Mr Davenport. I know you can! I'm sure of it.'

Charles felt blank, dry-mouthed, old. He had seen so much optimism turn to dust. He said, 'And if I fail? Imagine that. The position as now, one more operation down the road, one more load of hope that you won't want to let go. Will you want me to try again? And again? Until we scramble his brains forever?'

Moffat's eyes, behind his glasses, blinked feverishly. 'I only want one more chance.'

In theatre, probing amidst the detritus of an excised tumour, finding and sealing the leaking vessel, he found time to think. Martin Moffat was almost certainly doomed, whatever he did, so the operation in that sense was neither here nor there. But the principle gave concern. If he tried again, would he be pandering to wasted hopes? Was there really any chance of success? If not he would be wasting time and money simply to placate Moffat. There had to be some clinical justification.

He looked across the table at Perkins. 'The Moffat case. In your honest opinion, did I err on the side of caution? You've seen the video, should I have gone deeper and if so, how far?'

Perkins was taken aback. His advice had never been sought before. 'I don't think my opinion can possibly be valid, sir.'

'Nonetheless.'

'Perhaps – another millimetre? Or preferably, extend downwards a fraction. I remember thinking that at the time.'

Charles inserted a neat stitch. 'I wish you'd damn well said.'

'It was the first time, sir. Caution was the order of the day.'

'It isn't now. You know they want me to have another bash? General chorus of encouragement it is. Mixed with threats, of course. What do you think?'

Perkins blinked above his mask. He had sandy eyelashes, almost invisible against his skin. 'On balance it's probably worth a try.'

Charles sighed and sat back on his stool. Sitting like this put a strain on his back, he'd much rather stand. 'OK then. Book him in. Wait until my knee's better and I can get up to him. Fortnight on Friday. You can do that, Sister, can't you?'

'Right, sir. Absolutely.'

An air of celebration seemed to pervade the operating floor. Charles couldn't understand it. But then he saw that it emanated from Perkins, and realised that in taking his advice while putting right the registrar's error, he had inadvertently absolved him. What's more, everyone wanted to be on his team for the big operation. Nurses were arguing in the sluice, and Theatre Sister was looking smug. Charles sat in the rest room and stretched his leg. Just the vent to do now, and then he had to start on the day's stock of bangs, bumps and headaches. And the radiologist wanted to talk about cancer treatment, and he'd a paper to write – he felt totally dispirited.

Perkins came in and sat down in the chair opposite. He went very pink. 'My wife and I were wondering, sir, if you'd like to dine with us one evening.'

Oh damn, thought Charles. He was being pitied and

523

buttered up, all at the same time. 'Thank you,' he said thinly. 'Delightful. Next month, perhaps. When I'm a little less busy.'

'Yes, sir. Indeed. Of course. I'll talk to your secretary, shall I?'

'Yes. You do that.'

He ostentatiously opened a paper he didn't want to read. Perkins was humming cheerfully, but the only thing Charles wanted cheerfully to do was throttle him.

On the morning of the operation, Charles was awake with the dawn. He blamed the birds as much as anything, sitting on trees outside his window and singing like Pavarotti. He got out of bed and went through to the bathroom. He felt lousy today. When he looked in the glass all he could see was stubble and liverish eyes, testament to the whisky he was drinking these days. And why not? he thought aggressively. Who cared what he did? Celia was gone.

He felt better when he had cleaned his teeth. He put on a sweater and went out into the garden, and found pleasure in breathing in cold morning air. Once he had tried to grow vegetables, he thought, looking at the tangle of the plot. Once he had made plans for this house. Nothing had changed, he was here, the house was here, but the will had vanished.

The daffodils, refusing to accept the new order, were flowering in profusion. They weren't a flower he much liked usually, since they seemed to him to be determined to pretend to be plastic, but today he grabbed a handful and stuck them in a milk bottle in the kitchen. His own reasoning defeated him. Perhaps he wanted to raise a small fist at fate, to challenge what seemed Martin Moffat's inevitable destiny. Something had to come right for once.

He had an hour to waste. He went into the dusty sitting room and turned on the television, to watch again the video of the operation. Still he couldn't decide which way to extend his incision. Should it be deeper, longer, wider? There were arguments for all of those, which meant in essence that nobody knew.

The door bell rang. He switched off the video and got up, wondering who on earth it could be. In a pearl grey suit, with a silk tie and gold pin, was David Sheraton.

'Can I come in?'

'For five minutes. I'm operating today.'

'That's why I came early. It won't take long. I want the pearls.'

Charles felt a slight shock. He had forgotten the pearls. 'What makes you think I have them?'

'Come off it! Celia told me.'

Charles shot his cuffs and mechanically checked the links. 'She told me quite a few things, too. I don't like you much.'

'If I could just have the pearls. I'm her husband. They are mine, you know.'

'She meant them for her children. They're not going to you.'

David's pale face flushed. 'You haven't got any rights over this. I mean to have those pearls.'

'You can't prove they're yours, any more than you can prove that I've got them,' said Charles. He met the other man's eye in deliberate challenge.

David raised a finger. 'I warn you I'm not taking no for an answer. I know enough to make the Sunday papers crawl around with their tongues hanging out. Think about it.'

Charles walked pointedly to the door. But before he opened it he said, 'Let me ask you something. Did you ever love her? Really?'

A crack of laughter. David said, 'You really want to believe you're the one and only, don't you? The only one who loved her as she should be loved, the only one to be hurt. But I was there first, old boy. I knew her when she was like a young queen. No one could resist her. She could have any man she wanted, just for the asking.'

Charles said, 'You liked her affairs, didn't you? They were a turn-on. That's why you didn't mind about me.'

David looked at him for a moment, before lifting his shoulders in a Gallic shrug. 'That's the way it goes. She was a very sexy woman. If she had someone at a party, I'd make sure she had me on the way home. She'd give one hell of a performance. Guilt, you see. Had to pretend she'd been longing for me all night.'

'And you liked that?' Charles was frankly incredulous.

David laughed in his face. 'Come off it. Even you must realise she wasn't Miss Peaches and Cream.'

Rage blazed up in him. Charles drew back his fist and plunged it deep into the other man's face, relishing the impact, delighting in the collapse of the tissue he struck. It was a blow for Celia, a blow for revenge! Blood exploded from nose and smashed lip, and David fell away, gasping. But he made no move to strike back, and Charles just stood there, not trying to hit again. With that one blow he had done enough.

'That made me very happy,' he said softly.

David pulled out a handkerchief and put it to his face. 'Balance that happiness against what I'm going to do to you. It had better be worth it.'

Charles opened the door and David reeled out into the morning. A few drops of his blood lay sprinkled across the tiles of the kitchen floor and before he left for the hospital Charles cleaned them up, very thoroughly. The mark, cleaner than the murky surroundings, gleamed reproachfully. God, but he was letting things go.

For some reason he felt better. When he walked into the hospital, his knee no longer hurting, his head for once clear, he had a sense of anticipation for the coming task. This time he was going to do a quick, clean job. If the result was a disaster it would at least come after textbook surgery.

In the familiar surroundings of the operating floor some of his confidence ebbed. Images kept flashing into his mind. His first brain operation. His first day in hospital. His first day at school. Everything was reversed, stripping him of all the painfully acquired confidence. He could kill this boy today. If it was David Sheraton, he would kill him, and be glad of it.

Thankfully, rewardingly, once in theatre the routine carried him along. They put on Rhapsody in Blue again, and as always everyone started to hum. Theatre Sister gave him his favourite-shaped scalpel, with a little gesture that said she alone understood his needs.

'Thank you, Sister,' he said graciously, and she bridled a little. The nurses exchanged glances. Everyone knew she fancied Davenport like mad.

Perkins said, 'I watched the video again first thing. Are you going deeper, sir?'

'No. I'm following your line of thought. Longer.'

A gulp. 'Are you sure?'

'Don't tell me you've changed your mind, Perkins. When my whole surgical career hangs in the balance.'

A polite chuckle ran round the room. The anaesthetist said, 'It's just like last time. I'll try and keep one step ahead.'

Charles said, 'Good. Good. Perkins, will you try and keep that steady? No Sister, not the bloody big one! Thank you. Change the record, someone.'

Everyone began to relax. It was just another normal day. Some idiot put on selections from The Sound of Music and was roundly cursed, but even after it had finished everyone was left humming Edelweiss. The anaesthetist kept up a bass rendering of The Hills Are Alive With The Sound of Music, like a wayward bassoon. Charles said, 'There we are. That's the beggar. Happy with that, Perkins?'

'I don't know, sir. If you think—'

'Looks fine to me. Any changes anywhere?'

'Breathing's increased. Some eye response. You've been very quick.'

'Right. Let's leave it at that, then.'

He began to close up. The patient's hand, palm upwards, began to close. 'That happened last time, didn't it?' said Charles.

They all agreed that it had. But restlessness began to increase, until Charles was having difficulty working. 'Calm him down a bit,' he instructed. 'There's not so much bleeding this time. Let's get him closed and out of here.'

Even under pressure Charles's handiwork was neat and precise. At the end, with the new line of stitches exactly mimicking the old, Perkins said, 'Well done, sir.'

All Charles wanted was a drink. He wandered from the theatre, discarding this and that, while nurses caught things as they fell. A cup of tea was all that was on offer and he supposed it would have to do. He looked at the clock. Five hours. That wasn't so bad.

He slumped in a chair and let his head fall back. A headache was beginning somewhere in his temporal lobe, which in a patient could be a sign of a tumour, he supposed, although in him it was just tension. He closed his eyes for a moment, only for the door to crash back on its hinges. It was a nurse. 'He's awake, sir. He opened his eyes and spoke.'

Charles blinked. 'What did he say?'

'It was very slurred. I think he said he was cold.'

'And he's still awake? How long was it last time?'

'Only a few minutes, sir. Five at the most.'

'Right. Get the father in. It might be his last chance.'

He got heavily to his feet and went into the recovery room. Martin Moffat was strung up with drips and tubes, but despite them his head was turning rhythmically from side to side. Charles didn't like the look of that. 'Martin? Can you hear me?'

The head steadied for a moment. The eyes met his without recognition, but why should he know him? They had never met. 'You're in hospital,' explained Davenport. 'You've had an operation on your head. You'll feel better soon.'

Perkins arrived and began checking reflexes. Martin's legs, thin and white, jerked obediently. Behind him, the door opened and his father came in. He took his son's hand. 'Martin? Martin, it's me.'

The turning of the head ceased. Thickly, as if speaking through flannel, Martin said, 'Hello, Dad.'

Moffat's legs seemed to sink beneath him. He slid to a sitting position by his son's bed. 'Hello, Martin,' he managed.

Charles was holding fingers before the boy's face. 'How many? Quick now.'

'Don't know. Three. Hurts. What's that smell? Bread.'

Anosmia. Charles said, 'Perkins. Get moving, we may have a seizure.'

This theatre was always prepared. They injected straight into the canula in Martin's hand, and the convulsions, when they came, were muted. He groaned, his eyes glassy, and his father said, 'Martin? Martin, are you OK?'

Charles said, 'He'll sleep now. Seizures like this aren't uncommon after surgery. We've injured him, you see.'

'Yes. Yes.' Moffat stood up, unable to take his eyes off his son's face. Hands took him by the shoulders and gently eased him from the room. He could come back later, they promised. When Martin was more awake.

Between them, Charles and Perkins worked out a drug regime. If seizures were to be the order of the day the patient would have to be sedated until the brain had settled itself – if it ever did. He felt pessimistic all of a sudden. All the signs told of a patient who would not do well. But then Perkins said, 'I'm quite pleased really, aren't you, sir? We've got activity going, and that has to be good.' And Charles wondered if he was losing his perspective on things. If you lost it you wouldn't have the capacity to know.

He changed and looked at his watch. There was a meeting of the finance committee this afternoon, and he ought to look in. He wandered down, tired and irritable, and everyone looked up and welcomed him.

'Charles! Wonderful.' Even Sheila Duncombe, the lady gynaecologist, got up and poured him some tea, and as a confirmed feminist it was against her religion. Charles wondered if he was looking worse than he knew.

But it was something quite other. In his absence, and in expectation of the trust fund, they had finalised plans for expansion. The gynaecologist was to have a new suite of labour rooms, the heart men were to have a helipad for organ deliveries, even orthopaedics were excitedly planning a post-operative exercise gym. 'And what about my new ward?' said Charles quietly. 'Where is the neurological spend in all this?'

Mr James said, 'We did prioritise. And of course the Law Society Fund is bound to be neurology targeted. Under the circumstances—'

'You thought I could get by on jam tomorrow. May I remind you all that the money you're spending was generated neurologically?'

'But it was a general gift.'

'Not that general. I insist that we put my projects back on the table.'

Nobody said anything. Nobody moved. Charles felt the winds of treachery blowing about him on this fine spring day. He was too young, too ambitious and too successful. He had stolen the heart men's thunder, demanded money that others thought was theirs, and everyone would much prefer that he left Aireborough and went to work elsewhere.

James said, 'Your time with us has been – somewhat unconventional, hasn't it, Charles?'

'You knew when I came here that I wanted to develop my department. That I work closely with research teams. That I experiment!'

'In some very odd directions, if I may say so.' The gynaecologist looked at him over her glasses. A snigger ran round the table.

'This is a gathering of wolves,' said Charles.

He got up as if to leave, but stood for a moment looking down at them. 'Don't imagine you're going to get me out with threats,' he said easily. 'I don't frighten that easily. By the time you get any sort of disciplinary action up and running, Celia Sheraton will be very dead and your case will look like a lot of name-calling. And I've got a few friends where they count. So by all means make your plans and expand your empires, but at the end of the day, if I don't get my slice of the cake, I'll rake up hundreds of grateful patients and parade every one of them in my support. I shall be the white knight at the forefront of technology, while you lot grub around buying potted palms instead of patient care. You're going to put Aireborough back ten years. Think about it.'

He swept from the room and stormed down the corridor, more angry than he was prepared for. How dare they try and oust him in such a brutally amateurish way? He should have made more friends, of course. It wouldn't have hurt to canvass some support.

Footsteps were running after him. It was Sheila Duncombe, the gynaecologist. 'Charles! Charles, please wait. I want a word with you.'

He turned on his heel to face her. 'Yes? What now?'

She was tall, thin and unsentimental. She said, 'You're far too confrontational, you know. You could have talked them around. James thinks he can bully his way through, but nobody takes that seriously. It doesn't have to be a gunfight.'

'I didn't choose the ground,' said Charles grimly. 'You were offering nil expansion and disciplinary charges if I dared to object.'

'You ought to be disciplined,' said Sheila. 'You had an affair with a patient. Be honest!'

He said nothing, but simply looked away. A girl walked by, heavily pregnant, and Sheila Duncombe acknowledged her. 'Twins,' she remarked. 'Should be fun.'

Charles said, 'How is she?'

'As expected. Why don't you come and see?'

'No. No point. Is the baby—?'

'It's OK. No more than that. If the worst comes to the worst we'll put her on life support and do a section. But I don't hold out much hope.'

'No.'

He swallowed, but the tightness in his throat remained. Sheila said, 'This is very difficult for you, isn't it? You don't have to pretend.'

He said huskily, 'I've got very few friends around here. I can't expect people to understand.'

'Your staff are sticking by you. So you must have done something right.' Greatly daring, she rested a hand on his arm. 'Why don't you come and see her? It might help.'

He looked at her bleakly. 'All I wanted was to make her well. And all the things I could have done I didn't dare try. I loved her too much. I let my love destroy her. If she hadn't been pregnant – if I'd made her terminate—'

Sheila reached up and put her thick, workworn fingers gently on his mouth. 'There's no use thinking like that. I know things look bad, I know it's foolish to hope, but there could be a baby out of this! And if there is – that's your baby. No one else wants it. Don't you?'

He closed his eyes, on sudden tears. She waited until he had recovered himself and then said, 'Goodbye, Charles. Come down and see us soon.'

He turned and walked away.

Chapter Thirty-Six

It was almost eight in the evening when Charles came back to the hospital. Visiting time was ending and there was a stream of people coming out of the doors, their baskets empty, their faces slack. Two young girls were in the midst of the throng, and Charles recognised them at once. Ellen and Lucy. He went across.

'Hello, girls. Did you come by yourselves?'

'Mum brought us,' said Ellen. 'She's waiting in the car park. She didn't think we'd want her to come in.'

'That's very thoughtful of her.'

Lucy said, 'She doesn't mind so much now. Now that—'

'Yes,' said Charles. 'Now that Celia's dying.'

Ellen rubbed her cheek with the back of her hand. Although not a beautiful child normally, in this half light she had much in her of Celia. Her hair was as long and as lustrous, its colour hidden now by the twilight. Her hands had the same length and grace. Charles found the comparisons unpleasant and began to move away, but Ellen said, 'Please, Mr Davenport! Everyone says there's nothing that can be done. But she isn't dead, it's just like before! Can't you do something? You – you must want to.'

He said, 'It isn't the same as before. She's in a very deep coma. Her brain stem – the part of her brain that keeps everything alive – is gradually starting to fail.'

'So stop it,' said Lucy. 'Do an operation. It was on the news tonight, about someone you woke up after an operation.'

He blinked. 'On the news?'

Ellen nodded her agreement. 'This man came on and said it was his son. It was all about how brilliant you were, and we came tonight to see. We asked the nurse, but she said she

533

didn't know. We're not stupid, Mr Davenport! We know she's very ill. But – couldn't you try?'

He looked into their anxious faces. He couldn't answer the question. But even as he walked away they followed him. 'Why not?' demanded Lucy. 'You operated on this other man's son. Why not Celia?'

'Because she's pregnant. The baby would die.'

'It's going to die anyway, though. That's what the nurse thinks.'

'She shouldn't have told you that.'

'We asked. I think you're just being selfish. I think you're scared.'

He stopped, then. 'Of course I'm scared. Look, she didn't like what she found when she came back to life last time, do you really think she'd want to try again? Suppose she couldn't speak? Suppose she couldn't see?'

Lucy said, 'You must always have that problem when you operate.'

He felt a shock go through him. These girls were so bright, so like Celia. They had her full-frontal honesty. If there was any part in them of David he couldn't see it, thank God. 'Does your father know you're here?' he asked.

Ellen said, 'We had a row. He can't stop us.'

Lucy, tossing a belligerent head, said, 'He thinks he owns us, you know. He's like the police.'

He had a sudden urge to tell Celia about her daughters, to let her know just how proud she could be of them. She had felt unloved, her motherhood a failure, when it was nothing of the kind. Her daughters' loyalty transcended so much.

He said to the girls, 'It's time you were getting home. Isn't it school tomorrow?'

They nodded. He said, 'I wish you didn't have to face this. You're far too young.'

'I don't suppose it's better when you're old,' said Ellen.

Charles laughed, for the first time in weeks. What he wouldn't give for a daughter like Ellen. He would give – anything.

Sister Johnson was bristling when he entered her realm. 'That

534

man Moffat,' she said angrily. 'We should have known. Quite unprincipled. He went straight to the television people, he has no shame.'

'Did he say anything he shouldn't?'

'He should have said nothing at all! It was a stunt, you know. He wants the world aware of what you're doing here. He thinks publicity will make you treat his son more aggressively.'

Charles went to the boy's bed, in the prime position next to Sister's office. She kept her most precious charges there. 'I should think I've been quite aggressive enough. Has he stabilised?'

'Constant fitting for two hours. Better now. He's talking a little.'

'Is he? Martin? Martin, can you hear me?'

The eyes fluttered open. They were green, Charles realised. 'Hurt – everywhere,' came the whisper.

'Yes. You will. It won't last forever.'

'Want my mother.'

'Sister Johnson?'

She made a face. 'I'll try and persuade her. She was very nervous. In case he didn't pull through.'

'Well, I think he'll pull through,' said Charles, patting Martin's hand. 'You're going to be fine, old chap. Just fine.'

'Keep smelling bread.'

'Just one of those things. Keep his dosage up, Sister.'

He went with Sister into her office. 'He wakes up to find he's got epilepsy,' said Charles. 'Wonderful.'

'That isn't so serious,' said Sister. 'Mr Davenport, you're getting very silly. I don't know why these things bother you, they never used to.'

'What a prat I must have been.'

She looked at him severely. 'You were a good doctor and an excellent surgeon. Let's hope you can return to that happy condition. We'll have no more of this agonising! Now, are you going to operate on Mrs Sheraton or not?'

He jumped. They were all nagging at him! He felt like a beleaguered citadel, the defenders weak and downhearted.

He had last seen her the night they took her in, deeply

unconscious and hopelessly ill. Everyone had agreed it was only a matter of time. And time was passing, minute by minute, second by second. Apparently she still clung on. Why? Because of the baby? It must be that. Whatever will Celia still possessed was focused on surviving only long enough to give her baby life. She wouldn't last beyond that. She would stay only until that job was done.

Sister Johnson was looking at him. He swore at her under his breath, and her glasses glinted in amusement. She liked tormenting him, he decided. It was one of her keenest pleasures. 'The two cases are not the same,' he said defiantly.

'Obviously not. Which cases are? Principles remain, however.'

'You have none, Sister. You and Moffat are a pair.'

'Ah!' She pretended to be coy. 'You say the sweetest things.'

He flung out and down the stairs, into the car park and across the field, to the doors leading to maternity. It was the cosiest place in the hospital, all plants and comfortable sofas, with only a few posters about the dangers of smoking to disturb the expectant mothers' equilibrium. He realised he didn't know where to go and stopped a student nurse. 'Mrs Sheraton, please.'

'Oh. Yes, Mr Davenport.'

She scuttled along ahead of him, overawed by the great man he had become. He wondered when it had happened. It seemed only a moment since he had been less significant than she, fodder for the great machine that was a hospital. She stopped at a door and he said, 'Thank you, nurse. You can go now.'

And he waited until she was out of sight. Then he quietly opened the door.

She was lying very still. She was deathly pale, much paler than when he had first seen her. Without Sister Johnson's unremitting care she was losing weight, or perhaps it was the baby, taking it all. He took her hand and there was no response. She might have been dead already, except for the residual warmth in her palm. But her fingernails were growing still. She had the long, Lady of Shalott extremities he

536

remembered so well, before life and reality got to grips with her. They were mirrored now in Ellen, who was just setting out on womanhood.

Celia lay so very still. He put his hand on her belly, a small, too small mound. There was only the slightest movement. The life in this body was ebbing away, was only just enough to sustain the new life that clung to it.

He sat down by the bed and looked into Celia's face. He hated the loveliness of her, the ghostly perfection. These looks had moved him at first but they didn't any more. He wanted life in that face, he wanted lips that smiled, eyes that cried, skin that wrinkled and sagged with the passing years. She had done what she could to stay with him. He knew that now. No part of her had ever wanted this. If, in trying to make her live, he destroyed her, took away her dignity and her pleasure, left her useless, would she blame him? Surely not. That wasn't Celia. Her daughters drew their courage from her, it was something she possessed in full measure. Celia would not give up without a fight.

He rang the bell and summoned the nurse, demanding paper and pen to scrawl a note to Sheila Duncombe. 'I intend to operate. Decide best time, before or after section. Will liaise. Many thanks. CD.'

Then he went home and at last, thankfully, slept.

Sheila Duncombe knocked perfunctorily on the door of Charles's office, at the same time putting her head round and saying, 'May I come in?' He glanced up from his papers, glowering, but then he saw who it was.

'Oh. Sheila.'

'Yes.'

She sat down wearily. 'Any chance of a coffee? I had four deliveries last night, all of them tricky.'

He got up and poured her a cup from his own always bubbling machine. It was good and strong, although he lectured his patients often enough on the dangers of caffeine. 'You should go home to bed.'

'I will, it's a quiet day. But I wanted to tell you something. David Sheraton's refused his consent.'

He stood very still. But as she watched his colour changed to red, until even his eyes seemed bloodshot.

'Charles?' she said doubtfully.

He went to the window, taking a grip on the sill with white-knuckled hands. She realised he was furiously angry. 'What did he talk about? Letting her die with dignity?'

She nodded. 'He had it all off pat.'

'I bet he did. Did you talk to James? There are procedures for this sort of thing.'

She hesitated. 'I came here first. I'm anxious about the baby; if I'm going to do anything, I should do it now. And I didn't know how you'd feel about publicity.'

He turned away for a moment. Then he poured himself some coffee too. 'I've been skating on thin ice over this for so long I've started to believe I'll never fall through,' he said honestly. 'I'd be suspended at the very least. And I've got to do this operation!'

'I thought you weren't all that keen.'

'Did you?' He closed his eyes. 'If it was any other patient I'd do it at once. If it was any other operation I'd find someone else to have a go. The thing's a farce.'

She looked at him sardonically. 'Don't moan about it, you brought it on yourself. You men are all the same. You want to have your fun and get away scot free. I suppose it's heartening, really. Our career-mad trailblazer falling foul of the human heart. It makes the rest of us feel rather more secure.'

'Glad to be of service,' said Charles drily. He absently reached for the coffee pot and topped them both up. 'I'll talk to Sheraton.'

Sheila said, 'He's not a stupid man. You ought to be careful.'

Charles looked at her over his cup. It was a glance, no more than that, but she felt cold suddenly. Charles had mastered his rage, jamming it back under hatches with all the iron control in his possession, and there it stayed. Normal as he seemed, he was anything but. It was Sheraton who needed to take care.

When she left, summoned by bleeper to the sudden arrival of breech twins, Charles glanced at his watch. He was due to do a teaching round ten minutes ago, and he flung out of his office.

It would never do for his staff to conclude that this whole thing was getting to him. He must maintain the surface veneer of calm, controlled efficiency. When he found his small group of students shuffling their feet and waiting for him, he said, 'Well? What are you doing here? Did nobody think to go to the patient and begin examining him? After all this time I do expect some level of personal initiative!'

They all muttered anxious apologies, although until today they were under the impression that he would shoot anyone who touched his patients without his express permission. Nonetheless, their foot-tapping changed to humility, and Charles could begin his round.

The work seemed difficult today. He had never had any patience with students, but could usually manage a coherent dissertation on his theme. Today his mind wandered again and again, and after one long silence at the bed of a stroke patient he came back to the present to see his half-dozen disciples gazing at him like so many anxious camels. He said, 'You know, we never talk about the fundamentals, do we? What this is all about. You stand here and listen to me telling you about tests and pressures and clinical signs, but you never ask why. Why am I here, doing this? Why do you want to do it? We're all going to die of something, why not let the tumours and fractured skulls finish us off and spend our expertise in grief management? Some of our patients would definitely prefer to have died. Have you noticed that? Or are you all so well trained that you can't think beyond the obvious?'

One of the students said nervously, 'Aren't we talking quality of life, sir?'

'Yes. And quality of death. They're indefinable, and yet you're going to be asked to define them. I can't. I've been at this for twenty years and I still can't. You're all so bloody confident that all this is worthwhile, and I can't for the life of me see why.'

The patient, looking from under a sagging eyelid, said, 'That's all I bloody need. Just get me out of here and back to my allotment. I'll die planting lettuce and be damned to you!'

'There you are, sir,' said a student. 'We're here to help people like him plant lettuce.'

'To alleviate human misery,' said another. 'We can't always do it, but we have to try.'

'And you don't mind the risk of making things worse?' said Charles.

He felt very old, suddenly. Very old and very experienced. These bright, well brought up kids were so sure of themselves; they didn't know that life was all about losing that confidence. They would learn, as Charles had learned, that everything was much more difficult than they supposed, and in the end, much more simple.

He dismissed the students and walked out to his car. He felt as if he had taken a long time growing up. When he came to Aireborough his life had been directed quite firmly towards recognition and material success, to the exclusion of everything else. He had left behind friends and lovers, discarded all hangers-on, to get where he wanted to go. And he'd got there. Easily. His colleagues might dislike him but he had gained their admiration. The hierarchy might fear him but they knew what he was worth, until such time as that worth diminished. There was no space at the top for the failure or the embarrassment.

So now he stood precariously on his lonely pinnacle and knew that he'd chased the wrong dream. He'd helped patients because in helping them he'd helped himself. He'd made discoveries simply to further his own ambitions. And sometimes – perhaps only rarely – he'd used sick people for his own good and none of theirs. He hadn't ever expected to think that of himself. He did now.

He drove quickly, his mind very clear for once. He was taking a risk and he knew it. He glanced at his watch and saw that it wasn't yet four, so Braddock would be at work. He drove to his offices. He parked firmly in an empty executive space, and brushed the doorman's protestations aside. 'I have to see Mr Braddock. My name's Charles Davenport and it's urgent.'

There was a flurry at the desk, Charles's manner as much as his suit declared him to be a person of importance. He was whisked away upstairs, but would not be consigned to a sofa and kept waiting. 'Look, is Braddock here?' he demanded. 'I have to see him now.' An assistant tried to impede him but was summarily quelled.

A door opened. It was Edwin Braddock, neat, dapper, shooting his cuffs. 'Mr Davenport. Charles. Are you having difficulty? We're not used to having the great and the good descend on us without notice, we hardly know which way to turn.'

'Indeed. Look, I have to talk privately. It's about Celia.'

Braddock sighed. 'So I imagine. My dear, dear cousin. Come along in, do.' He ushered Charles into his room.

Charles looked about the vast office with distaste. 'I could fit a dozen patients in here. What do you use it all for? Golf?'

Edwin went to the drinks bar. 'Not one of my vices, I'm afraid. What can I offer you?'

'Scotch.'

The drink tasted of peat and heather moors. It was a very good malt. Charles sat down in one of the low, uncomfortable chairs, arms and legs sprawled like a gorilla in a nest. He hated modern furniture. 'Sheraton's trying to prevent Celia having treatment. He's refused his consent.'

Edwin poured himself a gin. 'He has the right. The trust only ever took command in the absence of David's instructions. Of course, David's been waiting for her to die for years. Life insurance.'

'What?'

'Oh. I thought perhaps you knew. Her life's insured for almost a million. You can't expect David to pass that up in favour of sentiment.'

'Good God.'

Charles finished his whisky, gathered his arms and legs together and stood up. He towered above Edwin, and saw at once that the other man resented it. He was a prickly mass of pride, about stature, manners, everything. 'Will you talk to David?' he asked. 'Look, I know you and Celia have disagreed in the past. But – but somehow, at heart I don't think you hate her.'

'I don't. I never have. When she was young I admired her beyond everything.'

'If you do this for her I'll make her drop any claim on the

estate,' said Charles. 'She won't need money, I'll look after her. You've got stuff on David that no one else has. Surely you can think of something that will make him consent.'

'You flatter me,' said Edwin. 'I don't know very much.'

'I'd lay money that it's more than enough.'

A pause. A considering glance. Edwin looked away.

He wasn't going to help, Charles could see that. He turned the heavy glass in his hand, noting the quality. Braddock was the total showman. Perhaps he was open to flattery. Charles said, 'You've surprised me, you know. If Celia's father could see the way you're running this place he might have left it to you after all.'

Edwin looked taken aback. 'Thank you. One does try.'

'If you do, it doesn't show. Look, I'd better be on my way. I'll go and see Sheraton, though I don't suppose it'll do any good. Tomorrow the whole damned thing will have to go public. And it could be too late.'

Edwin came with him to the door. 'How critical is the time?'

'I don't know. For the baby – well, it might be hours. For Celia – it's such a long shot I can't judge. I'm clutching at straws.'

Edwin stood at the door and didn't open it. 'She's a remarkable woman. What a shame it would be if the world lost the remarkable people and left the Sheratons of this world intact. If you want my advice I suggest a stick and carrot approach. Threats and then money – in whatever form you might possess a sizeable sum.'

'What sort of threat?'

'Oh God,' said Braddock. 'Oh God. If I must I must, I suppose. I'll call him at his office. I won't promise anything – but I'll call him.'

Charles found himself momentarily unable to speak. At last he said, 'This is very good of you. I'm – I'm very grateful.'

Edwin's pale, sharp face glanced up at him. 'So you should be. Please don't discuss this with anyone else. I shall deny it all.'

When he was alone, he lifted the telephone. There was a slight crackle on the line, and he wondered momentarily if someone might be listening in. It wasn't likely. Not everyone had his own devious mind. He dialled and waited. 'David? Edwin Braddock here. How are you? I was so sorry to hear about Celia.'

He leaned back in his chair, put his feet on the desk and talked.

Charles drove to Blantyre House at around nine. He had gone home, bathed, eaten and thought about drinking more whisky. But the bottle remained in the cupboard and Charles was resolutely sober. He felt clear-headed to the point of discomfort.

To his surprise Ellen opened the door. She was wearing a long black sweater over black tights, and looked elfin and nervous. 'Dad and Mum are having an awful fight,' she said lugubriously. 'They're in the library and they yell at us if we go in.'

Charles said, 'They'll yell even louder at me. Don't listen. Take Lucy and the dog and go for a walk.'

They called the chunky grey mutt and went off. Voices rose and fell in the library, the sounds of battle mixed with odd interludes of sensible talk. Charles rapped his knuckles on the polished oak of the door, turned the handle and went in.

David was standing by the fireplace, dishevelled, glass in hand. His face still bore the marks of Charles's assault. He looked old, thought Charles suddenly. It was a vision of how he would be in great age, eyes bleached to chalk and a face gone to bruised bone.

'Ellen let me in,' Charles said with unwonted diffidence.

Heather, in an old tweed skirt, was shaking with repressed sobs. 'I'm glad you're here, Charles. He's being impossible. I can't talk to him.'

'She means I won't do as she says,' said David, slurring his words a little. 'She wants me to give in. To be ruined. To have nothing left, not even this blasted house.'

Charles said, 'Is that all Celia's worth to you? Money?'

'For heaven's sake, man, Celia's dead! You're just pretending you can save her, you want to be God. There isn't any point. There isn't any damned point.'

Heather lifted her head. 'You haven't the right to decide,

David! She has to have the operation, she must. Then it really is up to God.'

He turned from them, his face tortured. It was more than money, thought Charles. Whatever Braddock had said to him had raised yet another ghost. Was it just the Will? What was David afraid of? 'Does Braddock know you tried to kill her?'

Heather shuddered and put her hands to her face. But David stared at him without speaking. A muscle twitched in his cheek.

Charles said, 'If you sign, I won't tell anyone. I've got the form here.

Heather said in a high, desperate voice, 'Don't be silly. It's a mistake. He never meant to hurt her.'

'He tried to drive her off the road and into the canal,' said Charles. 'No doubt he thought it would be good for her.'

'But – that wasn't me!' said David incredulously. 'Surely you don't believe it was?'

Charles was confused. If not that, what? Surely Braddock had threatened him? But he had also suggested money. He reached into his pocket and drew out the long, heavy, satin string of pearls. A few grains of rice fell from them on to the floor. 'Will you do it for these?' he asked quietly. 'Will you sign if I give you these?'

Heather reached out and touched them. 'They're beautiful. David, surely—'

'It isn't just the money!' said David urgently. 'You don't understand what it's been like. A haunting. A living, daily haunting. You want me to go back to that, never to be free. She won't come back to life. She'll lie there again, halfway between life and death, never letting go.'

Heather came to his side. She took David's hand in a gentle clasp. 'Please, David,' she said. 'If we're ever to be happy again, you must sign. We can't undo anything, we can only atone. You can't have her death on your conscience.'

He looked at her bleakly. 'What about her life?'

Slowly, grimly, he moved to the table and picked up the pen. Charles waited, tense with expectation. Still David didn't sign. He said in a slow, careful voice, 'It seems I must always be guilty. Whatever I do, I'm never free. Like a curse. You might as well know, I suppose. I'm sick of living with it. I've had her death on my conscience for the last ten years.' Then he bent and signed his name.

Late that night, Charles went to the hospital again. As always the corridors were quiet, but not deserted; the odd nurse, the odd sleepless figure, came and went, and now and then a doctor staggered by, a junior in the last stages of exhaustion. Charles walked on, soothed by the sameness, tonight as every night.

The Moffat boy was in a side ward now. Charles knocked softly and went in, but the patient wasn't asleep. He was propped up on pillows, anxious and slightly disorientated. 'Mum?' he said.

'It's me,' said Charles. 'Has your mother been?'

Moffat nodded. 'She comes every day.'

'Yes. When you're well she can take you home.'

'I want to go home.'

The room was full of flowers and cards. There was a jigsaw on a tray, hardly begun, and a pile of unread books, and a wicker basket, courtesy of occupational therapy and untouched since it left that department. 'Do you find much to do?' asked Charles, taking up the basket and expertly twisting a stem.

'I – I can't seem to think. Can't concentrate. They say I'll be better if – when—'

'You could be quite different in six months. Healing takes time.'

'I don't know.'

'Would you like a drink? I'll get nurse to make you something warm.'

'Yes. Thanks.'

Charles put down the basket and left. The nurse, a married woman doing the night shift and going home in the morning to a small baby, was kinder than need be. 'I'll go and sit with him,' she said. 'He likes company.'

Charles nodded. His thoughts were spinning wildly, and he knew he ought to postpone everything until the morning. But the form was burning a hole in his pocket. He had to deliver it at least to James's office, if not to James himself. Then he would telephone Sheila Duncombe and everything could begin.

But Moffat's face disturbed him, his voice, his anxiety. The boy was epileptic, and his intelligence seemed diminished. Before Celia, and if that was all, Charles would have hailed it as a major triumph, but if this was to be Celia – he was suddenly frightened. It was all such a risk.

Her room drew him like a magnet. The maternity unit was lively tonight, with expectant fathers hovering outside examination rooms, making faces at their wives through the doors. As Charles passed, Sheila Duncombe emerged from one such room. 'Hello,' she said. 'What are you doing here?'

'Visiting. I've got consent.'

'Oh. Well – that's good.'

They stood awkwardly together, and Charles said, 'Why don't you let the fathers in during examinations? I thought togetherness was all the rage.'

She grimaced. 'Not in my department. They're all such experts now, it's impossible. They order me to do forceps deliveries on perfectly normal presentations, so I keep them at bay at least until I've decided how we're getting on. Look, shall I come with you? I'm just hanging around for a while, to see if I'm needed. I came in to do a section, but the mother's getting on fine.'

He didn't want her, but he couldn't say no. She kept up a flow of earthy chatter, symptomatic of those in the baby business. 'Have you got any children?' he asked, and she shook her head.

'Couldn't. A pity, really. Sometimes I long to know what it's really like. Not like brains.'

'Sometimes like brains,' he conceded. 'But sometimes I think neurology is a very unnatural science.'

'A bit – cold?'

'Icy.'

She opened the door of Celia's room, saying, 'Hello, Mrs Sheraton. It's Dr Duncombe and Mr Davenport to see you. How are you feeling?'

Charles said nothing. Celia lay propped on pillows, a graven image of herself. Someone had plaited her hair in a long, golden rope, thicker by far than her wrist. She was so dreadfully thin.

'How is—?'

'The baby? A poor foetal heartbeat. If you've got consent I'll get everything ready for the morning.'

'And the chances?'

'You know as well as I do. At just twenty-three weeks, with a poor uterine environment, they can't be good. Will you attend?'

He nodded. 'We'll take her off your hands straight after.'

'Back to your cold, technical world. Poor girl.'

She reached out and touched Celia's hand. Charles thought how much he liked Sheila Duncombe. After all this, whatever happened after this, he should get to know her better. There were people in this hospital that could be his friends, if ever he took the trouble to make them such. He didn't have to remain forever in his cold, technical tower.

Sheila said, 'She's very lovely, isn't she? I saw you with her once. You looked – alive.'

He caught the connection at once. Was he trying to save her life – or his? He took hold of the long, golden plait, and it was living hair still. Through it he remembered her. The memory was painfully sweet.

Walking back through the hospital there was the punctured shrieking of the newborn. 'Mrs Aubrey's delivered,' said Sheila delightedly. 'I'll go in and congratulate. Super!' She paused at the door and looked back at Charles. 'Why don't you come?'

He grimaced. 'It would ruin my suit.'

'OK.' She fluttered her fingers. 'See you tomorrow, then. Theatre.'

The night stretched on, empty and so alone. Suddenly Charles turned and ran silently back through the corridors, back to Celia. He stood at the side of the bed, staring at the still face. Then he bent, and kissed her.

Chapter Thirty-Seven

The morning was dull and overcast, with drizzle threatening on the wind. Charles dressed with his usual care, glowering at himself in the bathroom mirror, prepared to see omens everywhere today, even in clouds. He would be less nervous if he himself was operating, he thought. He imagined every possible disaster.

As a last thought before he left, he went upstairs and fetched the small pink teddy he had bought and Celia had cuddled when she was ill and alone here. He had seen babies sometimes, impossibly small and weak, with just such a teddy tucked in the incubator with them. It was a sign that somebody cared. And he did.

By the time he reached the hospital it was raining. He splashed to the door, feeling more and more discouraged, and growled at everyone who dared to say hello. Perkins was waiting in maternity, and Charles looked at him in distaste. He had the happy, anticipatory air of someone who was enjoying himself, and why shouldn't he? It was an interesting case.

Sheila Duncombe was all scrubbed up. 'Hurry up, you two,' she urged. 'I do want to get on. Everything's ready.'

They were last into theatre. In Charles's terms, the place was primitive, with none of the gadgetry he used. Instead there were forceps and suction cups, oxygen bottles and stirrups, and of course an incubator. Charles turned his back on it right away.

'Everyone ready?' asked Sheila. 'Right, then. Let's have her in.'

The trolley made its silent entrance. Celia's hair was hidden beneath a cap. Under the harsh theatre lights her skin looked like bleached paper, and her belly, swollen and distended, the only substantial part of her. ⎯

'No need for anaesthesia,' said Sheila cheerfully. 'Come on, everyone, gather round. Let's get on.'

Some part of Charles's mind disconnected itself. He was able to watch and admire Sheila Duncombe's technique, so different from his own, so much more workmanlike. A wide, low, invasive incision. The skin peeled away, and the welling blood was instantly staunched. The paediatrician hovered, whistling between his teeth, and someone said, 'Her blood pressure's lousy. This kid's going to have it tough.'

Sheila seemed to rummage in Celia's insides. Charles almost laughed. It was years since he had seen one of these and he was reminded of an incompetent magician. Any minute now something would appear. A rabbit? A bunch of flowers? A baby?

When it came the creature was tiny, impossibly small. Its umbilicus was twice as thick as one of its legs. 'A girl,' said Sheila, in a noncommittal voice. 'There you are, everyone. A little girl.'

'Let's have her,' said the paediatrician, and at once the cord was cut and the child surrounded. Sheila set about repairing the damage she had caused. 'Now, Celia,' she said comfortably. 'You have a lovely little girl.'

'How heavy?' asked Charles.

'Barely a pound and a half, I should think.' Sheila glanced up at him. 'You knew she wouldn't have much chance.'

He nodded. Perkins was twitching at Sheila's elbow and she said sardonically, 'Do I take it you think you could do a better job, Mr Perkins? Is my needlework not to your taste?'

'Sorry, Dr Duncombe. We do things a little differently in neurosurgery.'

'I bet you do. No operation takes less than four hours. My patients haven't got four hours to waste, they've lives to lead. Now, I've just about finished. Are you taking over, Charles? I've had a word with Sister Johnson about our end of things, I'm sure she can cope. When do you hope to operate?'

He shrugged. 'A day or two. Perhaps more. We'll see how she comes out of this.'

She nodded, and the patient was prepared for transfer. As they walked out together, Sheila said, 'I'm sorry about the baby, Charles. I wish we could have kept her in better condition.'

'A real no-hoper, then?'

'I don't think you should bank on miracles, let's say.'

Charles had work to do. He strode purposefully back to his unit, forcing his mind to concentrate on the cases he needed to see. Two suspected tumours, one of which he thought was probably multiple sclerosis or something similar and not a tumour at all. There was too the interesting case of a man blind since birth, who might well have a brain lesion that would account for it. For a second the old Charles asserted himself; he had a vision of the headlines – 'Miracle Doctor Gave Me My Sight!' Now that would do him some good.

The morning rolled on, scooping him up and carrying him along. At lunch, a sandwich today, he deliberately avoided asking questions about Celia or the baby. He might well have gone on in ignorance had Sheila Duncombe not bleeped him. 'Charles?' she said when he came to the phone. 'Just to tell you the baby's still here. She's making a fight of it. Why don't you come down and see?'

'I'm desperately busy up here,' he said gruffly. 'Tomorrow perhaps.'

'Don't be such a stoic! Anyway, they want to baptise her and they need a name, so you'd better come down and see to it. Tomorrow won't do. We're waiting, Charles.'

He put down the phone, mentally cursing the woman. But he had half an hour to spare. More if he wanted, he wasn't operating. His sandwich turned to dust on his tongue, and he knew that if he didn't go, if he never went, there would be no end to his regret.

The special baby unit was a series of rooms, at the side of which ran a glass corridor. Concerned visitors could stand in the corridor and look in at the babies, stranded in their incubators, tubes everywhere. Charles knew that he could go in, but instead he went to the corridor. He wanted the protection of that firm glass wall.

But Ellen was there. She was standing with her hands

against the glass, her face remote and absorbed. Charles said, 'How did you know?'

She glanced up at him. 'I rang the hospital. I do every day. You should have told me. You promised you would.'

Charles said nothing. He turned and looked into the room, at the half a dozen glass boxes containing half a dozen sickly souls. They were all very, very small and one was absolutely tiny. A little girl, no bigger than Charles's hand. 'Is that her?' he said incredulously.

'Yes. She's so small.'

'I saw her born. She seemed bigger. My God, there's nothing there!'

Ellen said, 'I love her already. I can't bear it if she dies.'

Words of comfort rose to his lips, but he didn't utter them. Instead he said, 'They're not holding out any hope, you know. We're going to have to bear it.'

Ellen looked at him, and her eyes filled with swimming tears.

He didn't know what to do. She fished for a handkerchief and couldn't find one, so he gave her his own immaculate starched square. She took it and mopped her eyes.

'We can go in if you like,' said Charles.

She sniffed. 'I'd like that. You can't see her too well from here.'

They went round to the door, and Charles had a brief word with the nurse. She knew him well, he was often called in to pontificate on this or that neurological problem. She said, 'Little Baby Sheraton. We wanted to baptise her, but we haven't got a name.'

'Ellen's going to think of one,' said Charles. 'After all, she's the big sister.'

They went to the incubator and stood looking down. The baby seemed even smaller, covered in a faint brush of hair. Her breathing was rapid and seemed as if it must be painful, or at least painfully exhausting. Tiny eyelids flickered now and then. Tiny hands lay crumpled like pieces of screwed-up paper.

'They regulate her oxygen,' said Charles. 'She's too young

to breathe properly yet. Her systems are so undeveloped they have to be protected.'

'Babies younger than this have lived,' said Ellen desperately.

'Yes. Some have.'

The nurse came across and checked a tube. She said, 'Actually, she's doing better than we hoped. If she lasts a week and doesn't go back, she might be all right.'

'Please last a week, baby,' said Ellen, pressing her hands against the enclosing plastic box.

'I've rung for the priest,' said the nurse. 'All you have to do is give her a name.'

Charles and Ellen looked at one another. 'She's yours,' whispered Ellen. 'What do you want? Celia?'

He shuddered. 'No! Nothing like that. What's your favourite?'

Without a moment's hesitation, she said, 'Josephine. I always wanted to be Josephine.'

The priest came in. The blinds were drawn against the corridor, and the little room was shadowed. Soft bleeps and whistles came from the equipment, and the nurse opened the incubator a crack. 'What have you chosen?' asked the man.

Charles heard himself say, 'Josephine. Josephine Celia.'

'That's very pretty. I name this child Josephine Celia, in the name of the Father, the Son and the Holy Spirit.'

His thumb gently marked her forehead. The baby's eyes flickered a little more. 'Can I touch her?' asked Ellen, but the nurse shook her head. Charles suddenly remembered the toy, crammed into his pocket. He drew it out. 'You can give her this,' he said softly. And Ellen took it and laid it down, a foolish blob of pink fur in a sea of equipment. 'For Josephine,' she said.

Outside, in the car park, Charles discovered that Ellen had skipped school and come on the bus. Expecting her to take a taxi, he offered to drive her home, and she said, 'Actually I wanted to see my mother.'

'Not today,' said Charles. 'She'll look worse than ever and you'll be upset. Tomorrow.'

She nodded, as if accepting an invitation. 'OK.'

It seemed as if he was to take her home. She curled up in the front seat of the Jaguar, her face closed against intimate talk. Nonetheless he said, 'How are David and Heather? Have things settled down?'

She nodded, abstractedly. He knew she wasn't telling the truth. 'Do you know what they're rowing about?' he asked bluntly.

She turned to look at him. 'I didn't say they were.'

'Yes, you did. Be honest, Ellen. David's drinking and Heather's nerves are in shreds.'

'If you know so much, why ask me?'

He hesitated. She was a child, she might not understand. But he didn't believe that. Ellen was harbouring a secret. Choosing his words with care, he said, 'I know your father was somehow involved in your mother's car crash. The one that started this whole thing off. I don't know what he did and I don't say it was deliberate. I just want you to tell me what you know.'

She curled her knees up and hugged them to herself. Charles felt a great pity for her suddenly. So much anxiety, so much pain, trapped in that youthful frame. She said, 'He won't get into trouble, will he?'

'I don't know. I don't think so. Not after so long.'

She took a shuddering breath. If he could have spared her he would, he thought. He longed to free her from the chains of adult guilt. But he had to know. 'Ellen—'

'It wasn't on purpose!' Her hands clenched into tight balls, reflecting the agonising tension inside her. 'It was a mistake. Dad makes those all the time, he's always thinking about something else. They serviced the car at the works and something was wrong. There's a spring in the suspension – the car's unstable, you see. The spring works OK, but really the whole thing ought to be redesigned, and Dad can't afford it. So there's a spring, and if it's not fitted everything's slack and dangerous. Dad brought the car from the works and realised at once something was wrong. They hadn't fitted the spring. He – he didn't tell Celia. And at this party they were at, tennis or

554

something, he had a bit to drink and forgot. At least, he didn't quite forget. He told someone to tell her. They didn't. They can't have. And she crashed.'

Charles moved smoothly down a gear, and let the Jaguar zoom into the distance. Ellen closed her eyes and said, 'Don't.'

'You heard your father say all this?'

'Yes. I listened. Do you think it was bad?'

'What? Listening?'

'No.'

'If it happened like he says it did – then it wasn't bad. It was one of those things. One of those stupid, avoidable things.'

Ellen let out a long, relieved sigh. She said, 'I don't want Mum and Dad to break up. I want us to be happy again, and Celia to be well and the baby – I want it all to be settled. Dad isn't the same any more.'

'You ought to talk to him.'

'I can't. He thinks I'm a little girl. That's the trouble, you see. I grew up and saw all the things they wanted to keep hidden, and I can't tell them what I see because they think they're things I shouldn't know. Nobody likes clever kids. No one says so, but it's true.'

He stopped the car in a layby and sat for a moment, holding the wheel. Then he saw the girl's anxious face. 'It's all right, I'm not going to murder you,' he assured her. 'I just need to say this carefully. I love your mother very much. I'm sure you know that. And I'm going to operate on her. But the thing I want you to understand is that she's probably going to die. I never say that sort of thing to people normally, because they might ask why I'm operating in the first place, and sometimes it's pretty hard to know. Except that if I didn't there'd never be any progress. Or hope. And there is a little bit of that.'

Her face, young and very still, appalled him. He looked away. He said, 'Whatever happens, I want you to know that I'm on your side. Because I can't do more for Celia than help you and Lucy in any way you need.'

Ellen watched him beneath her thick fringe of hair. She was wary still, he could see. Finally, she nodded. 'I'll remember that.' But he thought she wouldn't. He was, after all, an outsider. What this girl needed more than anything was Celia. Her mother.

He switched on the engine and felt the warm hum of good tuning. 'I like this car,' said Ellen, snuggling down into her seat. Her secret told, the dragon vanquished, she was a child again. He drove her home.

Edwin awoke in his bed on Sunday morning at Linton Place, aware that for some reason he couldn't at once recall he was in a foul temper. Then he remembered. The Sunday papers. On Friday, at the London club, George Marlborough had come in.

Friday was spent in London, discussing the interminable problems that beset the Marlborough chain. Edwin had set in train a massive programme of refurbishment, and containing costs and keeping things running meant long and arduous meetings. Business extended into the evening, and treating himself, he put on his dinner jacket, went into the club and played host. It was fun, to be greeted deferentially, and to be talked about behind hands. Perhaps he drank a little too much. And he had a thing going with one of the croupiers, a French boy with a pleasant and refreshing attitude. No passion here, no protestations of love, just money and satisfaction.

There was nothing to warn him of trouble. Edwin moved from table to table, well-dressed, gracious, looking for all the world as if he had the breeding that George Marlborough had dissipated in florid overindulgence. The French boy grinned at him across the tables, the champagne flowed, a film star won two hundred pounds and told everyone the place was wonderful. And then, to everyone's surprise, Marlborough himself came in.

The irony of it was, he wasn't exactly a member any more. He had a card, one of the old ones, but he hadn't ever paid any sort of a subscription. But what could anyone do, when he turned up half drunk and half belligerent, waving money and demanding to gamble? They couldn't risk a scene in the street. There was a gossip columnist there and several photographers, as well as the camera-toting customers who weren't above selling the odd snap for thousands. So, rather than cause trouble, Edwin let him play, getting more drunk and more belligerent by the minute.

He behaved as the worst customers do, sloshing liquor and talking loudly, treading on people and hailing acquaintances who turned out to be people he didn't know. The final straw was his bleary fondling of one of the croupiers. She was a svelte creature with long black hair that reached almost to the hem of her dress, and Marlborough's big pudgy hand went up that dress like a crab to its lair. She shrieked – for which she was later reprimanded, Edwin expected more control than that – and Marlborough roared, 'What's the creature screaming for? She's for sale, isn't she? Place is becoming a bloody nunnery!'

Edwin went across, signalling to the girl to take herself off. 'If you wouldn't mind, Sir George,' he said politely, 'we'll call you a taxi.'

'I do mind! I do bloody mind! Club for queers is it now, only nancy boys welcome? That your totty, is it, the foreign bimbo in trousers?'

Edwin felt himself pale to the point of unconsciousness, holding himself upright through pure willpower. Before he could signal to his security men, Marlborough blathered on, yelling, 'You got the damned place by playing dirty, but I suppose that's your style, you dirty little bugger! Go in arse first! Anyone you haven't screwed around here? Never seen such a lot of tarts.'

At last Edwin found the strength to act. He nodded to security and the giants descended. Marlborough was borne through the crowd, still bawling: 'Aren't we making everything nice and pretty? What the queers like, is it? A lot of frills?'

The fuss died down, of course, as these things always do. Edwin stayed just long enough for it not to appear that he was running for cover. He drove straight back to Yorkshire, thoughts running wild in his head. Suppose it was reported? Suppose it was believed? Suppose his father saw it?

He dressed and shaved, and called the dogs for their walk, although it was still very early. There would be something in the papers, he supposed. He prayed for only a small, snide paragraph. The dogs frolicked in the morning dew, sending ducks squawking into the air, startled out of early morning tranquillity. Soon, everyone would know. He'd be branded a pariah.

He calmed during the walk, and began to think more rationally. It would all blow over. In a week everything would be forgotten. It was a little disturbance in a London club, nothing more. But his nerves still jangled and the jangling turned to sheer panic as he saw Tomul with the Sunday papers. He ran back to the house, the dogs barking all around him, sensing his agitation. Grabbing the papers without a word, he spread them out on the polished wood of the dining table. And his heart sank.

The headlines read 'Marlborough in Dirty Protest', 'Gay Times Ahead!' and 'Who's a Pretty Bimbo Then?' Large photographs of Marlborough being thrown out like a vast balloon were juxtaposed with snaps of Edwin and, behind him, the croupier, lips pursed.

What's more, on the inside pages of one of the quality Sundays was an exposé of the Braddock takeover. 'Whatever else may be said,' concluded the article euphemistically, 'Braddock's deals are always secret, mysterious and hard to follow. He can't be surprised if people assume the worst.'

The telephone rang. A reporter. Edwin hung up at once and told Tomul to answer the telephone until further notice. It rang incessantly, disrupting Edwin's thoughts. Could he sue? It wouldn't be wise. It would only create scandal.

The day dragged by, interminable. In the early evening there came a call from the gate. 'Edwin. It's me.'

'Father?'

'Who else did you expect? One of your boyfriends? Let me in at once.'

If only he could leave him there. If only he need never face this man. But, inevitably, there was no escape. His father's old, seldom-driven car made its erratic way through the park to the house, stammering to a stop at the foot of the steps. A large, liver-spotted hand wrestled with the door, ignoring the servants. The old man roared, 'Edwin! Assist me. Do your duty.'

Obediently Edwin went to help him up the steps.

His father smelled of cough medicine and unaired clothes. Touching him was repellent, thought Edwin, progressing unpleasantly into the library. The old man demanded a fire, a drink, some food. Only when all was to his satisfaction did he glower at his son and say, 'All right, Edwin. This is the last straw. Finally you've let me down.'

Davenport and Perkins stood looking at the pictures in front of them. 'There's something there,' said Charles. 'The more I look at it the more I think so.'

'But where did it come from? She hasn't any recent injury. The accident was ten years ago!'

'She's had odd attacks for ages now. There must be a lesion of some kind. Suppose it's been there for years, exerting a tiny amount of pressure every time her blood pressure rises. That would account for a great deal, wouldn't it? Pregnancy, with its added strain, finally caused her collapse. We have two problems here, then. Two causes of her condition. Two reasons to operate.'

Perkins giggled, and Charles felt his hackles rise. Would the man ever control that nervousness? 'When do you think, sir? We're pretty booked up.'

'Make it next week sometime. Invite a few people to come and watch – it should be fascinating.'

He was aware of the younger man's surprise. It irritated him. But what did they expect, that he would go to pieces? He was professional enough, surely, to separate the personal element here. If he couldn't there would be no point in operating at all. He was the only person in the country, probably in the world, practising this technique, and he owed it to himself to maintain his professionalism above everything – everything – else.

One of his juniors shuffled in, a young man who had tried to give a lumbar puncture to a patient with suspected intra-cranial pressure, which would have had much the same result as piercing a balloon with a pin. Fortunately a nurse had stood up to him and there had been something of a row. She had apparently told him, 'You can yell all you like, but old man Davenport is going to tear one of us limb from limb, and I'd much rather it was you – so leave this patient alone!' Now the moment had come for the ritual limb tearing. Charles looked at the frightened young man, remembering the days when he would probably have kicked him off his staff for anything so stupid. Was he going to give him a second chance? He was new. His sin was ignorance.

He sighed. 'Did you really think you could get by on my department without any work? And I don't mean fifteen-hour days. I mean getting your head in a book and learning!' He dragged a volume from a shelf and thrust it at the boy. 'Get stuck into this. Take the morning to find out what tests are appropriate and when. After that go and buy that nurse the biggest bunch of flowers you can find, to thank her for saving the patient's life and your career. In this department you don't do anything unless you're one hundred per cent sure, and if you ask Perkins or me you'll get credit that you won't get if you blunder on and make a mistake. We're not ogres. At least, Perkins isn't.' He turned back to studying yesterday's test results. The junior, who had certainly been expecting the sack, sidled out. Perkins moved restlessly and Charles said, 'I take it you think I'm getting soft.'

'Not at all, sir.'

Charles linked his hands on the papers in front of him. 'He could turn out really well. He's a nice bloke, the patients like him.'

'Are you sure that's important, sir?'

Charles fought his irritation. 'It isn't unimportant. There are no perfect doctors, Perkins, so we have to take what we've got and teach them the things they don't know. Accuracy for the slapdash, and empathy for the brutal technicians. We're in danger of kicking out all the nice blokes because technicians don't make mistakes. They just make everyone bloody miserable. We're going to give the juniors time, Perkins, and see if we can make something of them.'

Greatly daring, he said, 'Which sort were you, sir?'

'Before I reached my current state of perfection, you mean?' Charles grinned mirthlessly. 'The brutal bloody technician, of course. Let's get on.'

★ ★ ★

560

The buzzing of the telephone woke Charles from a deep sleep. His hand reached out automatically for the receiver, while his mind still struggled up from the depths.

'Mr Davenport? Are you there?'

He heaved himself up on an elbow. 'Yes. What time is it?'

'Half-past two. It's Mrs Sheraton. Respiration poor, blood pressure falling – I think we're losing her.'

A moment of frozen horror. 'Mr Davenport?'

'Yes. I'm here. Get the team together, we'll operate. I'll be there in half an hour. Less. Get her ready.'

'Yes sir.'

He flung out of bed and into the bathroom, to throw cold water on his face to try and wake up. It was a mistake. He started to shiver, his system reeling from the shock of so sudden an awakening. In the car he turned the heater on full and tried to gather his thoughts. She wasn't going to make it. She had sent baby Josephine off on her perilous voyage, and was now herself sinking beneath the waves. This operation was a last-ditch stand, a hopeless attempt. But at least he would see what he had been dealing with for so long. The enemy would at last be confronted.

His first sight of the patient was in theatre, and then he felt a great jolt of pain. Her hair was gone. The fragile beauty of her skull, naked and vulnerable, caught at his heart. He should of course have expected it, but the familiar face in its unfamiliar setting gave him the greatest shock. He had a momentary longing to be anywhere else, doing anything else. He shouldn't have to do this thing, it was asking too much.

'Did anyone save the hair?' he asked gruffly.

'Sister Johnson, sir,' said Perkins.

'Oh. Right.'

Everyone was gathering round, getting settled, ready to begin. The sense of urgency was almost palpable. He usually liked to wait a second, to gather his thoughts, focus his concentration. Not tonight. Unhesitating, almost brutal, he drew the blade of his scalpel down Celia's naked head.

The routine calmed him. The painstaking drilling and sawing. As he began to remove his careful trapdoor, he felt a thrill of expectation. Now, at last, he would see.

A piece of bone was out of place. It lay like a needle, point down in the tissue below. He had been looking for some mild abrasion, some skull deformity, not this.

'Why on earth did we never see it?' he demanded. 'When this is over, Perkins, get every X-ray and scan that's ever been done and see if we can find it.'

'Yes, sir.' Perkins almost chortled with glee. 'Look at it, sir. An absolutely specific point of pressure.'

It was firmly embedded. Like a fishhook, it resisted backward pressure. Only after twenty minutes of the gentlest teasing could it be persuaded to come free. Charles laid it carefully in a dish, while small spots of blood welled from the site of its extraction.

'How is she?'

'Very weak. But not getting much weaker.'

'OK. We'll go on.'

Now they were going deep into the brain. After the Moffat boy they were used to the procedure and could achieve some element of speed. One of the nurses yawned suddenly and Charles asked for the time. It was almost seven, nearly four hours since he began. Suddenly the anaesthetist said, 'Wait a minute. I don't like her.'

'Can't stop now,' said Charles. 'I'm nearly there.'

'Blood pressure's dropping.'

'Right. Give me three minutes.'

'You might not get it.'

'I know.'

He slid his tiny instrument into the slippery, fluid-saturated depths of Celia's brain. His cut must be swift and exact. If the substance that these few cells produced was the cause of all her pain, then its production must be curtailed. He visualised the Moffat boy, tried to duplicate the exact extent of his attack.

'She's going!'

'I'm out.'

He stood back for ten minutes and watched them struggle. Blood, injections, oxygen. It wasn't a new scenario, he was no stranger to the moment when you took off the gloves, tossed them down and told someone to see the relatives. He never knew what to say. He ought to learn, he thought, and imagined telling Ellen; Lucy. David, damn him, would cheer.

'OK,' said someone. 'We've got her. Are you ready, sir?'

'When you are. Right, Perkins, let's close up.'

The job was done. The patient, swathed in gauze no whiter than her face, was wheeled from the room. 'Well done, sir!' said Perkins enthusiastically.

Charles said, 'I think the object of the exercise is for the patient to survive, you know. It isn't enough to do a beautiful job.'

'It could become standard procedure, though, sir. Martin Moffat's doing remarkably well, under the circumstances. It really is an achievement. You'll have to write something for the *Lancet*.'

Charles looked at him sardonically. 'You write it, Perkins. I'll wait. Strange as it may seem, this time I'm taking it slowly.'

He went and drank tea in his room. He felt at peace and knew it was because he had done all he could, right to the end, and had shirked nothing. The lives of Celia and her baby were in other hands now. He could do no more.

Gradually, as the adrenalin subsided and weariness took its place, he began to feel different. A creeping, numbing sense of desolation began. His day, his future, stretched ahead like a limitless desert, with nothing in it of pleasure or peace. He whispered suddenly, 'I can't bear it!' and put his hand to his mouth to force back tears he hadn't shed since childhood. If Celia had never existed, he thought, he would have been happier. What you never have you never miss. But her life was coming to an end and he didn't know how he was going to go on by himself. He had lost the capacity for loneliness.

There was a knock on the door and he cleared his throat and pulled himself together. It was his secretary, with the morning mail and the papers. She had brought him a bacon sandwich as well, because everyone knew he'd been in theatre all night. The thought of it turned his stomach but he thanked her all the same, and when she'd gone he hid the thing under a file. But an item in the paper's Stop Press caught his eye: 'Peer Beaten To Death'. The hasty, smudged print beneath read cryptically, 'George Marlborough attacked in London. Dead.'

563

He felt absolute amazement, so much so that he forgot himself and resurrected the bacon sandwich. George Marlborough had attacked Braddock and Marlborough was dead. Scientific training notwithstanding he couldn't help but jump to a conclusion.

Chapter Thirty-Eight

The police were really very polite. Edwin gave them coffee. He said, 'I can assure you, my takeover of Marlborough was quite legal, Inspector. And if someone battered old George to death then good luck to them. He was a drunkard by anyone's standards.'

'You didn't like him very much, did you, sir?'

'I did not beat him to death, Inspector.'

'Do you have an alibi for three in the morning on Thursday?'

'No, I do not. Like ninety per cent of the population I was asleep in bed. Do you have anything that links me to the scene of the crime? Otherwise you might just as well indict anyone at all. Marlborough had enemies enough.'

'I wonder if you recognise this?'

It was a photograph. A photograph of a walking stick, with a distinctive handle cut in the shape of a man's head. The eyes were closed, the hair blown back, the nose and chin jutting forcefully from the stem. It was Edwin's.

'I – I have had a stick like that. I'm sure I still have. Don't tell me—'

'It is the murder weapon, sir. Found at the scene of the crime.'

'But I'm not stupid! Would I leave my own walking stick there? Obviously it can't be me.'

'Nonetheless, sir. You'd be amazed how often these things turn out to be obvious.'

Edwin refused to say another word, he had already said too much. He telephoned his lawyer, while the police began a systematic search of the house. Feodor and Tomul clung together in an excess of anxiety, and the policemen said to one another, 'Right lot we've got here!' At noon Edwin was arrested and formally charged.

David was in his office when Heather called. He was surprised, she very rarely came to the works. He got up, saying, 'Darling!', arms outstretched.

'Edwin Braddock's been arrested for murder.'

'What?' He dropped his arms, shocked. 'It's not Celia, is it? Is she dead?'

'No.' She sat down in a heap in a chair. She felt exhausted. 'Don't you ever think of anyone else? It's George Marl-borough. They think Edwin beat him to death.'

'A bit macho for him, I would have thought.'

'All the same. He's been charged.'

David looked at her critically. Without make-up, she was dressed in her usual drab tweeds. Her hair needed cutting and suddenly she looked like a tired, sad, middle-aged woman. She annoyed him. It was almost an insult to him that she took so little care. He couldn't remember the last time she'd smiled at him, or even laughed easily in his presence. They lived, all of them, in shadow.

He said, 'Why did you come to tell me this? You don't think I did it, do you?'

She shook her head. But he said, 'You do think it, don't you? What's happened to us, Heather? You think I'm capable of anything!'

'Aren't you? I thought I knew you. I thought you were a good man. And all these years you've been telling me lies.'

'I made a stupid mistake. An error. It was a chapter of errors. Someone in the works made a mistake and all I did was omit to make sure that Celia was told. That was all. I promise.'

'But you've felt guilty for ten long years. I don't believe your promises any more.'

He stared at her, mastering himself. 'What is it you think I did? Apart from murder George Marlborough.'

'Don't joke, David! I think you deliberately caused Celia's accident. You knew the car was unsafe, you wanted her to crash. Then, when she came back to life, you deliberately set

566

fire to the Sheraton, to frighten her. And I think you tried to kill her, at least once.'

'I didn't do any of those things.'

'Didn't you? Didn't you? I look in your face and I see the guilt! I see how you're waiting, day by day, for her to die! I used to think you loved her, but you wanted her dead ten years ago, and you're tired of waiting. I never knew you before, David. I thought – I thought you were just like me.'

He ducked his head. 'All right! I set fire to the Sheraton. I wanted the insurance money. If that was wrong then I'm sorry, but that's the full extent of my sinning! Heather, underneath everything I am like you.'

But his admission had fuelled all her doubts. She shrieked, 'You don't even like sleeping with me, do you? Even that was pretend.'

'No!' He was galvanised now, and leaped from his seat. He came to her and took hold of her hands, squeezing them and kneading them. 'I like what we have. It's good and pure and wholesome—'

'It's not what you had with Celia, though. Now she really excited you. You wanted something different from her.'

He drew back and looked at her. Two spots of colour rode high on her cheeks. They gave her the colour she had lacked. He said, 'If I'd known you liked that kind of thing, I'd have given it you. That's the trouble, isn't it? You're jealous. You want what Celia had.'

'I don't want anything but the truth!'

The truth? He didn't know what was true any more. You thought you knew what you had done, and why you had done it, but even that was only a guess. He had loved Celia, and he had hated her too. If that was what Heather wanted then she should have it. 'Come on, then,' he murmured. 'I'll show you the truth. There's no one at home, let's go there and be truthful with one another.' He gripped her arm, brutally resisting as she tried to make him let her go. 'No, you don't, there's no backing off now. You don't trust me. You want what Celia had. You want to see what I'm like. Well, Heather, I'll show you!'

567

He was on fire with anger. His fingers drilled into her flesh as he propelled her out to the car. Some of the men lifted their heads from their work and looked at one another, and Heather whispered, 'Will you stop it, David? You're making a scene.'

He pushed her into her seat, started the engine and gunned the Sheraton into a roaring departure.

At the house she said, 'I don't want this, David. Go back to work.'

'You do want it. You said you did.'

'I said nothing of the kind!'

'Get upstairs, Heather.'

She was afraid of him. His eyes were very pale, almost white. His hair seemed to fly in uncontrolled wisps around his head, and when he touched her his hands held no tenderness. He might have been touching wood.

In the bedroom he dragged at her tweed jacket. She began to take it off herself, but he wouldn't wait and ripped it from her shoulders. He tore her blouse. She said, 'Don't! It's my favourite, it's silk.'

'It's cheap silk. My wife shouldn't wear cheap clothes.'

'But I'm not your wife. You were so busy waiting for Celia's insurance you wouldn't marry me!'

She had flicked him on the raw. 'Do you really think that? God, Heather, how you must despise me.'

He took hold of her shoulders and threw her down on the bed, and she tried to wriggle away. He threw himself on top of her, pinning her down, his hands on her breasts, his knee forced up between her legs. He pressed against her opening, almost brutal.

'This is what I did to Celia,' he said breathlessly. 'Do you like it? Do you?'

'David, stop it. Please stop it.'

'Why? You think she had the best of it, the best of me. How much more do you want?'

'None of it. Please, David, stop!'

'Not yet.'

He pushed her skirt up and her underclothes down, ripping what would not give way. He knelt between her knees, and she felt utterly exposed. She was naked, vulnerable, opened up like a snail stripped of its shell. He closed his fingers in her pubic hair, a rough, painful caress. When he let her go he pulled himself free of his trousers, his sex like a solid thing, iron hard and unrelenting. She didn't expect him to stop now. She lay, tense as a bow, and watched him, the man that she loved, the man to whom she had given her trust. He came down on her and into her, hard, cruel, a male of the species taking his pleasure. And he wasn't even drunk!

She turned her face to the pillow, away from him, and began to cry. He heaved up and down, his body pounding into hers, punctuating each thrust with an animal grunt. She reached out and pulled the pillow over her face, wanting to smother it out. She wouldn't endure this. She couldn't. He slowed on her, and was still.

'Heather? Heather, don't.'

She lifted a tear-drenched face. 'Go on and finish. Why don't you? It's what you want.'

'I don't want to hurt you.'

'How can you say that now?'

He knew he should leave her, roll aside and be done. If he wanted to have anything left in his life then he should. But he was sick of dishonesty, sick of pretending. She ought to know what he was like. He put his face to hers, muttering, 'Don't mind it. I won't be long – I love you, Heather – I won't ever do this again—'

Stone cold, both inside and out, she felt his breath on her cheek, his hands on her skin, his climax deep inside her. As he subsided, gasping, a dead weight bearing her down, she wondered if she had ever really known him.

The thought haunted her through the next days, the apologies, the flowers. When Celia had her accident Heather had been so ready to accept him, she hadn't really thought further than that. Now she suspected everything, every motive, every chance occurrence. David, the man she had loved and cared for all these years, seemed suddenly a monster.

When the weekend came she couldn't face the family. She left, before ten, intending to go to the office, but found instead that she was driving aimlessly around. There seemed to be no one she could talk to, no one who could understand. Suddenly she thought of Charles.

She didn't know what she expected of the house. Chaos, perhaps. It would be no surprise if Charles had gone to pieces, living out his nightmare amidst tangled roses and dark windows. But he greeted her at the door, in jeans and sweatshirt, and the house was warm and rather stark. A pot of coffee bubbled on the stove.

She said, 'I hope I'm not spoiling your weekend.'

He said, 'I was working, actually. When you do new work you've got to write it up quite soon or you forget all the problems you had.'

'How's—' she hesitated, wondering how to phrase it.

'The baby? Celia? As you'd expect. Not good.'

'Surely the baby at least—'

He shook his head. 'I know Ellen keeps visiting. I wish she wouldn't. She's going to be so hurt.'

He looked so calm and rational. Heather was a little shocked. She sat at the table, taking the coffee he offered, watching him sprawl his long legs and rest a relaxed elbow. 'I thought you cared for her!' She hadn't meant to say it. But recently the control she exerted on her utterances seemed to have gone slack; she found herself saying anything sometimes.

In an iron voice he said, 'Do you want me to cry all night? Drink myself to death? Would that suit you better?'

'But you're just going on as before.'

He grimaced, and sipped his coffee. 'Not quite. But the changes don't show, thank God. I'm – different. I'm getting used to being alone again. There's never going to be anyone else.'

'That's silly! Of course there will be.'

He shrugged. 'If I wanted, I suppose. But I don't. If this has come to what it has then I'd rather live my life alone.'

'I wish David had,' said Heather. Then she flushed and added, 'I don't mean that!'

Charles felt a small, satisfying flicker of triumph. In his

570

heart of hearts he wanted David Sheraton to be miserable. That he should find it possible to be happy had been for Charles a sick joke. 'What's he done now?'

'Nothing! At least – everything. He tried to kill her.'

'Do you know that? For sure?'

'Why else would he be so guilty about her? After all these years?'

Charles sighed. Heather was so relentlessly black and white. And so, once, was he. 'I don't think he ever had the courage to try and kill her. He might have wanted to – briefly. But he never did anything. David's mixed up when it comes to women. He wants a mother and a lover and he can't accept them both in the same person. Even within the same decade. Celia was the lover, you're the mother. Sometimes he hates what Celia made him feel and do. Sometimes he wants more excitement from you. It isn't totally without precedent.'

'You do really believe that? You think he's – safe?'

Charles shrugged. 'As safe as anyone. We're all capable of more than we imagine, Heather. Even you.'

She laughed, shakily. 'Are you talking about Braddock? I suppose – it looks as if – I behaved very badly, didn't I?'

'Yes, Heather. You did.'

She looked down at her hands, the nails broken. She knew she looked a mess. If only she could get back to being the person she used to be, neat, disciplined, with none of these awkward, nagging doubts. She said, 'I don't know if I want to live with him any more. That's the truth of it. I want more than before. I want to be married, I want to be a mother. A real mother. Do you think I'm too old?'

He considered. 'Thirty-nine, aren't you? I'm no gynae-cologist but you could do it. Your body's a bit set in its ways after thirty-nine years of undisturbed living, so you'd certainly know what was happening, but if you wanted – do you really want David's child?'

'I don't know. I want my child. For me.'

She stayed for lunch, and he opened some white wine and made omelettes. Heather had the feeling that he was being patient with her, and she was surprised. Charles Davenport had never done anything that didn't immediately please him, not in her experience anyway. She was getting giggly on his wine when the doorbell rang. Charles raised his eyebrows. 'If things go on like this I shall have to dig a moat.' The bell rang again and he called, 'Come in! It's not locked.'

It was Edwin Braddock.

They were both stunned. Heather said at last, 'I thought you were in prison. For murder.'

Edwin said, 'How kind of you to give me the benefit of the doubt, Heather.'

Charles laughed. 'Don't mind her, she's drunk. Here, have a glass yourself. You look as if you need it.'

He did indeed. Immaculate as always, in pinstripe and starched shirt, the skin of his face was tight across the bones. He was pale to the point of greenness, and when he reached for his wine they saw that his hand was shaking.

'I take it you're on bail,' said Charles.

'Yes. For a huge sum. They really think it was me.'

'And was it?'

'No.'

He drank the wine thirstily, and Charles went to the fridge for another bottle. He brought some cheese too, and half a loaf, and Edwin picked at the food without appetite.

'You can't blame us all for suspecting you,' said Charles easily. 'Let's think of what's happened. Arson. Burglary. Kidnap. And several attempts to cause Celia to die in a car, not to mention the man who did die in that fire in Strasbourg.'

'An accident,' said Edwin. 'I explained it all to Celia.'

'Who isn't in a position to tell us that at the moment.' Charles leaned back in his chair. 'You don't get my vote of confidence.'

'I'm not asking for it.'

Some colour was returning to Edwin's cheeks. He drank some more wine, closing his eyes appreciatively. 'This is quite good. One doesn't expect doctors to have much of a palate. All that exposure to noxious substances.' He glanced up at them both. 'I don't want favours. Merely your dispassionate observations. The attempts on Celia's life were not mine. Who was really behind them? David?'

Heather gulped. Charles said, 'He's a possible. But I don't

quite think so. He doesn't have the guts.'

Edwin said, 'What about you, Heather? You hated her enough.'

Heather's colour came up. But she met Edwin's gaze for long enough to say, 'She's the girls' mother! I wouldn't. I – didn't. I won't say I didn't feel like murder sometimes, but I'm not that sort.'

'So few of us are,' said Edwin drily.

'Let's run down the list,' said Charles, enumerating events on his fingers. 'The Will. We know all about that. You and David worked together to get your hands on the loot. Very devious. Then, ten years later, a car goes on fire. Probably David. A house burns down. Down to you, old chap. Burglary. You again. Car chase that looks like kidnap. You?'

After a moment Edwin nodded. 'We didn't plan anything more than a short period of detention. She really was being tiresome. I feared for my entire fortune.'

'How terrible for you. Let me go on. The attempt to drive Celia into the canal. David? You?'

Edwin shook his head. 'I really don't know. Any more than I know who killed George Marlborough. And he was a man who deserved everything he got.'

'David didn't know George Marlborough,' said Heather testily. 'And you did. I'm sure the police have very good reason for charging you.'

Edwin said, 'Merely my walking stick. And I say again, it wasn't me.'

'So it was someone else,' said Heather, her logical mind clicking like a computer. 'Someone with a real grudge, who wanted to do you down once and for all. And it couldn't be Celia.'

'I agree,' said Edwin. 'Not even Celia, for all her remarkable qualities, could rise from a deathbed to commit murder. That's why I came here, Charles. I thought it might be you.'

Charles stared at him. 'Me?'

'Why not? You're more than ready to fight Celia's battles. It might be your idea of a last duty, so to speak. To get at me. My reward a prison cell, my heritage gone.' Edwin waved a hand theatrically and Charles began to laugh. 'It wasn't me,' he said.

'And any half good counsel could get you off if all the evidence they have is a walking stick.'

'My God, Charles, they convict people on anything nowadays! If it goes to trial I'm done for. You know what it's like. These days everyone wants to throw stones at people like me.'

Heather got unsteadily to her feet and went to make some coffee. There was an odd companionability about the gathering, sheltering from a cold grey world and a cold grey afternoon. All at once Edwin became amusing, telling tales of his father and old Joe Braddock. 'They loathed each other, you know. Never exchanged a civil word in forty years, but Joe kept on inviting us to the house, and we kept on going. Farcical.'

'I was scared of Joe,' confessed Heather. 'He was very polite, very formal, and I just knew that he hated my guts. Not because I was me, you understand. I wasn't Celia.'

They nibbled at cheese, and Charles fetched the brandy and gave everyone a tot. Something that was held tight inside him, something he hadn't even known was in a knot, began gradually to unravel. He felt a sense of ease, suddenly. Life was going to be possible after all. He didn't need to fight and struggle, to fill every hour with labour and give no time to thought. He could survive. He said, 'This is the first time I've enjoyed myself in months.'

Edwin said, 'This may be the last time I enjoy myself for years,' and they all laughed uproariously. It was a strange afternoon.

The telephone rang and Charles groaned. 'It's bound to be the hospital. Answer it will you, someone? It'll be some nurse checking up. I've a junior that no one believes. He makes life-threatening mistakes.'

'How wonderfully reassuring,' said Edwin thinly. 'When the constabulary beat me to jelly, remind me to avoid your hospital at all costs.'

'I'll go,' said Heather, and got to her feet. They heard the rise and fall of her voice in the hall.

'It's David,' said Charles. 'I bet he's tracked her down.'

'I really do have the greatest contempt for that man's

574

abilities,' said Edwin. 'For all her primitive values, Heather deserves better than that.'

She came back into the room. Something in her face alerted them. Charles felt the brandy rise up in his throat. He went to the sink and gripped the cold porcelain, suddenly wishing that they would go, that he could be alone to absorb whatever terrible thing had happened.

Heather said, 'Celia's awake.'

He didn't at first understand her. He lifted his head, like a lion waking from sleep, bemused and gruff. 'What did you say?'

'They asked me to tell you – Celia's awake. She spoke. They want you to go.'

Charles licked his lips, dry and tasting of brandy. He had been drinking but never felt more sober in his life. He found his keys, moving like an automaton, and became aware that Edwin and Heather were watching him. 'See yourselves out,' he said vaguely.

'Of course. Don't concern yourself.'

'No.'

When he'd gone Edwin and Heather looked at each other. 'Alone at last,' he said flippantly. 'God knows what happens now.'

Heather said, 'David won't get the insurance money. He needed it so!'

'My dear girl, even with the pearls?'

'We needed more. We need to expand.'

Edwin sighed. 'Don't you ever think, Heather, that David can dispose of more money to less purpose than any man in history? The King John of private enterprise.'

'You owe us! You know you do!'

'Don't be tiresome, my dear.'

Housewife to the last, Heather gathered up the cups and plates and washed them. Then she picked up her coat and made ready to go. 'What a mess everything's in,' she said suddenly. 'It's what comes of cheating, I suppose.'

'Not in the least,' retorted Edwin. 'It comes of denying the natural order of things. If Celia had died when she should there would be no problem at all.'

'We'd all just live on our ill-gotten gains,' said Heather. 'All of a sudden I feel sorry for Celia. She should never have been so rich.'

'She was rich all right,' mused Edwin. 'The fates can't abide such wealth as was hers. An abundance of beauty, sex and money. And we envious little people couldn't wait to take it all away.'

He poured himself another brandy, and stood in the kitchen, dapper even now. He would go soon, back to his house and his dogs. Although she was going back to turmoil, Heather envied him not at all.

Chapter Thirty-Nine

The nurse got up as Charles entered. He said, 'I'll watch her. I'll call you when I go.'

She nodded and he went to the bed. It was in shadow, a dim cavern in which dials glowed green and lights burned fiercely red. One hand lay outside the bedclothes, impossibly long and white. Charles touched the fingers and they closed on his.

'Hello, Celia.'

'Charles.'

Her voice grated, the vocal cords sore from long hours on a ventilator. He said, 'How do you feel?'

'Terrible. Ill. What have you done to me?'

'We delivered the baby by Caesarean section and then operated on your head.'

'The baby?'

'A little girl. Ellen named her Josephine. She's – she's in an incubator.'

A slow smile spread over Celia's face. 'Josephine,' she murmured. 'Can I see her?'

'No. She's very tiny. She can't be moved.'

'When I'm better then. I'll go to her.'

'Yes.'

He held her hand while a great thankfulness began in him, an emotion he could not express in this quiet, secluded place. The box into which he had crammed all his useless, difficult feelings had burst open and spilled everything once again. He reached out and touched the head upon the pillow, with fine gold fluff growing beyond the bandages.

'We cut your hair,' he said to her. 'But I love it like this.'

'Do you?' Her huge eyes blinked sleepily in the dim light. 'I thought I was dying,' she confided. 'I dreamed I was dead. I was only sad because of you.'

'Why?'

'You didn't know how much you meant to me. How important you were. Perhaps I didn't know until you were gone.'

'You told me once that you loved David and always would. You didn't care if he loved you back, it didn't matter. He was the one.'

She chuckled, and his heart felt as if it would burst. 'Did I really say that? You didn't believe me, did you?'

'No. I never believe things that don't suit me.'

'You autocrat, you.'

He bent his head and touched her lips with his own. A long slender arm reached up around his neck, too weak to do more than hold him with its negligible weight. When she blinked her lashes brushed his cheek, when he breathed she tasted the brandy he had drunk. 'I love you more than my life,' he whispered.

'I love you more than that,' she replied. 'Living's so hard, sometimes it's tempting to stop. I love you enough to keep on living when I'm so tired I could die.'

He sat for a while after she slept. He could not abandon the thought that she would slip away again at any moment. But the nurse came in to do her checks, and said, 'Isn't it exciting, sir? Two! You'll be famous.'

'They're probably the only two people in the country who need this treatment. It's a fringe thing, that's all.'

'Sister Johnson says you could revolutionise neurology. She says you'll always be remembered for your work.'

'Sister Johnson said that? Nurse, are you being facetious?'

'No, sir. It's what she said.'

'Good God.'

If the brandy had failed to affect him earlier, it was making up for it now. He felt drunk and incapable. He reeled from Celia's room into the brightness of the ward where Sister Johnson was parading with all her usual stiff-backed correctness. She was like the rhinoceros, thought Charles, overtaken by progress, its very existence under threat, but still

578

retaining the ability to thunder out of thickets and terrorise people.

'I'm glad you're looking pleased with yourself, Mr Davenport,' she said when she saw him. 'You're to be congratulated.'

'Thank you, Sister. We didn't deserve this one. She should have died.'

'Oh, I think you deserve it. You've turned into a very good doctor and an excellent surgeon.'

He took both her hands in his. 'Well done, Sister. When I think of the unpromising material you had to deal with, it's good to know you finally knocked it into shape.'

'Behave, Mr Davenport,' she said calmly. 'I appreciate your exuberance, but this isn't the place. Take yourself home.'

But he couldn't go home. He wanted to hover outside Celia's room, to experience every instant of her waking. Members of his team started to appear, and each one sought to congratulate him.

'Can we go public, sir?' asked Perkins.

'No! Definitely not. We don't want every sad and hopeless case ending up at our door. I'm writing an article for the *Lancet*. It's all that's necessary.'

Eyebrows were raised. This was a change of tune and no mistake from the days when Celia Sheraton was being exhibited on an overhead projector as a fifteen-foot nude. General chatter began about possibilities for the future, but the cacophony was suddenly stilled. Moffat had come in.

'Charles,' he said stiffly. 'Just to add my congratulations.'

'Thank you. How's Martin today?'

'Quite well. We're teaching him to eat with a spoon.'

'I did say—'

'Yes. It's a price we were willing to pay. We're hoping to have him home soon.'

'Does he want to go home?'

'Oh, yes.' There was a pause and Moffat looked embarrassed. 'It's as we hoped, you know,' he managed at last. 'We've got a second chance. And we're not going to make a mess of it this time.'

Charles nodded and made encouraging noises. Whatever

Sister Johnson said, he would never be good at this sort of thing. The easy pleasantries were never easy for him.

Suddenly Moffat said, 'It strengthens the case, of course. Celia's case. I'm sure we can win.'

Charles felt irritated by him. 'Can't we let that drop? It's only money. I'm sick of people talking about money.'

'She's going to need some means of support. We could try and settle. What about three million?'

'Nobody needs that much support,' said Charles sardonically.

'When the publicity starts it's bound to help,' said Moffat. 'When will she be fit for television?'

'Never,' said Charles. 'She's not going on television. She isn't a circus animal, to be exhibited!' Suddenly he'd had enough. His temper snapped. 'Get out of here, will you?' he roared, and bore down on Moffat, forcing him to back away. 'Be off with you, man. This is a hospital, not some money-grubbing law office!' He slammed the door on Moffat's retreat. At last.

His staff were hiding their amusement. Charles realised he had fulfilled all their expectations. If it amused them, he thought. But with Moffat gone he felt at a complete loose end.

'Is there anything to do?' he asked Perkins. 'A round or something?'

'It's visiting, sir.'

'Oh.'

He wandered off, disconsolate. What could he do during visiting hours when all he wanted was to shout and burst balloons? Visit someone. It was the only thing. Josephine. He set off for the special baby unit, purposeful at last.

Ellen was there. He beamed at her, putting out his hands to sweep her honeyed mass of hair into a pony-tail which he held on the top of her head. 'Hi, beautiful! Just to tell you your mum's awake. She talked to me.'

Ellen pushed at his hands and the hair fell in a tangle over her face. She threw handfuls away, spitting hair out of her mouth. 'You mean she's better? For good?'

'I don't know about that. For now. Very weak, of course,

but conscious. You don't know what it's been like, Ellen. If she'd recovered and been impaired – she wouldn't have thanked me. And I'd got so used to thinking it was all going to end, I can't believe that it isn't.'

'Can I see her?'

'Not yet, love. Tomorrow perhaps.'

The colour was flooding into Ellen's pale face. Charles thought how little he had considered the strain she was under. He never understood the pain people felt until afterwards. He thought of the baby, on which Ellen pinned all her hopes and he none. 'Let's go in and see Josephine,' he said. 'To celebrate.'

The nurse was difficult about Ellen, but Charles bullied her and she gave in. 'These women get so proprietorial,' he said in an undervoice. 'They think the babies are theirs.'

'Does the baby know she's ours, do you think?' asked Ellen. 'She might think she does belong to the nurse.'

They stood either side of the glass box, looking down at their tiny point of interest. She wasn't perceptibly bigger. From time to time her mouth made little sucking movements, and she swam against the mattress, like a badly designed fish.

'If I wasn't going to be a mechanic, I'd be a baby doctor,' said Ellen firmly.

'You could do worse,' said Charles. 'People are just complex machines.'

'Do you really think that?'

'No. Actually I don't. I could never fall in love with a machine.'

Ellen looked up at him and laughed. Charles felt his heart stir. He felt a great affection welling up in him, because Celia, the source of all his joy, was his again. At that moment he wanted to embrace the whole world.

Celia woke in the night and lay listening to the squeaks and buzzes of the machines that monitored her every function. She felt like a specimen in a laboratory, an experimental animal. She cleared her throat and the nurse rose from her seat at the bottom of the bed.

'Would you like a drink, Mrs Sheraton? Shall we clear your tubes?'

'No, thank you.'

She didn't know which part hurt most. When she moved her legs the scar in her stomach pulled, when she turned her head hair prickled against her scar, and when she lifted her arm her hand throbbed from the insertion of canulas into flat and resistant veins. But she was alive. That had to be good.

'How's my baby?' she asked. 'Have you seen her?'

'Not yet, no. She's quite famous. We don't often have them so small.'

'She is all right?'

'As far as I know. Shall I get someone to talk to you in the morning?'

'Yes, please.'

She lay back on her pillow. The night stretched ahead, quite limitless, and ordinarily she would be bored. Not tonight. She felt as if she was newly present in her body. Every thought and every movement seemed in some way strange and different. She began checking herself out, wriggling toes and fingers, closing first one eye and then the other. She held her tongue between her teeth and relished the sharp sensation. Both sides of her body were functioning, as far as she could tell. It was wonderful.

Someone came to the door. 'Phone call for you,' she said to the nurse. 'A friend.'

'I can't take it. I can't leave here.'

'She's OK, isn't she? He said it was urgent.'

'Can you hang on here then?'

'No, I've got to get back.'

'Damn! Look – I'll just be five minutes.'

They slipped out of the room and left Celia to herself. How delightful it was, she thought, to be unobserved. To be alone with her body. She was constantly watched, measured and stimulated. But the door opened again and she sighed. So brief a luxury.

'That was quick,' she said hoarsely. There was no reply. She turned her head a little on the pillow. It wasn't the nurse. Someone was coming to the bed, hat pulled down, feet shuffling on the floor. 'What do you want?' asked Celia. No answer. With a sense of terrible foreboding, she knew why this person had come.

Using all her strength she moved away across the bed, trying to urge her legs out and on to the floor. The electrodes on her breast came with her, trailing inelegantly on all sides, and the monitors peeped away happily, noting increased heart rate without alarm. Her feet met the cold floor, but she could not possibly stand. She crumpled in a heap, and the intruder swung like a robot in the dark, coming round the bed to get her.

'Get away from me!' she whispered hoarsely. 'Don't touch me!'

He was breathing heavily. She could smell him, alien in this sterile world. She must defend herself!

Reaching out feebly, desperately, she touched the drip stand at the side of her bed. She dragged at it with all her might, but her strength was puny and the stand quite strong. She reached up higher. If it would not fall it might support her. As she pulled above the centre of gravity, the stand crashed down. It missed Celia, it missed her attacker, but the monitor met its end. A shrill note of alarm ripped through the night. 'POWEEEE, POWEEEE,' it screamed.

Something crashed against the wall behind her head. The alarm shrieked on, 'POWEEEE, POWEEEE', the lights came on and her attacker was gone.

'Oh, my God, you fell out of bed,' said the nurse. 'The old man will kill me if Sister doesn't get there first. Oh my God!'

Celia gazed up at her with panic in her eyes. 'Someone was here! They tried to hurt me!'

'You fell, didn't you?'

'No. It was a man, didn't you see anyone? You must have done, he threw something against the wall.'

'There isn't anything here. I can't see anything.'

'You must!'

'Ouch! It's melted the paint. It's acid.'

It was the beginning of a long night. Security was called, who in turn called the police. All entrances to the hospital were guarded, but no one was found. Besides, who were they looking for? A man of some kind. Celia was moved to another room and a guard posted ouside her door. She insisted they call Mr Davenport.

He came with a sweater pulled on over his pyjamas and when she saw him Celia burst into tears. 'I don't know what he was going to do, Charles. He had acid!'

'Did he indeed?'

'Why is it still going on!'

He put his arm around her and soothed her, but he felt far from calm himself. 'Was it David? Edwin? Would you have known?'

'I don't know. It was dark. He didn't speak, just shuffled in.'

'Shuffled? Was he old, or disabled?'

'Possibly. But it could have been an act.'

'Why pretend, if you're going to kill someone?'

'In case someone came in. He smelled odd too.'

'Like?'

'I'm not sure. The sort of thing you use to rub on strains.'

It was all she could say. He went to look at her room and saw the paint burnt through to the plaster. He had no doubt at all that a moment more would have seen Celia with acid down her throat. The thought was nauseating.

As he went around the hospital, questioning anyone who might have seen something and getting no more than the police had, he felt the burn of his anger. It was mixed with outrage, the same feeling he had when a child came in, or a boy off a motorbike, with gross injuries which need not have happened at all. The body was so fragile, so utterly precious, and people conspired so easily in its destruction. And for someone to threaten Celia – after all this!

He went out to his car. He had to see David. Driving fast and furious he roared through the lanes and byways, startling owls and roaming foxes, careering up to the door of Blantyre House. He sounded his car's horn, urgent, demanding. All the lights came on, and in a minute or two David appeared at the top of the steps. He was fastening his dressing gown.

584

'What the hell do you think you're doing? Have you finally gone stark raving mad?'

'I don't know,' said Charles furiously. 'Possibly. Someone tried to kill Celia tonight and I want to know if it was you.'

'Is she all right?' It was Heather, and behind her the sleepy faces of the girls.

'She's OK. No thanks to anyone. A phone call took the nurse away long enough for someone to try and choke her with acid. He didn't touch her, thank God, but my first thought was of you. Where were you at about half-past two?'

Nobody said anything. All at once Heather turned away and burst into tears. 'They had a row,' supplied Ellen. 'Dad went out.'

David said, 'You can't possibly think I'd attack Celia with acid! I admit I was angry. But—'

'But nothing,' said Charles. 'You burned the Sheraton, didn't you? And what else?'

'Nothing else. I swear, nothing. Look, you can't prove it was me.'

'And you can't prove it wasn't.'

David seemed as if turned to stone. Only a muscle worked the point of his jaw. Heather's sobs punctuated the night, and Lucy said, 'Don't, Mum. Dad wouldn't do anything awful. I know he wouldn't.'

Ellen, cold and strained, said, 'Don't admit it, Dad! You're safe until you do.'

He turned to her, hands outstretched in pleading. 'I did nothing to hurt anyone tonight. I never meant to hurt your mother. My darling, darling girl, I want you to believe me. I caused your mother's accident. The fault was mine. But only because I told someone to tell her the car was dangerous and didn't tell her myself! At the time I wondered – I was so guilty. Sometimes I imagined I'd meant her to die. But I didn't. I loved her. I really did. Nobody should have to live with a mistake as long as I have!'

Charles stood silent. How clear it all was now. David had wrestled with his guilt over years, never knowing if his forgetfulness had been deliberate or not. It might have been.

585

And to add to it, he had tried to subvert Joe's Will, and ended up with nothing. So he pinned all his hopes on Celia's life policy, and she thwarted him then and didn't die. Whatever he did, whichever way he turned, he couldn't profit! The fates conspired to oppose him.

'When the accident happened,' he said quietly, 'who did you tell about the state of the car? Edwin? Celia's mother? Who?'

David rubbed a hand across his eyes. He was trembling like a leaf in autumn. 'Henry Braddock. Joe's brother. A cantankerous old bastard at the best of times, never got on with Joe. But he was always there, pushing Edwin on, trying to get his foot in the door.'

'Is he still alive?'

'Henry? Yes, I think so. He doesn't get about much now. Had a run-in with that arthritis drug – Opren, wasn't it? He doesn't go out in the light. Pretty bad deal, all in all.'

'Yes. It sounds it.'

Charles turned away. He was finished with David for tonight. Heather said, 'Are you going to tell the police, then?'

'What should I say? I don't think he was there tonight.'

'Then who was?'

'I don't know. Edwin, perhaps. I'll go there now.'

Ellen said, 'Don't. Or at least, not alone. He's got dogs.'

'I'm not scared of Edwin Braddock,' said Charles with a laugh. 'He's got one murder charge hanging over him as it is.'

'And another one wouldn't hurt,' said Heather. 'She's right, you shouldn't go alone. I'll come. I'll bring the dog.'

Charles protested but it wasn't any use. Heather insisted on coming, slippers, dressing gown and small grey dog included. It sat on the leather of the back seats, looking lugubrious and sleepy.

'This is just stupid,' complained Charles.

'It's only sensible to have a witness,' said Heather. 'We don't know what Edwin might be driven to. He's a very odd man.'

'We were drinking brandy with him, not twelve hours ago!'

'He's still ruthless.'

Sighing, Charles started the engine. Heather gripped her

586

seatbelt with nervous hands, and he was irritated with her. If she was going to lack courage he would rather go alone. He would rather go alone in any case.

When they reached Linton Place they buzzed and buzzed at the gates. After ten minutes or so a voice on the intercom said, 'Yiss? It is night. What you want?'

'I'm a doctor and a friend of Mr Braddock. My name is Charles Davenport and I have to see Mr Braddock at once.'

They waited, in silence, and Charles buzzed once again. The sky was lightening on the far horizon, a pale glow above the trees. At last the gates creaked open.

They were ushered into the library, the dog pressing close to Heather's legs. They found Edwin before a newly lit fire. He was wearing black silk pyjamas, as crisp as if they had but that minute been taken from their packet. 'Charles! Heather!' he exclaimed, coming towards them in welcome. 'What on earth has happened? You must be frozen. Tomul, fetch some tea. Or would you prefer cocoa? We can pretend we're at war.'

'We may be,' said Charles.

Edwin looked confused. 'What on earth do you mean? Has Celia – is Celia—'

'No,' said Charles. 'But she should be. Someone tried to force acid down her throat.'

'My God!'

Edwin fell back in amazement. It was a mistake. The action was too studied, too thought out. He had spent the time since the first buzz at the gate deciding how he would react. He had arranged a little theatre, with himself as the star. The anger which Charles thought he had suppressed bubbled up like a hot well of mud and burst forth into the air. 'You bastard!' he roared. 'You unprincipled bastard! You tried to murder her!'

He went for Edwin in a rush. Heather shrieked, and an Alsatian appeared from nowhere and leaped. Charles flung up an arm, but it took him in the chest and bore him down.

'No! No!' screamed Heather. Tip, the cross-bred bull terrier, went like a rocket across the floor. It hit the Alsatian full force, going straight for the throat, a fighting dog doing what suited him best. The Alsatian, too big and all mouth, found himself beset by a whirling, slashing dervish. The dogs spun away across the rug, a snarling mass.

'Get it off!' yelled Edwin. 'Get the brute off! He'll kill my Lupus.'

Charles got to his feet. He was bleeding from the hand. 'You call yours first,' he told Edwin.

'I'll catch him. I promise.'

Heather, hands to her chin, called, 'Tip! Tip, come!' And then, when the dog took no notice, 'Tip! Tip, will you come! Good boy!'

The dog ignored her. Edwin was wringing his hands, and blood flew in a rainbow arc from Tip's teeth. Greatly daring, Heather made a lunge for her dog, his feet scrabbling for a hold on the polished wood floor. With a last flurry of rage, he broke away. Heather caught him up and held him. 'I told you there'd be trouble,' she told Charles righteously.

Edwin was examining Lupus. 'He's ripped lumps out of him,' he said in a shaking voice. 'You shouldn't keep a brute like that.'

'Yours was the brute,' said Charles, wrapping his hand in his handkerchief.

'You attacked me. He was doing his duty. And I tell you again, whoever tried to kill Celia tonight wasn't me.'

Charles sighed wearily. He was tired of these endless denials. 'Someone tried to kill her,' he said tightly. 'Who do you suppose it was? The same person who knocked Marlborough on the head? Busy soul, isn't he?'

A voice from the door said, 'If you like.'

They all turned. A man was standing there. He was old and had once been tall. He had the deathly pallor of someone to whom daylight is a stranger, and the cramped and crabbed hands of the arthritic, shining with embrocation. Wintergreen. The smell Celia had recalled. 'Henry Braddock!' said Charles incredulously. 'You are Henry Braddock? Joe's brother.'

'His younger brother,' said Henry. 'He left me out of his Will, you know. I hadn't even got my compensation, but he left me out just the same. Mean bastard, my brother. His daughter was just like him. No family loyalty.'

'Father,' said Edwin, warningly.

'Shut up and let me speak!'

Charles said, 'It was you tonight. At the hospital.'

'Yes.'

'How much else? The initial crash, of course.'

Henry snorted. 'Hardly! A sin of omission, no more. But, as always, my brother proved unhelpful. If he could avoid helping someone he would. Kept the money all to himself. Never did a thing for Edwin. Not a damned thing. He got his deserts, of course, when he died. And I hope he's up there now, seeing it all. I got Edwin the money, I got him the firm, I got him everything. But he squanders it. He's a useless boy in many ways. Extravagant. And corrupt, of course. After all I've suffered, to have a pervert for a son!'

Edwin was crooning to his dog. He looked up and said, 'That's all you ever thought me, wasn't it? A pervert. You never saw anything else in me. Nothing of quality. Nothing to commend.'

'Don't whinge, boy. You've got brains, I'll give you that. My brains. But still you don't stand pressure.'

'What sort of pressure?' asked Charles. 'Murder charges? You killed Marlborough, didn't you? And implicated your son.'

Edwin said, 'He couldn't! He didn't! Not even he—'

'Why not me?' Henry swung his big head aggressively. 'Why not? The night's my own time. My only time. At night I can do what I want. It amused me to use your stick. The man was drunk, the thing was easy, and your stick was so good for the job. I worked in the mines as a boy, you know. Joe did too, it's where we got our strength. He never did a thing for me, never helped me to get out, never gave me a hand. And I knew if Edwin was made of anything, he'd find a way to get off. It was up to me to see that Edwin changed. To make him strong.'

His son's face was suffused with dark colour. 'You're a wicked old bastard!' he swore. 'You don't care what you put me through. You haven't a shred of conscience, an ounce of kindness! Who do you hate more? Me or Celia?'

The old man stared at him. 'I hate Celia. I despise you.'

Edwin choked back an hysterical laugh.

The old man stood, his head sunk between massive

589

shoulders. He seemed to have forgotten why he was there. After a moment he turned and shuffled away.

Charles tied a knot in his handkerchief with his teeth, staunching the blood. He looked at Edwin, slumped in a chair, despairing. 'How much did you know?'

He made a gesture. 'Some. Not enough. He tried to drive her into the canal. That was the first. He won't go to prison, of course. No one convicts madmen.'

'Did you use him to do what you wouldn't do yourself?'

Edwin lifted his shoulders in a weary, hopeless shrug. 'Others must be the judge of that. He turned on me in the end. Even me.'

The sun was rising as they left. It lit the lake with a thousand rays, and the birds began their chorus of morning joy. 'What happens now?' asked Heather.

Charles said, 'I'll tell the police. As Edwin says, the old man's probably mad. I doubt he'll stand trial. And we won't get Edwin either.'

Heather cradled the dog, sitting on her knee. He wore his usual slightly glum expression. 'Thank God it wasn't David.'

'Thank God for a lot of things. Including the dog.'

He ruffled the animal's ears. Heather remembered how much she had hated the dog when he came. It was a fault of hers, this dislike of change. She should open her mind, get used to different things, different situations. Her life was her own. She should live it, and not stand idly by while others decided her fate. She ought to be more like Celia.

Chapter Forty

Summer was in command of the day, in all its abundance. The trees, full of leaf but not yet dusty, stood like full-skirted sentinels against the sky. It was warm and would soon be hot, and Lucy and Ellen were squabbling about what they would wear. 'I don't want anyone to see my legs!' complained Lucy, who had taken against shorts.

'She's going through a stage,' said Ellen, world-weary.

'We'll be late if we don't hurry,' said Heather. She was frazzled and anxious, her pretty print dress already damp.

David, suddenly light-hearted, appeared with his ancient panama. 'Do I look the part, girls? Very Noel Coward.'

'We leave that to Edwin,' said Heather acidly.

The girls insisted on going in the Sheraton, although it was far too small. Heather had to have Tip on her lap, but she didn't mind that as much as the girls' incessant squabbling, as they fought for space in the tiny back seat.

'You're doing that on purpose, you brute!'

'Ouch! Now you've scarred me for life!'

'Shut up, girls,' said David easily. 'Mum's looking fragile.'

'How kind of you to notice.'

The gates of Linton Place stood wide to welcome them. Ellen, who had lately read Tolkien, said, 'There should be blackened reeds and pools of stagnant water. In a minute the sky will darken and we'll be sucked under the earth and lost!'

'You're horrible,' said Lucy.

Heather said tightly, 'Girls, will you please shut up!'

They had been invited to a picnic, and as they neared the house they saw long tables set out by the lake. White cloths fluttered in the breeze and the sunshine glinted on silver and crystal. There was even a flower arrangement on a pedestal.

'This is truly amazing,' said Ellen. 'The man's bonkers.'

'Don't say that now,' said Heather, setting her face in a rigid smile. 'If you say anything like that today I won't be responsible.'

'He definitely isn't,' said Ellen.

'Isn't what?' queried Lucy.

'Responsible.' Since Ellen had embarked so firmly on independence it was impossible to get the last word.

Edwin came out of the house to welcome them, running down the terrace steps like a character in a musical. 'Heather! David! The darling girls.'

'Hello, Uncle Edwin,' said Ellen and Lucy, dutifully. Lucy succumbed to nervous giggles.

'Isn't it going to be glorious? Feodor, champagne – Ellen can have some, can't she? What about you, Lucy? What's your poison?'

'Lemonade, please,' gasped Lucy.

'And for Ellen,' said Heather, and Ellen looked daggers.

Another car was driving through the park. Edwin said, 'Let's get our drinks before we're all upstaged by dear Celia.'

'What do you mean?' asked Ellen, pretending innocence.

'Have some champagne,' said Edwin.

Charles got out first. He was wearing khaki shorts but somehow managed to look amazingly good. Lucy began to feel better about her own attire, and stopped standing behind people. Ellen ran to the car.

'Are you all right? Have you got her?'

'We have indeed.'

Celia was wearing a wide-skirted dress in blue muslin, topped with a cartwheel hat. She looked glamorous and relaxed, reaching into the back of the car for the carrycot.

'Leave it alone,' said Charles. 'You're not supposed to lift things.'

'You can't have a baby and not lift things. Don't fuss, everyone.'

'Do as you're told.'

Charles moved her firmly out of the way and Celia stamped in irritation. 'I'll murder him one of these days!'

Edwin said, 'Please, Celia. Not in present company.' And she laughed.

They all crowded round the carrycot. Heather said nervously, 'Are you sure she ought to be here? In the open? She's so small.'

'She's huge compared with what she was,' said Ellen.

'We've got a doctor on hand,' said Celia easily, and Charles said, 'Don't rely on me. I know nothing at all about babies.'

Celia made a face. 'Now he tells me!'

The baby set up a small, crumpled moan. Celia lifted her from the carrycot and cradled her. 'See your big sisters,' she said. 'Aren't they lovely? Do you want to hold her, Lucy?'

'I don't know if I dare.'

Heather said, 'Lucy certainly shouldn't. She's far too clumsy.'

Celia said, 'Of course she isn't. Sit down, Lucy, and I'll give her to you.'

Charles said, 'What a lovely day it's going to be. What's in the food, Edwin? Hemlock?'

'That would be in the drink, surely? Let me offer you champagne.'

'How kind – I think. Will any of us get out of here alive? I warn you, I've left instructions with my solicitor.'

'Don't be tiresome, Charles. You medical men have the most leaden sense of humour.'

Celia went to sit on a rug. She took off her hat, letting the breeze ruffle the fine curls which were all she had as yet of hair. The sensation was delicious. She was beginning to think that she would spend all her life in ecstasy over the smallest things, from a warm bath, to the smell of coffee, to the feel of cold tiles beneath her feet. Life was so ordinary for most people. For her it was remarkable, in every tiny way.

Charles came to sit beside her. 'Right, everyone,' he said. 'Before we all get totally drunk, which I imagine is Edwin's intention, let's talk.'

'Tact, Charles,' murmured Edwin. 'Tact. We don't need to meet everything head-on, you know.'

'We do at this moment,' said Charles. 'Gather round. Now,

593

I've tried to reason with Celia but she's adamant. She wants her money.'

'And why not?' said Celia defiantly. 'I'm at least as good a custodian as any one of you. And it's my money.'

Charles quelled her with a look. 'The point is, do we go back to court, embarrass everyone, wash a lot of dirty linen and pay a lot of lawyers, or do you, Edwin, settle a fair sum? Three million's been suggested.'

Edwin choked on his champagne. 'What? I can't possibly afford three million.'

'I'd take it in shares,' said Celia. 'I've no wish to bankrupt you.'

'How kind,' said Edwin sarcastically.

'Yes.' She smiled at him. 'Isn't it?'

Somewhat pettishly, Edwin said, 'I do think you ought to be more grateful for your very existence, Celia. To utter a cliché, but one with substance, money isn't everything.'

'Then you won't mind giving me some,' she retorted. 'It is mine, Edwin. If necessary I shall make you all stand up in court and say exactly what happened when my father died.'

'And we'll counter with the little episode of the pearls.'

Celia chuckled. 'But I was ill, Edwin. Unbalanced by my experiences. And we should have to discuss your father, and his place in secure accommodation, and—'

'Oh, all right!' Edwin signalled to Feodor for more champagne. 'Three million it is. When I think of what would have happened to the business if I'd let David take it over, I think you should pay me!'

David said, 'Damn it all, will you stop treating me like some idiot? I've run a good business for nearly twenty years!'

'A business,' said Edwin. 'Not a good one. The trouble with you, David, is that you don't like money. You like spending it but you can't get accustomed to having it. Keeping it. Giving it treats. Money is a pet and should be regarded as such. To be loved and cherished.'

'Where are the pets?' asked Heather, looking nervously about.

'Locked away,' said Edwin. 'I heard you were bringing your boon companion. The thing should wear a muzzle.'

'I told you he was a monster,' said Ellen to Lucy, rather too loudly.

Heather coloured. 'She doesn't mean it.'

'I bet she does,' said Celia. 'You're going to have to work very hard the next few years, Edwin. I'm going to be watching you quite carefully. As an important shareholder, I'll expect high standards in every sphere of activity. No more accidents, if you please. Not even little ones. Not even a teensie weensie fire.'

Edwin gave a forced laugh.

Suddenly David said, 'Would you mind telling me why I was invited here today? Simply to be witness to your good fortune, Celia?'

She looked at him, her eyes very dark. He had the grace to look away. 'Do you really think I owe you?' she asked quietly. 'Honestly, now.'

'We were married a long time.'

'Six years. I don't count the next ten. I don't think we'd have stayed married, you know, whatever happened. We were so busy papering over the cracks. You resented my money, my father. I had my own ideas about Sheraton cars which you hated. And it all came out at parties. You've got Blantyre House, you can't really feel you should have more.'

David was very pale. 'I suffered for ten years, for ten long years—'

'Yes,' she admitted. 'I admit, it can't have been easy. For you or Heather.'

'Well.' David looked mollified. 'Some sense at last.'

'I'm sorry I was so difficult at first,' said Celia. 'It's very frightening to be unwanted.'

Heather said, 'Perhaps I owe an apology also. I made no attempt to understand. I'm sorry.'

'When you've all stopped being nice to one another,' said David urgently, 'I have to point out that I've got a business in desperate need of funds! You made me mortgage the house, Celia. We were getting along fine until then.'

'You were limping along,' she said. 'Have you managed to sell the pearls?'

He nodded. 'We got far less than we should.'

'I told you that. You wouldn't believe me. You never did.'

There was a silence. Celia felt a certain despair. She had loved David once. The love had been real, but she hadn't known the object of it. He wasn't what she had thought. In her youth, in her salad days, he had enthralled her. Not now. 'I'll give you the money,' she said. 'I'll bank on Edwin's good business sense and borrow against the shares. And I want a half share in Sheraton. I want to join in decision-making, not stand on the sidelines watching things go wrong.'

'Over my dead body!' flared David.

Celia laughed mirthlessly. 'It was almost over mine.'

Charles put a hand on her arm. 'You could always appoint a manager.'

She thought for a moment. 'Who?'

'Heather.'

'Me?' Heather looked dumbfounded.

Edwin said, 'You surprise me, Charles. You must come and dine one day. You're really quite astute. For a medical man.'

'We're not all entirely stupid, you know.'

'Blinkered. And so political. That's my objective view.'

'You're too kind.'

David said, 'Actually, that's a good idea. Heather's very organised, very sensible. Perhaps – I admit I've been distracted of late. If I could just get back to making a good car!'

'You don't like women meddling,' said Heather in surprise.

'I didn't like Celia meddling,' said David. 'It was the equivalent of selling out to Joe Braddock. We could do it, Heather. Couldn't we?'

Celia didn't wait for a reply. She said, 'Right then. That's settled. Heather will keep her eye on the finances at Sheraton on my behalf. There's just one other thing, David. I've got some papers for you to sign. Our divorce. I think it's time, don't you?'

'More than time,' he said fervently. 'To be quite honest, Celia—'

'What?' She fixed him with her steady blue gaze, daring him to curse her in front of the children. He dropped his eyes.

She felt sorry for him suddenly. David had always resented loving her. He had seen in her all the things he wanted in himself, and had thought that by marrying her he could have them. He wanted Braddock brains, Braddock money, Braddock recklessness. They had never been his. He didn't admire his own qualities, she thought suddenly. In his youth he had been a creative, intelligent, charming man.

Lunch passed in a haze of alcohol. Even the losers felt that at last everything had been resolved. It was a relief to have an end to conflict. Edwin lay back on a rug, giggling uncontrollably, gasping, 'At last I've got rid of the bloody old man. Thank God for that at least.'

Charles said, 'Was it his idea to destroy the Will?'

'Oh, yes.' Edwin propped himself up on an elbow. 'He'd been planning it for years. But he didn't get on with Celia's mother, so I was his stooge. Without me he couldn't have done a thing. He's spent years thinking I was his puppet.'

'And were you?'

Edwin laughed again. 'What do you think? I did what suited me. Kept him informed. You're lucky you ever got out of hospital in the first place, Celia. He might have paid you a visit.'

'He did,' said Celia. 'I thought I'd imagined it. A man came and took me out in a car. He was very pale and quiet and uncomfortable. I thought I knew who he was, and of course I did. It was Uncle Henry.'

David came and squatted on the edge of the rug. He looked at Edwin's sprawling, giggling figure with undisguised anger. 'You realise he killed your mother, Celia,' he said abruptly.

She blinked and sat up. 'Did you, Edwin? How?'

'I did nothing of the kind,' he said. 'I can't vouch for my father, of course. He had a great many pills for his condition. He might have called on her. But your mother had a heart attack, Celia, no more than that.'

'Charles?' She turned her eyes on him.

He shrugged. 'Anything's possible.'

'It was him,' said David. 'I always wondered. Between the time she called me and the time I arrived, someone did her in.'

'You can't prove a thing,' said Edwin. His voice was clear and cold. And suddenly Celia felt a great grief for her mother, and her mother's pain, and for David and for his. She put out

597

her hand and touched David's arm, but when he saw who touched him he shook her off. He wasn't hers any more, she thought. The parting, so long in coming, was complete.

Perhaps she had drunk too little. Everyone else was sleepy and garrulous. She got up, taking the the baby from her carrycot to go for a walk. Heather ran to catch up. 'Do you mind if I come?'

'No. Not at all.'

A light breeze was blowing. It stirred the hair against their cheeks and hustled their skirts. The air seemed sweet today. Every step away from the picnic seemed to be a step towards wellbeing. Celia cradled the tiny scrap of baby against her breast. She felt as if she had lived a hundred years, but had her youth again, with all its optimism and joy. The past was over, blown away with honesty and courage. Only a little time ago she had felt unaccountably cursed, but the good fairy had waved her wand and turned her curses into blessings. She would never again take her life for granted, she thought. Never again would she be so careless of her bounty.

They walked on around the lake. Ducks and swans eyed them speculatively, to see if they had any bread. 'Back to feeding the ducks,' said Celia happily. 'We used to go every day when the girls were tiny.'

'Is she quite all right?' asked Heather. 'The baby, I mean. She was so terribly early—'

Celia cut her off. 'We don't know yet. I think she'll be fine. I won't mind if she isn't, quite honestly, and neither will Charles. He adores her.'

Heather said, quietly, 'I should so like one of my own.'

Celia said nothing. They walked to the far end of the lake, where some past owner had built a little folly, where they rested on a stone bench, gazing out across trees and water, sky and hills. 'David isn't a bad man,' said Celia at last. 'He has his weaknesses, that's all. I was always wrong for him. Too – too everything. Rich. Wilful. Spoiled. You had ten good years together, you and he. I changed him, just as I did before. Made him less steady. Less kind. More envious.'

'Do you really think that? Or do you just want me to go on providing for your girls?'

Celia turned to her. 'Of course I want that. Because they want it. A happy, familiar, comfortable home, just like you gave them before. With a bit more money, of course.'

'You always were bloody mercenary!'

'Used to it. That's all.'

It was very quiet. Far away across the lake the girls were playing ball, and their cries floated across like those of rare and tuneful birds. Heather felt a grudging admiration for the woman beside her. She had survived what few could, with more grace than many. That she had no caution annoyed Heather still, who had too much. Celia would risk everything on a whim, Heather risked nothing on a certainty. Why didn't she just go ahead and get pregnant? She would have something of her own, then. Something no one could steal away.

If only she and David could make love again as they used to do. She felt a great longing for tenderness, a close and loving embrace. Celia was right. For ten years they had been happy. She must try for happiness again.

The baby was mewing restlessly. Celia said, 'I must take her back. She needs feeding so often you wouldn't believe.'

'Is Charles any help?'

'Charles?' Celia chuckled. 'I'm not sure. His medical training gets in the way. Charles likes machines, you see, and babies are fairly erratic mechanisms at the best of times. This child seems to thrive on confounding his carefully thought out systems. Poor Charles.'

Heather said, 'I never thought you and Charles were all that well suited, actually.'

'Didn't you?' Celia got up, ready to walk back. 'I like to think that we've transcended all the superficial things. You know, whether you like the same food or the same films. We don't. We never will. We don't even like the same people, because Charles hates almost everybody on principle. But if there was one person in the whole world that I thought was most like me, it would be him. We discovered each other, you see.'

'Twin souls,' said Heather caustically.

Celia turned, suddenly fierce. 'Yes, that's exactly it. And we

599

can't be the only ones. We had a reason to try, and found each other in the process. You ought not to put up with just getting on with David, you know. Take the time and the trouble to discover what sort of person he really is. He might be just like you.'

Slow colour rose in Heather's cheeks. They walked in silence back to the others.

Charles and Celia went home in the late afternoon. They bathed the baby together, fed her yet again, and put her down to sleep. She looked at them out of dark blue eyes already heavy.

'She looks like you,' said Celia. 'Your unamused stare.'

The baby's eyes drooped and closed in sleep. Charles put his hand on her mother's slender neck. 'Come to bed.'

It was the first time since the baby. They went into the square light room, which had once been so spartan and now was strewn with Celia's things, and stood by the tall double bed. Charles knew he was eager, knew he would be too quick. He knelt in front of her, and reached up under her skirt. She half lay on the bed, feeling him explore her, feeling his breath hot on her skin. She prayed for a gentle touch.

His tongue roamed over her in lazy delight. She gasped and fell back still more, her fingers opening and closing in his hair. She had never liked this, had never wanted it from anyone else. But a languor was spreading over her, silken threads taking power from her limbs, taking restlessness from her soul. She wanted nothing more than this. The feeling came, sharp and insistent, but instinctively she shied away. The scars in her womb had healed, but there were scars still in her mind. She feared the violence even of pleasure.

'No. No!' She pushed at him. He merely wrapped his arms around her thighs and pulled her, knees wide, on to him. Blood pounded in her head, his mouth was relentless, relentlessly soft. Her body abandoned control, she let out a cry of absolute release. He stood up as she came, and went into her. Her eyes flew open and she clutched at his shoulders, flinching instinctively. But she had no cause. There was no pain, she simply knew that she was full beyond measure. He gave a single thrust and erupted into her, the perfect, the inevitable end.

They were quiet together afterwards. The early evening light played across the bed, and Charles ran his hands through Celia's soft and childish curls. 'If you had died,' he said softly, 'I was going to give all this up and devote myself to science.'

'Am I depriving the world, then?' she murmured. 'What an evil woman I must be.'

He buried his head in her warm flesh. 'You made me kind,' he whispered.

'But kindness isn't really what I'm about. There's a lot of my father in me, Charles. I don't know how to be sweet.'

'Did I talk about sweetness? Compassion, then. You made me understand that the people I see every day are facing something terrible. I've been to the end of the world with you, and whatever they say, it's full of dragons and boiling mists. It's eternity. It's fear.'

She sat up, the better to look at him. 'You lose the fear when you're close, you know. There's a pull, almost a calling. Some part of you wants to go.'

He drew her back down to him. 'I don't ever want to let you go.'

She touched his face. 'That's what makes us stay. Don't credit me with more than my worth, Charles. I didn't teach you anything. You discovered yourself.'

As the evening wore on, the sun began to slide behind the trees, speckling the bed with diamonds of fragmented light. They lay together, at peace at last, while somewhere close at hand a baby began to stir. Celia opened her eyes and looked about her, seeing the colours and the light as if for the very first time. Her world was full of magic and joy. For her, at last, this was truly a new beginning.